THE VIRGINIANS
A TALE OF THE LAST CENTURY

By William Makepeace Thackeray

TO SIR HENRY MADISON, Chief Justice of Madras, this book is inscribed by an affectionate old friend.

London, September 7, 1859.

CHAPTER I. In which one of the Virginians visits home

On the library wall of one of the most famous writers of America, there hang two crossed swords, which his relatives wore in the great War of Independence. The one sword was gallantly drawn in the service of the king, the other was the weapon of a brave and honoured republican soldier. The possessor of the harmless trophy has earned for himself a name alike honoured in his ancestors' country and his own, where genius such as his has always a peaceful welcome.

The ensuing history reminds me of yonder swords in the historian's study at Boston. In the Revolutionary War, the subjects of this story, natives of America, and children of the Old Dominion, found themselves engaged on different sides in the quarrel, coming together peaceably at its conclusion, as brethren should, their love ever having materially diminished, however angrily the contest divided them. The colonel in scarlet, and the general in blue and buff, hang side by side in the wainscoted parlour of the Warringtons, in England, where a descendant of one of the brothers has shown their portraits to me, with many of the letters which they wrote, and the books and papers which belonged to them. In the Warrington family, and to distinguish them from other personages of that respectable race, these effigies have always gone by the name of "The Virginians"; by which name their memoirs are christened.

They both of them passed much time in Europe. They lived just on the verge of that Old World from which we are drifting away so swiftly. They were familiar with many varieties of men and fortune. Their lot brought them into contact with personages of whom we read only in books, who seem alive, as I read in the Virginians' letters regarding them, whose voices I almost fancy I hear, as I read the yellow pages written scores of years since, blotted with the boyish tears of disappointed passion, dutifully despatched after famous balls and ceremonies of the grand Old World, scribbled by camp-fires, or out of prison; nay, there is one that has a bullet through it, and of which a greater portion of the text is blotted out with the blood of the bearer.

These letters had probably never been preserved, but for the affectionate thrift of one person, to whom they never failed in their dutiful correspondence. Their mother kept all her sons' letters, from the very first, in which Henry, the younger of the twins, sends his love to his brother, then ill of a sprain at his grandfather's house of Castlewood, in Virginia, and thanks his grandpapa for a horse which he rides with his tutor, down to the last, "from my beloved son," which reached her but a few hours before her death. The venerable lady never visited Europe, save once with her parents in the reign of George the Second; took refuge in Richmond when the house of Castlewood was burned down during the war; and was called Madam Esmond ever after that event; never caring much for the name or family of Warrington, which she held in very slight estimation as compared to her own.

The letters of the Virginians, as the reader will presently see, from specimens to be shown to him, are by no means full. They are hints rather than descriptions—indications and outlines chiefly: it may be, that the present writer has mistaken the forms, and filled in the colour wrongly: but, poring over the documents, I have tried to imagine the situation of the writer, where he was, and by what persons surrounded. I have drawn the figures as I fancied they were; set down conversations as I think I might have heard them; and so, to the best of my ability, endeavoured to revivify the bygone times and people. With what success the task has been accomplished, with what profit or amusement to himself, the kind reader will please to determine.

One summer morning in the year 1756, and in the reign of his Majesty King George the Second, the Young Rachel, Virginian ship, Edward Franks master, came up the Avon river on her happy return from her annual voyage to the Potomac. She proceeded to Bristol with the tide, and moored in the stream as near as possible to Trail's wharf, to which she was consigned. Mr. Trail, her part owner, who could survey his ship from his counting-house windows, straightway took boat and came up her side. The owner of the Young Rachel, a large grave man in his own hair, and of a demure aspect, gave the hand of welcome to Captain Franks, who stood on his deck, and congratulated the captain upon the speedy and fortunate voyage which he had made. And, remarking that we ought to be thankful to Heaven for its mercies, he proceeded presently to business by asking particulars relative to cargo and passengers.

Franks was a pleasant man, who loved a joke. "We have," says he, "but yonder ugly negro boy, who is fetching the trunks, and a passenger who has the state cabin to himself."

Mr. Trail looked as if he would have preferred more mercies from Heaven. "Confound you, Franks, and your luck! The Duke William, which came in last week, brought fourteen, and she is not half of our tonnage."

"And this passenger, who has the whole cabin, don't pay nothin'," continued the Captain. "Swear now, it will do you good, Mr. Trail, indeed it will. I have tried the medicine."

"A passenger take the whole cabin and not pay? Gracious mercy, are you a fool, Captain Franks?"

"Ask the passenger himself, for here he comes." And, as the master spoke, a young man of some nineteen years of age came up the hatchway. He had a cloak and a sword under his arm, and was dressed in deep mourning, and called out, "Gumbo, you idiot, why don't you fetch the baggage out of the cabin? Well, shipmate, our journey is ended. You will see all the little folks to-night whom you have been talking about. Give my love to Polly, and Betty, and Little Tommy; not forgetting my duty to Mrs. Franks. I thought, yesterday, the voyage would never be done, and now I am almost sorry it is over. That little berth in my cabin looks very comfortable now I am going to leave it."

Mr. Trail scowled at the young passenger who had paid no money for his passage. He scarcely nodded his head to the stranger, when Captain Franks said, "This here gentleman is Mr. Trail, sir, whose name you have a-heerd of."

"It's pretty well known in Bristol, sir," says Mr. Trail, majestically.

"And this is Mr. Warrington, Madam Esmond Warrington's son, of Castlewood," continued the Captain.

The British merchant's hat was instantly off his head, and the owner of the beaver was making a prodigious number of bows as if a crown prince were before him.

"Gracious powers, Mr. Warrington! This is a delight, indeed! What a crowning mercy that your voyage should have been so prosperous! You must have my boat to go on shore. Let me cordially and respectfully welcome you to England: let me shake your hand as the son of my benefactress and patroness, Mrs. Esmond Warrington, whose name is known and honoured on Bristol 'Change, I warrant you. Isn't it, Franks?"

"There's no sweeter tobacco comes from Virginia, and no better brand than the Three Castles," says Mr. Franks, drawing a great brass tobacco-box from his pocket, and thrusting a quid into his jolly mouth. "You don't know what a comfort it is, sir! you'll take to it, bless you, as you grow older. Won't he, Mr. Trail? I wish you had ten shiploads of it instead of one. You might have ten shiploads: I've told Madam Esmond so; I've rode over her plantation; she treats me like a lord when I go to the house; she don't grudge me the best of wine, or keep me cooling my heels in the counting-room as some folks does" (with a look at Mr. Trail). "She is a real born lady, she is; and might have a thousand hogsheads as easy as her hundreds, if there were but hands enough."

"I have lately engaged in the Guinea trade, and could supply her ladyship with any number of healthy young negroes before next fall," said Mr. Trail, obsequiously.

"We are averse to the purchase of negroes from Africa," said the young gentleman, coldly. "My grandfather and my mother have always objected to it, and I do not like to think of selling or buying the poor wretches."

"It is for their good, my dear young sir! for their temporal and their spiritual good!" cried Mr. Trail. "And we purchase the poor creatures only for their benefit; let me talk this matter over with you at my own house. I can introduce you to a happy home, a Christian family, and a British merchant's honest fare. Can't I, Captain Franks?"

"Can't say," growled the Captain. "Never asked me to take bite or sup at your table. Asked me to psalm-singing once, and to hear Mr. Ward preach: don't care for them sort of entertainments."

Not choosing to take any notice of this remark, Mr. Trail continued in his low tone: "Business is business, my dear young sir, and I know, 'tis only my duty, the duty of all of us, to cultivate the fruits of the earth in their season. As the heir of Lady Esmond's estate—for I speak, I believe, to the heir of that great property?—"

The young gentleman made a bow.

"—I would urge upon you, at the very earliest moment, the propriety, the duty of increasing the ample means with which Heaven has blessed you. As an honest factor, I could not do otherwise; as a prudent man, should I scruple to speak of what will tend to your profit and mine? No, my dear Mr. George."

"My name is not George; my name is Henry," said the young man as he turned his head away, and his eyes filled with tears.

"Gracious powers! what do you mean, sir? Did you not say you were my lady's heir? and is not George Esmond Warrington, Esq.——"

"Hold your tongue, you fool!" cried Mr. Franks, striking the merchant a tough blow on his sleek sides, as the young lad turned away. "Don't you see the young gentleman a-swabbing his eyes, and note his black clothes?"

"What do you mean, Captain Franks, by laying your hand on your owners? Mr. George is the heir; I know the Colonel's will well enough."

"Mr. George is there," said the Captain, pointing with his thumb to the deck.

"Where?" cries the factor.

"Mr. George is there!" reiterated the Captain, again lifting up his finger towards the topmast, or the sky beyond. "He is dead a year, sir, come next 9th of July. He would go out with General Braddock on that dreadful business to the Belle Riviere. He and a thousand more never came back again. Every man of them was murdered as he fell. You know the Indian way, Mr. Trail?" And here the Captain passed his hand rapidly round his head. "Horrible! ain't it, sir? horrible! He was a fine young man, the very picture of this one; only his hair was black, which is now hanging in a bloody Indian wigwam. He was often and often on board of the Young Rachel, and would have his chests of books broke open on deck before they was landed. He was a shy and silent young gent: not like this one, which was the merriest, wildest young fellow, full of his songs and fun. He took on dreadful at the news; went to his bed, had that fever which lays so many of 'em by the heels along that swampy Potomac, but he's got better on the voyage: the voyage makes every one better; and, in course, the young gentleman can't be for ever a-crying after a brother who dies and leaves him a great fortune. Ever since we sighted Ireland he has been quite gay and happy, only he would go off at times, when he was most merry, saying, 'I wish my dearest Georgy could enjoy this here sight along with me, and when you mentioned the t'other's name, you see, he couldn't stand it.'" And the honest Captain's own eyes filled with tears, as he turned and looked towards the object of his compassion.

Mr. Trail assumed a lugubrious countenance befitting the tragic compliment with which he prepared to greet the young Virginian; but the latter answered him very curtly, declined his offers of hospitality, and only stayed in Mr. Trail's house long enough to drink a glass of wine and to take up a sum of money of which he stood in need. But he and Captain Franks parted on the very warmest terms, and all the little crew of the Young Rachel cheered from the ship's side as their passenger left it.

Again and again Harry Warrington and his brother had pored over the English map, and determined upon the course which they should take upon arriving at Home. All Americans who love the old country—and what gently-nurtured man or woman of Anglo-Saxon race does not?—have ere this rehearsed their English travels, and visited in fancy the spots with which their hopes, their parents' fond stories, their friends' descriptions, have rendered them familiar. There are few things to me more affecting in the history of the quarrel which divided the two great nations than the recurrence of that word Home, as used by the younger towards the elder country. Harry Warrington had his chart laid out. Before London, and its glorious temples of St. Paul's and St. Peter's; its grim Tower, where the brave and loyal had shed their blood, from Wallace down to Balmerino and Kilmarnock, pitied by gentle hearts; before the awful window of Whitehall, whence the martyr Charles had issued, to kneel once more, and then ascend to Heaven;—before Playhouses, Parks, and Palaces, wondrous resorts of wit, pleasure, and splendour;—before Shakspeare's Resting-place under the tall spire which rises by Avon, amidst the sweet Warwickshire pastures;—before Derby, and Falkirk, and Culloden, where the cause of honour and loyalty had fallen, it might be to rise no more: —before all these points of their pilgrimage there was one which the young Virginian brothers held even more sacred, and that was the home of their family,—that old Castlewood in Hampshire, about which their parents had talked so fondly. From Bristol to Bath, from Bath to Salisbury, to Winchester, to Hexton, to Home; they knew the way, and had mapped the journey many and many a time.

We must fancy our American traveller to be a handsome young fellow, whose suit of sables only made him look the more interesting. The plump landlady from her bar, surrounded by her china and punch-bowls, and stout gilded bottles of strong waters, and glittering rows of silver flagons, looked kindly after the young gentleman as he passed through the inn-hall from his post-chaise, and the obsequious chamberlain bowed him upstairs to the Rose or the Dolphin. The trim chambermaid dropped her best curtsey for his fee, and Gumbo, in the inn-kitchen, where the townsfolk drank their mug of ale by the great fire, bragged of his young master's splendid house in Virginia, and of the immense wealth to which he was heir. The postchaise whirled the traveller through the most delightful home-scenery his eyes had ever lighted on. If English landscape is pleasant to the American of the present day, who must needs contrast the rich woods and glowing pastures, and picturesque ancient villages of the old country with the rough aspect of his own, how much pleasanter must Harry Warrington's course have been, whose journeys had lain through swamps and forest solitudes from one Virginian ordinary to another log-house at the end of the day's route, and who now lighted suddenly upon the busy, happy, splendid scene of English summer? And the highroad, a hundred years ago, was not that grass-grown desert of the present time. It was alive with constant travel and traffic: the country towns and inns swarmed with life and gaiety. The ponderous waggon, with its bells and plodding team; the light post-coach that achieved the journey from the White Hart, Salisbury, to the Swan with Two Necks, London, in two days; the strings of packhorses that had not yet left the road; my lord's gilt postchaise-and-six, with the outriders galloping on ahead; the country squire's great coach and heavy Flanders mares; the farmers trotting to market, or the parson jolting to the cathedral town on Dumpling, his wife behind on the pillion—all these crowding sights and brisk people greeted the young traveller on his summer journey. Hodge, the farmer's boy, took off his hat, and Polly, the milkmaid, bobbed a curtsey, as the chaise whirled over the pleasant village-green, and the white-headed children lifted their chubby faces and cheered. The church-spires glistened with gold, the cottage-gables glared in sunshine, the great elms murmured in summer, or cast purple shadows over the grass. Young Warrington never had such a glorious day, or witnessed a scene so delightful. To be nineteen years of age, with high health, high spirits, and a full purse, to be making your first journey, and rolling through the country in a postchaise at nine miles an hour—O happy youth! almost it makes one young to think of him! But Harry was too eager to give more than a passing glance at the Abbey at Bath, or gaze with more than a moment's wonder at the mighty Minster at Salisbury. Until he beheld Home it seemed to him he had no eyes for any other place.

At last the young gentleman's postchaise drew up at the rustic inn on Castlewood Green, of which his grandsire had many a time talked to him, and which bears as its ensign, swinging from an elm near the inn porch, the Three Castles of the Esmond family. They had a sign, too, over the gateway of Castlewood House, bearing the same cognisance. This was the hatchment of Francis, Lord Castlewood, who now lay in the chapel hard by, his son reigning in his stead.

Harry Warrington had often heard of Francis, Lord Castlewood. It was for Frank's sake, and for his great love towards the boy, that Colonel Esmond determined to forgo his claim to the English estates and rank of his family, and retired to Virginia. The young man had led a wild youth; he had fought with distinction under Marlborough; he had married a foreign lady, and most lamentably adopted her religion. At one time he had been a Jacobite (for loyalty to the sovereign was ever hereditary in the Esmond family), but had received some slight or injury from the Prince, which had caused him to rally to King George's side. He had, on his second marriage, renounced the errors of Popery which he had temporarily embraced, and returned to the Established Church again. He had, from his constant support of the King and the Minister of the time being, been rewarded by his Majesty George II., and died an English peer. An earl's coronet now figured on the hatchment which hung over Castlewood gate—and there was an end of the jolly gentleman. Between Colonel Esmond, who had become his stepfather, and his lordship there had ever been a brief but affectionate correspondence—on the Colonel's part especially, who loved his stepson, and had a hundred stories to tell about him to his grandchildren. Madam Esmond, however, said she could see nothing in her half-brother. He was dull, except when he drank too much wine, and that, to be sure, was every day at dinner. Then he was boisterous, and his conversation not pleasant. He was good-looking—yes—a fine tall stout animal; she had rather her boys should follow a different model. In spite of the grandfather's encomium of the late lord, the boys had no very great respect for their kinsman's memory. The lads and their mother were staunch Jacobites, though having every respect for his present Majesty; but right was right, and nothing could make their hearts swerve from their allegiance to the descendants of the martyr Charles.

With a beating heart Harry Warrington walked from the inn towards the house where his grandsire's youth had been passed. The little village-green of Castlewood slopes down towards the river, which is spanned by an old bridge of a single broad arch, and from this the ground rises gradually towards the house, grey with many gables and buttresses, and backed by a darkling wood. An old man sate at the wicket on a stone bench in front of the great arched entrance to the house, over which the earl's hatchment was hanging. An old dog was crouched at the man's feet. Immediately above the ancient sentry at the gate was an open casement with some homely flowers in the window, from behind which good-humoured girls' faces were peeping. They were watching the young traveller dressed in black as he walked up gazing towards the castle, and the ebony attendant who followed the gentleman's steps also accoutred in mourning. So was he at the gate in mourning, and the girls when they came out had black ribbons.

To Harry's surprise, the old man accosted him by his name. "You have had a nice ride to Hexton, Master Harry, and the sorrel carried you well."

"I think you must be Lockwood," said Harry, with rather a tremulous voice, holding out his hand to the old man. His grandfather had often told him of Lockwood, and how he had accompanied the Colonel and the young Viscount in Marlborough's wars forty years ago. The veteran seemed puzzled by the mark of affection which Harry extended to him. The old dog gazed at the new-comer, and then went and put his head between his knees. "I have heard of you often. How did you know my name?"

"They say I forget most things," says the old man, with a smile; "but I ain't so bad as that quite. Only this mornin', when you went out, my darter says, 'Father, do you know why you have a black coat on?' 'In course I know why I have a black coat,' says I. 'My lord is dead. They say 'twas a foul blow, and Master Frank is my lord now, and Master Harry'—why, what have you done since you've went out this morning? Why, you have a-grow'd taller and changed your hair—though I know—I know you."

One of the young women had tripped out by this time from the porter's lodge, and dropped the stranger a pretty curtsey. "Grandfather sometimes does not recollect very well," she said, pointing to her head. "Your honour seems to have heard of Lockwood?"

"And you, have you never heard of Colonel Francis Esmond?"

"He was Captain and Major in Webb's Foot, and I was with him in two campaigns, sure enough," cries Lockwood. "Wasn't I, Ponto?"

"The Colonel as married Viscountess Rachel, my late lord's mother? and went to live amongst the Indians? We have heard of him. Sure we have his picture in our gallery, and hisself painted it."

"Went to live in Virginia, and died there seven years ago, and I am his grandson."

"Lord, your honour! Why, your honour's skin's as white as mine," cries Molly. "Grandfather, do you hear this? His honour is Colonel Esmond's grandson that used to send you tobacco, and his honour have come all the way from Virginia."

"To see you, Lockwood," says the young man, "and the family. I only set foot on English ground yesterday, and my first visit is for home. I may see the house, though the family are from home?" Molly dared to say Mrs. Barker would let his honour see the house, and Harry Warrington made his way across the court, seeming to know the place as well as if he had been born there, Miss Molly thought, who followed, accompanied by Mr. Gumbo making her a profusion of polite bows and speeches.

CHAPTER II. In which Harry has to pay for his Supper

Colonel Esmond's grandson rang for a while at his ancestors' house of Castlewood, before any one within seemed inclined to notice his summons. The servant, who at length issued from the door, seemed to be very little affected by the announcement that the visitor was a relation of the family. The family was away, and in their absence John cared very little for their relatives, but was eager to get back to his game at cards with Thomas in the window-seat. The housekeeper was busy getting ready for my lord and my lady, who were expected that evening. Only by strong entreaties could Harry gain leave to see my lady's sitting-room and the picture-room, where, sure enough, was a portrait of his grandfather in periwig and breastplate, the counterpart of their picture in Virginia, and a likeness of his grandmother, as Lady Castlewood, in a yet earlier habit of Charles II.'s time; her neck bare, her fair golden hair waving over her shoulders in ringlets which he remembered to have seen snowy white. From the contemplation of these sights the sulky housekeeper drove him. Her family was about to arrive. There was my lady the Countess, and my lord and his brother, and the young ladies, and the Baroness, who was to have the state bedroom. Who was the Baroness? The Baroness Bernstein, the young ladies' aunt. Harry wrote down his name on a paper from his own pocket-book, and laid it on a table in the hall. "Henry Esmond Warrington, of Castlewood, in Virginia, arrived in England yesterday—staying at the Three Castles in the village." The lackeys rose up from their cards to open the door to him, in order to get their "wails," and Gumbo quitted the bench at the gate, where he had been talking with old Lockwood, the porter, who took Harry's guinea, hardly knowing the meaning of the gift. During the visit to the home of his fathers, Harry had only seen little Polly's countenance that was the least unselfish or kindly: he walked away, not caring to own how disappointed he was, and what a damp had been struck upon him by the aspect of the place. They ought to have known him. Had any of them ridden up to his house in

Virginia, whether the master were present or absent, the guests would have been made welcome, and, in sight of his ancestors' hall, he had to go and ask for a dish of bacon and eggs at a country alehouse!

After his dinner, he went to the bridge and sate on it, looking towards the old house, behind which the sun was descending as the rooks came cawing home to their nests in the elms. His young fancy pictured to itself many of the ancestors of whom his mother and grandsire had told him. He fancied knights and huntsmen crossing the ford;—cavaliers of King Charles's days; my Lord Castlewood, his grandmother's first husband, riding out with hawk and hound. The recollection of his dearest lost brother came back to him as he indulged in these reveries, and smote him with a pang of exceeding tenderness and longing, insomuch that the young man hung his head and felt his sorrow renewed for the dear friend and companion with whom, until of late, all his pleasures and griefs had been shared. As he sate plunged in his own thoughts, which were mingled up with the mechanical clinking of the blacksmith's forge hard by, the noises of the evening, the talk of the rooks, and the calling of the birds round about—a couple of young men on horseback dashed over the bridge. One of them, with an oath, called him a fool, and told him to keep out of the way—the other, who fancied he might have jostled the foot-passenger, and possibly might have sent him over the parapet, pushed on more quickly when he reached the other side of the water, calling likewise to Tom to come on; and the pair of young gentlemen were up the hill on their way to the house before Harry had recovered himself from his surprise at their appearance, and wrath at their behaviour. In a minute or two, this advanced guard was followed by two livery servants on horseback, who scowled at the young traveller on the bridge a true British welcome of Curse you, who are you? After these, in a minute or two, came a coach-and-six, a ponderous vehicle having need of the horses which drew it, and containing three ladies, a couple of maids, and an armed man on a seat behind the carriage. Three handsome pale faces looked out at Harry Warrington as the carriage passed over the bridge, and did not return the salute which, recognising the family arms, he gave it. The gentleman behind the carriage glared at him haughtily. Harry felt terribly alone. He thought he would go back to Captain Franks. The Rachel and her little tossing cabin seemed a cheery spot in comparison to that on which he stood. The inn-folks did not know his name of Warrington. They told him that was my lady in the coach, with her stepdaughter, my Lady Maria, and her daughter, my Lady Fanny; and the young gentleman in the grey frock was Mr. William, and he with powder on the chestnut was my lord. It was the latter had sworn the loudest, and called him a fool; and it was the grey frock which had nearly galloped Harry into the ditch.

The landlord of the Three Castles had shown Harry a bedchamber, but he had refused to have his portmanteaux unpacked, thinking that, for a certainty, the folks of the great house would invite him to theirs. One, two, three hours passed, and there came no invitation. Harry was fain to have his trunks open at last, and to call for his slippers and gown. Just before dark, about two hours after the arrival of the first carriage, a second chariot with four horses had passed over the bridge, and a stout, high-coloured lady, with a very dark pair of eyes, had looked hard at Mr. Warrington. That was the Baroness Bernstein, the landlady said, my lord's aunt, and Harry remembered the first Lady Castlewood had come of a German family. Earl, and Countess, and Baroness, and postillions, and gentlemen, and horses, had all disappeared behind the castle gate, and Harry was fain to go to bed at last, in the most melancholy mood and with a cruel sense of neglect and loneliness in his young heart. He could not sleep, and, besides, ere long, heard a prodigious noise, and cursing, and giggling, and screaming from my landlady's bar, which would have served to keep him awake.

Then Gumbo's voice was heard without, remonstrating, "You cannot go in, sar—my master asleep, sar!" but a shrill voice, with many oaths, which Harry Warrington recognised, cursed Gumbo for a stupid, negro woolly-pate, and he was pushed aside, giving entrance to a flood of oaths into the room, and a young gentleman behind them.

"Beg your pardon, Cousin Warrington," cried the young blasphemer, "are you asleep? Beg your pardon for riding you over on the bridge. Didn't know you—course shouldn't have done it—thought it was a lawyer with a writ—dressed in black, you know. Gad! thought it was Nathan come to nab me." And Mr. William laughed incoherently. It was evident that he was excited with liquor.

"You did me great honour to mistake me for a sheriff's-officer, cousin," says Harry, with great gravity, sitting up in his tall nightcap.

"Gad! I thought it was Nathan, and was going to send you souse into the river. But I ask your pardon. You see I had been drinking at the Bell at Hexton, and the punch is good at the Bell at Hexton. Hullo! you, Davis! a bowl of punch; d'you hear?"

"I have had my share for to-night, cousin, and I should think you have," Harry continues, always in the dignified style.

"You want me to go, Cousin What's-your-name, I see," Mr. William said, with gravity. "You want me to go, and they want me to come, and I didn't want to come. I said, I'd see him hanged first,—that's what I said. Why should I trouble myself to come down all alone of an evening, and look after a fellow I don't care a pin for? Zackly what I said. Zackly what Castlewood said. Why the devil should he go down? Castlewood says, and so said my lady, but the Baroness would have you. It's all the Baroness's doing, and if she says a thing, it must be done; so you must just get up and come." Mr. Esmond delivered these words with the most amiable rapidity and indistinctness, running them into one another, and tacking about the room as he spoke. But the young Virginian was in great wrath. "I tell you what, cousin," he cried, "I won't move for the Countess, or for the Baroness, or for all the cousins in Castlewood." And when the landlord entered the chamber with the bowl of punch, which Mr. Esmond had ordered, the young gentleman in bed called out fiercely to the host, to turn that sot out of the room.

"Sot, you little tobacconist! Sot, you Cherokee!" screams out Mr. William. "Jump out of bed, and I'll drive my sword through your body. Why didn't I do it to-day when I took you for a bailiff—a confounded pettifogging bum-bailiff!" And he went on screeching more oaths and incoherencies, until the landlord, the drawer, the hostler, and all the folks of the kitchen were brought to lead him away. After which Harry Warrington closed his tent round him in sulky wrath, and, no doubt, finally went fast to sleep.

My landlord was very much more obsequious on the next morning when he met his young guest, having now fully learned his name and quality. Other messengers had come from the castle on the previous night to bring both the young gentlemen home, and poor Mr. William, it appeared, had returned in a wheelbarrow, being not altogether unaccustomed to that mode of conveyance. "He never remembers nothin' about it the next day. He is of a real kind nature, Mr. William," the landlord vowed, "and the men get crowns and half-crowns from him by saying that he beat them overnight when he was in liquor. He's the devil when he's tipsy, Mr. William, but when he is sober he is the very kindest of young gentlemen."

As nothing is unknown to writers of biographies of the present kind, it may be as well to state what had occurred within the walls of Castlewood House, whilst Harry Warrington was without, awaiting some token of recognition from his kinsmen. On their arrival at home the family had found the paper on which the lad's name was inscribed, and his appearance occasioned a little domestic council. My Lord Castlewood supposed that must have been the young gentleman whom they had seen on the bridge, and as they had not drowned him they must invite him. Let a man go down with the proper messages, let a servant carry a note. Lady Fanny thought it would be more civil if one of the brothers would go to their kinsman, especially considering the original greeting which they had given. Lord Castlewood had not the slightest objection to his brother William going—yes, William should go. Upon this Mr. William said (with a yet stronger expression) that he would be hanged if he would go. Lady Maria thought the young gentleman whom they had remarked at the bridge was a pretty fellow enough. Castlewood is dreadfully dull, I am sure neither of my brothers do anything to make it amusing. He may be vulgar—no doubt, he is vulgar—but let us see the American. Such was Lady Maria's opinion. Lady Castlewood was neither for inviting nor for refusing him, but for delaying. "Wait till your aunt comes, children; perhaps the Baroness won't like to see the young man; at least, let us consult her before we ask him." And so the hospitality to be offered by his nearest kinsfolk to poor Harry Warrington remained yet in abeyance.

At length the equipage of the Baroness Bernstein made its appearance, and whatever doubt there might be as to the reception of the Virginian stranger, there was no lack of enthusiasm in this generous family regarding their wealthy and powerful kinswoman. The state-chamber had already been prepared for her. The cook had arrived the previous day with instructions to get ready a supper for her such as her ladyship liked. The table sparkled with old plate, and was set in the oak dining-room with the pictures of the family round the walls. There was the late Viscount, his father, his mother, his sister —these two lovely pictures. There was his predecessor by Vandyck, and his Viscountess. There was Colonel Esmond, their relative in Virginia, about whose grandson the ladies and gentlemen of the Esmond family showed such a very moderate degree of sympathy.

The feast set before their aunt, the Baroness, was a very good one, and her ladyship enjoyed it. The supper occupied an hour or two, during which the whole Castlewood family were most attentive to their guest. The Countess pressed all the good dishes upon her, of which she freely partook: the butler no sooner saw her glass empty than he filled it with champagne: the young folks and their mother kept up the conversation, not so much by talking, as by listening appropriately to their friend. She was full of spirits and humour. She seemed to know everybody in Europe, and about those everybodies the wickedest stories. The Countess of Castlewood, ordinarily a very demure, severe woman, and a stickler for the proprieties, smiled at the very worst of these anecdotes; the girls looked at one another and laughed at the maternal signal; the boys giggled and roared with especial delight at their sisters' confusion. They also partook freely of the wine which the butler handed round, nor did they, or their guest, disdain the bowl of smoking punch, which was laid on the table after the supper. Many and many a night, the Baroness said, she had drunk at that table by her father's side. "That was his place," she pointed to the place where the Countess now sat. She saw none of the old plate. That was all melted to pay his gambling debts. She hoped, "Young gentlemen, that you don't play."

"Never, on my word," says Castlewood.

"Never, 'pon honour," says Will—winking at his brother.

The Baroness was very glad to hear they were such good boys. Her face grew redder with the punch; and she became voluble, might have been thought coarse, but that times were different, and those critics were inclined to be especially favourable.

She talked to the boys about their father, their grandfather—other men and women of the house. "The only man of the family was that," she said, pointing (with an arm that was yet beautifully round and white) towards the picture of the military gentleman in the red coat and cuirass, and great black periwig.

"The Virginian? What is he good for? I always thought he was good for nothing but to cultivate tobacco and my grandmother," says my lord, laughing.

She struck her hand upon the table with an energy that made the glasses dance. "I say he was the best of you all. There never was one of the male Esmonds that had more brains than a goose, except him. He was not fit for this wicked, selfish old world of ours, and he was right to go and live out of it. Where would your father have been, young people, but for him?"

"Was he particularly kind to our papa?" says Lady Maria.

"Old stories, my dear Maria!" cries the Countess. "I am sure my dear Earl was very kind to him in giving him that great estate in Virginia."

"Since his brother's death, the lad who has been here to-day is heir to that. Mr. Draper told me so! Peste! I don't know why my father gave up such a property."

"Who has been here to-day?" asked the Baroness, highly excited.

"Harry Esmond Warrington, of Virginia," my lord answered: "a lad whom Will nearly pitched into the river, and whom I pressed my lady the Countess to invite to stay here."

"You mean that one of the Virginian boys has been to Castlewood, and has not been asked to stay here?"

"There is but one of them, my dear creature," interposes the Earl. "The other, you know, has just been——"

"For shame, for shame!"

"Oh! it ain't pleasant, I confess, to be se——"

"Do you mean that a grandson of Henry Esmond, the master of this house, has been here, and none of you have offered him hospitality?"

"Since we didn't know it, and he is staying at the Castles?" interposes Will.

"That he is staying at the Inn, and you are sitting there!" cries the old lady. "This is too bad—call somebody to me. Get me my hood—I'll go to the boy myself. Come with me this instant, my Lord Castlewood."

The young man rose up, evidently in wrath. "Madame the Baroness of Bernstein," he said, "your ladyship is welcome to go; but as for me, I don't choose to have such words as 'shameful' applied to my conduct. I won't go and fetch the young gentleman from Virginia, and I propose to sit here and finish this bowl of punch. Eugene! Don't Eugene me, madam. I know her ladyship has a great deal of money, which you are desirous should remain in our amiable family. You want it more than I do. Cringe for it—I won't." And he sank back in his chair.

The Baroness looked at the family, who held their heads down, and then at my lord, but this time without any dislike. She leaned over to him and said rapidly in German, "I had unright when I said the Colonel was the only man of the family. Thou canst, if thou willest, Eugene." To which remark my lord only bowed.

"If you do not wish an old woman to go out at this hour of the night, let William, at least, go and fetch his cousin," said the Baroness.

"The very thing I proposed to him."

"And so did we—and so did we!" cried the daughters in a breath.

"I am sure, I only wanted the dear Baroness's consent!" said their mother, "and shall be charmed for my part to welcome our young relative."

"Will! Put on thy pattens and get a lantern, and go fetch the Virginian," said my lord.

"And we will have another bowl of punch when he comes," says William, who by this time had already had too much. And he went forth—how we have seen; and how he had more punch; and how ill he succeeded in his embassy.

The worthy lady of Castlewood, as she caught sight of young Harry Warrington by the river-side, must have seen a very handsome and interesting youth, and very likely had reasons of her own for not desiring his presence in her family. All mothers are not eager to encourage the visits of interesting youths of nineteen in families where there are virgins of twenty. If Harry's acres had been in Norfolk or Devon, in place of Virginia, no doubt the good Countess would have been rather more eager in her welcome. Had she wanted him she would have given him her hand readily enough. If our people of ton are selfish, at any rate they show they are selfish; and, being cold-hearted, at least have no hypocrisy of affection.

Why should Lady Castlewood put herself out of the way to welcome the young stranger? Because he was friendless? Only a simpleton could ever imagine such a reason as that. People of fashion, like her ladyship, are friendly to those who have plenty of friends. A poor lad, alone, from a distant country, with only very moderate means, and those not as yet in his own power, with uncouth manners very likely, and coarse provincial habits; was a great lady called upon to put herself out of the way for such a youth? Allons donc! He was quite as well at the alehouse as at the castle.

This, no doubt, was her ladyship's opinion, which her kinswoman, the Baroness Bernstein, who knew her perfectly well, entirely understood. The Baroness, too, was a woman of the world, and, possibly, on occasion, could be as selfish as any other person of fashion. She fully understood the cause of the deference which all the Castlewood family showed to her—mother, and daughter, and sons,—and being a woman of great humour, played upon the dispositions of the various members of this family, amused herself with their greedinesses, their humiliations, their artless respect for her money-box, and clinging attachment to her purse. They were not very rich; Lady Castlewood's own money was settled on her children. The two elder had inherited nothing but flaxen heads from their German mother, and a pedigree of prodigious distinction. But those who had money, and those who had none, were alike eager for the Baroness's; in this matter the rich are surely quite as greedy as the poor.

So if Madam Bernstein struck her hand on the table, and caused the glasses and the persons round it to tremble at her wrath, it was because she was excited with plenty of punch and champagne, which her ladyship was in the habit of taking freely, and because she may have had a generous impulse when generous wine warmed her blood, and felt indignant as she thought of the poor lad yonder, sitting friendless and lonely on the outside of his ancestors' door; not because she was specially angry with her relatives, who she knew would act precisely as they had done.

The exhibition of their selfishness and humiliation alike amused her, as did Castlewood's act of revolt. He was as selfish as the rest of the family, but not so mean; and, as he candidly stated, he could afford the luxury of a little independence, having tolerable estate to fall back upon.

Madam Bernstein was an early woman, restless, resolute, extraordinarily active for her age. She was up long before the languid Castlewood ladies (just home from their London routs and balls) had quitted their feather-beds, or jolly Will had slept off his various potations of punch. She was up, and pacing the green terraces that sparkled with the sweet morning dew, which lay twinkling, also, on a flowery wilderness of trim parterres, and on the crisp walls of the dark box hedges, under which marble fauns and dryads were cooling themselves, whilst a thousand birds sang, the fountains plashed and glittered in the rosy morning sunshine, and the rooks cawed from the great wood.

Had the well-remembered scene (for she had visited it often in childhood) a freshness and charm for her? Did it recall days of innocence and happiness, and did its calm beauty soothe or please, or awaken remorse in her heart? Her manner was more than ordinarily affectionate and gentle, when, presently, after pacing the walks for a half-hour, the person for whom she was waiting came to her. This was our young Virginian, to whom she had despatched an early billet by one of the Lockwoods. The note was signed B. Bernstein, and informed Mr. Esmond Warrington that his relatives at Castlewood, and among them a dear friend of his grandfather, were most anxious that he should come to "Colonel Esmond's house in England." And now, accordingly, the lad made his appearance, passing under the old Gothic doorway, tripping down the steps from one garden terrace to another, hat in hand, his fair hair blowing from his flushed cheeks, his slim figure clad in mourning. The handsome and modest looks, the comely face and person, of the young lad pleased the lady. He made her a low bow which would have done credit to Versailles. She held out a little hand to him, and, as his own palm closed over it, she laid the other hand softly on his ruffle. She looked very kindly and affectionately in the honest blushing face.

"I knew your grandfather very well, Harry," she said. "So you came yesterday to see his picture, and they turned you away, though you know the house was his of right?"

Harry blushed very red. "The servants did not know me. A young gentleman came to me last night," he said, "when I was peevish, and he, I fear, was tipsy. I spoke rudely to my cousin, and would ask his pardon. Your ladyship knows that in Virginia our manners towards strangers are different. I own I had expected another kind of welcome. Was it you, madam, who sent my cousin to me last night?"

"I sent him; but you will find your cousins most friendly to you to-day. You must stay here. Lord Castlewood would have been with you this morning, only I was so eager to see you. There will be breakfast in an hour; and meantime you must talk to me. We will send to the Three Castles for your servant and your baggage. Give me your arm. Stop, I dropped my cane when you came. You shall be my cane."

"My grandfather used to call us his crutches," said Harry.

"You are like him, though you are fair."

"You should have seen—you should have seen George," said the boy, and his honest eyes welled with tears. The recollection of his brother, the bitter pain of yesterday's humiliation, the affectionateness of the present greeting—all, perhaps, contributed to soften the lad's heart. He felt very tenderly and gratefully towards the lady who had received him so warmly. He was utterly alone and miserable a minute since, and here was a home and a kind hand held out to him. No wonder he clung to it. In the hour during which they talked together, the young fellow had poured out a great deal of his honest heart to the kind new-found friend; when the dial told breakfast-time, he wondered to think how much he had told her. She took him to the breakfast-room; she presented him to his aunt, the Countess, and bade him embrace his cousins. Lord Castlewood was frank and gracious enough. Honest Will had a headache, but was utterly unconscious of the proceedings of the past night. The ladies were very pleasant and polite, as ladies of their fashion know how to be. How should Harry Warrington, a simple truth-telling lad from a distant colony, who had only yesterday put his foot upon English shore, know that my ladies, so smiling and easy in demeanour, were furious against him, and aghast at the favour with which Madam Bernstein seemed to regard him?

She was folle of him, talked of no one else, scarce noticed the Castlewood young people, trotted with him over the house, and told him all its story, showed him the little room in the courtyard where his grandfather used to sleep, and a cunning cupboard over the fireplace which had been made in the time of the Catholic persecutions; drove out with him in the neighbouring country, and pointed out to him the most remarkable sites and houses, and had in return the whole of the young man's story.

This brief biography the kind reader will please to accept, not in the precise words in which Mr. Harry Warrington delivered it to Madam Bernstein, but in the form in which it has been cast in the Chapters next ensuing.

CHAPTER III. The Esmonds in Virginia

Henry Esmond, Esq., an office who had served with the rank of Colonel during the wars of Queen Anne's reign, found himself, at its close, compromised in certain attempts for the restoration of the Queen's family to the throne of these realms. Happily for itself, the nation preferred another dynasty; but some of the few opponents of the house of Hanover took refuge out of the three kingdoms, and amongst others, Colonel Esmond was counselled by his friends to go abroad. As Mr. Esmond sincerely regretted the part which he had taken, and as the august Prince who came to rule over England was the most pacable of sovereigns, in a very little time the Colonel's friends found means to make his peace.

Mr. Esmond, it has been said, belonged to the noble English family which takes its title from Castlewood, in the county of Hants; and it was pretty generally known that King James II. and his son had offered the title of

Marquis to Colonel Esmond and his father, and that the former might have assumed the (Irish) peerage hereditary in his family, but for an informality which he did not choose to set right. Tired of the political struggles in which he had been engaged, and annoyed by family circumstances in Europe, he preferred to establish himself in Virginia, where he took possession of a large estate conferred by King Charles I. upon his ancestor. Here Mr. Esmond's daughter and grandsons were born, and his wife died. This lady, when she married him, was the widow of the Colonel's kinsman, the unlucky Viscount Castlewood, killed in a duel by Lord Mohun, at the close of King William's reign.

Mr. Esmond called his American house Castlewood, from the patrimonial home in the old country. The whole usages of Virginia, indeed, were fondly modelled after the English customs. It was a loyal colony. The Virginians boasted that King Charles II. had been king in Virginia before he had been king in England. English king and English church were alike faithfully honoured there. The resident gentry were allied to good English families. They held their heads above the Dutch traders of New York, and the money-getting Roundheads of Pennsylvania and New England. Never were people less republican than those of the great province which was soon to be foremost in the memorable revolt against the British Crown.

The gentry of Virginia dwelt on their great lands after a fashion almost patriarchal. For its rough cultivation, each estate had a multitude of hands—of purchased and assigned servants—who were subject to the command of the master. The land yielded their food, live stock, and game. The great rivers swarmed with fish for the taking. From their banks the passage home was clear. Their ships took the tobacco off their private wharves on the banks of the Potomac or the James river, and carried it to London or Bristol,—bringing back English goods and articles of home manufacture in return for the only produce which the Virginian gentry chose to cultivate. Their hospitality was boundless. No stranger was ever sent away from their gates. The gentry received one another, and travelled to each other's houses, in a state almost feudal. The question of Slavery was not born at the time of which we write. To be the proprietor of black servants shocked the feelings of no Virginian gentleman; nor, in truth, was the despotism exercised over the negro race generally a savage one. The food was plenty; the poor black people lazy and not unhappy. You might have preached negro emancipation to Madam Esmond of Castlewood as you might have told her to let the horses run loose out of her stables; she had no doubt but that the whip and the corn-bag were good for both.

Her father may have thought otherwise, being of a sceptical turn on very many points, but his doubts did not break forth in active denial, and he was rather disaffected than rebellious. At one period, this gentleman had taken a part in active life at home, and possibly might have been eager to share its rewards; but in latter days he did not seem to care for them. A something had occurred in his life, which had cast a tinge of melancholy over all his existence. He was not unhappy—to those about him most kind—most affectionate, obsequious even to the women of his family, whom be scarce ever contradicted; but there had been some bankruptcy of his heart, which his spirit never recovered. He submitted to life, rather than enjoyed it, and never was in better spirits than in his last hours when he was going to lay it down.

Having lost his wife, his daughter took the management of the Colonel and his affairs; and he gave them up to her charge with an entire acquiescence. So that he had his books and his quiet, he cared for no more. When company came to Castlewood, he entertained them handsomely, and was of a very pleasant, sarcastical turn. He was not in the least sorry when they went away.

"My love, I shall not be sorry to go myself," he said to his daughter, "and you, though the most affectionate of daughters, will console yourself after a while. Why should I, who am so old, be romantic? You may, who are still a young creature." This he said, not meaning all he said, for the lady whom he addressed was a matter-of-fact little person, with very little romance in her nature.

After fifteen years' residence upon his great Virginian estate, affairs prospered so well with the worthy proprietor, that he acquiesced in his daughter's plans for the building of a mansion much grander and more durable than the plain wooden edifice in which he had been content to live, so that his heirs might have a habitation worthy of their noble name. Several of Madam Warrington's neighbours had built handsome houses for themselves; perhaps it was her ambition to take rank in the country, which inspired this desire for improved quarters. Colonel Esmond, of Castlewood, neither cared for quarters nor for quarterings. But his daughter had a very high opinion of the merit and antiquity of her lineage; and her sire, growing exquisitely calm and good-natured in his serene, declining years, humoured his child's peculiarities in an easy, bantering way,—nay, helped her with his antiquarian learning, which was not inconsiderable, and with his skill in the art of painting, of which he was a proficient. A knowledge of heraldry, a hundred years ago, formed part of the education of most noble ladies and gentlemen: during her visit to Europe, Miss Esmond had eagerly studied the family history and pedigrees, and returned thence to Virginia with a store of documents relative to her family on which she relied with implicit gravity and credence, and with the most edifying volumes then published in France and England, respecting the noble science. These works proved, to her perfect satisfaction, not only that the Esmonds were descended from noble Norman warriors, who came into England along with their victorious chief, but from native English of royal dignity: and two magnificent heraldic trees, cunningly painted by the hand of the Colonel, represented the family springing from the Emperor Charlemagne on the one hand, who was drawn in plate-armour, with his imperial mantle and diadem, and on the other from Queen Boadicea, whom the Colonel insisted upon painting in the light costume of an ancient British queen, with a prodigious gilded crown, a trifling mantle of furs, and a lovely symmetrical person, tastefully tattooed with figures of a brilliant blue tint. From these two illustrious stocks the family-tree rose until it united in the thirteenth century somewhere in the person of the fortunate Esmond who claimed to spring from both.

Of the Warrington family, into which she married, good Madam Rachel thought but little. She wrote herself Esmond Warrington, but was universally called Madam Esmond of Castlewood, when after her father's decease she came to rule over that domain. It is even to be feared that quarrels for precedence in the colonial society occasionally disturbed her temper; for though her father had had a marquis's patent from King James, which he had burned and disowned, she would frequently act as if that document existed and was in full force. She considered the English Esmonds of an inferior dignity to her own branch; and as for the colonial aristocracy, she made no scruple of asserting her superiority over the whole body of them. Hence quarrels and angry words, and even a scuffle or two, as we gather from her notes, at the Governor's assemblies at Jamestown. Wherefore recall the memory of these squabbles? Are not the persons who engaged in them beyond the reach of quarrels now, and has not the republic put an end to these social inequalities? Ere the establishment of Independence, there was no more aristocratic country in the world than Virginia; so the Virginians, whose history we have to narrate, were bred to have the fullest respect for the institutions of home, and the rightful king had not two more faithful little subjects than the young twins of Castlewood.

When the boys' grandfather died, their mother, in great state, proclaimed her eldest son George her successor and heir of the estate; and Harry, George's younger brother by half an hour, was always enjoined to respect his senior. All the household was equally instructed to pay him honour; the negroes, of whom there was a large and happy family, and the assigned servants from Europe, whose lot was made as bearable as it might be under the government of the lady of Castlewood. In the whole family there scarcely was a rebel save Mrs. Esmond's faithful friend and companion, Madam Mountain, and Harry's foster-mother, a faithful negro woman, who never could be made to understand why her child should not be first, who was handsomer, and stronger, and cleverer than his brother, as she vowed; though, in truth, there was scarcely any difference in the beauty, strength, or stature of the twins. In disposition, they were in many points exceedingly unlike; but in feature they resembled each other so closely, that but for the colour of their hair it had been difficult to distinguish them. In their beds, and when their heads were covered with those vast ribboned nightcaps which our great and little ancestors wore, it was scarcely possible for any but a nurse or mother to tell the one from the other child.

Howbeit alike in form, we have said that they differed in temper. The elder was peaceful, studious, and silent; the younger was warlike and noisy. He was quick at learning when he began, but very slow at beginning. No threats of the ferule would provoke Harry to learn in an idle fit, or would prevent George from helping his brother in his lesson. Harry was of a strong military turn, drilled the little negroes on the estate and caned them like a corporal, having many good boxing-matches with them, and never bearing malice if he was worsted;—whereas George was sparing of blows and gentle with all about him. As the custom in all families was, each of the boys had a special little servant assigned him; and it was a known fact that George, finding his little wretch of a blackamoor asleep on his master's bed, sat down beside it and brushed the flies off the child with a feather fan, to the horror of old Gumbo, the child's father, who found his young master so engaged, and to the indignation of Madam Esmond, who ordered the young negro off to the proper officer for a whipping. In vain George implored and entreated—burst into passionate tears, and besought a remission of the sentence. His mother was inflexible regarding the young rebel's punishment, and the little negro went off beseeching his young master not to cry.

A fierce quarrel between mother and son ensued out of this event. Her son would not be pacified. He said the punishment was a shame—a shame; that he was the master of the boy, and no one—no, not his mother,—had a right to touch him; that she might order him to be corrected, and that he would suffer the punishment, as he and Harry often had, but no one should lay a hand on his boy. Trembling with passionate rebellion against what he conceived the injustice of procedure, he vowed—actually shrieking out an oath, which shocked his fond mother and governor, who never before heard such language from the usually gentle child—that on the day he came of age he would set young Gumbo free—went to visit the child in the slaves' quarters, and gave him one of his own toys.

The young black martyr was an impudent, lazy, saucy little personage, who would be none the worse for a whipping, as the Colonel no doubt thought; for he acquiesced in the child's punishment when Madam Esmond insisted upon it, and only laughed in his good-natured way when his indignant grandson called out,

"You let mamma rule you in everything, grandpapa."

"Why, so I do," says grandpapa. "Rachel, my love, the way in which I am petticoat-ridden is so evident that even this baby has found it out."

"Then why don't you stand up like a man?" says little Harry', who always was ready to abet his brother.

Grandpapa looked queerly.

"Because I like sitting down best, my dear," he said. "I am an old gentleman, and standing fatigues me."

On account of a certain apish drollery and humour which exhibited itself in the lad, and a liking for some of the old man's pursuits, the first of the twins was the grandfather's favourite and companion, and would laugh and talk out all his infantine heart to the old gentleman, to whom the younger had seldom a word to say. George was a demure studious boy, and his senses seemed to brighten up in the library, where his brother was so gloomy. He knew the books before he could well-nigh carry them, and read in them long before he could understand them. Harry, on the other hand, was all alive in the stables or in the wood, eager for all parties of hunting and fishing, and promised to be a good sportsman from a very early age. Their grandfather's ship was sailing for Europe once when the boys were children, and they were asked, what present Captain Franks should bring them back? George was divided between books and a fiddle; Harry instantly declared for a little gun: and Madam Warrington (as she then was called) was hurt that her elder boy should have low tastes, and applauded the younger's choice as more worthy of his name and lineage. "Books, papa, I can fancy to be a good choice," she replied to her father, who tried to convince her that George had a right to his opinion, "though I am sure you must have pretty nigh all the books in the world already. But I never can desire—I may be wrong, but I never can desire—that my son, and the grandson of the Marquis of Esmond, should be a fiddler."

"Should be a fiddlestick, my dear," the old Colonel answered.

"Remember that Heaven's ways are not ours, and that each creature born has a little kingdom of thought of his own, which it is a sin in us to invade. Suppose George loves music? You can no more stop him than you can order a rose not to smell sweet, or a bird not to sing."

"A bird! A bird sings from nature; George did not come into the world with a fiddle in his hand," says Mrs. Warrington, with a toss of her head. "I am sure I hated the harpsichord when a chit at Kensington School, and only learned it to please my mamma. Say what you will, dear sir, I can not believe that this fiddling is work for persons of fashion."

"And King David who played the harp, my dear?"

"I wish my papa would read him more, and not speak about him in that way," said Mrs. Warrington.

"Nay, my dear, it was but by way of illustration," the father replied gently. It was Colonel Esmond's nature, as he has owned in his own biography, always to be led by a woman; and, his wife dead, he coaxed and dandled and spoiled his daughter; laughing at her caprices, but humouring them; making a joke of her prejudices, but letting them have their way; indulging, and perhaps increasing, her natural imperiousness of character, though it was his maxim that we can't change dispositions by meddling, and only make hypocrites of our children by commanding them over-much.

At length the time came when Mr. Esmond was to have done with the affairs of this life, and he laid them down as if glad to be rid of their burthen. We must not ring in an opening history with tolling bells, or preface it with a funeral sermon. All who read and heard that discourse, wondered where Parson Broadbent of Jamestown found the eloquence and the Latin which adorned it. Perhaps Mr. Dempster knew, the boys' Scotch tutor, who corrected the proofs of the oration, which was printed, by desire of his Excellency and many persons of honour, at Mr. Franklin's press in Philadelphia. No such sumptuous funeral had ever been seen in the country as that which Madam Esmond Warrington ordained for her father, who would have been the first to smile at that pompous grief. The little lads of Castlewood, almost smothered in black trains and hatbands, headed the procession, and were followed by my Lord Fairfax from Greenway Court, by his Excellency the Governor of Virginia (with his coach), by the Randolphs, the Careys, the Harrisons, the Washingtons, and many others, for the whole county esteemed the departed gentleman, whose goodness, whose high talents, whose benevolence and unobtrusive urbanity had earned for him the just respect of his neighbours. When informed of the event, the family of Colonel Esmond's stepson, the Lord Castlewood of Hampshire in England, asked to be at the charges of the marble slab which recorded the names and virtues of his lordship's mother and her husband; and after due time of preparation, the monument was set up, exhibiting the arms and coronet of the Esmonds, supported by a little chubby group of weeping cherubs, and reciting an epitaph which for once did not tell any falsehoods.

CHAPTER IV. In which Harry finds a New Relative

Kind friends, neighbours hospitable, cordial, even respectful,—an ancient name, a large estate and a sufficient fortune, a comfortable home, supplied with all the necessaries and many of the luxuries of life, and a troop of servants, black and white, eager to do your bidding; good health, affectionate children, and, let us humbly add, a good cook, cellar, and library—ought not a person in the possession of all these benefits to be considered very decently happy? Madam Esmond Warrington possessed all these causes for happiness; she reminded herself of them daily in her morning and evening prayers. She was scrupulous in her devotions, good to the poor, never knowingly did anybody a wrong. Yonder I fancy her enthroned in her principality of Castlewood, the country gentlefolks paying her court, the sons dutiful to her, the domestics tumbling over each other's black heels to do her bidding, the poor whites grateful for her bounty and implicitly taking her doses when they were ill, the smaller gentry always acquiescing in her remarks, and for ever letting her win at backgammon—well, with all these benefits, which are more sure than fate allots to most mortals, I don't think the little Princess Pocahontas, as she was called, was to be envied in the midst of her dominions. The Princess's husband, who was cut off in early life, was as well perhaps out of the way. Had he survived his marriage by many years, they would have quarrelled fiercely, or, he would infallibly have been a henpecked husband, of which sort there were a few specimens still extant a hundred years ago. The truth is, little Madam Esmond never came near man or woman, but she tried to domineer over them. If people obeyed, she was their very good friend; if they resisted, she fought and fought until she or they gave in. We are all miserable sinners that's a fact we acknowledge in public every Sunday—no one announced it in a more clear resolute voice than the little lady. As a mortal, she may have been in the wrong, of course; only she very seldom acknowledged the circumstance to herself, and to others never. Her father, in his old age, used to watch her freaks of despotism, haughtiness, and stubbornness, and amuse himself with them. She felt that his eye was upon her; his humour, of which quality she possessed little herself, subdued and bewildered her. But, the Colonel gone, there was nobody else whom she was disposed to obey,—and so I am rather glad for my part that I did not live a hundred years ago at Castlewood in Westmorland County in Virginia. I fancy, one would not have been too happy there. Happy, who is happy? Was not there a serpent in Paradise itself? and if Eve had been perfectly happy beforehand, would she have listened to him?

The management of the house of Castlewood had been in the hands of the active little lady long before the Colonel slept the sleep of the just. She now exercised a rigid supervision over the estate; dismissed Colonel Esmond's English factor and employed a new one; built, improved, planted, grew tobacco, appointed a new overseer, and imported a new tutor. Much as she loved her father, there were some of his maxims by which she was not inclined to abide. Had she not obeyed her papa and mamma during all their lives, as a dutiful daughter should? So ought all children to obey their parents, that their days might be long in the land. The little Queen domineered over her little dominion, and the Princes her sons were only her first subjects. Ere long she discontinued her husband's name of Warrington and went by the name of Madam Esmond in the country. Her family pretensions were known there. She had no objection to talk of the Marquis's title which King James had given to her father and grandfather. Her papa's enormous magnanimity might induce him to give up his titles and rank to the younger branch of the family, and to her half-brother, my Lord Castlewood and his children; but she and her sons were of the elder branch of the Esmonds, and she expected that they should be treated accordingly. Lord Fairfax was the only gentleman in the colony of Virginia to whom she would allow precedence over her. She insisted on the pas before all Lieutenant-Governors' and Judges' ladies; before the wife of the Governor of a colony she would, of course, yield as to the representative of the Sovereign. Accounts are extant, in the family papers and letters, of one or two tremendous battles which Madam fought with the wives of colonial dignitaries upon these questions of etiquette. As for her husband's family of Warrington, they were as naught in her eyes. She married an English baronet's younger son out of Norfolk to please her parents, whom she was always bound to obey. At the early age at which she married—a chit out of a boarding-school—she would have jumped overboard if her papa had ordered. "And that is always the way with the Esmonds," she said.

The English Warringtons were not over-much flattered by the little American Princess's behaviour to them, and her manner of speaking about them. Once a year a solemn letter used to be addressed to the Warrington family, and to her noble kinsmen the Hampshire Esmonds; but a Judge's lady with whom Madam Esmond had quarrelled returning to England out of Virginia chanced to meet Lady Warrington, who was in London with Sir Miles attending Parliament, and this person repeated some of the speeches which the Princess Pocahontas was in the habit of making regarding her own and her husband's English relatives, and my Lady Warrington, I suppose, carried the story to my Lady Castlewood; after which the letters from Virginia were not answered, to the surprise and wrath of Madam Esmond, who speedily left off writing also.

So this good woman fell out with her neighbours, with her relatives, and, as it must be owned, with her sons also.

A very early difference which occurred between the Queen and Crown Prince arose out of the dismissal of Mr. Dempster, the lad's tutor and the late Colonel's secretary. In her father's life Madam Esmond bore him with difficulty, or it should be rather said Mr. Dempster could scarce put up with her. She was jealous of books somehow, and thought your bookworms dangerous folks, insinuating bad principles. She had heard that Dempster was a Jesuit in disguise, and the poor fellow was obliged to go build himself a cabin in a clearing, and teach school and practise medicine where he could find customers among the sparse inhabitants of the province. Master George vowed he never would forsake his old tutor, and kept his promise. Harry had always loved fishing and sporting better than books, and he and the poor Dominie had never been on terms of close intimacy. Another cause of dispute presently ensued.

By the death of an aunt, and at his father's demise, the heir of Mr. George Warrington became entitled to a sum of six thousand pounds, of which their mother was one of the trustees. She never could be made to understand that she was not the proprietor, and not merely the trustee of this money; and was furious with the London lawyer, the other trustee, who refused to send it over at her order. "Is not all I have my sons'?" she cried, "and would I not cut myself into little pieces to serve them? With the six thousand pounds I would have bought Mr. Boulter's estate and negroes, which would have given us a good thousand pounds a year, and made a handsome provision for my Harry." Her young friend and neighbour, Mr. Washington of Mount Vernon, could not convince her that the London agent was right, and must not give up his trust except to those for whom he held it. Madam Esmond gave the London lawyer a piece of her mind, and, I am sorry to say, informed Mr. Draper that he was an insolent pettifogger, and deserved to be punished for doubting the honour of a mother and an Esmond. It must be owned that the Virginian Princess had a temper of her own.

George Esmond, her firstborn, when this little matter was referred to him, and his mother vehemently insisted that he should declare himself, was of the opinion of Mr. Washington, and Mr. Draper, the London lawyer. The boy said he could not help himself. He did not want the money: he would be very glad to think otherwise, and to give the money to his mother, if he had the power. But Madam Esmond would not hear any of these reasons. Feelings were her reasons. Here was a chance of making Harry's fortune—dear Harry, who was left with such a slender younger brother's; pittance—and the wretches in London would not help him; his own brother, who inherited all her papa's estate, would not help him. To think of a child of hers being so mean at fourteen year of age! etc. etc. Add tears, scorn, frequent innuendo, long estrangement, bitter outbreak, passionate appeals to Heaven, and the like, and we may fancy the widow's state of mind. Are there not beloved beings of the gentler sex who argue in the same way nowadays? The book of female logic is blotted all over with tears, and Justice in their courts is for ever in a passion.

This occurrence set the widow resolutely saving for her younger son, for whom, as in duty bound, she was eager to make a portion. The fine buildings were stopped which the Colonel had commenced at Castlewood, who had freighted ships from New York with Dutch bricks, and imported, at great charges, mantelpieces, carved cornice-work, sashes and glass, carpets and costly upholstery from home. No more books were bought. The agent had orders to discontinue sending wine. Madam Esmond deeply regretted the expense of a fine carriage which she had had from England, and only rode in it to church groaning in spirit, and crying to the sons opposite her, "Harry, Harry! I wish I had put by the money for thee, my poor portionless child—three hundred and eighty guineas of ready money to Messieurs Hatchett!"

"You will give me plenty while you live, and George will give me plenty when you die," says Harry, gaily.

"Not unless he changes in spirit, my dear," says the lady, with a grim glance at her elder boy. "Not unless Heaven softens his heart and teaches him charity, for which I pray day and night; as Mountain knows; do you not, Mountain?"

Mrs. Mountain, Ensign Mountain's widow, Madam Esmond's companion and manager, who took the fourth seat in the family coach on these Sundays, said, "Humph! I know you are always disturbing yourself and crying out about this legacy, and I don't see that there is any need."

"Oh no! no need!" cries the widow, rustling in her silks; "of course I have no need to be disturbed, because my eldest born is a disobedient son and an unkind brother—because he has an estate, and my poor Harry, bless him, but a mess of pottage."

George looked despairingly at his mother until he could see her no more for eyes welled up with tears. "I wish you would bless me, too, O my mother!" he said, and burst into a passionate fit of weeping. Harry's arms were in a moment round his brother's neck, and he kissed George a score of times.

"Never mind, George. I know whether you are a good brother or not. Don't mind what she says. She don't mean it."

"I do mean it, child," cries the mother. "Would to Heaven——"

"HOLD YOUR TONGUE, I SAY" roars out Harry. "It's a shame to speak so to him, ma'am."

"And so it is, Harry," says Mrs. Mountain, shaking his hand. "You never said a truer word in your life."

"Mrs. Mountain, do you dare to set my children against me?" cries the widow. "From this very day, madam——"

"Turn me and my child into the street? Do," says Mrs. Mountain. "That will be a fine revenge because the English lawyer won't give you the boy's money.

Find another companion who will tell you black is white, and flatter you: it is not my way, madam. When shall I go? I shan't be long a-packing. I did not bring much into Castlewood House, and I shall not take much out."

"Hush! the bells are ringing for church, Mountain. Let us try, if you please, and compose ourselves," said the widow, and she looked with eyes of extreme affection, certainly at one—perhaps at both—of her children. George kept his head down, and Harry, who was near, got quite close to him during the sermon, and sat with his arm round his brother's neck.

Harry had proceeded in his narrative after his own fashion, interspersing it with many youthful ejaculations, and answering a number of incidental questions asked by his listener. The old lady seemed never tired of hearing him. Her amiable hostess and her daughters came more than once, to ask if she would ride, or walk, or take a dish of tea, or play a game at cards; but all these amusements Madam Bernstein declined, saying that she found infinite amusement in Harry's conversation. Especially when any of the Castlewood family were present, she redoubled her caresses, insisted upon the lad speaking close to her ear, and would call out to the others, "Hush, my dears! I can't hear our cousin speak." And they would quit the room, striving still to look pleased.

"Are you my cousin, too?" asked the honest boy. "You see kinder than my other cousins."

Their talk took place in the wainscoted parlour, where the family had taken their meals in ordinary for at least two centuries past, and which, as we have said, was hung with portraits of the race. Over Madam Bernstein's great chair was a Kneller, one of the most brilliant pictures of the gallery, representing a young lady of three or four and twenty, in the easy flowing dress and loose robes of Queen Anne's time—a hand on a cushion near her, a quantity of auburn hair parted off a fair forehead, and flowing over pearly shoulders and a lovely neck. Under this sprightly picture the lady sate with her knitting-needles.

When Harry asked, "Are you my cousin, too?" she said, "That picture is by Sir Godfrey, who thought himself the greatest painter in the world. But he was not so good as Lely, who painted your grandmother—my—my Lady Castlewood, Colonel Esmond's wife; nor he so good as Sir Anthony Van Dyck, who painted your great-grandfather, yonder—and who looks, Harry, a much finer gentleman than he was. Some of us are painted blacker than we are. Did you recognise your grandmother in that picture? She had the loveliest fair hair and shape of any woman of her time."

"I fancied I knew the portrait from instinct, perhaps, and a certain likeness to my mother."

"Did Mrs. Warrington—I beg her pardon, I think she calls herself Madam or my Lady Esmond now———?"

"They call my mother so in our province," said the boy.

"Did she never tell you of another daughter her mother had in England, before she married your grandfather?"

"She never spoke of one."

"Nor your grandfather?"

"Never. But in his picture-books, which he constantly made for us children, he used to draw a head very like that above your ladyship. That, and Viscount Francis, and King James III., he drew a score of times, I am sure."

"And the picture over me reminds you of no one, Harry?"

"No, indeed."

"Ah! Here is a sermon!" says the lady, with a sigh. "Harry, that was my face once—yes, it was—and then I was called Beatrix Esmond. And your mother is my half-sister, child, and she has never even mentioned my name!"

CHAPTER V. Family Jars

As Harry Warrington related to his new-found relative the simple story of his adventures at home, no doubt Madam Bernstein, who possessed a great sense of humour and a remarkable knowledge of the world, formed her judgment respecting the persons and events described; and if her opinion was not in all respects favourable, what can be said but that men and women are imperfect, and human life not entirely pleasant or profitable? The court and city-bred lady recoiled at the mere thought of her American sister's countrified existence. Such a life would be rather wearisome to most city-bred ladies. But little Madam Warrington knew no better, and was satisfied with her life, as indeed she was with herself in general. Because you and I are epicures or dainty feeders, it does not follow that Hodge is miserable with his homely meal of bread and bacon. Madam Warrington had a life of duties and employments which might be humdrum, but at any rate were pleasant to her. She was a brisk little woman of business, and all the affairs of her large estate came under her cognisance. No pie was baked at Castlewood but her little finger was in it. She set the maids to their spinning, she saw the kitchen wenches at their work, she trotted afield on her pony, and oversaw the overseers and the negro hands as they worked in the tobacco-and corn-fields. If a slave was ill, she would go to his quarters in any weather, and doctor him with great resolution. She had a book full of receipts after the old fashion, and a closet where she distilled waters and compounded elixirs, and a medicine-chest which was the terror of her neighbours. They trembled to be ill, lest the little lady should be upon them with her decoctions and her pills.

A hundred years back there were scarce any towns in Virginia; the establishments of the gentry were little villages in which they and their vassals dwelt. Rachel Esmond ruled like a little queen in Castlewood; the princes, her neighbours, governed their estates round about. Many of these were rather needy potentates, living plentifully but in the roughest fashion, having numerous domestics whose liveries were often ragged; keeping open houses, and turning away no stranger from their gates; proud, idle, fond of all sorts of field sports as became gentlemen of good lineage. The widow of Castlewood was as hospitable as her neighbours, and a better economist than most of them. More than one, no doubt, would have had no objection to share her life-interest in the estate, and supply the place of papa to her boys. But where was the man good enough for a person of her ladyship's exalted birth? There was a talk of making the Duke of Cumberland viceroy, or even king, over America. Madam Warrington's gossips laughed, and said she was waiting for him. She remarked, with much gravity and dignity, that persons of as high birth as his Royal Highness had made offers of alliance to the Esmond family.

She had, as lieutenant under her, an officer's widow who has been before named, and who had been Madam Esmond's companion at school, as her late husband had been the regimental friend of the late Mr. Warrington. When the English girls at the Kensington Academy, where Rachel Esmond had her education, teased and tortured the little American stranger, and laughed at the princified airs which she gave herself from a very early age, Fanny Parker defended and befriended her. They both married ensigns in Kingsley's. They became tenderly attached to each other. It was "my Fanny" and "my Rachel" in the letters of the young ladies. Then, my Fanny's husband died in sad out-at-elbowed circumstances, leaving no provision for his widow and her infant; and, in one of his annual voyages, Captain Franks brought over Mrs. Mountain, in the Young Rachel, to Virginia.

There was plenty of room in Castlewood House, and Mrs. Mountain served to enliven the place. She played cards with the mistress: she had some knowledge of music, and could help the eldest boy in that way: she laughed and was pleased with the guests: she saw to the strangers' chambers, and presided over the presses and the linen. She was a kind, brisk, jolly-looking widow, and more than one unmarried gentleman of the colony asked her to change her name for his own. But she chose to keep that of Mountain, though, and perhaps because, it had brought her no good fortune. One marriage was enough for her, she said. Mr. Mountain had amiably spent her little fortune and his own. Her last trinkets went to pay his funeral; and, as long as Madam Warrington would keep her at Castlewood, she preferred a home without a husband to any which as yet had been offered to her in Virginia. The two ladies quarrelled plentifully; but they loved each other: they made up their differences: they fell out again, to be reconciled presently. When either of the boys was ill, each lady vied with the other in maternal tenderness and care. In his last days and illness, Mrs. Mountain's cheerfulness and kindness had been greatly appreciated by the Colonel, whose memory Madam Warrington regarded more than that of any living person. So that, year after year, when Captain Franks would ask Mrs. Mountain, in his pleasant way, whether she was going back with him that voyage? she would decline, and say that she proposed to stay a year more.

And when suitors came to Madam Warrington, as come they would, she would receive their compliments and attentions kindly enough, and asked more than one of these lovers whether it was Mrs. Mountain he came after? She would use her best offices with Mountain. Fanny was the best creature, was of a good English family, and would make any gentleman happy. Did the Squire declare it was to her and not her dependant that he paid his addresses; she would make him her gravest curtsey, say that she really had been utterly mistaken as to his views, and let him know that the daughter of the Marquis of Esmond lived for her people and her sons, and did not propose to change her condition. Have we not read how Queen Elizabeth was a perfectly sensible woman of business, and was pleased to inspire not only terror and awe, but love in the bosoms of her subjects? So the little Virginian princess had her favourites, and accepted their flatteries, and grew tired of them, and was cruel or kind to them as suited her wayward imperial humour. There was no amount of compliment which she would not graciously receive and take as her due. Her little foible was so well known that the wags used to practise upon it. Rattling Jack Firebrace of Henrico county had free quarters for months at Castlewood, and was a prime favourite with the lady there, because he addressed verses to her which he stole out of the pocket-books. Tom Humbold of Spotsylvania wagered fifty hogsheads against five that he would make her institute an order of knighthood, and won his wager.

The elder boy saw these freaks and oddities of his good mother's disposition, and chafed and raged at them privately. From very early days he revolted when flatteries and compliments were paid to the little lady, and strove to expose them with his juvenile satire; so that his mother would say gravely, "The Esmonds were always of a jealous disposition, and my poor boy takes after my father and mother in this." George hated Jack Firebrace and Tom Humbold, and all their like; whereas Harry went out sporting with them, and fowling, and fishing, and cock-fighting, and enjoyed all the fun of the country.

One winter, after their first tutor had been dismissed, Madam Esmond took them to Williamsburg, for such education as the schools and college there afforded, and there it was the fortune of the family to listen to the preaching of the famous Mr. Whitfield, who had come into Virginia, where the habits and preaching of the established clergy were not very edifying. Unlike many of the neighbouring provinces, Virginia was a Church of England colony: the clergymen were paid by the State and had glebes allotted to them; and, there being no Church of England bishop as yet in America, the colonists were obliged to import their divines from the mother-country. Such as came were not, naturally, of the very best or most eloquent kind of pastors. Noblemen's hangers-on, insolvent parsons who had quarrelled with justice or the bailiff, brought their stained cassocks into the colony in the hopes of finding a living there. No wonder that Whitfield's great voice stirred those whom harmless Mr. Broadbent, the Williamsburg chaplain, never could awaken. At first the boys were as much excited as their mother by Mr. Whitfield: they sang hymns, and listened to him with fervour, and, could he have remained long enough among them, Harry and George had both worn black coats probably instead of epaulettes. The simple boys communicated their experiences to one another, and were on the daily and nightly look-out for the sacred "call," in the hope or the possession of which such a vast multitude of Protestant England was thrilling at the time.

But Mr. Whitfield could not stay always with the little congregation of Williamsburg. His mission was to enlighten the whole benighted people of the Church, and from the East to the West to trumpet the truth and bid slumbering sinners awaken. However, he comforted the widow with precious letters, and promised to send her a tutor for her sons who should be capable of teaching them not only profane learning, but of strengthening and confirming them in science much more precious.

In due course, a chosen vessel arrived from England. Young Mr. Ward had a voice as loud as Mr. Whitfield's, and could talk almost as readily and for as long a time. Night and evening the hall sounded with his exhortations. The domestic negroes crept to the doors to listen to him. Other servants darkened the porch windows with their crisp heads to hear him discourse. It was over the black sheep of the Castlewood flock that Mr. Ward somehow had the most influence. These woolly lamblings were immensely affected by his exhortations, and, when he gave out the hymn, there was such a negro chorus about the house as might be heard across the Potomac—such a chorus as would never have been heard in the Colonel's time—for that worthy gentleman had a suspicion of all cassocks, and said he would never have any controversy with a clergyman but upon backgammon. Where money was wanted for charitable purposes no man was more ready, and the good, easy Virginian clergyman, who loved backgammon heartily, too, said that the worthy Colonel's charity must cover his other shortcomings.

Ward was a handsome young man. His preaching pleased Madam Esmond from the first, and, I daresay, satisfied her as much as Mr. Whitfield's. Of course it cannot be the case at the present day when they are so finely educated, but women, a hundred years ago, were credulous, eager to admire and believe, and apt to imagine all sorts of excellences in the object of their admiration. For weeks, nay, months, Madam Esmond was never tired of hearing Mr. Ward's great glib voice and voluble commonplaces: and, according to her wont, she insisted that her neighbours should come and listen to him, and ordered them to be converted. Her young favourite, Mr. Washington, she was especially anxious to influence; and again and again pressed him to come and stay at Castlewood and benefit by the spiritual advantages there to be obtained. But that young gentleman found he had particular business which called him home or away from home, and always ordered his horse of evenings when the time was coming for Mr. Ward's exercises. And—what boys are just towards their pedagogue?—the twins grew speedily tired and even rebellious under their new teacher.

They found him a bad scholar, a dull fellow, and ill-bred to boot. George knew much more Latin and Greek than his master, and caught him in perpetual blunders and false quantities. Harry, who could take much greater liberties than were allowed to his elder brother, mimicked Ward's manner of eating and talking, so that Mrs. Mountain and even Madam Esmond were forced to laugh, and little Fanny Mountain would crow with delight. Madam Esmond would have found the fellow out for a vulgar quack but for her sons' opposition, which she, on her part, opposed with her own indomitable will. "What matters whether he has more or less of profane learning?" she asked; "in that which is most precious, Mr. W. is able to be a teacher to all of us. What if his manners are a little rough? Heaven does not choose its elect from among the great and wealthy. I wish you knew one book, children, as well as Mr. Ward does. It is your wicked pride—the pride of all the Esmonds—which prevents you from listening to him. Go down on your knees in your chamber and pray to be corrected of that dreadful fault." Ward's discourse that evening was about Naaman the Syrian, and the pride he had in his native rivers of Abana and Pharpar, which he vainly imagined to be superior to the healing waters of Jordan—the moral being, that he, Ward, was the keeper and guardian of the undoubted waters of Jordan, and that the unhappy, conceited boys must go to perdition unless they came to him.

George now began to give way to a wicked sarcastic method, which, perhaps, he had inherited from his grandfather, and with which, when a quiet, skilful young person chooses to employ it, he can make a whole family uncomfortable. He took up Ward's pompous remarks and made jokes of them, so that that young divine chafed and almost choked over his great meals. He made Madam Esmond angry, and doubly so when he sent off Harry into fits of laughter. Her authority was defied, her officer scorned and insulted, her youngest child perverted, by the obstinate elder brother. She made a desperate and unhappy attempt to maintain her power.

The boys were fourteen years of age, Harry being taller and much more advanced than his brother, who was delicate, and as yet almost childlike in stature and appearance. The baculine method was a quite common mode of argument in those days. Sergeants, schoolmasters, slave-overseers, used the cane freely. Our little boys had been horsed many a day by Mr. Dempster, their Scotch tutor, in their grandfather's time; and Harry, especially, had got to be quite accustomed to the practice, and made very light of it. But, in the interregnum after Colonel Esmond's death, the cane had been laid aside, and the young gentlemen of Castlewood had been allowed to have their own way. Her own and her lieutenant's authority being now spurned by the youthful rebels, the unfortunate mother thought of restoring it by means of coercion. She took counsel of Mr. Ward. That athletic young pedagogue could easily find chapter and verse to warrant the course which he wished to pursue—in fact, there was no doubt about the wholesomeness of the practice in those clays. He had begun by flattering the boys, finding a good berth and snug quarters at Castlewood, and hoping to remain there.

But they laughed at his flattery, they scorned his bad manners, they yawned soon at his sermons; the more their mother favoured him, the more they disliked him; and so the tutor and the pupils cordially hated each other. Mrs. Mountain, who was the boys' friend, especially George's friend, whom she thought unjustly treated by his mother, warned the lads to be prudent, and that some conspiracy was hatching against them. "Ward is more obsequious than ever to your mamma. It turns my stomach, it does, to hear him flatter, and to see him gobble—the odious wretch! You must be on your guard, my poor boys—you must learn your lessons, and not anger your tutor. A mischief will come, I know it will. Your mamma was talking about you to Mr. Washington the other day, when I came into the room. I don't like that Major Washington, you know I don't. Don't say—O Mounty! Master Harry. You always stand up for your friends, you do. The Major is very handsome and tall, and he may be very good, but he is much too old a young man for me. Bless you, my dears, the quantity of wild oats your father sowed and my own poor Mountain when they were ensigns in Kingsley's, would fill sacks full! Show me Mr. Washington's wild oats, I say—not a grain! Well, I happened to step in last Tuesday, when he was here with your mamma; and I am sure they were talking about you, for he said, 'Discipline is discipline, and must be preserved. There can be but one command in a house, ma'am, and you must be the mistress of yours.'"

"The very words he used to me," cries Harry. "He told me that he did not like to meddle with other folks' affairs, but that our mother was very angry, dangerously angry, he said, and he begged me to obey Mr. Ward, and specially to press George to do so."

"Let him manage his own house, not mine," says George, very haughtily. And the caution, far from benefiting him, only rendered the lad more supercilious and refractory.

On the next day the storm broke, and vengeance fell on the little rebel's head. Words passed between George and Mr. Ward during the morning study. The boy was quite insubordinate and unjust: even his faithful brother cried out, and owned that he was in the wrong. Mr. Ward kept his temper—to compress, bottle up, cork down, and prevent your anger from present furious explosion, is called keeping your temper—and said he should speak upon this business to Madam Esmond. When the family met at dinner, Mr. Ward requested her ladyship to stay, and, temperately enough, laid the subject of dispute before her.

He asked Master Harry to confirm what he had said: and poor Harry was obliged to admit all the dominie's statements.

George, standing under his grandfather's portrait by the chimney, said haughtily that what Mr. Ward had said was perfectly correct.

"To be a tutor to such a pupil is absurd," said Mr. Ward, making a long speech, interspersed with many of his usual Scripture phrases, at each of which, as they occurred, that wicked young George smiled, and pished scornfully, and at length Ward ended by asking her honour's leave to retire.

"Not before you have punished this wicked and disobedient child," said Madam Esmond, who had been gathering anger during Ward's harangue, and especially at her son's behaviour.

"Punish!" says George.

"Yes, sir, punish! If means of love and entreaty fail, as they have with your proud heart, other means must be found to bring you to obedience. I punish you now, rebellious boy, to guard you from greater punishment hereafter. The discipline of this family must be maintained. There can be but one command in a house, and I must be the mistress of mine. You will punish this refractory boy, Mr. Ward, as we have agreed that you should do, and if there is the least resistance on his part, my overseer and servants will lend you aid."

In some such words the widow no doubt must have spoken, but with many vehement Scriptural allusions, which it does not become this chronicler to copy. To be for ever applying to the Sacred Oracles, and accommodating their sentences to your purpose—to be for ever taking Heaven into your confidence about your private affairs, and passionately calling for its interference in your family quarrels and difficulties—to be so familiar with its designs and schemes as to be able to threaten your neighbour with its thunders, and to know precisely its intentions regarding him and others who differ from your infallible opinion—this was the schooling which our simple widow had received from her impetuous young spiritual guide, and I doubt whether it brought her much comfort.

In the midst of his mother's harangue, in spite of it, perhaps, George Esmond felt he had been wrong. "There can be but one command in the house, and you must be mistress—I know who said those words before you," George said, slowly, and looking very white—"and—and I know, mother, that I have acted wrongly to Mr. Ward."

"He owns it! He asks pardon!" cries Harry. "That's right, George! That's enough: isn't it?"

"No, it is not enough!" cried the little woman. "The disobedient boy must pay the penalty of his disobedience. When I was headstrong, as I sometimes was as a child before my spirit was changed and humbled, my mamma punished me, and I submitted. So must George. I desire you will do your duty, Mr. Ward."

"Stop, mother!—you don't quite know what you are doing," George said, exceedingly agitated.

"I know that he who spares the rod spoils the child, ungrateful boy!" says Madam Esmond, with more references of the same nature, which George heard, looking very pale and desperate.

Upon the mantelpiece, under the Colonel's portrait, stood a china cup, by which the widow set great store, as her father had always been accustomed to drink from it. George suddenly took it, and a strange smile passed over his pale face.

"Stay one minute. Don't go away yet," he cried to his mother, who was leaving the room. "You—you are very fond of this cup, mother?"—and Harry looked at him, wondering. "If I broke it, it could never be mended, could it? All the tinkers' rivets would not make it a whole cup again. My dear old grandpapa's cup! I have been wrong. Mr. Ward, I ask pardon. I will try and amend."

The widow looked at her son indignantly, almost scornfully. "I thought," she said, "I thought an Esmond had been more of a man than to be afraid, and —" here she gave a little scream as Harry uttered an exclamation, and dashed forward with his hands stretched out towards his brother.

George, after looking at the cup, raised it, opened his hand, and let it fall on the marble slab below him. Harry had tried in vain to catch it.

"It is too late, Hal," George said. "You will never mend that again—never. Now, mother, I am ready, as it is your wish. Will you come and see whether I am afraid? Mr. Ward, I am your servant. Your servant? Your slave! And the next time I meet Mr. Washington, madam, I will thank him for the advice which he gave you."

"I say, do your duty, sir!" cried Mrs. Esmond, stamping her little foot. And George, making a low bow to Mr. Ward, begged him to go first out of the room to the study.

"Stop! For God's sake, mother, stop!" cried poor Hal. But passion was boiling in the little woman's heart, and she would not hear the boy's petition. "You only abet him, sir!" she cried.—"If I had to do it myself, it should be done!" And Harry, with sadness and wrath in his countenance, left the room by the door through which Mr. Ward and his brother had just issued.

The widow sank down on a great chair near it, and sat a while vacantly looking at the fragments of the broken cup. Then she inclined her head towards the door—one of half a dozen of carved mahogany which the Colonel had brought from Europe. For a while there was silence: then a loud outcry, which made the poor mother start.

In another minute Mr. Ward came out bleeding, from a great wound on his head, and behind him Harry, with flaring eyes, and brandishing a little couteau-de-chasse of his grandfather, which hung, with others of the Colonel's weapons, on the library wall.

"I don't care. I did it," says Harry. "I couldn't see this fellow strike my brother; and, as he lifted his hand, I flung the great ruler at him. I couldn't help it. I won't bear it; and, if one lifts a hand to me or my brother, I'll have his life," shouts Harry, brandishing the hanger.

The widow gave a great gasp and a sigh as she looked at the young champion and his victim. She must have suffered terribly during the few minutes of the boys' absence; and the stripes which she imagined had been inflicted on the elder had smitten her own heart. She longed to take both boys to it. She was not angry now. Very likely she was delighted with the thought of the younger's prowess and generosity. "You are a very naughty disobedient child," she said, in an exceedingly peaceable voice. "My poor Mr. Ward! What a rebel, to strike you! Papa's great ebony ruler, was it? Lay down that hanger, child. 'Twas General Webb gave it to my papa after the siege of Lille. Let me bathe your wound, my good Mr. Ward, and thank Heaven it was no worse. Mountain! Go fetch me some court-plaster out of the middle drawer in the japan cabinet. Here comes George. Put on your coat and waistcoat, child! You were going to take your punishment, sir, and that is sufficient. Ask pardon, Harry, of good Mr. Ward, for your wicked rebellious spirit,—I do, with all my heart, I am sure. And guard against your passionate nature, child—and pray to be forgiven. My son, O my son!" Here, with a burst of tears which she could no longer control, the little woman threw herself on the neck of her eldest-born; whilst Harry, laying the hanger down, went up very feebly to Mr. Ward, and said, "Indeed, I ask your pardon, sir. I couldn't help it; on my honour I couldn't; nor bear to see my brother struck."

The widow was scared, as after her embrace she looked up at George's pale face. In reply to her eager caresses, he coldly kissed her on the forehead, and separated from her. "You meant for the best, mother," he said, "and I was in the wrong. But the cup is broken; and all the king's horses and all the king's men cannot mend it. There—put the fair side outwards on the mantelpiece, and the wound will not show."

Again Madam Esmond looked at the lad, as he placed the fragments of the poor cup on the ledge where it had always been used to stand. Her power over him was gone. He had dominated her. She was not sorry for the defeat; for women like not only to conquer, but to be conquered; and from that day the young gentleman was master at Castlewood. His mother admired him as he went up to Harry, graciously and condescendingly gave Hal his hand, and said, "Thank you, brother!" as if he were a prince, and Harry a general who had helped him in a great battle.

Then George went up to Mr. Ward, who was still piteously bathing his eye and forehead in the water. "I ask pardon for Hal's violence, sir," George said, in great state. "You see, though we are very young, we are gentlemen, and cannot brook an insult from strangers. I should have submitted, as it was mamma's desire; but I am glad she no longer entertains it."

"And pray, sir, who is to compensate me?" says Mr. Ward; "who is to repair the insult done to me?"

"We are very young," says George, with another of his old-fashioned bows. "We shall be fifteen soon. Any compensation that is usual amongst gentlemen"

"This, sir, to a minister of the Word!" bawls out Ward, starting up, and who knew perfectly well the lads' skill in fence, having a score of times been foiled by the pair of them.

"You are not a clergyman yet. We thought you might like to be considered as a gentleman. We did not know."

"A gentleman! I am a Christian, sir!" says Ward, glaring furiously, and clenching his great fists.

"Well, well, if you won't fight, why don't you forgive?" says Harry. "If you don't forgive, why don't you fight? That's what I call the horns of a dilemma;" and he laughed his frank, jolly laugh.

But this was nothing to the laugh a few days afterwards, when, the quarrel having been patched up, along with poor Mr. Ward's eye, the unlucky tutor was holding forth according to his custom. He tried to preach the boys into respect for him, to reawaken the enthusiasm which the congregation had felt for him; he wrestled with their manifest indifference, he implored Heaven to warm their cold hearts again, and to lift up those who were falling back. All was in vain. The widow wept no more at his harangues, was no longer excited by his loudest tropes and similes, nor appeared to be much frightened by the very hottest menaces with which he peppered his discourse. Nay, she pleaded headache, and would absent herself of an evening, on which occasion the remainder of the little congregation was very cold indeed. One day, then, Ward, still making desperate efforts to get back his despised authority, was preaching on the beauty of subordination, the present lax spirit of the age, and the necessity of obeying our spiritual and temporal rulers. "For why, my dear friends," he nobly asked (he was in the habit of asking immensely dull questions, and straightway answering them with corresponding platitudes), "why are governors appointed, but that we should be governed? Why are tutors engaged, but that children should be taught?" (here a look at the boys). "Why are rulers———" Here he paused, looking with a sad, puzzled face at the young gentlemen. He saw in their countenances the double meaning of the unlucky word he had uttered, and stammered, and thumped the table with his fist. "Why, I say, are rulers———"

"Rulers," says George, looking at Harry.

"Rulers!" says Hal, putting his hand to his eye, where the poor tutor still bore marks of the late scuffle. Rulers, o-ho! It was too much. The boys burst out in an explosion of laughter. Mrs. Mountain, who was full of fun, could not help joining in the chorus; and little Fanny, who had always behaved very demurely and silently at these ceremonies, crowed again, and clapped her little hands at the others laughing, not in the least knowing the reason why.

This could not be borne. Ward shut down the book before him; in a few angry, but eloquent and manly words, said he would speak no more in that place; and left Castlewood not in the least regretted by Madam Esmond, who had doted on him three months before.

CHAPTER VI. The Virginians begin to see the World

After the departure of her unfortunate spiritual adviser and chaplain, Madam Esmond and her son seemed to be quite reconciled: but although George never spoke of the quarrel with his mother, it must have weighed upon the boy's mind very painfully, for he had a fever soon after the last recounted domestic occurrences, during which illness his brain once or twice wandered, when he shrieked out, "Broken! Broken! It never, never can be mended!" to the silent terror of his mother, who sate watching the poor child as he tossed wakeful upon his midnight bed. His malady defied her skill, and increased in spite of all the nostrums which the good widow kept in her closet and administered so freely to her people. She had to undergo another humiliation, and one day little Mr. Dempster beheld her at his door on horseback. She had ridden through the snow on her pony, to implore him to give his aid to her poor boy. "I shall bury my resentment, madam," said he, "as your ladyship buried your pride. Please God, I maybe time enough to help my dear young pupil!" So he put up his lancet, and his little provision of medicaments; called his only negro-boy after him, shut up his lonely hut, and once more returned to Castlewood. That night and for some days afterwards it seemed very likely that poor Harry would become heir of Castlewood; but by Mr. Dempster's skill the fever was got over, the intermittent attacks diminished in intensity, and George was restored almost to health again. A change of air, a voyage even to England, was recommended, but the widow had quarrelled with her children's relatives there, and owned with contrition that she had been too hasty. A journey to the north and east was determined on, and the two young gentlemen, with Mr. Dempster as their tutor, and a couple of servants to attend them, took a voyage to New York, and thence up the beautiful Hudson river to Albany, where they were received by the first gentry of the province, and thence into the French provinces, where they had the best recommendations, and were hospitably entertained by the French gentry. Harry camped with the Indians, and took furs and shot bears. George, who never cared for field-sports, and whose health was still delicate, was a special favourite with the French ladies, who were accustomed to see very few young English gentlemen speaking the French language so readily as our young gentlemen. George especially perfected his accent so as to be able to pass for a Frenchman. He had the bel air completely, every person allowed. He danced the minuet elegantly. He learned the latest imported French catches and songs, and played them beautifully on his violin, and would have sung them too but that his voice broke at this time, and changed from treble to bass; and, to the envy of poor Harry, who was absent on a bear-hunt, he even had an affair of honour with a young ensign of the regiment of Auvergne, the Chevalier de la Jabotiere, whom he pinked in the shoulder, and with whom he afterwards swore an eternal friendship. Madame de Mouchy, the superintendent's lady, said the mother was blest who had such a son, and wrote a complimentary letter to Madam Esmond upon Mr. George's behaviour. I fear, Mr. Whitfield would not have been over-pleased with the widow's elation on hearing of her son's prowess.

When the lads returned home at the end of ten delightful months, their mother was surprised at their growth and improvement. George especially was so grown as to come up to his younger-born brother. The boys could hardly be distinguished one from another, especially when their hair was powdered; but that ceremony being too cumbrous for country life, each of the gentlemen commonly wore his own hair, George his raven black, and Harry his light locks tied with a ribbon.

The reader who has been so kind as to look over the first pages of the lad's simple biography, must have observed that Mr. George Esmond was of a jealous and suspicious disposition, most generous and gentle and incapable of an untruth, and though too magnanimous to revenge, almost incapable of forgiving any injury. George left home with no goodwill towards an honourable gentleman, whose name afterwards became one of the most famous in the world; and he returned from his journey not in the least altered in his opinion of his mother's and grandfather's friend. Mr. Washington, though then but just of age, looked and felt much older. He always exhibited an extraordinary simplicity and gravity; he had managed his mother's and his family's affairs from a very early age, and was trusted by all his friends and the gentry of his county more than persons twice his senior.

Mrs. Mountain, Madam Esmond's friend and companion, who dearly loved the two boys and her patroness, in spite of many quarrels with the latter, and daily threats of parting, was a most amusing, droll letter-writer, and used to write to the two boys on their travels. Now, Mrs. Mountain was of a jealous turn likewise; especially she had a great turn for match-making, and fancied that everybody had a design to marry everybody else. There scarce came an unmarried man to Castlewood but Mountain imagined the gentleman had an eye towards the mistress of the mansion. She was positive that odious Mr. Ward intended to make love to the widow, and pretty sure the latter liked him. She knew that Mr. Washington wanted to be married, was certain that such a shrewd young gentleman would look out for a rich wife, and, as for the differences of ages, what matter that the Major (major was his rank in the militia) was fifteen years younger than Madam Esmond? They were used to such marriages in the family; my lady her mother was how many years older than the Colonel when she married him?—When she married him and was so jealous that she never would let the poor Colonel out of her sight. The poor Colonel! after his wife, he had been henpecked by his little daughter. And she would take after her mother, and marry again, be sure of that. Madam was a little chit of a woman, not five feet in her highest headdress and shoes, and Mr. Washington a great tall man of six feet two. Great tall men always married little chits of women: therefore, Mr. W. must be looking after the widow. What could be more clear than the deduction?

She communicated these sage opinions to her boy, as she called George, who begged her, for Heaven's sake, to hold her tongue. This she said she could do, but she could not keep her eyes always shut; and she narrated a hundred circumstances which had occurred in the young gentleman's absence, and which tended, as she thought, to confirm her notions. Had Mountain imparted these pretty suspicions to his brother? George asked sternly. No. George was her boy; Harry was his mother's boy. "She likes him best, and I like you best, George," cries Mountain. "Besides, if I were to speak to him, he would tell your mother in a minute. Poor Harry can keep nothing quiet, and then there would be a pretty quarrel between Madam and me!"

"I beg you to keep this quiet, Mountain," said Mr. George, with great dignity, "or you and I shall quarrel too. Neither to me nor to any one else in the world must you mention such an absurd suspicion."

Absurd! Why absurd? Mr. Washington was constantly with the widow. His name was forever in her mouth. She was never tired of pointing out his virtues and examples to her sons. She consulted him on every question respecting her estate and its management. She never bought a horse or sold a barrel of tobacco without his opinion. There was a room at Castlewood regularly called Mr. Washington's room. "He actually leaves his clothes here and his portmanteau when he goes away. Ah! George, George! One day will come when he won't go away," groaned Mountain, who, of course, always returned to the subject of which she was forbidden to speak. Meanwhile Mr. George adopted towards his mother's favourite a frigid courtesy, at which the honest gentleman chafed but did not care to remonstrate, or a stinging sarcasm, which he would break through as he would burst through so many brambles on those hunting excursions in which he and Harry Warrington rode so constantly together; whilst George, retreating to his tents, read mathematics, and French, and Latin, and sulked in his book-room more and more lonely.

Harry was away from home with some other sporting friends (it is to be feared the young gentleman's acquaintances were not all as eligible as Mr. Washington), when the latter came to pay a visit at Castlewood. He was so peculiarly tender and kind to the mistress there, and received by her with such special cordiality, that George Warrington's jealousy had well-nigh broken out in open rupture. But the visit was one of adieu, as it appeared.

Major Washington was going on a long and dangerous journey, quite to the western Virginia frontier and beyond it. The French had been for some time past making inroads into our territory. The government at home, as well as those of Virginia and Pennsylvania, were alarmed at this aggressive spirit of the Lords of Canada and Louisiana. Some of our settlers had already been driven from their holdings by Frenchmen in arms, and the governors of the British provinces were desirous to stop their incursions, or at any rate to protest against their invasion.

We chose to hold our American colonies by a law that was at least convenient for its framers. The maxim was, that whoever possessed the coast had a right to all the territory inland as far as the Pacific; so that the British charters only laid down the limits of the colonies from north to south, leaving them quite free from east to west. The French, meanwhile, had their colonies to the north and south, and aimed at connecting them by the Mississippi and the St. Lawrence and the great intermediate lakes and waters lying to the westward of the British possessions. In the year 1748, though peace was signed between the two European kingdoms, the colonial question remained unsettled, to be opened again when either party should be strong enough to urge it. In the year 1753, it came to an issue, on the Ohio river, where the British and French settlers met. To be sure, there existed other people besides French and British, who thought they had a title to the territory about which the children of their White Fathers were battling, namely, the native Indians and proprietors of the soil. But the logicians of St. James's and Versailles wisely chose to consider the matter in dispute as a European and not a Red-man's question, eliminating him from the argument, but employing his tomahawk as it might serve the turn of either litigant.

A company, called the Ohio Company, having grants from the Virginia government of lands along that river, found themselves invaded in their settlements by French military detachments, who roughly ejected the Britons from their holdings. These latter applied for protection to Mr. Dinwiddie, Lieutenant-Governor of Virginia, who determined upon sending an ambassador to the French commanding officer on the Ohio, demanding that the French should desist from their inroads upon the territories of his Majesty King George.

Young Mr. Washington jumped eagerly at the chance of distinction which this service afforded him, and volunteered to leave his home and his rural and professional pursuits in Virginia, to carry the governor's message to the French officer. Taking a guide, an interpreter, and a few attendants, and following the Indian tracks, in the fall of the year 1753, the intrepid young envoy made his way from Williamsburg almost to the shores of Lake Erie, and found the French commander at Fort le Boeuf. That officer's reply was brief: his orders were to hold the place and drive all the English from it. The French avowed their intention of taking possession of the Ohio. And with this rough answer the messenger from Virginia had to return through danger and difficulty, across lonely forest and frozen river, shaping his course by the compass, and camping at night in the snow by the forest fires.

Harry Warrington cursed his ill-fortune that he had been absent from home on a cock-fight, when he might have had chance of sport so much nobler; and on his return from his expedition, which he had conducted with an heroic energy and simplicity, Major Washington was a greater favourite than ever with the lady of Castlewood. She pointed him out as a model to both her sons. "Ah, Harry!" she would say, "think of you, with your cock-fighting and your racing-matches, and the Major away there in the wilderness, watching the French, and battling with the frozen rivers! Ah, George! learning may be a very good thing, but I wish my eldest son were doing something in the service of his country!"

"I desire no better than to go home and seek for employment, ma'am," says George. "You surely will not have me serve under Mr. Washington, in his new regiment, or ask a commission from Mr. Dinwiddie?"

"An Esmond can only serve with the king's commission," says Madam, "and as for asking a favour from Mr. Lieutenant-Governor Dinwiddie, I would rather beg my bread."

Mr. Washington was at this time raising such a regiment as, with the scanty pay and patronage of the Virginian government, he could get together, and proposed, with the help of these men-of-war, to put a more peremptory veto upon the French invaders than the solitary ambassador had been enabled to lay. A small force under another officer, Colonel Trent, had been already despatched to the west, with orders to fortify themselves so as to be able to resist any attack of the enemy. The French troops, greatly outnumbering ours, came up with the English outposts, who were fortifying themselves at a place on the confines of Pennsylvania where the great city of Pittsburg now stands. A Virginian officer with but forty men was in no condition to resist twenty times that number of Canadians, who appeared before his incomplete works. He was suffered to draw back without molestation; and the French, taking possession of his fort, strengthened it, and christened it by the name of the Canadian governor, Du Quesne. Up to this time no actual blow of war had been struck. The troops representing the hostile nations were in presence—the guns were loaded, but no one as yet had cried "Fire." It was strange, that in a savage forest of Pennsylvania, a young Virginian officer should fire a shot, and waken up a war which was to last for sixty years, which was to cover his own country and pass into Europe, to cost France her American colonies, to sever ours from us, and create the great Western republic; to rage over the Old World when extinguished in the New; and, of all the myriads engaged in the vast contest, to leave the prize of the greatest fame with him who struck the first blow!

He little knew of the fate in store for him. A simple gentleman, anxious to serve his king and do his duty, he volunteered for the first service, and executed it with admirable fidelity. In the ensuing year he took the command of the small body of provincial troops with which he marched to repel the Frenchmen. He came up with their advanced guard and fired upon them, killing their leader. After this he had himself to fall back with his troops, and was compelled to capitulate to the superior French force. On the 4th of July, 1754, the Colonel marched out with his troops from the little fort where he had hastily entrenched himself (and which they called Fort Necessity), gave up the place to the conqueror, and took his way home.

His command was over: his regiment disbanded after the fruitless, inglorious march and defeat. Saddened and humbled in spirit, the young officer presented himself after a while to his old friends at Castlewood. He was very young: before he set forth on his first campaign he may have indulged in exaggerated hopes of success, and uttered them. "I was angry when I parted from you," he said to George Warrington, holding out his hand, which the other eagerly took. "You seemed to scorn me and my regiment, George. I thought you laughed at us, and your ridicule made me angry. I boasted too much of what we would do."

"Nay, you have done your best, George," says the other, who quite forgot his previous jealousy in his old comrade's misfortune. "Everybody knows that a hundred and fifty starving men, with scarce a round of ammunition left, could not face five times their number perfectly armed, and everybody who knows Mr. Washington knows that he would do his duty. Harry and I saw the French in Canada last year. They obey but one will: in our provinces each governor has his own. They were royal troops the French sent against you..."

"Oh, but that some of ours were here!" cries Madam Esmond, tossing her head up. "I promise you a few good English regiments would make the white-coats run."

"You think nothing of the provincials: and I must say nothing now we have been so unlucky," said the Colonel, gloomily. "You made much of me when I was here before. Don't you remember what victories you prophesied for me—

how much I boasted myself very likely over your good wine? All those fine dreams are over now. 'Tis kind of your ladyship to receive a poor beaten fellow as you do:" and the young soldier hung down his head.

George Warrington, with his extreme acute sensibility, was touched at the other's emotion and simple testimony of sorrow under defeat. He was about to say something friendly to Mr. Washington, had not his mother, to whom the Colonel had been speaking, replied herself: "Kind of us to receive you, Colonel Washington!" said the widow. "I never heard that when men were unhappy, our sex were less their friends."

And she made the Colonel a very fine curtsey, which straightway caused her son to be more jealous of him than ever.

CHAPTER VII. Preparations for War

Surely no man can have better claims to sympathy than bravery, youth, good looks, and misfortune. Madam Esmond might have had twenty sons, and yet had a right to admire her young soldier. Mr. Washington's room was more than ever Mr. Washington's room now. She raved about him and praised him in all companies. She more than ever pointed out his excellences to her sons, contrasting his sterling qualities with Harry's love of pleasure (the wild boy!) and George's listless musings over his books. George was not disposed to like Mr. Washington any better for his mother's extravagant praises. He coaxed the jealous demon within him until he must have become a perfect pest to himself and all the friends round about him. He uttered jokes so deep that his simple mother did not know their meaning, but sate bewildered at his sarcasms, and powerless what to think of his moody, saturnine humour.

Meanwhile, public events were occurring which were to influence the fortunes of all our homely family. The quarrel between the French and English North Americans, from being a provincial, had grown to be a national, quarrel. Reinforcements from France had already arrived in Canada; and English troops were expected in Virginia. "Alas! my dear friend!" wrote Madame la Presidente de Mouchy, from Quebec, to her young friend George Warrington. "How contrary is the destiny to us! I see you quitting the embrace of an adored mother to precipitate yourself in the arms of Bellona. I see you pass wounded after combats. I hesitate almost to wish victory to our lilies when I behold you ranged under the banners of the Leopard. There are enmities which the heart does not recognise—ours assuredly are at peace among the tumults. All here love and salute you, as well as Monsieur the Bearhunter, your brother (that cold Hippolyte who preferred the chase to the soft conversation of our ladies!) Your friend, your enemy, the Chevalier de la Jabotiere, burns to meet on the field of Mars his generous rival. M. Du Quesne spoke of you last night at supper. M. Du Quesne, my husband, send affectuous remembrances to their young friend, with which are ever joined those of your sincere Presidente de Mouchy."

"The banner of the Leopard," of which George's fair correspondent wrote, was, indeed, flung out to the winds, and a number of the king's soldiers were rallied round it. It was resolved to wrest from the French all the conquests they had made upon British dominion. A couple of regiments were raised and paid by the king in America, and a fleet with a couple more was despatched from home under an experienced commander. In February, 1755, Commodore Keppel, in the famous ship Centurion, in which Anson had made his voyage round the world, anchored in Hampton Roads with two ships of war under his command, and having on board General Braddock, his staff, and a part of his troops. Mr. Braddock was appointed by the Duke. A hundred years ago the Duke of Cumberland was called The Duke par excellence in England—as another famous warrior has since been called. Not so great a Duke certainly was that first-named Prince as his party esteemed him, and surely not so bad a one as his enemies have painted him. A fleet of transports speedily followed Prince William's general, bringing stores, and men, and money in plenty.

The great man landed his troops at Alexandria on the Potomac river, and repaired to Annapolis in Maryland, where he ordered the governors of the different colonies to meet him in council, urging them each to call upon their respective provinces to help the common cause in this strait.

The arrival of the General and his little army caused a mighty excitement all through the provinces, and nowhere greater than at Castlewood. Harry was off forthwith to see the troops under canvas at Alexandria. The sight of their lines delighted him, and the inspiring music of their fifes and drums. He speedily made acquaintance with the officers of both regiments; he longed to join in the expedition upon which they were bound, and was a welcome guest at their mess.

Madam Esmond was pleased that her sons should have an opportunity of enjoying the society of gentlemen of good fashion from England. She had no doubt their company was improving, that the English gentlemen were very different from the horse-racing, cock-fighting Virginian squires, with whom Master Harry would associate, and the lawyers, and pettifoggers, and toad-eaters at the lieutenant-governor's table. Madam Esmond had a very keen eye for detecting flatterers in other folks' houses. Against the little knot of official people at Williamsburg she was especially satirical, and had no patience with their etiquettes and squabbles for precedence.

As for the company of the king's officers, Mr. Harry and his elder brother both smiled at their mamma's compliments to the elegance and propriety of the gentlemen of the camp. If the good lady had but known all, if she could but have heard their jokes and the songs which they sang over their wine and punch, if she could have seen the condition of many of them as they were carried away to their lodgings, she would scarce have been so ready to recommend their company to her sons. Men and officers swaggered the country round, and frightened the peaceful farm and village folk with their riot: the General raved and stormed against his troops for their disorder;

against the provincials for their traitorous niggardliness; the soldiers took possession almost as of a conquered country, they scorned the provincials, they insulted the wives even of their Indian allies, who had come to join the English warriors, upon their arrival in America, and to march with them against the French. The General was compelled to forbid the Indian women his camp. Amazed and outraged their husbands retired, and but a few months afterwards their services were lost to him, when their aid would have been most precious.

Some stories against the gentlemen of the camp, Madam Esmond might have heard, but she would have none of them. Soldiers would be soldiers, that everybody knew; those officers who came over to Castlewood on her son's invitation were most polite gentlemen, and such indeed was the case. The widow received them most graciously, and gave them the best sport the country afforded. Presently, the General himself sent polite messages to the mistress of Castlewood. His father had served with hers under the glorious Marlborough, and Colonel Esmond's name was still known and respected in England. With her ladyship's permission, General Braddock would have the honour of waiting upon her at Castlewood, and paying his respects to the daughter of so meritorious an officer.

If she had known the cause of Mr. Braddock's politeness, perhaps his compliments would not have charmed Madam Esmond so much. The Commander-in-Chief held levees at Alexandria, and among the gentry of the country, who paid him their respects, were our twins of Castlewood, who mounted their best nags, took with them their last London suits, and, with their two negro-boys, in smart liveries behind them, rode in state to wait upon the great man. He was sulky and angry with the provincial gentry, and scarce took any notice of the young gentlemen, only asking, casually, of his aide-de-camp at dinner, who the young Squire Gawkeys were in blue and gold and red waistcoats?

Mr. Dinwiddie, the Lieutenant-Governor of Virginia, the Agent from Pennsylvania, and a few more gentlemen, happened to be dining with his Excellency. "Oh!" says Mr. Dinwiddie, "those are the sons of the Princess Pocahontas;" on which, with a tremendous oath, the General asked, "Who the deuce was she?"

Dinwiddie, who did not love her, having indeed undergone a hundred pertnesses from the imperious little lady, now gave a disrespectful and ridiculous account of Madam Esmond, made merry with her pomposity and immense pretensions, and entertained General Braddock with anecdotes regarding her, until his Excellency fell asleep.

When he awoke, Dinwiddie was gone, but the Philadelphia gentleman was still at table, deep in conversation with the officers there present. The General took up the talk where it had been left when he fell asleep, and spoke of Madam Esmond in curt, disrespectful terms, such as soldiers were in the habit of using in those days, and asking, again, what was the name of the old fool about whom Dinwiddie had been talking? He then broke into expressions of contempt and wrath against the gentry, and the country in general.

Mr. Franklin of Philadelphia repeated the widow's name, took quite a different view of her character from that Mr. Dinwiddie had given, seemed to know a good deal about her, her father, and her estate; as, indeed, he did about every man or subject which came under discussion; explained to the General that Madam Esmond had beeves, and horses, and stores in plenty, which might be very useful at the present juncture, and recommended him to conciliate her by all means. The General had already made up his mind that Mr. Franklin was a very shrewd, intelligent person, and graciously ordered an aide-de-camp to invite the two young men to the next day's dinner. When they appeared he was very pleasant and good-natured; the gentlemen of the General's family made much of them. They behaved, as became persons of their name, with modesty and good-breeding; they returned home delighted with their entertainment, nor was their mother less pleased at the civilities which his Excellency had shown to her boys. In reply to Braddock's message, Madam Esmond penned a billet in her best style, acknowledging his politeness, and begging his Excellency to fix the time when she might have the honour to receive him at Castlewood.

We may be sure that the arrival of the army and the approaching campaign formed the subject of continued conversation in the Castlewood family. To make the campaign was the dearest wish of Harry's life. He dreamed only of war and battle; he was for ever with the officers at Williamsburg; he scoured and cleaned and polished all the guns and swords in the house; he renewed the amusements of his childhood, and had the negroes under arms. His mother, who had a gallant spirit, knew that the time was come when one of her boys must leave her and serve the king. She scarce dared to think on whom the lot should fall. She admired and respected the elder, but she felt that she loved the younger boy with all the passion of her heart.

Eager as Harry was to be a soldier, and with all his thoughts bent on that glorious scheme, he too scarcely dared to touch on the subject nearest his heart. Once or twice when he ventured on it with George, the latter's countenance wore an ominous look. Harry had a feudal attachment for his elder brother, worshipped him with an extravagant regard, and in all things gave way to him as the chief. So Harry saw, to his infinite terror, how George, too, in his grave way, was occupied with military matters. George had the wars of Eugene and Marlborough down from his bookshelves, all the military books of his grandfather, and the most warlike of Plutarch's lives. He and Dempster were practising with the foils again. The old Scotchman was an adept in the military art, though somewhat shy of saying where he learned it.

Madam Esmond made her two boys the bearers of the letter in reply to his Excellency's message, accompanying her note with such large and handsome presents for the General's staff and the officers of the two Royal Regiments, as caused the General more than once to thank Mr. Franklin for having been the means of bringing this welcome ally into the camp. "Would not one of the young gentlemen like to see the campaign?" the General asked. "A friend of theirs, who often spoke of them—Mr. Washington, who had been unlucky in the affair of last year—had already promised to join him as aide-de-camp, and his Excellency would gladly take another young Virginian gentleman into his family." Harry's eyes brightened and his face flushed at this offer. "He would like with all his heart to go!" he cried out. George said, looking hard at his younger brother, that one of them would be proud to attend his Excellency, whilst it would be the other's duty to take care of their mother at home. Harry allowed his senior to speak. His will was even still obedient to George's. However much he desired to go, he would not pronounce until George had declared himself. He longed so for the campaign, that the actual wish made him timid. He dared not speak on the matter as he went home with George. They rode for miles in silence, or strove to talk upon indifferent subjects; each knowing what was passing in the other's mind, and afraid to bring the awful question to an issue.

On their arrival at home the boys told their mother of General Braddock's offer. "I knew it must happen," she said; "at such a crisis in the country our family must come forward. Have you—have you settled yet which of you is to leave me?" and she looked anxiously from one to another, dreading to hear either name.

"The youngest ought to go, mother; of course I ought to go!" cries Harry, turning very red.

"Of course he ought," said Mrs. Mountain, who was present at their talk.

"There! Mountain says so! I told you so!" again cries Harry, with a sidelong look at George.

"The head of the family ought to go, mother," says George, sadly.

"No! no! you are ill, and have never recovered your fever. Ought he to go, Mountain?"

"You would make the best soldier, I know that, dearest Hal. You and George Washington are great friends, and could travel well together, and he does not care for me, nor I for him, however much he is admired in the family. But, you see, 'tis the law of Honour, my Harry." (He here spoke to his brother with a voice of extraordinary kindness and tenderness.) "The grief I have had in this matter has been that I must refuse thee. I must go. Had Fate given you the benefit of that extra half-hour of life which I have had before you, it would have been your lot, and you would have claimed your right to go first, you know you would."

"Yes, George," said poor Harry, "I own I should."

"You will stay at home, and take care of Castlewood and our mother. If anything happens to me, you are here to fill my place. I would like to give way, my dear, as you, I know, would lay down your life to serve me. But each of us must do his duty. What would our grandfather say if he were here?"

The mother looked proudly at her two sons. "My papa would say that his boys were gentlemen," faltered Madam Esmond, and left the young men, not choosing, perhaps, to show the emotion which was filling her heart. It was speedily known amongst the servants that Mr. George was going on the campaign. Dinah, George's foster-mother, was loud in her lamentations at losing him; Phillis, Harry's old nurse, was as noisy because Master George, as usual, was preferred over Master Harry. Sady, George's servant, made preparations to follow his master, bragging incessantly of the deeds which he would do, while Gumbo, Harry's boy, pretended to whimper at being left behind, though, at home, Gumbo was anything but a fire-eater.

But, of all in the house, Mrs. Mountain was the most angry at George's determination to go on the campaign. She had no patience with him. He did not know what he was doing by leaving home. She begged, implored, insisted that he should alter his determination; and vowed that nothing but mischief would come from his departure.

George was surprised at the pertinacity of the good lady's opposition. "I know, Mountain," said he, "that Harry would be the better soldier; but, after all, to go is my duty."

"To stay is your duty!" says Mountain, with a stamp of her foot.

"Why did not my mother own it when we talked of the matter just now?"

"Your mother!" says Mrs. Mountain, with a most gloomy, sardonic laugh; "your mother, my poor child!"

"What is the meaning of that mournful countenance, Mountain?"

"It may be that your mother wishes you away, George!" Mrs. Mountain continued, wagging her head. "It may be, my poor deluded boy, that you will find a father-in-law when you come back."

"What in heaven do you mean?" cried George, the blood rushing into his face.

"Do you suppose I have no eyes, and cannot see what is going on? I tell you, child, that Colonel Washington wants a rich wife. When you are gone, he will ask your mother to marry him, and you will find him master here when you come back. That is why you ought not to go away, you poor, unhappy, simple boy! Don't you see how fond she is of him? how much she makes of him? how she is always holding him up to you, to Harry, to everybody who comes here?"

"But he is going on the campaign, too," cried George.

"He is going on the marrying campaign, child!" insisted the widow.

"Nay; General Braddock himself told me that Mr. Washington had accepted the appointment of aide-de-camp."

"An artifice! an artifice to blind you, my poor child!" cries Mountain. "He will be wounded and come back—you will see if he does not. I have proofs of what I say to you—proofs under his own hand—look here!" And she took from her pocket a piece of paper in Mr. Washington's well-known handwriting.

"How came you by this paper?" asked George, turning ghastly pale.

"I—I found it in the Major's chamber!" says Mrs. Mountain, with a shamefaced look.

"You read the private letters of a guest staying in our house?" cried George. "For shame! I will not look at the paper!" And he flung it from him on to the fire before him.

"I could not help it, George; 'twas by chance, I give you my word, by the merest chance. You know Governor Dinwiddie is to have the Major's room, and the state-room is got ready for Mr. Braddock, and we are expecting ever so much company, and I had to take the things which the Major leaves here—he treats the house just as if it was his own already—into his new room, and this half-sheet of paper fell out of his writing-book, and I just gave one look at it by the merest chance, and when I saw what it was it was my duty to read it."

"Oh, you are a martyr to duty, Mountain!" George said grimly. "I dare say Mrs. Bluebeard thought it was her duty to look through the keyhole."

"I never did look through the keyhole, George. It's a shame you should say so! I, who have watched, and tended, and nursed you, like a mother; who have sate up whole weeks with you in fevers, and carried you from your bed to the sofa in these arms. There, sir, I don't want you there now. My dear Mountain, indeed! Don't tell me! You fly into a passion, and, call names, and wound my feelings, who have loved you like your mother—like your mother?—I only hope she may love you half as well. I say you are all ungrateful. My Mr. Mountain was a wretch, and every one of you is as bad."

There was but a smouldering log or two in the fireplace, and no doubt Mountain saw that the paper was in no danger as it lay amongst the ashes, or she would have seized it at the risk of burning her own fingers, and ere she uttered the above passionate defence of her conduct. Perhaps George was absorbed in his dismal thoughts; perhaps his jealousy overpowered him, for he did not resist any further when she stooped down and picked up the paper.

"You should thank your stars, child, that I saved the letter," cried she. "See! here are his own words, in his great big handwriting like a clerk. It was not my fault that he wrote them, or that I found them. Read for yourself, I say, George Warrington, and be thankful that your poor dear old Mounty is watching over you!"

Every word and letter upon the unlucky paper was perfectly clear. George's eyes could not help taking in the contents of the document before him. "Not a word of this, Mountain," he said, giving her a frightful look. "I—I will return this paper to Mr. Washington."

Mountain was scared at his face, at the idea of what she had done, and what might ensue. When his mother, with alarm in her countenance, asked him at dinner what ailed him that he looked so pale? "Do you suppose, madam," says he, filling himself a great bumper of wine, "that to leave such a tender mother as you does not cause me cruel grief?"

The good lady could not understand his words, his strange, fierce looks, and stranger laughter. He bantered all at the table; called to the servants and laughed at them, and drank more and more. Each time the door was opened, he turned towards it; and so did Mountain, with a guilty notion that Mr. Washington would step in.

CHAPTER VIII. In which George suffers from a Common Disease

On the day appointed for Madam Esmond's entertainment to the General, the house of Castlewood was set out with the greatest splendour; and Madam Esmond arrayed herself in a much more magnificent dress than she was accustomed to wear. Indeed, she wished to do every honour to her guest, and to make the entertainment—which, in reality, was a sad one to her—as pleasant as might be for her company. The General's new aide-de-camp was the first to arrive. The widow received him in the covered gallery before the house. He dismounted at the steps, and his servants led away his horses to the well-known quarters. No young gentleman in the colony was better mounted or a better horseman than Mr. Washington.

For a while ere the Major retired to divest himself of his riding-boots, he and his hostess paced the gallery in talk. She had much to say to him; she had to hear from him a confirmation of his own appointment as aide-de-camp to General Braddock, and to speak of her son's approaching departure. The negro servants bearing the dishes for the approaching feast were passing perpetually as they talked. They descended the steps down to the rough lawn in front of the house, and paced a while in the shade. Mr. Washington announced his Excellency's speedy approach, with Mr. Franklin of Pennsylvania in his coach.

This Mr. Franklin had been a common printer's boy, Mrs. Esmond had heard; a pretty pass things were coming to when such persons rode in the coach of the Commander-in-Chief! Mr. Washington said, a more shrewd and sensible gentleman never rode in coach or walked on foot. Mrs. Esmond thought the Major was too liberally disposed towards this gentleman; but Mr. Washington stoutly maintained against the widow that the printer was a most ingenious, useful, and meritorious man.

"I am glad, at least, that, as my boy is going to make the campaign, he will not be with tradesmen, but with gentlemen, with gentlemen of honour and fashion," says Madam Esmond, in her most stately manner.

Mr. Washington had seen the gentlemen of honour and fashion over their cups, and perhaps thought that all their sayings and doings were not precisely such as would tend to instruct or edify a young man on his entrance into life; but he wisely chose to tell no tales out of school, and said that Harry and George, now they were coming into the world, must take their share of good and bad, and hear what both sorts had to say.

"To be with a veteran officer of the finest army in the world," faltered the widow; "with gentlemen who have been bred in the midst of the Court; with friends of his Royal Highness, the Duke——"

The widow's friend only inclined his head. He did not choose to allow his countenance to depart from its usual handsome gravity.

"And with you, dear Colonel Washington, by whom my father always set such store. You don't know how much he trusted in you. You will take care of my boy, sir, will not you? You are but five years older, yet I trust to you more than to his seniors; my father always told the children, I alway bade them, to look up to Mr. Washington."

"You know I would have done anything to win Colonel Esmond's favour. Madam, how much would I not venture to merit his daughter's?"

The gentleman bowed with not too ill a grace. The lady blushed, and dropped one of the lowest curtsies. (Madam Esmond's curtsey was considered unrivalled over the whole province.) "Mr. Washington," she said, "will be always sure of a mother's affection, whilst he gives so much of his to her children." And so saying she gave him her hand, which he kissed with profound politeness. The little lady presently re-entered her mansion, leaning upon the tall young officer's arm. Here they were joined by George, who came to them, accurately powdered and richly attired, saluting his parent and his friend alike with low and respectful bows. Nowadays, a young man walks into his mother's room with hobnailed high-lows, and a wideawake on his head; and instead of making her a bow, puffs a cigar into her face.

But George, though he made the lowest possible bow to Mr. Washington and his mother, was by no means in good-humour with either of them. A polite smile played round the lower part of his countenance, whilst watchfulness and wrath glared out from the two upper windows. What had been said or done? Nothing that might not have been performed or uttered before the most decent, polite, or pious company. Why then should Madam Esmond continue to blush, and the brave Colonel to look somewhat red, as he shook his young friend's hand?

The Colonel asked Mr. George if he had had good sport? "No," says George, curtly. "Have you?" And then he looked at the picture of his father, which hung in the parlour.

The Colonel, not a talkative man ordinarily, straightway entered into a long description of his sport, and described where he had been in the morning, and what woods he had hunted with the king's officers; how many birds they had shot, and what game they had brought down. Though not a jocular man ordinarily, the Colonel made a long description of Mr. Braddock's heavy person and great boots, as he floundered through the Virginian woods, hunting, as they called it, with a pack of dogs gathered from various houses, with a pack of negroes barking as loud as the dogs, and actually shooting the deer when they came in sight of him. "Great God, sir!" says Mr. Braddock, puffing and blowing, "what would Sir Robert have said in Norfolk, to see a man hunting with a fowling-piece in his hand, and a pack of dogs actually laid on to a turkey!"

"Indeed, Colonel, you are vastly comical this afternoon!" cries Madam Esmond, with a neat little laugh, whilst her son listened to the story, looking more glum than ever. "What Sir Robert is there at Norfolk? Is he one of the newly arrived army-gentlemen?"

"The General meant Norfolk at home, madam, not Norfolk in Virginia," said Colonel Washington. "Mr. Braddock had been talking of a visit to Sir

Robert Walpole, who lived in that county, and of the great hunts the old Minister kept there, and of his grand palace, and his pictures at Houghton. I should like to see a good field and a good fox-chase at home better than any sight in the world," the honest sportsman added with a sigh.

"Nevertheless, there is good sport here, as I was saying," said young Esmond, with a sneer.

"What sport?" cries the other, looking at him.

"Why, sure you know, without looking at me so fiercely, and stamping your foot, as if you were going to charge me with the foils. Are you not the best sportsman of the country-side? Are there not all the fish of the field, and the beasts of the trees, and the fowls of the sea—no—the fish of the trees, and the beasts of the sea—and the—bah! You know what I mean. I mean shad, and salmon, and rock-fish, and roe-deer, and hogs, and buffaloes, and bisons, and elephants, for what I know. I'm no sportsman."

"No, indeed," said Mr. Washington, with a look of scarcely repressed scorn.

"Yes, I understand you. I am a milksop. I have been bred at my mamma's knee. Look at these pretty apron-strings, Colonel! Who would not like to be tied to them? See of what a charming colour they are! I remember when they were black—that was for my grandfather."

"And who would not mourn for such a gentleman?" said the Colonel, as the widow, surprised, looked at her son.

"And, indeed, I wish my grandfather were here, and would resurge, as he promises to do on his tombstone; and would bring my father, the Ensign, with him."

"Ah, Harry!" cries Mrs. Esmond, bursting into tears, as at this juncture her second son entered the room—in just such another suit, gold-corded frock, braided waistcoat, silver-hilted sword, and solitaire, as that which his elder brother wore. "Oh, Harry, Harry!" cries Madam Esmond, and flies to her younger son.

"What is it, mother?" asks Harry, taking her in his arms. "What is the matter, Colonel?"

"Upon my life, it would puzzle me to say," answered the Colonel, biting his lips.

"A mere question, Hal, about pink ribbons, which I think vastly becoming to our mother; as, no doubt, the Colonel does."

"Sir, will you please to speak for yourself?" cried the Colonel, bustling up, and then sinking his voice again.

"He speaks too much for himself," wept the widow.

"I protest I don't any more know the source of these tears, than the source of the Nile," said George, "and if the picture of my father were to begin to cry, I should almost as much wonder at the paternal tears. What have I uttered? An allusion to ribbons! Is there some poisoned pin in them, which has been struck into my mother's heart by a guilty fiend of a London mantua-maker? I professed to wish to be led in these lovely reins all my life long," and he turned a pirouette on his scarlet heels.

"George Warrington! what devil's dance are you dancing now?" asked Harry, who loved his mother, who loved Mr. Washington, but who, of all creatures, loved and admired his brother George.

"My dear child, you do not understand dancing—you care not for the politer arts—you can get no more music out of a spinet than by pulling a dead hog by the ear. By nature you were made for a man—a man of war—I do not mean a seventy-four, Colonel George, like that hulk which brought the hulking Mr. Braddock into our river. His Excellency, too, is a man of warlike turn, a follower of the sports of the field. I am a milksop, as I have had the honour to say."

"You never showed it yet. You beat that great Maryland man was twice your size," breaks out Harry.

"Under compulsion, Harry. 'Tis tuptu, my lad, or else 'tis tuptomai, as thy breech well knew when we followed school. But I am of a quiet turn, and would never lift my hand to pull a trigger, no, nor a nose, nor anything but a rose," and here he took and handled one of Madam Esmond's bright pink apron ribbons. "I hate sporting, which you and the Colonel love, and I want to shoot nothing alive, not a turkey, nor a titmouse, nor an ox, nor an ass, nor anything that has ears. Those curls of Mr. Washington's are prettily powdered."

The militia colonel, who had been offended by the first part of the talk, and very much puzzled by the last, had taken a modest draught from the great china bowl of apple-toddy which stood to welcome the guests in this as in all Virginian houses, and was further cooling himself by pacing the balcony in a very stately manner.

Again almost reconciled with the elder, the appeased mother stood giving a hand to each of her sons. George put his disengaged hand on Harry's shoulder. "I say one thing, George," says he with a flushing face.

"Say twenty things, Don Enrico," cries the other.

"If you are not fond of sporting and that, and don't care for killing game and hunting, being cleverer than me, why shouldst thou not stop at home and be quiet, and let me go out with Colonel George and Mr. Braddock?—that's what I say," says Harry, delivering himself of his speech.

The widow looked eagerly from the dark-haired to the fair-haired boy. She knew not from which she would like to part.

"One of our family must go because honneur oblige, and my name being number one, number one must go first," says George.

"Told you so," said poor Harry.

"One must stay, or who is to look after mother at home? We cannot afford to be both scalped by Indians or fricasseed by French."

"Fricasseed by French!" cries Harry; "the best troops of the world! Englishmen! I should like to see them fricasseed by the French!—What a mortal thrashing you will give them!" and the brave lad sighed to think he should not be present at the battue.

George sate down to the harpsichord and played and sang "Malbrouk s'en va-t-en guerre, Mironton, mironton, mirontaine," at the sound of which music the gentleman from the balcony entered. "I am playing 'God save the King,' Colonel, in compliment to the new expedition."

"I never know whether thou art laughing or in earnest," said the simple gentleman, "but surely methinks that is not the air."

George performed ever so many trills and quavers upon his harpsichord, and their guest watched him, wondering, perhaps, that a gentleman of George's condition could set himself to such an effeminate business. Then the Colonel took out his watch, saying that his Excellency's coach would be here almost immediately, and asking leave to retire to his apartment, and put himself in a fit condition to appear before her ladyship's company.

"Colonel Washington knows the way to his room pretty well," said George, from the harpsichord, looking over his shoulder, but never offering to stir.

"Let me show the Colonel to his chamber," cried the widow, in great wrath, and sailed out of the apartment, followed by the enraged and bewildered Colonel, as George continued crashing among the keys. Her high-spirited guest felt himself insulted, he could hardly say how; he was outraged and he could not speak; he was almost stifling with anger.

Harry Warrington remarked their friend's condition. "For heaven's sake, George, what does this all mean?" he asked his brother. "Why shouldn't he kiss her hand?" (George had just before fetched out his brother from their library, to watch this harmless salute.) "I tell you it is nothing but common kindness."

"Nothing but common kindness!" shrieked out George. "Look at that, Hal! Is that common kindness?" and he showed his junior the unlucky paper over which he had been brooding for some time. It was but a fragment, though the meaning was indeed clear without the preceding text.

The paper commenced: "... is older than myself, but I, again, am older than my years; and you know, dear brother, have ever been considered a sober person. All children are better for a father's superintendence, and her two, I trust, will find in me a tender friend and guardian."

"Friend and guardian! Curse him!" shrieked out George, clenching his fists —and his brother read on:

"... The flattering offer which General Braddock hath made me, will, of course, oblige me to postpone this matter until after the campaign. When we have given the French a sufficient drubbing, I shall return to repose under my own vine and fig-tree."

"He means Castlewood. These are his vines," George cries again, shaking his fist at the creepers sunning themselves on the wall.

"... Under my own vine and fig-tree; where I hope soon to present my dear brother to his new sister-in-law. She has a pretty Scripture name, which is..."— and here the document ended.

"Which is Rachel," George went on bitterly. "Rachel is by no means weeping for her children, and has every desire to be comforted. Now, Harry! Let us upstairs at once, kneel down as becomes us, and say, 'Dear papa, welcome to your house of Castlewood.'"

CHAPTER IX. Hospitalities

His Excellency the Commander-in-Chief set forth to pay his visit to Madam Esmond in such a state and splendour as became the first personage in all his Majesty's colonies, plantations, and possessions of North America. His guard of dragoons preceded him out of Williamsburg in the midst of an immense shouting and yelling of a loyal, and principally negro, population. The General rode in his own coach. Captain Talmadge, his Excellency's Master of the Horse, attended him at the door of the ponderous emblazoned vehicle, and riding by the side of the carriage during the journey from Williamsburg to Madam Esmond's house. Major Danvers, aide-de-camp, sate in the front of the carriage with the little postmaster from Philadelphia, Mr. Franklin, who, printer's boy as he had been, was a wonderful shrewd person, as his Excellency and the gentlemen of his family were fain to acknowledge, having a quantity of the most curious information respecting the colony, and regarding England too, where Mr. Franklin had been more than once. "'Twas extraordinary how a person of such humble origin should have acquired such a variety of learning and such a politeness of breeding too, Mr. Franklin!" his Excellency was pleased to observe, touching his hat graciously to the postmaster.

The postmaster bowed, said it had been his occasional good fortune to fall into the company of gentlemen like his Excellency, and that he had taken advantage of his opportunity to study their honours' manners, and adapt himself to them as far as he might. As for education, he could not boast much of that—his father being but in straitened circumstances, and the advantages small in his native country of New England: but he had done to the utmost of his power, and gathered what he could—he knew nothing like what they had in England.

Mr. Braddock burst out laughing, and said, "As for education, there were gentlemen of the army, by George, who didn't know whether they should spell bull with two b's or one. He had heard the Duke of Marlborough was no special good penman. He had not the honour of serving under that noble commander—his Grace was before his time—but he thrashed the French soundly, although he was no scholar."

Mr. Franklin said he was aware of both those facts.

"Nor is my Duke a scholar," went on Mr. Braddock—"aha, Mr. Postmaster, you have heard that, too—I see by the wink in your eye."

Mr. Franklin instantly withdrew the obnoxious or satirical wink in his eye, and looked in the General's jolly round face with a pair of orbs as innocent as a baby's. "He's no scholar, but he is a match for any French general that ever swallowed the English for fricassee de crapaud. He saved the crown for the best of kings, his royal father, his Most Gracious Majesty King George."

Off went Mr. Franklin's hat, and from his large buckled wig escaped a great halo of powder.

"He is the soldier's best friend, and has been the uncompromising enemy of all beggarly red-shanked Scotch rebels and intriguing Romish Jesuits who would take our liberty from us, and our religion, by George. His Royal Highness, my gracious master, is not a scholar neither, but he is one of the finest gentlemen in the world."

"I have seen his Royal Highness on horseback, at a review of the Guards, in Hyde Park," says Mr. Franklin. "The Duke is indeed a very fine gentleman on horseback."

"You shall drink his health to-day, Postmaster. He is the best of masters, the best of friends, the best of sons to his royal old father; the best of gentlemen that ever wore an epaulet."

"Epaulets are quite out of my way, sir," says Mr. Franklin, laughing. "You know I live in a Quaker City."

"Of course they are out of your way, my good friend. Every man to his business. You, and gentlemen of your class, to your books, and welcome. We don't forbid you; we encourage you. We, to fight the enemy and govern the country. Hey, gentlemen? Lord! what roads you have in this colony, and how this confounded coach plunges! Who have we here, with the two negro boys in livery? He rides a good gelding."

"It is Mr. Washington," says the aide-de-camp.

"I would like him for a corporal of the Horse Grenadiers," said the General. "He has a good figure on a horse. He knows the country too, Mr. Franklin."

"Yes, indeed."

"And is a monstrous genteel young man, considering the opportunities he has had. I should have thought he had the polish of Europe, by George I should."

"He does his best," says Mr. Franklin, looking innocently at the stout chief, the exemplar of English elegance, who sat swagging from one side to the other of the carriage, his face as scarlet as his coat—swearing at every other word; ignorant on every point off parade, except the merits of a bottle and the looks of a woman; not of high birth, yet absurdly proud of his no-ancestry; brave as a bulldog; savage, lustful, prodigal, generous; gentle in soft moods; easy of love and laughter; dull of wit; utterly unread; believing his country the first in the world, and he as good a gentleman as any in it. "Yes, he is mighty well for a provincial, upon my word. He was beat at Fort What-d'ye-call-um last year, down by the Thingamy river. What's the name on't, Talmadge?"

"The Lord knows, sir," says Talmadge; "and I dare say the Postmaster, too, who is laughing at us both."

"Oh, Captain!"

"Was caught in a regular trap. He had only militia and Indians with him. Good day, Mr. Washington. A pretty nag, sir. That was your first affair, last year?"

"That at Fort Necessity? Yes, sir," said the gentleman, gravely saluting, as he rode up, followed by a couple of natty negro grooms, in smart livery-coats and velvet hunting-caps. "I began ill, sir, never having been in action until that unlucky day."

"You were all raw levies, my good fellow. You should have seen our militia run from the Scotch, and be cursed to them. You should have had some troops with you."

"Your Excellency knows 'tis my passionate desire to see and serve with them," said Mr. Washington.

"By George, we shall try and gratify you, sir," said the General, with one of his usual huge oaths; and on the heavy carriage rolled towards Castlewood; Mr. Washington asking leave to gallop on ahead, in order to announce his Excellency's speedy arrival to the lady there.

The progress of the Commander-in-Chief was so slow, that several humbler persons who were invited to meet his Excellency came up with his carriage, and, not liking to pass the great man on the road, formed quite a procession in the dusty wake of his chariot-wheels. First came Mr. Dinwiddie, the Lieutenant-Governor of his Majesty's province, attended by his negro servants, and in company of Parson Broadbent, the jolly Williamsburg chaplain. These were presently joined by little Mr. Dempster, the young gentlemen's schoolmaster, in his great Ramillies wig, which he kept for occasions of state. Anon appeared Mr. Laws, the judge of the court, with Madam Laws on a pillion behind him, and their negro man carrying a box containing her ladyship's cap, and bestriding a mule. The procession looked so ludicrous, that Major Danvers and Mr. Franklin espying it, laughed outright, though not so loud as to disturb his Excellency, who was asleep by this time, bade the whole of this queer rearguard move on, and leave the Commander-in-Chief and his escort of dragoons to follow at their leisure. There was room for all at Castlewood when they came. There was meat, drink, and the best tobacco for his Majesty's soldiers; and laughing and jollity for the negroes; and a plenteous welcome for their masters.

The honest General required to be helped to most dishes at the table, and more than once, and was for ever holding out his glass for drink; Nathan's sangaree he pronounced to be excellent, and had drunk largely of it on arriving before dinner. There was cider, ale, brandy, and plenty of good Bordeaux wine, some which Colonel Esmond himself had brought home with him to the colony, and which was fit for ponteeficis coenis, said little Mr. Dempster, with a wink to Mr. Broadbent, the clergyman of the adjoining parish. Mr. Broadbent returned the wink and nod, and drank the wine without caring about the Latin, as why should he, never having hitherto troubled himself about the language? Mr. Broadbent was a gambling, guzzling, cock-fighting divine, who had passed much time in the Fleet Prison, at Newmarket, at Hockley-in-the-Hole; and having gone of all sorts of errands for his friend, Lord Cingbars, Lord Ringwood's son (my Lady Cingbars's waiting-woman being Mr. B.'s mother—I dare say the modern reader had best not be too particular regarding Mr. Broadbent's father's pedigree), had been of late sent out to a church-living in Virginia. He and young George had fought many a match of cocks together, taken many a roe in company, hauled in countless quantities of shad and salmon, slain wild geese and wild swans, pigeons and plovers, and destroyed myriads of canvas-backed ducks. It was said by the envious that Broadbent was the midnight poacher on whom Mr. Washington set his dogs, and whom he caned by the river-side at Mount Vernon. The fellow got away from his captor's grip, and scrambled to his boat in the dark; but Broadbent was laid up for two Sundays afterwards, and when he came abroad again had the evident remains of a black eye and a new collar to his coat. All the games at the cards had George Esmond and Parson Broadbent played together, besides hunting all the birds in the air, the beasts in the forest, and the fish of the sea. Indeed, when the boys rode together to get their reading with Mr. Dempster, I suspect that Harry stayed behind and took lessons from the other professor of European learning and accomplishments, —George going his own way, reading his own books, and, of course, telling no tales of his younger brother.

All the birds of the Virginia air, and all the fish of the sea in season were here laid on Madam Esmond's board to feed his Excellency and the rest of the English and American gentlemen. The gumbo was declared to be perfection (young Mr. George's black servant was named after this dish, being discovered behind the door with his head in a bowl of this delicious hotch-potch, by the late Colonel, and grimly christened on the spot), the shad were rich and fresh, the stewed terrapins were worthy of London aldermen (before George, he would like the Duke himself to taste them, his Excellency deigned to say), and indeed, stewed terrapins are worthy of any duke or even emperor. The negro-women have a genius for cookery, and in Castlewood kitchens there were adepts in the art brought up under the keen eye of the late and the present Madam Esmond. Certain of the dishes, especially the sweets and flan, Madam Esmond prepared herself with great neatness and dexterity; carving several of the principal pieces, as the kindly cumbrous fashion of the day was, putting up the laced lappets of her sleeves, and showing the prettiest round arms and small hands and wrists as she performed this ancient rite of a hospitality not so languid as ours. The old law of the table was that the mistress was to press her guests with a decent eagerness, to watch and see whom she could encourage to further enjoyment, to know culinary anatomic secrets, and execute carving operations upon fowls, fish, game, joints of meat, and so forth; to cheer her guests to fresh efforts, to whisper her neighbour, Mr. Braddock "I have kept for your Excellency the jowl of this salmon.—I will take no denial! Mr. Franklin, you drink only water, sir, though our cellar has wholesome wine which gives no headaches.—Mr. Justice, you love woodcock pie?"

"Because I know who makes the pastry," says Mr. Laws, the judge, with a profound bow. "I wish, madam, we had such a happy knack of pastry at home as you have at Castlewood. I often say to my wife, 'My dear, I wish you had

Madam Esmond's hand.'"

"It is a very pretty hand; I am sure others would like it too," says Mr. Postmaster of Boston, at which remark Mr. Esmond looks but half-pleased at the little gentleman.

"Such a hand for a light pie-crust," continues the Judge, "and my service to you, madam." And he thinks the widow cannot but be propitiated by this compliment. She says simply that she had lessons when she was at home in England for her education, and that there were certain dishes which her mother taught her to make, and which her father and sons both liked. She was very glad if they pleased her company. More such remarks follow: more dishes; ten times as much meat as is needful for the company. Mr. Washington does not embark in the general conversation much, but he and Mr. Talmadge, and Major Danvers, and the Postmaster, are deep in talk about roads, rivers, conveyances, sumpter-horses and artillery train; and the provincial militia Colonel has bits of bread laid at intervals on the table before him, and stations marked out, on which he has his finger, and regarding which he is talking to his brother aides-de-camp, till a negro servant, changing the courses, brushes off the Potomac with a napkin, and sweeps up the Ohio in a spoon.

At the end of dinner, Mr. Broadbent leaves his place and walks up behind the Lieutenant-Governor's chair, where he says grace, returning to his seat and resuming his knife and fork when this work of devotion is over. And now the sweets and puddings are come, of which I can give you a list, if you like; but what young lady cares for the puddings of to-day, much more for those which were eaten a hundred years ago, and which Madam Esmond had prepared for her guests with so much neatness and skill? Then, the table being cleared, Nathan, her chief manager, lays a glass to every person, and fills his mistress's. Bowing to the company, she says she drinks but one toast, but knows how heartily all the gentlemen present will join her. Then she calls, "His Majesty," bowing to Mr. Braddock, who with his aides-de-camp and the colonial gentlemen all loyally repeat the name of their beloved and gracious Sovereign. And hereupon, having drunk her glass of wine and saluted all the company, the widow retires between a row of negro servants, performing one of her very handsomest curtsies at the door.

The kind Mistress of Castlewood bore her part in the entertainment with admirable spirit, and looked so gay and handsome, and spoke with such cheerfulness and courage to all her company, that the few ladies who were present at the dinner could not but congratulate Madam Esmond upon the elegance of the feast, and especially upon her manner of presiding at it. But they were scarcely got to her drawing-room when her artificial courage failed her, and she burst into tears on the sofa by Mrs. Laws' side, just in the midst of a compliment from that lady. "Ah, madam!" she said, "it may be an honour, as you say, to have the King's representative in my house, and our family has received greater personages than Mr. Braddock. But he comes to take one of my sons away from me. Who knows whether my boy will return, or how? I dreamed of him last night as wounded, and quite white, with blood streaming from his side. I would not be so ill-mannered as to let my grief be visible before the gentlemen; but, my good Mrs. Justice, who has parted with children, and who has a mother's heart of her own, would like me none the better, if mine were very easy this evening."

The ladies administered such consolations as seemed proper or palatable to their hostess, who tried not to give way further to her melancholy, and remembered that she had other duties to perform, before yielding to her own sad mood. "It will be time enough, madam, to be sorry when they are gone," she said to the Justice's wife, her good neighbour. "My boy must not see me following him with a wistful face, and have our parting made more dismal by my weakness. It is good that gentlemen of his rank and station should show themselves where their country calls them. That has always been the way of the Esmonds, and the same Power which graciously preserved my dear father through twenty great battles in the Queen's time, I trust and pray, will watch over my son now his turn is come to do his duty." And, now, instead of lamenting her fate, or further alluding to it, I dare say the resolute lady sate down with her female friends to a pool of cards and a dish of coffee, whilst the gentlemen remained in the neighbouring parlour, still calling their toasts and drinking their wine. When one lady objected that these latter were sitting rather long, Madam Esmond said: "It would improve and amuse the boys to be with the English gentlemen. Such society was very rarely to be had in their distant province, and though their conversation sometimes was free, she was sure that gentleman and men of fashion would have regard to the youth of her sons, and say nothing before them which young people should not hear."

It was evident that the English gentlemen relished the good cheer provided for them. Whilst the ladies were yet at their cards, Nathan came in and whispered Mrs. Mountain, who at first cried out—"No! she would give no more—the common Bordeaux they might have, and welcome, if they still wanted more—but she would not give any more of the Colonel's." It appeared that the dozen bottles of particular claret had been already drunk up by the gentlemen, "besides ale, cider, Burgundy, Lisbon, and Madeira," says Mrs. Mountain, enumerating the supplies.

But Madam Esmond was for having no stint in the hospitality of the night. Mrs. Mountain was fain to bustle away with her keys to the sacred vault where the Colonel's particular Bordeaux lay, surviving its master, who, too, had long passed underground. As they went on their journey, Mrs. Mountain asked whether any of the gentlemen had had too much? Nathan thought Mister Broadbent was tipsy—he always tipsy; be then thought the General gentleman was tipsy; and he thought Master George was a lilly drunk.

"Master George!" cries Mrs. Mountain: "why, he will sit for days without touching a drop."

Nevertheless, Nathan persisted in his notion that Master George was a lilly drunk. He was always filling his glass, he had talked, he had sung, he had cut jokes, especially against Mr. Washington, which made Mr. Washington quite red and angry, Nathan said. "Well, well!" Mrs. Mountain cried eagerly; "it was right a gentleman should make himself merry in good company, and pass the bottle along with his friends." And she trotted to the particular Bordeaux cellar with only the more alacrity.

The tone of freedom and almost impertinence which young George Esmond had adopted of late days towards Mr. Washington had very deeply vexed and annoyed that gentleman. There was scarce half a dozen years' difference of age between him and the Castlewood twins;—but Mr. Washington had always been remarked for a discretion and sobriety much beyond his time of life, whilst the boys of Castlewood seemed younger than theirs. They had always been till now under their mother's anxious tutelage, and had looked up to their neighbour of Mount Vernon as their guide, director, friend—as, indeed, almost everybody seemed to do who came in contact with the simple and upright young man. Himself of the most scrupulous gravity and good breeding, in his communication with other folks he appeared to exact, or, at any rate, to occasion, the same behaviour. His nature was above levity and jokes: they seemed out of place when addressed to him. He was slow of comprehending them: and they slunk as it were abashed out of his society. "He always seemed great to me," says Harry Warrington, in one of his letters many years after the date of which we are writing; "and I never thought of him otherwise than of a hero. When he came over to Castlewood and taught us boys surveying, to see him riding to hounds was as if he was charging an army. If he fired a shot, I thought the bird must come down, and if be flung a net, the largest fish in the river were sure to be in it. His words were always few, but they were always wise; they were not idle, as our words are, they were grave, sober, and strong, and ready on occasion to do their duty. In spite of his antipathy to him, my brother respected and admired the General as much as I did—that is to say, more than any mortal man."

Mr. Washington was the first to leave the jovial party which were doing so much honour to Madam Esmond's hospitality. Young George Esmond, who had taken his mother's place when she left it, had been free with the glass and with the tongue. He had said a score of things to his guest which wounded and chafed the latter, and to which Mr. Washington could give no reply. Angry beyond all endurance, he left the table at length, and walked away through the open windows into the broad verandah or porch which belonged to Castlewood as to all Virginian houses.

Here Madam Esmond caught sight of her friend's tall frame as it strode up and down before the windows; and, the evening being warm, or her game over, she gave up her cards to one of the other ladies, and joined her good neighbour out of doors. He tried to compose his countenance as well as he could: it was impossible that he should explain to his hostess why and with whom he was angry.

"The gentlemen are long over their wine," she said; "gentlemen of the army are always fond of it."

"If drinking makes good soldiers, some yonder are distinguishing themselves greatly, madam," said Mr. Washington.

"And I dare say the General is at the head of his troops?"

"No doubt, no doubt," answered the Colonel, who always received this lady's remarks, playful or serious, with a peculiar softness and kindness. "But the General is the General, and it is not for me to make remarks on his Excellency's doings at table or elsewhere. I think very likely that military gentlemen born and bred at home are different from us of the colonies. We have such a hot sun, that we need not wine to fire our blood as they do. And drinking toasts seems a point of honour with them. Talmadge hiccupped to me—I should say, whispered to me just now, that an officer could no more refuse a toast than a challenge, and he said that it was after the greatest difficulty and dislike at first that he learned to drink. He has certainly overcome his difficulty with uncommon resolution."

"What, I wonder, can you talk of for so many hours?" asked the lady.

"I don't think I can tell you all we talk of, madam, and I must not tell tales out of school. We talked about the war, and of the force Mr. Contrecoeur has, and how we are to get at him. The General is for making the campaign in his coach, and makes light of it and the enemy. That we shall beat them, if we meet them, I trust there is no doubt."

"How can there be?" says the lady, whose father had served under Marlborough.

"Mr. Franklin, though he is only from New England," continued the gentleman, "spoke great good sense, and would have spoken more if the English gentlemen would let him; but they reply invariably that we are only raw provincials, and don't know what disciplined British troops can do. Had they not best hasten forwards and make turnpike roads and have comfortable inns ready for his Excellency at the end of the day's march?—'There's some sort of inns, I suppose,' says Mr. Danvers, 'not so comfortable as we have in England: we can't expect that.'—'No, you can't expect that,' says Mr. Franklin, who seems a very shrewd and facetious person. He drinks his water, and seems to laugh at the Englishmen, though I doubt whether it is fair for a water-drinker to sit by and spy out the weaknesses of gentlemen over their wine."

"And my boys? I hope they are prudent?" said the widow, laying her hand on her guest's arm. "Harry promised me, and when he gives his word, I can trust him for anything. George is always moderate. Why do you look so grave?"

"Indeed, to be frank with you, I do not know what has come over George in these last days," says Mr. Washington. "He has some grievance against me which I do not understand, and of which I don't care to ask the reason. He spoke to me before the gentlemen in a way which scarcely became him. We are going the campaign together, and 'tis a pity we begin such ill friends."

"He has been ill. He is always wild and wayward, and hard to understand. But he has the most affectionate heart in the world. You will bear with him, you will protect him—promise me you will."

"Dear lady, I will do so with my life," Mr. Washington said with great fervour. "You know I would lay it down cheerfully for you or any you love."

"And my father's blessing and mine go with you, dear friend!" cried the widow, full of thanks and affection.

As they pursued their conversation, they had quitted the porch under which they had first began to talk, and where they could hear the laughter and toasts of the gentlemen over their wine, and were pacing a walk on the rough lawn before the house. Young George Warrington, from his place at the head of the table in the dining-room, could see the pair as they passed to and fro, and had listened for some time past, and replied in a very distracted manner to the remarks of the gentlemen round about him, who were too much engaged with their own talk and jokes, and drinking, to pay much attention to their young host's behaviour. Mr. Braddock loved a song after dinner, and Mr. Danvers, his aide-de-camp, who had a fine tenor voice, was delighting his General with the latest ditty from Marybone Gardens, when George Warrington, jumping up, ran towards the window, and then returned and pulled his brother Harry by the sleeve, who sate with his back towards the window.

"What is it?" says Harry, who, for his part, was charmed, too, with the song and chorus.

"Come," cried George, with a stamp of his foot, and the younger followed obediently.

"What is it?" continued George, with a bitter oath. "Don't you see what it is? They were billing and cooing this morning; they are billing and cooing now before going to roost. Had we not better both go into the garden, and pay our duty to our mamma and papa?" and he pointed to Mr. Washington, who was taking the widow's hand very tenderly in his.

CHAPTER X. A Hot Afternoon

General Braddock and the other guests of Castlewood being duly consigned to their respective quarters, the boys retired to their own room, and there poured out to one another their opinions respecting the great event of the day. They would not bear such a marriage—no. Was the representative of the Marquises of Esmond to marry the younger son of a colonial family, who had been bred up as a land-surveyor? Castlewood, and the boys at nineteen years of age, handed over to the tender mercies of a stepfather of three-and-twenty! Oh, it was monstrous! Harry was for going straightway to his mother in her bedroom—where her black maidens were divesting her ladyship of the simple jewels and fineries which she had assumed in compliment to the feast—protesting against the odious match, and announcing that they would go home, live upon their little property there, and leave her for ever, if the unnatural union took place.

George advocated another way of stopping it, and explained his plan to his admiring brother. "Our mother," he said, "can't marry a man with whom one or both of us has been out on the field, and who has wounded us or killed us, or whom we have wounded or killed. We must have him out, Harry."

Harry saw the profound truth conveyed in George's statement, and admired his brother's immense sagacity. "No, George," says he, "you are right. Mother can't marry our murderer; she won't be as bad as that. And if we pink him he is done for. 'Cadit quaestio,' as Mr. Dempster used to say. Shall I send my boy with a challenge to Colonel George now?"

"My dear Harry," the elder replied, thinking with some complacency of his affair of honour at Quebec, "you are not accustomed to affairs of this sort."

"No," owned Harry, with a sigh, looking with envy and admiration on his senior.

"We can't insult a gentleman in our own house," continued George, with great majesty; "the laws of honour forbid such inhospitable treatment. But, sir, we can ride out with him, and, as soon as the park gates are closed, we can tell him our mind."

"That we can, by George!" cries Harry, grasping his brother's hand, "and that we will, too. I say, Georgy..." Here the lad's face became very red, and his brother asked him what he would say?

"This is my turn, brother," Harry pleaded. "If you go the campaign, I ought to have the other affair. Indeed, indeed, I ought." And he prayed for this bit of promotion.

"Again the head of the house must take the lead, my dear," George said, with a superb air. "If I fall, my Harry will avenge me. But I must fight George Washington, Hal: and 'tis best I should; for, indeed, I hate him the worst. Was it not he who counselled my mother to order that wretch, Ward, to lay hands on me?"

"Ah, George," interposed the more pacable younger brother, "you ought to forget and forgive."

"Forgive? Never, sir, as long as I remember. You can't order remembrance out of a man's mind; and a wrong that was a wrong yesterday must be a wrong to-morrow. I never, of my knowledge, did one to any man, and I never will suffer one, if I can help it. I think very ill of Mr. Ward, but I don't think so badly of him as to suppose he will ever forgive thee that blow with the ruler. Colonel Washington is our enemy, mine especially. He has advised one wrong against me, and he meditates a greater. I tell you, brother, we must punish him."

The grandsire's old Bordeaux had set George's ordinarily pale countenance into a flame. Harry, his brother's fondest worshipper, could not but admire George's haughty bearing and rapid declamation, and prepared himself, with his usual docility, to follow his chief. So the boys went to their beds, the elder conveying special injunctions to his junior to be civil to all the guests so long as they remained under the maternal roof on the morrow.

Good manners and a repugnance to telling tales out of school, forbid us from saying which of Madam Esmond's guests was the first to fall under the weight of her hospitality. The respectable descendants of Messrs. Talmadge and Danvers, aides-de-camp to his Excellency, might not care to hear how their ancestors were intoxicated a hundred years ago; and yet the gentlemen themselves took no shame in the fact, and there is little doubt they or their comrades were tipsy twice or thrice in the week. Let us fancy them reeling to bed, supported by sympathising negroes; and their vinous General, too stout a toper to have surrendered himself to a half-dozen bottles of Bordeaux, conducted to his chamber by the young gentlemen of the house, and speedily sleeping the sleep which friendly Bacchus gives. The good lady of Castlewood saw the condition of her guests without the least surprise or horror; and was up early in the morning, providing cooling drinks for their hot palates, which the servants carried to their respective chambers. At breakfast, one of the English officers rallied Mr. Franklin, who took no wine at all, and therefore refused the morning cool draught of toddy, by showing how the Philadelphia gentleman lost two pleasures, the drink and the toddy. The young fellow said the disease was pleasant and the remedy delicious, and laughingly proposed to continue repeating them both. The General's new American aide-de-camp, Colonel Washington, was quite sober and serene. The British officers vowed they must take him in hand, and teach him what the ways of the English army were; but the Virginian gentleman gravely said he did not care to learn that part of the English military education.

The widow, occupied as she had been with the cares of a great dinner, followed by a great breakfast on the morning ensuing, had scarce leisure to remark the behaviour of her sons very closely, but at least saw that George was scrupulously polite to her favourite, Colonel Washington, as to all the other guests of the house.

Before Mr. Braddock took his leave, he had a private audience of Madam Esmond, in which his Excellency formally offered to take her son into his family; and when the arrangements for George's departure were settled between his mother and future chief, Madam Esmond, though she might feel them, did not show any squeamish terrors about the dangers of the bottle, which she saw were amongst the severest and most certain which her son would have to face. She knew her boy must take his part in the world, and encounter his portion of evil and good. "Mr. Braddock is a perfect fine gentleman in the morning," she said stoutly to her aide-de-camp, Mrs. Mountain; "and though my papa did not drink, 'tis certain that many of the best company in England do." The jolly General good-naturedly shook hands with George, who presented himself to his Excellency after the maternal interview was over, and bade George welcome, and to be in attendance at Frederick three days hence; shortly after which time the expedition would set forth.

And now the great coach was again called into requisition, the General's escort pranced round it, the other guests and their servants went to horse. The lady of Castlewood attended his Excellency to the steps of the verandah in front of her house, the young gentlemen followed, and stood on each side of his coach-door. The guard trumpeter blew a shrill blast, the negroes shouted

"Huzzay, and God sabe de King," as Mr. Braddock most graciously took leave of his hospitable entertainers, and rolled away on his road to headquarters.

As the boys went up the steps, there was the Colonel once more taking leave of their mother. No doubt she had been once more recommending George to his namesake's care; for Colonel Washington said: "With my life. You may depend on me," as the lads returned to their mother and the few guests still remaining in the porch. The Colonel was booted and ready to depart. "Farewell, my dear Harry," he said. "With you, George, 'tis no adieu. We shall meet in three days at the camp."

Both the young men were going to danger, perhaps to death. Colonel Washington was taking leave of her, and she was to see him no more before the campaign. No wonder the widow was very much moved.

George Warrington watched his mother's emotion, and interpreted it with a pang of malignant scorn. "Stay yet a moment, and console our mamma," he said with a steady countenance, "only the time to get ourselves booted, and my brother and I will ride with you a little way, George." George Warrington had already ordered his horses. The three young men were speedily under way, their negro grooms behind them, and Mrs. Mountain, who knew she had made mischief between them and trembled for the result, felt a vast relief that Mr. Washington was gone without a quarrel with the brothers, without, at any rate, an open declaration of love to their mother.

No man could be more courteous in demeanour than George Warrington to his neighbour and namesake, the Colonel. The latter was pleased and surprised at his young friend's altered behaviour. The community of danger, the necessity of future fellowship, the softening influence of the long friendship which bound him to the Esmond family, the tender adieux which had just passed between him and the mistress of Castlewood, inclined the Colonel to forget the unpleasantness of the past days, and made him more than usually friendly with his young companion. George was quite gay and easy: it was Harry who was melancholy now: he rode silently and wistfully by his brother, keeping away from Colonel Washington, to whose side he used always to press eagerly before. If the honest Colonel remarked his young friend's conduct, no doubt he attributed it to Harry's known affection for his brother, and his natural anxiety to be with George now the day of their parting was so near.

They talked further about the war, and the probable end of the campaign: none of the three doubted its successful termination. Two thousand veteran British troops with their commander must get the better of any force the French could bring against them, if only they moved in decent time. The ardent young Virginian soldier had an immense respect for the experienced valour and tactics of the regular troops. King George II. had no more loyal subject than Mr. Braddock's new aide-de-camp.

So the party rode amicably together, until they reached a certain rude log-house, called Benson's, of which the proprietor, according to the custom of the day and country, did not disdain to accept money from his guests in return for hospitalities provided. There was a recruiting station here, and some officers and men of Halkett's regiment assembled, and here Colonel Washington supposed that his young friends would take leave of him.

Whilst their horses were baited, they entered the public room, and found a rough meal prepared for such as were disposed to partake. George Warrington entered the place with a particularly gay and lively air, whereas poor Harry's face was quite white and woebegone.

"One would think, Squire Harry, 'twas you who was going to leave home and fight the French and Indians, and not Mr. George," says Benson.

"I may be alarmed about danger to my brother," said Harry, "though I might bear my own share pretty well. 'Tis not my fault that I stay at home."

"No, indeed, brother," cries George.

"Harry Warrington's courage does not need any proof!" cries Mr. Washington.

"You do the family honour by speaking so well of us, Colonel," says Mr. George, with a low bow. "I dare say we can hold our own, if need be."

Whilst his friend was vaunting his courage, Harry looked, to say the truth, by no means courageous. As his eyes met his brother's, he read in George's look an announcement which alarmed the fond faithful lad. "You are not going to do it now?" he whispered his brother.

"Yes, now," says Mr. George, very steadily.

"For God's sake, let me have the turn. You are going on the campaign, you ought not to have everything—and there may be an explanation, George. We may be all wrong."

"Psha, how can we? It must be done now—don't be alarmed. No names shall be mentioned—I shall easily find a subject."

A couple of Halkett's officers, whom our young gentlemen knew, were sitting under the porch, with the Virginian toddy-bowl before them.

"What are you conspiring, gentlemen?" cried one of them. "Is it a drink?"

By the tone of their voices and their flushed cheeks, it was clear the gentlemen had already been engaged in drinking that morning.

"The very thing, sir," George said gaily. "Fresh glasses, Mr. Benson! What, no glasses? Then we must have at the bowl."

"Many a good man has drunk from it," says Mr. Benson; and the lads one after another, and bowing first to their military acquaintance, touched the bowl with their lips. The liquor did not seem to be much diminished for the boys' drinking, though George especially gave himself a toper's airs, and protested it was delicious after their ride. He called out to Colonel Washington, who was at the porch, to join his friends, and drink.

The lad's tone was offensive, and resembled the manner lately adopted by him, and which had so much chafed Mr. Washington. He bowed, and said he was not thirsty.

"Nay, the liquor is paid for," says George; "never fear, Colonel."

"I said I was not thirsty. I did not say the liquor was not paid for," said the young Colonel, drumming with his foot.

"When the King's health is proposed, an officer can hardly say no. I drink the health of his Majesty, gentlemen," cried George. "Colonel Washington can drink it or leave it. The King!"

This was a point of military honour. The two British officers of Halkett's, Captain Grace and Mr. Waring, both drank "The King." Harry Warrington drank "The King." Colonel Washington, with glaring eyes, gulped, too, a slight draught from the bowl.

Then Captain Grace proposed "The Duke and the Army," which toast there was likewise no gainsaying. Colonel Washington had to swallow "The Duke and the Army."

"You don't seem to stomach the toast, Colonel," said George.

"I tell you again, I don't want to drink," replied the Colonel. "It seems to me the Duke and the Army would be served all the better if their healths were not drunk so often."

"You are not up to the ways of regular troops as yet," said Captain Grace, with rather a thick voice.

"May be not, sir."

"A British officer," continues Captain Grace, with great energy but doubtful articulation, "never neglects a toast of that sort, nor any other duty. A man who refuses to drink the health of the Duke—hang me, such a man should be tried by a court-martial!"

"What means this language to me? You are drunk, sir!" roared Colonel Washington, jumping up, and striking the table with his fist.

"A cursed provincial officer say I'm drunk!" shrieks out Captain Grace. "Waring, do you hear that?"

"I heard it, sir!" cried George Warrington. "We all heard it. He entered at my invitation—the liquor called for was mine: the table was mine—and I am shocked to hear such monstrous language used at it as Colonel Washington has just employed towards my esteemed guest, Captain Waring."

"Confound your impudence, you infernal young jackanapes!" bellowed out Colonel Washington. "You dare to insult me before British officers, and find fault with my language? For months past, I have borne with such impudence from you, that if I had not loved your mother—yes, sir, and your good grandfather and your brother—I would—I would—" Here his words failed him, and the irate Colonel, with glaring eyes and purple face, and every limb quivering with wrath, stood for a moment speechless before his young enemy.

"You would what, sir?" says George, very quietly, "if you did not love my grandfather, and my brother, and my mother. You are making her petticoat a plea for some conduct of yours—you would do what, sir, may I ask again?"

"I would put you across my knee and whip you, you snarling little puppy, that's what I would do!" cried the Colonel, who had found breath by this time, and vented another explosion of fury.

"Because you have known us all our lives, and made our house your own, that is no reason you should insult either of us!" here cried Harry, starting up. "What you have said, George Washington, is an insult to me and my brother alike. You will ask pardon, sir!"

"Pardon?"

"Or give us the reparation that is due to gentlemen," continues Harry.

The stout Colonel's heart smote him to think that he should be at mortal quarrel or called upon to shed the blood of one of the lads he loved. As Harry stood facing him, with his fair hair, flushing cheeks, and quivering voice, an immense tenderness and kindness filled the bosom of the elder man. "I—I am bewildered," he said. "My words, perhaps, were very hasty. What has been the meaning of George's behaviour to me for months back? Only tell me, and, perhaps——"

The evil spirit was awake and victorious in young George Warrington: his black eyes shot out scorn and hatred at the simple and guileless gentleman before him. "You are shirking from the question, sir, as you did from the toast just now," he said. "I am not a boy to suffer under your arrogance. You have publicly insulted me in a public place, and I demand a reparation."

"In Heaven's name, be it!" says Mr. Washington, with the deepest grief in his face.

"And you have insulted me," continues Captain Grace, reeling towards him. "What was it he said? Confound the militia captain—colonel, what is he? You've insulted me! Oh, Waring! to think I should be insulted by a captain of militia!" And tears bedewed the noble Captain's cheek as this harrowing thought crossed his mind.

"I insult you, you hog!" the Colonel again yelled out, for he was little affected by humour, and had no disposition to laugh as the others had at the scene. And, behold, at this minute a fourth adversary was upon him.

"Great Powers, sir!" said Captain Waring, "are three affairs not enough for you, and must I come into the quarrel, too? You have a quarrel with these two young gentlemen."

"Hasty words, sir!" cries poor Harry once more.

"Hasty words, sir!" cries Captain Waring. "A gentleman tells another gentleman that he will put him across his knees and whip him, and you call those hasty words? Let me tell you if any man were to say to me, 'Charles Waring,' or 'Captain Waring, I'll put you across my knees and whip you,' I'd say, 'I'll drive my cheese-toaster through his body,' if he were as big as Goliath, I would. That's one affair with young Mr. George Warrington. Mr. Harry, of course, as a young man of spirit, will stand by his brother. That's two. Between Grace and the Colonel apology is impossible. And, now—run me through the body!—you call an officer of my regiment—of Halkett's, sir!—a hog before my face! Great heavens, sir! Mr. Washington, are you all like this in Virginia? Excuse me, I would use no offensive personality, as, by George! I will suffer none from any man! but, by Gad, Colonel! give me leave to tell you that you are the most quarrelsome man I ever saw in my life. Call a disabled officer of my regiment—for he is disabled, ain't you, Grace?—call him a hog before me! You withdraw it, sir—you withdraw it?"

"Is this some infernal conspiracy in which you are all leagued against me?"

shouted the Colonel. "It would seem as if I was drunk, and not you, as you all are. I withdraw nothing. I apologise for nothing. By heavens! I will meet one or half a dozen of you in your turn, young or old, drunk or sober."

"I do not wish to hear myself called more names," cried Mr. George Warrington. "This affair can proceed, sir, without any further insult on your part. When will it please you to give me the meeting?"

"The sooner the better, sir!" said the Colonel, fuming with rage.

"The sooner the better," hiccupped Captain Grace, with many oaths needless to print—(in those days, oaths were the customary garnish of all gentlemen's conversation)—and he rose staggering from his seat, and reeled towards his sword, which he had laid by the door, and fell as he reached the weapon. "The sooner the better!" the poor tipsy wretch again cried out from the ground, waving his weapon and knocking his own hat over his eyes.

"At any rate, this gentleman's business will keep cool till to-morrow," the militia Colonel said, turning to the other king's officer. "You will hardly bring your man out to-day, Captain Waring?"

"I confess that neither his hand nor mine are particularly steady," said Waring.

"Mine is!" cried Mr. Warrington, glaring at his enemy.

His comrade of former days was as hot and as savage. "Be it so—with what weapon, sir?" Washington said sternly.

"Not with small-swords, Colonel. We can beat you with them. You know that from our old bouts. Pistols had better be the word."

"As you please, George Warrington—and God forgive you, George! God pardon you, Harry! for bringing me into this quarrel," said the Colonel, with a face full of sadness and gloom.

Harry hung his head, but George continued with perfect calmness: "I, sir? It was not I who called names, who talked of a cane, who insulted a gentleman in a public place before gentlemen of the army. It is not the first time you have chosen to take me for a negro, and talked of the whip for me."

The Colonel started back, turning very red, and as if struck by a sudden remembrance.

"Great heavens, George! is it that boyish quarrel you are still recalling?"

"Who made you the overseer of Castlewood?" said the boy, grinding his teeth. "I am not your slave, George Washington, and I never will be. I hated you then, and I hate you now. And you have insulted me, and I am a gentleman, and so are you. Is that not enough?"

"Too much, only too much," said the Colonel, with a genuine grief on his face, and at his heart. "Do you bear malice too, Harry? I had not thought this of thee!"

"I stand by my brother," said Harry, turning away from the Colonel's look, and grasping George's hand. The sadness on their adversary's face did not depart. "Heaven be good to us! 'Tis all clear now," he muttered to himself. "The time to write a few letters, and I am at your service, Mr. Warrington," he said.

"You have your own pistols at your saddle. I did not ride out with any; but will send Sady back for mine. That will give you time enough, Colonel Washington?"

"Plenty of time, sir." And each gentleman made the other a low bow, and, putting his arm in his brother's, George walked away. The Virginian officer looked towards the two unlucky captains, who were by this time helpless with liquor. Captain Benson, the master of the tavern, was propping the hat of one of them over his head.

"It is not altogether their fault, Colonel," said my landlord, with a grim look of humour. "Jack Firebrace and Tom Humbold of Spotsylvania was here this morning, chanting horses with 'em. And Jack and Tom got 'em to play cards; and they didn't win—the British Captains didn't. And Jack and Tom challenged them to drink for the honour of Old England, and they didn't win at that game, neither, much. They are kind, free-handed fellows when they are sober, but they are a pretty pair of fools—they are."

"Captain Benson, you are an old frontier man, and an officer of ours, before you turned farmer and taverner. You will help me in this matter with yonder young gentlemen?" said the Colonel.

"I'll stand by and see fair play, Colonel. I won't have no hand in it, beyond seeing fair play. Madam Esmond has helped me many a time, tended my poor wife in her lying-in, and doctored our Betty in the fever. You ain't a-going to be very hard with them poor boys? Though I seen 'em both shoot: the fair one hunts well, as you know, but the old one's a wonder at an ace of spades."

"Will you be pleased to send my man with my valise, Captain, into any private room which you can spare me? I must write a few letters before this business comes on. God grant it were well over!" And the Captain led the Colonel into almost the only other room of his house, calling, with many oaths, to a pack of negro servants, to disperse thence, who were chattering loudly among one another, and no doubt discussing the quarrel which had just taken place. Edwin, the Colonel's man, returned with his master's portmanteau, and as he looked from the window, he saw Sady, George Warrington's negro, galloping away upon his errand, doubtless, and in the direction of Castlewood. The Colonel, young and naturally hot-headed, but the most courteous and scrupulous of men, and ever keeping his strong passions under guard, could not but think with amazement of the position in which he found, himself, and of the three, perhaps four enemies, who appeared suddenly before him, menacing his life. How had this strange series of quarrels been brought about? He had ridden away a few hours since from Castlewood, with his young companions, and, to all seeming, they were perfect friends. A shower of rain sends them into a tavern, where there are a couple of recruiting officers, and they are not seated for half an hour at a social table, but he has quarrelled with the whole company, called this one names, agreed to meet another in combat, and threatened chastisement to a third, the son of his most intimate friend!

CHAPTER XI. Wherein the two Georges prepare for Blood

The Virginian Colonel remained in one chamber of the tavern, occupied with gloomy preparations for the ensuing meeting; his adversary in the other room thought fit to make his testamentary dispositions, too, and dictated, by his obedient brother and secretary, a grandiloquent letter to his mother, of whom, and by that writing, he took a solemn farewell. She would hardly, he supposed, pursue the scheme which she had in view (a peculiar satirical emphasis was laid upon the scheme which she had in view), after the event of that morning, should he fall, as, probably, would be the case.

"My dear, dear George, don't say that!" cried the affrighted secretary.

"'As probably will be the case,'" George persisted with great majesty. "You know what a good shot Colonel George is, Harry. I, myself, am pretty fair at a mark, and 'tis probable that one or both of us will drop.—'I scarcely suppose you will carry out the intentions you have at present in view.'" This was uttered in a tone of still greater bitterness than George had used even in the previous phrase. Harry wept as he took it down.

"You see I say nothing; Madame Esmond's name does not even appear in the quarrel. Do you not remember in our grandfather's life of himself, how he says that Lord Castlewood fought Lord Mohun on a pretext of a quarrel at cards? and never so much as hinted at the lady's name, who was the real cause of the duel? I took my hint, I confess, from that, Harry. Our mother is not compromised in the—Why, child, what have you been writing, and who taught thee to spell?" Harry had written the last words "in view," in vew, and a great blot of salt water from his honest, boyish eyes may have obliterated some other bad spelling.

"I can't think about the spelling now, Georgy," whimpered George's clerk. "I'm too miserable for that. I begin to think, perhaps it's all nonsense, perhaps Colonel George never——"

"Never meant to take possession of Castlewood; never gave himself airs, and patronised us there; never advised my mother to have me flogged, never intended to marry her; never insulted me, and was insulted before the king's officers; never wrote to his brother to say we should be the better for his parental authority? The paper is there," cried the young man, slapping his breast-pocket, "and if anything happens to me, Harry Warrington, you will find it on my corse!"

"Write yourself, Georgy, I can't write," says Harry, digging his fists into his eyes, and smearing over the whole composition, bad spelling and all, with his elbows.

On this, George, taking another sheet of paper, sate down at his brother's place, and produced a composition in which he introduced the longest words, the grandest Latin quotations, and the most profound satire of which the youthful scribe was master. He desired that his negro boy, Sady, should be set free; that his Horace, a choice of his books, and, if possible, a suitable provision should be made for his affectionate tutor, Mr. Dempster; that his silver fruit-knife, his music-books, and harpsichord, should be given to little Fanny Mountain; and that his brother should take a lock of his hair, and wear it in memory of his ever fond and faithfully attached George. And he sealed the document with the seal of arms that his grandfather had worn.

"The watch, of course, will be yours," said George, taking out his grandfather's gold watch, and looking at it. "Why, two hours and a-half are gone! 'Tis time that Sady should be back with the pistols. Take the watch, Harry dear."

"It's no good!" cried out Harry, flinging his arms round his brother. "If he fights you, I'll fight him, too. If he kills my Georgy, —— him, he shall have a shot at me!" and the poor lad uttered more than one of those expressions, which are said peculiarly to affect recording angels, who have to take them down at celestial chanceries.

Meanwhile, General Braddock's new aide-de-camp had written five letters in his large resolute hand, and sealed them with his seal. One was to his mother, at Mount Vernon; one to his brother; one was addressed M. C. only; and one to his Excellency, Major-General Braddock. "And one, young gentleman, is for your mother, Madam Esmond," said the boys' informant.

Again the recording angel had to fly off with a violent expression, which parted from the lips of George Warrington. The chancery previously mentioned was crowded with such cases, and the messengers must have been for ever on the wing. But I fear for young George and his oath there was no excuse; for it was an execration uttered from a heart full of hatred, and rage, and jealousy.

It was the landlord of the tavern who communicated these facts to the young men. The Captain had put on his old militia uniform to do honour to the occasion, and informed the boys that the Colonel was walking up and down the garden a-waiting for 'em, and that the Reg'lars was a'most sober, too, by this time.

A plot of ground near the Captain's log-house had been enclosed with shingles, and cleared for a kitchen-garden; there indeed paced Colonel Washington, his hands behind his back, his head bowed down, a grave sorrow on his handsome face. The negro servants were crowded at the palings, and looking over. The officers under the porch had wakened up also, as their host remarked. Captain Waring was walking, almost steadily, under the balcony formed by the sloping porch and roof of the wooden house; and Captain Grace was lolling over the railing, with eyes which stared very much, though perhaps they did not see very clearly. Benson's was a famous rendezvous for cock-fights, horse-matches, boxing, and wrestling-matches, such as brought the Virginian country-folks together. There had been many brawls at Benson's, and men who came thither sound and sober, had gone thence with ribs broken and eyes gouged out. And squires, and farmers, and negroes, all participated in the sport.

There, then, stalked the tall young Colonel, plunged in dismal meditation.

There was no way out of his scrape, but the usual cruel one, which the laws of honour and the practice of the country ordered. Goaded into fury by the impertinence of a boy, he had used insulting words. The young man had asked for reparation. He was shocked to think that George Warrington's jealousy and revenge should have rankled in the young fellow so long but the wrong had been the Colonel's, and he was bound to pay the forfeit.

A great hallooing and shouting, such as negroes use, who love noise at all times, and especially delight to yell and scream when galloping on horseback, was now heard at a distance, and all the heads, woolly and powdered, were turned in the direction of this outcry. It came from the road over which our travellers had themselves passed three hours before, and presently the clattering of a horse's hoofs was heard, and now Mr. Sady made his appearance on his foaming horse, and actually fired a pistol off in the midst of a prodigious uproar from his woolly brethren. Then he fired another pistol off, to which noises Sady's horse, which had carried Harry Warrington on many a hunt, was perfectly accustomed; and now he was in the courtyard, surrounded by a score of his bawling comrades, and was descending amidst fluttering fowls and turkeys, kicking horses and shrieking frantic pigs; and brother-negroes crowded round him, to whom he instantly began to talk and chatter.

"Sady, sir, come here!" roars out Master Harry.

"Sady, come here! Confound you!" shouts Master George. (Again the recording angel is in requisition, and has to be off on one of his endless errands to the register office.) "Come directly, mas'r," says Sady, and resumes his conversation with his woolly brethren. He grins. He takes the pistols out of the holster. He snaps the locks. He points them at a grunter, which plunges through the farmyard. He points down the road, over which he has just galloped, and towards which the woolly heads again turn. He says again, "Comin', mas'r. Everybody a-comin'." And now, the gallop of other horses is heard. And who is yonder? Little Mr. Dempster, spurring and digging into his pony; and that lady in a riding-habit on Madam Esmond's little horse, can it be Madam Esmond? No. It is too stout. As I live it is Mrs. Mountain on Madam's grey!

"O Lor! O Golly! Hoop! Here dey come! Hurray!" A chorus of negroes rises up. "Here dey are!" Dr. Dempster and Mrs. Mountain have clattered into the yard, have jumped from their horses, have elbowed through the negroes, have rushed into the house, have run through it and across the porch, where the British officers are sitting in muzzy astonishment; have run down the stairs to the garden where George and Harry are walking, their tall enemy stalking opposite to them; and almost ere George Warrington has had time sternly to say, "What do you do here, madam?" Mrs. Mountain has flung her arms round his neck and cries: "Oh, George, my darling! It's a mistake! It's a mistake, and is all my fault!"

"What's a mistake?" asks George, majestically separating himself from the embrace.

75

"What is it, Mounty?" cries Harry, all of a tremble.

"That paper I took out of his portfolio, that paper I picked up, children; where the Colonel says he is going to marry a widow with two children. Who should it be but you, children, and who should it be but your mother?"

"Well?"

"Well, it's—it's not your mother. It's that little widow Custis whom the Colonel is going to marry. He'd always take a rich one; I knew he would. It's not Mrs. Rachel Warrington. He told Madam so to-day, just before he was going away, and that the marriage was to come off after the campaign. And—and your mother is furious, boys. And when Sady came for the pistols, and told the whole house how you were going to fight, I told him to fire the pistols off; and I galloped after him, and I've nearly broken my poor old bones in coming to you."

"I have a mind to break Mr. Sady's," growled George. "I specially enjoined the villain not to say a word."

"Thank God he did, brother!" said poor Harry. "Thank God he did!"

"What will Mr. Washington and those gentlemen think of my servant telling my mother at home that I was going to fight a duel?" asks Mr. George, still in wrath.

"You have shown your proofs before, George," says Harry, respectfully. "And, thank Heaven, you are not going to fight our old friend,—our grandfather's old friend. For it was a mistake and there is no quarrel now, dear, is there? You were unkind to him under a wrong impression."

"I certainly acted under a wrong impression," owns George, "but——"

"George! George Washington!" Harry here cries out, springing over the cabbage-garden towards the bowling-green, where the Colonel was stalking, and though we cannot hear him, we see him, with both his hands out, and with the eagerness of youth, and with a hundred blunders, and with love and affection thrilling in his honest voice we imagine the lad telling his tale to his friend.

There was a custom in those days which has disappeared from our manners now, but which then lingered. When Harry had finished his artless story, his friend the Colonel took him fairly to his arms, and held him to his heart: and his voice faltered as he said, "Thank God, thank God for this!"

"Oh, George," said Harry, who felt now how he loved his friend with all his heart, "how I wish I was going with you on the campaign!" The other pressed both the boy's hands, in a grasp of friendship, which each knew never would slacken.

Then the Colonel advanced, gravely holding out his hand to Harry's elder brother. Perhaps Harry wondered that the two did not embrace as he and the Colonel had just done. But, though hands were joined, the salutation was only formal and stern on both sides.

"I find I have done you a wrong, Colonel Washington," George said, "and must apologise, not for the error, but for much of my late behaviour which has resulted from it."

"The error was mine! It was I who found that paper in your room, and showed it to George, and was jealous of you, Colonel. All women are jealous," cried Mrs. Mountain.

"'Tis a pity you could not have kept your eyes off my paper, madam," said Mr. Washington. "You will permit me to say so. A great deal of mischief has come because I chose to keep a secret which concerned only myself and another person. For a long time George Warrington's heart has been black with anger against me, and my feeling towards him has, I own, scarce been more friendly. All this pain might have been spared to both of us, had my private papers only been read by those for whom they were written. I shall say no more now, lest my feelings again should betray me into hasty words. Heaven bless thee, Harry! Farewell, George! And take a true friend's advice, and try and be less ready to think evil of your friends. We shall meet again at the camp, and will keep our weapons for the enemy. Gentlemen! if you remember this scene to-morrow, you will know where to find me." And with a very stately bow to the English officers, the Colonel left the abashed company, and speedily rode away.

CHAPTER XII. News from the Camp

We must fancy that the parting between the brothers is over, that George has taken his place in Mr. Braddock's family, and Harry has returned home to Castlewood and his duty. His heart is with the army, and his pursuits at home offer the boy no pleasure. He does not care to own how deep his disappointment is, at being obliged to stay under the homely, quiet roof, now more melancholy than ever since George is away. Harry passes his brother's empty chamber with an averted face; takes George's place at the head of the table, and sighs as he drinks from his silver tankard. Madam Warrington calls the toast of "The King" stoutly every day; and, on Sundays, when Harry reads the service, and prays for all travellers by land and by water, she says, "We beseech Thee to hear us," with a peculiar solemnity. She insists on talking about George constantly, but quite cheerfully, and as if his return was certain. She walks into his vacant room, with head upright, and no outward signs of emotion. She sees that his books, linen, papers, etc., are arranged with care; talking of him with a very special respect, and specially appealing to the old servants at meals, and so forth, regarding things which are to be done "when Mr. George comes home." Mrs. Mountain is constantly on the whimper when George's name is mentioned, and Harry's face wears a look of the most ghastly alarm; but his mother's is invariably grave and sedate. She makes more blunders at piquet and backgammon than you would expect from her; and the servants find her awake and dressed, however early they may rise. She has prayed Mr. Dempster to come back into residence at Castlewood. She is not severe or haughty (as her wont certainly was) with any of the party, but quiet in her talk with them, and gentle in assertion and reply. She is for ever talking of her father and his campaigns, who came out of them all with no very severe wounds to hurt him; and so she hopes and trusts will her eldest son.

George writes frequent letters home to his brother, and, now the army is on its march, compiles a rough journal, which he forwards as occasion serves. This document is perused with great delight and eagerness by the youth to whom it is addressed, and more than once read out in family council, on the long summer nights, as Madam Esmond sits upright at her tea-table—(she never condescends to use the back of a chair)—as little Fanny Mountain is busy with her sewing, as Mr. Dempster and Mrs. Mountain sit over their cards, as the hushed old servants of the house move about silently in the gloaming, and listen to the words of the young master. Hearken to Harry Warrington reading out his brother's letter! As we look at the slim characters on the yellow page, fondly kept and put aside, we can almost fancy him alive who wrote and who read it—and yet, lo! they are as if they never had been; their portraits faint images in frames of tarnished gold. Were they real once, or are they mere phantasms? Did they live and die once? Did they love each other as true brothers, and loyal gentlemen? Can we hear their voices in the past? Sure I know Harry's, and yonder he sits in the warm summer evening, and reads his young brother's simple story:

"It must be owned that the provinces are acting scurvily by his Majesty King George II., and his representative here is in a flame of fury. Virginia is bad enough, and poor Maryland not much better, but Pennsylvania is worst of all. We pray them to send us troops from home to fight the French; and we promise to maintain the troops when they come. We not only don't keep our promise, and make scarce any provision for our defenders, but our people insist upon the most exorbitant prices for their cattle and stores, and actually cheat the soldiers who are come to fight their battles. No wonder the General swears, and the troops are sulky. The delays have been endless. Owing to the failure of the several provinces to provide their promised stores and means of locomotion, weeks and months have elapsed, during which time, no doubt, the French have been strengthening themselves on our frontier and in the forts they have turned us out of. Though there never will be any love lost between me and Colonel Washington, it must be owned that your favourite (I am not jealous, Hal) is a brave man and a good officer. The family respect him very much, and the General is always asking his opinion. Indeed, he is almost the only man who has seen the Indians in their war-paint, and I own I think he was right in firing upon Mons. Jumonville last year.

"There is to be no more suite to that other quarrel at Benson's Tavern than there was to the proposed battle between Colonel W. and a certain young gentleman who shall be nameless. Captain Waring wished to pursue it on coming into camp, and brought the message from Captain Grace, which your friend, who is as bold as Hector, was for taking up, and employed a brother aide-de-camp, Colonel Wingfield, on his side. But when Wingfield heard the circumstances of the quarrel, how it had arisen from Grace being drunk, and was fomented by Waring being tipsy, and how the two 44th gentlemen had chosen to insult a militia officer, he swore that Colonel Washington should not meet the 44th men; that he would carry the matter straightway to his Excellency, who would bring the two captains to a court-martial for brawling with the militia, and drunkenness, and indecent behaviour, and the captains were fain to put up their toasting-irons, and swallow their wrath. They were good-natured enough out of their cups, and ate their humble-pie with very good appetites at a reconciliation dinner which Colonel W. had with the 44th, and where he was as perfectly stupid and correct as Prince Prettyman need be. Hang him! He has no faults, and that's why I dislike him. When he marries that widow—ah me! what a dreary life she will have of it."

"I wonder at the taste of some men, and the effrontery of some women," says Madam Esmond, laying her teacup down. "I wonder at any woman who has been married once, so forgetting herself as to marry again! Don't you, Mountain?"

"Monstrous!" says Mountain, with a queer look.

Dempster keeps his eyes steadily fixed on his glass of punch. Harry looks as if he was choking with laughter, or with some other concealed emotion, but his mother says, "Go on, Harry! Continue with your brother's journal. He writes well: but, ah, will he ever be able to write like my papa?"

Harry resumes: "We keep the strictest order here in camp, and the orders against drunkenness and ill-behaviour on the part of the men are very severe. The roll of each company is called at morning, noon, and night, and a return of the absent and disorderly is given in by the officer to the commanding officer of the regiment, who has to see that they are properly punished. The men are punished, and the drummers are always at work. Oh, Harry, but it made one sick to see the first blood drawn from a great strong white back, and to hear the piteous yell of the poor fellow."

"Oh, horrid!" says Madam Esmond.

"I think I should have murdered Ward if he had flogged me. Thank Heaven he got off with only a crack of the ruler! The men, I say, are looked after carefully enough. I wish the officers were. The Indians have just broken up their camp, and retired in dudgeon, because the young officers were for ever drinking with the squaws—and—and—hum—ha." Here Mr. Harry pauses, as not caring to proceed with the narrative, in the presence of little Fanny, very likely, who sits primly in her chair by her mother's side, working her little sampler.

"Pass over that about the odious tipsy creatures," says Madam. And Harry commences, in a loud tone, a much more satisfactory statement: "Each regiment has Divine Service performed at the head of its colours every Sunday. The General does everything in the power of mortal man to prevent plundering, and to encourage the people round about to bring in provisions. He has declared soldiers shall be shot who dare to interrupt or molest the market-people. He has ordered the price of provisions to be raised a penny a pound, and has lent money out of his own pocket to provide the camp. Altogether, he is a strange compound, this General. He flogs his men without mercy, but he gives without stint. He swears most tremendous oaths in conversation, and tells stories which Mountain would be shocked to hear—"

"Why me?" asks Mountain; "and what have I to do with the General's silly stories?"

"Never mind the stories; and go on, Harry," cries the mistress of the house.

"—would be shocked to hear after dinner; but he never misses service. He adores his Great Duke, and has his name constantly on his lips. Our two regiments both served in Scotland, where I dare say Mr. Dempster knew the colour of their facings."

"We saw the tails of their coats, as well as their facings," growls the little Jacobite tutor.

"Colonel Washington has had the fever very smartly, and has hardly been well enough to keep up with the march. Had he not better go home and be nursed by his widow? When either of us is ill, we are almost as good friends again as ever. But I feel somehow as if I can't forgive him for having wronged him. Good Powers! How I have been hating him for these months past! Oh, Harry! I was in a fury at the tavern the other day, because Mountain came up so soon, and put an end to our difference. We ought to have burned a little gunpowder between us, and cleared the air. But though I don't love him, as you do, I know he is a good soldier, a good officer, and a brave, honest man; and, at any rate, shall love him none the worse for not wanting to be our stepfather."

"A stepfather, indeed!" cries Harry's mother. "Why, jealousy and prejudice have perfectly maddened the poor child! Do you suppose the Marquis of Esmond's daughter and heiress could not have found other stepfathers for her sons than a mere provincial surveyor? If there are any more such allusions in George's journal, I beg you skip 'em, Harry, my dear. About this piece of folly and blundering, there hath been quite talk enough already."

"'Tis a pretty sight," Harry continued, reading from his brother's journal, "to see a long line of redcoats, threading through the woods or taking their ground after the march. The care against surprise is so great and constant, that we defy prowling Indians to come unawares upon us, and our advanced sentries and savages have on the contrary fallen in with the enemy and taken a scalp or two from them. They are such cruel villains, these French and their painted allies, that we do not think of showing them mercy. Only think, we found but yesterday a little boy scalped but yet alive in a lone house, where his parents had been attacked and murdered by the savage enemy, of whom—so great is his indignation at their cruelty—our General has offered a reward of five pounds for all the Indian scalps brought in.

"When our march is over, you should see our camp, and all the care bestowed on it. Our baggage and our General's tents and guard are placed quite in the centre of the camp. We have outlying sentries by twos, by threes, by tens, by whole companies. At the least surprise, they are instructed to run in on the main body and rally round the tents and baggage, which are so arranged themselves as to be a strong fortification. Sady and I, you must know, are marching on foot now, and my horses are carrying baggage. The Pennsylvanians sent such rascally animals into camp that they speedily gave in. What good horses were left, 'twas our duty to give up: and Roxana has a couple of packs upon her back instead of her young master. She knows me right well, and whinnies when she sees me, and I walk by her side, and we have many a talk together on the march.

"July 4. To guard against surprises, we are all warned to pay especial attention to the beat of the drum; always halting when they hear the long roll beat, and marching at the beat of the long march. We are more on the alert regarding the enemy now. We have our advanced pickets doubled, and two sentries at every post. The men on the advanced pickets are constantly under arms, with fixed bayonets, all through the night, and relieved every two hours. The half that are relieved lie down by their arms, but are not suffered to leave their pickets. 'Tis evident that we are drawing very near to the enemy now. This packet goes out with the General's to Colonel Dunbar's camp, who is thirty miles behind us; and will be carried thence to Frederick, and thence to my honoured mother's house at Castlewood, to whom I send my duty, with kindest remembrances, as to all friends there, and how much love I need not say to my dearest brother from his affectionate—GEORGE E. WARRINGTON."

The whole land was now lying parched and scorching in the July heat. For ten days no news had come from the column advancing on the Ohio. Their march, though it toiled but slowly through the painful forest, must bring them ere long up with the enemy; the troops, led by consummate captains, were accustomed now to the wilderness, and not afraid of surprise. Every precaution had been taken against ambush. It was the outlying enemy who were discovered, pursued, destroyed, by the vigilant scouts and skirmishers of the British force. The last news heard was that the army had advanced considerably beyond the ground of Mr. Washington's discomfiture on the previous year, and two days after must be within a day's march of the French fort. About taking it no fears were entertained; the amount of the French reinforcements from Montreal was known. Mr. Braddock, with his two veteran regiments from Britain, and their allies of Virginia and Pennsylvania, were more than a match for any troops that could be collected under the white flag.

Such continued to be the talk, in the sparse towns of our Virginian province, at the gentry's houses, and the rough roadside taverns, where people met and canvassed the war. The few messengers who were sent back by the General reported well of the main force. 'Twas thought the enemy would not stand or defend himself at all. Had he intended to attack, he might have seized a dozen occasions for assaulting our troops at passes through which they had been allowed to go entirely free. So George had given up his favourite mare, like a hero as he was, and was marching afoot with the line? Madam Esmond vowed that he should have the best horse in Virginia or Carolina in place of Roxana. There were horses enough to be had in the provinces, and for money. It was only for the King's service that they were not forthcoming.

Although at their family meetings and repasts the inmates of Castlewood always talked cheerfully, never anticipating any but a triumphant issue to the campaign, or acknowledging any feeling of disquiet, yet, it must be owned they were mighty uneasy when at home, quitting it ceaselessly, and for ever on the trot from one neighbour's house to another in quest of news. It was prodigious how quickly reports ran and spread. When, for instance, a certain noted border warrior, called Colonel Jack, had offered himself and his huntsmen to the General, who had declined the ruffian's terms or his proffered service, the defection of Jack and his men was the talk of thousands of tongues immediately. The house negroes, in their midnight gallops about the country, in search of junketing or sweethearts, brought and spread news over amazingly wide districts. They had a curious knowledge of the incidents of the march for a fortnight at least after its commencement. They knew and laughed at the cheats practised on the army, for horses, provisions, and the like; for a good bargain over the foreigner was not an unfrequent or unpleasant practice among New Yorkers, Pennsylvanians, or Marylanders; though 'tis known that American folks have become perfectly artless and simple in later times, and never grasp, and never overreach, and are never selfish now. For three weeks after the army's departure, the thousand reports regarding it were cheerful; and when our Castlewood friends met at their supper, their tone was confident and their news pleasant.

But on the 10th of July a vast and sudden gloom spread over the province. A look of terror and doubt seemed to fall upon every face. Affrighted negroes wistfully eyed their masters and retired, and hummed and whispered with one another. The fiddles ceased in the quarters: the song and laugh of those cheery black folk were hushed. Right and left, everybody's servants were on the gallop for news. The country taverns were thronged with horsemen, who drank and cursed and brawled at the bars, each bringing his gloomy story. The army had been surprised. The troops had fallen into an ambuscade, and had been cut up almost to a man. All the officers were taken down by the French marksmen and the savages. The General had been wounded, and carried off the field in his sash. Four days afterwards the report was that the General was dead, and scalped by a French Indian.

Ah, what a scream poor Mrs. Mountain gave, when Gumbo brought this news from across the James River, and little Fanny sprang crying to her mother's arms! "Lord God Almighty, watch over us, and defend my boy!" said Mrs. Esmond, sinking down on her knees, and lifting her rigid hands to Heaven. The gentlemen were not at home when this rumour arrived, but they came in an hour or two afterwards, each from his hunt for news. The Scots tutor did not dare to look up and meet the widow's agonising looks. Harry Warrington was as pale as his mother. It might not be true about the manner of the General's death—but he was dead. The army had been surprised by Indians, and had fled, and been killed without seeing the enemy. An express had arrived from Dunbar's camp. Fugitives were pouring in there. Should he go and see? He must go and see. He and stout little Dempster armed themselves and mounted, taking a couple of mounted servants with them.

They followed the northward track which the expeditionary army had hewed out for itself, and at every step which brought them nearer to the scene of action, the disaster of the fearful day seemed to magnify. The day after the defeat a number of the miserable fugitives from the fatal battle of the 9th July had reached Dunbar's camp, fifty miles from the field. Thither poor Harry and his companions rode, stopping stragglers, asking news, giving money, getting from one and all the same gloomy tale—a thousand men were slain—two-thirds of the officers were down—all the General's aides-de-camp were hit. Were hit?—but were they killed? Those who fell never rose again. The tomahawk did its work upon them. O brother, brother! All the fond memories of their youth, all the dear remembrances of their childhood, the love and the laughter, the tender romantic vows which they had pledged to each other as lads, were recalled by Harry with pangs inexpressibly keen. Wounded men looked up and were softened by his grief: rough women melted as they saw the woe written on the handsome young face: the hardy old tutor could scarcely look at him for tears, and grieved for him even more than for his dear pupil who lay dead under the savage Indian knife.

CHAPTER XIII. Profitless Quest

At every step which Harry Warrington took towards Pennsylvania, the reports of the British disaster were magnified and confirmed. Those two famous regiments which had fought in the Scottish and Continental wars, had fled from an enemy almost unseen, and their boasted discipline and valour had not enabled them to face a band of savages and a few French infantry. The unfortunate commander of the expedition had shown the utmost bravery and resolution. Four times his horse had been shot under him. Twice he had been wounded, and the last time of the mortal hurt which ended his life three days after the battle. More than one of Harry's informants described the action to the poor lad,—the passage of the river, the long line of advance through the wilderness, the firing in front, the vain struggle of the men to advance, and the artillery to clear the way of the enemy; then the ambushed fire from behind every bush and tree, and the murderous fusillade, by which at least half of the expeditionary force had been shot down. But not all the General's suite were killed, Harry heard. One of his aides-de-camp, a Virginian gentleman, was ill of fever and exhaustion at Dunbar's camp.

One of them—but which? To the camp Harry hurried, and reached it at length. It was George Washington Harry found stretched in a tent there, and not his brother. A sharper pain than that of the fever Mr. Washington declared he felt, when he saw Harry Warrington, and could give him no news of George.

Mr. Washington did not dare to tell Harry all. For three days after the fight his duty had been to be near the General. On the fatal 9th of July, he had seen George go to the front with orders from the chief, to whose side he never returned. After Braddock himself died, the aide-de-camp had found means to retrace his course to the field. The corpses which remained there were stripped and horribly mutilated. One body he buried which he thought to be George Warrington's. His own illness was increased, perhaps occasioned, by the anguish which he underwent in his search for the unhappy young volunteer.

"Ah, George! If you had loved him you would have found him dead or alive," Harry cried out. Nothing would satisfy him but that he, too, should go to the ground and examine it. With money he procured a guide or two. He forded the river at the place where the army had passed over: he went from one end to the other of the dreadful field. It was no longer haunted by Indians now. The birds of prey were feeding on the mangled festering carcases. Save in his own grandfather, lying very calm, with a sweet smile on his lip, Harry had never yet seen the face of Death. The horrible spectacle of mutilation caused him to turn away with shudder and loathing. What news could the vacant woods, or those festering corpses lying under the trees, give the lad of his lost brother? He was for going, unarmed and with a white flag, to the French fort, whither, after their victory, the enemy had returned; but his guides refused to advance with him. The French might possibly respect them, but the Indians would not. "Keep your hair for your lady mother, my young gentleman," said the guide. "'Tis enough that she loses one son in this campaign."

When Harry returned to the English encampment at Dunbar's, it was his turn to be down with the fever. Delirium set in upon him, and he lay some time in the tent and on the bed from which his friend had just risen convalescent. For some days he did not know who watched him; and poor Dempster, who had tended him in more than one of these maladies, thought the widow must lose both her children; but the fever was so far subdued that the boy was enabled to rally somewhat, and get to horseback. Mr. Washington and Dempster both escorted him home. It was with a heavy heart, no doubt, that all three beheld once more the gates of Castlewood.

A servant in advance had been sent to announce their coming. First came Mrs. Mountain and her little daughter, welcoming Harry with many tears and embraces, but she scarce gave a nod of recognition to Mr. Washington; and the little girl caused the young officer to start, and turn deadly pale, by coming up to him with her hands behind her, and asking, "Why have you not brought George back too?" Harry did not hear. The sobs and caresses of his good friend and nurse luckily kept him from listening to little Fanny.

Dempster was graciously received by the two ladies. "Whatever could be done, we know you would do, Mr. Dempster," says Mrs. Mountain, giving him her hand. "Make a curtsey to Mr. Dempster, Fanny, and remember, child, to be grateful to all who have been friendly to our benefactors. Will it please you to take any refreshment before you ride, Colonel Washington?"

Mr. Washington had had a sufficient ride already, and counted as certainly upon the hospitality of Castlewood, as he would upon the shelter of his own house.

"The time to feed my horse, and a glass of water for myself, and I will trouble Castlewood hospitality no further," Mr. Washington said.

"Sure, George, you have your room here, and my mother is above-stairs getting it ready!" cries Harry. "That poor horse of yours stumbled with you, and can't go farther this evening."

"Hush! Your mother won't see him, child," whispered Mrs. Mountain.

"Not see George? Why, he is like a son of the house," cries Harry.

"She had best not see him. I don't meddle any more in family matters, child: but when the Colonel's servant rode in, and said you were coming, Madam Esmond left this room, my dear, where she was sitting reading Drelincourt, and said she felt she could not see Mr. Washington. Will you go to her?" Harry took his friend's arm, and excusing himself to the Colonel, to whom he said he would return in a few minutes, he left the parlour in which they had assembled, and went to the upper rooms, where Madam Esmond was.

He was hastening across the corridor, and, with an averted head, passing by one especial door, which he did not like to look at, for it was that of his brother's room; but as he came to it, Madam Esmond issued from it, and folded him to her heart, and led him in. A settee was by the bed, and a book of psalms lay on the coverlet. All the rest of the room was exactly as George had left it.

"My poor child! How thin thou art grown—how haggard you look! Never mind. A mother's care will make thee well again. 'Twas nobly done to go and brave sickness and danger in search of your brother. Had others been as faithful, he might be here now. Never mind, my Harry; our hero will come back to us,—I know he is not dead. One so good, and so brave, and so gentle, and so clever as he was, I know is not lost to us altogether." (Perhaps Harry thought within himself that his mother had not always been accustomed so to speak of her eldest son.) "Dry up thy tears, my dear! He will come back to us, I know he will come." And when Harry pressed her to give a reason for her belief, she said she had seen her father two nights running in a dream, and he had told her that her boy was a prisoner among the Indians.

Madam Esmond's grief had not prostrated her as Harry's had when first it fell upon him; it had rather stirred and animated her: her eyes were eager, her countenance angry and revengeful. The lad wondered almost at the condition in which he found his mother.

But when he besought her to go downstairs, and give a hand of welcome to George Washington, who had accompanied him, the lady's excitement painfully increased. She said she should shudder at touching his hand. She declared Mr. Washington had taken her son from her, she could not sleep under the same roof with him.

"He gave me his bed when I was ill, mother; and if our George is alive, how has George Washington a hand in his death? Ah! please God it be only as you say," cried Harry, in bewilderment.

"If your brother returns, as return he will, it will not be through Mr. Washington's help," said Madam Esmond. "He neither defended George on the field, nor would he bring him out of it."

"But he tended me most kindly in my fever," interposed Harry. "He was yet ill when he gave up his bed to me, and was thinking only of his friend, when any other man would have thought only of himself."

"A friend! A pretty friend!" sneers the lady. "Of all his Excellency's aides-de-camp, my gentleman is the only one who comes back unwounded. The brave and noble fall, but he, to be sure, is unhurt. I confide my boy to him, the pride of my life, whom he will defend with his, forsooth! And he leaves my George in the forest, and brings me back himself! Oh, a pretty welcome I must give him!"

"No gentleman," cried Harry, warmly, "was ever refused shelter under my grandfather's roof."

"Oh no—no gentleman!" exclaims the little widow; "let us go down, if you like, son, and pay our respects to this one. Will you please to give me your arm?" And taking an arm which was very little able to give her support, she walked down the broad stairs, and into the apartment where the Colonel sate.

She made him a ceremonious curtsey, and extended one of the little hands, which she allowed for a moment to rest in his. "I wish that our meeting had been happier, Colonel Washington," she said.

"You do not grieve more than I do that it is otherwise, madam," said the Colonel.

"I might have wished that the meeting had been spared, that I might not have kept you from friends whom you are naturally anxious to see,—that my boy's indisposition had not detained you. Home and his good nurse Mountain, and his mother and our good Doctor Dempster, will soon restore him. 'Twas scarce necessary, Colonel, that you, who have so many affairs on your hands, military and domestic, should turn doctor too."

"Harry was ill and weak, and I thought it was my duty to ride by him," faltered the Colonel.

"You yourself, sir, have gone through the fatigues and dangers of the campaign in the most wonderful manner," said the widow, curtseying again, and looking at him with her impenetrable black eyes.

"I wish to Heaven, madam, some one else had come back in my place!"

"Nay, sir, you have ties which must render your life more than ever valuable and dear to you, and duties to which, I know, you must be anxious to betake yourself. In our present deplorable state of doubt and distress, Castlewood can be a welcome place to no stranger, much less to you, and so I know, sir, you will be for leaving us ere long. And you will pardon me if the state of my own spirits obliges me for the most part to keep my chamber. But my friends here will bear you company as long as you favour us, whilst I nurse my poor Harry upstairs. Mountain, you will have the cedar-room on the ground-floor ready for Mr. Washington, and anything in the house is at his command.

Farewell, sir. Will you be pleased to present my compliments to your mother, who will be thankful to have her son safe and sound out of the war,—as also to my young friend Martha Custis, to whom and to whose children I wish every happiness. Come, my son!" and with these words, and another freezing curtsey, the pale little woman retreated, looking steadily at the Colonel, who stood dumb on the floor.

Strong as Madam Esmond's belief appeared to be respecting her son's safety, the house of Castlewood naturally remained sad and gloomy. She might forbid mourning for herself and family; but her heart was in black, whatever face the resolute little lady persisted in wearing before the world. To look for her son, was hoping against hope. No authentic account of his death had indeed arrived, and no one appeared who had seen him fall; but hundreds more had been so stricken on that fatal day, with no eyes to behold their last pangs, save those of the lurking enemy and the comrades dying by their side. A fortnight after the defeat, when Harry was absent on his quest, George's servant, Sady, reappeared wounded and maimed at Castlewood. But he could give no coherent account of the battle, only of his flight from the centre, where he was with the baggage. He had no news of his master since the morning of the action. For many days Sady lurked in the negro quarters away from the sight of Madam Esmond, whose anger he did not dare to face. That lady's few neighbours spoke of her as labouring under a delusion. So strong was it, that there were times when Harry and the other members of the little Castlewood family were almost brought to share in it. It seemed nothing strange to her, that her father out of another world should promise her her son's life. In this world or the next, that family sure must be of consequence, she thought. Nothing had ever yet happened to her sons, no accident, no fever, no important illness, but she had a prevision of it. She could enumerate half a dozen instances, which, indeed, her household was obliged more or less to confirm, how, when anything had happened to the boys at ever so great a distance, she had known of their mishap and its consequences. No, George was not dead; George was a prisoner among the Indians; George would come back and rule over Castlewood; as sure, as sure as his Majesty would send a great force from home to recover the tarnished glory of the British arms, and to drive the French out of the Americas.

As for Mr. Washington, she would never with her own goodwill behold him again. He had promised to protect George with his life. Why was her son gone and the Colonel alive? How dared he to face her after that promise, and appear before a mother without her son? She trusted she knew her duty. She bore illwill to no one: but as an Esmond, she had a sense of honour, and Mr. Washington had forfeited hers in letting her son out of his sight. He had to obey superior orders (some one perhaps objected)? Psha! a promise was a promise. He had promised to guard George's life with his own, and where was her boy? And was not the Colonel (a pretty Colonel, indeed!) sound and safe? Do not tell me that his coat and hat had shots through them! (This was her answer to another humble plea in Mr. Washington's behalf.) Can't I go into the study this instant and fire two shots with my papa's pistols through this paduasoy skirt,—and should I be killed? She laughed at the notion of death resulting from any such operation; nor was her laugh very pleasant to hear. The satire of people who have little natural humour is seldom good sport for bystanders. I think dull men's faceticae are mostly cruel.

So, if Harry wanted to meet his friend, he had to do so in secret, at court-houses, taverns, or various places of resort; or in their little towns, where the provincial gentry assembled. No man of spirit, she vowed, could meet Mr. Washington after his base desertion of her family. She was exceedingly excited when she heard that the Colonel and her son absolutely had met. What a heart must Harry have to give his hand to one whom she considered as little better than George's murderer! "For shame to say so! For shame upon you, ungrateful boy, forgetting the dearest, noblest, most perfect of brothers, for that tall, gawky, fox-hunting Colonel, with his horrid oaths! How can he be George's murderer, when I say my boy is not dead? He is not dead, because my instinct never deceived me: because, as sure as I see his picture now before me,—only 'tis not near so noble or so good as he used to look,—so surely two nights running did my papa appear to me in my dreams. You doubt about that, very likely? 'Tis because you never loved anybody sufficiently, my poor Harry; else you might have leave to see them in dreams, as has been vouchsafed to some."

"I think I loved George, mother," cried Harry. "I have often prayed that I might dream about him, and I don't."

"How you can talk, sir, of loving George, and then—go and meet your Mr. Washington at horse-races, I can't understand! Can you, Mountain?"

"We can't understand many things in our neighbours' characters. I can understand that our boy is unhappy, and that he does not get strength, and that he is doing no good here, in Castlewood, or moping at the taverns and court-houses with horse-coupers and idle company," grumbled Mountain in reply to her patroness; and, in truth, the dependant was right.

There was not only grief in the Castlewood House, but there was disunion. "I cannot tell how it came," said Harry, as he brought the story to an end, which we have narrated in the last two numbers, and which he confided to his new-found English relative, Madame de Bernstein; "but since that fatal day of July, last year, and my return home, my mother never has been the same woman. She seemed to love none of us as she used. She was for ever praising George, and yet she did not seem as if she liked him much when he was with us. She hath plunged, more deeply than ever, into her books of devotion, out of which she only manages to extract grief and sadness, as I think. Such a gloom has fallen over our wretched Virginian house of Castlewood, that we all grew ill, and pale as ghosts, who inhabited it. Mountain told me, madam, that, for nights, my mother would not close her eyes. I have had her at my bedside, looking so ghastly, that I have started from my own sleep, fancying a ghost before me. By one means or other she has wrought herself into a state of excitement which if not delirium, is akin to it. I was again and again struck down by the fever, and all the Jesuits' bark in America could not cure me. We have a tobacco-house and some land about the new town of Richmond, in our province, and went thither, as Williamsburg is no wholesomer than our own place; and there I mended a little, but still did not get quite well, and the physicians strongly counselled a sea-voyage. My mother, at one time, had thoughts of coming with me, but—" (and here the lad blushed and hung his head down) "—we did not agree very well, though I know we loved each other very heartily, and 'twas determined that I should see the world for myself. So I took passage in our ship from the James River, and was landed at Bristol. And 'twas only on the 9th of July, this year, at sea, as had been agreed between me and Madam Esmond, that I put mourning on for my dear brother."

So that little Mistress of the Virginian Castlewood, for whom, I am sure, we have all the greatest respect, had the knack of rendering the people round about her uncomfortable; quarrelled with those she loved best, and exercised over them her wayward jealousies and imperious humours, until they were not sorry to leave her. Here was money enough, friends enough, a good position, and the respect of the world; a house stored with all manner of plenty, and good things, and poor Harry Warrington was glad to leave them all behind him. Happy! Who is happy? What good in a stalled ox for dinner every day, and no content therewith? Is it best to be loved and plagued by those you love, or to have an easy, comfortable indifference at home; to follow your fancies, live there unmolested, and die without causing any painful regrets or tears?

To be sure, when her boy was gone, Madam Esmond forgot all these little tiffs and differences. To hear her speak of both her children, you would fancy they were perfect characters, and had never caused her a moment's worry or annoyance. These gone, Madam fell naturally upon Mrs. Mountain and her little daughter, and worried and annoyed them. But women bear with hard words more easily than men, are more ready to forgive injuries, or, perhaps, to dissemble anger. Let us trust that Madam Esmond's dependants found their life tolerable, that they gave her ladyship sometimes as good as they got, that if they quarrelled in the morning they were reconciled at night, and sate down to a tolerably friendly game at cards and an amicable dish of tea.

But, without the boys, the great house of Castlewood was dreary to the widow. She left an overseer there to manage her estates, and only paid the place an occasional visit. She enlarged and beautified her house in the pretty little city of Richmond, which began to grow daily in importance. She had company there, and card-assemblies, and preachers in plenty; and set up her little throne there, to which the gentlefolks of the province were welcome to come and bow. All her domestic negroes, who loved society as negroes will do, were delighted to exchange the solitude of Castlewood for the gay and merry little town; where, for a time, and while we pursue Harry Warrington's progress in Europe, we leave the good lady.

CHAPTER XIV. Harry in England

When the famous Trojan wanderer narrated his escapes and adventures to Queen Dido, her Majesty, as we read, took the very greatest interest in the fascinating story-teller who told his perils so eloquently. A history ensued, more pathetic than any of the previous occurrences in the life of Pius Aeneas, and the poor princess had reason to rue the day when she listened to that glib and dangerous orator. Harry Warrington had not pious Aeneas's power of speech, and his elderly aunt, we may presume, was by no means so soft-hearted as the sentimental Dido; but yet the lad's narrative was touching, as he delivered it with his artless eloquence and cordial voice; and more than once, in the course of his story, Madam Bernstein found herself moved to a softness to which she had very seldom before allowed herself to give way. There were not many fountains in that desert of a life—not many sweet, refreshing resting-places. It had been a long loneliness, for the most part, until this friendly voice came and sounded in her ears and caused her heart to beat with strange pangs of love and sympathy. She doted on this lad, and on this sense of compassion and regard so new to her. Save once, faintly, in very very early youth, she had felt no tender sentiment for any human being. Such a woman would, no doubt, watch her own sensations very keenly, and must have smiled after the appearance of this boy, to mark how her pulses rose above their ordinary beat. She longed after him. She felt her cheeks flush with happiness when he came near. Her eyes greeted him with welcome, and followed him with fond pleasure. "Ah, if she could have had a son like that, how she would have loved him!" "Wait," says Conscience, the dark scoffer mocking within her, "wait, Beatrix Esmond! You know you will weary of this inclination, as you have of all. You know, when the passing fancy has subsided, that the boy may perish, and you won't have a tear for him; or talk, and you weary of his stories; and that your lot in life is to be lonely—lonely." Well? suppose life be a desert? There are halting-places and shades, and refreshing waters; let us profit by them for to-day. We know that we must march when to-morrow comes, and tramp on our destiny onward.

She smiled inwardly, whilst following the lad's narrative, to recognise in his simple tales about his mother, traits of family resemblance. Madam Esmond was very jealous?—Yes, that Harry owned. She was fond of Colonel Washington? She liked him, but only as a friend, Harry declared. A hundred times he had heard his mother vow that she had no other feeling towards him. He was ashamed to have to own that he himself had been once absurdly jealous of the Colonel. "Well, you will see that my half-sister will never forgive him," said Madam Beatrix. "And you need not be surprised, sir, at women taking a fancy to men younger than themselves; for don't I dote upon you; and don't all these Castlewood people crevent with jealousy?"

However great might be their jealousy of Madame de Bernstein's new favourite, the family of Castlewood allowed no feeling of illwill to appear in their language or behaviour to their young guest and kinsman. After a couple of days' stay in the ancestral house, Mr. Harry Warrington had become Cousin Harry with young and middle-aged. Especially in Madame Bernstein's presence, the Countess of Castlewood was most gracious to her kinsman, and she took many amiable private opportunities of informing the Baroness how charming the young Huron was, of vaunting the elegance of his manners and appearance, and wondering how, in his distant province, the child should ever have learned to be so polite?

These notes of admiration or interrogation, the Baroness took with equal complacency (speaking parenthetically, and, for his own part, the present chronicler cannot help putting in a little respectful remark here, and signifying his admiration of the conduct of ladies towards one another, and of the things which they say, which they forbear to say, and which they say behind each other's backs. With what smiles and curtseys they stab each other! with what compliments they hate each other! with what determination of long-suffering they won't be offended! with what innocent dexterity they can drop the drop of poison into the cup of conversation, hand round the goblet, smiling, to the whole family to drink, and make the dear, domestic circle miserable!)—I burst out of my parenthesis. I fancy my Baroness and Countess smiling at each other a hundred years ago, and giving each other the hand or the cheek, and calling each other, My dear, My dear creature, My dear Countess, My dear Baroness, My dear sister—even, when they were most ready to fight.

"You wonder, my dear Maria, that the boy should be so polite?" cries Madame de Bernstein. "His mother was bred up by two very perfect gentlefolks. Colonel Esmond had a certain grave courteousness, and a grand manner, which I do not see among the gentlemen nowadays."

"Eh, my dear, we all of us praise our own time! My grandmamma used to declare there was nothing like Whitehall and Charles the Second."

"My mother saw King James the Second's court for a short while, and though not a court-educated person, as you know,—her father was a country clergyman—yet was exquisitely well-bred. The Colonel, her second husband, was a person of great travel and experience, as well as of learning, and had frequented the finest company of Europe. They could not go into their retreat and leave their good manners behind them, and our boy has had them as his natural inheritance."

"Nay, excuse me, my dear, for thinking you too partial about your mother. She could not have been that perfection which your filial fondness imagines. She left off liking her daughter—my dear creature, you have owned that she did—and I cannot fancy a complete woman who has a cold heart. No, no, my dear sister-in-law! Manners are very requisite, no doubt, and, for a country parson's daughter, your mamma was very well—I have seen many of the cloth who are very well. Mr. Sampson, our chaplain, is very well. Dr. Young is very well. Mr. Dodd is very well; but they have not the true air—as how should they? I protest, I beg pardon! I forgot my lord bishop, your ladyship's first choice. But, as I said before, to be a complete woman, one must have, what you have, what I may say and bless Heaven for, I think I have—a good heart. Without the affections, all the world is vanity, my love! I protest I only live, exist, eat, drink, rest, for my sweet, sweet children!—for my wicked Willy, for my self-willed Fanny, dear naughty loves!" (She rapturously kisses a bracelet on each arm which contains the miniature representations of those two young persons.) "Yes, Mimi! yes, Fanchon! you know I do, you dear, dear little things! and if they were to die, or you were to die, your poor mistress would die too!" Mimi and Fanchon, two quivering Italian greyhounds, jump into their lady's arms, and kiss her hands, but respect her cheeks, which are covered with rouge. "No, my dear! For nothing do I bless Heaven so much (though it puts me to excruciating torture very often) as for having endowed me with sensibility and a feeling heart!"

"You are full of feeling, dear Anna," says the Baroness. "You are celebrated for your sensibility. You must give a little of it to our American nephew—cousin—I scarce know his relationship."

"Nay, I am here but as a guest in Castlewood now. The house is my Lord Castlewood's, not mine, or his lordship's whenever he shall choose to claim it. What can I do for the young Virginian that has not been done? He is charming. Are we even jealous of him for being so, my dear? and though we see what a fancy the Baroness de Bernstein has taken for him, do your ladyship's nephews and nieces—your real nephews and nieces—cry out? My poor children might be mortified, for indeed, in a few hours, the charming young man has made as much way as my poor things have been able to do in all their lives: but are they angry? Willy hath taken him out to ride. This morning, was not Maria playing the harpsichord whilst my Fanny taught him the minuet? 'Twas a charming young group, I assure you, and it brought tears into my eyes to look at the young creatures. Poor lad! we are as fond of him as you are, dear Baroness!"

Now, Madame de Bernstein had happened, through her own ears or her maid's, to overhear what really took place in consequence of this harmless little scene. Lady Castlewood had come into the room where the young people were thus engaged in amusing and instructing themselves, accompanied by her son William, who arrived in his boots from the kennel.

"Bravi, bravi! Oh, charming!" said the Countess, clapping her hands, nodding with one of her best smiles to Harry Warrington, and darting a look at his partner, which my Lady Fanny perfectly understood; and so, perhaps, did my Lady Maria at her harpsichord, for she played with redoubled energy, and nodded her waving curls, over the chords.

"Infernal young Choctaw! Is he teaching Fanny the war-dance? and is Fan going to try her tricks upon him now?" asked Mr. William, whose temper was not of the best.

And that was what Lady Castlewood's look said to Fanny. "Are you going to try your tricks upon him now?"

She made Harry a very low curtsey, and he blushed, and they both stopped dancing, somewhat disconcerted. Lady Maria rose from the harpsichord and walked away.

"Nay, go on dancing, young people! Don't let me spoil sport, and let me play for you," said the Countess; and she sate down to the instrument and played.

"I don't know how to dance," says Harry, hanging his head down, with a blush that the Countess's finest carmine could not equal.

"And Fanny was teaching you? Go on teaching him, dearest Fanny!"

"Go on, do!" says William, with a sidelong growl.

"I—I had rather not show off my awkwardness in company," adds Harry, recovering himself. "When I know how to dance a minuet, be sure I will ask my cousin to walk one with me."

"That will be very soon, dear Cousin Warrington, I am certain," remarks the Countess, with her most gracious air.

"What game is she hunting now?" thinks Mr. William to himself, who cannot penetrate his mother's ways; and that lady, fondly calling her daughter to her elbow, leaves the room.

They are no sooner in the tapestried passage leading away to their own apartment, but Lady Castlewood's bland tone entirely changes. "You booby!" she begins to her adored Fanny. "You double idiot! What are you going to do with the Huron? You don't want to marry a creature like that, and be a squaw in a wigwam?"

"Don't, mamma!" gasps Lady Fanny. Mamma was pinching her ladyship's arm black-and-blue. "I am sure our cousin is very well," Fanny whimpers, "and you said so yourself."

"Very well! Yes; and heir to a swamp, a negro, a log-cabin and a barrel of tobacco! My Lady Frances Esmond, do you remember what your ladyship's rank is, and what your name is, and who was your ladyship's mother, when, at three days' acquaintance, you commence dancing—a pretty dance, indeed—with this brat out of Virginia?"

"Mr. Warrington is our cousin," pleads Lady Fanny.

"A creature come from nobody knows where is not your cousin! How do we know he is your cousin? He may be a valet who has taken his master's portmanteau, and run away in his postchaise."

"But Madame de Bernstein says he is our cousin," interposes Fanny; "and he is the image of the Esmonds."

"Madame de Bernstein has her likes and dislikes, takes up people and forgets people; and she chooses to profess a mighty fancy for this young man. Because she likes him to-day, is that any reason why she should like him to-morrow? Before company, and in your aunt's presence, your ladyship will please to be as civil to him as necessary; but, in private, I forbid you to see him or encourage him."

"I don't care, madam, whether your ladyship forbids me or not!" cries out Lady Fanny, wrought up to a pitch of revolt.

"Very good, Fanny! then I speak to my lord, and we return to Kensington. If I can't bring you to reason, your brother will."

At this juncture the conversation between mother and daughter stopped, or Madame de Bernstein's informer had no further means of hearing or reporting it.

It was only in after days that she told Harry Warrington a part of what she knew. At present he but saw that his kinsfolks received him not unkindly. Lady Castlewood was perfectly civil to him; the young ladies pleasant and pleased; my Lord Castlewood, a man of cold and haughty demeanour, was not more reserved towards Harry than to any of the rest of the family; Mr. William was ready to drink with him, to ride with him, to go to races with him, and to play cards with him. When he proposed to go away, they one and all pressed him to stay. Madame de Bernstein did not tell him how it arose that he was the object of such eager hospitality. He did not know what schemes he was serving or disarranging, whose or what anger he was creating. He fancied he was welcome because those around him were his kinsmen, and never thought that those could be his enemies out of whose cup he was drinking, and whose hand he was pressing every night and morning.

CHAPTER XV. A Sunday at Castlewood

The second day after Harry's arrival at Castlewood was a Sunday. The chapel appertaining to the castle was the village church. A door from the house communicated with a great state pew which the family occupied, and here after due time they all took their places in order, whilst a rather numerous congregation from the village filled the seats below. A few ancient dusty banners hung from the church roof; and Harry pleased himself in imagining that they had been borne by retainers of his family in the Commonwealth wars, in which, as he knew well, his ancestors had taken a loyal and distinguished part. Within the altar-rails was the effigy of the Esmond of the time of King James the First, the common forefather of all the group assembled in the family pew. Madame de Bernstein, in her quality of Bishop's widow, never failed in attendance, and conducted her devotions with a gravity almost as exemplary as that of the ancestor yonder, in his square beard and red gown, for ever kneeling on his stone hassock before his great marble desk and book, under his emblazoned shield of arms. The clergyman, a tall, high-coloured, handsome young man, read the service in a lively, agreeable voice, giving almost a dramatic point to the chapters of Scripture which he read. The music was good—one of the young ladies of the family touching the organ—and would have been better but for an interruption and something like a burst of laughter from the servants' pew, which was occasioned by Mr. Warrington's lacquey Gumbo, who, knowing the air given out for the psalm, began to sing it in a voice so exceedingly loud and sweet, that the whole congregation turned towards the African warbler; the parson himself put his handkerchief to his mouth, and the liveried gentlemen from London were astonished out of all propriety. Pleased, perhaps, with the sensation which he had created, Mr.

Gumbo continued his performance until it became almost a solo, and the voice of the clerk himself was silenced. For the truth is, that though Gumbo held on to the book, along with pretty Molly, the porter's daughter, who had been the first to welcome the strangers to Castlewood, he sang and recited by ear and not by note, and could not read a syllable of the verses in the book before him.

This choral performance over, a brief sermon in due course followed, which, indeed, Harry thought a deal too short. In a lively, familiar, striking discourse the clergyman described a scene of which he had been witness the previous week—the execution of a horse-stealer after Assizes. He described the man and his previous good character, his family, the love they bore one another, and his agony at parting from them. He depicted the execution in a manner startling, terrible, and picturesque. He did not introduce into his sermon the Scripture phraseology, such as Harry had been accustomed to hear it from those somewhat Calvinistic preachers whom his mother loved to frequent, but rather spoke as one man of the world to other sinful people, who might be likely to profit by good advice. The unhappy man just gone, had begun as a farmer of good prospects; he had taken to drinking, card-playing, horse-racing, cock-fighting, the vices of the age; against which the young clergyman was generously indignant. Then he had got to poaching and to horse-stealing, for which he suffered. The divine rapidly drew striking and fearful pictures of these rustic crimes. He startled his hearers by showing that the Eye of the Law was watching the poacher at midnight, and setting traps to catch the criminal. He galloped the stolen horse over highway and common, and from one county into another, but showed Retribution ever galloping after, seizing the malefactor in the country fair, carrying him before the justice, and never unlocking his manacles till he dropped them at the gallows-foot. Heaven be pitiful to the sinner! The clergyman acted the scene. He whispered in the criminal's ear at the cart. He dropped his handkerchief on the clerk's head. Harry started back as that handkerchief dropped. The clergyman had been talking for more than twenty minutes. Harry could have heard him for an hour more, and thought he had not been five minutes in the pulpit. The gentlefolks in the great pew were very much enlivened by the discourse. Once or twice, Harry, who could see the pew where the house servants sate, remarked these very attentive; and especially Gumbo, his own man, in an attitude of intense consternation. But the smockfrocks did not seem to heed, and clamped out of church quite unconcerned. Gaffer Brown and Gammer Jones took the matter as it came, and the rosy-cheeked, red-cloaked village lasses sate under their broad hats entirely unmoved. My lord, from his pew, nodded slightly to the clergyman in the pulpit, when that divine's head and wig surged up from the cushion.

"Sampson has been strong to-day," said his lordship. "He has assaulted the Philistines in great force."

"Beautiful, beautiful!" says Harry.

"Bet five to four it was his Assize sermon. He has been over to Winton to preach, and to see those dogs," cries William.

The organist had played the little congregation out into the sunshine. Only Sir Francis Esmond, temp. Jac. I., still knelt on his marble hassock, before his prayer-book of stone. Mr. Sampson came out of his vestry in his cassock, and nodded to the gentlemen still lingering in the great pew.

"Come up, and tell us about those dogs," says Mr. William, and the divine nodded a laughing assent.

The gentlemen passed out of the church into the gallery of their house, which connected them with that sacred building. Mr. Sampson made his way through the court, and presently joined them. He was presented by my lord to the Virginian cousin of the family, Mr. Warrington: the chaplain bowed very profoundly, and hoped Mr. Warrington would benefit by the virtuous example of his European kinsmen. Was he related to Sir Miles Warrington of Norfolk? Sir Miles was Mr. Warrington's father's elder brother. What a pity he had a son! 'Twas a pretty estate, and Mr. Warrington looked as if he would become a baronetcy, and a fine estate in Norfolk.

"Tell me about my uncle," cried Virginian Harry.

"Tell us about those dogs!" said English Will, in a breath.

"Two more jolly dogs, two more drunken dogs, saving your presence, Mr. Warrington, than Sir Miles and his son, I never saw. Sir Miles was a staunch friend and neighbour of Sir Robert's. He can drink down any man in the county, except his son and a few more. The other dogs about which Mr. William is anxious, for Heaven hath made him a prey to dogs and all kinds of birds, like the Greeks in the Iliad———"

"I know that line in the Iliad," says Harry, blushing. "I only know five more, but I know that one." And his head fell. He was thinking, "Ah, my dear brother George knew all the Iliad and all the Odyssey, and almost every book that was ever written besides!"

"What on earth" (only he mentioned a place under the earth) "are you talking about now?" asked Will of his reverence.

The chaplain reverted to the dogs and their performance. He thought Mr. William's dogs were more than a match for them. From dogs they went off to horses. Mr. William was very eager about the Six Year Old Plate at Huntingdon. "Have you brought any news of it, Parson?"

"The odds are five to four on Brilliant against the field," says the parson, gravely, "but, mind you, Jason is a good horse."

"Whose horse?" asks my lord.

"Duke of Ancaster's. By Cartouche out of Miss Langley," says the divine. "Have you horse-races in Virginia, Mr. Warrington?"

"Haven't we!" cries Harry; "but oh! I long to see a good English race!"

"Do you—do you—bet a little?" continues his reverence.

"I have done such a thing," replies Harry with a smile.

"I'll take Brilliant even against the field, for ponies with you, cousin!" shouts out Mr. William.

"I'll give or take three to one against Jason!" says the clergyman.

"I don't bet on horses I don't know," said Harry, wondering to hear the chaplain now, and remembering his sermon half an hour before.

"Hadn't you better write home, and ask your mother?" says Mr. William, with a sneer.

"Will, Will!" calls out my lord, "our cousin Warrington is free to bet, or not, as he likes. Have a care how you venture on either of them, Harry Warrington. Will is an old file, in spite of his smooth face, and as for Parson Sampson, I defy our ghostly enemy to get the better of him."

"Him and all his works, my lord!" said Mr. Sampson, with a bow.

Harry was highly indignant at this allusion to his mother. "I'll tell you what, cousin Will," he said, "I am in the habit of managing my own affairs in my own way, without asking any lady to arrange them for me. And I'm used to make my own bets upon my own judgment, and don't need any relations to select them for me, thank you. But as I am your guest, and, no doubt, you want to show me hospitality, I'll take your bet—there. And so Done and Done."

"Done," says Will, looking askance.

"Of course it is the regular odds that's in the paper which you give me, cousin?"

"Well, no, it isn't," growled Will. "The odds are five to four, that's the fact, and you may have 'em, if you like."

"Nay, cousin, a bet is a bet; and I take you, too, Mr. Sampson."

"Three to one against Jason. I lay it. Very good," says Mr. Sampson.

"Is it to be ponies too, Mr. Chaplain?" asks Harry with a superb air, as if he had Lombard Street in his pocket.

"No, no. Thirty to ten. It is enough for a poor priest to win."

"Here goes a great slice out of my quarter's hundred," thinks Harry. "Well, I shan't let these Englishmen fancy that I am afraid of them. I didn't begin, but for the honour of Old Virginia I won't go back."

These pecuniary transactions arranged, William Esmond went away scowling towards the stables, where he loved to take his pipe with the grooms; the brisk parson went off to pay his court to the ladies, and partake of the Sunday dinner which would presently be served. Lord Castlewood and Harry remained for a while together. Since the Virginian's arrival my lord had scarcely spoken with him. In his manners he was perfectly friendly, but so silent that he would often sit at the head of his table, and leave it without uttering a word.

"I suppose yonder property of yours is a fine one by this time?" said my lord to Harry.

"I reckon it's almost as big as an English county," answered Harry, "and the land's as good, too, for many things." Harry would not have the Old Dominion, nor his share in it, underrated.

"Indeed!" said my lord, with a look of surprise. "When it belonged to my father it did not yield much."

"Pardon me, my lord. You know how it belonged to your father," cried the youth, with some spirit. "It was because my grandfather did not choose to claim his right." [This matter is discussed in the Author's previous work, The Memoirs of Colonel Esmond.]

"Of course, of course," says my lord, hastily.

"I mean, cousin, that we of the Virginian house owe you nothing but our own," continued Harry Warrington; "but our own, and the hospitality which you are now showing me."

"You are heartily welcome to both. You were hurt by the betting just now?"

"Well," replied the lad, "I am sort o' hurt. Your welcome, you see, is different to our welcome, and that's the fact. At home we are glad to see a man, hold out a hand to him, and give him of our best. Here you take us in, give us beef and claret enough, to be sure, and don't seem to care when we come, or when we go. That's the remark which I have been making since I have been in your lordship's house; I can't help telling it out, you see, now 'tis on my mind; and I think I am a little easier now I have said it." And with this, the excited young fellow knocked a billiard-ball across the table, and then laughed, and looked at his elder kinsman.

"A la bonne heure! We are cold to the stranger within and without our gates. We don't take Mr. Harry Warrington into our arms, and cry when we see our cousin. We don't cry when he goes away—but do we pretend?"

"No, you don't. But you try to get the better of him in a bet," says Harry, indignantly.

"Is there no such practice in Virginia, and don't sporting men there try to overreach one another? What was that story I heard you telling our aunt, of the British officers and Tom somebody of Spotsylvania!"

"That's fair!" cries Harry. "That is, it's usual practice, and a stranger must look out. I don't mind the parson; if he wins, he may have, and welcome. But a relation! To think that my own blood cousin wants money out of me!"

"A Newmarket man would get the better of his father. My brother has been on the turf since he rode over to it from Cambridge. If you play at cards with him—and he will if you will let him—he will beat you if he can."

"Well, I'm ready!" cries Harry. "I'll play any game with him that I know, or I'll jump with him, or I'll ride with him, or I'll row with him, or I'll wrestle with him, or I'll shoot with him—there—now."

The senior was greatly entertained, and held out his hand to the boy. "Anything, but don't fight with him," said my lord.

"If I do, I'll whip him! hanged if I don't!" cried the lad. But a look of surprise and displeasure on the nobleman's part recalled him to better sentiments. "A hundred pardons, my lord!" he said, blushing very red, and seizing his cousin's hand. "I talked of ill manners, being angry and hurt just now; but 'tis doubly ill-mannered of me to show my anger, and boast about my prowess to my own host and kinsman. It's not the practice with us Americans to boast, believe me, it's not."

"You are the first I ever met," says my lord, with a smile, "and I take you at your word. And I give you fair warning about the cards, and the betting, that is all, my boy."

"Leave a Virginian alone! We are a match for most men, we are," resumed the boy.

Lord Castlewood did not laugh. His eyebrows only arched for a moment, and his grey eyes turned towards the ground. "So you can bet fifty guineas, and afford to lose them? So much the better for you, cousin. Those great Virginian estates yield a great revenue, do they?"

"More than sufficient for all of us—for ten times as many as we are now," replied Harry. ("What, he is pumping me," thought the lad.)

"And your mother makes her son and heir a handsome allowance?"

"As much as ever I choose to draw, my lord!" cried Harry.

"Peste! I wish I had such a mother!" cried my lord. "But I have only the advantage of a stepmother, and she draws me. There is the dinner-bell. Shall we go into the eating-room?" And taking his young friend's arm, my lord led him to the apartment where that meal was waiting.

Parson Sampson formed the delight of the entertainment, and amused the ladies with a hundred agreeable stories. Besides being chaplain to his lordship, he was a preacher in London, at the new chapel in Mayfair, for which my Lady Whittlesea (so well known in the reign of George I.) had left an endowment. He had the choicest stories of all the clubs and coteries—the very latest news of who had run away with whom—the last bon-mot of Mr. Selwyn—the last wild bet of March and Rockingham. He knew how the old king had quarrelled with Madame Walmoden, and the Duke was suspected of having a new love; who was in favour at Carlton House with the Princess of Wales, and who was hung last Monday, and how well he behaved in the cart. My lord's chaplain poured out all this intelligence to the amused ladies and the delighted young provincial, seasoning his conversation with such plain terms and lively jokes as made Harry stare, who was newly arrived from the colonies, and unused to the elegances of London life. The ladies, old and young, laughed quite cheerfully at the lively jokes. Do not be frightened, ye fair readers of the present day! We are not going to outrage your sweet modesties, or call blushes on your maiden cheeks. But 'tis certain that their ladyships at Castlewood never once thought of being shocked, but sate listening to the parson's funny tales, until the chapel bell, clinking for afternoon service, summoned his reverence away for half an hour. There was no sermon. He would be back in the drinking of a bottle of Burgundy. Mr. Will called a fresh one, and the chaplain tossed off a glass ere he ran out.

Ere the half-hour was over, Mr. Chaplain was back again bawling for another bottle. This discussed, they joined the ladies, and a couple of card-tables were set out, as, indeed, they were for many hours every day, at which the whole of the family party engaged. Madame de Bernstein could beat any one of her kinsfolk at piquet, and there was only Mr. Chaplain in the whole circle who was at all a match for her ladyship.

In this easy manner the Sabbath-day passed. The evening was beautiful, and there was talk of adjourning to a cool tankard and a game of whist in a summer-house; but the company voted to sit indoors, the ladies declaring they thought the aspect of three honours in their hand, and some good court-cards, more beautiful than the loveliest scene of nature; and so the sun went behind the elms, and still they were at their cards; and the rooks came home cawing their evensong, and they never stirred except to change partners; and the chapel clock tolled hour after hour unheeded, so delightfully were they spent over the pasteboard; and the moon and stars came out; and it was nine o'clock, and the groom of the chambers announced that supper was ready.

Whilst they sate at that meal, the postboy's twanging horn was heard, as he trotted into the village with his letter-bag. My lord's bag was brought in presently from the village, and his letters, which he put aside, and his newspaper which he read. He smiled as he came to a paragraph, looked at his Virginian cousin, and handed the paper over to his brother Will, who by this time was very comfortable, having had pretty good luck all the evening, and a great deal of liquor.

"Read that, Will," says my lord.

Mr. William took the paper, and, reading the sentence pointed out by his brother, uttered an exclamation which caused all the ladies to cry out.

"Gracious heavens, William! What has happened?" cries one or the other fond sister.

"Mercy, child, why do you swear so dreadfully?" asks the young man's fond mamma.

"What's the matter?" inquires Madame de Bernstein, who has fallen into a doze after her usual modicum of punch and beer.

"Read it, Parson!" says Mr. William, thrusting the paper over to the chaplain, and looking as fierce as a Turk.

"Bit, by the Lord!" roars the chaplain, dashing down the paper.

"Cousin Harry, you are in luck," said my lord, taking up the sheet, and reading from it. "The Six Year Old Plate at Huntingdon was won by Jason, beating Brilliant, Pytho, and Ginger. The odds were five to four on Brilliant against the field, three to one against Jason, seven to two against Pytho, and twenty to one against Ginger."

"I owe you a half-year's income of my poor living, Mr. Warrington," groaned the parson. "I will pay when my noble patron settles with me."

"A curse upon the luck!" growls Mr. William; "that comes of betting on a Sunday,"—and he sought consolation in another great bumper.

"Nay, cousin Will. It was but in jest," cried Harry. "I can't think of taking my cousin's money."

"Curse me, sir, do you suppose, if I lose, I can't pay?" asks Mr. William; "and that I want to be beholden to any man alive? That is a good joke. Isn't it, Parson?"

"I think I have heard better," said the clergyman; to which William replied, "Hang it, let us have another bowl."

Let us hope the ladies did not wait for this last replenishment of liquor, for it is certain they had had plenty already during the evening.

CHAPTER XVI. In which Gumbo shows Skill with the Old English Weapon

Our young Virginian having won these sums of money from his cousin and the chaplain, was in duty bound to give them a chance of recovering their money, and I am afraid his mamma and other sound moralists would scarcely approve of his way of life. He plays at cards a great deal too much. Besides the daily whist or quadrille with the ladies, which set in soon after dinner at three o'clock, and lasted until supper-time, there occurred games involving the gain or loss of very considerable sums of money, in which all the gentlemen, my lord included, took part. Since their Sunday's conversation, his lordship was more free and confidential with his kinsman than he had previously been, betted with him quite affably, and engaged him at backgammon and piquet. Mr. William and the pious chaplain liked a little hazard; though this diversion was enjoyed on the sly, and unknown to the ladies of the house, who had exacted repeated promises from cousin Will that he would not lead the Virginian into mischief, and that he would himself keep out of it. So Will promised as much as his aunt or his mother chose to demand from him, gave them his word that he would never play—no, never; and when the family retired to rest, Mr. Will would walk over with a dice-box and a rum-bottle to cousin Harry's quarters, where he, and Hal, and his reverence would sit and play until daylight.

When Harry gave to Lord Castlewood those flourishing descriptions of the maternal estate in America, he had not wished to mislead his kinsman, or to boast, or to tell falsehoods, for the lad was of a very honest and truth-telling nature; but, in his life at home, it must be owned that the young fellow had had acquaintance with all sorts of queer company,—horse-jockeys, tavern loungers, gambling and sporting men, of whom a great number were found in his native colony. A landed aristocracy, with a population of negroes to work their fields, and cultivate their tobacco and corn, had little other way of amusement than in the hunting-field, or over the cards and the punch-bowl. The hospitality of the province was unbounded: every man's house was his neighbour's; and the idle gentlefolks rode from one mansion to another, finding in each pretty much the same sport, welcome, and rough plenty. The Virginian squire had often a barefooted valet, and a cobbled saddle; but there was plenty of corn for the horses, and abundance of drink and venison for the master within the tumble-down fences, and behind the cracked windows of the hall. Harry had slept on many a straw mattress, and engaged in endless jolly night-bouts over claret and punch in cracked bowls till morning came, and it was time to follow the hounds. His poor brother was of a much more sober sort, as the lad owned with contrition. So it is that Nature makes folks; and some love books and tea, and some like Burgundy and a gallop across country. Our young fellow's tastes were speedily made visible to his friends in

England. None of them were partial to the Puritan discipline; nor did they like Harry the worse for not being the least of a milksop. Manners, you see, were looser a hundred years ago; tongues were vastly more free-and-easy; names were named, and things were done, which we should screech now to hear mentioned. Yes, madam, we are not as our ancestors were. Ought we not to thank the Fates that have improved our morals so prodigiously, and made us so eminently virtuous?

So, keeping a shrewd keen eye upon people round about him, and fancying, not incorrectly, that his cousins were disposed to pump him, Harry Warrington had thought fit to keep his own counsel regarding his own affairs, and in all games of chance or matters of sport was quite a match for the three gentlemen into whose company he had fallen. Even in the noble game of billiards he could hold his own after a few days' play with his cousins and their revered pastor. His grandfather loved the game, and had over from Europe one of the very few tables which existed in his Majesty's province of Virginia. Nor, though Mr. Will could beat him at the commencement, could he get undue odds out of the young gamester. After their first bet, Harry was on his guard with Mr. Will, and cousin William owned, not without respect, that the American was his match in most things, and his better in many. But though Harry played so well that he could beat the parson, and soon was the equal of Will, who of course could beat both the girls, how came it, that in the contests with these, especially with one of them, Mr. Warrington frequently came off second? He was profoundly courteous to every being who wore a petticoat; nor has that traditional politeness yet left his country. All the women of the Castlewood establishment loved the young gentleman. The grim housekeeper was mollified by him: the fat cook greeted him with blowsy smiles; the ladies'-maids, whether of the French or the English nation, smirked and giggled in his behalf; the pretty porter's daughter at the lodge had always a kind word in reply to his. Madame de Bernstein took note of all these things, and, though she said nothing, watched carefully the boy's disposition and behaviour.

Who can say how old Lady Maria Esmond was? Books of the Peerage were not so many in those days as they are in our blessed times, and I cannot tell to a few years, or even a lustre or two. When Will used to say she was five-and-thirty, he was abusive, and, besides, was always given to exaggeration. Maria was Will's half-sister. She and my lord were children of the late Lord Castlewood's first wife, a German lady, whom, 'tis known, my lord married in the time of Queen Anne's wars. Baron Bernstein, who married Maria's Aunt Beatrix, Bishop Tusher's widow, was also a German, a Hanoverian nobleman, and relative of the first Lady Castlewood. If my Lady Maria was born under George I., and his Majesty George II. had been thirty years on the throne, how could she be seven-and-twenty, as she told Harry Warrington she was? "I am old, child," she used to say. She used to call Harry "child" when they were alone. "I am a hundred years old. I am seven-and-twenty. I might be your mother almost." To which Harry would reply, "Your ladyship might be the mother of all the cupids, I am sure. You don't look twenty, on my word you do Dot!"

Lady Maria looked any age you liked. She was a fair beauty with a dazzling white and red complexion, an abundance of fair hair which flowed over her shoulders, and beautiful round arms which showed to uncommon advantage when she played at billiards with cousin Harry. When she had to stretch across the table to make a stroke, that youth caught glimpses of a little ankle, a little clocked stocking, and a little black satin slipper with a little red heel, which filled him with unutterable rapture, and made him swear that there never was such a foot, ankle, clocked stocking, satin slipper in the world. And yet, oh, you foolish Harry! your mother's foot was ever so much more slender, and half an inch shorter, than Lady Maria's. But, somehow, boys do not look at their mammas' slippers and ankles with rapture.

No doubt Lady Maria was very kind to Harry when they were alone. Before her sister, aunt, stepmother, she made light of him, calling him a simpleton, a chit, and who knows what trivial names? Behind his back, and even before his face, she mimicked his accent, which smacked somewhat of his province. Harry blushed and corrected the faulty intonation, under his English monitresses. His aunt pronounced that they would soon make him a pretty fellow.

Lord Castlewood, we have said, became daily more familiar and friendly with his guest and relative. Till the crops were off the ground there was no sporting, except an occasional cock-match at Winchester, and a bull-baiting at Hexton Fair. Harry and Will rode off to many jolly fairs and races round about the young Virginian was presented to some of the county families—the Henleys of the Grange, the Crawleys of Queen's Crawley, the Redmaynes of Lionsden, and so forth. The neighbours came in their great heavy coaches, and passed two or three days in country fashion. More of them would have come, but for the fear all the Castlewood family had of offending Madame de Bernstein. She did not like country company; the rustical society and conversation annoyed her. "We shall be merrier when my aunt leaves us," the young folks owned. "We have cause, as you may imagine, for being very civil to her. You know what a favourite she was with our papa? And with reason. She got him his earldom, being very well indeed at Court at that time with the King and Queen. She commands here naturally, perhaps a little too much. We are all afraid of her: even my elder brother stands in awe of her, and my stepmother is much more obedient to her than she ever was to my papa, whom she ruled with a rod of iron. But Castlewood is merrier when our aunt is not here. At least we have much more company. You will come to us in our gay days, Harry, won't you? Of course you will: this is your home, sir. I was so pleased—oh, so pleased—when my brother said he considered it was your home!"

A soft hand is held out after this pretty speech, a pair of very well preserved blue eyes look exceedingly friendly. Harry grasps his cousin's hand with ardour. I do not know what privilege of cousinship he would not like to claim, only he is so timid. They call the English selfish and cold. He at first thought his relatives were so: but how mistaken he was! How kind and affectionate they are, especially the Earl,—and dear, dear Maria! How he wishes he could recall that letter which he had written to Mrs. Mountain and his mother, in which he hinted that his welcome had been a cold one! The Earl his cousin was everything that was kind, had promised to introduce him to London society, and present him at Court, and at White's. He was to consider Castlewood as his English home. He had been most hasty in his judgment regarding his relatives in Hampshire. All this, with many contrite expressions, he wrote in his second despatch to Virginia. And he added, for it hath been hinted that the young gentleman did not spell at this early time with especial accuracy, "My cousin, the Lady Maria, is a perfect Angle."

"Ille praeter omnes angulus ridet," muttered little Mr. Dempster, at home in Virginia.

"The child can't be falling in love with his angle, as he calls her!" cries out Mountain.

"Pooh, pooh! my niece Maria is forty!" says Madam Esmond. "I perfectly well recollect her when I was at home—a great, gawky, carroty creature, with a foot like a pair of bellows." Where is truth, forsooth, and who knoweth it? Is Beauty beautiful, or is it only our eyes that make it so? Does Venus squint? Has she got a splay-foot, red hair, and a crooked back? Anoint my eyes, good Fairy Puck, so that I may ever consider the Beloved Object a paragon! Above all, keep on anointing my mistress's dainty peepers with the very strongest ointment, so that my noddle may ever appear lovely to her, and that she may continue to crown my honest ears with fresh roses!

Now, not only was Harry Warrington a favourite with some in the drawing-room, and all the ladies of the servants'-hall, but, like master like man, his valet Gumbo was very much admired and respected by very many of the domestic circle. Gumbo had a hundred accomplishments. He was famous as a fisherman, huntsman, blacksmith. He could dress hair beautifully, and improved himself in the art under my lord's own Swiss gentleman. He was great at cooking many of his Virginian dishes, and learned many new culinary secrets from my lord's French man. We have heard how exquisitely and melodiously he sang at church; and he sang not only sacred but secular music, often inventing airs and composing rude words after the habit of his people. He played the fiddle so charmingly, that he set all the girls dancing in Castlewood Hall, and was ever welcome to a gratis mug of ale at the Three Castles in the village, if he would but bring his fiddle with him. He was good-natured and loved to play for the village children: so that Mr. Warrington's negro was a universal favourite in all the Castlewood domain.

Now it was not difficult for the servants'-hall folks to perceive that Mr. Gumbo was a liar, which fact was undoubted in spite of all his good qualities. For instance, that day at church, when he pretended to read out of Molly's psalm-book, he sang quite other words than those which were down in the book, of which he could not decipher a syllable. And he pretended to understand music, whereupon the Swiss valet brought him some, and Master

Gumbo turned the page upside down. These instances of long-bow practice daily occurred, and were patent to all the Castlewood household. They knew Gumbo was a liar, perhaps not thinking the worse of him for this weakness; but they did not know how great a liar he was, and believed him much more than they had any reason for doing, and because, I suppose, they liked to believe him.

Whatever might be his feelings of wonder and envy on first viewing the splendour and comforts of Castlewood, Mr. Gumbo kept his sentiments to himself, and examined the place, park, appointments, stables, very coolly. The horses, he said, were very well, what there were of them; but at Castlewood in Virginia they had six times as many, and let me see, fourteen eighteen grooms to look after them. Madam Esmond's carriages were much finer than my lord's,—great deal more gold on the panels. As for her gardens, they covered acres, and they grew every kind of flower and fruit under the sun. Pineapples and peaches? Pineapples and peaches were so common, they were given to pigs in his country. They had twenty forty gardeners, not white gardeners, all black gentlemen, like hisself. In the house were twenty forty gentlemen in livery, besides women-servants—never could remember how many women-servants,—dere were so many: tink dere were fifty women-servants—all Madam Esmond's property, and worth ever so many hundred pieces of eight apiece. How much was a piece of eight? Bigger than a guinea, a piece of eight was. Tink, Madam Esmond have twenty thirty thousand guineas a year,—have whole rooms full of gold and plate. Came to England in one of her ships; have ever so many ships, Gumbo can't count how many ships; and estates, covered all over with tobacco and negroes, and reaching out for a week's journey. Was Master Harry heir to all this property? Of course, now Master George was killed and scalped by the Indians. Gumbo had killed ever so many Indians, and tried to save Master George, but he was Master Harry's boy,—and Master Harry was as rich,—oh, as rich as ever he like. He wore black now, because Master George was dead; but you should see his chests full of gold clothes, and lace, and jewels at Bristol. Of course, Master Harry was the richest man in all Virginia, and might have twenty sixty servants; only he liked travelling with one best, and that one, it need scarcely be said, was Gumbo.

This story was not invented at once, but gradually elicited from Mr. Gumbo, who might have uttered some trifling contradictions during the progress of the narrative, but by the time he had told his tale twice or thrice in the servants'-hall or the butler's private apartment, he was pretty perfect and consistent in his part, and knew accurately the number of slaves Madam Esmond kept, and the amount of income which she enjoyed. The truth is, that as four or five blacks are required to do the work of one white man, the domestics in American establishments are much more numerous than in ours; and, like the houses of most other Virginian landed proprietors, Madam Esmond's mansion and stables swarmed with negroes.

Mr. Gumbo's account of his mistress's wealth and splendour was carried to my lord by his lordship's man, and to Madame de Bernstein and my ladies by their respective waiting-women, and, we may be sure, lost nothing in the telling. A young gentleman in England is not the less liked because he is reputed to be the heir to vast wealth and possessions; when Lady Castlewood came to hear of Harry's prodigious expectations, she repented of her first cool reception of him, and of having pinched her daughter's arm till it was black-and-blue for having been extended towards the youth in too friendly a manner. Was it too late to have him back into those fair arms? Lady Fanny was welcome to try, and resumed the dancing-lessons. The Countess would play the music with all her heart. But, how provoking! that odious, sentimental Maria would always insist upon being in the room; and, as sure as Fanny walked in the gardens or the park, so sure would her sister come trailing after her. As for Madame de Bernstein, she laughed, and was amused at the stories of the prodigious fortune of her Virginian relatives. She knew her half-sister's man of business in London, and very likely was aware of the real state of Madame Esmond's money matters; but she did not contradict the rumours which Gumbo and his fellow-servants had set afloat; and was not a little diverted by the effect which these reports had upon the behaviour of the Castlewood family towards their young kinsman.

"Hang him! Is he so rich, Molly?" said my lord to his elder sister. "Then good-bye to our chances with your aunt. The Baroness will be sure to leave him all her money to spite us, and because he doesn't want it. Nevertheless, the lad is a good lad enough, and it is not his fault being rich, you know."

"He is very simple and modest in his habits for one so wealthy," remarks Maria.

"Rich people often are so," says my lord. "If I were rich, I often think I would be the greatest miser, and live in rags and on a crust. Depend on it there is no pleasure so enduring as money-getting. It grows on you, and increases with old age. But because I am as poor as Lazarus, I dress in purple and fine linen, and fare sumptuously every day."

Maria went to the book-room and got the History of Virginia, by R. B. Gent —and read therein what an admirable climate it was, and how all kinds of fruit and corn grew in that province, and what noble rivers were those of Potomac and Rappahannoc, abounding in all sorts of fish. And she wondered whether the climate would agree with her, and whether her aunt would like her? And Harry was sure his mother would adore her, so would Mountain. And when he was asked about the number of his mother's servants, he said, they certainly had more servants than are seen in England—he did not know how many. But the negroes did not do near as much work as English servants did hence the necessity of keeping so great a number. As for some others of Gumbo's details which were brought to him, he laughed and said the boy was wonderful as a romancer, and in telling such stories he supposed was trying to speak out for the honour of the family.

So Harry was modest as well as rich! His denials only served to confirm his relatives' opinion regarding his splendid expectations. More and more the Countess and the ladies were friendly and affectionate with him. More and more Mr. Will betted with him, and wanted to sell him bargains. Harry's simple dress and equipage only served to confirm his friends' idea of his wealth. To see a young man of his rank and means with but one servant, and without horses or a carriage of his own—what modesty! When he went to London he would cut a better figure? Of course he would. Castlewood would introduce him to the best society in the capital, and he would appear as he ought to appear at St. James's. No man could be more pleasant, wicked, lively, obsequious than the worthy chaplain, Mr. Sampson. How proud he would be if he could show his young friend a little of London life!—if he could warn rogues off him, and keep him out of the way of harm! Mr. Sampson was very kind: everybody was very kind. Harry liked quite well the respect that was paid to him. As Madam Esmond's son he thought perhaps it was his due: and took for granted that he was the personage which his family imagined him to be. How should he know better, who had never as yet seen any place but his own province, and why should he not respect his own condition when other people respected it so? So all the little knot of people at Castlewood House, and from these the people in Castlewood village, and from thence the people in the whole county, chose to imagine that Mr. Harry Esmond Warrington was the heir of immense wealth, and a gentleman of very great importance, because his negro valet told lies about him in the servants'-hall.

Harry's aunt, Madame de Bernstein, after a week or two, began to tire of Castlewood and the inhabitants of that mansion, and the neighbours who came to visit them. This clever woman tired of most things and people sooner or later. So she took to nodding and sleeping over the chaplain's stories, and to doze at her whist and over her dinner, and to be very snappish and sarcastic in her conversation with her Esmond nephews and nieces, hitting out blows at my lord and his brother the jockey, and my ladies, widowed and unmarried, who winced under her scornful remarks, and bore them as they best might. The cook, whom she had so praised on first coming, now gave her no satisfaction; the wine was corked; the house was damp, dreary, and full of draughts; the doors would not shut, and the chimneys were smoky. She began to think the Tunbridge waters were very necessary for her, and ordered the doctor, who came to her from the neighbouring town of Hexton, to order those waters for her benefit.

"I wish to heaven she would go!" growled my lord, who was the most independent member of his family. "She may go to Tunbridge, or she may go to Bath, or she may go to Jericho, for me."

"Shall Fanny and I come with you to Tunbridge, dear Baroness?" asked Lady Castlewood of her sister-in-law.

"Not for worlds, my dear! The doctor orders me absolute quiet, and if you came I should have the knocker going all day, and Fanny's lovers would never be out of the house," answered the Baroness, who was quite weary of Lady Castlewood's company.

"I wish I could be of any service to my aunt!" said the sentimental Lady Maria, demurely.

"My good child, what can you do for me? You cannot play piquet so well as my maid, and I have heard all your songs till I am perfectly tired of them! One of the gentlemen might go with me: at least make the journey, and see me safe from highwaymen."

"I'm sure, ma'am, I shall be glad to ride with you," said Mr. Will.

"Oh, not you! I don't want you, William," cried the young man's aunt. "Why do not you offer, and where are your American manners, you ungracious Harry Warrington? Don't swear, Will, Harry is much better company than you are, and much better ton too, sir."

"Tong, indeed! Confound his tong," growled envious Will to himself.

"I dare say I shall be tired of him, as I am of other folks," continued the Baroness. "I have scarcely seen Harry at all in these last days. You shall ride with me to Tunbridge, Harry!"

At this direct appeal, and to no one's wonder more than that of his aunt, Mr. Harry Warrington blushed, and hemmed and ha'd and at length said, "I have promised my cousin Castlewood to go over to Hexton Petty Sessions with him to-morrow. He thinks I should see how the Courts here are conducted—and—and—the partridge-shooting will soon begin, and I have promised to be here for that, ma'am." Saying which words, Harry Warrington looked as red as a poppy, whilst Lady Maria held her meek face downwards, and nimbly plied her needle.

"You actually refuse to go with me to Tunbridge Wells?" called out Madame Bernstein, her eyes lightening, and her face flushing up with anger, too.

"Not to ride with you, ma'am; that I will do with all my heart; but to stay there—I have promised..."

"Enough, enough, sir! I can go alone, and don't want your escort," cried the irate old lady, and rustled out of the room.

The Castlewood family looked at each other with wonder. Will whistled. Lady Castlewood glanced at Fanny, as much as to say, His chance is over. Lady Maria never lifted up her eyes from her tambour-frame.

CHAPTER XVII. On the Scent

Young Harry Warrington's act of revolt came so suddenly upon Madame de Bernstein, that she had no other way of replying to it, than by the prompt outbreak of anger with which we left her in the last chapter. She darted two fierce glances at Lady Fanny and her mother as she quitted the room. Lady Maria over her tambour-frame escaped without the least notice, and scarcely lifted up her head from her embroidery, to watch the aunt retreating, or the looks which mamma-in-law and sister threw at one another.

"So, in spite of all, you have, madam?" the maternal looks seemed to say.

"Have what?" asked Lady Fanny's eyes. But what good in looking innocent? She looked puzzled. She did not look one-tenth part as innocent as Maria. Had she been guilty, she would have looked not guilty much more cleverly;

and would have taken care to study and compose a face so as to be ready to suit the plea. Whatever was the expression of Fanny's eyes, mamma glared on her as if she would have liked to tear them out.

But Lady Castlewood could not operate upon the said eyes then and there, like the barbarous monsters in the stage-direction in King Lear. When her ladyship was going to tear out her daughter's eyes, she would retire smiling, with an arm round her dear child's waist, and then gouge her in private.

"So you don't fancy going with the old lady to Tunbridge Wells?" was all she said to Cousin Warrington, wearing at the same time a perfectly well-bred simper on her face.

"And small blame to our cousin!" interposed my lord. (The face over the tambour-frame looked up for one instant.) "A young fellow must not have it all idling and holiday. Let him mix up something useful with his pleasures, and go to the fiddles and pump-rooms at Tunbridge or the Bath later. Mr. Warrington has to conduct a great estate in America: let him see how ours in England are carried on. Will hath shown him the kennel and the stables; and the games in vogue, which I think, cousin, you seem to play as well as your teachers. After harvest we will show him a little English fowling and shooting: in winter we will take him out a-hunting. Though there has been a coolness between us and our aunt-kinswoman in Virginia, yet we are of the same blood. Ere we send our cousin back to his mother, let us show him what an English gentleman's life at home is. I should like to read with him as well as sport with him, and that is why I have been pressing him of late to stay and bear me company."

My lord spoke with such perfect frankness that his mother-in-law and half-brother and sister could not help wondering what his meaning could be. The three last-named persons often held little conspiracies together, and caballed or grumbled against the head of the house. When he adopted that frank tone, there was no fathoming his meaning: often it would not be discovered until months had passed. He did not say, "This is true," but, "I mean that this statement should be accepted and believed in my family." It was then a thing convenue, that my Lord Castlewood had a laudable desire to cultivate the domestic affections, and to educate, amuse, and improve his young relative; and that he had taken a great fancy to the lad, and wished that Harry should stay for some time near his lordship.

"What is Castlewood's game now?" asked William of his mother and sister as they disappeared into the corridors. "Stop! By George, I have it!"

"What, William?"

"He intends to get him to play, and to win the Virginia estate back from him. That's what it is!"

"But the lad has not got the Virginia estate to pay, if he loses," remarks mamma.

"If my brother has not some scheme in view, may I be———."

"Hush! Of course he has a scheme in view. But what is it?"

"He can't mean Maria—Maria is as old as Harry's mother," muses Mr.

William.

"Pooh! with her old face and sandy hair and freckled skin! Impossible!" cries Lady Fanny, with somewhat of a sigh.

"Of course, your ladyship had a fancy for the Iroquois, too!" cried mamma.

"I trust I know my station and duty better, madam! If I had liked him, that is no reason why I should marry him. Your ladyship hath taught me as much as that."

"My Lady Fanny!"

"I am sure you married our papa without liking him. You have told me so a thousand times!"

"And if you did not love our father before marriage, you certainly did not fall in love with him afterwards," broke in Mr. William, with a laugh. "Fan and I remember how our honoured parents used to fight. Don't us, Fan? And our brother Esmond kept the peace."

"Don't recall those dreadful low scenes, William!" cries mamma. "When your father took too much drink, he was like a madman; and his conduct should be a warning to you, sir, who are fond of the same horrid practice."

"I am sure, madam, you were not much the happier for marrying the man you did not like, and your ladyship's title hath brought very little along with it," whimpered out Lady Fanny. "What is the use of a coronet with the jointure of a tradesman's wife?—how many of them are richer than we are? There is come lately to live in our Square, at Kensington, a grocer's widow from London Bridge, whose daughters have three gowns where I have one; and who, though they are waited on but by a man and a couple of maids, I know eat and drink a thousand times better than we do with our scraps of cold meat on our plate, and our great flaunting, trapesing, impudent, lazy lacqueys!"

"He! he! glad I dine at the palace, and not at home!" said Mr. Will. (Mr. Will, through his aunt's interest with Count Puffendorff, Groom of the Royal {and Serene Electoral} Powder-Closet, had one of the many small places at Court, that of Deputy Powder.)

"Why should I not be happy without any title except my own?" continued Lady Frances. "Many people are. I dare say they are even happy in America."

"Yes!—with a mother-in-law who is a perfect Turk and Tartar, for all I hear —with Indian war-whoops howling all around you and with a danger of losing your scalp, or of being eat up by a wild beast every time you went to church."

"I wouldn't go to church," said Lady Fanny.

"You'd go with anybody who asked you, Fan!" roared out Mr. Will: "and so would old Maria, and so would any woman, that's the fact." And Will laughed at his own wit.

"Pray, good folks, what is all your merriment about?" here asked Madame Bernstein, peeping in on her relatives from the tapestried door which led into the gallery where their conversation was held.

Will told her that his mother and sister had been having a fight (which was not a novelty, as Madame Bernstein knew), because Fanny wanted to marry their cousin, the wild Indian, and my lady Countess would not let her. Fanny protested against this statement. Since the very first day when her mother had told her not to speak to the young gentleman, she had scarcely exchanged two words with him. She knew her station better. She did not want to be scalped by wild Indians, or eat up by bears.

Madame de Bernstein looked puzzled. "If he is not staying for you, for whom is he staying?" she asked. "At the houses to which he has been carried, you have taken care not to show him a woman that is not a fright or in the nursery; and I think the boy is too proud to fall in love with a dairymaid, Will."

"Humph! That is a matter of taste, ma'am," says Mr. William, with a shrug of his shoulders.

"Of Mr. William Esmond's taste, as you say; but not of yonder boy's. The Esmonds of his grandfather's nurture, sir, would not go a-courting in the kitchen."

"Well, ma'am, every man to his taste, I say again. A fellow might go farther and fare worse than my brother's servants'-hall, and besides Fan, there's only the maids or old Maria to choose from."

"Maria! Impossible!" And yet, as she spoke the very words, a sudden thought crossed Madame Bernstein's mind, that this elderly Calypso might have captivated her young Telemachus. She called to mind half a dozen instances in her own experience of young men who had been infatuated by old women. She remembered how frequent Harry Warrington's absences had been of late—absences which she attributed to his love for field sports. She remembered how often, when he was absent, Maria Esmond was away too. Walks in cool avenues, whisperings in garden temples, or behind clipt hedges, casual squeezes of the hand in twilight corridors, or sweet glances and ogles in meetings on the stairs,—a lively fancy, an intimate knowledge of the world, very likely a considerable personal experience in early days, suggested all these possibilities and chances to Madame de Bernstein, just as she was saying that they were impossible.

"Impossible, ma'am! I don't know," Will continued. "My mother warned Fan off him."

"Oh, your mother did warn Fanny off?"

"Certainly, my dear Baroness!"

"Didn't she? Didn't she pinch Fanny's arm black-and-blue? Didn't they fight about it?"

"Nonsense, William! For shame, William!" cry both the implicated ladies in a breath.

"And now, since we have heard how rich he is, perhaps it is sour grapes, that is all. And now, since he is warned off the young bird, perhaps he is hunting the old one, that's all. Impossible why impossible? You know old Lady Suffolk, ma'am?"

"William, how can you speak about Lady Suffolk to your aunt?"

A grin passed over the countenance of the young gentleman. "Because Lady

Suffolk was a special favourite at Court? Well, other folks have succeeded her."

"Sir!" cries Madame de Bernstein, who may have had her reasons to take offence.

"So they have, I say; or who, pray, is my Lady Yarmouth now? And didn't old Lady Suffolk go and fall in love with George Berkeley, and marry him when she was ever so old? Nay, ma'am, if I remember right—and we hear a deal of town-talk at our table—Harry Estridge went mad about your ladyship when you were somewhat rising twenty; and would have changed your name a third time if you would but have let him."

This allusion to an adventure of her own later days, which was, indeed, pretty notorious to all the world, did not anger Madame de Bernstein, like Will's former hint about his aunt having been a favourite at George the Second's Court; but, on the contrary, set her in good-humour.

"Au fait," she said, musing, as she played a pretty little hand on the table, and no doubt thinking about mad young Harry Estridge; "'tis not impossible, William, that old folks, and young folks, too, should play the fool."

"But I can't understand a young fellow being in love with Maria," continued Mr. William, "however he might be with you, ma'am. That's oter shose, as our French tutor used to say. You remember the Count, ma'am; he! he!—and so does Maria!"

"William!"

"And I dare say the Count remembers the bastinado Castlewood had given to him. A confounded French dancing-master calling himself a count, and daring to fall in love in our family! Whenever I want to make myself uncommonly agreeable to old Maria, I just say a few words of parly voo to her. She knows what I mean."

"Have you abused her to your cousin, Harry Warrington?" asked Madame de Bernstein.

"Well—I know she is always abusing me—and I have said my mind about her," said Will.

"Oh, you idiot!" cried the old lady. "Who but a gaby ever spoke ill of a woman to her sweetheart? He will tell her everything, and they both will hate you."

"The very thing, ma'am!" cried Will, bursting into a great laugh. "I had a sort of a suspicion, you see, and two days ago, as we were riding together, I told Harry Warrington a bit of my mind about Maria;—why shouldn't I, I say? She is always abusing me, ain't she, Fan? And your favourite turned as red as my plush waistcoat—wondered how a gentleman could malign his own flesh and blood, and, trembling all over with rage, said I was no true Esmond."

"Why didn't you chastise him, sir, as my lord did the dancing-master?" cried Lady Castlewood.

"Well, mother,—you see that at quarter-staff there's two sticks used," replied Mr. William; "and my opinion is, that Harry Warrington can guard his own head uncommonly well. Perhaps that is one of the reasons why I did not offer to treat my cousin to a caning. And now you say so, ma'am, I know he has told

Maria. She has been looking battle, murder, and sudden death at me ever since. All which shows——" and here he turned to his aunt.

"All which shows what?"

"That I think we are on the right scent; and that we've found Maria—the old fox!" And the ingenuous youth here clapped his hand to his mouth, and gave a loud halloo.

How far had this pretty intrigue gone? now was the question. Mr. Will said, that at her age, Maria would be for conducting matters as rapidly as possible, not having much time to lose. There was not a great deal of love lost between Will and his half-sister.

"Who would sift the matter to the bottom? Scolding one party or the other was of no avail. Threats only serve to aggravate people in such cases. I never was in danger but once, young people," said Madame de Bernstein, "and I think that was because my poor mother contradicted me. If this boy is like others of his family, the more we oppose him, the more entete he will be; and we shall never get him out of his scrape."

"Faith, ma'am, suppose we leave him in it?" grumbled Will. "Old Maria and I don't love each other too much, I grant you; but an English earl's daughter is good enough for an American tobacco-planter, when all is said and done."

Here his mother and sister broke out. They would not hear of such a union. To which Will answered, "You are like the dog in the manger. You don't want the man yourself, Fanny"

"I want him, indeed!" cries Lady Fanny, with a toss of her head.

"Then why grudge him to Maria? I think Castlewood wants her to have him."

"Why grudge him to Maria, sir?" cried Madame de Bernstein, with great energy. "Do you remember who the poor boy is, and what your house owes to his family? His grandfather was the best friend your father ever had, and gave up this estate, this title, this very castle, in which you are conspiring against the friendless Virginian lad, that you and yours might profit by it. And the reward for all this kindness is, that you all but shut the door on the child when he knocks at it, and talk of marrying him to a silly elderly creature who might be his mother! He shan't marry her."

"The very thing we were saying and thinking, my dear Baroness!" interposes Lady Castlewood. "Our part of the family is not eager about the match, though my lord and Maria may be."

"You would like him for yourself, now that you hear he is rich—and may be richer, young people, mind you that," cried Madam Beatrix, turning upon the other women.

"Mr. Warrington may be ever so rich, madam, but there is no need why your ladyship should perpetually remind us that we are poor," broke in Lady Castlewood, with some spirit. "At least there is very little disparity in Fanny's age and Mr. Harry's; and you surely will be the last to say that a lady of our name and family is not good enough for any gentleman born in Virginia or elsewhere."

"Let Fanny take an English gentleman, Countess, not an American. With such a name and such a mother to help her, and with all her good looks and accomplishments, sure, she can't fail of finding a man worthy of her. But from what I know about the daughters of this house, and what I imagine about our young cousin, I am certain that no happy match could be made between them."

"What does my aunt know about me?" asked Lady Fanny, turning very red.

"Only your temper, my dear. You don't suppose that I believe all the tittle-tattle and scandal which one cannot help hearing in town? But the temper and early education are sufficient. Only fancy one of you condemned to leave St. James's and the Mall, and live in a plantation surrounded by savages! You would die of ennui, or worry your husband's life out with your ill-humour. You are born, ladies, to ornament courts—not wigwams. Let this lad go back to his wilderness with a wife who is suited to him."

The other two ladies declared in a breath that, for their parts, they desired no better, and, after a few more words, went on their way, while Madame de Bernstein, lifting up her tapestried door, retired into her own chamber. She saw all the scheme now; she admired the ways of women, calling a score of little circumstances back to mind. She wondered at her own blindness during the last few days, and that she should not have perceived the rise and progress of this queer little intrigue. How far had it gone? was now the question. Was Harry's passion of the serious and tragical sort, or a mere fire of straw which a day or two would burn out? How deeply was he committed? She dreaded the strength of Harry's passion, and the weakness of Maria's. A woman of her age is so desperate, Madame Bernstein may have thought, that she will make any efforts to secure a lover. Scandal, bah! She will retire and be a princess in Virginia, and leave the folks in England to talk as much scandal as they choose.

Is there always, then, one thing which women do not tell to one another, and about which they agree to deceive each other? Does the concealment arise from deceit or modesty? A man, as soon as he feels an inclination for one of the other sex, seeks for a friend of his own to whom he may impart the delightful intelligence. A woman (with more or less skill) buries her secret away from her kind. For days and weeks past, had not this old Maria made fools of the whole house,—Maria, the butt of the family?

I forbear to go into too curious inquiries regarding the Lady Maria's antecedents. I have my own opinion about Madame Bernstein's. A hundred years ago people of the great world were not so straitlaced as they are now, when everybody is good, pure, moral, modest; when there is no skeleton in anybody's closet; when there is no scheming; no slurring over old stories; when no girl tries to sell herself for wealth, and no mother abets her. Suppose my Lady Maria tries to make her little game, wherein is her ladyship's great eccentricity?

On these points no doubt the Baroness de Bernstein thought, as she communed with herself in her private apartment.

CHAPTER XVIII. An Old Story

As my Lady Castlewood and her son and daughter passed through one door of the saloon where they had all been seated, my Lord Castlewood departed by another issue; and then the demure eyes looked up from the tambour-frame on which they had persisted hitherto in examining the innocent violets and jonquils. The eyes looked up at Harry Warrington, who stood at an ancestral portrait under the great fireplace. He had gathered a great heap of blushes (those flowers which bloom so rarely after gentlefolks' springtime), and with them ornamented his honest countenance, his cheeks, his forehead, nay, his youthful ears.

"Why did you refuse to go with our aunt, cousin?" asked the lady of the tambour frame.

"Because your ladyship bade me stay," answered the lad.

"I bid you stay! La! child! What one says in fun, you take in earnest! Are all you Virginian gentlemen so obsequious as to fancy every idle word a lady says is a command? Virginia must be a pleasant country for our sex if it be so!"

"You said—when—when we walked in the terrace two nights since,—O heaven!" cried Harry, with a voice trembling with emotion.

"Ah, that sweet night, cousin!" cries the Tambour-frame.

"Whe—whe—when you gave me this rose from your own neck,"—roared out Harry, pulling suddenly a crumpled and decayed vegetable from his waistcoat—"which I will never part with—with, no, by heavens, whilst this heart continues to beat! You said, 'Harry, if your aunt asks you to go away, you will go, and if you go, you will forget me.'—Didn't you say so?"

"All men forget!" said the Virgin, with a sigh.

"In this cold selfish country they may, cousin, not in ours," continues Harry, yet in the same state of exaltation—"I had rather have lost an arm almost than refused the old lady. I tell you it went to my heart to say no to her, and she so kind to me, and who had been the means of introducing me to—to—O heaven!"

(Here a kick to an intervening spaniel, which flies yelping from before the fire, and a rapid advance on the tambour-frame.) "Look here, cousin! If you were to bid me jump out of yonder window, I should do it; or murder, I should do it."

"La! but you need not squeeze one's hand so, you silly child!" remarks Maria.

"I can't help it—we are so in the south. Where my heart is, I can't help speaking my mind out, cousin—and you know where that heart is! Ever since that evening—that—O heaven! I tell you I have hardly slept since—I want to do something—to distinguish myself—to be ever so great. I wish there was giants, Maria, as I have read of in—in books, that I could go and fight 'em. I wish you was in distress, that I might help you, somehow. I wish you wanted my blood, that I might spend every drop of it for you. And when you told me not to go with Madame Bernstein..."

"I tell thee, child? never."

"I thought you told me. You said you knew I preferred my aunt to my cousin, and I said then what I say now, 'Incomparable Maria! I prefer thee to all the women in the world and all the angels in Paradise—and I would go anywhere, were it to dungeons, if you ordered me!' And do you think I would not stay anywhere, when you only desired that I should be near you?" he added, after a moment's pause.

"Men always talk in that way—that is,—that is, I have heard so," said the spinster, correcting herself; "for what should a country-bred woman know about you creatures? When you are near us, they say you are all raptures and flames and promises and I don't know what; when you are away, you forget all about us."

"But I think I never want to go away as long as I live," groaned out the young man. "I have tired of many things; not books and that, I never cared for study much, but games and sports which I used to be fond of when I was a boy. Before I saw you, it was to be a soldier I most desired; I tore my hair with rage when my poor dear brother went away instead of me on that expedition in which we lost him. But now, I only care for one thing in the world, and you know what that is."

"You silly child! don't you know I am almost old enough to be...?"

"I know—I know! but what is that to me? Hasn't your br...—well, never mind who, some of 'em-told me stories against you, and didn't they show me the Family Bible, where all your names are down, and the dates of your birth?"

"The cowards! Who did that?" cried out Lady Maria. "Dear Harry, tell me who did that? Was it my mother-in-law, the grasping, odious, abandoned, brazen harpy? Do you know all about her? How she married my father in his cups—the horrid hussey!—and..."

"Indeed it wasn't Lady Castlewood," interposed the wondering Harry.

"Then it was my aunt," continued the infuriate lady. "A pretty moralist, indeed! A bishop's widow, forsooth, and I should like to know whose widow before and afterwards. Why, Harry, she intrigue: with the Pretender, and with the Court of Hanover, and, I dare say, would with the Court of Rome and the Sultan of Turkey if she had had the means. Do you know who her second husband was? A creature who..."

"But our aunt never spoke a word against you," broke in Harry, more and more amazed at the nymph's vehemence.

She checked her anger. In the inquisitive countenance opposite to her she thought she read some alarm as to the temper which she was exhibiting.

"Well, well! I am a fool," she said. "I want thee to think well of me, Harry!"

A hand is somehow put out and seized and, no doubt, kissed by the rapturous youth. "Angel!" he cries, looking into her face with his eager, honest eyes.

Two fish-pools irradiated by a pair of stars would not kindle to greater warmth than did those elderly orbs into which Harry poured his gaze. Nevertheless, he plunged into their blue depths, and fancied he saw heaven in their calm brightness. So that silly dog (of whom Aesop or the Spelling-book used to tell us in youth) beheld a beef-bone in the pond, and snapped at it, and lost the beef-bone he was carrying. O absurd cur! He saw the beefbone in his own mouth reflected in the treacherous pool, which dimpled, I dare say, with ever so many smiles, coolly sucked up the meat, and returned to its usual placidity. Ah! what a heap of wreck lie beneath some of those quiet surfaces! What treasures we have dropped into them! What chased golden dishes, what precious jewels of love, what bones after bones, and sweetest heart's flesh! Do not some very faithful and unlucky dogs jump in bodily, when they are swallowed up heads and tails entirely? When some women come to be dragged, it is a marvel what will be found in the depths of them. Cavete, canes! Have a care how ye lap that water. What do they want with us, the mischievous siren sluts? A green-eyed Naiad never rests until she has inveigled a fellow under the water; she sings after him, she dances after him; she winds round him, glittering tortuously; she warbles and whispers dainty secrets at his cheek, she kisses his feet, she leers at him from out of her rushes: all her beds sigh out, "Come, sweet youth! Hither, hither, rosy Hylas!" Pop goes Hylas. (Surely the fable is renewed for ever and ever?) Has his captivator any pleasure? Doth she take any account of him? No more than a fisherman landing at Brighton does of one out of a hundred thousand herrings.... The last time. Ulysses rowed by the Sirens' bank, he and his men did not care though a whole shoal of them were singing and combing their longest locks. Young Telemachus was for jumping overboard: but the tough old crew held the silly, bawling lad. They were deaf, and could not hear his bawling nor the sea-nymphs' singing. They were dim of sight, and did not see how lovely the witches were. The stale, old, leering witches! Away with ye! I dare say you have painted your cheeks by this time; your wretched old songs are as out of fashion as Mozart, and it is all false hair you are combing!

   In the last sentence you see Lector Benevolus and Scriptor Doctissimus figure as tough old Ulysses and his tough old Boatswain, who do not care a quid of tobacco for any Siren at Sirens' Point; but Harry Warrington is green Telemachus, who, be sure, was very unlike the soft youth in the good Bishop of Cambray's twaddling story. He does not see that the siren paints the lashes from under which she ogles him; will put by into a box when she has done the ringlets into which she would inveigle him; and if she eats him, as she proposes to do, will crunch his bones with a new set of grinders just from the dentist's, and warranted for mastication. The song is not stale to Harry Warrington, nor the voice cracked or out of tune that sings it. But—but—oh, dear me, Brother Boatswain! Don't you remember how pleasant the opera was when we first heard it? Cosi fan tutti was its name—Mozart's music. Now, I dare say, they have other words, and other music, and other singers and fiddlers, and another great crowd in the pit. Well, well, Cosi fan tutti is still upon the bills, and they are going on singing it over and over and over.

Any man or woman with a pennyworth of brains, or the like precious amount of personal experience, or who has read a novel before, must, when Harry pulled out those faded vegetables just now, have gone off into a digression of his own, as the writer confesses for himself he was diverging whilst he has been writing the last brace of paragraphs. If he sees a pair of lovers whispering in a garden alley or the embrasure of a window, or a pair of glances shot across the room from Jenny to the artless Jessamy, he falls to musing on former days when, etc. etc. These things follow each other by a general law, which is not as old as the hills, to be sure, but as old as the people who walk up and down them. When, I say, a lad pulls a bunch of amputated and now decomposing greens from his breast and falls to kissing it, what is the use of saying much more? As well tell the market-gardener's name from whom the slip-rose was bought—the waterings, clippings, trimmings, manurings, the plant has undergone—as tell how Harry Warrington came by it. Rose, elle a vecu la vie des roses, has been trimmed, has been watered, has been potted, has been sticked, has been cut, worn, given away, transferred to yonder boy's pocket-book and bosom, according to the laws and fate appertaining to roses.

And how came Maria to give it to Harry? And how did he come to want it and to prize it so passionately when he got the bit of rubbish? Is not one story as stale as the other? Are not they all alike? What is the use, I say, of telling them over and over? Harry values that rose because Maria has ogled him in the old way; because she has happened to meet him in the garden in the old way; because he has taken her hand in the old way; because they have whispered to one another behind the old curtain (the gaping old rag, as if everybody could not peep through it!); because, in this delicious weather, they have happened to be early risers and go into the park; because dear Goody Jenkins in the village happened to have a bad knee, and my lady Maria went to read to her, and gave her calves'-foot jelly, and because somebody, of course, must carry the basket. Whole chapters might have been written to chronicle all these circumstances, but A quoi bon? The incidents of life, and love-making especially, I believe to resemble each other so much, that I am surprised, gentlemen and ladies, you read novels any more. Psha! Of course that rose in young Harry's pocket-book had grown, and had budded, and had bloomed, and was now rotting, like other roses. I suppose you will want me to say that the young fool kissed it next? Of course he kissed it. What were lips made for, pray, but for smiling and simpering, and (possibly) humbugging, and kissing, and opening to receive mutton-chops, cigars, and so forth? I cannot write this part of the story of our Virginians, because Harry did not dare to write it himself to anybody at home, because, if he wrote any letters to Maria (which, of course, he did, as they were in the same house, and might meet each other as much as they liked), they were destroyed; because he afterwards chose to be very silent about the story, and we can't have it from her ladyship, who never told the truth about anything. But cui bono? I say again. What is the good of telling the story? My gentle reader, take your story: take mine. To-morrow it shall be Miss Fanny's, who is just walking away with her doll to the schoolroom and the governess (poor victim! she has a version of it in her desk): and next day it shall be Baby's, who is bawling out on the stairs for his bottle.

Maria might like to have and exercise power over the young Virginian; but she did not want that Harry should quarrel with his aunt for her sake, or that Madame de Bernstein should be angry with her. Harry was not the Lord of Virginia yet: he was only the Prince, and the Queen might marry and have other Princes, and the laws of primogeniture might not be established in Virginia, qu'en savait elle? My lord her brother and she had exchanged no words at all about the delicate business. But they understood each other, and the Earl had a way of understanding things without speaking. He knew his Maria perfectly well: in the course of a life of which not a little had been spent in her brother's company and under his roof, Maria's disposition, ways, tricks, faults, had come to be perfectly understood by the head of the family; and she would find her little schemes checked or aided by him, as to his lordship seemed good, and without need of any words between them. Thus three days before, when she happened to be going to see that poor dear old Goody, who was ill with the sore knee in the village (and when Harry Warrington happened to be walking behind the elms on the green too), my lord with his dogs about him, and his gardener walking after him, crossed the court, just as Lady Maria was tripping to the gate-house—and his lordship called his sister, and said: "Molly, you are going to see Goody Jenkins. You are a charitable soul, my dear. Give Gammer Jenkins this half-crown for me—unless our cousin, Warrington, has already given her money. A pleasant walk to you. Let her want for nothing." And at supper, my lord asked Mr. Warrington many questions about the poor in Virginia, and the means of maintaining them, to which the young gentleman gave the best answers he might. His lordship wished that in the old country there were no more poor people than in the new: and recommended Harry to visit the poor and people of every degree, indeed, high and low—in the country to look at the agriculture, in the city at the manufactures and municipal institutions—to which edifying advice Harry acceded with becoming modesty and few words, and Madame Bernstein nodded approval over her piquet with the chaplain. Next day, Harry was in my lord's justice-room: the next day he was out ever so long with my lord on the farm—and coming home, what does my lord do, but look in on a sick tenant? I think Lady Maria was out on that day, too; she had been reading good books to that poor dear Goody Jenkins, though I don't suppose Madame Bernstein ever thought of asking about her niece.

"CASTLEWOOD, HAMPSHIRE, ENGLAND, August 5, 1757.

"MY DEAR MOUNTAIN—At first, as I wrote, I did not like Castlewood, nor my cousins there, very much. Now, I am used to their ways, and we begin to understand each other much better. With my duty to my mother, tell her, I hope, that considering her ladyship's great kindness to me, Madam Esmond will be reconciled to her half-sister, the Baroness de Bernstein. The Baroness, you know, was my Grandmamma's daughter by her first husband, Lord Castlewood (only Grandpapa really was the real lord); however, that was not his, that is, the other Lord Castlewood's fault, you know, and he was very kind to Grandpapa, who always spoke most kindly of him to us as you know.

"Madame the Baroness Bernstein first married a clergyman, Reverend Mr. Tusher, who was so learned and good, and such a favourite of his Majesty, as was my aunt too, that he was made a Bishop. When he died, Our gracious King continued his friendship to my aunt; who married a Hanoverian nobleman, who occupied a post at the Court—and, I believe, left the Baroness very rich. My cousin, my Lord Castlewood, told me so much about her, and I am sure I have found from her the greatest kindness and affection.

"The (Dowiger) Countess Castlewood and my cousins Will and Lady Fanny have been described per last, that went by the Falmouth packet on the 20th ult. The ladies are not changed since then. Me and Cousin Will are very good friends. We have rode out a good deal. We have had some famous cocking matches at Hampton and Winton. My cousin is a sharp blade, but I think I have shown him that we in Virginia know a thing or two. Reverend Mr. Sampson, chaplain of the famaly, most excellent preacher, without any biggatry.

"The kindness of my cousin the Earl improves every day, and by next year's ship I hope my mother will send his lordship some of our best roll tobacco (for tennants) and hamms. He is most charatable to the poor. His sister, Lady Maria, equally so. She sits for hours reading good books to the sick: she is most beloved in the village."

"Nonsense!" said a lady to whom Harry submitted his precious manuscript. "Why do you flatter me, cousin?"

"You are beloved in the village and out of it," said Harry, with a knowing emphasis, "and I have flattered you, as you call it, a little more still, farther on."

"There is a sick old woman there, whom Madam Esmond would like, a most raligious, good, old lady.

"Lady Maria goes very often to read to her; which, she says, gives her comfort. But though her Ladyship hath the sweetest voice, both in speaking and singeing (she plays the church organ, and singes there most beautifully), I cannot think Gammer Jenkins can have any comfort from it, being very deaf, by reason of her great age. She has her memory perfectly, however, and remembers when my honoured Grandmother Rachel Lady Castlewood lived here. She says, my Grandmother was the best woman in the whole world, gave her a cow when she was married, and cured her husband, Gaffer Jenkins, of the collects, which he used to have very bad. I suppose it was with the Pills and Drops which my honoured Mother put up in my boxes, when I left dear Virginia. Having never been ill since, have had no use for the pills. Gumbo hath, eating and drinking a great deal too much in the Servants' Hall. The next angel to my Grandmother (N.B. I think I spelt angel wrong per last), Gammer Jenkins says, is Lady Maria, who sends her duty to her Aunt in Virginia, and remembers her, and my Grandpapa and Grandmamma when they were in Europe, and she was a little girl. You know they have Grandpapa's picture here, and I live in the very rooms which he had, and which are to be called mine, my Lord Castlewood says.

"Having no more to say, at present, I close with best love and duty to

my honoured Mother, and with respects to Mr. Dempster, and a kiss for

Fanny, and kind remembrances to Old Gumbo, Nathan, Old and Young Dinah,

and the pointer dog and Slut, and all friends, from their well-wisher

"HENRY ESMOND WARRINGTON."

"Have wrote and sent my duty to my Uncle Warrington in Norfolk. No anser as yet."

"I hope the spelling is right, cousin?" asked the author of the letter, from the critic to whom he showed it.

"'Tis quite well enough spelt for any person of fashion," answered Lady Maria, who did not choose to be examined too closely regarding the orthography.

"One word 'Angel,' I know, I spelt wrong in writing to my mamma, but I have learned a way of spelling it right, now."

"And how is that, sir?"

"I think 'tis by looking at you, cousin;" saying which words, Mr. Harry made her ladyship a low bow, and accompanied the bow by one of his best blushes, as if he were offering her a bow and a bouquet.

CHAPTER XIX. Containing both Love and Luck

At the next meal, when the family party assembled, there was not a trace of displeasure in Madame de Bernstein's countenance, and her behaviour to all the company, Harry included, was perfectly kind and cordial. She praised the cook this time, declared the fricassee was excellent, and that there were no eels anywhere like those in the Castlewood moats; would not allow that the wine was corked, or hear of such extravagance as opening a fresh bottle for a useless old woman like her; gave Madam Esmond Warrington, of Virginia, as her toast, when the new wine was brought, and hoped Harry had brought away his mamma's permission to take back an English wife with him. He did not remember his grandmother; her, Madame de Bernstein's, dear mother? The Baroness amused the company with numerous stories of her mother, of her beauty and goodness, of her happiness with her second husband, though the wife was so much older than Colonel Esmond. To see them together was delightful, she had heard. Their attachment was celebrated all through the country. To talk of disparity in marriages was vain after that. My Lady Castlewood and her two children held their peace whilst Madame Bernstein prattled. Harry was enraptured, and Maria surprised. Lord Castlewood was puzzled to know what sudden freak or scheme had occasioned this prodigious amiability on the part of his aunt; but did not allow the slightest expression of solicitude or doubt to appear on his countenance, which wore every mark of the most perfect satisfaction.

The Baroness's good-humour infected the whole family; not one person at table escaped a gracious word from her. In reply to some compliment to Mr. Will, when that artless youth uttered an expression of satisfaction and surprise at his aunt's behaviour, she frankly said: "Complimentary, my dear! Of course I am. I want to make up with you for having been exceedingly rude to everybody this morning. When I was a child, and my father and mother were alive, and lived here, I remember I used to adopt exactly the same behaviour. If I had been naughty in the morning, I used to try and coax my parents at night. I remember in this very room, at this very table—oh, ever so many hundred years ago!—so coaxing my father, and mother, and your grandfather, Harry Warrington; and there were eels for supper, as we have had them to-night, and it was that dish of collared eels which brought the circumstance back to my mind. I had been just as wayward that day, when I was seven years old, as I am to-day, when I am seventy, and so I confess my sins, and ask to be forgiven, like a good girl."

"I absolve your ladyship!" cried the chaplain, who made one of the party.

"But your reverence does not know how cross and ill-tempered I was. I scolded my sister, Castlewood: I scolded her children, I boxed Harry Warrington's ears: and all because he would not go with me to Tunbridge Wells."

"But I will go, madam; I will ride with you with all the pleasure in life," said Mr. Warrington.

"You see, Mr. Chaplain, what good, dutiful children they all are. 'Twas I alone who was cross and peevish. Oh, it was cruel of me to treat them so! Maria, I ask your pardon, my dear."

"Sure, madam, you have done me no wrong," says Maria to this humble suppliant.

"Indeed, I have, a very great wrong, child! Because I was weary of myself, I told you that your company would be wearisome to me. You offered to come with me to Tunbridge, and I rudely refused you."

"Nay, ma'am, if you were sick, and my presence annoyed you...

"But it will not annoy me! You were most kind to say that you would come. I do, of all things, beg, pray, entreat, implore, command that you will come."

My lord filled himself a glass, and sipped it. Most utterly unconscious did his lordship look. This, then, was the meaning of the previous comedy.

"Anything which can give my aunt pleasure, I am sure, will delight me," said Maria, trying to look as happy as possible.

"You must come and stay with me, my dear, and I promise to be good and good-humoured. My dear lord, you will spare your sister to me?"

"Lady Maria Esmond is quite of age to judge for herself about such a matter," said his lordship, with a bow. "If any of us can be of use to you, madam, you sure ought to command us." Which sentence, being interpreted, no doubt meant, "Plague take the old woman! She is taking Maria away in order to separate her from this young Virginian."

"Oh, Tunbridge will be delightful!" sighed Lady Maria.

"Mr. Sampson will go and see Goody Jones for you," my lord continued.

Harry drew pictures with his finger on the table. What delights had he not been speculating on? What walks, what rides, what interminable conversations, what delicious shrubberies and sweet sequestered summer-houses, what poring over music-books, what moonlight, what billing and cooing, had he not imagined! Yes, the day was coming. They were all departing—my Lady Castlewood to her friends, Madame Bernstein to her waters—and he was to be left alone with his divine charmer—alone with her and unutterable rapture! The thought of the pleasure was maddening. That these people were all going away. That he was to be left to enjoy that heaven—to sit at the feet of that angel and kiss the hem of that white robe. O Gods! 'twas too great bliss to be real! "I knew it couldn't be," thought poor Harry. "I knew something would happen to take her from me."

"But you will ride with us to Tunbridge, nephew Warrington, and keep us from the highwaymen?" said Madame de Bernstein.

Harry Warrington hoped the company did not see how red he grew. He tried to keep his voice calm and without tremor. Yes, he would ride with their ladyships, and he was sure they need fear no danger. Danger! Harry felt he would rather like danger than not. He would slay ten thousand highwaymen if they approached his mistress's coach. At least, he would ride by that coach, and now and again see her eyes at the window. He might not speak to her, but he should be near her. He should press the blessed hand at the inn at night, and feel it reposing on his as he led her to the carriage at morning. They would be two whole days going to Tunbridge, and one day or two he might stay there. Is not the poor wretch who is left for execution at Newgate thankful for even two or three days of respite?

You see, we have only indicated, we have not chosen to describe, at length, Mr. Harry Warrington's condition, or that utter depth of imbecility into which the poor young wretch was now plunged. Some boys have the complaint of love favourably and gently. Others, when they get the fever, are sick unto death with it; or, recovering, carry the marks of the malady down with them to the grave, or to remotest old age. I say, it is not fair to take down a young fellow's words when he is raging in that delirium. Suppose he is in love with a woman twice as old as himself; have we not all read of the young gentleman who committed suicide in consequence of his fatal passion for Mademoiselle Ninon de l'Enclos who turned out to be his grandmother? Suppose thou art making an ass of thyself, young Harry Warrington, of Virginia! are there not people in England who heehaw too? Kick and abuse him, you who have never brayed; but bear with him, all honest fellow-cardophagi: long-eared messmates, recognise a brother-donkey!

"You will stay with us for a day or two at the Wells," Madame Bernstein continued. "You will see us put into our lodgings. Then you can return to Castlewood and the partridge-shooting, and all the fine things which you and my lord are to study together."

Harry bowed an acquiescence. A whole week of heaven! Life was not altogether a blank, then.

"And as there is sure to be plenty of company at the Wells, I shall be able to present you," the lady graciously added.

"Company! ah! I shan't need company," sighed out Harry. "I mean that I shall be quite contented in the company of you two ladies," he added, eagerly; and no doubt Mr. Will wondered at his cousin's taste.

As this was to be the last night of cousin Harry's present visit to Castlewood, cousin Will suggested that he, and his reverence, and Warrington should meet at the quarters of the latter and make up accounts, to which process, Harry, being a considerable winner in his play transactions with the two gentlemen, had no objection. Accordingly, when the ladies retired for the night, and my lord withdrew—as his custom was—to his own apartments, the three gentlemen all found themselves assembled in Mr. Harry's little room before the punch-bowl, which was Will's usual midnight companion.

But Will's method of settling accounts was by producing a couple of fresh packs of cards, and offering to submit Harry's debt to the process of being doubled or acquitted. The poor chaplain had no more ready cash than Lord Castlewood's younger brother. Harry Warrington wanted to win the money of neither. Would he give pain to the brother of his adored Maria, or allow any one of her near kinsfolk to tax him with any want of generosity or forbearance? He was ready to give them their revenge, as the gentlemen proposed. Up to midnight he would play with them for what stakes they chose to name. And so they set to work, and the dice-box was rattled and the cards shuffled and dealt.

Very likely he did not think about the cards at all. Very likely he was thinking;—"At this moment, my beloved one is sitting with her beauteous golden locks outspread under the fingers of her maid. Happy maid! Now she is on her knees, the sainted creature, addressing prayers to that Heaven which is the abode of angels like her. Now she has sunk to rest behind her damask curtains. Oh, bless, bless her!" "You double us all round? I will take a card upon each of my two. Thank you, that will do—a ten—now, upon the other, a queen,—two natural vingt-et-uns, and as you doubled us you owe me so-and-so."

I imagine volleys of oaths from Mr. William, and brisk pattering of imprecations from his reverence, at the young Virginian's luck. He won because he did not want to win. Fortune, that notoriously coquettish jade, came to him, because he was thinking of another nymph, who possibly was as fickle. Will and the chaplain may have played against him, solicitous constantly to increase their stakes, and supposing that the wealthy Virginian wished to let them recover all their losings. But this was by no means Harry Warrington's notion. When he was at home he had taken a part in scores of such games as these (whereby we may be led to suppose that he kept many little circumstances of his life mum from his lady mother), and had learned to play and pay. And as he practised fair play towards his friends he expected it from them in return.

"The luck does seem to be with me, cousin," he said, in reply to some more oaths and growls of Will, "and I am sure I do not want to press it; but you don't suppose I'm going to be such a fool as to fling it away altogether? I have quite a heap of your promises on paper by this time. If we are to go on playing, let us have the dollars on the table, if you please; or, if not the money, the worth of it."

"Always the way with you rich men," grumbled Will. "Never lend except on security—always win because you are rich."

"Faith, cousin, you have been of late for ever flinging my riches into my face. I have enough for my wants and for my creditors."

"Oh, that we could all say as much!" groaned the chaplain. "How happy we, and how happy the duns would be! What have we got to play against our conqueror? There is my new gown, Mr. Warrington. Will you set me five pieces against it? I have but to preach in stuff if I lose. Stop! I have a Chrysostom, a Foxe's Martyrs, a Baker's Chronicle, and a cow and her calf. What shall we set against these?"

"I will bet one of cousin Will's notes for twenty pounds," cried Mr. Warrington, producing one of those documents.

"Or I have my brown mare, and will back her red against your honour's notes of hand, but against ready money."

"I have my horse. I will back my horse against you for fifty," bawls out Will.

Harry took the offers of both gentlemen. In the course of ten minutes the horse and the bay mare had both changed owners. Cousin William swore more fiercely than ever. The parson dashed his wig to the ground, and emulated his pupil in the loudness of his objurgations. Mr. Harry Warrington was quite calm, and not the least elated by his triumph. They had asked him to play, and he had played. He knew he should win. O beloved slumbering angel! he thought, am I not sure of victory when you are kind to me? He was looking out from his window towards the casement on the opposite side of the court, which he knew to be hers. He had forgot about his victims and their groans, and ill-luck, ere they crossed the court. Under yonder brilliant flickering star, behind yonder casement where the lamp was burning faintly, was his joy, and heart, and treasure.

CHAPTER XX. Facilis Descensus

Whilst the good old Bishop of Cambray, in his romance lately mentioned, described the disconsolate condition of Calypso at the departure of Ulysses, I forget whether he mentioned the grief of Calypso's lady's maid on taking leave of Odysseus's own gentleman. The menials must have wept together in the kitchen precincts whilst the master and mistress took a last wild embrace in the drawing-room; they must have hung round each other in the fore-cabin, whilst their principals broke their hearts in the grand saloon. When the bell rang for the last time, and Ulysses's mate bawled, "Now! any one for shore!" Calypso and her female attendant must have both walked over the same plank, with beating hearts and streaming eyes; both must have waved pocket-handkerchiefs (of far different value and texture), as they stood on the quay, to their friends on the departing vessel, whilst the people on the land, and the crew crowding in the ship's bows, shouted hip, hip, huzzay (or whatever may be the equivalent Greek for the salutation) to all engaged on that voyage. But the point to be remembered is, that if Calypso ne pouvait se consoler, Calypso's maid ne pouvait se consoler non plus. They had to walk the same plank of grief, and feel the same pang of separation; on their return home, they might not use pocket-handkerchiefs of the same texture and value, but the tears, no doubt, were as salt and plentiful which one shed in her marble halls, and the other poured forth in the servants' ditto.

Not only did Harry Warrington leave Castlewood a victim to love, but Gumbo quitted the same premises a prey to the same delightful passion. His wit, accomplishments, good-humour, his skill in dancing, cookery, and music, had endeared him to the whole female domestic circle. More than one of the men might be jealous of him, but the ladies all were with him. There was no such objection to the poor black men then in England as has obtained since among white-skinned people. Theirs was a condition not perhaps of equality, but they had a sufferance and a certain grotesque sympathy from all; and from women, no doubt, a kindness much more generous. When Ledyard and Parke, in Blackmansland, were persecuted by the men, did they not find the black women pitiful and kind to them? Women are always kind towards our sex. What (mental) negroes do they not cherish? what (moral) hunchbacks do they not adore? what lepers, what idiots, what dull drivellers, what misshapen monsters (I speak figuratively) do they not fondle and cuddle? Gumbo was treated by the women as kindly as many people no better than himself: it was only the men in the servants'-hall who rejoiced at the Virginian lad's departure. I should like to see him taking leave. I should like to see Molly housemaid stealing to the terrace-gardens in the grey dawning to cull a wistful posy. I should like to see Betty kitchenmaid cutting off a thick lock of her chestnut ringlets which she proposed to exchange for a woolly token from young Gumbo's pate. Of course he said he was regum progenies, a descendant of Ashantee kings. In Caffraria, Connaught and other places now inhabited by hereditary bondsmen, there must have been vast numbers of these potent sovereigns in former times, to judge from their descendants now extant.

At the morning announced for Madame de Bernstein's departure, all the numerous domestics of Castlewood crowded about the doors and passages, some to have a last glimpse of her ladyship's men and the fascinating Gumbo, some to take leave of her ladyship's maid, all to waylay the Baroness and her nephew for parting fees, which it was the custom of that day largely to distribute among household servants. One and the other gave liberal gratuities to the liveried society, to the gentlemen in black and ruffles, and to the swarm of female attendants. Castlewood was the home of the Baroness's youth; and as for her honest Harry, who had not only lived at free charges in the house, but had won horses and money—or promises of money—from his cousin and the unlucky chaplain, he was naturally of a generous turn, and felt that at this moment he ought not to stint his benevolent disposition. "My mother, I know," he thought, "will wish me to be liberal to all the retainers of the Esmond family." So he scattered about his gold pieces to right and left, and as if he had been as rich as Gumbo announced him to be. There was no one who came near him but had a share in his bounty. From the major-domo to the shoeblack, Mr. Harry had a peace-offering for them all. To the grim housekeeper in her still-room, to the feeble old porter in his lodge, he distributed some token of his remembrance. When a man is in love with one woman in a family, it is astonishing how fond he becomes of every person connected with it. He ingratiates himself with the maids; he is bland with the butler; he interests himself about the footman; he runs on errands for the daughters; he gives advice and lends money to the young son at college; he pats little dogs which he would kick otherwise; he smiles at old stories which would make him break out in yawns, were they uttered by any one but papa; he drinks sweet port wine for which he would curse the steward and the whole committee of a club; he bears even with the cantankerous old maiden aunt; he beats time when darling little Fanny performs her piece on the piano; and smiles when wicked, lively little Bobby upsets the coffee over his shirt.

Harry Warrington, in his way, and according to the customs of that age, had for a brief time past (by which I conclude that only for a brief time had his love been declared and accepted) given to the Castlewood family all these artless testimonies of his affection for one of them. Cousin Will should have won back his money and welcome, or have won as much of Harry's own as the lad could spare. Nevertheless, the lad, though a lover, was shrewd, keen, and fond of sport and fair play, and a judge of a good horse when he saw one. Having played for and won all the money which Will had, besides a great number of Mr. Esmond's valuable autographs, Harry was very well pleased to win Will's brown horse—that very quadruped which had nearly pushed him into the water on the first evening of his arrival at Castlewood. He had seen the horse's performance often, and in the midst of all his passion and romance, was not sorry to be possessed of such a sound, swift, well-bred hunter and roadster. When he had gazed at the stars sufficiently as they shone over his mistress's window, and put her candle to bed, he repaired to his own dormitory, and there, no doubt, thought of his Maria and his horse with youthful satisfaction, and how sweet it would be to have one pillioned on the other, and to make the tour of all the island on such an animal with such a pair of white arms round his waist. He fell asleep ruminating on these things, and meditating a million of blessings on his Maria, in whose company he was to luxuriate at least for a week more.

In the early morning poor Chaplain Sampson sent over his little black mare by the hands of his groom, footman, and gardener, who wept and bestowed a great number of kisses on the beast's white nose as he handed him over to Gumbo. Gumbo and his master were both affected by the fellow's sensibility; the negro servant showing his sympathy by weeping, and Harry by producing a couple of guineas, with which he astonished and speedily comforted the chaplain's boy. Then Gumbo and the late groom led the beast away to the stable, having commands to bring him round with Mr. William's horse after breakfast, at the hour when Madam Bernstein's carriages were ordered.

So courteous was he to his aunt, or so grateful for her departure, that the master of the house even made his appearance at the morning meal, in order to take leave of his guests. The ladies and the chaplain were present—the only member of the family absent was Will: who, however, left a note for his cousin, in which Will stated, in exceedingly bad spelling, that he was obliged to go away to Salisbury Races that morning, but that he had left the horse which his cousin won last night, and which Tom, Mr. Will's groom, would hand over to Mr. Warrington's servant. Will's absence did not prevent the rest of the party from drinking a dish of tea amicably, and in due time the carriages rolled into the courtyard, the servants packed them with the Baroness's multiplied luggage, and the moment of departure arrived.

A large open landau contained the stout Baroness and her niece; a couple of men-servants mounting on the box before them with pistols and blunderbusses ready in event of a meeting with highwaymen. In another carriage were their ladyships' maids, and another servant in guard of the trunks, which, vast and numerous as they were, were as nothing compared to the enormous baggage-train accompanying a lady of the present time. Mr. Warrington's modest valises were placed in this second carriage under the maid's guardianship, and Mr. Gumbo proposed to ride by the window for the chief part of the journey.

My lord, with his stepmother and Lady Fanny, accompanied their kinswoman to the carriage steps, and bade her farewell with many dutiful embraces. Her Lady Maria followed in a riding-dress, which Harry Warrington thought the most becoming costume in the world. A host of servants stood around, and begged Heaven bless her ladyship. The Baroness's departure was known in the village, and scores of the folks there stood waiting under the trees outside the gates, and huzzayed and waved their hats as the ponderous vehicles rolled away.

Gumbo was gone for Mr. Warrington's horses, as my lord, with his arm under his young guest's, paced up and down the court. "I hear you carry away some of our horses out of Castlewood?" my lord said.

Harry blushed. "A gentleman cannot refuse a fair game at the cards," he said. "I never wanted to play, nor would have played for money had not my cousin William forced me. As for the chaplain, it went to my heart to win from him, but he was as eager as my cousin."

"I know—I know! There is no blame to you, my boy. At Rome you can't help doing as Rome does; and I am very glad that you have been able to give Will a lesson. He is mad about play—would gamble his coat off his back—and I and the family have had to pay his debts ever so many times. May I ask how much you have won of him?"

"Well, some eighteen pieces the first day or two, and his note for a hundred and twenty more, and the brown horse, sixty—that makes nigh upon two hundred. But, you know, cousin, all was fair, and it was even against my will that we played at all. Will ain't a match for me, my lord—that is the fact. Indeed he is not."

"He is a match for most people, though," said my lord. "His brown horse, I think you said?"

"Yes. His brown horse—Prince William, out of Constitution. You don't suppose I would set him sixty against his bay, my lord?"

"Oh, I didn't know. I saw Will riding out this morning; most likely I did not remark what horse he was on. And you won the black mare from the parson?"

"For fourteen. He will mount Gumbo very well. Why does not the rascal come round with the horses?" Harry's mind was away to lovely Maria. He longed to be trotting by her side.

"When you get to Tunbridge, cousin Harry, you must be on the look-out against sharper players than the chaplain and Will. There is all sorts of queer company at the Wells."

"A Virginian learns pretty well to take care of himself, my lord, says Harry, with a knowing nod.

"So it seems! I recommend my sister to thee, Harry. Although she is not a baby in years, she is as innocent as one. Thou wilt see that she comes to no mischief?"

"I will guard her with my life, my lord!" cries Harry.

"Thou art a brave fellow. By the way, cousin, unless you are very fond of Castlewood, I would in your case not be in a great hurry to return to this lonely, tumble-down old house. I want myself to go to another place I have, and shall scarce be back here till the partridge-shooting. Go you and take charge of the women, of my sister and the Baroness, will you?"

"Indeed I will," said Harry, his heart beating with happiness at the thought.

"And I will write thee word when you shall bring my sister back to me. Here come the horses. Have you bid adieu to the Countess and Lady Fanny? They are kissing their hands to you from the music-room balcony."

Harry ran up to bid these ladies a farewell. He made that ceremony very brief, for he was anxious to be off to the charmer of his heart; and came downstairs to mount his newly-gotten steed, which Gumbo, himself astride on the parson's black mare, held by the rein.

There was Gumbo on the black mare, indeed, and holding another horse. But it was a bay horse, not a brown—a bay horse with broken knees—an aged, worn-out quadruped.

"What is this?" cries Harry.

"Your honour's new horse," says the groom, touching his cap.

"This brute?" exclaims the young gentleman, with one or more of those expressions then in use in England and Virginia. "Go and bring me round Prince William, Mr. William's horse, the brown horse."

"Mr. William have rode Prince William this morning away to Salisbury Races. His last words was, 'Sam, saddle my bay horse, Cato, for Mr. Warrington this morning. He is Mr. Warrington's horse now. I sold him to him last night.' And I know your honour is bountiful: you will consider the groom."

My lord could not help breaking into a laugh at these words of Sam the groom, whilst Harry, for his part, indulged in a number more of those remarks which politeness does not admit of our inserting here.

"Mr. William said he never could think of parting with the Prince under a hundred and twenty," said the groom, looking at the young man.

Lord Castlewood only laughed the more. "Will has been too much for thee, Harry Warrington."

"Too much for me, my lord! So may a fellow with loaded dice throw sixes, and be too much for me. I do not call this betting, I call it ch———"

"Mr. Warrington! Spare me bad words about my brother, if you please. Depend on it, I will take care that you are righted. Farewell. Ride quickly, or your coaches will be at Farnham before you;" and waving him an adieu, my lord entered into the house, whilst Harry and his companion rode out of the courtyard. The young Virginian was much too eager to rejoin the carriages and his charmer, to remark the unutterable love and affection which Gumbo shot from his fine eyes towards a young creature in the porter's lodge.

When the youth was gone, the chaplain and my lord sate down to finish their breakfast in peace and comfort. The two ladies did not return to this meal.

"That was one of Will's confounded rascally tricks," says my lord. "If our cousin breaks Will's head I should not wonder."

"He is used to the operation, my lord, and yet," adds the chaplain, with a grin, "when we were playing last night, the colour of the horse was not mentioned. I could not escape, having but one: and the black boy has ridden off on him. The young Virginian plays like a man, to do him justice."

"He wins because he does not care about losing. I think there can be little doubt but that he is very well to do. His mother's law-agents are my lawyers, and they write that the property is quite a principality, and grows richer every year."

"If it were a kingdom I know whom Mr. Warrington would make queen of it," said the obsequious chaplain.

"Who can account for taste, parson?" asks his lordship, with a sneer. "All men are so. The first woman I was in love with myself was forty; and as jealous as if she had been fifteen. It runs in the family. Colonel Esmond (he in scarlet and the breastplate yonder) married my grandmother, who was almost old enough to be his. If this lad chooses to take out an elderly princess to Virginia, we must not balk him."

"'Twere a consummation devoutly to be wished!" cries the chaplain. "Had I not best go to Tunbridge Wells myself, my lord, and be on the spot, and ready to exercise my sacred function in behalf of the young couple?"

"You shall have a pair of new nags, parson, if you do," said my lord. And with this we leave them peaceable over a pipe of tobacco after breakfast.

Harry was in such a haste to join the carriages that he almost forgot to take off his hat, and acknowledge the cheers of the Castlewood villagers: they all liked the lad, whose frank cordial ways and honest face got him a welcome in most places. Legends were still extant in Castlewood, of his grandparents, and how his grandfather, Colonel Esmond, might have been Lord Castlewood, but would not. Old Lockwood at the gate often told of the Colonel's gallantry in Queen Anne's wars. His feats were exaggerated, the behaviour of the present family was contrasted with that of the old lord and lady: who might not have been very popular in their time, but were better folks than those now in possession. Lord Castlewood was a hard landlord: perhaps more disliked because he was known to be poor and embarrassed than because he was severe. As for Mr. Will, nobody was fond of him. The young gentleman had had many brawls and quarrels about the village, had received and given broken heads, had bills in the neighbouring towns which he could not or would not pay; had been arraigned before the magistrates for tampering with village girls, and waylaid and cudgelled by injured husbands, fathers, sweethearts. A hundred years ago his character and actions might have been described at length by the painter of manners; but the Comic Muse, nowadays, does not lift up Molly Seagrim's curtain; she only indicates the presence of some one behind it, and passes on primly, with expressions of horror, and a fan before her eyes. The village had heard how the young Virginian squire had beaten Mr. Will at riding, at jumping, at shooting, and finally at card-playing, for everything is known; and they respected Harry all the more for this superiority. Above all, they admired him on account of the reputation of enormous wealth which Gumbo had made for his master. This fame had travelled over the whole county, and was preceding him at this moment on the boxes of Madame Bernstein's carriages, from which the valets, as they descended at the inns to bait, spread astounding reports of the young Virginian's rank and splendour. He was a prince in his own country. He had gold mines, diamond mines, furs, tobaccos, who knew what, or how much? No wonder the honest Britons cheered him and respected him for his prosperity, as the noble-hearted fellows always do. I am surprised city corporations did not address him, and offer gold boxes with the freedom of the city—he was so rich. Ah, a proud thing it is to be a Briton, and think that there is no country where prosperity is so much respected as in ours; and where success receives such constant affecting testimonials of loyalty!

So, leaving the villagers bawling, and their hats tossing in the air, Harry spurred his sorry beast, and galloped, with Gumbo behind him, until he came up with the cloud of dust in the midst of which his charmer's chariot was enveloped. Penetrating into this cloud, he found himself at the window of the carriage. The Lady Maria had the back seat to herself; by keeping a little behind the wheels, he could have the delight of seeing her divine eyes and smiles. She held a finger to her lip. Madame Bernstein was already dozing on her cushions. Harry did not care to disturb the old lady. To look at his cousin was bliss enough for him. The landscape around him might be beautiful, but what did he heed it? All the skies and trees of summer were as nothing compared to yonder face; the hedgerow birds sang no such sweet music as her sweet monosyllables.

The Baroness's fat horses were accustomed to short journeys, easy paces, and plenty of feeding; so that, ill as Harry Warrington was mounted, he could, without much difficulty, keep pace with his elderly kinswoman. At two o'clock they baited for a couple of hours for dinner. Mr. Warrington paid the landlord generously. What price could be too great for the pleasure which he enjoyed in being near his adored Maria, and having the blissful chance of a conversation with her, scarce interrupted by the soft breathing of Madame de Bernstein, who, after a comfortable meal, indulged in an agreeable half-hour's slumber? In voices soft and low, Maria and her young gentleman talked over and over again those delicious nonsenses which people in Harry's condition never tire of hearing and uttering.

They were going to a crowded watering-place, where all sorts of beauty and fashion would be assembled; timid Maria was certain that amongst the young beauties, Harry would discover some, whose charms were far more worthy to occupy his attention, than any her homely face and figure could boast of. By all the gods, Harry vowed that Venus herself could not tempt him from her side. It was he who for his part had occasion to fear. When the young men of fashion beheld his peerless Maria they would crowd round her car; they would cause her to forget the rough and humble American lad who knew nothing of fashion or wit, who had only a faithful heart at her service.

Maria smiles, she casts her eyes to heaven, she vows that Harry knows nothing of the truth and fidelity of women; it is his sex, on the contrary, which proverbially is faithless, and which delights to play with poor female hearts. A scuffle ensues; a clatter is heard among the knives and forks of the dessert; a glass tumbles over and breaks. An "Oh!" escapes from the innocent lips of Maria, The disturbance has been caused by the broad cuff of Mr. Warrington's coat, which has been stretched across the table to seize Lady Maria's hand, and has upset the wine-glass in so doing. Surely nothing could be more natural, or indeed necessary, than that Harry, upon hearing his sex's honour impeached, should seize upon his fair accuser's hand, and vow eternal fidelity upon those charming fingers?

What a part they play, or used to play, in love-making, those hands! How quaintly they are squeezed at that period of life! How they are pushed into conversation! what absurd vows and protests are palmed off by their aid! What good can there be in pulling and pressing a thumb and four fingers? I fancy I see Alexis laugh, who is haply reading this page by the side of Araminta. To talk about thumbs indeed!... Maria looks round, for her part, to see if Madame Bernstein has been awakened by the crash of glass; but the old lady slumbers quite calmly in her arm-chair, so her niece thinks there can be no harm in yielding to Harry's gentle pressure.

The horses are put to: Paradise is over—at least until the next occasion. When my landlord enters with the bill, Harry is standing quite at a distance from his cousin, looking from the window at the cavalcade gathering below. Madame Bernstein wakes up from her slumber, smiling and quite unconscious. With what profound care and reverential politeness Mr. Warrington hands his aunt to her carriage! how demure and simple looks Lady Maria as she follows! Away go the carriages, in the midst of a profoundly bowing landlord and waiters; of country-folks gathered round the blazing inn-sign; of shopmen gazing from their homely little doors; of boys and market-folks under the colonnade of the old town-hall; of loungers along the gabled street. "It is the famous Baroness Bernstein. That is she, the old lady in the capuchin. It is the rich young American who is just come from Virginia, and is worth millions and millions. Well, sure, he might have a better horse." The cavalcade disappears, and the little town lapses into its usual quiet. The landlord goes back to his friends at the club, to tell how the great folks are going to sleep at The Bush, at Farnham, to-night.

The inn dinner had been plentiful, and all the three guests of the inn had done justice to the good cheer. Harry had the appetite natural to his period of life. Maria and her aunt were also not indifferent to a good dinner: Madame Bernstein had had a comfortable nap after hers, which had no doubt helped her to bear all the good things of the meal—the meat pies, and the fruit pies, and the strong ale, and the heady port wine. She reclined at ease on her seat of the landau, and looked back affably, and smiled at Harry and exchanged a little talk with him as he rode by the carriage side. But what ailed the beloved being who sate with her back to the horses? Her complexion, which was exceedingly fair, was further ornamented with a pair of red cheeks, which Harry took to be natural roses. (You see, madam, that your surmises regarding the Lady Maria's conduct with her cousin are quite wrong and uncharitable, and that the timid lad had made no such experiments as you suppose, in order to ascertain whether the roses were real or artificial. A kiss, indeed! I blush to think you should imagine that the present writer could indicate anything so shocking!) Maria's bright red cheeks, I say still, continued to blush as it seemed with a strange metallic bloom: but the rest of her face, which had used to rival the lily in whiteness, became of a jonquil colour. Her eyes stared round with a ghastly expression. Harry was alarmed at the agony depicted in the charmer's countenance; which not only exhibited pain, but was exceedingly unbecoming. Madame Bernstein also at length remarked her niece's indisposition, and asked her if sitting backwards in the carriage made her ill, which poor Maria confessed to be the fact. On this, the elder lady was forced to make room for her niece on her own side, and, in the course of the drive to Farnham, uttered many gruff, disagreeable, sarcastic remarks to her fellow-traveller, indicating her great displeasure that Maria should be so impertinent as to be ill on the first day of a journey.

When they reached the Bush Inn at Farnham, under which name a famous inn has stood in Farnham town for these three hundred years—the dear invalid retired with her maid to her bedroom: scarcely glancing a piteous look at Harry as she retreated, and leaving the lad's mind in a strange confusion of dismay and sympathy. Those yellow, yellow cheeks, those livid wrinkled eyelids, that ghastly red—how ill his blessed Maria looked! And not only how ill, but how—away, horrible thought, unmanly suspicion! He tried to shut the idea out from his mind. He had little appetite for supper, though the jolly Baroness partook of that repast as if she had had no dinner; and certainly as if she had no sympathy with her invalid niece.

She sent her major-domo to see if Lady Maria would have anything from the table. The servant brought back word that her ladyship was still very unwell, and declined any refreshment.

"I hope she intends to be well to-morrow morning," cried Madame Bernstein, rapping her little hand on the table. "I hate people to be ill in an inn, or on a journey. Will you play piquet with me, Harry?"

Harry was happy to be able to play piquet with his aunt. "That absurd Maria!" says Madame Bernstein, drinking from a great glass of negus, "she takes liberties with herself. She never had a good constitution. She is forty-one years old. All her upper teeth are false, and she can't eat with them. Thank Heaven, I have still got every tooth in my head. How clumsily you deal, child!"

Deal clumsily indeed! Had a dentist been extracting Harry's own grinders at that moment, would he have been expected to mind his cards and deal them neatly? When a man is laid on the rack at the Inquisition, is it natural that he should smile and speak politely and coherently to the grave, quiet Inquisitor? Beyond that little question regarding the cards, Harry's Inquisitor did not show the smallest disturbance. Her face indicated neither surprise, nor triumph, nor cruelty. Madame Bernstein did not give one more stab to her niece that night: but she played at cards, and prattled with Harry, indulging in her favourite talk about old times, and parting from him with great cordiality and good-humour. Very likely he did not heed her stories. Very likely other thoughts occupied his mind. Maria is forty-one years old, Maria has false ——. Oh, horrible, horrible! Has she a false eye? Has she false hair? Has she a wooden leg? I envy not that boy's dreams that night.

Madame Bernstein, in the morning, said she had slept as sound as a top. She had no remorse, that was clear. (Some folks are happy and easy in mind when their victim is stabbed and done for.) Lady Maria made her appearance at the breakfast-table, too. Her ladyship's indisposition was fortunately over: her aunt congratulated her affectionately on her good looks. She sate down to her breakfast. She looked appealingly in Harry's face. He remarked, with his usual brilliancy and originality, that he was very glad her ladyship was better. Why, at the tone of his voice, did she start, and again gaze at him with frightened eyes? There sate the Chief Inquisitor, smiling, perfectly calm, eating ham and muffins. O poor writhing, rack-rent victim! O stony Inquisitor! O Baroness

Bernstein! It was cruel! cruel!

Round about Farnham the hops were gloriously green in the sunshine, and the carriages drove through the richest, most beautiful country. Maria insisted upon taking her old seat. She thanked her dear aunt. It would not in the least incommode her now. She gazed, as she had done yesterday, in the face of the young knight riding by the carriage side. She looked for those answering signals which used to be lighted up in yonder two windows, and told that love was burning within. She smiled gently at him, to which token of regard he tried to answer with a sickly grin of recognition. Miserable youth! Those were not false teeth he saw when she smiled. He thought they were, and they tore and lacerated him.

And so the day sped on—sunshiny and brilliant overhead, but all over clouds for Harry and Maria. He saw nothing: he thought of Virginia: he remembered how he had been in love with Parson Broadbent's daughter at Jamestown, and how quickly that business had ended. He longed vaguely to be at home again. A plague on all these cold-hearted English relations! Did they not all mean to trick him? Were they not all scheming against him? Had not that confounded Will cheated him about the horse?

At this very juncture, Maria gave a scream so loud and shrill that Madame Bernstein woke, that the coachman pulled his horses up, and the footman beside him sprang down from his box in a panic.

"Let me out! let me out!" screamed Maria. "Let me go to him! let me go to him!"

"What is it?" asked the Baroness.

It was that Will's horse had come down on his knees and nose, had sent his rider over his head, and Mr. Harry, who ought to have known better, was lying on his own face quite motionless.

Gumbo, who had been dallying with the maids of the second carriage, clattered up, and mingled his howls with Lady Maria's lamentations. Madame Bernstein descended from her landau, and came slowly up, trembling a good deal.

"He is dead—he is dead!" sobbed Maria.

"Don't be a goose, Maria!" her aunt said. "Ring at that gate, some one!"

Will's horse had gathered himself up and stood perfectly quiet after his feat: but his late rider gave not the slightest sign of life.

CHAPTER XXI. Samaritans

Lest any tender-hearted reader should be in alarm for Mr. Harry Warrington's safety, and fancy that his broken-kneed horse had carried him altogether out of this life and history, let us set her mind easy at the beginning of this chapter by assuring her that nothing very serious has happened. How can we afford to kill off our heroes, when they are scarcely out of their teens, and we have not reached the age of manhood of the story? We are in mourning already for one of our Virginians, who has come to grief in America; surely we cannot kill off the other in England? No, no. Heroes are not despatched with such hurry and violence unless there is a cogent reason for making away with them. Were a gentleman to perish every time a horse came down with him, not only the hero, but the author of this chronicle would have gone under ground, whereas the former is but sprawling outside it, and will be brought to life again as soon as he has been carried into the house where Madame de Bernstein's servants have rung the bell.

And to convince you that at least this youngest of the Virginians is still alive, here is an authentic copy of a letter from the lady into whose house he was taken after his fall from Mr. Will's brute of a broken-kneed horse, and in whom he appears to have found a kind friend:

"TO MRS. ESMOND WARRINGTON, OF CASTLEWOOD

"At her House at Richmond, in Virginia

"If Mrs. Esmond Warrington of Virginia can call to mind twenty-three years ago, when Miss Rachel Esmond was at Kensington Boarding School, she may perhaps remember Miss Molly Benson, her class-mate, who has forgotten all the little quarrels which they used to have together (in which Miss Molly was very often in the wrong), and only remembers the generous, high-spirited, sprightly, Miss Esmond, the Princess Pocahontas, to whom so many of our school-fellows paid court.

"Dear madam! I cannot forget that you were dear Rachel once upon a time, as I was your dearest Molly. Though we parted not very good friends when you went home to Virginia, yet you know how fond we once were. I still, Rachel, have the gold etui your papa gave me when he came to our speech-day at Kensington, and we two performed the quarrel of Brutus and Cassius out of Shakspeare; and 'twas only yesterday morning I was dreaming that we were both called up to say our lesson before the awful Miss Hardwood, and that I did not know it, and that as usual Miss Rachel Esmond went above me. How well remembered those old days are! How young we grow as we think of them! I remember our walks and our exercises, our good King and Queen as they walked in Kensington Gardens, and their court following them, whilst we of Miss Hardwood's school curtseyed in a row. I can tell still what we had for dinner on each day of the week, and point to the place where your garden was, which was always so much better kept than mine. So was Miss Esmond's chest of drawers a model of neatness, whilst mine were in a sad condition. Do you remember how we used to tell stories in the dormitory, and Madame Hibou, the French governess, would come out of bed and interrupt us with her hooting? Have you forgot the poor dancing-master, who told us he had been waylaid by assassins, but who was beaten, it appears, by my lord your brother's footmen? My dear, your cousin, the Lady Maria Esmond (her papa was, I think, but Viscount Castlewood in those times), has just been on a visit to this house, where you may be sure I did not recall those sad times to her remembrance, about which I am now chattering to Mrs. Esmond.

"Her ladyship has been staying here, and another relative of yours, the Baroness of Bernstein, and the two ladies are both gone on to Tunbridge Wells; but another and dearer relative still remains in my house, and is sound asleep, I trust, in the very next room, and the name of this gentleman is Mr. Henry Esmond Warrington. Now, do you understand how you come to hear from an old friend? Do not be alarmed, dear madam! I know you are thinking at this moment, 'My boy is ill. That is why Miss Molly Benson writes to me.' No, my dear; Mr. Warrington was ill yesterday, but to-day he is very comfortable; and our doctor, who is no less a person than my dear husband, Colonel Lambert, has blooded him, has set his shoulder, which was dislocated, and pronounces that in two days more Mr. Warrington will be quite ready to take the road.

"I fear I and my girls are sorry that he is so soon to be well. Yesterday evening, as we were at tea, there came a great ringing at our gate, which disturbed us all, as the bell very seldom sounds in this quiet place, unless a passing beggar pulls it for charity; and the servants, running out, returned with the news, that a young gentleman, who had a fall from his horse, was lying lifeless on the road, surrounded by the friends in whose company he was travelling. At this, my Colonel (who is sure the most Samaritan of men!) hastens away, to see how he can serve the fallen traveller, and presently, with the aid of the servants, and followed by two ladies, brings into the house such a pale, lifeless, beautiful, young man! Ah, my dear, how I rejoice to think that your child has found shelter and succour under my roof! that my husband has saved him from pain and fever, and has been the means of restoring him to you and health! We shall be friends again now, shall we not? I was very ill last year, and 'twas even thought I should die. Do you know, that I often thought of you then, and how you had parted from me in anger so many years ago? I began then a foolish note to you, which I was too sick to finish, to tell you that if I went the way appointed for us all, I should wish to leave the world in charity with every single being I had known in it.

"Your cousin, the Right Honourable Lady Maria Esmond, showed a great deal of maternal tenderness and concern for her young kinsman after his accident. I am sure she hath a kind heart. The Baroness de Bernstein, who is of an advanced age, could not be expected to feel so keenly as we young people; but was, nevertheless, very much moved and interested until Mr. Warrington was restored to consciousness, when she said she was anxious to get on towards Tunbridge, whither she was bound, and was afraid of all things to lie in a place where there was no doctor at hand. My Aesculapius laughingly said, he would not offer to attend upon a lady of quality, though he would answer for his young patient. Indeed, the Colonel, during his campaigns, has had plenty of practice in accidents of this nature, and I am certain, were we to call in all the faculty for twenty miles round, Mr. Warrington could get no better treatment. So, leaving the young gentleman to the care of me and my daughters, the Baroness and her ladyship took their leave of us, the latter very loth to go. When he is well enough, my Colonel will ride with him as far as

Westerham, but on his own horses, where an old army-comrade of Mr. Lambert's resides. And, as this letter will not take the post for Falmouth until, by God's blessing, your son is well and perfectly restored, you need be under no sort of alarm for him whilst under the roof of, madam, your affectionate, humble servant, MARY LAMBERT.

"P.S. Thursday.

"I am glad to hear (Mr. Warrington's coloured gentleman hath informed our people of the gratifying circumstance) that Providence hath blessed Mrs. Esmond with such vast wealth, and with an heir so likely to do credit to it. Our present means are amply sufficient, but will be small when divided amongst our survivors. Ah, dear madam! I have heard of your calamity of last year. Though the Colonel and I have reared many children (five), we have lost two, and a mother's heart can feel for yours! I own to you, mine yearned to your boy to-day, when (in a manner inexpressibly affecting to me and Mr. Lambert) he mentioned his dear brother. 'Tis impossible to see your son, and not to love and regard him. I am thankful that it has been our lot to succour him in his trouble, and that in receiving the stranger within our gates we should be giving hospitality to the son of an old friend."

Nature has written a letter of credit upon some men's faces, which is honoured almost wherever presented. Harry Warrington's countenance was so stamped in his youth. His eyes were so bright, his cheek so red and healthy, his look so frank and open, that almost all who beheld him, nay, even those who cheated him, trusted him. Nevertheless, as we have hinted, the lad was by no means the artless stripling he seemed to be. He was knowing enough with all his blushing cheeks; perhaps more wily and wary than he grew to be in after-age. Sure, a shrewd and generous man (who has led an honest life and has no secret blushes for his conscience) grows simpler as he grows older; arrives at his sum of right by more rapid processes of calculation; learns to eliminate false arguments more readily, and hits the mark of truth with less previous trouble of aiming, and disturbance of mind. Or is it only a senile delusion, that some of our vanities are cured with our growing years, and that we become more just in our perceptions of our own and our neighbour's shortcomings? ... I would humbly suggest that young people, though they look prettier, have larger eyes, and not near so many wrinkles about their eyelids, are often as artful as some of their elders. What little monsters of cunning your frank schoolboys are! How they cheat mamma! how they hoodwink papa! how they humbug the housekeeper! how they cringe to the big boy for whom they fag at school! what a long lie and five years' hypocrisy and flattery is their conduct towards Dr. Birch! And the little boys' sisters? Are they any better, and is it only after they come out in the world that the little darlings learn a trick or two?

You may see, by the above letter of Mrs. Lambert, that she, like all good women (and, indeed, almost all bad women), was a sentimental person; and, as she looked at Harry Warrington laid in her best bed, after the Colonel had bled him and clapped in his shoulder, as holding by her husband's hand she beheld the lad in a sweet slumber, murmuring a faint inarticulate word or two in his sleep, a faint blush quivering on his cheek, she owned he was a pretty lad indeed, and confessed with a sort of compunction that neither of her two boys—Jack who was at Oxford, and Charles who was just gone back to school after the Bartlemytide holidays—was half so handsome as the Virginian. What a good figure the boy had! and when papa bled him, his arm was as white as any lady's!

"Yes, as you say, Jack might have been as handsome but for the small-pox: and as for Charley———" "Always took after his papa, my dear Molly," said the Colonel, looking at his own honest face in a little looking-glass with a cut border and a japanned frame, by which the chief guests of the worthy gentleman and lady had surveyed their patches and powder, or shaved their hospitable beards.

"Did I say so, my love?" whispered Mrs. Lambert, looking rather scared.

"No; but you thought so, Mrs. Lambert."

"How can you tell one's thoughts so, Martin?" asks the lady.

"Because I am a conjurer, and because you tell them yourself, my dear," answered her husband. "Don't be frightened: he won't wake after that draught I gave him. Because you never see a young fellow but you are comparing him with your own. Because you never hear of one but you are thinking which of our girls he shall fall in love with and marry."

"Don't be foolish, sir," says the lady, putting a hand up to the Colonel's lips. They have softly trodden out of their guest's bedchamber by this time, and are in the adjoining dressing-closet, a snug little wainscoted room looking over gardens, with India curtains, more Japan chests and cabinets, a treasure of china, and a most refreshing odour of fresh lavender.

"You can't deny it, Mrs. Lambert," the Colonel resumes; "as you were looking at the young gentleman just now, you were thinking to yourself which of my girls will he marry? Shall it be Theo, or shall it be Hester? And then you thought of Lucy who was at boarding-school."

"There is no keeping anything from you, Martin Lambert," sighs the wife.

"There is no keeping it out of your eyes, my dear. What is this burning desire all you women have for selling and marrying your daughters? We men don't wish to part with 'em. I am sure, for my part, I should not like yonder young fellow half as well if I thought he intended to carry one of my darlings away with him."

"Sure, Martin, I have been so happy myself," says the fond wife and mother, looking at her husband with her very best eyes, "that I must wish my girls to do as I have done, and be happy, too!"

"Then you think good husbands are common, Mrs. Lambert, and that you may walk any day into the road before the house and find one shot out at the gate like a sack of coals?"

"Wasn't it providential, sir, that this young gentleman should be thrown over his horse's head at our very gate, and that he should turn out to be the son of my old schoolfellow and friend?" asked the wife. "There is something more than accident in such cases, depend upon that, Mr. Lambert!"

"And this was the stranger you saw in the candle three nights running, I suppose?"

"And in the fire, too, sir; twice a coal jumped out close by Theo. You may sneer, sir, but these things are not to be despised. Did I not see you distinctly coming back from Minorca, and dream of you at the very day and hour when you were wounded in Scotland?"

"How many times have you seen me wounded, when I had not a scratch, my dear? How many times have you seen me ill when I had no sort of hurt? You are always prophesying, and 'twere very hard on you if you were not sometimes right. Come! Let us leave our guest asleep comfortably, and go down and give the girls their French lesson."

So saying, the honest gentleman put his wife's arm under his, and they descended together the broad oak staircase of the comfortable old hall, round which hung the effigies of many foregone Lamberts, worthy magistrates, soldiers, country gentlemen, as was the Colonel whose acquaintance we have just made. The Colonel was a gentleman of pleasant, waggish humour. The French lesson which he and his daughters conned together was a scene out of Monsieur Moliere's comedy of "Tartuffe," and papa was pleased to be very facetious with Miss Theo, by calling her Madam, and by treating her with a great deal of mock respect and ceremony. The girls read together with their father a scene or two of his favourite author (nor were they less modest in those days, though their tongues were a little more free), and papa was particularly arch and funny as he read from Orgon's part in that celebrated play:

"ORGON.
Or sus, nous voila bien. J'ai, Mariane, en vous
Reconnu de tout temps un esprit assez doux,
Et de tout temps aussi vous m'avez ete chere.

MARIANE.
Je suis fort redevable a cet amour de pere.

ORGON.
Fort bien. Que dites-vous de Tartuffe notre hote?

MARIANE.
Qui? Moi?

ORGON.
Vous. Voyez bien comme vous repondrez.

MARIANE.
Helas! J'en dirai, moi, tout ce que vous voudrez!
(Mademoiselle Mariane laughs and blushes in spite of herself, whilst reading

this line.)
      ORGON.
   C'est parler sagement. Dites-moi donc, ma fille,
   Qu'en toute sa personne un haut merite brille,
   Qu'il touche votre coeur, et qu'il vous seroit doux
   De le voir par men choix devenir votre epoux!"

"Have we not read the scene prettily, Elmire?" says the Colonel, laughing, and turning round to his wife.

Elmira prodigiously admired Orgon's reading, and so did his daughters, and almost everything besides which Mr. Lambert said or did. Canst thou, O friendly reader, count upon the fidelity of an artless and tender heart or two, and reckon among the blessings which Heaven hath bestowed on thee the love of faithful women! Purify thine own heart, and try to make it worthy theirs. On thy knees, on thy knees, give thanks for the blessing awarded thee! All the prizes of life are nothing compared to that one. All the rewards of ambition, wealth, pleasure, only vanity and disappointment—grasped at greedily and fought for fiercely, and, over and over again, found worthless by the weary winners. But love seems to survive life, and to reach beyond it. I think we take it with us past the grave. Do we not still give it to those who have left us? May we not hope that they feel it for us, and that we shall leave it here in one or two fond bosoms, when we also are gone?

And whence, or how, or why, pray, this sermon? You see I know more about this Lambert family than you do to whom I am just presenting them: as how should you who never heard of them before! You may not like my friends; very few people do like strangers to whom they are presented with an outrageous flourish of praises on the part of the introducer. You say (quite naturally), What? Is this all? Are these the people he is so fond of? Why, the girl's not a beauty—the mother is good-natured, and may have been good-looking once, but she has no trace of it now—and, as for the father, he is quite an ordinary man. Granted but don't you acknowledge that the sight of an honest man, with an honest, loving wife by his side, and surrounded by loving and obedient children, presents something very sweet and affecting to you? If you are made acquainted with such a person, and see the eager kindness of the fond faces round about him, and that pleasant confidence and affection which beams from his own, do you mean to say you are not touched and gratified? If you happen to stay in such a man's house, and at morning or evening see him and his children and domestics gathered together in a certain name, do you not join humbly in the petitions of those servants, and close them with a reverent Amen? That first night of his stay at Oakhurst, Harry Warrington, who had had a sleeping potion, and was awake sometimes rather feverish, thought he heard the Evening Hymn, and that his dearest brother George was singing it at home, in which delusion the patient went off again to sleep.

CHAPTER XXII. In Hospital

Sinking into a sweet slumber, and lulled by those harmonious sounds, our young patient passed a night of pleasant unconsciousness, and awoke in the morning to find a summer sun streaming in at the window, and his kind host and hostess smiling at his bed-curtains. He was ravenously hungry, and his doctor permitted him straightway to partake of a mess of chicken, which the doctor's wife told him had been prepared by the hands of one of her daughters.

One of her daughters? A faint image of a young person—of two young persons—with red cheeks and black waving locks, smiling round his couch, and suddenly departing thence, soon after he had come to himself, arose in the young man's mind. Then, then, there returned the remembrance of a female—lovely, it is true, but more elderly—certainly considerably older—and with f——. Oh, horror and remorse! He writhed with anguish, as a certain recollection crossed him. An immense gulf of time gaped between him and the past. How long was it since he had heard that those pearls were artificial,—that those golden locks were only pinchbeck? A long, long time ago, when he was a boy, an innocent boy. Now he was a man,—quite an old man. He had been bled copiously; he had a little fever; he had had nothing to eat for very many hours; he had a sleeping-draught, and a long, deep slumber after.

"What is it, my dear child?" cries kind Mrs. Lambert, as he started.

"Nothing, madam; a twinge in my shoulder," said the lad. "I speak to my host and hostess? Sure you have been very kind to me."

"We are old friends, Mr. Warrington. My husband, Colonel Lambert, knew your father, and I and your mamma were schoolgirls together at Kensington. You were no stranger to us when your aunt and cousin told us who you were."

"Are they here?" asked Harry, looking a little blank.

"They must have lain at Tunbridge Wells last night. They sent a horseman from Reigate yesterday for news of you."

"Ah! I remember," says Harry, looking at his bandaged arm.

"I have made a good cure of you, Mr. Warrington. And now Mrs. Lambert and the cook must take charge of you."

"Nay; Theo prepared the chicken and rice, Mr. Lambert," said the lady. "Will Mr. Warrington get up after he has had his breakfast? We will send your valet to you."

"If howling proves fidelity, your man must be a most fond, attached creature," says Mr. Lambert.

"He let your baggage travel off after all in your aunt's carriage," said Mrs. Lambert. "You must wear my husband's linen, which, I dare say, is not so fine as yours."

"Pish, my dear! my shirts are good shirts enough for any Christian," cries the Colonel.

"They are Theo's and Hester's work," says mamma. At which her husband arches his eyebrows and looks at her. "And Theo hath ripped and sewed your sleeve to make it quite comfortable for your shoulder," the lady added.

"What beautiful roses!" cries Harry, looking at a fine China vase full of them that stood on the toilet-table, under the japan-framed glass.

"My daughter Theo cut them this morning. Well, Mr. Lambert? She did cut them!"

I suppose the Colonel was thinking that his wife introduced Theo too much into the conversation, and trod on Mrs. Lambert's slipper, or pulled her robe, or otherwise nudged her into a sense of propriety.

"And I fancied I heard some one singing the Evening Hymn very sweetly last night—or was it only a dream?" asked the young patient.

"Theo again, Mr. Warrington!" said the Colonel, laughing. "My servants said your negro man began to sing it in the kitchen as if he was a church organ."

"Our people sing it at home, sir. My grandpapa used to love it very much. His wife's father was a great friend of good Bishop Ken, who wrote it; and—and my dear brother used to love it too;" said the boy, his voice dropping.

It was then, I suppose, that Mrs. Lambert felt inclined to give the boy a kiss. His little accident, illness and recovery, the kindness of the people round about him, had softened Harry Warrington's heart, and opened it to better influences than those which had been brought to bear on it for some six weeks past. He was breathing a purer air than that tainted atmosphere of selfishness, and worldliness, and corruption, into which he had been plunged since his arrival in England. Sometimes the young man's fate, or choice, or weakness, leads him into the fellowship of the giddy and vain; happy he, whose lot makes him acquainted with the wiser company, whose lamps are trimmed, and whose pure hearts keep modest watch.

The pleased matron left her young patient devouring Miss Theo's mess of rice and chicken, and the Colonel seated by the lad's bedside. Gratitude to his hospitable entertainers, and contentment after a comfortable meal, caused in Mr. Warrington a very pleasant condition of mind and body. He was ready to talk now more freely than usually was his custom; for, unless excited by a strong interest or emotion, the young man was commonly taciturn and cautious in his converse with his fellows, and was by no means of an imaginative turn. Of books our youth had been but a very remiss student, nor were his remarks on such simple works as he had read, very profound or valuable; but regarding dogs, horses, and the ordinary business of life, he was a far better critic; and, with any person interested in such subjects, conversed on them freely enough.

Harry's host, who had considerable shrewdness, and experience of books, and cattle, and men, was pretty soon able to take the measure of his young guest in the talk which they now had together. It was now, for the first time, the Virginian learned that Mrs. Lambert had been an early friend of his mother's, and that the Colonel's own father had served with Harry's grandfather, Colonel Esmond, in the famous wars of Queen Anne. He found himself in a friend's country. He was soon at ease with his honest host, whose manners were quite simple and cordial, and who looked and seemed perfectly a gentleman, though he wore a plain fustian coat, and a waistcoat without a particle of lace.

"My boys are both away," said Harry's host, "or they would have shown you the country when you got up, Mr. Warrington. Now you can only have the company of my wife and her daughters. Mrs. Lambert hath told you already about one of them, Theo, our eldest, who made your broth, who cut your roses, and who mended your coat. She is not such a wonder as her mother imagines her to be: but little Theo is a smart little housekeeper, and a very good and cheerful lass, though her father says it."

"It is very kind of Miss Lambert to take so much care for me," says the young patient.

"She is no kinder to you than to any other mortal, and doth but her duty." Here the Colonel smiled. "I laugh at their mother for praising our children," he said, "and I think I am as foolish about them myself. The truth is, God hath given us very good and dutiful children, and I see no reason why I should disguise my thankfulness for such a blessing. You have never a sister, I think?"

"No, sir, I am alone now," Mr. Warrington said.

"Ay, truly, I ask your pardon for my thoughtlessness. Your man hath told our people what befell last year. I served with Braddock in Scotland; and hope he mended before he died. A wild fellow, sir, but there was a fund of truth about the man, and no little kindness under his rough swaggering manner. Your black fellow talks very freely about his master and his affairs. I suppose you permit him these freedoms as he rescued you——"

"Rescued me?" cries Mr. Warrington.

"From ever so many Indians on that very expedition. My Molly and I did not know we were going to entertain so prodigiously wealthy a gentleman. He saith that half Virginia belongs to you; but if the whole of North America were yours, we could but give you our best."

"Those negro boys, sir, lie like the father of all lies. They think it is for our honour to represent us as ten times as rich as we are. My mother has what would be a vast estate in England, and is a very good one at home. We are as well off as most of our neighbours, sir, but no better; and all our splendour is in Mr. Gumbo's foolish imagination. He never rescued me from an Indian in his life, and would run away at the sight of one, as my poor brother's boy did on that fatal day when he fell."

"The bravest man will do so at unlucky times," said the Colonel. "I myself saw the best troops in the world run at Preston, before a ragged mob of Highland savages."

"That was because the Highlanders fought for a good cause, sir."

"Do you think," asks Harry's host, "that the French Indians had the good cause in the fight of last year?"

"The scoundrels! I would have the scalp of every murderous redskin among 'em!" cried Harry, clenching his fist. "They were robbing and invading the British territories, too. But the Highlanders were fighting for their king."

"We, on our side, were fighting for our king; and we ended by winning the battle," said the Colonel, laughing.

"Ah!" cried Harry; "if his Royal Highness the Prince had not turned back at Derby, your king and mine, now, would be his Majesty King James the Third!"

"Who made such a Tory of you, Mr. Warrington?" asked Lambert.

"Nay, sir, the Esmonds were always loyal!" answered the youth. "Had we lived at home, and twenty years sooner, brother and I often and often agreed that our heads would have been in danger. We certainly would have staked them for the king's cause."

"Yours is better on your shoulders than on a pole at Temple Bar. I have seen them there, and they don't look very pleasant, Mr. Warrington."

"I shall take off my hat, and salute them, whenever I pass the gate," cried the young man, "if the king and the whole court are standing by!"

"I doubt whether your relative, my Lord Castlewood, is as staunch a supporter of the king over the water," said Colonel Lambert, smiling: "or your aunt, the Baroness of Bernstein, who left you in our charge. Whatever her old partialities may have been, she has repented of them; she has rallied to our side, landed her nephews in the Household, and looks to find a suitable match for her nieces. If you have Tory opinions, Mr. Warrington, take an old soldier's advice, and keep them to yourself."

"Why, sir, I do not think that you will betray me!" said the boy.

"Not I, but others might. You did not talk in this way at Castlewood? I mean the old Castlewood which you have just come from."

"I might be safe amongst my own kinsmen, surely, sir!" cried Harry.

"Doubtless. I would not say no. But a man's own kinsmen can play him slippery tricks at times, and he finds himself none the better for trusting them. I mean no offence to you or any of your family; but lacqueys have ears as well as their masters, and they carry about all sorts of stories. For instance, your black fellow is ready to tell all he knows about you, and a great deal more besides, as it would appear."

"Hath he told about the broken-kneed horse?" cried out Harry, turning very red.

"To say truth, my groom seemed to know something of the story, and said it was a shame a gentleman should sell another such a brute; let alone a cousin. I am not here to play the Mentor to you, or to carry about servants' tittle-tattle. When you have seen more of your cousins, you will form your own opinion of them; meanwhile, take an old soldier's advice, I say again, and be cautious with whom you deal, and what you say."

Very soon after this little colloquy, Mr. Lambert's guest rose, with the assistance of Gumbo, his valet, to whom he, for the hundredth time at least, promised a sound caning if ever he should hear that Gumbo had ventured to talk about his affairs again in the servants'-hall,—which prohibition Gumbo solemnly vowed and declared he would for ever obey; but I dare say he was chattering the whole of the Castlewood secrets to his new friends of Colonel Lambert's kitchen; for Harry's hostess certainly heard a number of stories concerning him which she could not prevent her housekeeper from telling;

though of course I would not accuse that worthy lady, or any of her sex or ours, of undue curiosity regarding their neighbours' affairs. But how can you prevent servants talking, or listening when the faithful attached creatures talk to you?

Mr. Lambert's house stood on the outskirts of the little town of Oakhurst, which, if he but travels in the right direction, the patient reader will find on the road between Farnham and Reigate,—and Madame Bernstein's servants naturally pulled at the first bell at hand, when the young Virginian met with his mishap. A few hundred yards farther, was the long street of the little old town, where hospitality might have been found under the great swinging ensigns of a couple of tuns, and medical relief was to be had, as a blazing gilt pestle and mortar indicated. But what surgeon could have ministered more cleverly to a patient than Harry's host, who tended him without a fee, or what Boniface could make him more comfortably welcome?

Two tall gates, each surmounted by a couple of heraldic monsters, led from the highroad up to a neat, broad stone terrace, whereon stood Oakhurst House; a square brick building, with windows faced with stone, and many high chimneys, and a tall roof surmounted by a fair balustrade. Behind the house stretched a large garden, where there was plenty of room for cabbages as well as roses to grow; and before the mansion, separated from it by the highroad, was a field of many acres, where the Colonel's cows and horses were at grass. Over the centre window was a carved shield supported by the same monsters who pranced or ramped upon the entrance-gates; and a coronet over the shield. The fact is, that the house had been originally the jointure-house of Oakhurst Castle, which stood hard by,—its chimneys and turrets appearing over the surrounding woods, now bronzed with the darkest foliage of summer. Mr. Lambert's was the greatest house in Oakhurst town; but the Castle was of more importance than all the town put together. The Castle and the jointure-house had been friends of many years' date. Their fathers had fought side by side in Queen Anne's wars. There were two small pieces of ordnance on the terrace of the jointure-house, and six before the Castle, which had been taken out of the same privateer, which Mr. Lambert and his kinsman and commander, Lord Wrotham, had brought into Harwich in one of their voyages home from Flanders with despatches from the great Duke.

His toilet completed with Mr. Gumbo's aid, his fair hair neatly dressed by that artist, and his open ribboned sleeve and wounded shoulder supported by a handkerchief which hung from his neck, Harry Warrington made his way out of the sick-chamber, preceded by his kind host, who led him first down a broad oak stair, round which hung many pikes and muskets of ancient shape, and so into a square marble-paved room, from which the living-rooms of the house branched off. There were more arms in this hall-pikes and halberts of ancient date, pistols and jack-boots of more than a century old, that had done service in Cromwell's wars, a tattered French guidon which had been borne by a French gendarme at Malplaquet, and a pair of cumbrous Highland broadswords, which, having been carried as far as Derby, had been flung away on the fatal field of Culloden. Here were breastplates and black morions of Oliver's troopers, and portraits of stern warriors in buff jerkins and plain bands and short hair. "They fought against your grandfathers and King Charles, Mr. Warrington," said Harry's host. "I don't hide that. They rode to join the Prince of Orange at Exeter. We were Whigs, young gentleman, and something more. John Lambert, the Major-General, was a kinsman of our house, and we were all more or less partial to short hair and long sermons. You do not seem to like either?" Indeed, Harry's face manifested signs of anything but pleasure whilst he examined the portraits of the Parliamentary heroes. "Be not alarmed, we are very good Churchmen now. My eldest son will be in orders ere long. He is now travelling as governor to my Lord Wrotham's son in Italy, and as for our women, they are all for the Church, and carry me with 'em. Every woman is a Tory at heart. Mr. Pope says a rake, but I think t'other is the more charitable word. Come, let us go see them," and, flinging open the dark oak door, Colonel Lambert led his young guest into the parlour where the ladies were assembled.

"Here is Miss Hester," said the Colonel, "and this is Miss Theo, the soup-maker, the tailoress, the harpsichord-player, and the songstress, who set you to sleep last night. Make a curtsey to the gentleman, young ladies! Oh, I forgot, and Theo is the mistress of the roses which you admired a short while since in your bedroom. I think she has kept some of them in her cheeks."

In fact, Miss Theo was making a profound curtsey and blushing most modestly as her papa spoke. I am not going to describe her person,—though we shall see a great deal of her in the course of this history. She was not a particular beauty. Harry Warrington was not over head and ears in love with her at an instant's warning, and faithless to—to that other individual with whom, as we have seen, the youth had lately been smitten. Miss Theo had kind eyes and a sweet voice; a ruddy freckled cheek and a round white neck, on which, out of a little cap such as misses wore in those times, fell rich curling clusters of dark brown hair. She was not a delicate or sentimental-looking person. Her arms, which were worn bare from the elbow like other ladies' arms in those days, were very jolly and red. Her feet were not so miraculously small but that you could see them without a telescope. There was nothing waspish about her waist. This young person was sixteen years of age, and looked older. I don't know what call she had to blush so when she made her curtsey to the stranger. It was such a deep ceremonial curtsey as you never see at present. She and her sister both made these "cheeses" in compliment to the new comer, and with much stately agility.

As Miss Theo rose up out of this salute, her papa tapped her under the chin (which was of the double sort of chins), and laughingly hummed out the line which he had read the day. "Eh bien! que dites-vous, ma fille, de notre hote?"

"Nonsense, Mr. Lambert!" cries mamma.

"Nonsense is sometimes the best kind of sense in the world," said Colonel Lambert. His guest looked puzzled.

"Are you fond of nonsense?" the Colonel continued to Harry, seeing by the boy's face that the latter had no great love or comprehension of his favourite humour. "We consume a vast deal of it in this house. Rabelais is my favourite reading. My wife is all for Mr. Fielding and Theophrastus. I think Theo prefers Tom Brown, and Mrs. Hetty here loves Dean Swift."

"Our papa is talking what he loves," says Miss Hetty.

"And what is that, miss?" asks the father of his second daughter.

"Sure, sir, you said yourself it was nonsense," answers the young lady, with a saucy toss of her head.

"Which of them do you like best, Mr. Warrington?" asked the honest Colonel.

"Which of whom, sir?"

"The Curate of Meudon, or the Dean of St. Patrick's, or honest Tom, or Mr. Fielding?"

"And what were they, sir?"

"They! Why, they wrote books."

"Indeed, sir. I never heard of either one of 'em," said Harry, hanging down his head. "I fear my book-learning was neglected at home, sir. My brother had read every book that ever was wrote, I think. He could have talked to you about 'em for hours together."

With this little speech Mrs. Lambert's eyes turned to her daughter, and Miss Theo cast hers down and blushed.

"Never mind, honesty is better than books any day, Mr. Warrington!" cried the jolly Colonel. "You may go through the world very honourably without reading any of the books I have been talking of, and some of them might give you more pleasure than profit."

"I know more about horses and dogs than Greek and Latin, sir. We most of us do in Virginia," said Mr. Warrington.

"You are like the Persians; you can ride and speak the truth."

"Are the Prussians very good on horseback, sir? I hope I shall see their king and a campaign or two, either with 'em or against 'em," remarked Colonel Lambert's guest. Why did Miss Theo look at her mother, and why did that good woman's face assume a sad expression?

Why? Because young lasses are bred in humdrum country towns, do you suppose they never indulge in romances? Because they are modest and have never quitted mother's apron, do you suppose they have no thoughts of their own? What happens in spite of all those precautions which the King and Queen take for their darling princess, those dragons, and that impenetrable forest, and that castle of steel? The fairy prince penetrates the impenetrable forest, finds the weak point in the dragon's scale armour, and gets the better of all the ogres who guard the castle of steel. Away goes the princess to him. She knew him at once. Her bandboxes and portmanteaux are filled with her best clothes and all her jewels. She has been ready ever so long.

That is in fairy tales, you understand—where the blessed hour and youth always arrive, the ivory horn is blown at the castle gate; and far off in her beauteous bower the princess hears it, and starts up, and knows that there is the right champion. He is always ready. Look! how the giants' heads tumble off as, falchion in hand, he gallops over the bridge on his white charger! How should that virgin, locked up in that inaccessible fortress, where she has never seen any man that was not eighty, or humpbacked, or her father, know that there were such beings in the world as young men? I suppose there's an instinct. I suppose there's a season. I never spoke for my part to a fairy princess, or heard as much from any unenchanted or enchanting maiden. Ne'er a one of them has ever whispered her pretty little secrets to me, or perhaps confessed them to herself, her mamma, or her nearest and dearest confidante. But they will fall in love. Their little hearts are constantly throbbing at the window of expectancy on the lookout for the champion. They are always hearing his horn. They are for ever on the tower looking out for the hero. Sister Ann, Sister Ann, do you see him? Surely 'tis a knight with curling mustachios, a flashing scimitar, and a suit of silver armour. Oh no! it is only a costermonger with his donkey and a pannier of cabbage! Sister Ann, Sister Ann, what is that cloud of dust? Oh, it is only a farmer's man driving a flock of pigs from market. Sister Ann, Sister Ann, who is that splendid warrior advancing in scarlet and gold? He nears the castle, he clears the drawbridge, he lifts the ponderous hammer at the gate. Ah me, he knocks twice! 'Tis only the postman with a double letter from Northamptonshire! So it is we make false starts in life. I don't believe there is any such thing known as first love—not within man's or woman's memory. No male or female remembers his or her first inclination any more than his or her own christening. What? You fancy that your sweet mistress, your spotless spinster, your blank maiden just out of the schoolroom, never cared for any but you? And she tells you so? Oh, you idiot! When she was four years old she had a tender feeling towards the Buttons who brought the coals up to the nursery, or the little sweep at the crossing, or the music-master, or never mind whom. She had a secret longing towards her brother's schoolfellow, or the third charity boy at church, and if occasion had served, the comedy enacted with you had been performed along with another. I do not mean to say that she confessed this amatory sentiment, but that she had it. Lay down this page, and think how many and many and many a time you were in love before you selected the present Mrs. Jones as the partner of your name and affections!

So, from the way in which Theo held her head down, and exchanged looks with her mother, when poor unconscious Harry called the Persians the Prussians, and talked of serving a campaign with them, I make no doubt she was feeling ashamed, and thinking within herself, "Is this the hero with whom my mamma and I have been in love for these twenty-four hours, and whom we have endowed with every perfection? How beautiful, pale, and graceful he looked yesterday as he lay on the ground! How his curls fell over his face! How sad it was to see his poor white arm, and the blood trickling from it when papa bled him! And now he is well and amongst us, he is handsome certainly, but oh, is it possible he is—he is stupid?" When she lighted the lamp and looked at him, did Psyche find Cupid out; and is that the meaning of the old allegory? The wings of love drop off at this discovery. The fancy can no more soar and disport in skyey regions, the beloved object ceases at once to be celestial, and remains plodding on earth, entirely unromantic and substantial.

CHAPTER XXIII. Holidays

Mrs. Lambert's little day-dream was over. Miss Theo and her mother were obliged to confess in their hearts that their hero was but an ordinary mortal. They uttered few words on the subject, but each knew the other's thoughts as people who love each other do; and mamma, by an extra tenderness and special caressing manner towards her daughter, sought to console her for her disappointment. "Never mind, my dear"—the maternal kiss whispered on the filial cheek—"our hero has turned out to be but an ordinary mortal, and none such is good enough for my Theo. Thou shalt have a real husband ere long, if there be one in England. Why, I was scarce fifteen when your father saw me at the Bury Assembly, and while I was yet at school, I used to vow that I never would have any other man. If Heaven gave me such a husband—the best man in the whole kingdom—sure it will bless my child equally, who deserves a king if she fancies him!" Indeed, I am not sure that Mrs. Lambert—who, of course, knew the age of the Prince of Wales, and was aware how handsome and good a young prince he was—did not expect that he too would come riding by her gate, and perhaps tumble down from his horse there, and be taken into the house, and be cured, and cause his royal grandpapa to give Martin Lambert a regiment, and fall in love with Theo.

The Colonel for his part, and his second daughter, Miss Hetty, were on the laughing, scornful, unbelieving side. Mamma was always match-making. Indeed, Mrs. Lambert was much addicted to novels, and cried her eyes out over them with great assiduity. No coach ever passed the gate, but she expected a husband for her girls would alight from it and ring the bell. As for Miss Hetty, she allowed her tongue to wag in a more than usually saucy way: she made a hundred sly allusions to their guest. She introduced Prussia and Persia into their conversation with abominable pertness and frequency. She asked whether the present King of Prussia was called the Shaw or the Sophy, and how far it was from Ispahan to Saxony, which his Majesty was at present invading, and about which war papa was so busy with his maps and his newspapers? She brought down the Persian Tales from her mamma's closet, and laid them slily on the table in the parlour where the family sate. She would not marry a Persian prince for her part; she would prefer a gentleman who might not have more than one wife at a time. She called our young Virginian Theo's gentleman, Theo's prince. She asked her mamma if she wished her, Hetty, to take the other visitor, the black prince, for herself? Indeed, she rallied her sister and her mother unceasingly on their sentimentalities, and would never stop until she had made them angry, when she would begin to cry herself, and kiss them violently one after the other, and coax them back into good-humour. Simple Harry Warrington, meanwhile, knew nothing of all the jokes, the tears, quarrels, reconciliations, hymeneal plans, and so forth, of which he was the innocent occasion. A hundred allusions to the Prussians and Persians were shot at him, and those Parthian arrows did not penetrate his hide at all. A Shaw? A Sophy? Very likely he thought a Sophy was a lady, and would have deemed it the height of absurdity that a man with a great black beard should have any such name. We fall into the midst of a quiet family: we drop like a stone, say, into a pool,—we are perfectly compact and cool, and little know the flutter and excitement we make there, disturbing the fish, frightening the ducks, and agitating the whole surface of the water. How should Harry know the effect which his sudden appearance produced in this little, quiet, sentimental family? He thought quite well enough of himself on many points, but was diffident as yet regarding women, being of that age when young gentlemen require encouragement and to be brought forward, and having been brought up at home in very modest and primitive relations towards the other sex. So Miss Hetty's jokes played round the lad, and he minded them no more than so many summer gnats. It was not that he was stupid, as she certainly thought him: he was simple, too much occupied with himself and his own honest affairs to think of others. Why, what tragedies, comedies, interludes, intrigues, farces, are going on under our noses in friends' drawing-rooms where we visit every day, and we remain utterly ignorant, self-satisfied, and blind! As these sisters sate and combed their flowing ringlets of nights, or talked with each other in the great bed where, according to the fashion of the day, they lay together, how should Harry know that he had so great a share in their thoughts, jokes, conversation? Three days after his arrival, his new and hospitable friends were walking with him in my Lord Wrotham's fine park, where they were free to wander; and here, on a piece of water, they came to some swans, which the young ladies were in the habit of feeding with bread. As the birds approached the young women, Hetty said, with a queer look at her mother and sister, and then a glance at her father, who stood by, honest, happy, in a red waistcoat,—Hetty said: "Mamma's swans are something like these, papa."

"What swans, my dear?" says mamma.

"Something like, but not quite. They have shorter necks than these, and are, scores of them, on our common," continues Miss Hetty. "I saw Betty plucking one in the kitchen this morning. We shall have it for dinner, with apple-sauce and——"

"Don't be a little goose!" says Miss Theo.

"And sage and onions. Do you love swan, Mr. Warrington?"

"I shot three last winter on our river," said the Virginian gentleman. "Ours are not such white birds as these—they eat very well, though." The simple youth had not the slightest idea that he himself was an allegory at that very time, and that Miss Hetty was narrating a fable regarding him. In some exceedingly recondite Latin work I have read that, long before Virginia was discovered, other folks were equally dull of comprehension.

So it was a premature sentiment on the part of Miss Theo—that little tender flutter of the bosom which we have acknowledged she felt on first beholding the Virginian, so handsome, pale, and bleeding. This was not the great passion which she knew her heart could feel. Like the birds, it had wakened and begun to sing at a false dawn. Hop back to thy perch, and cover thy head with thy wing, thou tremulous little fluttering creature! It is not yet light, and roosting is as yet better than singing. Anon will come morning, and the whole sky will redden, and you shall soar up into it and salute the sun with your music.

One little phrase, some three-and-thirty lines back, perhaps the fair and suspicious reader has remarked: "Three days after his arrival, Harry was walking with," etc. etc. If he could walk—which it appeared he could do perfectly well—what business had he to be walking with anybody but Lady Maria Esmond on the Pantiles, Tunbridge Wells? His shoulder was set: his health was entirely restored: he had not even a change of coats, as we have seen, and was obliged to the Colonel for his raiment. Surely a young man in such a condition had no right to be lingering on at Oakhurst, and was bound by every tie of duty and convenience, by love, by relationship, by a gentle heart waiting for him, by the washerwoman finally, to go to Tunbridge. Why did he stay behind, unless he was in love with either of the young ladies (and we say he wasn't)? Could it be that he did not want to go? Hath the gracious reader understood the meaning of the mystic S with which the last chapter commences, and in which the designer has feebly endeavoured to depict the notorious Sinbad the Sailor, surmounted by that odious old man of the sea? What if Harry Warrington should be that sailor, and his fate that choking, deadening, inevitable old man? What if for two days past he has felt those knees throttling him round the neck? if his fell aunt's purpose is answered, and if his late love is killed as dead by her poisonous communications as fair Rosamond was by her royal and legitimate rival? Is Hero then lighting the lamp up, and getting ready the supper, whilst Leander is sitting comfortably with some other party, and never in the least thinking of taking to the water? Ever since that coward's blow was struck in Lady Maria's back by her own relative, surely kind hearts must pity her ladyship. I know she has faults—ay, and wears false hair and false never mind what. But a woman in distress, shall we not pity her—a lady of a certain age, are we going to laugh at her because of her years? Between her old aunt and her unhappy delusion, be sure my Lady Maria Esmond is having no very pleasant time of it at Tunbridge Wells. There is no one to protect her. Madam Beatrix has her all to herself. Lady Maria is poor, and hopes for money from her aunt. Lady Maria has a secret or two which the old woman knows, and brandishes over her. I for one am quite melted and grow soft-hearted as I think of her. Imagine her alone, and a victim to that old woman! Paint to yourself that antique Andromeda (if you please we will allow that rich flowing head of hair to fall over her shoulders) chained to a rock on Mount Ephraim, and given up to that dragon of a Baroness! Succour, Perseus! Come quickly with thy winged feet and flashing falchion! Perseus is not in the least hurry. The dragon has her will of Andromeda for day after day.

Harry Warrington, who would not have allowed his dislocated and mended shoulder to keep him from going out hunting, remained day after day contentedly at Oakhurst, with each day finding the kindly folks who welcomed him more to his liking. Perhaps he had never, since his grandfather's death, been in such good company. His lot had lain amongst fox-hunting Virginian squires, with whose society he had put up very contentedly, riding their horses, living their lives, and sharing their punch-bowls. The ladies of his own and mother's acquaintance were very well bred, and decorous, and pious, no doubt, but somewhat narrow-minded. It was but a little place, his home, with its pompous ways, small etiquettes and punctilios, small flatteries, small conversations and scandals. Until he had left the place, some time after, he did not know how narrow and confined his life had been there. He was free enough personally. He had dogs and horses, and might shoot and hunt for scores of miles round about: but the little lady-mother domineered at home, and when there he had to submit to her influence and breathe her air.

Here the lad found himself in the midst of a circle where everything about him was incomparably gayer, brighter, and more free. He was living with a man and woman who had seen the world, though they lived retired from it, who had both of them happened to enjoy from their earliest times the use not only of good books, but of good company—those live books, which are such pleasant and sometimes such profitable reading. Society has this good at least: that it lessens our conceit, by teaching us our insignificance, and making us acquainted with our betters. If you are a young person who read this, depend upon it, sir or madam, there is nothing more wholesome for you than to acknowledge and to associate with your superiors. If I could, I would not have my son Thomas first Greek and Latin prize boy, first oar, and cock of the school. Better for his soul's and body's welfare that he should have a good place, not the first—a fair set of competitors round about him, and a good thrashing now and then, with a hearty shake afterwards of the hand which administered the beating. What honest man that can choose his lot would be a prince, let us say, and have all society walking backwards before him, only obsequious household-gentlemen to talk to, and all mankind mum except when your High Mightiness asks a question and gives permission to speak? One of the great benefits which Harry Warrington received from this family, before whose gate Fate had shot him, was to begin to learn that he was a profoundly ignorant young fellow, and that there were many people in the world far better than he knew himself to be. Arrogant a little with some folks, in the company of his superiors he was magnanimously docile. We have seen how faithfully he admired his brother at home, and his friend, the gallant young Colonel of Mount Vernon: of the gentlemen, his kinsmen at Castlewood, he had felt himself at least the equal. In his new acquaintance at Oakhurst he found a man who had read far more books than Harry could pretend to judge of, who had seen the world and come unwounded out of it, as he had out of the dangers and battles which he had confronted, and who had goodness and honesty written on his face and breathing from his lips, for which qualities our brave lad had always an instinctive sympathy and predilection.

As for the women, they were the kindest, merriest, most agreeable he had as yet known. They were pleasanter than Parson Broadbent's black-eyed daughter at home, whose laugh carried as far as a gun. They were quite as well-bred as the Castlewood ladies, with the exception of Madam Beatrix (who, indeed, was as grand as an empress on some occasions). But somehow, after a talk with Madam Beatrix, and vast amusement and interest in her stories, the lad would come away as with a bitter taste in his mouth, and fancy all the world wicked round about him. They were not in the least squeamish; and laughed over pages of Mr. Fielding, and cried over volumes of Mr. Richardson, containing jokes and incidents which would make Mrs. Grundy's hair stand on end, yet their merry prattle left no bitterness behind it: their tales about this neighbour and that were droll, not malicious; the curtseys and salutations with which the folks of the little neighbouring town received them, how kindly and cheerful! their bounties how cordial! Of a truth it is good to be with good people. How good Harry Warrington did not know at the time, perhaps, or until subsequent experience showed him contrasts, or caused him to feel remorse. Here was a tranquil, sunshiny day of a life that was to be agitated and stormy—a happy hour or two to remember. Not much happened during the happy hour or two. It was only sweet sleep, pleasant waking, friendly welcome, serene pastime. The gates of the old house seemed to shut the wicked world out somehow, and the inhabitants within to be better, and purer, and kinder than other people. He was not in love; oh no! not the least, either with saucy Hetty or generous Theodosia but when the time came for going away, he fastened on both their hands, and felt an immense regard for them. He thought he should like to know their brothers, and that they must be fine fellows; and as for Mrs. Lambert, I believe she was as sentimental at his departure as if he had been the last volume of Clarissa Harlowe.

"He is very kind and honest," said Theo, gravely, as, looking from the terrace, they saw him and their father and servants riding away on the road to Westerham.

"I don't think him stupid at all now," said little Hetty; "and, mamma, I think, he is very like a swan indeed."

"It felt just like one of the boys going to school," said mamma.

"Just like it," said Theo, sadly.

"I am glad he has got papa to ride with him to Westerham," resumed Miss Hetty, "and that he bought Farmer Briggs's horse. I don't like his going to those Castlewood people. I am sure that Madame Bernstein is a wicked old woman. I expected to see her ride away on her crooked stick."

"Hush, Hetty!"

"Do you think she would float if they tried her in the pond, as poor old mother Hely did at Elmhurst? The other old woman seemed fond of him—I mean the one with the fair tour. She looked very melancholy when she went away; but Madame Bernstein whisked her off with her crutch, and she was obliged to go. I don't care, Theo. I know she is a wicked woman. You think everybody good, you do, because you never do anything wrong yourself."

"My Theo is a good girl," says the mother, looking fondly at both her daughters.

"Then why do we call her a miserable sinner?"

"We are all so, my love," said mamma.

"What, papa too? You know you don't think so," cries Miss Hester. And to allow this was almost more than Mrs. Lambert could afford.

"What was that you told John to give to Mr. Warrington's black man?"

Mamma owned, with some shamefacedness, it was a bottle of her cordial water and a cake which she had bid Betty make. "I feel quite like a mother to him, my dears, I can't help owning it,—and you know both our boys still like one of our cakes to take to school or college with them."

CHAPTER XXIV. From Oakhurst to Tunbridge

Having her lily handkerchief in token of adieu to the departing travellers, Mrs. Lambert and her girls watched them pacing leisurely on the first few hundred yards of their journey, and until such time as a tree-clumped corner of the road hid them from the ladies' view. Behind that clump of limes the good matron had many a time watched those she loved best disappear. Husband departing to battle and danger, sons to school, each after the other had gone on his way behind yonder green trees, returning as it pleased Heaven's will at his good time, and bringing pleasure and love back to the happy little family. Besides their own instinctive nature (which to be sure aids wonderfully in the matter), the leisure and contemplation attendant upon their home life serve to foster the tenderness and fidelity of our women. The men gone, there is all day to think about them, and to-morrow and to-morrow—when there certainly will be a letter—and so on. There is the vacant room to go look at, where the boy slept last night, and the impression of his carpet bag is still on the bed. There is his whip hung up in the hall, and his fishing-rod and basket—mute memorials of the brief bygone pleasures. At dinner there comes up that cherry-tart, half of which our darling ate at two o'clock in spite of his melancholy, and with a choking little sister on each side of him. The evening prayer is said without that young scholar's voice to utter the due responses. Midnight and silence come, and the good mother lies wakeful, thinking how one of the dear accustomed brood is away from the nest. Morn breaks, home and holidays have passed away, and toil and labour have begun for him. So those rustling limes formed, as it were, a screen between the world and our ladies of the house at Oakhurst. Kind-hearted Mrs. Lambert always became silent and thoughtful, if by chance she and her girls walked up to the trees in the absence of the men of the family. She said she would like to carve their names up on the grey silvered trunks, in the midst of true-lovers' knots, as was then the kindly fashion; and Miss Theo, who had an exceeding elegant turn that way, made some verses regarding the trees, which her delighted parent transmitted to a periodical of those days.

"Now we are out of sight of the ladies," says Colonel Lambert, giving a parting salute with his hat, as the pair of gentlemen trotted past the limes in question. "I know my wife always watches at her window until we are round this corner. I hope we shall have you seeing the trees and the house again, Mr. Warrington; and the boys being at home, mayhap there will be better sport for you."

"I never want to be happier, sir, than I have been," replied Mr. Warrington; "and I hope you will let me say, that I feel as if I am leaving quite old friends behind me."

"The friend at whose house we shall sup to-night hath a son, who is an old friend of our family, too; and my wife, who is an inveterate marriage-monger, would have made a match between him and one of my girls, but that the Colonel hath chosen to fall in love with somebody else."

"Ah!" sighed Mr. Warrington.

"Other folks have done the same thing. There were brave fellows before Agamemnon."

"I beg your pardon, sir. Is the gentleman's name—Aga——? I did not quite gather it," meekly inquired the young traveller.

"No, his name is James Wolfe," cried the Colonel, smiling. "He is a young fellow still, or what we call so, being scarce thirty years old. He is the youngest lieutenant-colonel in the army, unless, to be sure, we except a few scores of our nobility, who take rank before us common folk."

"Of course of course!" says the Colonel's young companion with true colonial notions of aristocratic precedence.

"And I have seen him commanding captains, and very brave captains, who were thirty years his seniors, and who had neither his merit nor his good fortune. But, lucky as he hath been, no one envies his superiority, for, indeed, most of us acknowledge that he is our superior. He is beloved by every man of our old regiment and knows every one of them. He is a good scholar as well as a consummate soldier, and a master of many languages."

"Ah, sir!" said Harry Warrington, with a sigh of great humility; "I feel that I have neglected my own youth sadly; and am come to England but an ignoramus. Had my dear brother been alive, he would have represented our name and our colony, too, better than I can do. George was a scholar; George was a musician; George could talk with the most learned people in our country, and I make no doubt would have held his own here. Do you know, sir, I am glad to have come home, and to you especially, if but to learn how ignorant I am."

"If you know that well, 'tis a great gain already," said the Colonel, with a smile.

"At home, especially of late, and since we lost my brother, I used to think myself a mighty fine fellow, and have no doubt that the folks round about flattered me. I am wiser now,—that is, I hope I am,—though perhaps I am wrong, and only bragging again. But you see, sir, the gentry in our colony don't know very much, except about dogs and horses, and betting and games. I wish I knew more about books, and less about them."

"Nay. Dogs and horses are very good books, too, in their way, and we may read a deal of truth out of 'em. Some men are not made to be scholars, and may be very worthy citizens and gentlemen in spite of their ignorance. What call have all of us to be especially learned or wise, or to take a first place in the world? His Royal Highness is commander, and Martin Lambert is colonel, and Jack Hunt, who rides behind yonder, was a private soldier, and is now a very honest, worthy groom. So as we all do our best in our station, it matters not much whether that be high or low. Nay, how do we know what is high and what is low? and whether Jack's currycomb, or my epaulets, or his Royal Highness's baton, may not turn out to be pretty equal? When I began life, et militavi non sine—never mind what—I dreamed of success and honour; now I think of duty, and yonder folks, from whom we parted a few hours ago. Let us trot on, else we shall not reach Westerham before nightfall."

At Westerham the two friends were welcomed by their hosts, a stately matron, an old soldier, whose recollections and services were of five-and-forty years back, and the son of this gentleman and lady, the Lieutenant-Colonel of Kingsley's regiment, that was then stationed at Maidstone, whence the Colonel had come over on a brief visit to his parents. Harry looked with some curiosity at this officer, who, young as he was, had seen so much service, and obtained a character so high. There was little of the beautiful in his face. He was very lean and very pale; his hair was red, his nose and cheek-bones were high; but he had a fine courtesy towards his elders, a cordial greeting towards his friends, and an animation in conversation which caused those who heard him to forget, even to admire, his homely looks.

Mr. Warrington was going to Tunbridge? Their James would bear him company, the lady of the house said, and whispered something to Colonel Lambert at supper, which occasioned smiles and a knowing wink or two from that officer. He called for wine, and toasted "Miss Lowther." "With all my heart," cried the enthusiastic Colonel James, and drained his glass to the very last drop. Mamma whispered her friend how James and the lady were going to make a match, and how she came of the famous Lowther family of the North.

"If she was the daughter of King Charlemagne," cries Lambert, "she is not too good for James Wolfe, or for his mother's son."

"Mr. Lambert would not say so if he knew her," the young Colonel declared.

"Oh, of course, she is the priceless pearl, and you are nothing," cries mamma. "No. I am of Colonel Lambert's opinion; and, if she brought all Cumberland to you for a jointure, I should say it was my James's due. That is the way with 'em, Mr. Warrington. We tend our children through fevers, and measles, and whooping-cough, and small-pox; we send them to the army and can't sleep at night for thinking; we break our hearts at parting with 'em, and have them at home only for a week or two in the year, or maybe ten years, and, after all our care, there comes a lass with a pair of bright eyes, and away goes our boy, and never cares a fig for us afterwards."

"And pray, my dear, how did you come to marry James's papa?" said the elder Colonel Wolfe. "And why didn't you stay at home with your parents?"

"Because James's papa was gouty, and wanted somebody to take care of him, I suppose; not because I liked him a bit," answers the lady: and so with much easy talk and kindness the evening passed away.

On the morrow, and with many expressions of kindness and friendship for his late guest, Colonel Lambert gave over the young Virginian to Mr. Wolfe's charge, and turned his horse's head homewards, while the two gentlemen sped towards Tunbridge Wells. Wolfe was in a hurry to reach the place, Harry Warrington was, perhaps, not quite so eager: nay, when Lambert rode towards his own home, Harry's thoughts followed him with a great deal of longing desire to the parlour at Oakhurst, where he had spent three days in happy calm. Mr. Wolfe agreed in all Harry's enthusiastic praises of Mr. Lambert, and of his wife, and of his daughters, and of all that excellent family. "To have such a good name, and to live such a life as Colonel Lambert's," said Wolfe, "seem to me now the height of human ambition."

"And glory and honour?" asked Warrington, "are those nothing? and would you give up the winning of them?"

"They were my dreams once," answered the Colonel, who had now different ideas of happiness, "and now my desires are much more tranquil. I have followed arms ever since I was fourteen years of age. I have seen almost every kind of duty connected with my calling. I know all the garrison towns in this country, and have had the honour to serve wherever there has been work to be done during the last ten years. I have done pretty near the whole of a soldier's duty, except, indeed, the command of an army, which can hardly be hoped for by one of my years; and now, methinks, I would like quiet, books to read, a wife to love me, and some children to dandle on my knee. I have imagined some such Elysium for myself, Mr. Warrington. True love is better than glory; and a tranquil fireside, with the woman of your heart seated by it, the greatest good the gods can send to us."

Harry imagined to himself the picture which his comrade called up. He said "Yes," in answer to the other's remark; but, no doubt, did not give a very cheerful assent, for his companion observed upon the expression of his face.

"You say 'Yes' as if a fireside and a sweetheart were not particularly to your taste."

"Why, look you, Colonel, there are other things which a young fellow might like to enjoy. You have had sixteen years of the world: and I am but a few months away from my mother's apron-strings. When I have seen a campaign or two, or six, as you have: when I have distinguished myself like Mr. Wolfe, and made the world talk of me, I then may think of retiring from it."

To these remarks, Mr. Wolfe, whose heart was full of a very different matter, replied by breaking out in a further encomium of the joys of marriage; and a special rhapsody upon the beauties and merits of his mistress—a theme intensely interesting to himself, though not so, possibly, to his hearer, whose views regarding a married life, if he permitted himself to entertain any, were somewhat melancholy and despondent. A pleasant afternoon brought them to the end of their ride; nor did any accident or incident accompany it, save, perhaps, a mistake which Harry Warrington made at some few miles' distance from Tunbridge Wells, where two horsemen stopped them, whom Harry was for charging, pistol in hand, supposing them to be highwaymen. Colonel Wolfe, laughing, bade Mr. Warrington reserve his fire, for these folks were only innkeepers' agents, and not robbers (except in their calling). Gumbo, whose horse ran away with him at this particular juncture, was brought back after a great deal of bawling on his master's part, and the two gentlemen rode into the little town, alighted at their inn, and then separated, each in quest of the ladies whom he had come to visit.

Mr. Warrington found his aunt installed in handsome lodgings, with a guard of London lacqueys in her anteroom, and to follow her chair when she went abroad. She received him with the utmost kindness. His cousin, my Lady Maria, was absent when he arrived: I don't know whether the young gentleman was unhappy at not seeing her: or whether he disguised his feelings, or whether Madame de Bernstein took any note regarding them.

A beau in a rich figured suit, the first specimen of the kind Harry had seen, and two dowagers with voluminous hoops and plenty of rouge, were on a visit to the Baroness when her nephew made his bow to her. She introduced the young man to these personages as her nephew, the young Croesus out of Virginia, of whom they had heard. She talked about the immensity of his estate, which was as large as Kent; and, as she had read, infinitely more fruitful. She mentioned how her half-sister, Madam Esmond, was called Princess Pocahontas in her own country. She never tired in her praises of mother and son, of their riches and their good qualities. The beau shook the young man by the hand, and was delighted to have the honour to make his acquaintance. The ladies praised him to his aunt so loudly that the modest youth was fain to blush at their compliments. They went away to inform the Tunbridge society of the news of his arrival. The little place was soon buzzing with accounts of the wealth, the good breeding, and the good looks of the Virginian.

"You could not have come at a better moment, my dear," the Baroness said to her nephew, as her visitors departed with many curtseys and congees. "Those three individuals have the most active tongues in the Wells. They will trumpet your good qualities in every company where they go. I have introduced you to a hundred people already, and, Heaven help me! have told all sorts of fibs about the geography of Virginia in order to describe your estate. It is a prodigious large one, but I am afraid I have magnified it. I have filled it with all sorts of wonderful animals, gold mines, spices; I am not sure I have not said diamonds. As for your negroes, I have given your mother armies of them, and, in fact, represented her as a sovereign princess reigning over a magnificent dominion. So she has a magnificent dominion: I cannot tell to a few hundred thousand pounds how much her yearly income is, but I have no doubt it is a very great one. And you must prepare, sir, to be treated here as the heir-apparent of this royal lady. Do not let your head be turned. From this day forth you are going to be flattered as you have never been flattered in your life."

"And to what end, ma'am?" asked the young gentleman. "I see no reason why I should be reputed so rich, or get so much flattery."

"In the first place, sir, you must not contradict your old aunt, who has no desire to be made a fool of before her company. And as for your reputation, you must know we found it here almost ready-made on our arrival. A London newspaper has somehow heard of you, and come out with a story of the immense wealth of a young gentleman from Virginia lately landed, and a nephew of my Lord Castlewood. Immensely wealthy you are, and can't help yourself. All the world is eager to see you. You shall go to church to-morrow morning, and see how the whole congregation will turn away from its books and prayers, to worship the golden calf in your person. You would not have had me undeceive them, would you, and speak ill of my own flesh and blood?"

"But how am I bettered by this reputation for money?" asked Harry.

"You are making your entry into the world, and the gold key will open most of its doors to you. To be thought rich is as good as to be rich. You need not spend much money. People will say that you hoard it, and your reputation for avarice will do you good rather than harm. You'll see how the mothers will smile upon you, and the daughters will curtsey! Don't look surprised! When I was a young woman myself I did as all the rest of the world did, and tried to better myself by more than one desperate attempt at a good marriage. Your poor grandmother, who was a saint upon earth to be sure, bating a little jealousy, used to scold me, and called me worldly. Worldly, my dear! So is the world worldly; and we must serve it as it serves us; and give it nothing for nothing. Mr. Henry Esmond Warrington—I can't help loving the two first names, sir, old woman as I am, and that I tell you—on coming here or to London, would have been nobody. Our protection would have helped him but little. Our family has little credit, and, entre nous, not much reputation. I suppose you know that Castlewood was more than suspected in '45, and hath since ruined himself by play?"

Harry had never heard about Lord Castlewood or his reputation.

"He never had much to lose, but he has lost that and more: his wretched estate is eaten up with mortgages. He has been at all sorts of schemes to raise money:—my dear, he has been so desperate at times, that I did not think my diamonds were safe with him; and have travelled to and from Castlewood without them. Terrible, isn't it, to speak so of one's own nephew? But you are my nephew, too, and not spoiled by the world yet, and I wish to warn you of its wickedness. I heard of your play-doings with Will and the chaplain, but they could do you no harm,—nay, I am told you had the better of them. Had you played with Castlewood, you would have had no such luck: and you would have played, had not an old aunt of yours warned my Lord Castlewood to keep his hands off you."

"What, ma'am, did you interfere to preserve me?"

"I kept his clutches off from you: be thankful that you are come out of that ogre's den with any flesh on your bones! My dear, it has been the rage and passion of all our family. My poor silly brother played; both his wives played, especially the last one, who has little else to live upon now but her nightly assemblies in London, and the money for the cards. I would not trust her at Castlewood alone with you: the passion is too strong for them, and they would fall upon you, and fleece you; and then fall upon each other, and fight for the plunder. But for his place about the Court my poor nephew hath nothing, and that is Will's fortune, too, sir, and Maria's and her sister's."

"And are they, too, fond of the cards?"

"No; to do poor Molly justice, gaming is not her passion: but when she is amongst them in London, little Fanny will bet her eyes out of her head. I know what the passion is, sir: do not look so astonished; I have had it, as I had the measles when I was a child. I am not cured quite. For a poor old woman there is nothing left but that. You will see some high play at my card-tables to-night. Hush! my dear. It was that I wanted, and without which I moped so at Castlewood! I could not win of my nieces or their mother. They would not pay if they lost. 'Tis best to warn you, my dear, in time, lest you should be shocked by the discovery. I can't live without the cards, there's the truth!"

A few days before, and while staying with his Castlewood relatives, Harry, who loved cards, and cock-fighting, and betting, and every conceivable sport himself, would have laughed very likely at this confession. Amongst that family into whose society he had fallen, many things were laughed at, over which some folks looked grave. Faith and honour were laughed at; pure lives were disbelieved; selfishness was proclaimed as common practice; sacred duties were sneeringly spoken of, and vice flippantly condoned. These were no Pharisees: they professed no hypocrisy of virtue, they flung no stones at discovered sinners:—they smiled, shrugged their shoulders, and passed on. The members of this family did not pretend to be a whit better than their neighbours, whom they despised heartily; they lived quite familiarly with the folks about whom and whose wives they told such wicked, funny stories; they took their share of what pleasure or plunder came to hand, and lived from day to day till their last day came for them. Of course there are no such people now; and human nature is very much changed in the last hundred years. At any rate, card-playing is greatly out of mode: about that there can be no doubt: and very likely there are not six ladies of fashion in London who know the difference between Spadille and Manille.

"How dreadfully dull you must have found those humdrum people at that village where we left you—but the savages were very kind to you, child!" said Madame de Bernstein, patting the young man's cheek with her pretty old hand.

"They were very kind; and it was not at all dull, ma'am, and I think they are some of the best people in the world," said Harry, with his face flushing up. His aunt's tone jarred upon him. He could not bear that any one should speak or think lightly of the new friends whom he had found. He did not want them in such company.

The old lady, imperious and prompt to anger, was about to resent the check she had received, but a second thought made her pause. "Those two girls," she thought, "a sick-bed—an interesting stranger—of course he has been falling in love with one of them." Madame Bernstein looked round with a mischievous glance at Lady Maria, who entered the room at this juncture.

CHAPTER XXV. New Acquaintances

Cousin Maria made her appearance, attended by a couple of gardener's boys bearing baskets of flowers, with which it was proposed to decorate Madame de Bernstein's drawing-room against the arrival of her ladyship's company. Three footmen in livery, gorgeously laced with worsted, set out twice as many card-tables. A major-domo in black and a bag, with fine laced ruffles; and looking as if he ought to have a sword by his side, followed the lacqueys bearing fasces of wax candles, which he placed a pair on each card-table, and in the silver sconces on the wainscoted wall that was now gilt with the slanting rays of the sun, as was the prospect of the green common beyond, with its rocks and clumps of trees and houses twinkling in the sunshine. Groups of many-coloured figures in hoops and powder and brocade sauntered over the green, and dappled the plain with their shadows. On the other side from the Baroness's windows you saw the Pantiles, where a perpetual fair was held, and heard the clatter and buzzing of the company. A band of music was here performing for the benefit of the visitors to the Wells. Madame Bernstein's chief sitting-room might not suit a recluse or a student, but for those who liked bustle, gaiety, a bright cross light, and a view of all that was going on in the cheery busy place, no lodging could be pleasanter. And when the windows were lighted up, the passengers walking below were aware that her ladyship was at home and holding a card-assembly, to which an introduction was easy enough. By the way, in speaking of the past, I think the night-life of society a hundred years since was rather a dark life. There was not one wax-candle for ten which we now see in a lady's drawing-room: let alone gas and the wondrous new illuminations of clubs. Horrible guttering tallow smoked and stunk in passages. The candle-snuffer was a notorious officer in the theatre. See Hogarth's pictures: how dark they are, and how his feasts are, as it were, begrimed with tallow! In "Marriage a la Mode," in Lord Viscount Squanderfield's grand saloons, where he and his wife are sitting yawning before the horror-stricken steward when their party is over—there are but eight candles—one on each card-table, and half a dozen in a brass chandelier.

If Jack Briefless convoked his friends to oysters and beer in his chambers, Pump Court, he would have twice as many. Let us comfort ourselves by thinking that Louis Quatorze in all his glory held his revels in the dark, and bless Mr. Price and other Luciferous benefactors of mankind, for banishing the abominable mutton of our youth.

So Maria with her flowers (herself the fairest flower), popped her roses, sweet-williams, and so forth, in vases here and there, and adorned the apartment to the best of her art. She lingered fondly over this bowl and that dragon jar, casting but sly timid glances the while at young cousin Harry, whose own blush would have become any young woman, and you might have thought that she possibly intended to outstay her aunt; but that Baroness, seated in her arm-chair, her crooked tortoiseshell stick in her hand, pointed the servants imperiously to their duty; rated one and the other soundly: Tom for having a darn in his stocking; John for having greased his locks too profusely out of the candle-box; and so forth—keeping a stern domination over them. Another remark concerning poor Jeames of a hundred years ago: Jeames slept two in a bed, four in a room, and that room a cellar very likely, and he washed in a trough such as you would hardly see anywhere in London now out of the barracks of her Majesty's Foot Guards.

If Maria hoped a present interview, her fond heart was disappointed. "Where are you going to dine, Harry?" asks Madame de Bernstein. "My niece Maria and I shall have a chicken in the little parlour—I think you should go to the best ordinary. There is one at the White Horse at three, we shall hear his bell in a minute or two. And you will understand, sir, that you ought not to spare expense, but behave like Princess Pocahontas's son. Your trunks have been taken over to the lodging I have engaged for you. It is not good for a lad to be always hanging about the aprons of two old women. Is it, Maria?"

"No," says her ladyship, dropping her meek eyes; whilst the other lady's glared in triumph. I think Andromeda had been a good deal exposed to the Dragon in the course of the last five or six days: and if Perseus had cut the latter's cruel head off he would have committed not unjustifiable monstricide. But he did not bare sword or shield; he only looked mechanically at the lacqueys in tawny and blue as they creaked about the room.

"And there are good mercers and tailors from London always here to wait on the company at the Wells. You had better see them, my dear, for your suit is not of the very last fashion—a little lace———"

"I can't go out of mourning, ma'am," said the young man, looking down at his sables.

"Ho, sir," cried the lady, rustling up from her chair and rising on her cane, "wear black for your brother till you are as old as Methuselah, if you like. I am sure I don't want to prevent you. I only want you to dress, and to do like other people, and make a figure worthy of your name."

"Madam," said Mr. Warrington with great state, "I have not done anything to disgrace it that I know."

Why did the old Woman stop and give a little start as if she had been struck?

Let bygones be bygones. She and the boy had a score of little passages of this kind in which swords were crossed and thrusts rapidly dealt or parried. She liked Harry none the worse for his courage in facing her. "Sure a little finer linen than that shirt you wear will not be a disgrace to you, sir," she said, with rather a forced laugh.

Harry bowed and blushed. It was one of the homely gifts of his Oakhurst friends. He felt pleased somehow to think he wore it; thought of the new friends, so good, so pure, so simple, so kindly, with immense tenderness, and felt, while invested in this garment, as if evil could not touch him. He said he would go to his lodging, and make a point of returning arrayed in the best linen he had.

"Come back here, sir," said Madame Bernstein, "and if our company has not arrived, Maria and I will find some ruffles for you!" And herewith, under a footman's guidance, the young fellow walked off to his new lodgings.

Harry found not only handsome and spacious apartments provided for him, but a groom in attendance waiting to be engaged by his honour, and a second valet, if he was inclined to hire one to wait upon Mr. Gumbo. Ere he had been many minutes in his rooms, emissaries from a London tailor and bootmaker waited him with the cards and compliments of their employers, Messrs. Regnier and Tull; the best articles in his modest wardrobe were laid out by Gumbo, and the finest linen with which his thrifty Virginian mother had provided him. Visions of the snow-surrounded home in his own country, of the crackling logs and the trim quiet ladies working by the fire, rose up before him. For the first time a little thought that the homely clothes were not quite smart enough, the home-worked linen not so fine as it might be, crossed the young man's mind. That he should be ashamed of anything belonging to him or to Castlewood! That was strange. The simple folks there were only too well satisfied with all things that were done, or said, or produced at Castlewood; and Madam Esmond, when she sent her son forth on his travels, thought no young nobleman need be better provided. The clothes might have fitted better and been of a later fashion, to be sure—but still the young fellow presented a comely figure enough when he issued from his apartments, his toilet over; and Gumbo calling a chair, marched beside it, until they reached the ordinary where the young gentleman was to dine.

Here he expected to find the beau whose acquaintance he had made a few hours before at his aunt's lodging, and who had indicated to Harry that the White Horse was the most modish place for dining at the Wells, and he mentioned his friend's name to the host: but the landlord and waiters leading him into the room with many smiles and bows assured his honour that his honour did not need any other introduction than his own, helped him to hang up his coat and sword on a peg, asked him whether he would drink Burgundy, Pontac, or champagne to his dinner, and led him to a table.

Though the most fashionable ordinary in the village, the White Horse did not happen to be crowded on this day. Monsieur Barbeau, the landlord, informed Harry that there was a great entertainment at Summer Hill, which had taken away most of the company; indeed, when Harry entered the room, there were but four other gentlemen in it. Two of these guests were drinking wine, and had finished their dinner: the other two were young men in the midst of their meal, to whom the landlord, as he passed, must have whispered the name of the new-comer, for they looked at him with some appearance of interest, and made him a slight bow across the table as the smiling host bustled away for Harry's dinner.

Mr. Warrington returned the salute of the two gentlemen, who bade him welcome to Tunbridge, and hoped he would like the place upon better acquaintance. Then they smiled and exchanged waggish looks with each other, of which Harry did not understand the meaning, nor why they cast knowing glances at the two other guests over their wine.

One of these persons was in a somewhat tarnished velvet coat with a huge queue and bag, and voluminous ruffles and embroidery. The other was a little beetle-browed, hook-nosed, high-shouldered gentleman, whom his opposite companion addressed as milor, or my lord, in a very high voice. My lord, who was sipping the wine before him, barely glanced at the new-comer, and then addressed himself to his own companion.

"And so you know the nephew of the old woman—the Croesus who comes to arrive?"

"You're thrown out there, Jack!" says one young gentleman to the other.

"Never could manage the lingo," said Jack. The two elders had begun to speak in the French language.

"But assuredly, my dear lord!" says the gentleman with the long queue.

"You have shown energy, my dear Baron! He has been here but two hours. My people told me of him only as I came to dinner."

"I knew him before!—I have met him often in London with the Baroness and my lord, his cousin," said the Baron.

A smoking soup for Harry here came in, borne by the smiling host. "Behold, sir! Behold a potage of my fashion!" says my landlord, laying down the dish and whispering to Harry the celebrated name of the nobleman opposite. Harry thanked Monsieur Barbeau in his own language, upon which the foreign gentleman, turning round, grinned most graciously at Harry, and said, "Fous bossedez notre langue barfaidement, monsieur." Mr. Warrington had never heard the French language pronounced in that manner in Canada. He bowed in return to the foreign gentleman.

"Tell me more about the Croesus, my good Baron," continued his lordship, speaking rather superciliously to his companion, and taking no notice of Harry, which perhaps somewhat nettled the young man.

"What will you, that I tell you, my dear lord? Croesus is a youth like other youths; he is tall, like other youths; he is awkward, like other youths; he has black hair, as they all have who come from the Indies. Lodgings have been taken for him at Mrs. Rose's toy-shop."

"I have lodgings there too," thought Mr. Warrington. "Who is Croesus they are talking of? How good the soup is!"

"He travels with a large retinue," the Baron continued, "four servants, two postchaises, and a pair of outriders. His chief attendant is a black man who saved his life from the savages in America, and who will not hear, on any account, of being made free. He persists in wearing mourning for his elder brother from whom he inherits his principality."

"Could anything console you for the death of yours, Chevalier?" cried out the elder gentleman.

"Milor! his property might," said the Chevalier, "which you know is not small."

"Your brother lives on his patrimony—which you have told me is immense —you by your industry, my dear Chevalier."

"Milor!" cries the individual addressed as Chevalier.

"By your industry or your esprit,—how much more noble! Shall you be at the Baroness's to-night? She ought to be a little of your parents, Chevalier?"

"Again I fail to comprehend your lordship," said the other gentleman, rather sulkily.

"Why, she is a woman of great wit—she is of noble birth—she has undergone strange adventures—she has but little principle (there you happily have the advantage of her). But what care we men of the world? You intend to go and play with the young Creole, no doubt, and get as much money from him as you can. By the way, Baron, suppose he should be a guet-apens, that young Creole? Suppose our excellent friend has invented him up in London, and brings him down with his character for wealth to prey upon the innocent folks here?"

"J'y ai souvent pense, milor," says the little Baron, placing his finger to his nose very knowingly, "that Baroness is capable of anything."

"A Baron—a Baroness, que voulez-vous, my friend? I mean the late lamented husband. Do you know who he was?"

"Intimately. A more notorious villain never dealt a card. At Venice, at Brussels, at Spa, at Vienna—the gaols of every one of which places he knew. I knew the man, my lord."

"I thought you would. I saw him at the Hague, where I first had the honour of meeting you, and a more disreputable rogue never entered my doors. A minister must open them to all sorts of people, Baron,—spies, sharpers, ruffians of every sort."

"Parbleu, milor, how you treat them!" says my lord's companion.

"A man of my rank, my friend—of the rank I held then—of course, must see all sorts of people—entre autres your acquaintance. What his wife could want with such a name as his I can't conceive."

"Apparently, it was better than the lady's own."

"Effectively! So I have heard of my friend Paddy changing clothes with the scarecrow. I don't know which name is the most distinguished, that of the English bishop or the German baron."

"My lord," cried the other gentleman, rising and laying his hand on a large star on his coat, "you forget that I, too, am a Baron and a Chevalier of the

Holy Roman———"

"———Order of the Spur!—not in the least, my dear knight and baron! You will have no more wine? We shall meet at Madame de Bernstein's to-night." The knight and baron quitted the table, felt in his embroidered pockets, as if for money to give the waiter, who brought him his great laced hat, and waving that menial off with a hand surrounded by large ruffles and blazing rings, he stalked away from the room.

It was only when the person addressed as my lord had begun to speak of the bishop's widow and the German baron's wife that Harry Warrington was aware how his aunt and himself had been the subject of the two gentlemen's conversation. Ere the conviction had settled itself on his mind, one of the speakers had quitted the room, and the other, turning to a table at which two gentlemen sate, said, "What a little sharper it is! Everything I said about Bernstein relates mutato nomine to him. I knew the fellow to be a spy and a rogue. He has changed his religion I don't know how many times. I had him turned out of the Hague myself when I was ambassador, and I know he was caned in Vienna."

"I wonder my Lord Chesterfield associates with such a villain!" called out Harry from his table. The other couple of diners looked at him. To his surprise the nobleman so addressed went on talking.

"There cannot be a more fieffe coquin than this Poellnitz. Why, Heaven be thanked, he has actually left me my snuff-box! You laugh?—the fellow is capable of taking it." And my lord thought it was his own satire at which the young men were laughing.

"You are quite right, sir," said one of the two diners, turning to Mr. Warrington, "though, saving your presence, I don't know what business it is of yours. My lord will play with anybody who will set him. Don't be alarmed, he is as deaf as a post, and did not hear a word that you said; and that's why my lord will play with anybody who will put a pack of cards before him, and that is the reason why he consorts with this rogue."

"Faith, I know other noblemen who are not particular as to their company," says Mr. Jack.

"Do you mean because I associate with you? I know my company, my good friend, and I defy most men to have the better of me."

Not having paid the least attention to Mr. Warrington's angry interruption, my lord opposite was talking in his favourite French with Monsieur Barbeau, the landlord, and graciously complimenting him on his dinner. The host bowed again and again; was enchanted that his Excellency was satisfied: had not forgotten the art which he had learned when he was a young man in his Excellency's kingdom of Ireland. The salmi was to my lord's liking? He had just served a dish to the young American seigneur who sate opposite, the gentleman from Virginia.

"To whom?" My lord's pale face became red for a moment, as he asked this question, and looked towards Harry Warrington, opposite to him.

"To the young gentleman from Virginia who has just arrived, and who perfectly possesses our beautiful language!" says Mr. Barbeau, thinking to kill two birds, as it were, with this one stone of a compliment.

"And to whom your lordship will be answerable for language reflecting upon my family, and uttered in the presence of these gentlemen," cried out Mr. Warrington, at the top of his voice, determined that his opponent should hear.

"You must go and call into his ear, and then he may perchance hear you," said one of the younger guests.

"I will take care that his lordship shall understand my meaning, one way or other," Mr. Warrington said, with much dignity; "and will not suffer calumnies regarding my relatives to be uttered by him or any other man!"

Whilst Harry was speaking, the little nobleman opposite to him did not hear him, but had time sufficient to arrange his own reply. He had risen, passing his handkerchief once or twice across his mouth, and laying his slim fingers on the table. "Sir," said he, "you will believe, on the word of a gentleman, that I had no idea before whom I was speaking, and it seems that my acquaintance, Monsieur de Poellnitz, knew you no better than myself. Had I known you, believe me that I should have been the last man in the world to utter a syllable that should give you annoyance; and I tender you my regrets and apologies, before my Lord March and Mr. Morris here present."

To these words, Mr. Warrington could only make a bow, and mumble out a few words of acknowledgment: which speech having made believe to hear, my lord made Harry another very profound bow, and saying he should have the honour of waiting upon Mr. Warrington at his lodgings, saluted the company, and went away.

CHAPTER XXVI. In which we are at a very Great Distance from Oakhurst

Within the precinct of the White Horse Tavern, and coming up to the windows of the eating-room, was a bowling-green, with a table or two, where guests might sit and partake of punch or tea. The three gentlemen having come to an end of their dinner about the same time, Mr. Morris proposed that they should adjourn to the Green, and there drink a cool bottle. "Jack Morris would adjourn to the Dust Hole, as a pretext for a fresh drink," said my lord. On which Jack said he supposed each gentleman had his own favourite way of going to the deuce. His weakness, he owned, was a bottle.

"My Lord Chesterfield's deuce is deuce-ace," says my Lord March. "His lordship can't keep away from the cards or dice."

"My Lord March has not one devil, but several devils. He loves gambling, he loves horse-racing, he loves betting, he loves drinking, he loves eating, he loves money, he loves women; and you have fallen into bad company, Mr. Warrington, when you lighted upon his lordship. He will play you for every acre you have in Virginia."

"With the greatest pleasure in life, Mr. Warrington!" interposes my lord.

"And for all your tobacco, and for all your spices, and for all your slaves, and for all your oxen and asses, and for everything that is yours."

"Shall we begin now? Jack, you are never without a dice-box or a bottle-screw. I will set Mr. Warrington for what he likes."

"Unfortunately, my lord, the tobacco, and the slaves, and the asses, and the oxen, are not mine, as yet. I am just of age, and my mother, scarce twenty years older, has quite as good chance of long life as I have."

"I will bet you that you survive her. I will pay you a sum now against four times the sum to be paid at her death. I will set you a fair sum over this table against the reversion of your estate in Virginia at the old lady's departure. What do you call your place?"

"Castlewood."

"A principality, I hear it is. I will bet that its value has been exaggerated ten times at least amongst the quidnuncs here. How came you by the name of Castlewood?—you are related to my lord? Oh, stay: I know,—my lady, your mother, descends from the real head of the house. He took the losing side in '15. I have had the story a dozen times from my old Duchess. She knew your grandfather. He was friend of Addison and Steele, and Pope and Milton, I dare say, and the bigwigs. It is a pity he did not stay at home, and transport the other branch of the family to the plantations."

"I have just been staying at Castlewood with my cousin there," remarked Mr. Warrington.

"Hm! Did you play with him? He's fond of pasteboard and bones."

"Never, but for sixpences and a pool of commerce with the ladies."

"So much the better for both of you. But you played with Will Esmond if he was at home? I will lay ten to one you played with Will Esmond."

Harry blushed, and owned that of an evening his cousin and he had had a few games at cards.

"And Tom Sampson, the chaplain," cried Jack Morris, "was he of the party? I wager that Tom made a third, and the Lord deliver you from Tom and Will Esmond together!"

"Nay; the truth is, I won of both of them," said Mr. Warrington.

"And they paid you? Well, miracles will never cease!"

"I did not say anything about miracles," remarked Mr. Harry, smiling over his wine.

"And you don't tell tales out of school—the volto sciolto—hey, Mr. Warrington?" says my lord.

"I beg your pardon," said downright Harry, "French is the only language besides my own of which I know a little."

"My Lord March has learned Italian at the Opera, and a pretty penny his lessons have cost him," remarked Jack Morris. "We must show him the Opera—mustn't we, March?"

"Must we, Morris?" said my lord, as if he only half liked the other's familiarity.

Both of the two gentlemen were dressed alike, in small scratch-wigs without powder, in blue frocks with plate buttons, in buckskins and riding-boots, in little hats with a narrow cord of lace, and no outward mark of fashion.

"I don't care about the Opera much, my lord," says Harry, warming with his wine; "but I should like to go to Newmarket, and long to see a good English hunting-field."

"We will show you Newmarket and the hunting-field, sir. Can you ride pretty well?"

"I think I can," Harry said; "and I can shoot pretty well, and jump some."

"What's your weight? I bet you we weigh even, or I weigh most. I bet you Jack Morris beats you at birds or a mark, at five-and-twenty paces. I bet you I jump farther than you on flat ground, here on this green."

"I don't know Mr. Morris's shooting—I never saw either gentleman before —but I take your bets, my lord, at what you please," cries Harry, who by this time was more than warm with Burgundy.

"Ponies on each!" cried my lord.

"Done and done!" cried my lord and Harry together. The young man thought it was for the honour of his country not to be ashamed of any bet made to him.

"We can try the last bet now, if your feet are pretty steady," said my lord, springing up, stretching his arms and limbs, and looking at the crisp, dry grass. He drew his boots off, then his coat and waistcoat, buckling his belt round his waist, and flinging his clothes down to the ground.

Harry had more respect for his garments. It was his best suit. He took off the velvet coat and waistcoat, folded them up daintily, and, as the two or three tables round were slopped with drink, went to place the clothes on a table in the eating-room, of which the windows were open.

Here a new guest had entered; and this was no other than Mr. Wolfe, who was soberly eating a chicken and salad, with a modest pint of wine. Harry was in high spirits. He told the Colonel he had a bet with my Lord March—would Colonel Wolfe stand him halves? The Colonel said he was too poor to bet. Would he come out and see fair play? That he would with all his heart. Colonel Wolfe set down his glass, and stalked through the open window after his young friend.

"Who is that tallow-faced Put with the carroty hair?" says Jack Morris, on whom the Burgundy had had its due effect.

Mr. Warrington explained that this was Lieutenant-Colonel Wolfe, of the 20th Regiment.

"Your humble servant, gentlemen!" says the Colonel, making the company a rigid military bow.

"Never saw such a figure in my life!" cries Jack Morris. "Did you—March?"

"I beg your pardon, I think you said March?" said the Colonel, looking very much surprised.

"I am the Earl of March, sir, at Colonel Wolfe's service," said the nobleman, bowing. "My friend, Mr. Morris, is so intimate with me, that, after dinner, we are quite like brothers."

Why is not all Tunbridge Wells by to hear this? thought Morris. And he was so delighted that he shouted out, "Two to one on my lord!"

"Done!" calls out Mr. Warrington; and the enthusiastic Jack was obliged to cry "Done!" too.

"Take him, Colonel," Harry whispers to his friend.

But the Colonel said he could not afford to lose, and therefore could not hope to win.

"I see you have won one of our bets already, Mr. Warrington," my Lord March remarked. "I am taller than you by an inch or two, but you are broader round the shoulders."

"Pooh, my dear Will! I bet you you weigh twice as much as he does!" cries Jack Morris.

"Done, Jack!" says my lord, laughing. "The bets are all ponies. Will you take him, Mr. Warrington?"

"No, my dear fellow—one's enough," says Jack.

"Very good, my dear fellow," says my lord; "and now we will settle the other wager."

Having already arrayed himself in his best silk stockings, black satin-net breeches, and neatest pumps, Harry did not care to take off his shoes as his antagonist had done, whose heavy riding-boots and spurs were, to be sure, little calculated for leaping. They had before them a fine even green turf of some thirty yards in length, enough for a run and enough for a jump. A gravel walk ran around this green, beyond which was a wall and gate-sign—a field azure, bearing the Hanoverian White Horse rampant between two skittles proper, and for motto the name of the landlord and of the animal depicted.

My lord's friend laid a handkerchief on the ground as the mark whence the leapers were to take their jump, and Mr. Wolfe stood at the other end of the grass-plat to note the spot where each came down. "My lord went first," writes Mr. Warrington, in a letter to Mrs. Mountain, at Castlewood, Virginia, still extant. "He was for having me take the lead; but, remembering the story about the Battel of Fontanoy which my dearest George used to tell, I says, 'Monseigneur le Comte, tirez le premier, s'il vous play.' So he took his run in his stocken feet, and for the honour of Old Virginia, I had the gratafacation of beating his lordship by more than two feet—viz., two feet nine inches—me jumping twenty-one feet three inches, by the drawer's measured tape, and his lordship only eighteen six. I had won from him about my weight before (which I knew the moment I set my eye upon him). So he and Mr. Jack paid me these two betts. And with my best duty to my mother—she will not be displeased with me, for I bett for the honor of the Old Dominion, and my opponent was a nobleman of the first quality, himself holding two Erldomes, and heir to a Duke. Betting is all the rage here, and the bloods and young fellows of fashion are betting away from morning till night.

"I told them—and that was my mischief perhaps—that there was a gentleman at home who could beat me by a good foot; and when they asked who it was, and I said Col. G. Washington, of Mount Vernon—as you know he can, and he's the only man in his county or mine that can do it—Mr. Wolfe asked me ever so many questions about Col. G. W., and showed that he had heard of him, and talked over last year's unhappy campane as if he knew every inch of the ground, and he knew the names of all our rivers, only he called the Potowmac Pottamac, at which we had a good laugh at him. My Lord of March and Ruglen was not in the least ill-humour about losing, and he and his friend handed me notes out of their pocket-books, which filled mine that was getting very empty, for the vales to the servants at my cousin Castlewood's house and buying a horse at Oakhurst have very nearly put me on the necessity of making another draft upon my honoured mother or her London or Bristol agent."

These feats of activity over, the four gentlemen now strolled out of the tavern garden into the public walk, where, by this time, a great deal of company was assembled: upon whom Mr. Jack, who was of a frank and free nature, with a loud voice, chose to make remarks that were not always agreeable. And here, if my Lord March made a joke, of which his lordship was not sparing, Jack roared, "Oh, ho, ho! Oh, good Gad! Oh, my dear earl! Oh, my dear lord, you'll be the death of me!" "It seemed as if he wished everybody to know," writes Harry sagaciously to Mrs. Mountain, "that his friend and companion was an Erl!"

There was, indeed, a great variety of characters who passed. M. Poellnitz, no finer dressed than he had been at dinner, grinned, and saluted with his great laced hat and tarnished feathers. Then came by my Lord Chesterfield, in a pearl-coloured suit, with his blue ribbon and star, and saluted the young men in his turn.

"I will back the old boy for taking his hat off against the whole kingdom, and France either," says my Lord March. "He has never changed the shape of that hat of his for twenty years. Look at it. There it goes again! Do you see that great, big, awkward, pock-marked, snuff-coloured man, who hardly touches his clumsy beaver in reply. D—— his confounded impudence—do you know who that is?"

"No, curse him! Who is it, March?" asks Jack, with an oath.

"It's one Johnson, a Dictionary-maker, about whom my Lord Chesterfield wrote some most capital papers, when his dixonary was coming out, to patronise the fellow. I know they were capital. I've heard Horry Walpole say so, and he knows all about that kind of thing. Confound the impudent schoolmaster!"

"Hang him, he ought to stand in the pillory!" roars Jack.

"That fat man he's walking with is another of your writing fellows,—a printer,—his name is Richardson; he wrote Clarissa, you know."

"Great heavens! my lord, is that the great Richardson? Is that the man who wrote Clarissa?" called out Colonel Wolfe and Mr. Warrington, in a breath.

Harry ran forward to look at the old gentleman toddling along the walk with a train of admiring ladies surrounding him.

"Indeed, my very dear sir," one was saying, "you are too great and good to live in such a world; but sure you were sent to teach it virtue!"

"Ah, my Miss Mulso! Who shall teach the teacher?" said the good, fat old man, raising a kind, round face skywards. "Even he has his faults and errors! Even his age and experience does not prevent him from stumbl——. Heaven bless my soul, Mr. Johnson! I ask your pardon if I have trodden on your corn."

"You have done both, sir. You have trodden on the corn, and received the pardon," said Mr. Johnson, and went on mumbling some verses, swaying to and fro, his eyes turned towards the ground, his hands behind him, and occasionally endangering with his great stick the honest, meek eyes of his companion-author.

"They do not see very well, my dear Mulso," he says to the young lady, "but such as they are, I would keep my lash from Mr. Johnson's cudgel. Your servant, sir." Here he made a low bow, and took off his hat to Mr. Warrington, who shrank back with many blushes, after saluting the great author. The great author was accustomed to be adored. A gentler wind never puffed mortal vanity. Enraptured spinsters flung tea-leaves round him, and incensed him with the coffee-pot. Matrons kissed the slippers they had worked for him. There was a halo of virtue round his nightcap. All Europe had thrilled, panted, admired, trembled, wept, over the pages of the immortal little, kind, honest man with the round paunch. Harry came back quite glowing and proud at having a bow from him. "Ah!" says he, "my lord, I am glad to have seen him!"

"Seen him! why, dammy, you may see him any day in his shop, I suppose?" says Jack, with a laugh.

"My brother declared that he, and Mr. Fielding, I think, was the name, were the greatest geniuses in England; and often used to say, that when we came to Europe, his first pilgrimage would be to Mr. Richardson," cried Harry, always impetuous, honest, and tender, when he spoke of the dearest friend.

"Your brother spoke like a man," cried Mr. Wolfe, too, his pale face likewise flushing up. "I would rather be a man of genius, than a peer of the realm."

"Every man to his taste, Colonel," says my lord, much amused. "Your enthusiasm—I don't mean anything personal—refreshes me, on my honour it does."

"So it does me—by gad—perfectly refreshes me," cries Jack

"So it does Jack—you see—it actually refreshes Jack! I say, Jack, which would you rather be?—a fat old printer, who has written a story about a confounded girl and a fellow that ruins her,—or a peer of Parliament with ten thousand a year?"

"March—my Lord March, do you take me for a fool?" says Jack, with a tearful voice. "Have I done anything to deserve this language from you?"

"I would rather win honour than honours: I would rather have genius than wealth. I would rather make my name than inherit it, though my father's, thank God, is an honest one," said the young Colonel. "But pardon me, gentlemen," and here making, them a hasty salutation, he ran across the parade towards a young and elderly lady and a gentleman, who were now advancing.

"It is the beautiful Miss Lowther. I remember now," says my lord. "See! he takes her arm! The report is, he is engaged to her."

"You don't mean to say such a fellow is engaged to any of the Lowthers of the North?" cries out Jack. "Curse me, what is the world come to, with your printers, and your half-pay ensigns, and your schoolmasters, and your infernal nonsense?"

The Dictionary-maker, who had shown so little desire to bow to my Lord Chesterfield, when that famous nobleman courteously saluted him, was here seen to take off his beaver, and bow almost to the ground, before a florid personage in a large round hat, with bands and a gown, who made his appearance in the Walk. This was my Lord Bishop of Salisbury, wearing complacently the blue riband and badge of the Garter, of which Noble Order his lordship was prelate.

Mr. Johnson stood, hat in hand, during the whole time of his conversation with Dr. Gilbert; who made many flattering and benedictory remarks to Mr. Richardson, declaring that he was the supporter of virtue, the preacher of sound morals, the mainstay of religion, of all which points the honest printer himself was perfectly convinced.

Do not let any young lady trip to her grandpapa's bookcase in consequence of this eulogium, and rashly take down Clarissa from the shelf. She would not care to read the volumes, over which her pretty ancestresses wept and thrilled a hundred years ago; which were commended by divines from pulpits and belauded all Europe over. I wonder, are our women more virtuous than their grandmothers, or only more squeamish? If the former, then Miss Smith of New York is certainly more modest than Miss Smith of London, who still does not scruple to say that tables, pianos, and animals have legs. Oh, my faithful, good old Samuel Richardson! Hath the news yet reached thee in Hades that thy sublime novels are huddled away in corners, and that our daughters may no more read Clarissa than Tom Jones? Go up, Samuel, and be reconciled with thy brother-scribe, whom in life thou didst hate so. I wonder whether a century hence the novels of to-day will be hidden behind locks and wires, and make pretty little maidens blush?

"Who is yonder queer person in the high headdress of my grandmother's time, who stops and speaks to Mr. Richardson?" asked Harry, as a fantastically dressed lady came up, and performed a curtsey and a compliment to the bowing printer.

Jack Morris nervously struck Harry a blow in the side with the butt end of his whip. Lord March laughed.

"Yonder queer person is my gracious kinswoman, Katharine, Duchess of Dover and Queensberry, at your service, Mr. Warrington. She was a beauty price! She is changed now, isn't she? What an old Gorgon it is! She is a great patroness of your book-men and when that old frump was young, they actually made verses about her."

The Earl quitted his friends for a moment to make his bow to the old Duchess, Jack Morris explaining to Mr. Warrington how, at the Duke's death, my Lord of March and Ruglen would succeed to his cousin's dukedoms.

"I suppose," says Harry, simply, "his lordship is here in attendance upon the old lady?"

Jack burst into a loud laugh.

"Oh yes! very much! exactly!" says he. "Why, my dear fellow, you don't mean to say you haven't heard about the little Opera-dancer?"

"I am but lately arrived in England, Mr. Morris," said Harry, with a smile, "and in Virginia, I own, we have not heard much about the little Opera-dancer."

Luckily for us, the secret about the little Opera-dancer never was revealed, for the young men's conversation was interrupted by a lady in a cardinal cape, and a hat by no means unlike those lovely headpieces which have returned into vogue a hundred years after the date of our present history, who made a profound curtsey to the two gentlemen and received their salutation in return. She stopped opposite to Harry; she held out her hand, rather to his wonderment:

"Have you so soon forgotten me, Mr. Warrington?" she said.

Off went Harry's hat in an instant. He started, blushed, stammered, and called out Good Heavens! as if there had been any celestial wonder in the circumstance! It was Lady Maria come out for a walk. He had not been thinking about her. She was, to say truth, for the moment so utterly out of the young gentleman's mind, that her sudden re-entry there and appearance in the body startled Mr. Warrington's faculties, and caused those guilty blushes to crowd into his cheeks.

No. He was not even thinking of her! A week ago—a year, a hundred years ago it seemed—he would not have been surprised to meet her anywhere. Appearing from amidst darkling shrubberies, gliding over green garden terraces, loitering on stairs or corridors, hovering even in his dreams, all day or all night, bodily or spiritually, he had been accustomed to meet her. A week ago his heart used to beat. A week ago, and at the very instant when he jumped out of his sleep, there was her idea smiling on him. And it was only last Tuesday that his love was stabbed and slain, and he not only had left off mourning for her, but had forgotten her!

"You will come and walk with me a little?" she said. "Or would you like the music best? I dare say you will like the music best."

"You know," said Harry, "I don't care about any music much, except"—he was thinking of the evening hymn—"except of your playing." He turned very red again as he spoke, he felt he was perjuring himself horribly.

The poor lady was agitated herself by the flutter and agitation which she saw in her young companion. Gracious Heaven! Could that tremor and excitement mean that she was mistaken, and that the lad was still faithful? "Give me your arm, and let us take a little walk," she said, waving round a curtsey to the other two gentlemen: "my aunt is asleep after her dinner." Harry could not but offer the arm, and press the hand that lay against his heart. Maria made another fine curtsey to Harry's bowing companions, and walked off with her prize. In her griefs, in her rages, in the pains and anguish of wrong and desertion, how a woman remembers to smile, curtsey, caress, dissemble! How resolutely they discharge the social proprieties; how they have a word, or a hand, or a kind little speech or reply for the passing acquaintance who crosses unknowing the path of the tragedy, drops a light airy remark or two (happy self-satisfied rogue!) and passes on. He passes on, and thinks that woman was rather pleased with what I said. "That joke I made was rather neat. I do really think Lady Maria looks rather favourably at me, and she's a dev'lish fine woman, begad she is!" O you wiseacre! Such was Jack Morris's observation and case as he walked away leaning on the arm of his noble friend, and thinking the whole Society of the Wells was looking at him. He had made some exquisite remarks about a particular run of cards at Lady Flushington's the night before, and Lady Maria had replied graciously and neatly, and so away went Jack perfectly happy.

The absurd creature! I declare we know nothing of anybody (but that for my part I know better and better every day). You enter smiling to see your new acquaintance, Mrs. A. and her charming family. You make your bow in the elegant drawing-room of Mr. and Mrs. B.? I tell you that in your course through life you are for ever putting your great clumsy foot upon the mute invisible wounds of bleeding tragedies. Mrs. B.'s closets for what you know are stuffed with skeletons. Look there under the sofa-cushion. Is that merely Missy's doll, or is it the limb of a stifled Cupid peeping out? What do you suppose are those ashes smouldering in the grate?—Very likely a suttee has been offered up there just before you came in: a faithful heart has been burned out upon a callous corpse, and you are looking on the cineri doloso. You see B. and his wife receiving their company before dinner. Gracious powers! Do you know that that bouquet which she wears is a signal to Captain C., and that he will find a note under the little bronze Shakespeare on the mantelpiece in the study? And with all this you go up and say some uncommonly neat thing (as you fancy) to Mrs. B. about the weather (clever dog!), or about Lady E.'s last party (fashionable buck!), or about the dear children in the nursery (insinuating rogue!). Heaven and earth, my good sir, how can you tell that B. is not going to pitch all the children out of the nursery window this very night, or that his lady has not made an arrangement for leaving them, and running off with the Captain? How do you know that those footmen are not disguised bailiffs?—that yonder large-looking butler (really a skeleton) is not the pawnbroker's man? and that there are not skeleton rotis and entrees under every one of the covers? Look at their feet peeping from under the tablecloth. Mind how you stretch out your own lovely little slippers, madam, lest you knock over a rib or two. Remark the death's-head moths fluttering among the flowers. See, the pale winding-sheets gleaming in the wax-candles! I know it is an old story, and especially that this preacher has yelled vanitas vanitatum five hundred times before. I can't help always falling upon it, and cry out with particular loudness and wailing, and become especially melancholy, when I see a dead love tied to a live love. Ha! I look up from my desk, across the street: and there come in Mr. and Mrs. D. from their walk in Kensington Gardens. How she hangs on him! how jolly and happy he looks, as the children frisk round! My poor dear benighted Mrs. D., there is a Regent's Park as well as a Kensington Gardens in the world. Go in, fond wretch! Smilingly lay before him what you know he likes for dinner. Show him the children's copies and the reports of their masters. Go with Missy to the piano, and play your artless duet together; and fancy you are happy!

There go Harry and Maria taking their evening walk on the common, away from the village which is waking up from its after-dinner siesta, and where the people are beginning to stir and the music to play. With the music Maria knows Madame de Bernstein will waken: with the candles she must be back to the tea-table and the cards. Never mind. Here is a minute. It may be my love is dead, but here is a minute to kneel over the grave and pray by it. He certainly was not thinking about her: he was startled and did not even know her. He was laughing and talking with Jack Morris and my Lord March. He is twenty years younger than she. Never mind. To-day is to-day in which we are all equal. This moment is ours. Come, let us walk a little way over the heath, Harry. She will go, though she feels a deadly assurance that he will tell her all is over between them, and that he loves the dark-haired girl at Oakhurst.

CHAPTER XXVII. Plenus Opus Aleae

"Let me hear about those children, child, whom I saw running about at the house where they took you in, poor dear boy, after your dreadful fall?" says Maria, as they paced the common. "Oh, that fall, Harry! I thought I should have died when I saw it! You needn't squeeze one's arm so. You know you don't care for me?"

"The people are the very best, kindest, dearest people I have ever met in the world," cries Mr. Warrington. "Mrs. Lambert was a friend of my mother when she was in Europe for her education. Colonel Lambert is a most accomplished gentleman, and has seen service everywhere. He was in Scotland with his Royal Highness, in Flanders, at Minorca. No natural parents could be kinder than they were to me. How can I show my gratitude to them? I want to make them a present: I must make them a present," says Harry, clapping his hand into his pocket, which was filled with the crisp spoils of Morris and March.

"We can go to the toy-shop, my dear, and buy a couple of dolls for the children," says Lady Maria. "You would offend the parents by offering anything like payment for their kindness."

"Dolls for Hester and Theo! Why, do you think a woman is not woman till she is forty, Maria?" (The arm under Harry's here gave a wince perhaps,—ever so slight a wince.) "I can tell you Miss Hester by no means considers herself a child, and Miss Theo is older than her sister. They know ever so many languages. They have read books—oh! piles and piles of books! They play on the harpsichord and sing together admirable; and Theo composes, and sings songs of her own."

"Indeed! I scarcely saw them. I thought they were children. They looked quite childish. I had no idea they had all these perfections, and were such wonders of the world."

"That's just the way with you women! At home, if me or George praised a woman, Mrs. Esmond, and Mountain, too, would be sure to find fault with her!" cries Harry.

"I am sure I would find fault with no one who is kind to you, Mr. Warrington," sighed Maria, "though you are not angry with me for envying them because they had to take care of you when you were wounded and ill—whilst I—I had to leave you?"

"You dear good Maria!"

"No, Harry! I am not dear and good. There, sir, you needn't be so pressing in your attentions. Look! There is your black man walking with a score of other wretches in livery. The horrid creatures are going to fuddle at the tea-garden, and get tipsy like their masters. That dreadful Mr. Morris was perfectly tipsy when I came to you, and frightened you so."

"I had just won great bets from both of them. What shall I buy for you, my dear cousin?" And Harry narrated the triumphs which he had just achieved. He was in high spirits: he laughed, he bragged a little. "For the honour of Virginia I was determined to show them what jumping was," he said. "With a little practice I think I could leap two foot farther."

Maria was pleased with the victories of her young champion. "But you must beware about play, child," she said. "You know it hath been the ruin of our family. My brother Castlewood, Will, our poor father, our aunt, Lady Castlewood herself, they have all been victims to it: as for my Lord March, he is the most dreadful gambler and the most successful of all the nobility."

"I don't intend to be afraid of him, nor of his friend Mr. Jack Morris neither," says Harry, again fingering the delightful notes. "What do you play at Aunt Bernstein's? Cribbage, all-fours, brag, whist, commerce, piquet, quadrille? I'm ready at any of 'em. What o'clock is that striking—sure 'tis seven!"

"And you want to begin now," said the plaintive Maria. "You don't care about walking with your poor cousin. Not long ago you did."

"Hey! Youth is youth, cousin!" cried Mr. Harry, tossing up his head, "and a young fellow must have his fling!" and he strutted by his partner's side, confident, happy, and eager for pleasure. Not long ago he did like to walk with her. Only yesterday, he liked to be with Theo and Hester, and good Mrs. Lambert; but pleasure, life, gaiety, the desire to shine and to conquer, had also their temptations for the lad, who seized the cup like other lads, and did not care to calculate on the headache in store for the morning. Whilst he and his cousin were talking, the fiddles from the open orchestra on the Parade made a great tuning and squeaking, preparatory to their usual evening concert. Maria knew her aunt was awake again, and that she must go back to her slavery. Harry never asked about that slavery, though he must have known it, had he taken the trouble to think. He never pitied his cousin. He was not thinking about her at all. Yet when his mishap befell him, she had been wounded far more cruelly than he was. He had scarce ever been out of her thoughts, which of course she had had to bury under smiling hypocrisies, as is the way with her sex. I know, my dear Mrs. Grundy, you think she was an old fool? Ah! do you suppose fools' caps do not cover grey hair, as well as jet or auburn? Bear gently with our elderly fredaines, O you Minerva of a woman! Or perhaps you are so good and wise that you don't read novels at all. This I know, that there are late crops of wild oats, as well as early harvests of them; and (from observation of self and neighbour) I have an idea that the avena fatua grows up to the very last days of the year.

Like worldly parents anxious to get rid of a troublesome child, and go out to their evening party, Madame Bernstein and her attendants had put the sun to bed, whilst it was as yet light, and had drawn the curtains over it, and were busy about their cards and their candles, and their tea and negus, and other refreshments. One chair after another landed ladies at the Baroness's door, more or less painted, patched, brocaded. To these came gentlemen in gala raiment. Mr. Poellnitz's star was the largest, and his coat the most embroidered of all present. My Lord of March and Ruglen, when he made his appearance, was quite changed from the individual with whom Harry had made acquaintance at the White Horse. His tight brown scratch was exchanged for a neatly curled feather top, with a bag and grey powder, his jockey-dress and leather breeches replaced by a rich and elegant French suit. Mr. Jack Morris had just such another wig and a suit of stuff as closely as possible resembling his lordship's. Mr. Wolfe came in attendance upon his beautiful mistress, Miss Lowther, and her aunt who loved cards, as all the world did. When my Lady Maria Esmond made her appearance, 'tis certain that her looks belied Madame Bernstein's account of her. Her shape was very fine, and her dress showed a great deal of it. Her complexion was by nature exceeding fair, and a dark frilled ribbon, clasped by a jewel, round her neck, enhanced its snowy whiteness. Her cheeks were not redder than those of other ladies present, and the roses were pretty openly purchased by everybody at the perfumery-shops. An artful patch or two, it was supposed, added to the lustre of her charms. Her hoop was not larger than the iron contrivances which ladies of the present day hang round their persons; and we may pronounce that the costume, if absurd in some points, was pleasing altogether. Suppose our ladies took to wearing of bangles and nose-rings? I dare say we should laugh at the ornaments, and not dislike them, and lovers would make no difficulty about lifting up the ring to be able to approach the rosy lips underneath.

As for the Baroness de Bernstein, when that lady took the pains of making a grand toilette, she appeared as an object, handsome still, and magnificent, but melancholy, and even somewhat terrifying to behold. You read the past in some old faces, while some others lapse into mere meekness and content. The fires go quite out of some eyes, as the crow's-feet pucker round them; they flash no longer with scorn, or with anger, or love; they gaze, and no one is melted by their sapphire glances; they look, and no one is dazzled. My fair young reader, if you are not so perfect a beauty as the peerless Lindamira, Queen of the Ball; if, at the end of it, as you retire to bed, you meekly own that you have had but two or three partners, whilst Lindamira has had a crowd round her all night—console yourself with thinking that, at fifty, you will look as kind and pleasant as you appear now at eighteen. You will not have to lay down your coach-and-six of beauty and see another step into it, and walk yourself through the rest of life. You will have to forgo no long-accustomed homage; you will not witness and own the depreciation of your smiles. You will not see fashion forsake your quarter; and remain all dust, gloom, cobwebs within your once splendid saloons, and placards in your sad windows, gaunt, lonely, and to let! You may not have known any grandeur, but you won't feel any desertion. You will not have enjoyed millions, but you will have escaped bankruptcy. "Our hostess," said my Lord Chesterfield to his friend in a confidential whisper, of which the utterer did not in the least know the loudness, "puts me in mind of Covent Garden in my youth. Then it was the court end of the town, and inhabited by the highest fashion. Now, a nobleman's house is a gaming-house, or you may go in with a friend and call for a bottle."

"Hey! a bottle and a tavern are good things in their way," says my Lord March, with a shrug of his shoulders. "I was not born before the Georges came in, though I intend to live to a hundred. I never knew the Bernstein but as an old woman; and if she ever had beauty, hang me if I know how she spent it."

"No, hang me, how did she spend it?" laughs out Jack Morris.

"Here's a table! Shall we sit down and have a game?—Don't let the Frenchman come in. He won't pay. Mr. Warrington, will you take a card?" Mr. Warrington and my Lord Chesterfield found themselves partners against Mr. Morris and the Earl of March. "You have come too late, Baron," says the elder nobleman to the other nobleman who was advancing. "We have made our game. What, have you forgotten Mr. Warrington of Virginia—the young gentleman whom you met in London?"

"The young gentleman whom I met at Arthur's Chocolate House had black hair, a little cocked nose, and was by no means so fortunate in his personal appearance as Mr. Warrington," said the Baron, with much presence of mind. "Warrington, Dorrington, Harrington? We of the continent cannot retain your insular names. I certify that this gentleman is not the individual of whom I spoke at dinner." And, glancing kindly upon him, the old beau sidled away to a farther end of the room, where Mr. Wolfe and Miss Lowther were engaged in deep conversation in the embrasure of a window. Here the Baron thought fit to engage the Lieutenant-Colonel upon the Prussian manual exercise, which had lately been introduced into King George II.'s army—a subject with which Mr. Wolfe was thoroughly familiar, and which no doubt would have interested him at any other moment but that. Nevertheless the old gentleman uttered his criticisms and opinions, and thought he perfectly charmed the two persons to whom he communicated them.

At the commencement of the evening the Baroness received her guests personally, and as they arrived engaged them in talk and introductory courtesies. But as the rooms and tables filled, and the parties were made up, Madame de Bernstein became more and more restless, and finally retreated with three friends to her own corner, where a table specially reserved for her was occupied by her major-domo. And here the old lady sate down resolutely, never changing her place or quitting her game till cock-crow. The charge of receiving the company devolved now upon my Lady Maria, who did not care for cards, but dutifully did the honours of the house to her aunt's guests, and often rustled by the table where her young cousin was engaged with his three friends.

"Come and cut the cards for us," said my Lord March to her ladyship as she passed on one of her wistful visits. "Cut the cards and bring us luck, Lady Maria! We have had none to-night, and Mr. Warrington is winning everything."

"I hope you are not playing high, Harry?" said the lady, timidly.

"Oh no, only sixpences," cried my lord, dealing.

"Only sixpences," echoed Mr. Morris, who was Lord March's partner. But Mr. Morris must have been very keenly alive to the value of sixpence, if the loss of a few such coins could make his round face look so dismal. My Lord Chesterfield sate opposite Mr. Warrington, sorting his cards. No one could say, by inspecting that calm physiognomy, whether good or ill fortune was attending his lordship.

Some word, not altogether indicative of delight, slipped out of Mr. Morris's lips, on which his partner cried out, "Hang it, Morris, play your cards, and hold your tongue!" Considering they were only playing for sixpences, his lordship, too, was strangely affected.

Maria, still fondly lingering by Harry's chair, with her hand at the back of it, could see his cards, and that a whole covey of trumps was ranged in one corner. She had not taken away his luck. She was pleased to think she had cut that pack which had dealt him all those pretty trumps. As Lord March was dealing, he had said in a quiet voice to Mr. Warrington, "The bet as before, Mr. Warrington, or shall we double it?"

"Anything you like, my lord," said Mr. Warrington, very quietly.

"We will say, then,—shillings."

"Yes, shillings," says Mr. Warrington, and the game proceeded.

The end of the day's, and some succeeding days' sport may be gathered from the following letter, which was never delivered to the person to whom it was addressed, but found its way to America in the papers of Mr. Henry Warrington:

"TUNBRIDGE WELLS, August 10, 1756.

"DEAR GEORGE—As White's two bottles of Burgundy and a pack of cards constitute all the joys of your life, I take for granted that you are in London at this moment, preferring smoke and faro to fresh air and fresh haystacks. This will be delivered to you by a young gentleman with whom I have lately made acquaintance, and whom you will be charmed to know. He will play with you at any game for any stake, up to any hour of the night, and drink any reasonable number of bottles during the play. Mr. Warrington is no other than the Fortunate Youth about whom so many stories have been told in the Public Advertiser and other prints. He has an estate in Virginia as big as Yorkshire, with the incumbrance of a mother, the reigning Sovereign; but, as the country is unwholesome, and fevers plentiful, let us hope that Mrs. Esmond will die soon, and leave this virtuous lad in undisturbed possession. She is aunt of that polisson of a Castlewood, who never pays his play-debts, unless he is more honourable in his dealings with you than he has been with me. Mr. W. is de bonne race. We must have him of our society, if it be only that I may win my money back from him.

"He has had the devil's luck here, and has been winning everything, whilst his old card-playing beldam of an aunt has been losing. A few nights ago, when I first had the ill-luck to make his acquaintance, he beat me in jumping (having practised the art amongst the savages, and running away from bears in his native woods); he won bets off me and Jack Morris about my weight; and at night, when we sat down to play, at old Bernstein's, he won from us all round. If you can settle our last Epsom account please hand over to Mr. Warrington 350 pounds, which I still owe him, after pretty well emptying my pocket-book. Chesterfield has dropped six hundred to him, too; but his lordship does not wish to have it known, having sworn to give up play and live cleanly. Jack Morris, who has not been hit as hard as either of us, and can afford it quite as well, for the fat chuff has no houses nor train to keep up, and all his misbegotten father's money in hand, roars like a bull of Bashan about his losses. We had a second night's play, en petit comite, and Barbeau served us a fair dinner in a private room. Mr. Warrington holds his tongue like a gentleman, and none of us have talked about our losses; but the whole place does, for us. Yesterday the Cattarina looked as sulky as thunder, because I would not give her a diamond necklace, and says I refuse her because I have lost five thousand to the Virginian. My old Duchess of Q. has the very same story, besides knowing to a fraction what Chesterfield and Jack have lost.

"Warrington treated the company to breakfast and music at the rooms; and you should have seen how the women tore him to pieces. That fiend of a Cattarina ogled him out of my vis-a-vis, and under my very nose, yesterday, as we were driving to Penshurst, and I have no doubt has sent him a billet-doux ere this. He shot Jack Morris all to pieces at a mark: we shall try him with partridges when the season comes.

"He is a fortunate fellow, certainly. He has youth (which is not deboshed by evil courses in Virginia, as ours is in England); he has good health, good looks, and good luck.

"In a word, Mr. Warrington has won our money in a very gentlemanlike manner; and, as I like him, and wish to win some of it back again, I put him under your worship's saintly guardianship. Adieu! I am going to the North, and shall be back for Doncaster.

"Yours ever, dear George,

"M. et R."

"To George Augustus Selwyn, Esq., at White's Chocolate House, St. James's Street."

CHAPTER XXVIII. The Way of the World

Our young Virginian found himself, after two or three days at Tunbridge Wells, by far the most important personage in that merry little watering-place. No nobleman in the place inspired so much curiosity. My Lord Bishop of Salisbury himself was scarce treated with more respect. People turned round to look after Harry as he passed, and country-folks stared at him as they came into market. At the rooms, matrons encouraged him to come round to them, and found means to leave him alone with their daughters, most of whom smiled upon him. Everybody knew, to an acre and a shilling, the extent of his Virginian property, and the amount of his income. At every tea-table in the Wells, his winnings at play were told and calculated. Wonderful is the knowledge which our neighbours have of our affairs! So great was the interest and curiosity which Harry inspired, that people even smiled upon his servant, and took Gumbo aside and treated him with ale and cold meat, in order to get news of the young Virginian. Mr. Gumbo fattened under the diet, became a leading member of the Society of Valets in the place, and lied more enormously than ever. No party was complete unless Mr. Warrington attended it. The lad was not a little amused and astonished by this prosperity, and bore his new honours pretty well. He had been bred at home to think too well of himself, and his present good fortune no doubt tended to confirm his self-satisfaction. But he was not too much elated. He did not brag about his victories or give himself any particular airs. In engaging in play with the gentlemen who challenged him, he had acted up to his queer code of honour. He felt as if he was bound to meet them when they summoned him, and that if they invited him to a horse-race, or a drinking-bout, or a match at cards, for the sake of Old Virginia he must not draw back. Mr. Harry found his new acquaintances ready to try him at all these sports and contests. He had a strong head, a skilful hand, a firm seat, an unflinching nerve. The representative of Old Virginia came off very well in his friendly rivalry with the mother-country.

Madame de Bernstein, who got her fill of cards every night, and, no doubt, repaired the ill-fortune of which we heard in the last chapter, was delighted with her nephew's victories and reputation. He had shot with Jack Morris and beat him; he had ridden a match with Mr. Scamper and won it. He played tennis with Captain Batts, and, though the boy had never tried the game before, in a few days he held his own uncommonly well. He had engaged in play with those celebrated gamesters, my Lords of Chesterfield and March; and they both bore testimony to his coolness, gallantry, and good breeding. At his books Harry was not brilliant certainly; but he could write as well as a great number of men of fashion; and the naivete of his ignorance amused the old lady. She had read books in her time, and could talk very well about them with bookish people: she had a relish for humour and delighted in Moliere and Mr. Fielding, but she loved the world far better than the library, and was never so interested in any novel but that she would leave it for a game of cards. She superintended with fond pleasure the improvements of Harry's toilette: rummaged out fine laces for his ruffles and shirt, and found a pretty diamond-brooch for his frill. He attained the post of prime favourite of all her nephews and kinsfolk. I fear Lady Maria was only too well pleased at the lad's successes, and did not grudge him his superiority over her brothers; but those gentlemen must have quaked with fear and envy when they heard of Mr. Warrington's prodigious successes, and the advance which he had made in their wealthy aunt's favour.

After a fortnight of Tunbridge, Mr. Harry had become quite a personage. He knew all the good company in the place. Was it his fault if he became acquainted with the bad likewise? Was he very wrong in taking the world as he found it, and drinking from that sweet sparkling pleasure-cup, which was filled for him to the brim? The old aunt enjoyed his triumphs, and for her part only bade him pursue his enjoyments. She was not a rigorous old moralist, nor, perhaps, a very wholesome preceptress for youth. If the Cattarina wrote him billets-doux, I fear Aunt Bernstein would have bade him accept the invitations: but the lad had brought with him from his colonial home a stock of modesty which he still wore along with the honest homespun linen. Libertinism was rare in those thinly-peopled regions from which he came. The vices of great cities were scarce known or practised in the rough towns of the American continent. Harry Warrington blushed like a girl at the daring talk of his new European associates: even Aunt Bernstein's conversation and jokes astounded the young Virginian, so that the worldly old woman would call him Joseph, or simpleton.

But, however innocent he was, the world gave him credit for being as bad as other folks. How was he to know that he was not to associate with that saucy Cattarina? He had seen my Lord March driving her about in his lordship's phaeton. Harry thought there was no harm in giving her his arm, and parading openly with her in the public walks. She took a fancy to a trinket at the toy-shop; and, as his pockets were full of money, he was delighted to make her a present of the locket, which she coveted. The next day it was a piece of lace: again Harry gratified her. The next day it was something else: there was no end to Madame Cattarina's fancies: but here the young gentleman stopped, turning off her request with a joke and a laugh. He was shrewd enough, and not reckless or prodigal, though generous. He had no idea of purchasing diamond drops for the petulant little lady's pretty ears.

But who was to give him credit for his Modesty? Old Bernstein insisted upon believing that her nephew was playing Don Juan's part, and supplanting my Lord March. She insisted the more when poor Maria was by; loving to stab the tender heart of that spinster, and enjoying her niece's piteous silence and discomfiture.

"Why, my dear," says the Baroness, "boys will be boys, and I don't want Harry to be the first milksop in his family!" The bread which Maria ate at her aunt's expense choked her sometimes. O me, how hard and indigestible some women know how to make it!

Mr. Wolfe was for ever coming over from Westerham to pay court to the lady of his love; and, knowing that the Colonel was entirely engaged in that pursuit, Mr. Warrington scarcely expected to see much of him, however much he liked that officer's conversation and society. It was different from the talk of the ribald people round about Harry. Mr. Wolfe never spoke of cards, or horses' pedigrees; or bragged of his performances in the hunting-field; or boasted of the favours of women; or retailed any of the innumerable scandals of the time. It was not a good time. That old world was more dissolute than ours. There was an old king with mistresses openly in his train, to whom the great folks of the land did honour. There was a nobility, many of whom were mad and reckless in the pursuit of pleasure; there was a looseness of words and acts which we must note, as faithful historians, without going into particulars, and needlessly shocking honest readers. Our young gentleman had lighted upon some of the wildest of these wild people, and had found an old relative who lived in the very midst of the rout.

Harry then did not remark how Colonel Wolfe avoided him, or when they casually met, at first, notice the Colonel's cold and altered demeanour. He did not know the stories that were told of him. Who does know the stories that are told of him? Who makes them? Who are the fathers of those wondrous lies? Poor Harry did not know the reputation he was getting; and that, whilst he was riding his horse and playing his game and taking his frolic, he was passing amongst many respectable persons for being the most abandoned and profligate and godless of young men.

Alas, and alas! to think that the lad whom we liked so, and who was so gentle and quiet when with us, so simple and so easily pleased, should be a hardened profligate, a spendthrift, a confirmed gamester, a frequenter of abandoned women! These stories came to honest Colonel Lambert at Oakhurst: first one bad story, then another, then crowds of them, till the good man's kind heart was quite filled with grief and care, so that his family saw that something annoyed him. At first he would not speak on the matter at all, and put aside the wife's fond queries. Mrs. Lambert thought a great misfortune had happened; that her husband had been ruined; that he had been ordered on a dangerous service; that one of the boys was ill, disgraced, dead; who can resist an anxious woman, or escape the cross-examination of the conjugal pillow? Lambert was obliged to tell a part of what he knew about

Harry Warrington. The wife was as much grieved and amazed as her husband had been. From papa's and mamma's bedroom the grief, after being stifled for a while under the bed-pillows there, came downstairs. Theo and Hester took the complaint after their parents, and had it very bad. O kind, little, wounded hearts! At first Hester turned red, flew into a great passion, clenched her little fists, and vowed she would not believe a word of the wicked stories; but she ended by believing them. Scandal almost always does master people; especially good and innocent people. Oh, the serpent they had nursed by their fire! Oh, the wretched, wretched boy! To think of his walking about with that horrible painted Frenchwoman, and giving her diamond necklaces, and parading his shame before all the society at the Wells! The three ladies having cried over the story, and the father being deeply moved by it, took the parson into their confidence. In vain he preached at church next Sunday his favourite sermon about scandal, and inveighed against our propensity to think evil. We repent we promise to do so no more; but when the next bad story comes about our neighbour we believe it. So did those kind, wretched Oakhurst folks believe what they heard about poor Harry Warrington.

Harry Warrington meanwhile was a great deal too well pleased with himself to know how ill his friends were thinking of him, and was pursuing a very idle and pleasant, if unprofitable, life, without having the least notion of the hubbub he was creating, and the dreadful repute in which he was held by many good men. Coming out from a match at tennis with Mr. Batts, and pleased with his play and all the world, Harry overtook Colonel Wolfe, who had been on one of his visits to the lady of his heart. Harry held out his hand, which the Colonel took, but the latter's salutation was so cold, that the young man could not help remarking it, and especially noting how Mr. Wolfe, in return for a fine bow from Mr. Batts's hat, scarcely touched his own with his forefinger. The tennis Captain walked away looking somewhat disconcerted, Harry remaining behind to talk with his friend of Westerham. Mr. Wolfe walked by him for a while, very erect, silent, and cold.

"I have not seen you these many days," says Harry.

"You have had other companions," remarks Mr. Wolfe, curtly.

"But I had rather be with you than any of them," cries the young man.

"Indeed I might be better company for you than some of them," says the other.

"Is it Captain Batts you mean?" asked Harry.

"He is no favourite of mine, I own; he bore a rascally reputation when he was in the army, and I doubt has not mended it since he was turned out. You certainly might find a better friend than Captain Batts. Pardon the freedom which I take in saying so," says Mr. Wolfe, grimly.

"Friend! he is no friend: he only teaches me to play tennis: he is hand-in-glove with my lord, and all the people of fashion here who play."

"I am not a man of fashion," says Mr. Wolfe.

"My dear Colonel, what is the matter? Have I angered you in any way? You speak almost as if I had, and I am not conscious of having done anything to forfeit your regard," said Mr. Warrington.

"I will be free with you, Mr. Warrington," said the Colonel, gravely, "and tell you with frankness that I don't like some of your friends!"

"Why, sure, they are men of the first rank and fashion in England," cries Harry, not choosing to be offended with his companion's bluntness.

"Exactly, they are men of too high rank and too great fashion for a hard-working poor soldier like me; and if you continue to live with such, believe me, you will find numbers of us humdrum people can't afford to keep such company. I am here, Mr. Warrington, paying my addresses to an honourable lady. I met you yesterday openly walking with a French ballet-dancer, and you took off your hat. I must frankly tell you, that I had rather you would not take off your hat when you go out in such company."

"Sir," said Mr. Warrington, growing very red, "do you mean that I am to forgo the honour of Colonel Wolfe's acquaintance altogether?"

"I certainly shall request you to do so when you are in company with that person," said Colonel Wolfe, angrily; but he used a word not to be written at present, though Shakespeare puts it in the mouth of Othello.

"Great heavens! what a shame it is to speak so of any woman!" cries Mr. Warrington. "How dare any man say that that poor creature is not honest?"

"You ought to know best, sir," says the other, looking at Harry with some surprise, "or the world belies you very much."

"What ought I to know best? I see a poor little French dancer who is come hither with her mother, and is ordered by the doctors to drink the waters. I know that a person of my rank in life does not ordinarily keep company with people of hers; but really, Colonel Wolfe, are you so squeamish? Have I not heard you say that you did not value birth, and that all honest people ought to be equal? Why should I not give this little unprotected woman my arm? there are scarce half a dozen people here who can speak a word of her language. I can talk a little French, and she is welcome to it; and if Colonel Wolfe does not choose to touch his hat to me, when I am walking with her, by George he may leave it alone," cried Harry, flushing up.

"You don't mean to say," says Mr. Wolfe, eyeing him, "that you don't know the woman's character?"

"Of course, sir, she is a dancer, and, I suppose, no better or worse than her neighbours. But I mean to say that, had she been a duchess, or your grandmother, I couldn't have respected her more."

"You don't mean to say that you did not win her at dice, from Lord March?"

"At what?"

"At dice, from Lord March. Everybody knows the story. Not a person at the Wells is ignorant of it. I heard it but now, in the company of that good old Mr. Richardson, and the ladies were saying that you would be a character for a colonial Lovelace."

"What on earth else have they said about me?" asked Harry Warrington; and such stories as he knew the Colonel told. The most alarming accounts of his own wickedness and profligacy were laid before him. He was a corrupter of virtue, an habitual drunkard and gamester, a notorious blasphemer and freethinker, a fitting companion for my Lord March, finally, and the company into whose society he had fallen. "I tell you these things," said Mr. Wolfe, "because it is fair that you should know what is said of you, and because I do heartily believe, from your manner of meeting the last charge brought against you, that you are innocent of most of the other counts. I feel, Mr. Warrington, that I, for one, have been doing you a wrong; and sincerely ask you to pardon me."

Of course, Harry was eager to accept his friend's apology, and they shook hands with sincere cordiality this time. In respect of most of the charges brought against him, Harry rebutted them easily enough: as for the play, he owned to it. He thought that a gentleman should not refuse a fair challenge from other gentlemen, if his means allowed him: and he never would play beyond his means. After winning considerably at first, he could afford to play large stakes, for he was playing with other people's money. Play, he thought, was fair,—it certainly was pleasant. Why, did not all England, except the Methodists, play? Had he not seen the best company at the Wells over the cards—his aunt amongst them?

Mr. Wolfe made no immediate comment upon Harry's opinion as to the persons who formed the best company at the Wells, but he frankly talked with the young man, whose own frankness had won him, and warned him that the life he was leading might be the pleasantest, but surely was not the most profitable of lives. "It can't be, sir," said the Colonel, "that a man is to pass his days at horse-racing and tennis, and his nights carousing or at cards. Sure, every man was made to do some work: and a gentleman, if he has none, must make some. Do you know the laws of your country, Mr. Warrington? Being a great proprietor, you will doubtless one day be a magistrate at home. Have you travelled over the country, and made yourself acquainted with its trades and manufactures? These are fit things for a gentleman to study, and may occupy him as well as a cock-fight or a cricket-match. Do you know anything of our profession? That, at least, you will allow, is a noble one; and, believe me, there is plenty in it to learn, and suited, I should think, to you. I speak of it rather than of books and the learned professions, because, as far as I can judge, your genius does not lie that way. But honour is the aim of life," cried Mr. Wolfe, "and every man can serve his country one way or the other. Be sure, sir, that idle bread is the most dangerous of all that is eaten; that cards and pleasure may be taken by way of pastime after work, but not instead of work, and all day. And do you know, Mr. Warrington, instead of being the Fortunate Youth, as all the world calls you, I think you are rather Warrington the Unlucky, for you are followed by daily idleness, daily flattery, daily temptation, and the Lord, I say, send you a good, deliverance out of your good fortune."

But Harry did not like to tell his aunt that afternoon why it was he looked so grave. He thought he would not drink, but there were some jolly fellows at the ordinary who passed the bottle round; and he meant not to play in the evening, but a fourth was wanted at his aunt's table, and how could he resist?

He was the old lady's partner several times during the night, and he had Somebody's own luck to be sure; and once more he saw the dawn, and feasted on chickens and champagne at sunrise.

CHAPTER XXIX. In which Harry continues to enjoy Otium sine Dignitate

Whilst there were card-players enough to meet her at her lodgings and the assembly-rooms, Madame de Bernstein remained pretty contentedly at the Wells, scolding her niece, and playing her rubber. At Harry's age almost all places are pleasant, where you can have lively company, fresh air, and your share of sport and diversion. Even all pleasure is pleasant at twenty. We go out to meet it with alacrity, speculate upon its coming, and when its visit is announced, count the days until it and we shall come together. How very gently and coolly we regard it towards the close of Life's long season! Madam, don't you recollect your first ball; and does not your memory stray towards that happy past, sometimes, as you sit ornamenting the wall whilst your daughters are dancing? I, for my part, can remember when I thought it was delightful to walk three miles and back in the country to dine with old Captain Jones. Fancy liking to walk three miles, now, to dine with Jones and drink his half-pay port! No doubt it was bought from the little country-town wine-merchant, and cost but a small sum; but 'twas offered with a kindly welcome, and youth gave it a flavour which no age of wine or man can impart to it nowadays. Viximus nuper. I am not disposed to look so severely upon young Harry's conduct and idleness, as his friend the stern Colonel of the Twentieth Regiment. O blessed idleness! Divine lazy nymph! Reach me a novel as I lie in my dressing-gown at three o'clock in the afternoon; compound a sherry-cobbler for me, and bring me a cigar! Dear slatternly, smiling Enchantress! They may assail thee with bad names—swear thy character away, and call thee the Mother of Evil; but, for all that, thou art the best company in the world!

My Lord of March went away to the North; and my Lord Chesterfield, finding the Tunbridge waters did no good to his deafness, returned to his solitude at Blackheath; but other gentlemen remained to sport and take their pleasure, and Mr. Warrington had quite enough of companions at his ordinary at the White Horse. He soon learned to order a French dinner as well as the best man of fashion out of St. James's; could talk to Monsieur Barbeau, in Monsieur B.'s native language, much more fluently than most other folks,— discovered a very elegant and decided taste in wines, and could distinguish between Clos Vougeot and Romande with remarkable skill. He was the young King of the Wells, of which the general frequenters were easygoing men of the world, who were by no means shocked at that reputation for gallantry and extravagance which Harry had got, and which had so frightened Mr. Wolfe.

Though our Virginian lived amongst the revellers, and swam and sported in the same waters with the loose fish, the boy had a natural shrewdness and honesty which kept him clear of the snares and baits which are commonly set for the unwary. He made very few foolish bets with the jolly idle fellows round about him, and the oldest hands found it difficult to take him in. He engaged in games outdoors and in, because he had a natural skill and aptitude for them, and was good to hold almost any match with any fair competitor. He was scrupulous to play only with those gentlemen whom he knew, and always to settle his own debts on the spot. He would have made but a very poor figure at a college examination; though he possessed prudence and fidelity, keen, shrewd perception, great generosity, and dauntless personal courage.

And he was not without occasions for showing of what stuff he was made. For instance, when that unhappy little Cattarina, who had brought him into so much trouble, carried her importunities beyond the mark at which Harry thought his generosity should stop, he withdrew from the advances of the Opera-House Siren with perfect coolness and skill, leaving her to exercise her blandishments upon some more easy victim. In vain the mermaid's hysterical mother waited upon Harry, and vowed that a cruel bailiff had seized all her daughter's goods for debt, and that her venerable father was at present languishing in a London gaol. Harry declared that between himself and the bailiff there could be no dealings, and that because he had had the good fortune to become known to Mademoiselle Cattarina, and to gratify her caprices by presenting her with various trinkets and knick-knacks for which she had a fancy, he was not bound to pay the past debts of her family, and must decline being bail for her papa in London, or settling her outstanding accounts at Tunbridge. The Cattarina's mother first called him a monster and an ingrate, and then asked him, with a veteran smirk, why he did not take pay for the services he had rendered to the young person? At first, Mr. Warrington could not understand what the nature of the payment might be: but when that matter was explained by the old woman, the honest lad rose up in horror, to think that a woman should traffic in her child's dishonour, told her that he came from a country where the very savages would recoil from such a bargain; and, having bowed the old lady ceremoniously to the door, ordered Gumbo to mark her well, and never admit her to his lodgings again. No doubt she retired breathing vengeance against the Iroquois: no Turk or Persian, she declared, would treat a lady so: and she and her daughter retreated to London as soon as their anxious landlord would let them. Then Harry had his perils of gaming, as well as his perils of gallantry. A man who plays at bowls, as the phrase is, must expect to meet with rubbers. After dinner at the ordinary, having declined to play piquet any further with Captain Batts, and being roughly asked his reason for refusing, Harry fairly told the Captain that he only played with gentlemen who paid, like himself: but expressed himself so ready to satisfy Mr. Batts, as soon as their outstanding little account was settled, that the Captain declared himself satisfied d'avance, and straightway left the Wells without paying Harry or any other creditor. Also he had an occasion to show his spirit by beating a chairman who was rude to old Miss Whiffler one evening as she was going to the assembly: and finding that the calumny regarding himself and that unlucky opera-dancer was repeated by Mr. Hector Buckler, one of the fiercest frequenters of the Wells, Mr. Warrington stepped up to Mr. Buckler in the pump-room, where the latter was regaling a number of water-drinkers with the very calumny, and publicly informed Mr. Buckler that the story was a falsehood, and that he should hold any person accountable to himself who henceforth uttered it. So that though our friend, being at Rome, certainly did as Rome did, yet he showed himself to be a valorous and worthy Roman; and, hurlant avec les loups, was acknowledged by Mr. Wolfe himself to be as brave as the best of the wolves.

If that officer had told Colonel Lambert the stories which had given the latter so much pain, we may be sure that when Mr. Wolfe found his young friend was innocent, he took the first opportunity to withdraw the odious charges against him. And there was joy among the Lamberts, in consequence of the lad's acquittal—something, doubtless, of that pleasure, which is felt by higher natures than ours, at the recovery of sinners. Never had the little family been so happy—no, not even when they got the news of Brother Tom winning his scholarship—as when Colonel Wolfe rode over with the account of the conversation which he had with Harry Warrington. "Hadst thou brought me a regiment, James, I think I should not have been better pleased," said Mr. Lambert. Mrs. Lambert called to her daughters who were in the garden, and kissed them both when they came in, and cried out the good news to them. Hetty jumped for joy, and Theo performed some uncommonly brilliant operations upon the harpsichord that night; and when Dr. Boyle came in for his backgammon, he could not, at first, account for the illumination in all their faces, until the three ladies, in a happy chorus, told him how right he had been in his sermon, and how dreadfully they had wronged that poor dear, good young Mr. Warrington.

"What shall we do, my dear?" says the Colonel to his wife. "The hay is in, the corn won't be cut for a fortnight,—the horses have nothing to do. Suppose we..." And here he leans over the table and whispers in her ear.

"My dearest Martin! The very thing!" cries Mrs. Lambert, taking her husband's hand and pressing it.

"What's the very thing, mother?" cries young Charley, who is home for his Bartlemytide holidays.

"The very thing is to go to supper. Come, Doctor! We will have a bottle of wine to-night, and drink repentance to all who think evil."

"Amen," says the Doctor; "with all my heart!" And with this the worthy family went to their supper.

CHAPTER XXX. Contains a Letter to Virginia

Having repaired one day to his accustomed dinner at the White Horse ordinary, Mr. Warrington was pleased to see amongst the faces round the table the jolly, good-looking countenance of Parson Sampson, who was regaling the company when Harry entered, with stories and bons-mots, which kept them in roars of laughter. Though he had not been in London for some months, the parson had the latest London news, or what passed for such with the folks at the ordinary: what was doing in the King's house at Kensington; and what in the Duke's in Pall Mall: how Mr. Byng was behaving in prison, and who came to him: what were the odds at Newmarket, and who was the last reigning toast in Covent Garden;—the jolly chaplain could give the company news upon all these points,—news that might not be very accurate indeed, but was as good as if it were for the country gentlemen who heard it. For suppose that my Lord Viscount Squanderfield was ruining himself for Mrs. Polly, and Sampson called her Mrs. Lucy? that it was Lady Jane who was in love with the actor, and not Lady Mary? that it was Harry Hilton, of the Horse Grenadiers, who had the quarrel with Chevalier Solingen, at Marybone Garden, and not Tommy Ruffler, of the Foot Guards? The names and dates did not matter much. Provided the stories were lively and wicked, their correctness was of no great importance; and Mr. Sampson laughed and chattered away amongst his country gentlemen, charmed them with his spirits and talk, and drank his share of one bottle after another, for which his delighted auditory persisted in calling. A hundred years ago, the Abbe Parson, the clergyman who frequented the theatre, the tavern, the racecourse, the world of fashion, was no uncommon character in English society: his voice might be heard the loudest in the hunting-field; he could sing the jolliest song at the Rose or the Bedford Head, after the play was over at Covent Garden, and could call a main as well as any at the gaming-table.

It may have been modesty, or it may have been claret, which caused his reverence's rosy face to redden deeper, but when he saw Mr. Warrington enter, he whispered "Maxima debetur" to the laughing country squire who sat next him in his drab coat and gold-laced red waistcoat, and rose up from his chair and ran, nay, stumbled forward, in his haste to greet the Virginian: "My dear sir, my very dear sir, my conqueror of spades, and clubs, and hearts, too, I am delighted to see your honour looking so fresh and well," cries the chaplain.

Harry returned the clergyman's greeting with great pleasure: he was glad to see Mr. Sampson; he could also justly compliment his reverence upon his cheerful looks and rosy gills.

The squire in the drab coat knew Mr. Warrington; he made a place beside himself; he called out to the parson to return to his seat on the other side, and to continue his story about Lord Ogle and the grocer's wife in———. Where he did not say, for his sentence was interrupted by a shout and an oath addressed to the parson for treading on his gouty toe.

The chaplain asked pardon, hurriedly turned round to Mr. Warrington, and informed him, and the rest of the company indeed, that my Lord Castlewood sent his affectionate remembrances to his cousin, and had given special orders to him (Mr. Sampson) to come to Tunbridge Wells and look after the young gentleman's morals; that my Lady Viscountess and my Lady Fanny were gone to Harrogate for the waters; that Mr. Will had won his money at Newmarket, and was going on a visit to my Lord Duke; that Molly the housemaid was crying her eyes out about Gumbo, Mr. Warrington's valet;—in fine, all the news of Castlewood and its neighbourhood. Mr. Warrington was beloved by all the country round, Mr. Sampson told the company, managing to introduce the names of some persons of the very highest rank into his discourse. "All Hampshire had heard of his successes at Tunbridge, successes of every kind," says Mr. Sampson, looking particularly arch; my lord hoped, their ladyships hoped, Harry would not be spoilt for his quiet Hampshire home.

The guests dropped off one by one, leaving the young Virginian to his bottle of wine and the chaplain.

"Though I have had plenty," says the jolly chaplain, "that is no reason why I should not have plenty more," and he drank toast after toast, and bumper after bumper, to the amusement of Harry, who always enjoyed his society.

By the time when Sampson had had his "plenty more," Harry, too, was become specially generous, warm-hearted, and friendly. A lodging—why should Mr. Sampson go to the expense of an inn, when there was a room at Harry's quarters? The chaplain's trunk was ordered thither, Gumbo was bidden to make Mr. Sampson comfortable—most comfortable; nothing would satisfy Mr. Warrington but that Sampson should go down to his stables and see his horses; he had several horses now; and when at the stable Sampson recognised his own horse which Harry had won from him; and the fond beast whinnied with pleasure, and rubbed his nose against his old master's coat; Harry rapped out a brisk energetic expression or two, and vowed by Jupiter that Sampson should have his old horse back again: he would give him to Sampson, that he would; a gift which the chaplain accepted by seizing Harry's hand, and blessing him,—by flinging his arms round the horse's neck, and weeping for joy there, weeping tears of Bordeaux and gratitude. Arm-in-arm the friends walked to Madame Bernstein's from the stable, of which they brought the odours into her ladyship's apartment. Their flushed cheeks and brightened eyes showed what their amusement had been. Many gentlemen's cheeks were in the habit of flushing in those days, and from the same cause.

Madame Bernstein received her nephew's chaplain kindly enough. The old lady relished Sampson's broad jokes and rattling talk from time to time, as she liked a highly-spiced dish or a new entree composed by her cook, upon its two or three first appearances. The only amusement of which she did not grow tired, she owned, was cards. "The cards don't cheat," she used to say. "A bad hand tells you the truth to your face: and there is nothing so flattering in the world as a good suite of trumps." And when she was in a good humour, and sitting down to her favourite pastime, she would laughingly bid her nephew's chaplain say grace before the meal. Honest Sampson did not at first care to take a hand at Tunbridge Wells. Her ladyship's play was too high for him, he would own, slapping his pocket with a comical piteous look, and its contents had already been handed over to the fortunate youth at Castlewood. Like most persons of her age, and indeed her sex, Madame Bernstein was not prodigal of money. I suppose it must have been from Harry Warrington, whose heart was overflowing with generosity as his purse with guineas, that the chaplain procured a small stock of ready coin, with which he was presently enabled to appear at the card-table.

Our young gentleman welcomed Mr. Sampson to his coin, as to all the rest of the good things which he had gathered about him. 'Twas surprising how quickly the young Virginian adapted himself to the habits of life of the folks amongst whom he lived. His suits were still black, but of the finest cut and quality. "With a star and ribbon, and his stocking down, and his hair over his shoulder, he would make a pretty Hamlet," said the gay old Duchess Queensberry. "And I make no doubt he has been the death of a dozen Ophelias already, here and amongst the Indians," she added, thinking not at all the worse of Harry for his supposed successes among the fair. Harry's lace and linen were as fine as his aunt could desire. He purchased fine shaving-plate of the toy-shop women, and a couple of magnificent brocade bedgowns, in which his worship lolled at ease, and sipped his chocolate of a morning. He had swords and walking-canes, and French watches with painted backs and diamond settings, and snuff boxes enamelled by artists of the same cunning nation. He had a levee of grooms, jockeys, tradesmen, daily waiting in his anteroom, and admitted one by one to him and Parson Sampson, over his chocolate, by Gumbo, the groom of the chambers. We have no account of the number of men whom Mr. Gumbo now had under him. Certain it is that no single negro could have taken care of all the fine things which Mr. Warrington now possessed, let alone the horses and the postchaise which his honour had bought. Also Harry instructed himself in the arts which became a gentleman in those days. A French fencing-master, and a dancing-master of the same nation, resided at Tunbridge during that season when Harry made his appearance: these men of science the young Virginian sedulously frequented, and acquired considerable skill and grace in the peaceful and warlike accomplishments which they taught. Ere many weeks were over he could handle the foils against his master or any frequenter of the fencing-school,— and, with a sigh, Lady Maria (who danced very elegantly herself) owned that there was no gentleman at court who could walk a minuet more gracefully than Mr. Warrington. As for riding, though Mr. Warrington took a few lessons on the great horse from a riding-master who came to Tunbridge, he declared that their own Virginian manner was well enough for him, and that he saw no one amongst the fine folks and the jockeys who could ride better than his friend Colonel George Washington of Mount Vernon.

The obsequious Sampson found himself in better quarters than he had enjoyed for ever so long a time. He knew a great deal of the world, and told a great deal more, and Harry was delighted with his stories, real or fancied. The man of twenty looks up to the man of thirty, admires the latter's old jokes, stale puns, and tarnished anecdotes, that are slopped with the wine of a hundred dinner-tables. Sampson's town and college pleasantries were all new and charming to the young Virginian. A hundred years ago,—no doubt there are no such people left in the world now,—there used to be grown men in London who loved to consort with fashionable youths entering life; to tickle their young fancies with merry stories; to act as Covent Garden Mentors and masters of ceremonies at the Round-house; to accompany lads to the gaming-table, and perhaps have an understanding with the punters; to drink lemonade to Master Hopeful's Burgundy, and to stagger into the streets with perfectly cool heads when my young lord reeled out to beat the watch. Of this, no doubt, extinct race, Mr. Sampson was a specimen: and a great comfort it is to think (to those who choose to believe the statement) that in Queen Victoria's reign there are no flatterers left, such as existed in the reign of her royal great-grandfather, no parasites pandering to the follies of young men; in fact, that all the toads have been eaten off the face of the island (except one or two that are found in stones, where they have lain perdus these hundred years), and the toad-eaters have perished for lack of nourishment.

With some sauces, as I read, the above-mentioned animals are said to be exceedingly fragrant, wholesome, and savoury eating. Indeed, no man could look more rosy and healthy, or flourish more cheerfully, than friend Sampson upon the diet. He became our young friend's confidential leader, and, from the following letter, which is preserved in the Warrington correspondence, it will be seen that Mr. Harry not only had dancing and fencing masters, but likewise a tutor, chaplain, and secretary:—

TO MRS. ESMOND WARRINGTON OF CASTLEWOOD AT HER HOUSE AT RICHMOND, VIRGINIA

Mrs. Bligh's Lodgings, Pantiles, Tunbridge Wells,

"August 25th, 1756.

"HONOURED MADAM—Your honoured letter of 20 June, per Mr. Trail of Bristol, has been forwarded to me duly, and I have to thank your goodness and kindness for the good advice which you are pleased to give me, as also for the remembrances of dear home, which I shall love never the worse for having been to the home of our ancestors in England.

"I writ you a letter by the last monthly packet, informing my honoured mother of the little accident I had on the road hither, and of the kind friends who I found and whom took me in. Since then I have been profiting of the fine weather and the good company here, and have made many friends among our nobility, whose acquaintance I am sure you will not be sorry that I should make. Among their lordships I may mention the famous Earl of Chesterfield, late Ambassador to Holland, and Viceroy of the Kingdom of Ireland; the Earl of March and Ruglen, who will be Duke of Queensberry at the death of his Grace; and her Grace the Duchess, a celebrated beauty of the Queen's time, when she remembers my grandpapa at Court. These and many more persons of the first fashion attend my aunt's assemblies, which are the most crowded at this crowded place. Also on my way hither I stayed at Westerham, at the house of an officer, Lieut.-Gen. Wolfe, who served with my grandfather and General Webb in the famous wars of the Duke of Marlborough. Mr. Wolfe has a son, Lieut.-Col. James Wolfe, engaged to be married to a beautiful lady now in this place, Miss Lowther of the North—and though but 30 years old he is looked up to as much as any officer in the whole army, and has served with honour under his Royal Highness the Duke wherever our arms have been employed.

"I thank my honoured mother for announcing to me that a quarter's allowance of 52l. 10s. will be paid me by Mr. Trail. I am in no present want of cash, and by practising a rigid economy, which will be necessary (as I do not disguise) for the maintenance of horses, Gumbo, and the equipage and apparel requisite for a young gentleman of good family, hope to be able to maintain my credit without unduly trespassing upon yours. The linnen and clothes which I brought with me will with due care last for some years—as you say. 'Tis not quite so fine as worn here by persons of fashion, and I may have to purchase a few very fine shirts for great days: but those I have are excellent for daily wear.

"I am thankful that I have been quite without occasion to use your excellent family pills. Gumbo hath taken them with great benefit, who grows fat and saucy upon English beef, ale, and air. He sends his humble duty to his mistress, and prays Mrs. Mountain to remember him to all his fellow-servants, especially Dinah and Lily, for whom he has bought posey-rings at Tunbridge Fair.

"Besides partaking of all the pleasures of the place, I hope my honoured mother will believe that I have not been unmindful of my education. I have had masters in fencing and dancing, and my Lord Castlewood's chaplain, the Reverend Mr. Sampson, having come hither to drink the waters, has been so good as to take a vacant room at my lodging. Mr. S. breakfasts with me, and we read together of a morning—he saying that I am not quite such a dunce as I used to appear at home. We have read in Mr. Rapin's History, Dr. Barrow's Sermons, and, for amusement, Shakspeare, Mr. Pope's Homer, and (in French) the translation of an Arabian Work of Tales, very diverting. Several men of learning have been staying here besides the persons of fashion; and amongst the former was Mr. Richardson, the author of the famous books which you and Mountain and my dearest brother used to love so. He was pleased when I told him that his works were in your closet in Virginia, and begged me to convey his respectful compliments to my lady-mother. Mr. R. is a short fat man, with little of the fire of genius visible in his eye or person.

"My aunt and my cousin, the Lady Maria, desire their affectionate compliments to you, and with best regards for Mountain, to whom I enclose a note, I am,—Honoured madam, your dutiful son, H. ESMOND WARRINGTON."

Note in Madam Esmond's Handwriting,

"From my son. Received October 15 at Richmond. Sent 16 jars preserved peaches, 224 lbs. best tobacco, 24 finest hams, per Royal William of Liverpool, 8 jars peaches, 12 hams for my nephew, the Rt. Honourable the Earl of Castlewood. 4 jars, 6 hams for the Baroness Bernstein, ditto ditto for Mrs. Lambert of Oakhurst, Surrey, and 1/2 cwt. tobacco. Packet of Infallible

Family Pills for Gumbo. My Papa's large silver-gilt shoe-buckles for H., and red silver-laced saddle-cloth."

II. (enclosed in No. I.)

"For Mrs. Mountain.

"What do you mien, you silly old Mountain, by sending an order for your poor old divadends dew at Xmas? I'd have you to know I don't want your 7l. 10, and have toar your order up into 1000 bitts. I've plenty of money. But I'm obleaged to you all same. A kiss to Fanny from—Your loving HARRY."

Note in Madam Esmond's Handwriting

"This note, which I desired M. to show to me, proves that she hath a good heart, and that she wished to show her gratitude to the family, by giving up her half-yearly divd. (on L500 3 per ct.) to my boy. Hence I reprimanded her very slightly for daring to send money to Mr. E. Warrington, unknown to his mother. Note to Mountain not so well spelt as letter to me.

"Mem. to write to Revd. Mr. Sampson desire to know what theolog. books he reads with H. Recommend Law, Baxter, Drelincourt.—Request H. to say his catechism to Mr. S., which he has never quite been able to master. By next ship peaches (3), tobacco 1/2 cwt. Hams for Mr. S."

The mother of the Virginians and her sons have long long since passed away. So how are we to account for the fact, that of a couple of letters sent under one enclosure and by one packet, one should be well spelt, and the other not entirely orthographical? Had Harry found some wonderful instructor, such as exists in the present lucky times, and who would improve his writing in six lessons? My view of the case, after deliberately examining the two notes, is this: No. 1, in which there appears a trifling grammatical slip ("the kind, friends who I found and whom took me in"), must have been re-written from a rough copy which had probably undergone the supervision of a tutor or friend. The more artless composition, No. 2, was not referred to the scholar who prepared No. 1 for the maternal eye, and to whose corrections of "who" and "whom" Mr. Warrington did not pay very close attention. Who knows how he may have been disturbed? A pretty milliner may have attracted Harry's attention out of window—a dancing bear with pipe and tabor may have passed along the common—a jockey come under his windows to show off a horse there? There are some days when any of us may be ungrammatical and spell ill. Finally, suppose Harry did not care to spell so elegantly for Mrs. Mountain as for his lady-mother, what affair is that of the present biographer, century, reader? And as for your objection that Mr. Warrington, in the above communication to his mother, showed some little hypocrisy and reticence in his dealings with that venerable person, I dare say, young folks, you in your time have written more than one prim letter to your papas and mammas in which not quite all the transactions of your lives were narrated, or if narrated, were exhibited in the most favourable light for yourselves—I dare say, old folks! you, in your time, were not altogether more candid. There must be a certain distance between me and my son Jacky. There must be a respectful, an amiable, a virtuous hypocrisy between us. I do not in the least wish that he should treat me as his equal, that he should contradict me, take my arm-chair, read the newspaper first at breakfast, ask unlimited friends to dine when I have a party of my own, and so forth. No; where there is not equality there must be hypocrisy. Continue to be blind to my faults; to hush still as mice when I fall asleep after dinner; to laugh at my old jokes; to admire my sayings; to be astonished at the impudence of those unbelieving reviewers; to be dear filial humbugs, O my children! In my castle I am king. Let all my royal household back before me. 'Tis not their natural way of walking, I know: but a decorous, becoming, and modest behaviour highly agreeable to me. Away from me they may do, nay, they do do, what they like. They may jump, skip, dance, trot, tumble over heads and heels, and kick about freely, when they are out of the presence of my majesty. Do not then, my dear young friends, be surprised at your mother and aunt when they cry out, "Oh, it was highly immoral and improper of Mr. Warrington to be writing home humdrum demure letters to his dear mamma, when he was playing all sorts of merry pranks!"—but drop a curtsey, and say, "Yes, dear grandmamma (or aunt, as may be), it was very wrong of him: and I suppose you never had your fun when you were young." Of course, she didn't! And the sun never shone, and the blossoms never budded, and the blood never danced, and the fiddles never sang, in her spring-time. Eh, Babet! mon lait de poule et mon bonnet de nuit! Ho, Betty! my gruel and my slippers! And go, ye frisky, merry little souls! and dance, and have your merry little supper of cakes and ale!

CHAPTER XXXI. The Bear and the Leader

Our candid readers know the real state of the case regarding Harry Warrington and that luckless Cattarina; but a number of the old ladies at Tunbridge Wells supposed the Virginian to be as dissipated as any young English nobleman of the highest quality, and Madame de Bernstein was especially incredulous about her nephew's innocence. It was the old lady's firm belief that Harry was leading not only a merry life, but a wicked one, and her wish was father to the thought that the lad might be no better than his neighbours. An old Roman herself, she liked her nephew to do as Rome did. All the scandal regarding Mr. Warrington's Lovelace adventures she eagerly and complacently accepted. We have seen how, on one or two occasions, he gave tea and music to the company at the Wells; and he was so gallant and amiable to the ladies (to ladies of a much better figure and character than the unfortunate Cattarina), that Madame Bernstein ceased to be disquieted regarding the silly love affair which had had a commencement at Castlewood, and relaxed in her vigilance over Lady Maria. Some folks—many old folks—are too selfish to interest themselves long about the affairs of their neighbours. The Baroness had her trumps to think of, her dinners, her twinges of rheumatism: and her suspicions regarding Maria and Harry, lately so lively, now dozed, and kept a careless, unobservant watch. She may have thought that the danger was over, or she may have ceased to care whether it existed or not, or that artful Maria, by her conduct, may have quite cajoled, soothed, and misguided the old Dragon, to whose charge she was given over. At Maria's age, nay, earlier indeed, maidens have learnt to be very sly, and at Madame Bernstein's time of life dragons are not so fierce and alert. They cannot turn so readily, some of their old teeth have dropped out, and their eyes require more sleep than they needed in days when they were more active, venomous, and dangerous. I, for my part, know a few female dragons, de par le monde, and, as I watch them and remember what they were, admire the softening influence of years upon these whilom destroyers of man- and woman-kind. Their scales are so soft that any knight with a moderate power of thrust can strike them: their claws, once strong enough to tear out a thousand eyes, only fall with a feeble pat that scarce raises the skin: their tongues, from their toothless old gums, dart a venom which is rather disagreeable than deadly. See them trailing their languid tails, and crawling home to their caverns at roosting-time! How weak are their powers of doing injury! their maleficence how feeble! How changed are they since the brisk days when their eyes shot wicked fire; their tongue spat poison; their breath blasted reputation; and they gobbled up a daily victim at least!

If the good folks at Oakhurst could not resist the testimony which was brought to them regarding Harry's ill-doings, why should Madame Bernstein, who in the course of her long days had had more experience of evil than all the Oakhurst family put together, be less credulous than they? Of course every single old woman of her ladyship's society believed every story that was told about Mr. Harry Warrington's dissipated habits, and was ready to believe as much more ill of him as you please. When the little dancer went back to London, as she did, it was because that heartless Harry deserted her. He deserted her for somebody else, whose name was confidently given,—whose name?—whose half-dozen names the society at Tunbridge Wells would whisper about; where there congregated people of all ranks and degrees, women of fashion, women of reputation, of demi-reputation, of virtue, of no virtue,—all mingling in the same rooms, dancing to the same fiddles, drinking out of the same glasses at the Wells, and alike in search of health, or society, or pleasure. A century ago, and our ancestors, the most free or the most straitlaced, met together at a score of such merry places as that where our present scene lies, and danced, and frisked, and gamed, and drank at Epsom, Bath, Tunbridge, Harrogate, as they do at Homburg and Baden now.

Harry's bad reputation, then, comforted his old aunt exceedingly, and eased her mind in respect to the boy's passion for Lady Maria. So easy was she in her mind, that when the chaplain said he came to escort her ladyship home, Madame Bernstein did not even care to part from her niece. She preferred rather to keep her under her eye, to talk to her about her wicked young cousin's wild extravagances, to whisper to her that boys would be boys, to confide to Maria her intention of getting a proper wife for Harry,—some one of a suitable age,—some one with a suitable fortune,—all which pleasantries poor Maria had to bear with as much fortitude as she could muster.

There lived, during the last century, a certain French duke and marquis, who distinguished himself in Europe, and America likewise, and has obliged posterity by leaving behind him a choice volume of memoirs, which the gentle reader is specially warned not to consult. Having performed the part of Don Juan in his own country, in ours, and in other parts of Europe, he has kindly noted down the names of many court-beauties who fell victims to his powers of fascination; and very pleasant reading no doubt it must be for the grandsons and descendants of the fashionable persons amongst whom our brilliant nobleman moved, to find the names of their ancestresses adorning M. le Duc's sprightly pages, and their frailties recorded by the candid writer who caused them.

In the course of the peregrinations of this nobleman, he visited North America, and, as had been his custom in Europe, proceeded straightway to fall in love. And curious it is to contrast the elegant refinements of European society, where, according to monseigneur, he had but to lay siege to a woman in order to vanquish her, with the simple lives and habits of the colonial folks, amongst whom this European enslaver of hearts did not, it appears, make a single conquest. Had he done so, he would as certainly have narrated his victories in Pennsylvania and New England, as he described his successes in this and his own country. Travellers in America have cried out quite loudly enough against the rudeness and barbarism of transatlantic manners; let the present writer give the humble testimony of his experience that the conversation of American gentlemen is generally modest, and, to the best of his belief, the lives of the women pure.

We have said that Mr. Harry Warrington brought his colonial modesty along with him to the old country; and though he could not help hearing the free talk of the persons amongst whom he lived, and who were men of pleasure and the world, he sat pretty silent himself in the midst of their rattle; never indulged in double entendre in his conversation with women; had no victories over the sex to boast of; and was shy and awkward when he heard such narrated by others.

This youthful modesty Mr. Sampson had remarked during his intercourse with the lad at Castlewood, where Mr. Warrington had more than once shown himself quite uneasy whilst cousin Will was telling some of his choice stories; and my lord had curtly rebuked his brother, bidding him keep his jokes for the usher's table at Kensington, and not give needless offence to their kinsman. Hence the exclamation of "Reverentia pueris," which the chaplain had addressed to his neighbour at the ordinary on Harry's first appearance there. Mr. Sampson, if he had not strength sufficient to do right himself, at least had grace enough not to offend innocent young gentlemen by his cynicism.

The chaplain was touched by Harry's gift of the horse; and felt a genuine friendliness towards the lad. "You see, sir," says he, "I am of the world, and must do as the rest of the world does. I have led a rough life, Mr. Warrington, and can't afford to be more particular than my neighbours. Video meliora, deteriora sequor, as we said at college. I have got a little sister, who is at boarding-school, not very far from here, and, as I keep a decent tongue in my head when I am talking with my little Patty, and expect others to do as much, sure I may try and do as much by you."

The chaplain was loud in his praises of Harry to his aunt, the old Baroness. She liked to hear him praised. She was as fond of him as she could be of anything; was pleased in his company, with his good looks, his manly courageous bearing, his blushes, which came so readily, his bright eyes, his deep youthful voice. His shrewdness and simplicity constantly amused her; she would have wearied of him long before, had he been clever, or learned, or witty, or other than he was. "We must find a good wife for him, Chaplain," she said to Mr. Sampson. "I have one or two in my eye, who, I think, will suit him. We must set him up here; he never will bear going back to his savages again, or to live with his little Methodist of a mother."

Now about this point Mr. Sampson, too, was personally anxious, and had also a wife in his eye for Harry. I suppose he must have had some conversations with his lord at Castlewood, whom we have heard expressing some intention of complimenting his chaplain with a good living or other provision, in event of his being able to carry out his lordship's wishes regarding a marriage for Lady Maria. If his good offices could help that anxious lady to a husband, Sampson was ready to employ them: and he now waited to see in what most effectual manner he could bring his influence to bear.

Sampson's society was most agreeable, and he and his young friend were intimate in the course of a few hours. The parson rejoiced in high spirits, good appetite, good humour; pretended to no sort of squeamishness, and indulged in no sanctified hypocritical conversation; nevertheless, he took care not to shock his young friend by any needless outbreaks of levity or immorality of talk, initiating his pupil, perhaps from policy, perhaps from compunction, only into the minor mysteries, as it were; and not telling him the secrets with which the unlucky adept himself was only too familiar. With Harry, Sampson was only a brisk, lively, jolly companion, ready for any drinking bout, or any sport, a cock-fight, a shooting-match, a game at cards, or a gallop across the common; but his conversation was decent, and he tried much more to amuse the young man, than to lead him astray. The chaplain was quite successful: he had immense animal spirits as well as natural wit, and aptitude as well as experience in that business of toad-eater which had been his calling and livelihood from his very earliest years,—ever since he first entered college as a servitor, and cast about to see by whose means he could make his fortune in life. That was but satire just now, when we said there were no toad-eaters left in the world. There are many men of Sampson's profession now, doubtless; nay, little boys at our public schools are sent thither at the earliest age, instructed by their parents, and put out apprentices to toad-eating. But the flattery is not so manifest as it used to be a hundred years since. Young men and old have hangers-on, and led captains, but they assume an appearance of equality, borrow money, or swallow their toads in private, and walk abroad arm-in-arm with the great man, and call him by his name without his title. In those good old times, when Harry Warrington first came to Europe, a gentleman's toad-eater pretended to no airs of equality at all; openly paid court to his patron, called him by that name to other folks, went on his errands for him,—any sort of errands which the patron might devise,—called him sir in speaking to him, stood up in his presence until bidden to sit down, and flattered him ex officio. Mr. Sampson did not take the least shame in speaking of Harry as his young patron,—as a young Virginian nobleman recommended to him by his other noble patron, the Earl of Castlewood. He was proud of appearing at Harry's side, and as his humble retainer, in public talked about him to the company, gave orders to Harry's tradesmen, from whom, let us hope, he received a percentage in return for his recommendations, performed all the functions of aide-de-camp—others, if our young gentleman demanded them from the obsequious divine, who had gaily discharged the duties of ami du prince to ever so many young men of fashion, since his own entrance into the world. It must be confessed that, since his arrival in Europe, Mr. Warrington had not been uniformly lucky in the friendships which he had made.

"What a reputation, sir, they have made for you in this place!" cries Mr. Sampson, coming back from the coffee-house to his patron. "Monsieur de Richelieu was nothing to you!"

"How do you mean, Monsieur de Richelieu?—Never was at Minorca in my life," says downright Harry, who had not heard of those victories at home, which made the French duke famous.

Mr. Sampson explained. The pretty widow Patcham who had just arrived was certainly desperate about Mr. Warrington: her way of going on at the rooms, the night before, proved that. As for Mrs. Hooper, that was a known case, and the Alderman had fetched his wife back to London for no other reason. It was the talk of the whole Wells.

"Who says so?" cries out Harry, indignantly. "I should like to meet the man who dares say so, and confound the villain!"

"I should not like to show him to you," says Mr. Sampson, laughing. "It might be the worse for him."

"It's a shame to speak with such levity about the character of ladies or of gentlemen either," continues Mr. Warrington, pacing up and down the room in a fume.

"So I told them," says the chaplain, wagging his head and looking very much moved and very grave, though, if the truth were known, it had never come into his mind at all to be angry at hearing charges of this nature against Harry.

"It's a shame, I say, to talk away the reputation of any man or woman as people do here. Do you know, in our country, a fellow's ears would not be safe; and a little before I left home, three brothers shot down a man, for having spoken ill of their sister."

"Serve the villain right!" cries Sampson.

"Already they have had that calumny about me set a-going here, Sampson,—about me and the poor little French dancing-girl."

"I have heard," says Mr. Sampson, shaking powder out of his wig.

"Wicked; wasn't it?"

"Abominable."

"They said the very same thing about my Lord March. Isn't it shameful?"

"Indeed it is," says Mr. Sampson, preserving a face of wonderful gravity.

"I don't know what I should do if these stories were to come to my mother's ears. It would break her heart, I do believe it would. Why, only a few days before you came, a military friend of mine, Mr. Wolfe, told me how the most horrible lies were circulated about me. Good heavens! What do they think a gentleman of my name and country can be capable of—I a seducer of women? They might as well say I was a horse-stealer or a housebreaker. I vow if I hear any man say so, I'll have his ears!"

"I have read, sir, that the Grand Seignior of Turkey has bushels of ears sometimes sent in to him," says Mr. Sampson, laughing. "If you took all those that had heard scandal against you or others, what basketsful you would fill!"

"And so I would, Sampson, as soon as look at 'em:—any fellow's who said a word against a lady or a gentleman of honour!" cries the Virginian.

"If you'll go down to the Well, you'll find a harvest of 'em. I just came from there. It was the high tide of Scandal. Detraction was at its height. And you may see the nymphas discentes and the aures satyrorum acutas," cries the chaplain, with a shrug of his shoulders.

"That may be as you say, Sampson," Mr. Warrington replies, "but if ever I hear any man speak against my character I'll punish him. Mark that."

"I shall be very sorry for his sake, that I should; for you'll mark him in a way he won't like, sir; and I know you are a man of your word."

"You may be sure of that, Sampson. And now shall we go to dinner, and afterwards to my Lady Trumpington's tea?"

"You know, sir, I can't resist a card or a bottle," says Mr. Sampson. "Let us have the last first and then the first shall come last." And with this the two gentlemen went off to their accustomed place of refection.

That was an age in which wine-bibbing was more common than in our politer time; and, especially since the arrival of General Braddock's army in his native country, our young Virginian had acquired rather a liking for the filling of bumpers and the calling of toasts; having heard that it was a point of honour among the officers never to decline a toast or a challenge. So Harry and his chaplain drank their claret in peace and plenty, naming, as the simple custom was, some favourite lady with each glass.

The chaplain had reasons of his own for desiring to know how far the affair between Harry and my Lady Maria had gone; whether it was advancing, or whether it was ended; and he and his young friend were just warm enough with the claret to be able to talk with that great eloquence, that candour, that admirable friendliness, which good wine taken in rather injudicious quantity inspires. O kindly harvests of the Aquitanian grape! O sunny banks of

Garonne! O friendly caves of Gledstane and Morol, where the dusky flasks lie recondite! May we not say a word of thanks for all the pleasure we owe you? Are the Temperance men to be allowed to shout in the public places? are the Vegetarians to bellow "Cabbage for ever?" and may we modest Enophilists not sing the praises of our favourite plant? After the drinking of good Bordeaux wine, there is a point (I do not say a pint) at which men arrive, when all the generous faculties of the soul are awakened and in full vigour; when the wit brightens and breaks out in sudden flashes; when the intellects are keenest; when the pent-up words and confined thoughts get a night-rule, and rush abroad and disport themselves; when the kindliest affection, come out and shake hands with mankind, and the timid Truth jumps up naked out of his well and proclaims himself to all the world. How, by the kind influence of the wine-cup, we succour the poor and humble! How bravely we rush to the rescue of the oppressed! I say, in the face of all the pumps which ever spouted, that there is a moment in a bout of good wine at which, if a man could but remain, wit, wisdom, courage, generosity, eloquence, happiness were his; but the moment passes, and that other glass somehow spoils the state of beatitude. There is a headache in the morning; we are not going into Parliament for our native town; we are not going to shoot those French officers who have been speaking disrespectfully of our country; and poor Jeremy Diddler calls about eleven o'clock for another half-sovereign, and we are unwell in bed, and can't see him, and send him empty away.

Well, then, as they sate over their generous cups, the company having departed, and the bottle of claret being brought in by Monsieur Barbeau, the chaplain found himself in an eloquent state, with a strong desire for inculcating sublime moral precepts whilst Harry was moved by an extreme longing to explain his whole private history, and to impart all his present feelings to his new friend. Mark that fact. Why must a man say everything that comes uppermost in his noble mind, because, forsooth, he has swallowed a half-pint more wine than he ordinarily drinks? Suppose I had committed a murder (of course I allow the sherry, and champagne at dinner), should I announce that homicide somewhere about the third bottle (in a small party of men) of claret at dessert? Of course: and hence the fidelity to water-gruel announced a few pages back.

"I am glad to hear what your conduct has really been with regard to the Cattarina, Mr. Warrington; I am glad from my soul," says the impetuous chaplain. "The wine is with you. You have shown that you can bear down calumny, and resist temptation. Ah! my dear sir, men are not all so fortunate. What famous good wine this is!" and he sucks up a glass with "A toast from you, my dear sir, if you please?"

"I give you 'Miss Fanny Mountain, of Virginia,'" says Mr. Warrington, filling a bumper as his thoughts fly straightway, ever so many thousand miles, to home.

"One of your American conquests, I suppose?" says the chaplain.

"Nay, she is but ten years old, and I have never made any conquests at all in

Virginia, Mr. Sampson," says the young gentleman.

"You are like a true gentleman, and don't kiss and tell, sir."

"I neither kiss nor tell. It isn't the custom of our country, Sampson, to ruin girls, or frequent the society of low women. We Virginian gentlemen honour women: we don't wish to bring them to shame," cries the young toper, looking very proud and handsome. "The young lady whose name I mentioned hath lived in our family since her infancy, and I would shoot the man who did her a wrong;—by Heaven, I would!"

"Your sentiments do you honour! Let me shake hands with you! I will shake hands with you, Mr. Warrington," cried the enthusiastic Sampson. "And let me tell you 'tis the grasp of honest friendship offered you, and not merely the poor retainer paying court to the wealthy patron. No! with such liquor as this, all men are equal;—faith, all men are rich, whilst it lasts! and Tom Sampson is as wealthy with his bottle as your honour with all the acres of your principality!"

"Let us have another bottle of riches," says Harry, with a laugh. "Encore du cachet jaune, mon bon Monsieur Barbeau!" and exit Monsieur Barbeau to the caves below.

"Another bottle of riches! Capital, capital! How beautifully you speak French, Mr. Harry!"

"I do speak it well," says Harry. "At least, when I speak, Monsieur Barbeau understands me well enough."

"You do everything well, I think. You succeed in whatever you try. That is why they have fancied here you have won the hearts of so many women, sir."

"There you go again about the women! I tell you I don't like these stories about women. Confound me, Sampson, why is a gentleman's character to be blackened so?"

"Well, at any rate, there is one, unless my eyes deceive me very much indeed, sir!" cries the chaplain.

"Whom do you mean?" asked Harry, flushing very red.

"Nay, I name no names. It isn't for a poor chaplain to meddle with his betters' doings, or to know their thoughts," says Mr. Sampson.

"Thoughts! what thoughts, Sampson?"

"I fancied I saw, on the part of a certain lovely and respected lady at Castlewood, a preference exhibited. I fancied, on the side of a certain distinguished young gentleman, a strong liking manifested itself: but I may have been wrong, and ask pardon."

"Oh, Sampson, Sampson!" broke out the young man. "I tell you I am miserable. I tell you I have been longing for some one to confide in, or ask advice of. You do know, then, that there has been something going on—something between me and—help Mr. Sampson, Monsieur Barbeau—and—and some one else?"

"I have watched it this month past," says the chaplain.

"Confound me, sir, do you mean you have been a spy on me?" says the other hotly.

"A spy! You made little disguise of the matter, Mr. Warrington, and her ladyship wasn't a much better hand at deceiving. You were always together. In the shrubberies, in the walks, in the village, in the galleries of the house,—you always found a pretext for being together, and plenty of eyes besides mine watched you."

"Gracious powers! What did you see, Sampson?" cries the lad.

"Nay, sir, 'tis forbidden to kiss and tell. I say so again," says the chaplain.

The young man turned very red. "Oh, Sampson!" he cried, "can I—can I confide in you?"

"Dearest sir—dear generous youth—you know I would shed my heart's blood for you!" exclaimed the chaplain, squeezing his patron's hand, and turning a brilliant pair of eyes ceilingwards.

"Oh, Sampson! I tell you I am miserable. With all this play and wine, whilst I have been here, I tell you I have been trying to drive away care. I own to you that when we were at Castlewood there were things passed between a certain lady and me."

The parson gave a slight whistle over his glass of Bordeaux.

"And they've made me wretched, those things have. I mean, you see, that if a gentleman has given his word, why, it's his word, and he must stand by it, you know. I mean that I thought I loved her,—and so I do very much, and she's a most dear, kind, darling, affectionate creature, and very handsome, too, —quite beautiful; but then, you know, our ages, Sampson! Think of our ages, Sampson! She's as old as my mother!"

"Who would never forgive you."

"I don't intend to let anybody meddle in my affairs, not Madam Esmond nor anybody else," cries Harry: "but you see, Sampson, she is old—and, oh, hang it! Why did Aunt Bernstein tell me———?"

"Tell you what?"

"Something I can't divulge to anybody, something that tortures me!"

"Not about the—the———" the chaplain paused: he was going to say about her ladyship's little affair with the French dancing-master; about other little anecdotes affecting her character. But he had not drunk wine enough to be quite candid, or too much, and was past the real moment of virtue.

"Yes, yes, every one of 'em false—every one of 'em!" shrieks out Harry.

"Great powers, what do you mean?" asks his friend.

"These, sir, these!" says Harry, beating a tattoo on his own white teeth. "I didn't know it when I asked her. I swear I didn't know it. Oh, it's horrible—it's horrible! and it has caused me nights of agony, Sampson. My dear old grandfather had a set a Frenchman at Charleston made them for him, and we used to look at 'em grinning in a tumbler, and when they were out, his jaws used to fall in—I never thought she had 'em."

"Had what, sir?" again asked the chaplain.

"Confound it, sir, don't you see I mean teeth?" says Harry, rapping the table.

"Nay, only two."

"And how the devil do you know, sir?" asks the young man, fiercely.

"I—I had it from her maid. She had two teeth knocked out by a stone which cut her lip a little, and they have been replaced."

"Oh, Sampson, do you mean to say they ain't all sham ones?" cries the boy.

"But two, sir, at least so Peggy told me, and she would just as soon have blabbed about the whole two-and-thirty—the rest are as sound as yours, which are beautiful."

"And her hair, Sampson, is that all right, too?" asks the young gentleman.

"'Tis lovely—I have seen that. I can take my oath to that. Her ladyship can sit upon it; and her figure is very fine; and her skin is as white as snow; and her heart is the kindest that ever was; and I know, that is I feel sure, it is very tender about you, Mr. Warrington."

"Oh, Sampson! Heaven, Heaven bless you! What a weight you've taken off my mind with those—those—never mind them! Oh, Sam! How happy—that is, no, no—ob, how miserable I am! She's as old as Madam Esmond—by George she is—she's as old as my mother. You wouldn't have a fellow marry a woman as old as his mother? It's too bad: by George it is. It's too bad." And here, I am sorry to say, Harry Esmond Warrington, Esquire, of Castlewood, in Virginia, began to cry. The delectable point, you see, must have been passed several glasses ago.

"You don't want to marry her, then?" asks the chaplain.

"What's that to you, sir? I've promised her, and an Esmond—a Virginia Esmond mind that—Mr. What's-your-name—Sampson—has but his word!" The sentiment was noble, but delivered by Harry with rather a doubtful articulation.

"Mind you, I said a Virginia Esmond," continued poor Harry, lifting up his finger. "I don't mean the younger branch here. I don't mean Will, who robbed me about the horse, and whose bones I'll break. I give you Lady Maria—Heaven bless her, and Heaven bless you, Sampson, and you deserve to be a bishop, old boy!"

"There are letters between you, I suppose?" says Sampson.

"Letters! Dammy, she's always writing me letters!—never lets me into a window but she sticks one in my cuff. Letters! that is a good idea! Look here! Here's letters!" And he threw down a pocket-book containing a heap of papers of the poor lady's composition.

"Those are letters, indeed. What a post-bag!" says the chaplain.

"But any man who touches them—dies—dies on the spot!" shrieks Harry, starting from his seat, and reeling towards his sword; which he draws, and then stamps with his foot, and says, "Ha! ha!" and then lunges at M. Barbeau, who skips away from the lunge behind the chaplain, who looks rather alarmed. I know we could have had a much more exciting picture than either of those we present of Harry this month, and the lad, with his hair dishevelled, raging about the room flamberge au vent, and pinking the affrighted innkeeper and chaplain, would have afforded a good subject for the pencil. But oh, to think of him stumbling over a stool, and prostrated by an enemy who has stole away his brains! Come, Gumbo! and help your master to bed!

CHAPTER XXXII. In which a Family Coach is ordered

Our pleasing duty now is to divulge the secret which Mr. Lambert whispered in his wife's ear at the close of the antepenultimate chapter, and the publication of which caused such great pleasure to the whole of the Oakhurst family. As the hay was in, the corn not ready for cutting, and by consequence the farm horses disengaged, why, asked Colonel Lambert, should they not be put into the coach, and should we not all pay a visit to Tunbridge Wells, taking friend Wolfe at Westerham on our way?

Mamma embraced this proposal, and I dare say the honest gentleman who made it. All the children jumped for joy. The girls went off straightway to get together their best calamancoes, paduasoys, falbalas, furbelows, capes, cardinals, sacks, negligees, solitaires, caps, ribbons, mantuas, clocked stockings, and high-heeled shoes, and I know not what articles of toilet. Mamma's best robes were taken from the presses, whence they only issued on rare, solemn occasions, retiring immediately afterwards to lavender and seclusion; the brave Colonel produced his laced hat and waistcoat and silver-hilted hanger; Charley rejoiced in a rasee holiday suit of his father's, in which the Colonel had been married, and which Mrs. Lambert cut up, not without a pang. Ball and Dumpling had their tails and manes tied with ribbon, and Chump, the old white cart-horse, went as unicorn leader, to help the carriage-horses up the first hilly five miles of the road from Oakhurst to Westerham. The carriage was an ancient vehicle, and was believed to have served in the procession which had brought George I. from Greenwich to London, on his first arrival to assume the sovereignty of these realms. It had belonged to Mr. Lambert's father, and the family had been in the habit of regarding it, ever since they could remember anything, as one of the most splendid coaches in the three kingdoms. Brian, coachman, and—must it also be owned?—ploughman, of the Oakhurst family, had a place on the box, with Mr. Charley by his side. The precious clothes were packed in imperials on the roof. The Colonel's pistols were put in the pockets of the carriage, and the blunderbuss hung behind the box, in reach of Brian, who was an old soldier. No highwayman, however, molested the convoy; not even an innkeeper levied contributions on Colonel Lambert, who, with a slender purse and a large family, was not to be plundered by those or any other depredators on the king's highway; and a reasonable cheap modest lodging had been engaged for them by young Colonel Wolfe, at the house where he was in the habit of putting up, and whither he himself accompanied them on horseback.

It happened that these lodgings were opposite Madame Bernstein's; and as the Oakhurst family reached their quarters on a Saturday evening, they could see chair after chair discharging powdered beaux and patched and brocaded beauties at the Baroness's door, who was holding one of her many card-parties. The sun was not yet down (for our ancestors began their dissipations at early hours, and were at meat, drink, or cards, any time after three o'clock in the afternoon until any time in the night or morning), and the young country ladies and their mother from their window could see the various personages as they passed into the Bernstein rout. Colonel Wolfe told the ladies who most of the characters were. 'Twas almost as delightful as going to the party themselves, Hetty and Theo thought, for they not only could see the guests arriving, but look into the Baroness's open casements and watch many of them there. Of a few of the personages we have before had a glimpse. When the Duchess of Queensberry passed, and Mr. Wolfe explained who she was, Martin Lambert was ready with a score of lines about "Kitty, beautiful and young," from his favourite Mat Prior.

"Think that that old lady was once like you, girls!" cries the Colonel.

"Like us, papa? Well, certainly we never set up for being beauties!" says Miss Hetty, tossing up her little head.

"Yes, like you, you little baggage; like you at this moment, who want to go to that drum yonder:—

    'Inflamed with rage at sad restraint
      Which wise mamma ordained,
    And sorely vexed to play the saint
      Whilst wit and beauty reigned.'"

"We were never invited, papa; and I am sure if there's no beauty more worth seeing than that, the wit can't be much worth the hearing," again says the satirist of the family.

"Oh, but he's a rare poet, Mat Prior!" continues the Colonel; "though, mind you, girls, you'll skip over all the poems I have marked with a cross. A rare poet! and to think you should see one of his heroines! 'Fondness prevailed, mamma gave way' (she always will, Mrs. Lambert!)—

    'Fondness prevailed, mamma gave way,
      Kitty at heart's desire
    Obtained the chariot for a day,
      And set the world on fire!'"

"I am sure it must have been very inflammable," says mamma.

"So it was, my dear, twenty years ago, much more inflammable than it is now," remarks the Colonel.

"Nonsense, Mr. Lambert," is mamma's answer.

"Look, look!" cries Hetty, running forward and pointing to the little square, and the covered gallery, where was the door leading to Madame Bernstein's apartments, and round which stood a crowd of street urchins, idlers, and yokels, watching the company.

"It's Harry Warrington!" exclaims Theo, waving a handkerchief to the young Virginian: but Warrington did not see Miss Lambert. The Virginian was walking arm-in-arm with a portly clergyman in a crisp rustling silk gown, and the two went into Madame de Bernstein's door.

"I heard him preach a most admirable sermon here last Sunday," says Mr.

Wolfe; "a little theatrical, but most striking and eloquent."

"You seem to be here most Sundays, James," says Mrs. Lambert.

"And Monday, and soon till Saturday," adds the Colonel. "See, Harry has beautified himself already, hath his hair in buckle, and I have no doubt is going to the drum too."

"I had rather sit quiet generally of a Saturday evening," says sober Mr. Wolfe; "at any rate, away from card-playing and scandal; but I own, dear Mrs. Lambert, I am under orders. Shall I go across the way and send Mr. Warrington to you?"

"No, let him have his sport. We shall see him to-morrow. He won't care to be disturbed amidst his fine folks by us country-people," said meek Mrs. Lambert.

"I am glad he is with a clergyman who preaches so well," says Theo, softly; and her eyes seemed to say, You see, good people, he is not so bad as you thought him, and as I, for my part, never believed him to be. "The clergyman has a very kind, handsome face."

"Here comes a greater clergyman," cries Mr. Wolfe. "It is my Lord of Salisbury, with his blue ribbon, and a chaplain behind him."

"And whom a mercy's name have we here?" breaks in Mrs. Lambert, as a sedan-chair, covered with gilding, topped with no less than five earl's coronets, carried by bearers in richly laced clothes, and preceded by three footmen in the same splendid livery, now came up to Madame de Bernstein's door. The Bishop, who had been about to enter, stopped, and ran back with the most respectful bows and curtseys to the sedan-chair, giving his hand to the lady who stepped thence.

"Who on earth is this?" asks Mrs. Lambert.

"Sprechen sie Deutsch? Ja, meinherr. Nichts verstand," says the waggish Colonel.

"Pooh, Martin."

"Well, if you can't understand High Dutch, my love, how can I help it? Your education was neglected at school. Can you understand heraldry?—I know you can."

"I make." cries Charley, reciting the shield, "three merions on a field or, with an earl's coronet."

"A countess's coronet, my son. The Countess of Yarmouth, my son."

"And pray who is she?"

"It hath ever been the custom of our sovereigns to advance persons of distinction to honour," continues the Colonel, gravely, "and this eminent lady hath been so promoted by our gracious monarch, to the rank of Countess of this kingdom."

"But why, papa?" asked the daughters together.

"Never mind, girls!" said mamma.

But that incorrigible Colonel would go on.

"Y, my children, is one of the last and the most awkward letters of the whole alphabet. When I tell you stories, you are always saying Why. Why should my Lord Bishop be cringing to that lady? Look at him rubbing his fat hands together, and smiling into her face! It's not a handsome face any longer. It is all painted red and white like Scaramouch's in the pantomime. See, there comes another blue-riband, as I live. My Lord Bamborough. The descendant of the Hotspurs. The proudest man in England. He stops, he bows, he smiles; he is hat in hand, too. See, she taps him with her fan. Get away, you crowd of little blackguard boys, and don't tread on the robe of the lady whom the King delights to honour."

"But why does the King honour her?" ask the girls once more.

"There goes that odious last letter but one! Did you ever hear of her Grace the Duchess of Kendal? No. Of the Duchess of Portsmouth? Non plus. Of the Duchess of La Valliore? Of Fair Rosamond, then?"

"Hush, papa! There is no need to bring blushes on the cheeks of my dear ones, Martin Lambert!" said the mother, putting her finger to her husband's lips.

"'Tis not I; it is their sacred Majesties who are the cause of the shame," cries the son of the old republican. "Think of the bishops of the Church and the proudest nobility of the world cringing and bowing before that painted High Dutch Jezebel. Oh, it's a shame! a shame!"

"Confusion!" here broke out Colonel Wolfe, and making a dash at his hat, ran from the room. He had seen the young lady whom he admired and her guardian walking across the Pantiles on foot to the Baroness's party, and they came up whilst the Countess of Yarmouth-Walmoden was engaged in conversation with the two lords spiritual and temporal, and these two made the lowest reverences and bows to the Countess, and waited until she had passed in at the door on the Bishop's arm.

Theo turned away from the window with a sad, almost awestricken face. Hetty still remained there, looking from it with indignation in her eyes, and a little red spot on each cheek.

"A penny for little Hetty's thoughts," says mamma, coming to the window to lead the child away.

"I am thinking what I should do if I saw papa bowing to that woman," says Hetty.

Tea and a hissing kettle here made their appearance, and the family sate down to partake of their evening meal,—leaving, however, Miss Hetty, from her place, command of the window, which she begged her brother not to close. That young gentleman had been down amongst the crowd to inspect the armorial bearings of the Countess's and other sedans, no doubt, and also to invest sixpence in a cheese-cake, by mamma's order and his own desire, and he returned presently with this delicacy wrapped up in a paper.

"Look, mother," he comes back and says, "do you see that big man in brown beating all the pillars with a stick? That is the learned Mr. Johnson. He comes to the Friars sometimes to see our master. He was sitting with some friends just now at the tea-table before Mrs. Brown's tart-shop. They have tea there, twopence a cup; I heard Mr. Johnson say he had had seventeen cups—that makes two-and-tenpence—what a sight of money for tea!"

"What would you have, Charley?" asks Theo.

"I think I would have cheese-cakes," says Charley, sighing, as his teeth closed on a large slice, "and the gentleman whom Mr. Johnson was with," continues Charley, with his mouth quite full, "was Mr. Richardson who wrote——"

"Clarissa!" cry all the women in a breath, and run to the window to see their favourite writer. By this time the sun was sunk, the stars were twinkling overhead, and the footman came and lighted the candles in the Baroness's room opposite our spies.

Theo and her mother were standing together looking from their place of observation. There was a small illumination at Mrs. Brown's tart- and tea-shop, by which our friends could see one lady getting Mr. Richardson's hat and stick, and another tying a shawl round his neck, after which he walked home.

"Oh dear me! he does not look like Grandison!" cries Theo.

"I rather think I wish we had not seen him, my dear," says mamma, who has been described as a most sentimental woman and eager novel-reader; and here again they were interrupted by Miss Hetty, who cried:

"Never mind that little fat man, but look yonder, mamma."

And they looked yonder. And they saw, in the first place, Mr. Warrington undergoing the honour of a presentation to the Countess of Yarmouth, who was still followed by the obsequious peer and prelate with blue ribands. And now the Countess graciously sate down to a card-table, the Bishop and the Earl and a fourth person being her partners. And now Mr. Warrington came into the embrasure of the window with a lady whom they recognised as the lady whom they had seen for a few minutes at Oakhurst.

"How much finer he is!" remarks mamma.

"How he is improved in his looks! What has he done to himself?" asks Theo.

"Look at his grand lace frills and rules! My dear, he has not got on our shirts any more," cries the matron.

"What are you talking about, girls?" asks papa, reclining on his sofa, where, perhaps, he was dozing after the fashion of honest house-fathers.

The girls said how Harry Warrington was in the window, talking with his cousin Lady Maria Esmond.

"Come away!" cries papa. "You have no right to be spying the young fellow. Down with the curtains, I say!"

And down the curtains went, so that the girls saw no more of Madame Bernstein's guests or doings for that night.

I pray you be not angry at my remarking, if only by way of contrast between these two opposite houses, that while Madame Bernstein and her guests—bishop, dignitaries, noblemen, and what not—were gambling or talking scandal, or devouring champagne and chickens (which I hold to be venial sin), or doing honour to her ladyship the king's favourite, the Countess of Yarmouth-Walmoden, our country friends in their lodgings knelt round their table, whither Mr. Brian the coachman came as silently as his creaking shoes would let him, whilst Mr. Lambert, standing up, read in a low voice, a prayer that Heaven would lighten their darkness and defend them from the perils of that night, and a supplication that it would grant the request of those two or three gathered together.

Our young folks were up betimes on Sunday morning, and arrayed themselves in those smart new dresses which were to fascinate the Tunbridge folks, and, with the escort of brother Charley, paced the little town, and the quaint Pantiles, and the pretty common, long ere the company was at breakfast, or the bells had rung to church. It was Hester who found out where Harry Warrington's lodging must be, by remarking Mr. Gumbo in an undress, with his lovely hair in curl-papers, drawing a pair of red curtains aside, and opening a window-sash, whence he thrust his head and inhaled the sweet morning breeze. Mr. Gumbo did not happen to see the young people from Oakhurst, though they beheld him clearly enough. He leaned gracefully from the window; he waved a large feather brush, with which he condescended to dust the furniture of the apartment within; he affably engaged in conversation with a cherry-cheeked milkmaid, who was lingering under the casement, and kissed his lily hand to her. Gumbo's hand sparkled with rings, and his person was decorated with a profusion of jewellery—gifts, no doubt, of the fair who appreciated the young African. Once or twice more before breakfast-time the girls passed near that window. It remained opened, but the room behind it was blank. No face of Harry Warrington appeared there. Neither spoke to the other of the subject on which both were brooding. Hetty was a little provoked with Charley, who was clamorous about breakfast, and told him he was always thinking of eating. In reply to her sarcastic inquiry, he artlessly owned he should like another cheese-cake, and good-natured Theo, laughing, said she had a sixpence, and if the cake-shop were open of a Sunday morning Charley should have one. The cake-shop was open: and Theo took out her little purse, netted by her dearest friend at school, and containing her pocket-piece, her grandmother's guinea, her slender little store of shillings—nay, some copper money at one end; and she treated Charley to the meal which he loved.

A great deal of fine company was at church. There was that funny old Duchess, and old Madame Bernstein, with Lady Maria at her side; and Mr. Wolfe, of course, by the side of Miss Lowther, and singing with her out of the same psalm-book; and Mr. Richardson with a bevy of ladies. One of them is Miss Fielding, papa tells them after church, Harry Fielding's sister. "Oh, girls, what good company he was! And his books are worth a dozen of your milksop Pamelas and Clarissas, Mrs. Lambert: but what woman ever loved true humour? And there was Mr. Johnson sitting amongst the charity children. Did you see how he turned round to the altar at the Belief, and upset two or three of the scared little urchins in leather breeches? And what a famous sermon Harry's parson gave, didn't he? A sermon about scandal. How, he touched up some of the old harridans who were seated round! Why wasn't Mr. Warrington at church? It was a shame he wasn't at church."

"I really did not remark whether he was there or not," says Miss Hetty, tossing her head up.

But Theo, who was all truth, said, "Yes, I thought of him, and was sorry he was not there; and so did you think of him, Hetty."

"I did no such thing, miss," persists Hetty.

"Then why did you whisper to me it was Harry's clergyman who preached?"

"To think of Mr. Warrington's clergyman is not to think of Mr. Warrington. It was a most excellent sermon, certainly, and the children sang most dreadfully out of tune. And there is Lady Maria at the window opposite, smelling at the roses; and that is Mr. Wolfe's step, I know his great military tramp. Right left—right left! How do you do, Colonel Wolfe?"

"Why do you look so glum, James?" asks Colonel Lambert, good-naturedly. "Has the charmer been scolding thee, or is thy conscience pricked by the sermon. Mr. Sampson, isn't the parson's name? A famous preacher, on my word!"

"A pretty preacher, and a pretty practitioner!" says Mr. Wolfe, with a shrug of his shoulders.

"Why, I thought the discourse did not last ten minutes, and madam did not sleep one single wink during the sermon, didst thou, Molly?"

"Did you see when the fellow came into church?" asked the indignant Colonel Wolfe. "He came in at the open door of the common, just in time, and as the psalm was over."

"Well, he had been reading the service probably to some sick person; there are many here," remarks Mrs. Lambert.

"Reading the service! Oh, my good Mrs. Lambert! Do you know where I found him? I went to look for your young scapegrace of a Virginian."

"His own name is a very pretty name, I'm sure," cries out Hetty. "It isn't Scapegrace! It is Henry Esmond Warrington, Esquire."

"Miss Hester, I found the parson in his cassock, and Henry Esmond Warrington, Esquire, in his bedgown, at a quarter before eleven o'clock in the morning, when all the Sunday bells were ringing, and they were playing over a game of piquet they had had the night before!"

"Well, numbers of good people play at cards of a Sunday. The King plays at cards of a Sunday."

"Hush, my dear!"

"I know he does," says Hetty, "with that painted person we saw yesterday—that Countess what-d'you-call-her?"

"I think, my dear Miss Hester, a clergyman had best take to God's books instead of the Devil's books on that day—and so I took the liberty of telling your parson." Hetty looked as if she thought it was a liberty which Mr. Wolfe had taken. "And I told our young friend that I thought he had better have been on his way to church than there in his bedgown."

"You wouldn't have Harry go to church in a dressing-gown and nightcap, Colonel Wolfe? That would be a pretty sight, indeed!" again says Hetty, fiercely.

214

"I would have my little girl's tongue not wag quite so fast," remarks papa, patting the girl's flushed little cheek.

"Not speak when a friend is attacked, and nobody says a word in his favour? No; nobody!"

Here the two lips of the little mouth closed on each other: the whole little frame shook: the child flung a parting look of defiance at Mr. Wolfe, and went out of the room, just in time to close the door, and burst out crying on the stair.

Mr. Wolfe looked very much discomfited. "I am sure, Aunt Lambert, I did not intend to hurt Hester's feelings."

"No, James," she said, very kindly—the young officer used to call her Aunt Lambert in quite early days—and she gave him her hand.

Mr. Lambert whistled his favourite tune of "Over the hills and far away," with a drum accompaniment performed by his fingers on the window. "I say, you mustn't whistle on Sunday, papa!" cries the artless young gown-boy from Grey Friars; and then suggested that it was three hours from breakfast, and he should like to finish Theo's cheese-cake.

"Oh, you greedy child!" cries Theo. But here, hearing a little exclamatory noise outside, she ran out of the room, closing the door behind her. And we will not pursue her. The noise was that sob which broke from Hester's panting, overloaded heart; and, though we cannot see, I am sure the little maid flung herself on her sister's neck, and wept upon Theo's kind bosom.

Hetty did not walk out in the afternoon when the family took the air on the common, but had a headache and lay on her bed, where her mother watched her. Charley had discovered a comrade from Grey Friars: Mr. Wolfe of course paired off with Miss Lowther: and Theo and her father, taking their sober walk in the Sabbath sunshine, found Madame Bernstein basking on a bench under a tree, her niece and nephew in attendance. Harry ran up to greet his dear friends: he was radiant with pleasure at beholding them—the elder ladies were most gracious to the Colonel and his wife, who had so kindly welcomed their Harry.

How noble and handsome he looked! Theo thought: she called him by his Christian name, as if he were really her brother. "Why did we not see you sooner to-day, Harry?" she asked.

"I never thought you were here, Theo."

"But you might have seen us if you wished."

"Where?" asked Harry.

"There, sir," she said, pointing to the church. And she held her hand up as if in reproof; but a sweet kindness beamed in her honest face. Ah, friendly young reader, wandering on the world and struggling with temptation, may you also have one or two pure hearts to love and pray for you!

CHAPTER XXXIII. Contains a Soliloquy by Hester

Martin Lambert's first feeling, upon learning the little secret which his younger daughter's emotion had revealed, was to be angry with the lad who had robbed his child's heart away from him and her family. "A plague upon all scapegraces, English or Indian!" cried the Colonel to his wife. "I wish this one had broke his nose against any doorpost but ours."

"Perhaps we are to cure him of being a scapegrace, my dear," says Mrs. Lambert, mildly interposing, "and the fall at our door hath something providential in it. You laughed at me, Mr. Lambert, when I said so before; but if Heaven did not send the young gentleman to us, who did? And it may be for the blessing and happiness of us all that he came, too."

"It's hard, Molly!" groaned the Colonel. "We cherish and fondle and rear 'em: we tend them through sickness and health: we toil and we scheme: we hoard away money in the stocking, and patch our own old coats: if they've a headache we can't sleep for thinking of their ailment; if they have a wish or fancy, we work day and night to compass it, and 'tis darling daddy and dearest pappy, and whose father is like ours? and so forth. On Tuesday morning I am king of my house and family. On Tuesday evening Prince Whippersnapper makes his appearance, and my reign is over. A whole life is forgotten and forsworn for a pair of blue eyes, a pair of lean shanks, and a head of yellow hair."

"'Tis written that we women should leave all to follow our husband. I think our courtship was not very long, dear Martin!" said the matron, laying her hand on her husband's arm.

"'Tis human nature, and what can you expect of the jade?" sighed the Colonel.

"And I think I did my duty to my husband, though I own I left my papa for him," added Mrs. Lambert, softly.

"Excellent wench! Perdition catch my soul! but I do love thee, Molly!" says the good Colonel; "but, then, mind you, your father never did me; and if ever I am to have sons-in-law———"

"Ever, indeed! Of course my girls are to have husbands, Mr. Lambert!" cries mamma.

"Well, when they come, I'll hate them, madam, as your father did me; and quite right too, for taking his treasure away from him."

"Don't be irreligious and unnatural, Martin Lambert! I say you are unnatural, sir!" continues the matron.

"Nay, my dear, I have an old tooth in my left jaw, here; and 'tis natural that the tooth should come out. But when the toothdrawer pulls it, 'tis natural that I should feel pain. Do you suppose, madam, that I don't love Hetty better than any tooth in my head?" asks Mr. Lambert. But no woman was ever averse to the idea of her daughter getting a husband, however fathers revolt against the invasion of the son-in-law. As for mothers and grandmothers, those good folks are married over again in the marriage of their young ones; and their souls attire themselves in the laces and muslins of twenty-forty years ago; the postillion's white ribbons bloom again, and they flutter into the postchaise, and drive away. What woman, however old, has not the bridal favours and raiment stowed away, and packed in lavender, in the inmost cupboards of her heart?

"It will be a sad thing, parting with her," continued Mrs. Lambert, with a sigh.

"You have settled that point already, Molly," laughs the Colonel. "Had I not best go out and order raisins and corinths for the wedding-cake?"

"And then I shall have to leave the house in their charge when I go to her, you know, in Virginia. How many miles is it to Virginia, Martin? I should think it must be thousands of miles."

"A hundred and seventy-three thousand three hundred and ninety-one and three-quarters, my dear, by the near way," answers Lambert, gravely; "that through Prester John's country. By the other route, through Persia———"

"Oh, give me the one where there is the least of the sea, and your horrid ships, which I can't bear!" cries the Colonel's spouse. "I hope Rachel Esmond and I shall be better friends. She had a very high spirit when we were girls at school."

"Had we not best go about the baby-linen, Mrs. Martin Lambert?" here interposed her wondering husband. Now, Mrs. Lambert, I dare say, thought there was no matter for wonderment at all, and had remarked some very pretty lace caps and bibs in Mrs. Bobbinit's toy-shop. And on that Sunday afternoon, when the discovery was made, and while little Hetty was lying upon her pillow with feverish cheeks, closed eyes, and a piteous face, her mother looked at the child with the most perfect ease of mind, and seemed to be rather pleased than otherwise at Hetty's woe.

The girl was not only unhappy, but enraged with herself for having published her secret. Perhaps she had not known it until the sudden emotion acquainted her with her own state of mind; and now the little maid chose to be as much ashamed as if she had done a wrong, and been discovered in it. She was indignant with her own weakness, and broke into transports of wrath against herself. She vowed she never would forgive herself for submitting to such a humiliation. So the young pard, wounded by the hunter's dart, chafes with rage in the forest, is angry with the surprise of the rankling steel in her side, and snarls and bites at her sister-cubs, and the leopardess, her spotted mother.

Little Hetty tore and gnawed, and growled, so that I should not like to have been her fraternal cub, or her spotted dam or sire. "What business has any young woman," she cried out, "to indulge in any such nonsense? Mamma, I ought to be whipped, and sent to bed. I know perfectly well that Mr. Warrington does not care a fig about me. I dare say he likes French actresses and the commonest little milliner-girl in the toy-shop better than me. And so he ought, and so they are better than me. Why, what a fool I am to burst out crying like a ninny about nothing, and because Mr. Wolfe said Harry played cards of a Sunday! I know he is not clever, like papa. I believe he is stupid—I am certain he is stupid: but he is not so stupid as I am. Why, of course, I can't marry him. How am I to go to America, and leave you and Theo? Of course, he likes somebody else, at America, or at Tunbridge, or at Jericho, or somewhere. He is a prince in his own country, and can't think of marrying a poor half-pay officer's daughter, with twopence to her fortune. Used not you to tell me how, when I was a baby, I cried and wanted the moon? I am a baby now, a most absurd, silly, little baby—don't talk to me, Mrs. Lambert, I am. Only there is this to be said, he don't know anything about it, and I would rather cut my tongue out than tell him."

Dire were the threats with which Hetty menaced Theo, in case her sister should betray her. As for the infantile Charley, his mind being altogether set on cheese-cakes, he had not remarked or been moved by Miss Hester's emotion; and the parents and the kind sister of course all promised not to reveal the little maid's secret.

"I begin to think it had been best for us to stay at home," sighed Mrs. Lambert to her husband.

"Nay, my dear," replied the other. "Human nature will be human nature; surely Hetty's mother told me herself that she had the beginning of a liking for a certain young curate before she fell over head and ears in love with a certain young officer of Kingsley's. And as for me, my heart was wounded in a dozen places ere Miss Molly Benson took entire possession of it. Our sons and daughters must follow in the way of their parents before them, I suppose. Why, but yesterday, you were scolding me for grumbling at Miss Het's precocious fancies. To do the child justice, she disguises her feelings entirely, and I defy Mr. Warrington to know from her behaviour how she is disposed towards him."

"A daughter of mine and yours, Martin," cries the mother, with great dignity, "is not going to fling herself at a gentleman's head!"

"Neither herself nor the teacup, my dear," answers the Colonel. "Little Miss Het treats Mr. Warrington like a vixen. He never comes to us, but she boxes his ears in one fashion or t'other. I protest she is barely civil to him; but, knowing what is going on in the young hypocrite's mind, I am not going to be angry at her rudeness."

"She hath no need to be rude at all, Martin; and our girl is good enough for any gentleman in England or America. Why, if their ages suit, shouldn't they marry after all, sir?"

"Why, if he wants her, shouldn't he ask her, my dear? I am sorry we came. I am for putting the horses into the carriage, and turning their heads towards home again."

But mamma fondly said, "Depend on it, my dear, that these matters are wisely ordained for us. Depend upon it, Martin, it was not for nothing that Harry Warrington was brought to our gate in that way; and that he and our children are thus brought together again. If that marriage has been decreed in Heaven, a marriage it will be."

"At what age, Molly, I wonder, do women begin and leave off match-making? If our little chit falls in love and falls out again, she will not be the first of her sex, Mrs. Lambert. I wish we were on our way home again, and, if I had my will, would trot off this very night."

"He has promised to drink his tea here to-night. You would not take away our child's pleasure, Martin?" asked the mother, softly.

In his fashion, the father was not less good-natured. "You know, my dear," says Lambert, "that if either of 'em had a fancy to our ears, we would cut them off and serve them in a fricassee."

Mary Lambert laughed at the idea of her pretty little delicate ears being so served. When her husband was most tender-hearted, his habit was to be most grotesque. When he pulled the pretty little delicate ear, behind which the matron's fine hair was combed back, wherein twinkled a shining line or two of silver, I dare say he did not hurt her much. I dare say she was thinking of the soft, well-remembered times of her own modest youth and sweet courtship. Hallowed remembrances of sacred times! If the sight of youthful love is pleasant to behold, how much more charming the aspect of the affection that has survived years, sorrows, faded beauty perhaps, and life's doubts, differences, trouble!

In regard of her promise to disguise her feelings for Mr. Warrington in that gentleman's presence, Miss Hester was better, or worse if you will, than her word. Harry not only came to take tea with his friends, but invited them for the next day to an entertainment at the Rooms, to be given in their special honour.

"A dance, and given for us!" cries Theo. "Oh, Harry, how delightful! I wish we could begin this very minute!"

"Why, for a savage Virginian, I declare, Harry Warrington, thou art the most civilised young man possible!" says the Colonel. "My dear, shall we dance a minuet together?"

"We have done such a thing before, Martin Lambert!" says the soldier's fond wife. Her husband hums a minuet tune; whips a plate from the tea-table, and makes a preparatory bow and flourish with it as if it were a hat, whilst madam performs her best curtsey.

Only Hetty, of the party, persists in looking glum and displeased. "Why, child, have you not a word of thanks to throw to Mr. Warrington?" asks Theo of her sister.

"I never did care for dancing much," says Hetty. "What is the use of standing up opposite a stupid man, and dancing down a room with him?"

"Merci du compliment!" says Mr. Warrington.

"I don't say that you are stupid—that is—that is, I—I only meant country dances," says Hetty, biting her lips, as she caught her sister's eye. She remembered she had said Harry was stupid, and Theo's droll humorous glance was her only reminder.

But with this Miss Hetty chose to be as angry as if it had been quite a cruel rebuke. "I hate dancing—there—I own it," she says, with a toss of her head.

"Nay, you used to like it well enough, child!!" interposes her mother.

"That was when she was a child: don't you see she is grown up to be an old woman?" remarks Hetty's father. "Or perhaps Miss Hester has got the gout?"

"Fiddle!" says Hester, snappishly, drubbing with her little feet.

"What's a dance without a fiddle?" says imperturbed papa.

Darkness has come over Harry Warrington's face. "I come to try my best, and give them pleasure and a dance," he thinks, "and the little thing tells me she hates dancing. We don't practise kindness, or acknowledge hospitality so in our country. No—nor speak to our parents so, neither." I am afraid, in this particular usages have changed in the United States during the last hundred years, and that the young folks there are considerably Hettified.

Not content with this, Miss Hester must proceed to make such fun of all the company at the Wells, and especially of Harry's own immediate pursuits and companions, that the honest lad was still further pained at her behaviour; and, when he saw Mrs. Lambert alone, asked how or in what he had again offended, that Hester was so angry with him? The kind matron felt more than ever well disposed towards the boy, after her daughter's conduct to him. She would have liked to tell the secret which Hester hid so fiercely. Theo, too, remonstrated with her sister in private; but Hester would not listen to the subject, and was as angry in her bedroom, when the girls were alone, as she had been in the parlour before her mother's company. "Suppose he hates me?" says she. "I expect he will. I hate myself, I do, and scorn myself for being such an idiot. How ought he to do otherwise than hate me? Didn't I abuse him, call him goose, all sorts of names? And know he is not clever all the time. I know I have better wits than he has. It is only because he is tall, and has blue eyes, and a pretty nose that I like him. What an absurd fool a girl must be to like a man merely because he has a blue nose and hooked eyes! So I am a fool, and I won't have you say a word to the contrary, Theo!"

Now Theo thought that her little sister, far from being a fool, was a wonder of wonders, and that if any girl was worthy of any prince in Christendom, Hetty was that spinster. "You are silly sometimes, Hetty," says Theo, "that is when you speak unkindly to people who mean you well, as you did to Mr. Warrington at tea to-night. When he proposed to us his party at the Assembly Rooms, and nothing could be more gallant of him, why did you say you didn't care for music, or dancing, or tea? You know you love them all!"

"I said it merely to vex myself, Theo, and annoy myself, and whip myself, as I deserve, child. And, besides, how can you expect such an idiot as I am to say anything but idiotic things? Do you know, it quite pleased me to see him angry. I thought, ah! now I have hurt his feelings! Now he will say, Hetty Lambert is an odious little set-up, sour-tempered vixen. And that will teach him, and you, and mamma, and papa, at any rate, that I am not going to set my cap at Mr. Harry. No; our papa is ten times as good as he is. I will stay by our papa, and if he asked me to go to Virginia with him to-morrow, I wouldn't, Theo. My sister is worth all the Virginians that ever were made since the world began."

And here, I suppose, follow osculations between the sisters, and mother's knock comes to the door, who has overheard their talk through the wainscot, and calls out, "Children, 'tis time to go to sleep." Theo's eyes close speedily, and she is at rest; but ob, poor little Hetty! Think of the hours tolling one after another, and the child's eyes wide open, as she lies tossing and wakeful with the anguish of the new wound!

"It is a judgment upon me," she says, "for having thought and spoke scornfully of him. Only, why should there be a judgment upon me? I was only in fun. I knew I liked him very much all the time: but I thought Theo liked him too, and I would give up anything for my darling Theo. If she had, no tortures should ever have drawn a word from me—I would have got a rope-ladder to help her to run away with Harry, that I would, or fetched the clergyman to marry them. And then I would have retired alone, and alone, and alone, and taken care of papa and mamma, and of the poor in the village, and have read sermons, though I hate 'em, and would have died without telling a word—not a word—and I shall die soon, I know I shall." But when the dawn rises, the little maid is asleep, nestling by her sister, the stain of a tear or two upon her flushed downy cheek.

Most of us play with edged tools at some period of our lives, and cut ourselves accordingly. At first the cut hurts and stings, and down drops the knife, and we cry out like wounded little babies as we are. Some very very few and unlucky folks at the game cut their heads sheer off, or stab themselves mortally, and perish outright, and there is an end of them. But,—heaven help us!—many people have fingered those ardentes sagittas which Love sharpens on his whetstone, and are stabbed, scarred, pricked, perforated, tattooed all over with the wounds, who recovered, and live to be quite lively. Wir auch have tasted das irdische Glueck; we also have gelebt and—und so weiter. Warble your death-song, sweet Thekla! Perish off the face of the earth, poor pulmonary victim, if so minded! Had you survived to a later period of life, my dear, you would have thought of a sentimental disappointment without any reference to the undertaker. Let us trust there is no present need of a sexton for Miss Hetty. But meanwhile, the very instant she wakes, there, tearing at her little heart, will that Care be, which has given her a few hours' respite, melted, no doubt, by her youth and her tears.

CHAPTER XXXIV. In which Mr. Warrington treats the Company with Tea and a Ball

Generous with his very easily gotten money, hospitable and cordial to all, our young Virginian, in his capacity of man of fashion, could not do less than treat his country friends to an entertainment at the Assembly Rooms, whither, according to the custom of the day, he invited almost all the remaining company at the Wells. Card-tables were set in one apartment, for all those who could not spend an evening without the pastime then common to all European society: a supper with champagne in some profusion and bowls of negus was prepared in another chamber: the large assembly-room was set apart for the dance, of which enjoyment Harry Warrington's guests partook in our ancestors' homely fashion. I cannot fancy that the amusement was especially lively. First, minuets were called, two or three of which were performed by as many couple. The spinsters of the highest rank in the assembly went out for the minuet, and my Lady Maria Esmond, being an earl's daughter, and the person of the highest rank present (with the exception of Lady Augusta Crutchley, who was lame), Mr. Warrington danced the first minuet with his cousin, acquitting himself to the satisfaction of the whole room, and performing much more elegantly than Mr. Wolfe, who stood up with Miss Lowther. Having completed the dance with Lady Maria, Mr. Warrington begged Miss Theo to do him the honour of walking the next minuet, and accordingly Miss Theo, blushing and looking very happy, went through her exercise to the great delight of her parents and the rage of Miss Humpleby, Sir John Humpleby's daughter, of Liphook, who expected, at least, to have stood up next after my Lady Maria. Then, after the minuets, came country dances, the music being performed by a harp, fiddle, and flageolet, perched in a little balcony, and thrumming through the evening rather feeble and melancholy tunes. Take up an old book of music, and play a few of those tunes now, and one wonders how people at any time could have found the airs otherwise than melancholy. And yet they loved and frisked and laughed and courted to that sad accompaniment. There is scarce one of the airs that has not an amari aliquid, a tang of sadness. Perhaps it is because they are old and defunct, and their plaintive echoes call out to us from the limbo of the past, whither they have been consigned for this century. Perhaps they were gay when they were alive; and our descendants when they hear—well, never mind names—when they hear the works of certain maestri now popular, will say: Bon Dieu, is this the music which amused our forefathers?

Mr. Warrington had the honour of a duchess's company at his tea-drinking —Colonel Lambert's and Mr. Prior's heroine, the Duchess of Queensberry. And though the duchess carefully turned her back upon a countess who was present, laughed loudly, glanced at the latter over her shoulder, and pointed at her with her fan, yet almost all the company pushed, and bowed, and cringed, and smiled, and backed before this countess, scarcely taking any notice of her Grace of Queensberry and her jokes, and her fan, and her airs. Now this countess was no other than the Countess of Yarmouth-Walmoden, the lady whom his Majesty George the Second, of Great Britain, France, and Ireland, King, Defender of the Faith, delighted to honour. She had met Harry Warrington in the walks that morning, and had been mighty gracious to the young Virginian. She had told him they would have a game at cards that night; and purblind old Colonel Blinkinsop, who fancied the invitation had been addressed to him, had made the profoundest of bows. "Pooh! pooh!" said the Countess of England and Hanover, "I don't mean you. I mean the young Firshinian!" And everybody congratulated the youth on his good fortune. At night, all the world, in order to show their loyalty, doubtless, thronged round my Lady Yarmouth; my Lord Bamborough was eager to make her parti at quadrille. My Lady Blanche Pendragon, that model of virtue; Sir Lancelot Quintain, that pattern of knighthood and valour; Mr. Dean of Ealing, that exemplary divine and preacher; numerous gentlemen, noblemen, generals, colonels, matrons, and spinsters of the highest rank, were on the watch for a smile from her, or eager to jump up and join her card-table. Lady Maria waited upon her with meek respect, and Madame de Bernstein treated the Hanoverian lady with profound gravity and courtesy.

Harry's bow had been no lower than hospitality required; but, such as it was, Miss Hester chose to be indignant with it. She scarce spoke a word to her partner during their dance together; and when he took her to the supper-room for refreshment she was little more communicative. To enter that room they had to pass by Madame Walmoden's card-table, who good-naturedly called out to her host as he was passing, and asked him if his "breddy liddle bardner liked tanzing?"

"I thank your ladyship, I don't like tanzing, and I don't like cards," says Miss Hester, tossing up her head; and, dropping a curtsey like a "cheese," she strutted away from the Countess's table.

Mr. Warrington was very much offended. Sarcasm from the young to the old pained him: flippant behaviour towards himself hurt him. Courteous in his simple way to all persons whom he met, he expected a like politeness from them. Hetty perfectly well knew what offence she was giving; could mark the displeasure reddening on her partner's honest face, with a sidelong glance of her eye; nevertheless she tried to wear her most ingenuous smile; and, as she came up to the sideboard where the refreshments were set, artlessly said:

"What a horrid, vulgar old woman that is; don't you think so?"

"What woman?" asked the young man.

"That German woman—my Lady Yarmouth—to whom all the men are bowing and cringing."

"Her ladyship has been very kind to me," says Harry, grimly. "Won't you have some of this custard?"

"And you have been bowing to her, too! You look as if your negus was not nice," harmlessly continues Miss Hetty.

"It is not very good negus," says Harry, with a gulp.

"And the custard is bad too! I declare 'tis made with bad eggs!" cries Miss Lambert.

"I wish, Hester, that the entertainment and the company had been better to your liking," says poor Harry.

"'Tis very unfortunate; but I dare say you could not help it," cries the young woman, tossing her little curly head.

Mr. Warrington groaned in spirit, perhaps in body, and clenched his fists and his teeth. The little torturer artlessly continued, "You seem disturbed: shall we go to my mamma?"

"Yes, let us go to your mamma," cries Mr. Warrington, with glaring eyes and a "Curse you, why are you always standing in the way?" to an unlucky waiter.

"La! Is that the way you speak in Virginia?" asks Miss Pertness.

"We are rough there sometimes, madam, and can't help being disturbed," he says slowly, and with a quiver in his whole frame, looking down upon her with fire flashing out of his eyes. Hetty saw nothing distinctly afterwards, and until she came to her mother. Never had she seen Harry look so handsome or so noble.

"You look pale, child!" cries mamma, anxious, like all pavidae matres.

"'Tis the cold—no, I mean the heat. Thank you, Mr. Warrington." And she makes him a faint curtsey, as Harry bows a tremendous bow, and walks elsewhere amongst his guests. He hardly knows what is happening at first, so angry is he.

He is aroused by another altercation, between his aunt and the Duchess of Queensberry. When the royal favourite passed the Duchess, her Grace gave her Ladyship an awful stare out of eyes that were not so bright now as they had been in the young days when they "set the world on fire;" turned round with an affected laugh to her neighbour, and shot at the jolly Hanoverian lady a ceaseless fire of giggles and sneers. The Countess pursued her game at cards, not knowing, or not choosing, perhaps, to know how her enemy was gibing at her. There had been a feud of many years' date between their Graces of Queensberry and the family on the throne.

"How you all bow down to the idol! Don't tell me! You are as bad as the rest, my good Madame Bernstein!" the Duchess says. "Ah, what a true Christian country this is! and how your dear first husband, the Bishop, would have liked to see such a sight!"

"Forgive me, if I fail quite to understand your Grace."

"We are both of us growing old, my good Bernstein, or, perhaps, we won't understand when we don't choose to understand. That is the way with us women, my good young Iroquois."

"Your Grace remarked, that it was a Christian country," said Madame de Bernstein, "and I failed to perceive the point of the remark."

"Indeed, my good creature, there is very little point in it! I meant we were such good Christians, because we were so forgiving. Don't you remember reading, when you were young, or your husband the Bishop reading, when he was in the pulpit, how when a woman amongst the Jews was caught doing wrong, the Pharisees were for stoning her out of hand? Far from stoning such a woman now, look, how fond we are of her! Any man in this room would go round it on his knees if yonder woman bade him. Yes, Madame Walmoden, you may look up from your cards with your great painted face, and frown with your great painted eyebrows at me. You know I am talking about you; and intend to go on talking about you, too. I say any man here would go round the room on his knees, if you bade him!"

"I think, madam, I know two or three who wouldn't!" says Mr. Warrington, with some spirit.

"Quick, let me hug them to my heart of hearts!" cries the old Duchess. "Which are they? Bring 'em to me, my dear Iroquois! Let us have a game of four—of honest men and women; that is to say, if we can find a couple more partners, Mr. Warrington!"

"Here are we three," says the Baroness Bernstein, with a forced laugh; "let us play a dummy."

"Pray, madam, where is the third?" asks the old Duchess, looking round.

"Madam!" cries out the other elderly lady, "I leave your Grace to boast of your honesty, which I have no doubt is spotless: but I will thank you not to doubt mine before my own relatives and children!"

"See how she fires up at a word! I am sure, my dear creature, you are quite as honest as most of the company," says the Duchess.

"Which may not be good enough for her Grace the Duchess of Queensberry and Dover, who, to be sure, might have stayed away in such a case, but it is the best my nephew could get, madam, and his best he has given you. You look astonished, Harry, my dear—and well you may. He is not used to our ways, madam."

"Madam, he has found an aunt who can teach him our ways, and a great deal more!" cries the Duchess, rapping her fan.

"She will teach him to try and make all his guests welcome, old or young, rich or poor. That is the Virginian way, isn't it, Harry? She will tell him, when Catherine Hyde is angry with his old aunt, that they were friends as girls, and ought not to quarrel now they are old women. And she will not be wrong, will she, Duchess?" And herewith the one dowager made a superb curtsey to the other, and the battle just impending between them passed away.

"Egad, it was like Byng and Galissoniere!" cried Chaplain Sampson, as Harry talked over the night's transactions with his tutor next morning. "No power on earth, I thought, could have prevented those two from going into action!"

"Seventy-fours at least—both of 'em!" laughs Harry.

"But the Baroness declined the battle, and sailed out of fire with inimitable skill."

"Why should she be afraid? I have heard you say my aunt is as witty as any woman alive, and need fear the tongue of no dowager in England."

"Hem! Perhaps she had good reasons for being peaceable!" Sampson knew very well what they were, and that poor Bernstein's reputation was so hopelessly flawed and cracked, that any sarcasms levelled at Madame Walmoden were equally applicable to her.

"Sir," cried Harry, in great amazement, "you don't mean to say there is anything against the character of my aunt, the Baroness de Bernstein!"

The chaplain looked at the young Virginian with such an air of utter wonderment, that the latter saw there must be some history against his aunt, and some charge which Sampson did not choose to reveal. "Good heavens!" Harry groaned out, "are there two then in the family, who are——?"

"Which two?" asked the chaplain.

But here Harry stopped, blushing very red. He remembered, and we shall presently have to state, whence he had got his information regarding the other family culprit, and bit his lip, and was silent.

"Bygones are always unpleasant things, Mr. Warrington," said the chaplain; "and we had best hold our peace regarding them. No man or woman can live long in this wicked world of ours without some scandal attaching to them, and I fear our excellent Baroness has been no more fortunate than her neighbours. We cannot escape calumny, my dear young friend! You have had sad proof enough of that in your brief stay amongst us. But we can have clear consciences, and that is the main point!" And herewith the chaplain threw his handsome eyes upward, and tried to look as if his conscience was as white as the ceiling.

"Has there been anything very wrong, then, about my Aunt Bernstein?" continued Harry, remembering how at home his mother had never spoken of the Baroness.

"O sancta simplicitas!" the chaplain muttered to himself. "Stories, my dear sir, much older than your time or mine. Stories such as were told about everybody, de me, de te; you know with what degree of truth in your own case."

"Confound the villain! I should like to hear any scoundrel say a word against the dear old lady," cries the young gentleman. "Why, this world, parson, is full of lies and scandal!"

"And you are just beginning to find it out, my dear sir," cries the clergyman, with his most beatified air. "Whose character has not been attacked? My lord's, yours, mine,—every one's. We must bear as well as we can, and pardon to the utmost of our power."

"You may. It's your cloth, you know; but, by George, I won't!" cries Mr. Warrington, and again goes down the fist with a thump on the table. "Let any fellow say a word in my hearing against that dear old creature, and I'll pull his nose, as sure as my name is Harry Esmond. How do you do, Colonel Lambert? You find us late again, sir. Me and his reverence kept it up pretty late with some of the young fellows, after the ladies went away. I hope the dear ladies are well, sir?" and here Harry rose, greeting his friend the Colonel very kindly, who had come to pay him a morning visit, and had entered the room followed by Mr. Gumbo (the latter preferred walking very leisurely about all the affairs of life), just as Harry—suiting the action to the word—was tweaking the nose of Calumny.

"The ladies are purely. Whose nose were you pulling when I came in, Mr. Warrington?" says the Colonel, laughing.

"Isn't it a shame, sir? The parson, here, was telling me that there are villains here who attack the character of my aunt, the Baroness of Bernstein!"

"You don't mean to say so!" cries Mr. Lambert.

"I tell Mr. Harry that everybody is calumniated!" says the chaplain, with a clerical intonation; but, at the same time, he looks at Colonel Lambert and winks, as much as to say, "He knows nothing—keep him in the dark."

The Colonel took the hint. "Yes," says he, "the jaws of slander are for ever wagging. Witness that story about the dancing-girl, that we all believed against you, Harry Warrington."

"What, all, sir?"

"No, not all. One didn't—Hetty didn't. You should have heard her standing up for you, Harry, t'other day, when somebody—a little bird—brought us another story about you; about a game at cards on Sunday morning, when you and a friend of yours might have been better employed." And here there was a look of mingled humour and reproof at the clergyman.

"Faith, I own it, sir!" says the chaplain. "It was mea culpa, mea maxima—no, mea minima culpa, only the rehearsal of an old game at piquet, which we had been talking over."

"And did Miss Hester stand up for me?" says Harry.

"Miss Hester did. But why that wondering look?" asks the Colonel.

"She scolded me last night like—like anything," says downright Harry. "I never heard a young girl go on so. She made fun of everybody—hit about at young and old—so that I couldn't help telling her, sir, that in our country, leastways in Virginia (they say the Yankees are very pert), young people don't speak of their elders so. And, do you know, sir, we had a sort of a quarrel, and I'm very glad you've told me she spoke kindly of me," says Harry, shaking his friend's hand, a ready boyish emotion glowing in his cheeks and in his eyes.

"You won't come to much hurt if you find no worse enemy than Hester, Mr. Warrington," said the girl's father, gravely, looking not without a deep thrill of interest at the flushed face and moist eyes of his young friend. "Is he fond of her?" thought the Colonel. "And how fond? 'Tis evident he knows nothing, and Miss Het has been performing some of her tricks. He is a fine, honest lad, and God bless him!" And Colonel Lambert looked towards Harry with that manly, friendly kindness which our lucky young Virginian was not unaccustomed to inspire, for he was comely to look at, prone to blush, to kindle, nay, to melt, at a kind story. His laughter was cheery to hear: his eyes shone confidently: his voice spoke truth.

"And the young lady of the minuet? She distinguished herself to perfection: the whole room admired," asked the courtly chaplain. "I trust Miss—Miss ———"

"Miss Theodosia is perfectly well, and ready to dance at this minute with your reverence," says her father. "Or stay, Chaplain, perhaps you only dance on Sunday?" The Colonel then turned to Harry again. "You paid your court very neatly to the great lady, Mr. Flatterer. My Lady Yarmouth has been trumpeting your praises at the Pump Room. She says she has got a leedel boy in Hannover dat is wery like you, and you are a sharming young mans."

"If her ladyship were a queen, people could scarcely be more respectful to her," says the chaplain.

"Let us call her a vice-queen, parson," says the Colonel, with a twinkle of his eye.

"Her Majesty pocketed forty of my guineas at quadrille," cries Mr. Warrington, with a laugh.

"She will play you on the same terms another day. The Countess is fond of play, and she wins from most people," said the Colonel, drily. "Why don't you bet her ladyship five thousand on a bishopric, parson? I have heard of a clergyman who made such a bet, and who lost it, and who paid it, and who got the bishopric.

"Ah! who will lend me the five thousand? Will you, sir? asked the chaplain.

"No, sir! I won't give her five thousand to be made Commander-in-Chief or Pope of Rome," says the Colonel, stoutly. "I shall fling no stones at the woman; but I shall bow no knee to her, as I see a pack of rascals do. No offence—I don't mean you. And I don't mean Harry Warrington, who was quite right to be civil to her, and to lose his money with good-humour. Harry, I am come to bid thee farewell, my boy. We have had our pleasuring—my money is run out, and we must jog back to Oakhurst. Will you ever come and see the old place again?"

"Now, sir, now! I'll ride back with you!" cries Harry, eagerly.

"Why—no—not now," says the Colonel, in a hurried manner. "We haven't got room—that is, we're—we're expecting some friends." ["The Lord forgive me for the lie!" he mutters.] "But—but you'll come to us when—when Tom's at home—yes, when Tom's at home. That will be famous fun—and I'd have you to know, sir, that my wife and I love you sincerely, sir—and so do the girls, however much they scold you. And if you ever are in a scrape—and such things have happened, Mr. Chaplain! you will please to count upon me. Mind that, sir!"

And the Colonel was for taking leave of Harry then and there, on the spot, but the young man followed him down the stairs, and insisted upon saying good-bye to his dear ladies.

Instead, however, of proceeding immediately to Mr. Lambert's lodging, the two gentlemen took the direction of the common, where, looking from Harry's windows, Mr. Sampson saw the pair in earnest conversation. First, Lambert smiled and looked roguish. Then, presently, at a farther stage of the talk, he flung up both his hands and performed other gestures indicating surprise and agitation.

"The boy is telling him," thought the chaplain. When Mr. Warrington came back in an hour, he found his reverence deep in the composition of a sermon. Harry's face was grave and melancholy; he flung down his hat, buried himself in a great chair, and then came from his lips something like an execration.

"The young ladies are going, and our heart is affected?" said the chaplain, looking up from his manuscript.

"Heart!" sneered Harry.

"Which of the young ladies is the conqueror, sir? I thought the youngest's eyes followed you about at your ball."

"Confound the little termagant!" broke out Harry. "What does she mean by being so pert to me? She treats me as if I was a fool!"

"And no man is, sir, with a woman!" said the scribe of the sermon.

"Ain't they, Chaplain?" And Harry growled out more naughty words expressive of inward disquiet.

"By the way, have you heard anything of your lost property?" asked the chaplain, presently looking up from his pages.

Harry said "No!" with another word, which I would not print for the world.

"I begin to suspect, sir, that there was more money than you like to own in that book. I wish I could find some."

"There were notes in it," said Harry, very gloomily, "and—and papers that I am very sorry to lose. What the deuce has come of it? I had it when we dined together."

"I saw you put it in your pocket," cried the chaplain. "I saw you take it out and pay at the toy-shop a bill for a gold thimble and workbox for one of your young ladies. Of course you have asked there, sir?"

"Of course I have," says Mr. Warrington, plunged in melancholy.

"Gumbo put you to bed—at least, if I remember right. I was so cut myself that I scarce remember anything. Can you trust those black fellows, sir?"

"I can trust him with my head. With my head?" groaned out Mr. Warrington, bitterly., "I can't trust myself with it."

"'Oh, that a man should put an enemy into his mouth to steal away his brains!'"

"You may well call it an enemy, Chaplain. Hang it, I have a great mind to make a vow never to drink another drop! A fellow says anything when he is in drink."

The chaplain laughed. "You, sir," he said, "are close enough!" And the truth was, that, for the last few days, no amount of wine would unseal Mr. Warrington's lips, when the artless Sampson by chance touched on the subject of his patron's loss.

"And so the little country nymphs are gone, or going, sir?" asked the chaplain. "They were nice, fresh little things; but I think the mother was the finest woman of the three. I declare, a woman at five-and-thirty or so is at her prime. What do you say, sir?"

Mr. Warrington looked, for a moment, askance at the clergyman. "Confound all women, I say!" muttered the young misogynist. For which sentiment every well-conditioned person will surely rebuke him.

CHAPTER XXXV. Entanglements

Our good Colonel had, no doubt, taken counsel with his good wife, and they had determined to remove their little Hetty as speedily as possible out of the reach of the charmer. In complaints such as that under which the poor little maiden was supposed to be suffering, the remedy of absence and distance often acts effectually with men; but I believe women are not so easily cured by the alibi treatment. Some of them will go away ever so far, and forever so long, and the obstinate disease hangs by them, spite of distance or climate. You may whip, abuse, torture, insult them, and still the little deluded creatures will persist in their fidelity. Nay, if I may speak, after profound and extensive study and observation, there are few better ways of securing the faithfulness and admiration of the beautiful partners of our existence than a little judicious ill-treatment, a brisk dose of occasional violence as an alterative, and, for general and wholesome diet, a cooling but pretty constant neglect. At sparing intervals administer small quantities of love and kindness; but not every day, or too often, as this medicine, much taken, loses its effect. Those dear creatures who are the most indifferent to their husbands, are those who are cloyed by too much surfeiting of the sugar-plums and lollipops of Love. I have known a young being, with every wish gratified, yawn in her adoring husband's face, and prefer the conversation and petits soins of the merest booby and idiot; whilst, on the other hand, I have seen Chloe,—at whom Strephon has flung his bootjack in the morning, or whom he has cursed before the servants at dinner,—come creeping and fondling to his knee at tea-time, when he is comfortable after his little nap and his good wine; and pat his head and play him his favourite tunes; and, when old John, the butler, or old Mary, the maid, comes in with the bed-candles, look round proudly, as much as to say, Now, John, look how good my dearest Henry is! Make your game, gentlemen, then! There is the coaxing, fondling, adoring line, when you are henpecked, and Louisa is indifferent, and bored out of her existence. There is the manly, selfish, effectual system, where she answers to the whistle and comes in at "Down Charge;" and knows her master; and frisks and fawns about him; and nuzzles at his knees; and "licks the hand that's raised"—that's raised to do her good, as (I quote from memory) Mr. Pope finely observes. What used the late lamented O'Connell to say, over whom a grateful country has raised such a magnificent testimonial? "Hereditary bondsmen," he used to remark, "know ye not, who would be free, themselves must strike the blow?" Of course you must, in political as in domestic circles. So up with your cudgels, my enslaved, injured boys!

Women will be pleased with these remarks, because they have such a taste for humour and understand irony; and I should not be surprised if young Grubstreet, who corresponds with three penny papers and describes the persons and conversation of gentlemen whom he meets at his "clubs," will say, "I told you so! He advocates the thrashing of women! He has no nobility of soul! He has no heart!" Nor have I, my eminent young Grubstreet! any more than you have ears. Dear ladies! I assure you I am only joking in the above remarks,—I do not advocate the thrashing of your sex at all,—and, as you can't understand the commonest bit of fun, beg leave flatly to tell you, that I consider your sex a hundred times more loving and faithful than ours.

So, what is the use of Hetty's parents taking her home, if the little maid intends to be just as fond of Harry absent as of Harry present? Why not let her see him before Ball and Dobbin are put to, and say, "Good-bye, Harry! I was very wilful and fractious last night, and you were very kind: but good-bye, Harry!" She will show no special emotion: she is so ashamed of her secret, that she will not betray it. Harry is too much preoccupied to discover it for himself. He does not know what grief is lying behind Hetty's glances, or hidden under the artifice of her innocent young smiles. He has, perhaps, a care of his own. He will part from her calmly, and fancy she is happy to get back to her music and her poultry and her flower-garden.

He did not even ride part of the way homewards by the side of his friend's carriage. He had some other party arranged for, that afternoon, and when he returned thence, the good Lamberts were gone from Tunbridge Wells. There were their windows open, and the card in one of them signifying that the apartments were once more to let. A little passing sorrow at the blank aspect of the rooms lately enlivened by countenances so frank and friendly, may have crossed the young gentleman's mind; but he dines at the White Horse at four o'clock, and eats his dinner and calls fiercely for his bottle. Poor little Hester will choke over her tea about the same hour when the Lamberts arrive to sleep at the house of their friends at Westerham. The young roses will be wan in her cheeks in the morning, and there will be black circles round her eyes. It was the thunder: the night was hot: she could not sleep: she will be better when she gets home again the next day. And home they come. There is the gate where he fell. There is the bed he lay in, the chair in which he used to sit—what ages seem to have passed! What a gulf between to-day and yesterday! Who is that little child calling her chickens, or watering her roses yonder? Are she and that girl the same Hester Lambert? Why, she is ever so much older than Theo now—Theo, who has always been so composed, and so clever, and so old for her age. But in a night or two Hester has lived—oh, long, long years! So have many besides: and poppy and mandragora will never medicine them to the sweet sleep they tasted yesterday.

Maria Esmond saw the Lambert cavalcade drive away, and felt a grim relief. She looks with hot eyes at Harry when he comes into his aunt's card-tables, flushed with Barbeau's good wine. He laughs, rattles in reply to his aunt, who asks him which of the girls is his sweetheart? He gaily says he loves them both like sisters. He has never seen a better gentleman, nor better people, than the Lamberts. Why is Lambert not a general? He has been a most distinguished officer: his Royal Highness the Duke is very fond of him. Madame Bernstein says that Harry must make interest with Lady Yarmouth for his protege.

"Elle ravvole de fous, cher bedid anche!" says Madame Bernstein, mimicking the Countess's German accent. The Baroness is delighted with her boy's success. "You carry off the hearts of all the old women, doesn't he, Maria?" she says, with a sneer at her niece, who quivers under the stab.

"You were quite right, my dear, not to perceive that she cheated at cards, and you play like a grand seigneur," continues Madame de Bernstein.

"Did she cheat?" cries Harry, astonished. "I am sure, ma'am, I saw no unfair play."

"No more did I, my dear, but I am sure she cheated. Bah! every woman cheats, I and Maria included, when we can get a chance. But when you play with the Walmoden, you don't do wrong to lose in moderation; and many men cheat in that way. Cultivate her. She has taken a fancy to your beaux yeux. Why should your Excellency not be Governor of Virginia, sir? You must go and pay your respects to the Duke and his Majesty at Kensington. The Countess of Yarmouth will be your best friend at court."

"Why should you not introduce me, aunt?" asked Harry.

The old lady's rouged cheek grew a little redder. "I am not in favour at Kensington," she said. "I may have been once; and there are no faces so unwelcome to kings as those they wish to forget. All of us want to forget something or somebody. I dare say our ingenu here would like to wipe a sum or two off the slate. Wouldst thou not, Harry?"

Harry turned red, too, and so did Maria, and his aunt laughed one of those wicked laughs which are not altogether pleasant to hear. What meant those guilty signals on the cheeks of her nephew and niece? What account was scored upon the memory of either, which they were desirous to efface? I fear Madame Bernstein was right, and that most folks have some ugly reckonings written up on their consciences, which we were glad to be quit of.

Had Maria known one of the causes of Harry's disquiet, the middle-aged spinster would have been more unquiet still. For some days he had missed a pocket-book. He had remembered it in his possession on that day when he drank so much claret at the White Horse, and Gumbo carried him to bed. He sought for it in the morning, but none of his servants had seen it. He had inquired for it at the White Horse, but there were no traces of it. He could not cry the book, and could only make very cautious inquiries respecting it. He must not have it known that the book was lost. A pretty condition of mind Lady Maria Esmond would be in, if she knew that the outpourings of her heart were in the hands of the public! The letters contained all sorts of disclosures: a hundred family secrets were narrated by the artless correspondent: there were ever so much satire and abuse of persons with whom she and Mr. Warrington came in contact. There were expostulations about his attentions to other ladies. There was scorn, scandal, jokes, appeals, protests of eternal fidelity; the usual farrago, dear madam, which you may remember you wrote to your Edward, when you were engaged to him, and before you became Mrs. Jones. Would you like those letters to be read by any one else? Do you recollect what you said about the Miss Browns in two or three of those letters, and the unfavourable opinion you expressed of Mrs. Thompson's character? Do you happen to recall the words which you used regarding Jones himself, whom you subsequently married (for in consequence of disputes about the settlements your engagement with Edward was broken off)? and would you like Mr. J. to see those remarks? You know you wouldn't. Then be pleased to withdraw that imputation which you have already cast in your mind upon Lady Maria Esmond. No doubt her letters were very foolish, as most love-letters are, but it does not follow that there was anything wrong in them. They are foolish when written by young folks to one another, and how much more foolish when written by an old man to a young lass, or by an old lass to a young lad! No wonder Lady Maria should not like her letters to be read. Why, the very spelling—but that didn't matter so much in her ladyship's days, and people are just as foolish now, though they spell better. No, it is not the spelling which matters so much; it is the writing at all. I for one, and for the future, am determined never to speak or write my mind out regarding anything or anybody. I intend to say of every woman that she is chaste and handsome; of every man that he is handsome, clever, and rich; of every book that it is delightfully interesting; of Snobmore's manners that they are gentlemanlike; of Screwby's dinners that they are luxurious; of Jawkins's conversation that it is lively and amusing; of Xantippe, that she has a sweet temper; of Jezebel, that her colour is natural; of Bluebeard, that he really was most indulgent to his wives, and that very likely they died of bronchitis. What? a word against the spotless Messalina? What an unfavourable view of human nature! What? King Cheops was not a perfect monarch? Oh, you railer at royalty and slanderer of all that is noble and good! When this book is concluded, I shall change the jaundiced livery which my books have worn since I began to lisp in numbers, have rose-coloured coats for them with cherubs on the cover, and all the characters within shall be perfect angels.

Meanwhile we are in a society of men and women, from whose shoulders no sort of wings have sprouted as yet, and who, without any manner of doubt, have their little failings. There is Madame Bernstein: she has fallen asleep after dinner, and eating and drinking too much,—those are her ladyship's little failings. Mr. Harry Warrington has gone to play a match at billiards with Count Caramboli: I suspect idleness is his failing. That is what Mr. Chaplain Sampson remarks to Lady Maria, as they are talking together in a low tone, so as not to interrupt Aunt Bernstein's doze in the neighbouring room.

"A gentleman of Mr. Warrington's means can afford to be idle," says Lady Maria. "Why, sure you love cards and billiards yourself, my good Mr. Sampson?"

"I don't say, madam, my practice is good, only my doctrine is sound," says Mr. Chaplain with a sigh. "This young gentleman should have some employment. He should appear at court, and enter the service of his country, as befits a man of his station. He should settle down, and choose a woman of a suitable rank as his wife." Sampson looks in her ladyship's face as he speaks.

"Indeed, my cousin is wasting his time," says Lady Maria, blushing slightly.

"Mr. Warrington might see his relatives of his father's family," suggests Mr. Chaplain.

"Suffolk country boobies drinking beer and hallooing after foxes! I don't see anything to be gained by his frequenting them, Mr. Sampson!"

"They are of an ancient family, of which the chief has been knight of the shire these hundred years," says the chaplain. "I have heard Sir Miles hath a daughter of Mr. Harry's age—and beauty, too."

"I know nothing, sir, about Sir Miles Warrington, and his daughters, and his beauties!" cries Maria, in a fluster.

"The Baroness stirred—no—her ladyship is in a sweet sleep," says the chaplain, in a very soft voice. "I fear, madam, for your ladyship's cousin, Mr. Warrington. I fear for his youth; for designing persons who may get about him; for extravagances, follies, intrigues even into which he will be led, and into which everybody will try to tempt him. His lordship, my kind patron, bade me to come and watch over him, and I am here accordingly, as your ladyship knoweth. I know the follies of young men. Perhaps I have practised them myself. I own it with a blush," adds Mr. Sampson with much unction—not, however, bringing the promised blush forward to corroborate the asserted repentance.

"Between ourselves, I fear Mr. Warrington is in some trouble now, madam," continues the chaplain, steadily looking at Lady Maria.

"What, again?" shrieks the lady.

"Hush! Your ladyship's dear invalid!" whispers the chaplain again pointing towards Madame Bernstein. "Do you think your cousin has any partiality for any—any member of Mr. Lambert's family? for example, Miss Lambert?"

"There is nothing between him and Miss Lambert," says Lady Maria.

"Your ladyship is certain?"

"Women are said to have good eyes in such matters, my good Sampson," says my lady, with an easy air. "I thought the little girl seemed to be following him."

"Then I am at fault once more," the frank chaplain said. "Mr. Warrington said of the young lady, that she ought to go back to her doll, and called her a pert, stuck-up little hussy."

"Ah!" sighed Lady Maria, as if relieved by the news.

"Then, madam, there must be somebody else," said the chaplain. "Has he confided nothing to your ladyship?"

"To me, Mr. Sampson? What? Where? How?" exclaims Maria.

"Some six days ago, after we had been dining at the White Horse, and drinking too freely, Mr. Warrington lost a pocket-book containing letters."

"Letters?" gasps Lady Maria.

"And probably more money than he likes to own," continues Mr. Sampson, with a grave nod of the head. "He is very much disturbed about the book. We have both made cautious inquiries about it. We have——Gracious powers, is your ladyship ill?"

Here my Lady Maria gave three remarkably shrill screams, and tumbled off her chair.

"I will see the Prince. I have a right to see him. What's this?—Where am I?—What's the matter?" cries Madame Bernstein, waking up from her sleep. She had been dreaming of old days, no doubt. The old lady shook in all her limbs—her face was very much flushed. She stared about wildly a moment, and then tottered forward on her tortoiseshell cane. "What—what's the matter?" she asked again. "Have you killed her, sir?"

"Some sudden qualm must have come over her ladyship. Shall I cut her laces, madam? or send for a doctor?" cries the chaplain, with every look of innocence and alarm.

"What has passed between you, sir?" asked the old lady, fiercely.

"I give you my honour, madam, I have done I don't know what. I but mentioned that Mr. Warrington had lost a pocket-book containing letters, and my lady swooned, as you see."

Madame Bernstein dashed water on her niece's face. A feeble moan told presently that the lady was coming to herself.

The Baroness looked sternly after Mr. Sampson, as she sent him away on his errand for the doctor. Her aunt's grim countenance was of little comfort to poor Maria when she saw it on waking up from her swoon.

"What has happened?" asked the younger lady, bewildered and gasping.

"H'm! You know best what has happened, madam, I suppose. What hath happened before in our family?" cried the old Baroness, glaring at her niece with savage eyes.

"Ah, yes! the letters have been lost—ach lieber Himmel!" And Maria, as she would sometimes do, when much moved, began to speak in the language of her mother.

"Yes! the seal has been broken, and the letters have been lost, 'tis the old story of the Esmonds," cried the elder, bitterly.

"Seal broken, letters lost? What do you mean,—aunt?" asked Maria, faintly.

"I mean that my mother was the only honest woman that ever entered the family!" cried the Baroness, stamping her foot. "And she was a parson's daughter of no family in particular, or she would have gone wrong, too. Good heavens! is it decreed that we are all to be...?"

"To be what, madam?" cried Maria.

"To be what my Lady Queensberry said we were last night. To be what we are! You know the word for it!" cried the indignant old woman. "I say, what has come to the whole race? Your father's mother was an honest woman, Maria. Why did I leave her? Why couldn't you remain so?"

"Madam!" exclaims Maria, "I declare, before Heaven, I am as——"

"Bah! Don't madam me! Don't call heaven to witness—there's nobody by! And if you swore to your innocence till the rest of your teeth dropped out of your mouth, my Lady Maria Esmond, I would not believe you!"

"Ah! it was you told him!" gasped Maria. She recognised an arrow out of her aunt's quiver.

"I saw some folly going on between you and the boy, and I told him that you were as old as his mother. Yes, I did! Do you suppose I am going to let Henry Esmond's boy fling himself and his wealth away upon such a battered old rock as you? The boy shan't be robbed and cheated in our family. Not a shilling of mine shall any of you have if he comes to any harm amongst you.

"Ah! you told him!" cried Maria, with a sudden burst of rebellion. "Well, then! I'd have you to know that I don't care a penny, madam, for your paltry money! I have Mr. Harry Warrington's word—yes, and his letters—and I know he will die rather than break it."

"He will die if he keeps it!" (Maria shrugged her shoulders.)

"But you don't care for that—you've no more heart——"

"Than my father's sister, madam!" cries Maria again. The younger woman, ordinarily submissive, had turned upon here persecutor.

"Ah! Why did not I marry an honest man?" said the of lady, shaking her head sadly. "Henry Esmond was noble and good, and perhaps might have made me so. But no, no—we have all got the taint in us—all! You don't mean to sacrifice this boy, Maria?"

"Madame ma tante, do you take me for a fool at my age?" asks Maria.

"Set him free! I'll give you five thousand pounds—in my—in my will, Maria. I will, on my honour!"

"When you were young, and you liked Colonel Esmond, you threw him aside for an earl, and the earl for a duke?"

"Yes."

"Eh! Bon sang ne peut mentir! I have no money, I have no friends. My father was a spendthrift, my brother is a beggar. I have Mr. Warrington's word, and I know, madam, he will keep it. And that's what I tell your ladyship!" cries Lady Maria with a wave of her hand. "Suppose my letters are published to all the world to-morrow? Apres? I know they contain things I would as lieve not tell. Things not about me alone. Comment! Do you suppose there are no stories but mine in the family? It is not my letters that I am afraid of, so long as I have his, madam. Yes, his and his word, and I trust them both."

"I will send to my merchant, and give you the money now, Maria," pleaded the old lady.

"No, I shall have my pretty Harry, and ten times five thousand pounds!" cries Maria.

"Not till his mother's death, madam, who is just your age!"

"We can afford to wait, aunt. At my age, as you say, I am not so eager as young chits for a husband."

"But to wait my sister's death, at least, is a drawback?"

"Offer me ten thousand pounds, Madam Tusher, and then we will see!" cries Maria.

"I have not so much money in the world, Maria," said the old lady.

"Then, madam, let me make what I can for myself!" says Maria.

"Ah, if he heard you?"

"Apres? I have his word. I know he will keep it. I can afford to wait, madam," and she flung out of the room, just as the chaplain returned. It was Madame Bernstein who wanted cordials now. She was immensely moved and shocked by the news which had been thus suddenly brought to her.

CHAPTER XXXVI. Which seems to mean Mischief

Though she had clearly had the worst of the battle described in the last chapter, the Baroness Bernstein, when she next met her niece showed no rancour or anger. "Of course, my Lady Maria," she said, "you can't suppose that I, as Harry Warrington's near relative, can be pleased at the idea of his marrying a woman who is as old as his mother, and has not a penny to her fortune; but if he chooses to do so silly a thing, the affair is none of mine; and I doubt whether I should have been much inclined to be taken au serieux with regard to that offer of five thousand pounds which I made in the heat of our talk. So it was already at Castlewood that this pretty affair was arranged? Had I known how far it had gone, my dear, I should have spared some needless opposition. When a pitcher is broken, what railing can mend it?"

"Madam!" here interposed Maria.

"Pardon me—I mean nothing against your ladyship's honour or character, which, no doubt, are quite safe. Harry says so, and you say so—what more can one ask?"

"You have talked to Mr. Warrington, madam?"

"And he has owned that he made you a promise at Castlewood: that you have it in his writing."

"Certainly I have, madam!" says Lady Maria.

"Ah!" (the elder lady did not wince at this). "And I own, too, that at first I put a wrong construction upon the tenor of your letters to him. They implicate other members of the family——"

"Who have spoken most wickedly of me, and endeavoured to prejudice me in every way in my dear Mr. Warrington's eyes. Yes, madam, I own I have written against them, to justify myself."

"But, of course, are pained to think that any wretch should get possession of stories to the disadvantage of our family, and make them public scandal. Hence your disquiet just now."

"Exactly so," said Lady Maria. "From Mr. Warrington I could have nothing concealed henceforth, and spoke freely to him. But that is a very different thing from wishing all the world to know the disputes of a noble family."

"Upon my word, Maria, I admire you, and have done you injustice. These—these twenty years, let us say."

"I am very glad, madam, that you end by doing me justice at all," said the niece.

"When I saw you last night, opening the ball with my nephew, can you guess what I thought of, my dear?"

"I really have no idea what the Baroness de Bernstein thought of," said Lady Maria, haughtily.

"I remembered that you had performed to that very tune with the dancing-master at Kensington, my dear!"

"Madam, it was an infamous calumny."

"By which the poor dancing-master got a cudgelling for nothing!"

"It is cruel and unkind, madam, to recall that calumny—and I shall beg to decline living any longer with any one who utters it," continued Maria, with great spirit.

"You wish to go home? I can fancy you won't like Tunbridge. It will be very hot for you if those letters are found."

"There was not a word against you in them, madam: about that I can make your mind easy."

"So Harry said, and did your ladyship justice. Well, my dear, we are tired of one another, and shall be better apart for a while."

"That is precisely my own opinion," said Lady Maria, dropping a curtsey.

"Mr. Sampson can escort you to Castlewood. You and your maid can take a postchaise."

"We can take a postchaise, and Mr. Sampson can escort me," echoed the younger lady. "You see, madam, I act like a dutiful niece."

"Do you know, my dear, I have a notion that Sampson has got the letters?" said the Baroness, frankly.

"I confess that such a notion has passed through my own mind."

"And you want to go home in the chaise, and coax the letters from him! Delilah! Well, they can be no good to me, and I trust you may get them. When will you go? The sooner the better, you say? We are women of the world, Maria. We only call names when we are in a passion. We don't want each other's company; and we part on good terms. Shall we go to my Lady Yarmouth's? 'Tis her night. There is nothing like a change of scene after one of those little nervous attacks you have had, and cards drive away unpleasant thoughts better than any doctor."

Lady Maria agreed to go to Lady Yarmouth's cards, and was dressed and ready first, awaiting her aunt in the drawing-room. Madame Bernstein, as she came down, remarked Maria's door was left open. "She has the letters upon her," thought the old lady. And the pair went off to their entertainment in their respective chairs, and exhibited towards each other that charming cordiality and respect which women can show after, and even during, the bitterest quarrels.

That night, on their return from the Countess's drum, Mrs. Brett, Madame Bernstein's maid, presented herself to my Lady Maria's call, when that lady rang her hand-bell upon retiring to her room. Betty, Mrs. Brett was ashamed to say, was not in a fit state to come before my lady. Betty had been a-junketing and merry-making with Mr. Warrington's black gentleman, with my Lord Bamborough's valet, and several more ladies and gentlemen of that station, and the liquor—Mrs. Brett was shocked to own it—had proved too much for Mrs. Betty. Should Mrs. Brett undress my lady? My lady said she would undress without a maid, and gave Mrs. Brett leave to withdraw. "She has the letters in her stays," thought Madame Bernstein. They had bidden each other an amicable good-night on the stairs.

Mrs. Betty had a scolding the next morning, when she came to wait on her mistress, from the closet adjoining Lady Maria's apartment, in which Betty lay. She owned, with contrition, her partiality for rum-punch, which Mr. Gumbo had the knack of brewing most delicate. She took her scolding with meekness, and, having performed her usual duties about her lady's person, retired.

Now Betty was one of the Castlewood girls who had been so fascinated by Gumbo, and was a very good-looking, blue-eyed lass, upon whom Mr. Case, Madame Bernstein's confidential man, had also cast the eyes of affection. Hence, between Messrs. Gumbo and Case, there had been jealousies and even quarrels; which had caused Gumbo, who was of a peaceful disposition, to be rather shy of the Baroness's gentlemen, the chief of whom vowed he would break the bones, or have the life of Gumbo, if he persisted in his attentions to Mrs. Betty.

But on the night of the rum-punch, though Mr. Case found Gumbo and Mrs. Betty whispering in the doorway, in the cool breeze, and Gumbo would have turned pale with fear had he been able so to do, no one could be more gracious than Mr. Case. It was he who proposed the bowl of punch, which was brewed and drunk in Mrs. Betty's room, and which Gumbo concocted with exquisite skill. He complimented Gumbo on his music. Though a sober man ordinarily, he insisted upon more and more drinking, until poor Mrs. Betty was reduced to the state which occasioned her ladyship's just censure.

As for Mr. Case himself, who lay out of the house, he was so ill with the punch, that he kept his bed the whole of the next day, and did not get strength to make his appearance, and wait on his ladies, until supper-time; when his mistress good-naturedly rebuked him, saying that it was not often he sinned in that way.

"Why, Case, I could have made oath it was you I saw on horseback this morning galloping on the London road," said Mr. Warrington, who was supping with his relatives.

"Me! law bless you, sir! I was a-bed, and I thought my head would come off with the aching. I ate a bit at six o'clock, and drunk a deal of small beer, and I am almost my own man again now. But that Gumbo, saving your honour's presence, I won't taste none of his punch again." And the honest major-domo went on with his duties among the bottles and glasses.

As they sate after their meal, Madame Bernstein was friendly enough. She prescribed strong fortifying drinks for Maria, against the recurrence of her fainting fits. The lady had such attacks not unfrequently. She urged her to consult her London physician, and to send up an account of her case by Harry. By Harry! asked the lady. Yes. Harry was going for two days on an errand for his aunt to London. "I do not care to tell you, my dear, that it is on business which will do him good. I wish Mr. Draper to put him into my will, and as I am going travelling upon a round of visits when you and I part, I think, for security, I shall ask Mr. Warrington to take my trinket-box in his postchaise to London with him, for there have been robberies of late, and I have no fancy for being stopped by highwaymen."

Maria looked blank at the notion of the young gentleman's departure, but hoped that she might have his escort back to Castlewood, whither her elder brother had now returned. "Nay," says his aunt, "the lad hath been tied to our apron-strings long enough. A day in London will do him no harm. He can perform my errand for me and be back with you by Saturday."

"I would offer to accompany Mr. Warrington, but I preach on Friday before her ladyship," says Mr. Sampson. He was anxious that my Lady Yarmouth should judge of his powers as a preacher; and Madame Bernstein had exerted her influence with the king's favourite to induce her to hear the chaplain.

Harry relished the notion of a rattling journey to London, and a day or two of sport there. He promised that his pistols were good, and that he would hand the diamonds over in safety to the banker's strong-room. Would he occupy his aunt's London house? No, that would be a dreary lodging with only a housemaid and a groom in charge of it. He would go to the Star and Garter in Pall Mall, or to an inn in Covent Garden. "Ah! I have often talked over that journey," said Harry, his countenance saddening.

"And with whom, sir?" asked Lady Maria.

"With one who promised to make it with me," said the young man, thinking, as he always did, with an extreme tenderness of the lost brother.

"He has more heart, my good Maria, than some of us!" says Harry's aunt, witnessing his emotion. Uncontrollable gusts of grief would, not unfrequently, still pass over our young man. The parting from his brother; the scene and circumstances of George's fall last year; the recollection of his words, or of some excursion at home which they had planned together; would recur to him and overcome him. "I doubt, madam," whispered the chaplain, demurely, to Madame Bernstein, after one of these bursts of sorrow, "whether some folks in England would suffer quite so much at the death of their elder brother."

But, of course, this sorrow was not to be perpetual; and we can fancy Mr. Warrington setting out on his London journey eagerly enough, and very gay and happy, if it must be owned, to be rid of his elderly attachment. Yes. There was no help for it. At Castlewood, on one unlucky evening, he had made an offer of his heart and himself to his mature cousin, and she had accepted the foolish lad's offer. But the marriage now was out of the question. He must consult his mother. She was the mistress for life of the Virginian property. Of course she would refuse her consent to such a union. The thought of it was deferred to a late period. Meanwhile, it hung like a weight round the young man's neck, and caused him no small remorse and disquiet.

No wonder that his spirits rose more gaily as he came near London, and that he looked with delight from his postchaise windows upon the city as he advanced towards it. No highwayman stopped our traveller on Blackheath. Yonder are the gleaming domes of Greenwich, canopied with woods. There is the famous Thames, with its countless shipping; there actually is the Tower of London. "Look, Gumbo! There is the Tower!" "Yes, master," says Gumbo, who has never heard of the Tower; but Harry has, and remembers how he has read about it in Howell's Medulla, and how he and his brother used to play at the Tower, and he thinks with delight now, how he is actually going to see the armour and the jewels and the lions. They pass through Southwark and over that famous London Bridge, which was all covered with houses like a street two years ago. Now there is only a single gate left, and that is coming down. Then the chaise rolls through the city; and, "Look, Gumbo, that is Saint Paul's!" "Yes, master; Saint Paul's," says Gumbo, obsequiously, but little struck by the beauties of the architecture. And so by the well-known course we reach the Temple, and Gumbo and his master look up with awe at the rebel heads on Temple Bar.

The chaise drives to Mr. Draper's chambers in Middle Temple Lane, where

Harry handed the precious box over to Mr. Draper, and a letter from his aunt, which the gentleman read with some interest seemingly, and carefully put away. He then consigned the trinket-box to his strong closet, went into the adjoining room, taking his clerk with him, and then was at Mr. Warrington's service to take him to an hotel. An hotel in Covent Garden was fixed upon as the best place for his residence. "I shall have to keep you for two or three days, Mr. Warrington," the lawyer said. "I don't think the papers which the Baroness wants can be ready until then. Meanwhile, I am at your service to see the town. I live out of it myself, and have a little box at Camberwell, where I shall be proud to have the honour of entertaining Mr. Warrington; but a young man, I suppose, will like his inn and his liberty best, sir?"

Harry said yes, he thought the inn would be best; and the postchaise, and a clerk of Mr. Draper's inside, was despatched to the Bedford, whither the two gentlemen agreed to walk on foot.

Mr. Draper and Mr. Warrington sat and talked for a while. The Drapers, father and son, had been lawyers time out of mind to the Esmond family, and the attorney related to the young gentleman numerous stories regarding his ancestors of Castlewood. Of the present Earl Mr. Draper was no longer the agent: his father and his lordship had had differences, and his lordship's business had been taken elsewhere: but the Baroness was still their honoured client, and very happy indeed was Mr. Draper to think that her ladyship was so well disposed towards her nephew.

As they were taking their hats to go out, a young clerk of the house stopped his principal in the passage, and said: "If you please, sir, them papers of the Baroness was given to her ladyship's man, Mr. Case, two days ago."

"Just please to mind your own business, Mr. Brown," said the lawyer, rather sharply. "This way, Mr. Warrington. Our Temple stairs are rather dark. Allow me to show you the way."

Harry saw Mr. Draper darting a Parthian look of anger at Mr. Brown. "So it was Case I saw on the London Road two days ago," he thought. "What business brought the old fox to London?" Wherewith, not choosing to be inquisitive about other folks' affairs, he dismissed the subject from his mind.

Whither should they go first? First, Harry was for going to see the place where his grandfather and Lord Castlewood had fought a duel fifty-six years ago, in Leicester Field. Mr. Draper knew the place well, and all about the story. They might take Covent Garden on their way to Leicester Field, and see that Mr. Warrington was comfortably lodged. "And order dinner," says Mr. Warrington. No, Mr. Draper could not consent to that. Mr. Warrington must be so obliging as to honour him on that day. In fact, he had made so bold as to order a collation from the Cock. Mr. Warrington could not decline an invitation so pressing, and walked away gaily with his friend, passing under that arch where the heads were, and taking off his hat to them, much to the lawyer's astonishment.

"They were gentlemen who died for their king, sir. My dear brother George and I always said we would salute 'em when we saw 'em," Mr. Warrington said.

"You'll have a mob at your heels if you do, sir," said the alarmed lawyer.

"Confound the mob, sir," said Mr. Harry, loftily, but the passers-by, thinking about their own affairs, did not take any notice of Mr. Warrington's conduct; and he walked up the thronging Strand, gazing with delight upon all he saw, remembering, I dare say, for all his life after, the sights and impressions there presented to him, but maintaining a discreet reserve; for he did not care to let the lawyer know how much he was moved, or the public perceive that he was a stranger. He did not hear much of his companion's talk, though the latter chattered ceaselessly on the way. Nor was Mr. Draper displeased by the young Virginian's silent and haughty demeanour. A hundred years ago a gentleman was a gentleman, and his attorney his very humble servant.

The chamberlain at the Bedford showed Mr. Warrington to his rooms, bowing before him with delightful obsequiousness, for Gumbo had already trumpeted his master's greatness, and Mr. Draper's clerk announced that the new-comer was a "high fellar." Then, the rooms surveyed, the two gentlemen went to Leicester Field, Mr. Gumbo strutting behind his master: and, having looked at the scene of his grandsire's wound, and poor Lord Castlewood's tragedy, they returned to the Temple to Mr. Draper's chambers.

Who was that shabby-looking big man Mr. Warrington bowed to as they went out after dinner for a walk in the gardens? That was Mr. Johnson, an author, whom he had met at Tunbridge Wells. "Take the advice of a man of the world, sir," says Mr. Draper, eyeing the shabby man of letters very superciliously; "the less you have to do with that kind of person, the better. The business we have into our office about them literary men is not very pleasant, I can tell you." "Indeed!" says Mr. Warrington. He did not like his new friend the more as the latter grew more familiar. The theatres were shut. Should they go to Sadler's Wells? or Marybone Gardens? or Ranelagh? or how? "Not Ranelagh," says Mr. Draper, "because there's none of the nobility in town;" but, seeing in the newspaper that at the entertainment at Sadler's Wells, Islington, there would be the most singular kind of diversion on eight hand-bells by Mr. Franklyn, as well as the surprising performances of Signora Catherina, Harry wisely determined that he would go to Marybone Gardens, where they had a concert of music, a choice of tea, coffee, and all sorts of wines, and the benefit of Mr. Draper's ceaseless conversation. The lawyer's obsequiousness only ended at Harry's bedroom door, where, with haughty grandeur, the young gentleman bade his talkative host good night.

The next morning Mr. Warrington, arrayed in his brocade bedgown, took his breakfast, read the newspaper, and enjoyed his ease in his inn. He read in the paper news from his own country. And when he saw the words, Williamsburg, Virginia, June 7th, his eyes grew dim somehow. He had just had letters by that packet of June 7th, but his mother did not tell how—"A great number of the principal gentry of the colony have associated themselves under the command of the Honourable Peyton Randolph, Esquire, to march to the relief of their distressed fellow-subjects, and revenge the cruelties of the French and their barbarous allies. They are in a uniform: viz., a plain blue frock, nanquin or brown waistcoats and breeches, and plain hats. They are armed each with a light firelock, a brace of pistols, and a cutting sword."

"Ah, why ain't we there, Gumbo?" cried out Harry.

"Why ain't we dar?" shouted Gumbo.

"Why am I here, dangling at women's trains?" continued the Virginian.

"Think dangling at women's trains very pleasant, Master Harry!" says the materialistic Gumbo, who was also very little affected by some further home news which his master read, viz., that The Lovely Sally, Virginia ship, had been taken in sight of port by a French privateer.

And now, reading that the finest mare in England, and a pair of very genteel bay geldings, were to be sold at the Bull Inn, the lower end of Hatton Garden, Harry determined to go and look at the animals, and inquired his way to the place. He then and there bought the genteel bay geldings, and paid for them with easy generosity. He never said what he did on that day, being shy of appearing like a stranger; but it is believed that he took a coach and went to Westminster Abbey, from which he bade the coachman drive him to the Tower, then to Mrs. Salmon's Waxwork, then to Hyde Park and Kensington Palace; then he had given orders to go to the Royal Exchange, but catching a glimpse of Covent Garden, on his way to the Exchange, he bade Jehu take him to his inn, and cut short his enumeration of places to which he had been, by flinging the fellow a guinea.

Mr. Draper had called in his absence, and said he would come again; but Mr. Warrington, having dined sumptuously by himself, went off nimbly to Marybone Gardens again, in the same noble company.

As he issued forth the next day, the bells of St. Paul's, Covent Garden, were ringing for morning prayers, and reminded him that friend Sampson was going to preach his sermon. Harry smiled. He had begun to have a shrewd and just opinion of the value of Mr. Sampson's sermons.

CHAPTER XXXVII. In which various Matches are fought

Reading in the London Advertiser, which was served to his worship with his breakfast, an invitation to all lovers of manly British sport to come and witness a trial of skill between the great champions Sutton and Figg, Mr. Warrington determined upon attending these performances, and accordingly proceeded to the Wooden House, in Marybone Fields, driving thither the pair of horses which he had purchased on the previous day. The young charioteer did not know the road very well, and veered and tacked very much more than was needful upon his journey from Covent Garden, losing himself in the green lanes behind Mr. Whitfield's round Tabernacle of Tottenham Road, and the fields in the midst of which Middlesex Hospital stood. He reached his destination at length, however, and found no small company assembled to witness the valorous achievements of the two champions.

A crowd of London blackguards was gathered round the doors of this temple of British valour; together with the horses and equipages of a few persons of fashion, who came, like Mr. Warrington, to patronise the sport. A variety of beggars and cripples hustled round the young gentleman, and whined to him for charity. Shoeblack-boys tumbled over each other for the privilege of blacking his honour's boots; nosegay-women and flying fruiterers plied Mr. Gumbo with their wares; piemen, pads, tramps, strollers of every variety, hung round the battle-ground. A flag was flying upon the building; and, on to the stage in front, accompanied by a drummer and a horn-blower, a manager repeatedly issued to announce to the crowd that the noble English sports were just about to begin.

Mr. Warrington paid his money, and was accommodated with a seat in a gallery commanding a perfect view of the platform whereon the sports were performed; Mr. Gumbo took his seat in the amphitheatre below; or, when tired, issued forth into the outer world to drink a pot of beer, or play a game at cards with his brother-lacqueys, and the gentlemen's coachmen on the boxes of the carriages waiting without. Lacqueys, liveries, footmen—the old society was encumbered with a prodigious quantity of these. Gentlemen or women could scarce move without one, sometimes two or three, vassals in attendance. Every theatre had its footman's gallery: an army of the liveried race hustled around every chapel-door: they swarmed in anterooms: they sprawled in halls and on landings: they guzzled, devoured, debauched, cheated, played cards, bullied visitors for vails:—that noble old race of footmen is well-nigh gone. A few thousand of them may still be left among us. Grand, tall, beautiful, melancholy, we still behold them on levee days, with their nosegays and their buckles, their plush and their powder. So have I seen in America specimens, nay camps and villages, of Red Indians. But the race is doomed. The fatal decree has gone forth, and Uncas with his tomahawk and eagle's plume, and Jeames with his cocked hat and long cane, are passing out of the world where they once walked in glory.

Before the principal combatants made their appearance, minor warriors and exercises were exhibited. A boxing-match came off, but neither of the men were very game or severely punished, so that Mr. Warrington and the rest of the spectators had but little pleasure out of that encounter. Then ensued some cudgel-playing; but the heads broken were of so little note, and the wounds given so trifling and unsatisfactory, that no wonder the company began to hiss, grumble, and show other signs of discontent. "The masters, the masters!" shouted the people, whereupon those famous champions at length thought fit to appear.

The first who walked up the steps to the stage was the intrepid Sutton, sword in hand, who saluted the company with his warlike weapon, making an especial bow and salute to a private box or gallery in which sate a stout gentleman, who was seemingly a person of importance. Sutton was speedily followed by the famous Figg, to whom the stout gentleman waved a hand of approbation. Both men were in their shirts, their heads were shaven clean, but bore the cracks and scars of many former glorious battles. On his burly sword-arm, each intrepid champion wore an "armiger," or ribbon of his colour. And now the gladiators shook hands, and, as a contemporary poet says: "The word it was bilboe." [The antiquarian reader knows the pleasant poem in the sixth volume of Dodsley's Collection, in which the above combat is described.]

At the commencement of the combat the great Figg dealt a blow so tremendous at his opponent, that had it encountered the other's honest head, that comely noddle would have been shorn off as clean as the carving-knife chops the carrot. But Sutton received his adversary's blade on his own sword, whilst Figg's blow was delivered so mightily that the weapon brake in his hands, less constant than the heart of him who wielded it. Other sword were now delivered to the warriors. The first blood drawn spouted from the panting side of Figg amidst a yell of delight from Sutton's supporters; but the veteran appealing to his audience, and especially, as it seemed, to the stout individual in the private gallery, showed that his sword broken in the previous encounter had caused the wound.

Whilst the parley occasioned by this incident was going on, Mr. Warrington saw a gentleman in a riding-frock and plain scratch-wig enter the box devoted to the stout personage, and recognised with pleasure his Tunbridge Wells friend, my Lord of March and Ruglen. Lord March, who was by no means prodigal of politeness seemed to show singular deference to the stout gentleman, and Harry remarked how his lordship received, with a profound bow, some bank-bills which the other took out from a pocket-book and handed to him. Whilst thus engaged, Lord March spied out our Virginian, and, his interview with the stout personage finished, my lord came over to Harry's gallery and warmly greeted his young friend. They sat and beheld the combat waging with various success, but with immense skill and valour on both sides. After the warriors had sufficiently fought with swords, they fell to with the quarter-staff, and the result of this long and delightful battle was, that victory remained with her ancient champion Figg.

Whilst the warriors were at battle, a thunderstorm had broken over the building, and Mr. Warrington gladly enough accepted a seat in my Lord March's chariot, leaving his own phaeton to be driven home by his groom. Harry was in great delectation with the noble sight he had witnessed: be pronounced this indeed to be something like sport, and of the best he had seen since his arrival in England: and, as usual, associating any pleasure which he enjoyed with the desire that the dear companion of his boyhood should share the amusement in common with him, he began by sighing out, "I wish..." then he stopped. "No, I don't," says he.

"What do you wish and what don't you wish?" asks Lord March.

"I was thinking, my lord, of my elder brother, and wished he had been with me. We had promised to have our sport together at home, you see; and many's the time we talked of it. But he wouldn't have liked this rough sort of sport, and didn't care for fighting, though he was the bravest lad alive."

"Oh! he was the bravest lad alive, was he?" asks my lord, lolling on his cushion, and eyeing his Virginian friend with some curiosity.

"You should have seen him in a quarrel with a very gallant officer, our friend —an absurd affair, but it was hard to keep George off him. I never saw a fellow so cool, nor more savage and determined, God help me. Ah! I wish for the honour of the country, you know, that he could have come here instead of me, and shown you a real Virginian gentleman."

"Nay, sir, you'll do very well. What is this I hear of Lady Yarmouth taking you into favour?" said the amused nobleman.

"I will do as well as another. I can ride, and, I think, I can shoot better than George; but then my brother had the head, sir, the head!" says Harry, tapping his own honest skull. "Why, I give you my word, my lord, that he had read almost every book that was ever written; could play both on the fiddle and harpsichord, could compose poetry and sermons most elegant. What can I do? I am only good to ride and play at cards, and drink Burgundy." And the penitent hung down his head. "But them I can do as well as most fellows, you see. In fact, my lord, I'll back myself," he resumed, to the other's great amusement.

Lord March relished the young man's naivete, as the jaded voluptuary still to the end always can relish the juicy wholesome mutton-chop. "By Gad, Mr. Warrington," says he, "you ought to be taken to Exeter 'Change, and put in a show."

"And for why?"

"A gentleman from Virginia who has lost his elder brother and absolutely regrets him. The breed ain't known in this country. Upon my honour and conscience, I believe that you would like to have him back again."

"Believe!" cries the Virginian, growing red in the face.

"That is, you believe you believe you would like him back again. But depend on it you wouldn't. 'Tis not in human nature, sir; not as I read it, at least. Here are some fine houses we are coming to. That at the corner is Sir Richard Littleton's, that great one was my Lord Bingley's. 'Tis a pity they do nothing better with this great empty space of Cavendish Square than fence it with these unsightly boards. By George! I don't know where the town's running. There's Montagu House made into a confounded Don Saltero's museum, with books and stuffed birds and rhinoceroses. They have actually run a cursed cut —New Road they call it—at the back of Bedford House Gardens, and spoilt the Duke's comfort, though, I guess, they will console him in the pocket. I don't know where the town will stop. Shall we go down Tyburn Road and the Park, or through Swallow Street, and into the habitable quarter of the town? We can dine at Pall Mall, or, if you like, with you; and we can spend the evening as you like—with the Queen of Spades, or..."

"With the Queen of Spades, if your lordship pleases," says Mr. Warrington, blushing. So the equipage drove to his hotel in Covent Garden, where the landlord came forward with his usual obsequiousness, and recognising my Lord of March and Ruglen, bowed his wig on to my lord's shoes in his humble welcomes to his lordship. A rich young English peer in the reign of

George the Second; a wealthy patrician in the reign of Augustus; which would you rather have been? There is a question for any young gentlemen's debating-clubs of the present day.

The best English dinner which could be produced, of course, was at the service of the young Virginian and his noble friend. After dinner came wine in plenty, and of quality good enough even for the epicurean earl. Over the wine there was talk of going to see the fireworks at Vauxhall, or else of cards. Harry, who had never seen a firework beyond an exhibition of a dozen squibs at Williamsburg on the fifth of November (which he thought a sublime display), would have liked the Vauxhall, but yielded to his guest's preference for piquet; and they were very soon absorbed in that game.

Harry began by winning as usual; but, in the course of a half-hour, the luck turned and favoured my Lord March, who was at first very surly when Mr. Draper, Mr. Warrington's man of business, came bowing into the room, where he accepted Harry's invitation to sit and drink. Mr. Warrington always asked everybody to sit and drink, and partake of his best. Had he a crust, he would divide it; had he a haunch, he would share it; had he a jug of water, he would drink about with a kindly spirit; had he a bottle of Burgundy, it was gaily drunk with a thirsty friend. And don't fancy the virtue is common. You read of it in books, my dear sir, and fancy that you have it yourself because you give six dinners of twenty people and pay your acquaintance all round; but the welcome, the friendly spirit, the kindly heart? Believe me, these are rare qualities in our selfish world. We may bring them with us from the country when we are young, but they mostly wither after transplantation, and droop and perish in the stifling London air.

Draper did not care for wine very much, but it delighted the lawyer to be in the company of a great man. He protested that he liked nothing better than to see piquet played by two consummate players and men of fashion; and, taking a seat, undismayed by the sidelong scowls of his lordship, surveyed the game between the gentlemen. Harry was not near a match for the experienced player of the London clubs. To-night, too, Lord March held better cards to aid his skill.

What their stakes were was no business of Mr. Draper's. The gentlemen said they would play for shillings, and afterwards counted up their gains and losses, with scarce any talking, and that in an undertone. A bow on both sides, a perfectly grave and polite manner on the part of each, and the game went on.

But it was destined to a second interruption, which brought an execration from Lord March's lips. First was heard a scuffling without—then a whispering—then an outcry as of a woman in tears, and then, finally, a female rushed into the room, and produced that explosion of naughty language from Lord March.

"I wish your women would take some other time for coming, confound 'em," says my lord, laying his cards down in a pet.

"What, Mrs. Betty!" cried Harry.

Indeed it was no other than Mrs. Betty, Lady Maria's maid; and Gumbo stood behind her, his fine countenance beslobbered with tears.

"What has happened?" asks Mr. Warrington, in no little perturbation of spirit. "The Baroness is well?"

"Help! help! sir, your honour!" ejaculates Mrs. Betty, and proceeds to fall on her knees.

"Help whom?"

A howl ensues from Gumbo.

"Gumbo! you scoundrel! has anything happened between Mrs. Betty and you?" asks the black's master.

Mr. Gumbo steps back with great dignity, laying his hand on his heart, and saying, "No, sir; nothing hab happened 'twix' this lady and me."

"It's my mistress, sir," cries Betty. "Help! help! here's the letter she have wrote, sir! They have gone and took her, sir!"

"Is it only that old Molly Esmond? She's known to be over head and heels in debt! Dry your eyes in the next room, Mrs. Betty, and let me and Mr. Warrington go on with our game," says my lord, taking up his cards.

"Help! help her!" cries Betty again. "Oh, Mr. Harry! you won't be a-going on with your cards, when my lady calls out to you to come and help her! Your honour used to come quick enough when my lady used to send me to fetch you at Castlewood!"

"Confound you! can't you hold your tongue?" says my lord, with more choice words and oaths.

But Betty would not cease weeping, and it was decreed that Lord March was to cease winning for that night. Mr. Warrington rose from his seat, and made for the bell, saying:

"My dear lord, the game must be over for to-night. My relative writes to me in great distress, and I am bound to go to her."

"Curse her! Why couldn't she wait till to-morrow?" cries my lord, testily.

Mr. Warrington ordered a postchaise instantly. His own horses would take him to Bromley.

"Bet you, you don't do it within the hour! bet you, you don't do it within five quarters of an hour! bet you four to one—or I'll take your bet, which you please—that you're not robbed on Blackheath! Bet you, you are not at Tunbridge Wells before midnight!" cries Lord March.

"Done!" says Mr. Warrington. And my lord carefully notes down the terms of the four wagers in his pocket-book.

Lady Maria's letter ran as follows:—

"MY DEAR COUSIN—I am fell into a trapp, which I perceive the machinations of villians. I am a prisner. Betty will tell you all. Ah, my Henrico! come to the resque of your MOLLY."

In half an hour after the receipt of this missive, Mr. Warrington was in his postchaise and galloping over Westminster Bridge on the road to succour his kinswoman.

CHAPTER XXXVIII. Sampson and the Philistines

My happy chance in early life led me to become intimate with a respectable person who was born in a certain island, which is pronounced to be the first gem of the ocean by, no doubt, impartial judges of maritime jewellery. The stories which that person imparted to me regarding his relatives who inhabited the gem above-mentioned, were such as used to make my young blood curdle with horror to think there should be so much wickedness in the world. Every crime which you can think of; the entire Ten Commandments broken in a general smash; such rogueries and knaveries as no storyteller could invent; such murders and robberies as Thurtell or Turpin scarce ever perpetrated;— were by my informant accurately remembered, and freely related, respecting his nearest kindred, to any one who chose to hear him. It was a wonder how any of the family still lived out of the hulks. Me brother Tim had brought his fawther's gree hairs with sorrow to the greeve; me brother Mick had robbed the par'sh church repaytedly; me sisther Annamaroia had jilted the Captain and run off with the Ensign, forged her grandmother's will, and stole the spoons, which Larry the knife-boy was hanged for. The family of Atreus was as nothing compared to the race of O'What-d'ye-call-'em, from which my friend sprung; but no power on earth would, of course, induce me to name the country whence he came.

How great then used to be my naif astonishment to find these murderers, rogues, parricides, habitual forgers of bills of exchange, and so forth, every now and then writing to each other as "my dearest brother," "my dearest sister," and for months at a time living on the most amicable terms! With hands reeking with the blood of his murdered parents, Tim would mix a screeching tumbler, and give Maria a glass from it. With lips black with the perjuries he had sworn in court respecting his grandmother's abstracted testament, or the murder of his poor brother Thady's helpless orphans, Mick would kiss his sister Julia's bonny cheek, and they would have a jolly night, and cry as they talked about old times, and the dear old Castle What-d'ye-call-'em, where they were born, and the fighting Onetyoneth being quartered there, and the Major proposing for Cyaroloine, and the tomb of their seented mother (who had chayted them out of the propertee). Heaven bless her soul! They used to weep and kiss so profusely at meeting and parting, that it was touching to behold them. At the sight of their embraces one forgot those painful little stories, and those repeated previous assurances that, did they tell all, they could hang each other all round.

What can there be finer than forgiveness? What more rational than, after calling a man by every bad name under the sun, to apologise, regret hasty expressions, and so forth, withdraw the decanter (say) which you have flung at your enemy's head, and be friends as before? Some folks possess this admirable, this angellike gift of forgiveness. It was beautiful, for instance, to see our two ladies at Tunbridge Wells forgiving one another, smiling, joking, fondling almost in spite of the hard words of yesterday—yes, and forgetting bygones, though they couldn't help remembering them perfectly well. I wonder, can you and I do as much? Let us strive, my friend, to acquire this pacable, Christian spirit. My belief is that you may learn to forgive bad language employed to you; but, then, you must have a deal of practice, and be accustomed to hear and use it. You embrace after a quarrel and mutual bad language. Heaven bless us! Bad words are nothing when one is accustomed to them, and scarce need ruffle the temper on either side.

So the aunt and niece played cards very amicably together, and drank to each other's health, and each took a wing of the chicken, and pulled a bone of the merry-thought, and (in conversation) scratched their neighbours', not each other's, eyes out. Thus we have read how the Peninsular warriors, when the bugles sang truce, fraternised and exchanged tobacco-pouches and wine, ready to seize their firelocks and knock each other's heads off when the truce was over; and thus our old soldiers, skilful in war, but knowing the charms of a quiet life, laid their weapons down for the nonce, and hob-and-nobbed gaily together. Of course, whilst drinking with Jack Frenchman, you have your piece handy to blow his brains out if he makes a hostile move: but, meanwhile, it is A votre sante, mon camarade! Here's to you, mounseer! and everything is as pleasant as possible. Regarding Aunt Bernstein's threatened gout? The twinges had gone off. Maria was so glad! Maria's fainting fits? She had no return of them. A slight recurrence last night. The Baroness was so sorry! Her niece must see the best doctor, take everything to fortify her, continue to take the steel, even after she left Tunbridge. How kind of Aunt Bernstein to offer to send some of the bottled waters after her! Suppose Madame Bernstein says in confidence to her own woman, "Fainting fits!—pooh!—epilepsy! inherited from that horrible scrofulous German mother!" What means have we of knowing the private conversation of the old lady and her attendant? Suppose Lady Maria orders Mrs. Betty, her ladyship's maid, to taste every glass of medicinal water, first declaring that her aunt is capable of poisoning her? Very likely such conversations take place. These are but precautions—these are the firelocks which our old soldiers have at their sides, loaded and cocked, but at present lying quiet on the grass.

Having Harry's bond in her pocket, the veteran Maria did not choose to press for payment. She knew the world too well for that. He was bound to her, but she gave him plenty of day-rule, and leave of absence on parole. It was not her object needlessly to chafe and anger her young slave. She knew the difference of ages, and that Harry must have his pleasures and diversions. "Take your ease and amusement, cousin," says Lady Maria. "Frisk about, pretty little mousekin," says grey Grimalkin, purring in the corner, and keeping watch with her green eyes. About all that Harry was to see and do on his first visit to London, his female relatives had of course talked and joked. Both of the ladies knew perfectly what were a young gentleman's ordinary amusements in those days, and spoke of them with the frankness which characterised those easy times.

Our wily Calypso consoled herself, then, perfectly, in the absence of her young wanderer, and took any diversion which came to hand. Mr. Jack Morris, the gentleman whom we have mentioned as rejoicing in the company of Lord March and Mr. Warrington, was one of these diversions. To live with titled personages was the delight of Jack Morris's life; and to lose money at cards to an earl's daughter was almost a pleasure to him. Now, the Lady Maria Esmond was an earl's daughter who was very glad to win money. She obtained permission to take Mr. Morris to the Countess of Yarmouth's assembly, and played cards with him—and so everybody was pleased.

Thus the first eight-and-forty hours after Mr. Warrington's departure passed pretty cheerily at Tunbridge Wells, and Friday arrived, when the sermon was to be delivered which we have seen Mr. Sampson preparing. The company at the Wells were ready enough to listen to it. Sampson had a reputation for being a most amusing and eloquent preacher; and if there were no breakfast, conjurer, dancing bears, concert going on, the good Wells folk would put up with a sermon. He knew Lady Yarmouth was coming, and what a power she had in the giving of livings and the dispensing of bishoprics, the Defender of the Faith of that day having a remarkable confidence in her ladyship's opinion upon these matters;—and so we may be sure that Mr. Sampson prepared his very best discourse for her hearing. When the Great Man is at home at the Castle, and walks over to the little country church, in the park, bringing the Duke, the Marquis, and a couple of Cabinet Ministers with him, has it ever been your lot to sit among the congregation, and watch Mr. Trotter the curate and his sermon? He looks anxiously at the Great Pew; he falters as he gives out his text, and thinks, "Ah! perhaps his lordship may give me a living!" Mrs. Trotter and the girls look anxiously at the Great Pew too, and watch the effects of papa's discourse—the well-known favourite discourse—upon the big-wigs assembled. Papa's first nervousness is over: his noble voice clears, warms to his sermon: he kindles: he takes his pocket-handkerchief out: he is coming to that exquisite passage which has made them all cry at the parsonage: he has begun it! Ah! What is that humming noise, which fills the edifice, and causes hob-nailed Melibaeus to grin at smock-frocked Tityrus? It is the Right Honourable Lord Naseby snoring in the pew by the fire! And poor Trotter's visionary mitre disappears with the music.

Sampson was the domestic chaplain of Madame Bernstein's nephew. The two ladies of the Esmond family patronised the preacher. On the day of the sermon, the Baroness had a little breakfast in his honour, at which Sampson made his appearance, rosy and handsome, with a fresh-flowered wig, and a smart, rustling, new cassock, which he had on credit from some church-admiring mercer at the Wells. By the side of his patronesses, their ladyships' lacqueys walking behind them with their great gilt prayer-books, Mr. Sampson marched from breakfast to church. Every one remarked how well the Baroness Bernstein looked; she laughed, and was particularly friendly with her niece; she had a bow and a stately smile for all, as she moved on, with her tortoiseshell cane. At the door there was a dazzling conflux of rank and fashion—all the fine company of the Wells trooping in; and her ladyship of

Yarmouth, conspicuous with vermilion cheeks, and a robe of flame-coloured taffeta. There were shabby people present, besides the fine company, though these latter were by far the most numerous. What an odd-looking pair, for instance, were those in ragged coats, one of them with his carroty hair appearing under his scratch-wig, and who entered the church just as the organ stopped! Nay, he could not have been a Protestant, for he mechanically crossed himself as he entered the place, saying to his comrade, "Bedad, Tim, I forgawt!" by which I conclude that the individual came from an island which has been mentioned at the commencement of this chapter. Wherever they go a rich fragrance of whisky spreads itself. A man may be a heretic, but possess genius: these Catholic gentlemen have come to pay homage to Mr. Sampson.

Nay, there are not only members of the old religion present, but disciples of a creed still older. Who are those two individuals with hooked noses and sallow countenances, who worked into the church in spite of some little opposition on the part of the beadle? Seeing the greasy appearance of these Hebrew strangers, Mr. Beadle was for denying them admission. But one whispered into his ear, "We wants to be conwerted, gov'nor!" another slips money into his hand,—Mr. Beadle lifts up the mace with which he was barring the doorway, and the Hebrew gentlemen enter. There goes the organ! the doors have closed. Shall we go in, and listen to Mr. Sampson's sermon, or lie on the grass without?

Preceded by that beadle in gold lace, Sampson walked up to the pulpit, as rosy and jolly a man as you could wish to see. Presently, when he surged up out of his plump pulpit cushion, why did his Reverence turn as pale as death? He looked to the western church-door—there, on each side of it, were those horrible Hebrew caryatides. He then looked to the vestry-door, which was hard by the rector's pew, in which Sampson had been sitting during the service, alongside of their ladyships his patronesses. Suddenly a couple of perfumed Hibernian gentlemen slipped out of an adjacent seat, and placed themselves on a bench close by that vestry-door and rector's pew, and so sate till the conclusion of the sermon, with eyes meekly cast down to the ground. How can we describe that sermon, if the preacher himself never knew how it came to an end?

Nevertheless, it was considered an excellent sermon. When it was over, the fine ladies buzzed into one another's ears over their pews, and uttered their praise and comments. Madame Walmoden, who was in the next pew to our friends, said it was bewdiful, and made her dremble all over. Madame Bernstein said it was excellent. Lady Maria was pleased to think that the family chaplain should so distinguish himself. She looked up at him, and strove to catch his reverence's eye, as he still sate in his pulpit; she greeted him with a little wave of the hand and flutter of her handkerchief. He scarcely seemed to note the compliment; his face was pale, his eyes were looking yonder, towards the font, where those Hebrews still remained. The stream of people passed by them—in a rush, when they were lost to sight,—in a throng—in a march of twos and threes—in a dribble of one at a time. Everybody was gone. The two

Hebrews were still there by the door.

The Baroness de Bernstein and her niece still lingered in the rector's pew, where the old lady was deep in conversation with that gentleman.

"Who are those horrible men at the door? and what a smell of spirits there is!" cries Lady Maria, to Mrs. Brett, her aunt's woman, who had attended the two ladies.

"Farewell, doctor; you have a darling little boy: is he to be a clergyman, too?" asks Madame de Bernstein. "Are you ready, my dear?" And the pew is thrown open, and Madame Bernstein, whose father was only a viscount, insists that her niece, Lady Maria, who was an earl's daughter, should go first out of the pew.

As she steps forward, those individuals whom her ladyship designated as two horrible men, advance. One of them pulls a long strip of paper out of his pocket, and her ladyship starts and turns pale. She makes for the vestry, in a vague hope that she can clear the door and close it behind her. The two whiskified gentlemen are up with her, however; one of them actually lays his hand on her shoulder, and says:

"At the shuit of Misthress Pincott, of Kinsington, mercer, I have the honour of arresting your leedyship. Me neem is Costigan, madam, a poor gentleman of Oireland, binding to circumstances and forced to follow a disagrayable profession. Will your leedyship walk, or shall me man go fetch a cheer?"

For reply Lady Maria Esmond gives three shrieks, and falls swooning to the ground. "Keep the door, Mick!" shouts Mr. Costigan. "Best let in no one else, madam," he says, very politely, to Madame de Bernstein. "Her ladyship has fallen in a feenting fit, and will recover here, at her aise."

"Unlace her, Brett!" cries the old lady, whose eyes twinkle oddly; and as soon as that operation is performed, Madame Bernstein seizes a little bag suspended by a hair chain, which Lady Maria wears round her neck, and snips the necklace in twain. "Dash some cold water over her face, it always recovers her!" says the Baroness. "You stay with her, Brett. How much is your suit gentlemen?"

Mr. Costigan says, "The deem we have against her leedyship for one hundred and thirty-two pounds, in which she is indebted to Misthress Eliza Pincott"

Meanwhile, where is the Reverend Mr. Sampson? Like the fabled opossum we have read of, who, when he spied the unerring gunner from his gum-tree, said: "It's no use Major, I will come down," so Sampson gave himself up to his pursuers. "At whose suit, Simons?" he sadly asked. Sampson knew Simons: they had met many a time before.

"Buckleby Cordwainer," says Mr. Simons.

"Forty-eight pound and charges, I know," says Mr. Sampson, with a sigh. "I haven't got the money. What officer is there here?" Mr. Simons's companion, Mr. Lyons, here stepped forward, and said his house was most convenient, and often used by gentlemen, and he should be most happy and proud to accommodate his reverence.

Two chairs happened to be in waiting outside the chapel. In those two chairs my Lady Maria Esmond and Mr. Sampson placed themselves, and went to Mr. Lyons's residence, escorted by the gentlemen to whom we have just been introduced.

Very soon after the capture the Baroness Bernstein sent Mr. Case, her confidential servant, with a note to her niece, full of expressions of the most ardent affection: but regretting that her heavy losses at cards rendered the payment of such a sum as that in which Lady Maria stood indebted quite impossible. She had written off to Mrs. Pincott, by that very post, however, to entreat her to grant time, and as soon as ever she had an answer, would not fail to acquaint her dear unhappy niece.

Mrs. Betty came over to console her mistress: and the two poor women cast about for money enough to provide a horse and chaise for Mrs. Betty, who had very nearly come to misfortune, too. Both my Lady Maria and her maid had been unlucky at cards, and could not muster more than eighteen shillings between them: so it was agreed that Betty should sell a gold chain belonging to her lady, and with the money travel to London. Now, Betty took the chain to the very toy-shop man who had sold it to Mr. Warrington, who had given it to his cousin; and the toy-shop man, supposing that she had stolen the chain, was for bringing in a constable to Betty. Hence, she had to make explanations, and to say how her mistress was in durance; and, ere the night closed, all Tunbridge Wells knew that my Lady Maria Esmond was in the hands of bailiffs. Meanwhile, however, the money was found, and Mrs. Betty whisked up to London in search of the champion in whom the poor prisoner confided.

"Don't say anything about that paper being gone! Oh, the wretch, the wretch! She shall pay it me!" I presume that Lady Maria meant her aunt by the word "wretch." Mr. Sampson read a sermon to her ladyship, and they passed the evening over revenge and backgammon; with well-grounded hopes that Harry Warrington would rush to their rescue as soon as ever he heard of their mishap.

Though, ere the evening was over, every soul at the Wells knew what had happened to Lady Maria, and a great deal more; though they knew she was taken in execution, the house where she lay, the amount—nay, ten times the amount—for which she was captured, and that she was obliged to pawn her trinkets to get a little money to keep her in jail; though everybody said that old fiend of a Bernstein was at the bottom of the business, of course they were all civil and bland in society; and, at my Lady Trumpington's cards that night, where Madame Bernstein appeared, and as long as she was within hearing, not a word was said regarding the morning's transactions. Lady Yarmouth asked the Baroness news of her breddy nephew, and heard Mr. Warrington was in London. My Lady Maria was not coming to Lady Trumpington's that evening? My Lady Maria was indisposed, had fainted at church that morning, and was obliged to keep her room. The cards were dealt, the fiddles sang, the wine went round, the gentlefolks talked, laughed, yawned, chattered, the footmen waylaid the supper, the chairmen drank and swore, the stars climbed the sky, just as though no Lady Maria was imprisoned, and no poor Sampson arrested. 'Tis certain, dearly beloved brethren, that the little griefs, stings, annoyances, which you and I feel acutely in our own persons, don't prevent our neighbours from sleeping; and that when we slip out of the world the world does not miss us. Is this humiliating to our vanity? So much the better. But, on the other hand, is it not a comfortable and consoling truth? And mayn't we be thankful for our humble condition? If we were not selfish—passez-moi le mot, s.v.p.—and if we had to care for other people's griefs as much as our own, how intolerable human life would be! If my neighbour's tight boot pinched my corn; if the calumny uttered against Jones set Brown into fury; if Mrs. A's death plunged Messrs. B, C, D, E, F, into distraction, would there be any bearing of the world's burthen? Do not let us be in the least angry or surprised if all the company played on, and were happy, although Lady Maria had come to grief. Countess, the deal is with you! Are you going to Stubblefield to shoot as usual, Sir John? Captain, we shall have you running off to the Bath after the widow! So the clatter goes on; the lights burns; the beaux and the ladies flirt, laugh, ogle; the prisoner rages in his cell; the sick man tosses on his bed.

Perhaps Madame de Bernstein stayed at the assembly until the very last, not willing to allow the company the chance of speaking of her as soon as her back should be turned. Ah, what a comfort it is, I say again, that we have backs, and that our ears don't grow on them! He that has ears to hear, let him stuff them with cotton. Madame Bernstein might have heard folks say it was heartless of her to come abroad, and play at cards, and make merry when her niece was in trouble. As if she could help Maria by staying at home, indeed! At her age, it is dangerous to disturb an old lady's tranquillity. "Don't tell me!" says Lady Yarmouth. "The Bernstein would play at cards over her niece's coffin. Talk about her heart! who ever said she had one? That old spy lost it to the Chevalier a thousand years ago, and has lived ever since perfectly well without one. For how much is the Maria put in prison? If it were only a small sum we would pay it, it would vex her aunt so. Find out, Fuchs, in the morning, for how much Lady Maria Esmond is put in prison." And the faithful Fuchs bowed, and promised to do her Excellency's will.

Meanwhile, about midnight, Madame de Bernstein went home, and presently fell into a sound sleep, from which she did not wake up until a late hour of the morning, when she summoned her usual attendant, who arrived with her ladyship's morning dish of tea. If I told you she took a dram with it, you would be shocked. Some of our great-grandmothers used to have cordials in their "closets." Have you not read of the fine lady in Walpole, who said, "If I drink more, I shall be 'muckibus!'?" As surely as Mr. Gough is alive now, our ancestresses were accustomed to partake pretty freely of strong waters.

So, having tipped off the cordial, Madame Bernstein rouses and asks Mrs. Brett the news.

"He can give it you," says the waiting-woman, sulkily.

"He? Who?"

Mrs. Brett names Harry, and says Mr. Warrington arrived about midnight yesterday—and Betty, my Lady Maria's maid, was with him. "And my Lady Maria sends your ladyship her love and duty, and hopes you slept well," says Brett.

"Excellently, poor thing! Is Betty gone to her?"

"No; she is here," says Mrs. Brett.

"Let me see her directly," cries the old lady.

"I'll tell her," replies the obsequious Brett, and goes away upon her mistress's errand, leaving the old lady placidly reposing on her pillows. Presently, two pairs of high-heeled shoes are heard pattering over the deal floor of the bedchamber. Carpets were luxuries scarcely known in bedrooms of those days.

"So, Mrs. Betty, you were in London yesterday?" calls Bernstein from her curtains.

"It is not Betty—it is I! Good morning, dear aunt! I hope you slept well?" cries a voice which made old Bernstein start on her pillow. It was the voice of Lady Maria, who drew the curtains aside, and dropped her aunt a low curtsey. Lady Maria looked very pretty, rosy, and happy. And with the little surprise incident at her appearance through Madame Bernstein's curtains, I think we may bring this chapter to a close.

CHAPTER XXXIX. Harry to the Rescue

"My dear Lord March" (wrote Mr. Warrington from Tunbridge Wells, on Saturday morning, the 25th August, 1756): "This is to inform you (with satisfaction) that I have one all our three betts. I was at Bromley two minutes within the hour; my new horses kep a-going at a capital rate. I drove them myself, having the postilion by me to show me the way, and my black man inside with Mrs. Betty. Hope they found the drive very pleasant. We were not stopped on Blackheath, though two fellows on horseback rode up to us, but not liking the looks of our countenantses, rode off again; and we got into Tunbridge Wells (where I transacted my business) at forty-five minutes after eleven. This makes me quitts with your lordship after yesterday's piquet, which I shall be very happy to give your revenge, and am—

"Your most obliged, faithful servant,

"H. ESMOND WARRINGTON."

And now, perhaps, the reader will understand by what means Lady Maria Esmond was enabled to surprise her dear aunt in her bed on Saturday morning, and walk out of the house of captivity. Having despatched Mrs. Betty to London, she scarcely expected that her emissary would return on the day of her departure; and she and the chaplain were playing their cards at

256

midnight, after a small refection which the bailiff's wife had provided for them, when the rapid whirling of wheels was heard approaching their house, and caused the lady to lay her trumps down, and her heart to beat with more than ordinary emotion. Whirr came the wheels—the carriage stopped at the very door: there was a parley at the gate: then appeared Mrs. Betty, with a face radiant with joy, though her eyes were full of tears; and next, who is that tall young gentleman who enters? Can any of my readers guess? Will they be very angry if I say that the chaplain slapped down his cards with a huzzay, whilst Lady Maria, turning as white as a sheet, rose up from her chair, tottered forward a step or two, and, with an hysterical shriek, flung herself in her cousin's arms? How many kisses did he give her? If they were mille, deinde centum, dein mille altera, dein secunda centum, and so on, I am not going to cry out. He had come to rescue her. She knew he would; he was her champion, her preserver from bondage and ignominy. She wept a genuine flood of tears upon his shoulder, and as she reclines there, giving way to a hearty emotion, I protest I think she looks handsomer than she has looked during the whole course of this history. She did not faint this time; she went home, leaning lovingly on her cousin's arm, and may have had one or two hysterical outbreaks in the night; but Madame Bernstein slept soundly, and did not hear her.

"You are both free to go home," were the first words Harry said. "Get my lady's hat and cardinal, Betty, and, Chaplain, we'll smoke a pipe together at our lodgings, it will refresh me after my ride." The chaplain, who, too, had a great deal of available sensibility, was very much overcome; he burst into tears as he seized Harry's hand, and kissed it, and prayed God to bless his dear, generous, young patron. Mr. Warrington felt a glow of pleasure thrill through his frame. It is good to be able to help the suffering and the poor; it is good to be able to turn sorrow into joy. Not a little proud and elated was our young champion, as, with his hat cocked, he marched by the side of his rescued princess. His feelings came out to meet him, as it were, and beautiful happinesses with kind eyes and smiles danced before him, and clad him in a robe of honour, and scattered flowers on his path, and blew trumpets and shawms of sweet gratulation, calling, "Here comes the conqueror! Make way for the champion!" And so they led him up to the king's house, and seated him in the hall of complacency, upon the cushions of comfort. And yet it was not much he had done. Only a kindness. He had but to put his hand in his pocket, and with an easy talisman, drive off the dragon which kept the gate, and cause the tyrant to lay down his axe, who had got Lady Maria in execution. Never mind if his vanity is puffed up; he is very good-natured; he has rescued two unfortunate people, and pumped tears of goodwill and happiness out of their eyes:—and if he brags a little to-night, and swaggers somewhat to the chaplain, and talks about London, and Lord March, and White's, and Almack's, with the air of a macaroni, I don't think we need like him much the less.

Sampson continued to be prodigiously affected. This man had a nature most easily worked upon, and extraordinarily quick to receive pain and pleasure, to tears, gratitude, laughter, hatred, liking. In his preaching profession he had educated and trained his sensibilities so that they were of great use to him; he was for the moment what he acted. He wept quite genuine tears, finding that he could produce them freely. He loved you whilst he was with you; he had a real pang of grief as he mingled his sorrow with the widow or orphan; and, meeting Jack as he came out of the door, went to the tavern opposite, and laughed and roared over the bottle. He gave money very readily, but never repaid when he borrowed. He was on this night in a rapture of gratitude and flattery towards Harry Warrington. In all London, perhaps, the unlucky Fortunate Youth could not have found a more dangerous companion.

To-night he was in his grateful mood, and full of enthusiasm for the benefactor who had released him from durance. With each bumper his admiration grew stronger. He exalted Harry as the best and noblest of men, and the complacent young simpleton, as we have said, was disposed to take these praises as very well deserved. "The younger branch of our family," said Mr. Harry, with a superb air, "have treated you scurvily; but, by Jove, Sampson my boy, I'll stand by you!" At a certain period of Burgundian excitement Mr. Warrington was always very eloquent respecting the splendour of his family. "I am very glad I was enabled to help you in your strait. Count on me whenever you want me, Sampson. Did you not say you had a sister at boarding-school? You will want money for her, sir. Here is a little bill which may help to pay her schooling." And the liberal young fellow passed a bank-note across to the chaplain.

Again the man was affected to tears. Harry's generosity smote him.

"Mr. Warrington," he said, putting the bank-note a short distance from him, "I—I don't deserve your kindness—by George, I don't!" and he swore an oath to corroborate his passionate assertion.

"Psha!" says Harry. "I have plenty more of 'em. There was no money in that confounded pocket-book which I lost last week."

"No, sir. There was no money!" says Mr. Sampson, dropping his head.

"Hallo! How do you know, Mr. Chaplain?" asks the young gentleman.

"I know because I am a villain, sir. I am not worthy of your kindness. I told you so. I found the book, sir, that night, when you had too much wine at Barbeau's."

"And read the letters?" asked Mr. Warrington, starting up and turning very red.

"They told me nothing I did not know, sir," said the chaplain "You have had spies about you whom you little suspect—from whom you are much too young and simple to be able to keep your secret."

"Are those stories about Lady Fanny, and my cousin Will and his doings, true then?" inquired Harry.

"Yes, they are true," sighed the chaplain. "The house of Castlewood has not been fortunate, sir, since your honour's branch, the elder branch, left it."

"Sir, you don't dare for to breathe a word against my Lady Maria?" Harry cried out.

"Oh, not for worlds!" says Mr. Sampson, with a queer look at his young friend. "I may think she is too old for your honour, and that 'tis a pity you should not have a wife better suited to your age, though I admit she looks very young for hers, and hath every virtue and accomplishment."

"She is too old, Sampson, I know she is," says Mr. Warrington, with much majesty; "but she has my word, and you see, sir, how fond she is of me. Go bring me the letters, sir, which you found, and let me try and forgive you for having seized upon them."

"My benefactor, let me try and forgive myself!" cries Mr. Sampson, and departed towards his chamber, leaving his young patron alone over his wine.

Sampson returned presently, looking very pale. "What has happened, sir?" says Harry, with an imperious air.

The chaplain held out a pocket-book. "With your name in it, sir," he said.

"My brother's name in it," says Harry; "it was George who gave it to me."

"I kept it in a locked chest, sir, in which I left it this morning before I was taken by those people. Here is the book, sir, but the letters are gone. My trunk and valise have also been tampered with. And I am a miserable, guilty man, unable to make you the restitution which I owe you." Sampson looked the picture of woe as he uttered these sentiments. He clasped his hands together, and almost knelt before Harry in an attitude the most pathetic.

Who had been in the rooms in Mr. Sampson's and Mr. Warrington's absence? The landlady was ready to go on her knees, and declare that nobody had come in: nor, indeed, was Mr. Warrington's chamber in the least disturbed, nor anything abstracted from Mr. Sampson's scanty wardrobe and possessions, except those papers of which he deplored the absence.

Whose interest was it to seize them? Lady Maria's? The poor woman had been a prisoner all day, and during the time when the capture was effected.

She certainly was guiltless of the rape of the letters. The sudden seizure of the two—Case, the house-steward's secret journey to London,—Case, who knew the shoemaker at whose house Sampson lodged in London, and all the secret affairs of the Esmond family,—these points, considered together and separately, might make Mr. Sampson think that the Baroness Bernstein was at the bottom of this mischief. But why arrest Lady Maria? The chaplain knew nothing as yet about that letter which her ladyship had lost; for poor Maria had not thought it necessary to confide her secret to him.

As for the pocket-book and its contents, Mr. Harry was so swollen up with self-satisfaction that evening, at winning his three bets, at rescuing his two friends, at the capital premature cold supper of partridges and ancient Burgundy which obsequious Monsieur Barbeau had sent over to the young gentleman's lodgings, that he accepted Sampson's vows of contrition, and solemn promises of future fidelity, and reached his gracious hand to the chaplain, and condoned his offence. When the latter swore his great gods, that henceforth he would be Harry's truest, humblest friend and follower, and at any moment would be ready to die for Mr. Warrington, Harry said, majestically, "I think, Sampson, you would; I hope you would. My family—the

Esmond family—has always been accustomed to have faithful friends round about 'em—and to reward 'em too. The wine's with you, Chaplain. What toast do you call, sir?"

"I call a blessing on the house of Esmond-Warrington!" cries the chaplain, with real tears in his eyes.

"We are the elder branch, sir. My grandfather was the Marquis of Esmond," says Mr. Harry, in a voice noble but somewhat indistinct. "Here's to you, Chaplain—and I forgive you, sir—and God bless you, sir—and if you had been took for three times as much, I'd have paid it. Why, what's that I see through the shutters? I am blest if the sun hasn't risen again! We have no need of candles to go to bed, ha, ha!" And once more extending his blessing to his chaplain, the young fellow went off to sleep.

About noon Madame de Bernstein sent over a servant to say that she would be glad if her nephew would come over and drink a dish of chocolate with her, whereupon our young friend rose and walked to his aunt's lodgings. She remarked, not without pleasure, some alteration in his toilette: in his brief sojourn in London he had visited a tailor or two, and had been introduced by my Lord March to some of his lordship's purveyors and tradesmen.

Aunt Bernstein called him "my dearest child," and thanked him for his noble, his generous behaviour to dear Maria. What a shock that seizure in church had been to her! A still greater shock that she had lost three hundred only on the Wednesday night to Lady Yarmouth, and was quite a sec. "Why," said the Baroness, "I had to send Case to London to my agent to get me money to pay—I could not leave Tunbridge in her debt."

"So Case did go to London?" says Mr. Harry.

"Of course he did: the Baroness de Bernstein can't afford to say she is court d'argent. Canst thou lend me some, child?"

"I can give your ladyship twenty-two pounds," said Harry, blushing very red: "I have but forty-four left till I get my Virginian remittances. I have bought horses and clothes, and been very extravagant, aunt."

"And rescued your poor relations in distress, you prodigal good boy. No, child, I do not want thy money. I can give thee some. Here is a note upon my agent for fifty pounds, vaurien! Go and spend it, and be merry! I dare say thy mother will repay me, though she does not love me." And she looked quite affectionate, and held out a pretty hand, which the youth kissed.

"Your mother did not love me, but your mother's father did once. Mind, sir, you always come to me when you have need of me."

When bent on exhibiting them, nothing could exceed Beatrix Bernstein's grace or good-humour. "I can't help loving you, child," she continued, "and yet I am so angry with you that I have scarce the patience to speak to you. So you have actually engaged yourself to poor Maria, who is as old as your mother? What will Madam Esmond say? She may live three hundred years, and you will not have wherewithal to support yourselves."

"I have ten thousand pounds from my father, of my own, now my poor brother is gone," said Harry, "that will go some way."

260

"Why, the interest will not keep you in card-money."

"We must give up cards," says Harry.

"It is more than Maria is capable of. She will pawn the coat off your back to play. The rage for it runs in all my brother's family—in me too, I own it. I warned you. I prayed you not to play with them, and now a lad of twenty to engage himself to a woman of forty-two!—to write letters on his knees and signed with his heart's blood (which he spells like hartshorn), and say that he will marry no other woman than his adorable cousin, Lady Maria Esmond. Oh! it's cruel—cruel!"

"Great heavens! madam, who showed you my letter?" asked Harry, burning with a blush again.

"An accident. She fainted when she was taken by those bailiffs. Brett cut her laces for her; and when she was carried off, poor thing, we found a little sachet on the floor, which I opened, not knowing in the least what it contained. And in it was Mr. Harry Warrington's precious letter. And here, sir, is the case."

A pang shot through Harry's heart. "Great heavens! why didn't she destroy it?" he thought.

"I—I will give it back to Maria," he said, stretching out his hand for the little locket.

"My dear, I have burned the foolish letter," said the old lady.

"If you choose to betray me I must take the consequence. If you choose to write another, I cannot help thee. But, in that case, Harry Esmond, I had rather never see thee again. Will you keep my secret? Will you believe an old woman who loves you and knows the world better than you do? I tell you, if you keep that foolish promise, misery and ruin are surely in store for you. What is a lad like you in the hands of a wily woman of the world, who makes a toy of you? She has entrapped you into a promise, and your old aunt has cut the strings and set you free. Go back again! Betray me if you will, Harry."

"I am not angry with you, aunt—I wish I were," said Mr. Warrington, with very great emotion. "I—I shall not repeat what you told me."

"Maria never will, child—mark my words!" cried the old lady, eagerly. "She will never own that she has lost that paper. She will tell you that she has it."

"But I am sure she—she is very fond of me; you should have seen her last night," faltered Harry.

"Must I tell more stories against my own flesh and blood?" sobs out the Baroness. "Child, you do not know her past life!"

"And I must not, and I will not!" cries Harry, starting up. "Written or said—it does not matter which! But my word is given; they may play with such things in England, but we gentlemen of Virginia don't break 'em. If she holds me to my word, she shall have me. If we are miserable, as I dare say we shall be, I'll take a firelock, and go join the King of Prussia, or let a ball put an end to me."

"I—I have no more to say. Will you be pleased to ring that bell? I—I wish you a good morning, Mr. Warrington," and dropping a very stately curtsey, the old lady rose on her tortoiseshell stick, and turned towards the door. But, as she made her first step, she put her hand to her heart, sank on the sofa again, an shed the first tears that had dropped for long years from Beatrix Esmond's eyes.

Harry was greatly moved, too. He knelt down by her. He seized her cold hand, and kissed it. He told her, in his artless way, how very keenly he had felt her love for him, and how, with all his heart, he returned it. "Ah, aunt!" said he, "you don't know what a villain I feel myself. When you told me, just now how that paper was burned—oh! I was ashamed to think how glad I was." He bowed his comely head over her hand. She felt hot drops from his eyes raining on it. She had loved this boy. For half a century past—never, perhaps, in the course of her whole worldly life, had she felt a sensation so tender and so pure. The hard heart was wounded now, softened, overcome. She put her two hands on his shoulders, and lightly kissed his forehead.

"You will not tell her what I have done, child?" she said.

He declared never! never! And demure Mrs. Brett, entering at her mistress's summons, found the nephew and aunt in this sentimental attitude.

CHAPTER XL. In which Harry pays off an Old Debt, and incurs some New Ones

Our Tunbridge friends were now weary of the Wells, and eager to take their departure. When the autumn should arrive, Bath was Madame de Bernstein's mark. There were more cards, company, life, there. She would reach it after paying a few visits to her country friends. Harry promised, with rather a bad grace, to ride with Lady Maria and the chaplain to Castlewood. Again they passed by Oakhurst village, and the hospitable house where Harry had been so kindly entertained. Maria made so many keen remarks about the young ladies of Oakhurst, and their setting their caps at Harry, and the mother's evident desire to catch him for one of them, that, somewhat in a pet, Mr. Warrington said he would pass his friends' door, as her ladyship disliked and abused them; and was very haughty and sulky that evening at the inn where they stopped, some few miles farther on the road. At supper, my Lady Maria's smiles brought no corresponding good-humour to Harry's face; her tears (which her ladyship had at command) did not seem to create the least sympathy from Mr. Warrington; to her querulous remarks he growled a surly reply; and my lady was obliged to go to bed at length without getting a single tete-a-tete with her cousin,—that obstinate chaplain, as if by order, persisting in staying in the room. Had Harry given Sampson orders to remain? She departed with a sigh. He bowed her to the door with an obstinate politeness, and consigned her to the care of the landlady and her maid.

What horse was that which galloped out of the inn-yard ten minutes after Lady Maria had gone to her chamber? An hour after her departure from their supper-room, Mrs. Betty came in for her lady's bottle of smelling-salts, and found Parson Sampson smoking a pipe alone. Mr. Warrington was gone to bed—was gone to fetch a walk in the moonlight—how should he know where Mr. Harry was? Sampson answered, in reply to the maid's interrogatories. Mr. Warrington was ready to set forward the next morning, and took his place by the side of Lady Maria's carriage. But his brow was black—the dark spirit was still on him. He hardly spoke to her during the journey. "Great heavens! she must have told him that she stole it!" thought Lady Maria within her own mind.

The fact is, that, as they were walking up that steep hill which lies about three miles from Oakhurst, on the Westerham road, Lady Maria Esmond, leaning on her fond youth's arm, and indeed very much in love with him, had warbled into his ear the most sentimental vows, protests, and expressions of affection. As she grew fonder, he grew colder. As she looked up in his face, the sun shone down upon hers, which, fresh and well-preserved as it was, yet showed some of the lines and wrinkles of twoscore years; and poor Harry, with that arm leaning on his, felt it intolerably weighty, and by no means relished his walk up the hill. To think that all his life, that drag was to be upon him! It was a dreary look forward and he cursed the moonlight walk, and the hot evening, and the hot wine which had made him give that silly pledge by which he was fatally bound.

Maria's praises and raptures annoyed Harry beyond measure. The poor thing poured out scraps of the few plays which she knew that had reference to her case, and strove with her utmost power to charm her young companion. She called him, over and over again, her champion, her Henrico, her preserver, and vowed that his Molinda would be ever, ever faithful to him. She clung to him. "Ah, child! have I not thy precious image, thy precious hair, thy precious writing here?" she said, looking in his face. "Shall it not go with me to the grave? It would, sir, were I to meet with unkindness from my Henrico!" she sighed out.

Here was a strange story! Madame Bernstein had given him the little silken case—she had burned the hair and the note which the case contained, and Maria had it still on her heart! It was then, at the start which Harry gave, as she was leaning on his arm—at the sudden movement as if he would drop hers—that Lady Maria felt her first pang of remorse that she had told a fib, or rather, that she was found out in telling a fib, which is a far more cogent reason for repentance. Heaven help us! if some people were to do penance for telling lies, would they ever be out of sackcloth and ashes?

Arrived at Castlewood, Mr. Harry's good-humour was not increased. My lord was from home; the ladies also were away; the only member of the family whom Harry found, was Mr. Will, who returned from partridge-shooting just as the chaise and cavalcade reached the gate, and who turned very pale when he saw his cousin, and received a sulky scowl of recognition from the young Virginian.

Nevertheless, he thought to put a good face on the matter, and they met at supper, where, before my Lady Maria, their conversation was at first civil, but not lively. Mr. Will had been to some races? To several. He had been pretty successful in his bets? Mr. Warrington hopes. Pretty well. "And you have brought back my horse sound?" asked Mr. Warrington.

"Your horse! what horse?" asked Mr. Will.

"What horse? my horse!" says Mr. Harry, curtly.

"Protest I don't understand you," says Will.

"The brown horse for which I played you, and which I won of you the night before you rode away upon it," says Mr. Warrington, sternly. "You remember the horse, Mr. Esmond."

"Mr. Warrington, I perfectly well remember playing you for a horse, which my servant handed over to you on the day of your departure."

"The chaplain was present at our play. Mr. Sampson, will you be umpire between us?" Mr. Warrington said, with much gentleness.

"I am bound to decide that Mr. Warrington played for the brown horse," says Mr. Sampson.

"Well, he got the other one," said sulky Mr. Will, with a grin.

"And sold it for thirty shillings!" said Mr. Warrington, always preserving his calm tone.

Will was waggish. "Thirty shillings? and a devilish good price, too, for the broken-kneed old rip. Ha, ha!"

"Not a word more. 'Tis only a question about a bet, my dear Lady Maria. Shall I serve you some more chicken?" Nothing could be more studiously courteous and gay than Mr. Warrington was, so long as the lady remained in the room. When she rose to go, Harry followed her to the door, and closed it upon her with the most courtly bow of farewell. He stood at the closed door for a moment, and then he bade the servants retire. When those menials were gone, Mr. Warrington locked the heavy door before them, and pocketed the key.

As it clicked in the lock, Mr. Will, who had been sitting over his punch, looking now and then askance at his cousin, asked, with one of the oaths which commonly garnished his conversation, what the—Mr. Warrington meant by that?

"I guess there's going to be a quarrel," said Mr. Warrington, blandly, "and there is no use in having these fellows look on at rows between their betters."

"Who is going to quarrel here, I should like to know?" asked Will, looking very pale, and grasping a knife.

"Mr. Sampson, you were present when I played Mr. Will fifty guineas against his brown horse?"

"Against his horse!" bawls out Mr. Will.

"I am not such a something fool as you take me for," says Mr. Warrington, "although I do come from Virginia!" And he repeated his question: "Mr. Sampson, you were here when I played the Honourable William Esmond, Esquire, fifty guineas against his brown horse?"

"I must own it, sir," says the chaplain, with a deprecatory look towards his lord's brother.

"I don't own no such a thing," says Mr. Will, with rather a forced laugh.

"No, sir: because it costs you no more pains to lie than to cheat," said Mr. Warrington, walking up to his cousin. "Hands off, Mr. Chaplain, and see fair play! Because you are no better than a—ha!——"

No better than a what we can't say, and shall never know, for as Harry uttered the exclamation, his dear cousin flung a wine bottle at Mr. Warrington's head, who bobbed just in time, so that the missile flew across the room, and broke against the wainscot opposite, breaking the face of a pictured ancestor of the Esmond family, and then itself against the wall, whence it spirted a pint of good port wine over the chaplain's face and flowered wig. "Great heavens, gentlemen, I pray you to be quiet!" cried the parson, dripping with gore.

But gentlemen are not inclined at some moments to remember the commands of the Church. The bottle having failed, Mr. Esmond seized the large silver-handled knife and drove at his cousin. But Harry caught up the other's right hand with his left, as he had seen the boxers do at Marybone; and delivered a rapid blow upon Mr. Esmond's nose, which sent him reeling up against the oak panels, and I dare say caused him to see ten thousand illuminations. He dropped his knife in his retreat against the wall, which his rapid antagonist kicked under the table.

Now Will, too, had been at Marybone and Hockley-in-the-Hole, and after a gasp for breath and a glare over his bleeding nose at his enemy, he dashed forward his head as though it had been a battering-ram, intending to project it into Mr. Henry Warrington's stomach.

This manoeuvre Harry had seen, too, on his visit to Marybone, and amongst the negroes upon the maternal estate, who would meet in combat like two concutient cannon-balls, each harder than the other. But Harry had seen and marked the civilised practice of the white man. He skipped aside, and, saluting his advancing enemy with a tremendous blow on the right ear, felled him, so that he struck his head against the heavy oak table and sank lifeless to the ground.

"Chaplain, you will bear witness that it has been a fair fight!" said Mr. Warrington, still quivering with the excitement of the combat, but striving with all his might to restrain himself and look cool. And he drew the key from his pocket and opened the door in the lobby, behind which three or four servants were gathered. A crash of broken glass, a cry, a shout, an oath or two, had told them that some violent scene was occurring within, and they entered, and behold two victims bedabbled with red—the chaplain bleeding port wine, and the Honourable William Esmond, Esquire, stretched in his own gore.

"Mr. Sampson will bear witness that I struck fair, and that Mr. Esmond hit the first blow," said Mr. Warrington. "Undo his neckcloth, somebody—he may be dead; and get a fleam, Gumbo, and bleed him. Stop! He is coming to himself! Lift him up, you, and tell a maid to wash the floor."

Indeed, in a minute, Mr. Will did come to himself. First his eyes rolled about, or rather, I am ashamed to say, his eye, one having been closed by Mr. Warrington's first blow. First, then, his eye rolled about; then he gasped and uttered an inarticulate moan or two, then he began to swear and curse very freely and articulately.

"He is getting well," said Mr. Warrington.

"Oh, praise be Mussy!" sighs the sentimental Betty.

"Ask him, Gumbo, whether he would like any more?" said Mr. Warrington, with a stern humour.

"Massa Harry say, wool you like any maw?" asked obedient Gumbo, bowing over the prostrate gentleman.

"No, curse you, you black devil!" says Mr. Will, hitting up at the black object before him. ("So he nearly cut my tongue in to in my mouf!" Gumbo explained to the pitying Betty.) "No, that is, yes! You infernal Mohock! Why does not somebody kick him out of the place?"

"Because nobody dares, Mr. Esmond," says Mr. Warrington, with great state, arranging his ruffles—his ruffled ruffles.

"And nobody won't neither," growled the men. They had all grown to love Harry, whereas Mr. Will had nobody's good word.

"We know all's fair, sir. It ain't the first time Master William have been served so."

"And I hope it won't be the last," cries shrill Betty. "To go for to strike a poor black gentleman so!"

Mr. Will had gathered himself up by this time, had wiped his bleeding face with a napkin, and was skulking off to bed.

"Surely it's manners to say good night to the company. Good night, Mr. Esmond," says Mr. Warrington, whose jokes, though few, were not very brilliant; but the honest lad relished the brilliant sally and laughed at it inwardly.

"He's ad his zopper, and he goes to baid!" says Betty, in her native dialect, at which everybody laughed outright, except Mr. William, who went away leaving a black fume of curses, as it were, rolling out of that funnel, his mouth.

It must be owned that Mr. Warrington continued to be witty the next morning. He sent a note to Mr. Will begging to know whether he was for a ride to town or anywheres else. If he was for London, that he would friten the highwaymen on Hounslow Heath, and look a very genteel figar at the Chocolate House. Which letter, I fear, Mr. Will received with his usual violence, requesting the writer to go to some place—not Hounslow.

And, besides the parley between Will and Harry, there comes a maiden simpering to Mr. Warrington's door, and Gumbo advances, holding something white and triangular in his ebon fingers.

Harry knew what it was well enough. "Of course it's a letter," groans he. Molinda greets her Enrico, etc. etc. etc. No sleep has she known that night, and so forth, and so forth, and so forth. Has Enrico slept well in the halls of his fathers? und so weiter, und so weiter. He must never never quaril and be so cruel again. Kai ta loipa. And I protest I shan't quote any more of this letter. Ah, tablets, golden once,—are ye now faded leaves? Where is the juggler who transmuted you, and why is the glamour over?

After the little scandal with cousin Will, Harry's dignity would not allow him to stay longer at Castlewood: he wrote a majestic letter to the lord of the mansion, explaining the circumstances which had occurred, and, as he called in Parson Sampson to supervise the document, no doubt it contained none of those eccentricities in spelling which figured in his ordinary correspondence at this period. He represented to poor Maria, that after blackening the eye and damaging the nose of a son of the house, he should remain in it with a very bad grace; and she was forced to acquiesce in the opinion that, for the present, his absence would best become him. Of course, she wept plentiful tears at parting with him. He would go to London, and see younger beauties: he would find none, none who would love him like his fond Maria. I fear Mr. Warrington did not exhibit any profound emotion on leaving her: nay, he cheered up immediately after he crossed Castlewood Bridge, and made his horses whisk over the road at ten miles an hour: he sang to them to go along: he nodded to the pretty girls by the roadside: he chucked my landlady under the chin: he certainly was not inconsolable. Truth is, he longed to be back in London again, to make a figure at St. James's, at Newmarket, wherever the men of fashion congregated. All that petty Tunbridge society of women and card-playing seemed child's-play to him now he had tasted the delight of London life.

By the time he reached London again, almost all the four-and-forty pounds which we have seen that he possessed at Tunbridge had slipped out of his pocket, and further supplies were necessary. Regarding these he made himself presently easy. There were the two sums of 5000 pounds in his own and his brother's name, of which he was the master. He would take up a little money, and with a run or two of good luck at play he could easily replace it. Meantime he must live in a manner becoming his station, and it must be explained to Madam Esmond that a gentleman of his rank cannot keep fitting company, and appear as becomes him in society, upon a miserable pittance of two hundred a year.

Mr. Warrington sojourned at the Bedford Coffee-House as before, but only for a short while. He sought out proper lodgings at the Court end of the town, and fixed on some apartments in Bond Street, where he and Gumbo installed themselves, his horses standing at a neighbouring livery-stable. And now tailors, mercers, and shoemakers were put in requisition. Not without a pang of remorse, he laid aside his mourning and figured in a laced hat and waistcoat. Gumbo was always dexterous in the art of dressing hair, and with a little powder flung into his fair locks Mr. Warrington's head was as modish as that of any gentleman in the Mall. He figured in the Ring in his phaeton. Reports of his great wealth had long since preceded him to London, and not a little curiosity was excited about the fortunate Virginian.

Until our young friend could be balloted for at the proper season, my Lord March had written down his name for the club at White's Chocolate-House, as a distinguished gentleman from America. There were as yet but few persons of fashion in London, but with a pocket full of money at one-and-twenty, a young fellow can make himself happy even out of the season; and Mr. Harry was determined to enjoy.

He ordered Mr. Draper, then, to sell five hundred pounds of his stock. What would his poor mother have said had she known that the young spendthrift was already beginning to dissipate his patrimony? He dined at the tavern, he supped at the club, where Jack Morris introduced him, with immense eulogiums, to such gentlemen as were in town. Life and youth and pleasure were before him, the wine was set a-running, and the eager lad was greedy to drink. Do you see, far away in the west yonder, the pious widow at her prayers for her son? Behind the trees at Oakhurst a tender little heart, too, is beating for him, perhaps. When the Prodigal Son was away carousing, were not love and forgiveness still on the watch for him?

Amongst the inedited letters of the late Lord Orford, there is one which the present learned editor, Mr. Peter Cunningbam, has omitted from his collection, doubting possibly the authenticity of the document. Nay, I myself have only seen a copy of it in the Warrington papers in Madam Esmond's prim handwriting, and noted "Mr. H. Walpole's account of my son Henry at London, and of Baroness Tusher,—wrote to General Conway."

"ARLINGTON STREET, Friday Night.

"I have come away, child, for a day or two from my devotions to our Lady of Strawberry. Have I not been on my knees to her these three weeks, and aren't the poor old joints full of rheumatism? A fit took me that I would pay London a visit, that I would go to Vauxhall and Ranelagh. Quoi! May I not have my rattle as well as other elderly babies? Suppose, after being so long virtuous, I take a fancy to cakes and ale, shall your reverence say nay to me? George Selwyn and Tony Storer and your humble servant took boat at Westminster t'other night. Was it Tuesday?—no, Tuesday I was with their Graces of Norfolk, who are just from Tunbridge—it was Wednesday. How should I know? Wasn't I dead drunk with a whole pint of lemonade I took at White's?

"The Norfolk folk had been entertaining me on Tuesday with the account of a young savage Iroquois, Choctaw, or Virginian, who has lately been making a little noise in our quarter of the globe. He is an offshoot of that disreputable family of Esmond, Castlewood, of whom all the men are gamblers and spendthrifts, and all the women—well, I shan't say the word, lest Lady Ailesbury should be looking over your shoulder. Both the late lords, my father told me, were in his pay, and the last one, a beau of Queen Anne's reign, from a viscount advanced to be an earl through the merits and intercession of his notorious old sister Bernstein, late Tusher, nee Esmond—a great beauty, too, of her day, a favourite of the old Pretender. She sold his secrets to my papa, who paid her for them; and being nowise particular in her love for the Stuarts, came over to the august Hanoverian house at present reigning over us. 'Will Horace Walpole's tongue never stop scandal?' says your wife over your shoulder. I kiss your ladyship's hand. I am dumb. The Bernstein is a model of virtue. She had no good reasons for marrying her father's chaplain. Many of the nobility omit the marriage altogether. She wasn't ashamed of being Mrs. Tusher, and didn't take a German Baroncino for a second husband, whom nobody out of Hanover ever saw. The Yarmouth bears no malice. Esther and Vashti are very good friends, and have been cheating each other at Tunbridge at cards all the summer.

"'And what has all this to do with the Iroquois?' says your ladyship. The Iroquois has been at Tunbridge, too—not cheating, perhaps, but winning vastly. They say he has bled Lord March of thousands—Lord March, by whom so much blood hath been shed, that he has quarrelled with everybody, fought with everybody, rode over everybody, been fallen in love with by everybody's wife except Mr. Conway's, and not excepting her present Majesty, the Countess of England, Scotland, France and Ireland, Queen of Walmoden and Yarmouth, whom Heaven preserve to us.

"You know an offensive little creature, de par le monde, one Jack Morris, who skips in and out of all the houses of London. When we were at Vauxhall, Mr. Jack gave us a nod under the shoulder of a pretty young fellow enough, on whose arm he was leaning, and who appeared hugely delighted with the enchantments of the garden. Lord, how he stared at the fireworks! Gods, how he huzzayed at the singing of a horrible painted wench who shrieked the ears off my head! A twopenny string of glass beads and a strip of tawdry cloth are treasures in Iroquois-land, and our savage valued them accordingly.

"A buzz went about the place that this was the fortunate youth. He won three hundred at White's last night very genteelly from Rockingham and my precious nephew, and here he was bellowing and huzzaying over the music so as to do you good to hear. I do not love a puppet-show, but I love to treat children to one, Miss Conway! I present your ladyship my compliments, and hope we shall go and see the dolls together.

"When the singing woman came down from her throne, Jack Morris must introduce my Virginian to her. I saw him blush up to the eyes, and make her, upon my word, a very fine bow, such as I had no idea was practised in wigwams. 'There is a certain jenny squaw about her, and that's why the savage likes her,' George said—a joke certainly not as brilliant as a firework. After which it seemed to me that the savage and the savages retired together.

"Having had a great deal too much to eat and drink three hours before, my partners must have chicken and rack-punch at Vauxhall, where George fell asleep straightway, and for my sins I must tell Tony Storer what I knew about this Virginian's amiable family, especially some of the Bernstein's antecedents, and the history of another elderly beauty of the family, a certain Lady Maria, who was au mieux with the late Prince of Wales. What did I say? I protest not half of what I knew, and of course not a tenth part of what I was going to tell, for who should start out upon us but my savage, this time quite red in the face; and in his war paint. The wretch had been drinking fire-water in the next box!

"He cocked his hat, clapped his hand to his sword, asked which of the gentleman was it that was maligning his family? so that I was obliged to entreat him not to make such a noise, lest he should wake my friend, Mr. George Selwyn. And I added, 'I assure you, sir, I had no idea that you were near me, and most sincerely apologise for giving you pain.'

"The Huron took his hand off his tomahawk at this pacific rejoinder, made a bow not ungraciously, said he could not, of course, ask more than an apology from a gentleman of my age (Merci, monsieur!), and, hearing the name of Mr. Selwyn, made another bow to George, and said he had a letter to him from Lord March, which he had had the ill-fortune to mislay. George has put him up for the club, it appears, in conjunction with March, and no doubt these three lambs will fleece each other. Meanwhile, my pacified savage sate down with us, and buried the hatchet in another bowl of punch, for which these gentlemen must call. Heaven help us! 'Tis eleven o'clock, and here comes Bedson with my gruel! H. W.

"To the Honourable. H. S. Conway."

CHAPTER XLI. Rake's Progress

People were still very busy in Harry Warrington's time (not that our young gentleman took much heed of the controversy) in determining the relative literary merits of the ancients and the moderns; and the learned, and the world with them, indeed, pretty generally pronounced in favour of the former. The moderns of that day are the ancients of ours, and we speculate upon them in the present year of grace, as our grandchildren, a hundred years hence, will give their judgment about us. As for your book-learning, O respectable ancestors (though, to be sure, you have the mighty Gibbon with you), I think you will own that you are beaten, and could point to a couple of professors at Cambridge and Glasgow who know more Greek than was to be had in your time in all the universities of Europe, including that of Athens, if such an one existed. As for science, you were scarce more advanced than those heathen to whom in literature you owned yourselves inferior. And in public and private morality? Which is the better, this actual year 1858, or its predecessor a century back? Gentlemen of Mr. Disraeli's House of Commons! has every one of you his price, as in Walpole's or Newcastle's time, —or (and that is the delicate question) have you almost all of you had it? Ladies, I do not say that you are a society of Vestals—but the chronicle of a hundred years since contains such an amount of scandal, that you may be thankful you did not live in such dangerous times. No: on my conscience, I believe that men and women are both better; not only that the Susannas are more numerous, but that the Elders are not nearly so wicked. Did you ever hear of such books as Clarissa, Tom Jones, Roderick Random; paintings by contemporary artists, of the men and women, the life and society, of their day? Suppose we were to describe the doings of such a person as Mr. Lovelace or my Lady Bellaston, or that wonderful "Lady of Quality" who lent her memoirs to the author of Peregrine Pickle. How the pure and outraged

Nineteenth Century would blush, scream, run out of the room, call away the young ladies, and order Mr. Mudie never to send one of that odious author's books again! You are fifty-eight years old, madam, and it may be that you are too squeamish, that you cry out before you are hurt, and when nobody had any intention of offending your ladyship. Also, it may be that the novelist's art is injured by the restraints put upon him as many an honest, harmless statue at St. Peter's and the Vatican is spoiled by the tin draperies in which ecclesiastical old women have swaddled the fair limbs of the marble. But in your prudery there is reason. So there is in the state censorship of the Press. The page may contain matter dangerous to bonos mores. Out with your scissors, censor, and clip off the prurient paragraph! We have nothing for it but to submit. Society, the despot, has given his imperial decree. We may think the statue had been seen to greater advantage without the tin drapery; we may plead that the moral were better might we recite the whole fable. Away with him—not a word! I never saw the pianofortes in the United States with the frilled muslin trousers on their legs; but, depend on it, the muslin covered some of the notes as well as the mahogany, muffled the music, and stopped the player.

To what does this prelude introduce us? I am thinking of Harry Warrington, Esquire, in his lodgings in Bond Street, London, and of the life which he and many of the young bucks of fashion led in those times, and how I can no more take my faire young reader into them, than Lady Squeams can take her daughter to Cremorne Gardens on an ordinary evening. My dear Miss Diana (psha! I know you are eight-and-thirty, although you are so wonderfully shy, and want to make us believe you have just left off schoolroom dinners and a pinafore), when your grandfather was a young man about town, and a member of one of the clubs at White's, and dined at Pontac's off the feasts provided by Braund and Lebeck, and rode to Newmarket with March and Rockingham, and toasted the best in England with Gilly Williams and George Selwyn (and didn't understand George's jokes, of which, indeed, the flavour has very much evaporated since the bottling)—the old gentleman led a life of which your noble aunt (author of Legends of the Squeams's; or, Fair Fruits of a Family Tree) has not given you the slightest idea.

It was before your grandmother adopted those serious views for which she was distinguished during her last long residence at Bath, and after Colonel Tibbalt married Miss Lye, the rich soap-boiler's heiress, that her ladyship's wild oats were sown. When she was young, she was as giddy as the rest of the genteel world. At her house in Hill Street, she had ten card-tables on Wednesdays and Sunday evenings, except for a short time when Ranelagh was open on Sundays. Every night of her life she gambled for eight, nine, ten hours. Everybody else in society did the like. She lost; she won; she cheated; she pawned her jewels; who knows what else she was not ready to pawn, so as to find funds to supply her fury for play? What was that after-supper duel at the Shakspeare's Head in Covent Garden, between your grandfather and Colonel Tibbalt: where they drew swords and engaged only in the presence of Sir John Screwby, who was drunk under the table? They were interrupted by

Mr. John Fielding's people, and your grandfather was carried home to Hill Street wounded in a chair. I tell you those gentlemen in powder and ruffles, who turned out the toes of their buckled pumps so delicately, were terrible fellows. Swords were perpetually being drawn; bottles after bottles were drunk; oaths roared unceasingly in conversation; tavern-drawers and watchmen were pinked and maimed; chairmen belaboured; citizens insulted by reeling pleasure-hunters. You have been to Cremorne with proper "vouchers" of course? Do you remember our great theatres thirty years ago? You were too good to go to a play. Well, you have no idea what the playhouses were, or what the green boxes were, when Garrick and Mrs. Pritchard were playing before them! And I, for my children's sake, thank that good Actor in his retirement who was the first to banish that shame from the theatre. No, madam, you are mistaken; I do not plume myself on my superior virtue. I do not say you are naturally better than your ancestress in her wild, rouged, gambling, flaring tearing days; or even than poor Polly Fogle, who is just taken up for shoplifting, and would have been hung for it a hundred years ago. Only, I am heartily thankful that my temptations are less, having quite enough to do with those of the present century.

So, if Harry Warrington rides down to Newmarket to the October meeting, and loses or wins his money there; if he makes one of a party at the Shakspeare or Bedford Head; if he dines at White's ordinary, and sits down to macco and lansquenet afterwards; if he boxes the watch, and makes his appearance at the Roundhouse; if he turns out for a short space a wild dissipated, harum-scarum young Harry Warrington; I, knowing the weakness of human nature, am not going to be surprised; and, quite aware of my own shortcomings, don't intend to be very savage at my neighbour's. Mr. Sampson was: in his chapel in Long Acre he whipped Vice tremendously; gave Sin no quarter; out-cursed Blasphemy with superior Anathemas; knocked Drunkenness down, and trampled on the prostrate brute wallowing in the gutter; dragged out conjugal Infidelity, and pounded her with endless stones of rhetoric—and, after service, came to dinner at the Star and Garter, made a bowl of punch for Harry and his friends at the Bedford Head, or took a hand at whist at Mr. Warrington's lodgings or my Lord March's, or wherever there was a supper and good company for him.

I often think, however, in respect of Mr. Warrington's doings at this period of his coming to London, that I may have taken my usual degrading and uncharitable views of him—for, you see, I have not uttered a single word of virtuous indignation against his conduct, and if it was not reprehensible, have certainly judged him most cruelly. O the Truthful, O the Beautiful, O Modesty, O Benevolence, O Pudor, O Mores, O Blushing Shame, O Namby Pamby—each with your respective capital letters to your honoured names! O Niminy, O Piminy! how shall I dare for to go for to say that a young man ever was a young man?

No doubt, dear young lady, I am calumniating Mr. Warrington according to my heartless custom. As a proof here is a letter out of the Warrington collection, from Harry to his mother in which there is not a single word that would lead you to suppose he was leading a wild life. And such a letter from an only son to a fond and exemplary parent, we know must be true:—

"BOND STREET, LONDON, October 25, 1756.

"HONORD MADAM—I take up my pen to acknowledge your honored favor of 10 July per Lively Virginia packet, which has duly come to hand, forwarded by our Bristol agent, and rejoice to hear that the prospect of the crops is so good. 'Tis Tully who says that agriculture is the noblest pursuit; how delightful when that pursuit is also prophetable!

"Since my last, dated from Tunbridge Wells, one or two insadence have occurred of which it is nessasery [This word has been much operated upon with the penknife, but is left sic, no doubt to the writer's satisfaction.] I should advise my honored Mother. Our party there broke up end of August: the partridge-shooting commencing. Baroness Bernstein, whose kindness to me has been most invariable, has been to Bath, her usual winter resort, and has made me a welcome present of a fifty-pound bill. I rode back with Rev. Mr. Sampson, whose instruction I find most valluble, and my cousin, Lady Maria, to Castlewood. [Could Parson Sampson have been dictating the above remarks to Mr. Warrington?] I paid a flying visit on the way to my dear kind friends Col. and Mrs. Lambert, Oakhurst House, who send my honored mother their most affectionate remembrances. The youngest Miss Lambert, I grieve to say, was dellicate; and her parents in some anxiety.

"At Castlewood I lament to state my stay was short, owing to a quarrel with my cousin William. He is a young man of violent passions, and alas! addicted to liquor, when he has no controul over them. In a triffling dispute about a horse, high words arose between us, and he aymed a blow at me or its equivulent—which my Grandfathers my honored mothers child could not brook. I rejoyned, and feld him to the ground, whents he was carried almost sencelis to bed. I sent to enquire after his health in the morning: but having no further news of him, came away to London where I have been ever since with brief intavles of absence.

"Knowing you would wish me to see my dear Grandfathers University of Cambridge, I rode thither lately in company with some friends, passing through part of Harts, and lying at the famous bed of Ware. The October meeting was just begun at Cambridge when I went. I saw the students in their gownds and capps, and rode over to the famous Newmarket Heath, where there happened to be some races—my friend Lord Marchs horse Marrowbones by Cleaver coming off winner of a large steak. It was an amusing day—the jockeys, horses, etc., very different to our poor races at home—the betting awful—the richest noblemen here mix with the jox, and bett all round. Cambridge pleased me: especially King's College Chapel, of a rich but elegant Gothick.

"I have been out into the world, and am made member of the Club at White's, where I meet gentlemen of the first fashion. My Lords Rockingham, Carlisle, Orford, Bolingbroke, Coventry are of my friends, introduced to me by my Lord March, of whom I have often wrote before. Lady Coventry is a fine woman, but thinn. Every lady paints here, old and young; so, if you and Mountain and Fanny wish to be in fashion, I must send you out some roogepots: everybody plays—eight, ten, card-tables at every house on every receiving-night. I am sorry to say all do not play fair, and some do not pay fair. I have been obliged to sit down, and do as Rome does, and have actually seen ladies whom I could name take my counters from before my face!

"One day, his regiment the 20th being paraded in St. James's Park, a friend of mine, Mr. Wolfe, did me the honour to present me to his Royal Highness the Captain-General, who was most gracious; a fat, jolly Prince, if I may speak so without disrespect, reminding me in his manner of that unhappy General Braddock; whom we knew to our sorrow last year. When he heard my name, and how dearest George had served and fallen in Braddock's unfortunate campaign, he talked a great deal with me; asked why a young fellow like me did not serve too; why I did not go to the King of Prussia, who was a great General, and see a campaign or two; and whether that would not be better than dawdling about at routs and card-parties in London? I said, I would like to go with all my heart, but was an only son now, on leave from my mother, and belonged to our estate in Virginia. His Royal Highness said, Mr. Braddock had wrote home accounts of Mrs. Esmond's loyalty, and that he would gladly serve me. Mr. Wolfe and I have waited on him since, at his Royal Highness's house in Pall Mall. The latter, who is still quite a young man, made the Scots campaign with his Highness, whom Mr. Dempster loves so much at home. To be sure, he was too severe: if anything can be top severe against rebels in arms.

"Mr. Draper has had half the Stock, my late Papa's property, transferred to my name. Until there can be no doubt of that painful loss in our family which I would give my right hand to replace, the remaining stock must remain in the trustees' name in behalf of him who inherited it. Ah, dear mother! There is no day, scarce any hour, when I don't think of him. I wish he were by me often. I feel like as if I was better when I am thinking of him, and would like, for the honour of my family, that he was representing of it here instead of— Honored madam, your dutiful and affectionate son, HENRY ESMOND WARRINGTON."

"P.S.—I am like your sex, who always, they say, put their chief news in a poscrip. I had something to tell you about a person to whom my heart is engaged. I shall write more about it, which there is no hurry. Safice she is a nobleman's daughter, and her family as good as our own."

"CLARGIS STREET, LONDON, October 23, 1756.

"I think, my good sister, we have been all our lives a little more than kin and less than kind, to use the words of a poet whom your dear father loved dearly. When you were born in our Western Principallitie, my mother was not as old as Isaac's; but even then I was much more than old enough to be yours. And though she gave you all she could leave or give, including the little portion of love that ought to have been my share, yet, if we can have good will for one another, we may learn to do without affection: and some little kindness you owe me, for your son's sake; as well as your father's, whom I loved and admired more than any man I think ever I knew in this world: he was greater than almost all, though he made no noyse in it. I have seen very many who have, and, believe me, have found but few with such good heads and good harts as Mr. Esmond.

"Had we been better acquainted, I might have given you some advice regarding your young gentleman's introduction to Europe, which you would have taken or not, as people do in this world. At least you would have sed afterwards, 'What she counselled me was right, and had Harry done as Madam Beatrix wisht, it had been better for him.' My good sister, it was not for you to know, or for me to whom you never wrote to tell you, but your boy in coming to England and Castlewood found but ill friends there; except one, an old aunt, of whom all kind of evil hath been spoken and sed these fifty years past —and not without cawse too, perhaps.

"Now, I must tell Harry's mother what will doubtless scarce astonish her, that almost everybody who knows him loves him. He is prudent of his tongue, generous of his money, as bold as a lyon, with an imperious domineering way that sets well upon him; you know whether he is handsome or not: my dear, I like him none the less for not being over witty or wise, and never cared for your sett-the-Thames afire gentlemen, who are so much more clever than their neighbours. Your father's great friend, Mr. Addison, seemed to me but a supercillious prig, and his follower, Sir Dick Steele, was not pleasant in his cupps, nor out of 'em. And (revenons a luy) your Master Harry will certainly, pot burn the river up with his wits. Of book-learning he is as ignorant as any lord in England, and for this I hold him none the worse. If Heaven have not given him a turn that way, 'tis of no use trying to bend him.

"Considering the place he is to hold in his own colony when he returns, and the stock he comes from, let me tell you, that he hath not means enough allowed him to support his station, and is likely to make the more depence from the narrowness of his income—from sheer despair breaking out of all bounds, and becoming extravagant, which is not his turn. But he likes to live as well as the rest of his company, and, between ourselves, has fell into some of the finist and most rakish in England. He thinks 'tis for the honour of the family not to go back, and many a time calls for ortolans and champaign when he would as leaf dine with a stake and a mugg of beer. And in this kind of spirit I have no doubt from what he hath told me in his talk (which is very naif, as the French say), that his mamma hath encouraged him in his high opinion of himself. We women like our belongings to have it, however little we love to pay the cost. Will you have your ladd make a figar in London? Trebble his allowance at the very least, and his Aunt Bernstein (with his honored mamma's permission) will add a little more on to whatever summ you give him. Otherwise he will be spending the little capital I learn he has in this country, which, when a ladd once begins to manger, there is very soon an end to the loaf. Please God, I shall be able to leave Henry Esmond's grandson something at my death; but my savings are small, and the pension with which my gracious Sovereign hath endowed me dies with me. As for feu M. de Bernstein, he left only debt at his decease: the officers of his Majesty's Electoral Court of Hannover are but scantily paid.

"A lady who is at present very high in his Majesty's confidence hath taken a great phancy to your ladd, and will take an early occasion to bring him to the Sovereign's favorable notice. His Royal Highness the Duke he hath seen. If live in America he must, why should not Mr. Esmond Warrington return as Governor of Virginia, and with a title to his name? That is what I hope for him.

"Meanwhile, I must be candid with you, and tell you I fear he hath entangled himself here in a very silly engagement. Even to marry an old woman for money is scarce pardonable—the game ne valant gueres la chandelle—Mr. Bernstein, when alive, more than once assured me of this fact, and I believe him, poor gentleman! to engage yourself to an old woman without money, and to marry her merely because you have promised her, this seems to me a follie which only very young lads fall into, and I fear Mr. Warrington is one. How, or for what consideration, I know not, but my niece Maria Esmond hath escamote a promise from Harry. He knows nothing of her antecedens, which I do. She hath laid herself out for twenty husbands these twenty years past. I care not how she hath got the promise from him. 'Tis a sin and a shame that a woman more than forty years old should surprize the honour of a child like that, and hold him to his word. She is not the woman she pretends to be. A horse jockey (he saith) cannot take him in—but a woman!

"I write this news to you advisedly, displeasant as it must be. Perhaps 'twill bring you to England: but I would be very cautious, above all, very gentle, for the bitt will instantly make his high spirit restive. I fear the property is entailed, so that threats of cutting him off from it will not move Maria. Otherwise I know her to be so mercenary that (though she really hath a great phancy for this handsome ladd) without money she would not hear of him. All I could, and more than I ought, I have done to prevent the match. What and more I will not say in writing; but that I am, for Henry Esmond's sake, his grandson's sincerest friend, and madam,—Your faithful sister and servant, BEATRIX BARONESS DE BERNSTEIN.

"To Mrs. Esmond Warrington of Castlewood, in Virginia."

On the back of this letter is written, in Madam Esmond's hand, "My sister Bernstein's letter, received with Henry's December 24 on receipt of which it was determined my son should instantly go home."

CHAPTER XLII. Fortunatus Nimium

Though Harry Warrington persisted in his determination to keep that dismal promise which his cousin had extracted from him, we trust no benevolent reader will think so ill of him as to suppose that the engagement was to the young fellow's taste, and that he would not be heartily glad to be rid of it. Very likely the beating administered to poor Will was to this end; and Harry may have thought, "A boxing-match between us is sure to bring on a quarrel with the family; in the quarrel with the family, Maria may take her brother's side. I, of course, will make no retraction or apology. Will, in that case, may call me to account, when I know which is the better man. In the midst of the feud, the agreement may come to an end, and I may be a free man once more."

So honest Harry laid his train, and fired it: but, the explosion over, no harm was found to be done, except that William Esmond's nose was swollen, and his eye black for a week. He did not send a challenge to his cousin, Harry Warrington; and, in consequence, neither killed Harry, nor was killed by him. Will was knocked down, and he got up again. How many men of sense would do the same, could they get their little account settled in a private place, with nobody to tell how the score was paid! Maria by no means took her family's side in the quarrel, but declared for her cousin, as did my lord, when advised of the disturbance. Will had struck the first blow, Lord Castlewood said, by the chaplain's showing. It was not the first or the tenth time he had been found quarrelling in his cups. Mr. Warrington only showed a proper spirit in resenting the injury, and it was for Will, not for Harry, to ask pardon.

Harry said he would accept no apology as long as his horse was not returned or his bet paid. The chronicler has not been able to find out, from any of the papers which have come under his view, how that affair of the bet was finally arranged; but 'tis certain the cousins presently met in the houses of various friends, and without mauling each other.

Maria's elder brother had been at first quite willing that his sister, who had remained unmarried for so many years, and on the train of whose robe, in her long course over the path of life, so many briars, so much mud, so many rents and stains had naturally gathered, should marry with any bridegroom who presented himself, and if with a gentleman from Virginia, so much the better. She would retire to his wigwam in the forest, and there be disposed of. In the natural course of things, Harry would survive his elderly bride, and might console himself or not, as he preferred, after her departure.

But, after an interview with Aunt Bernstein, which his lordship had on his coming to London, he changed his opinion: and even went so far as to try and dissuade Maria from the match; and to profess a pity for the young fellow who was made to undergo a life of misery on account of a silly promise given at one-and-twenty!

Misery, indeed! Maria was at a loss to know why he was to be miserable. Pity, forsooth! My lord at Castlewood had thought it was no pity at all. Maria knew what pity meant. Her brother had been with Aunt Bernstein: Aunt Bernstein had offered money to break this match off. She understood what my lord meant, but Mr. Warrington was a man of honour, and she could trust him. Away, upon this, walks my lord to White's, or to whatever haunts he frequented. It is probable that his sister had guessed too accurately what the nature of his conversation wit Madame Bernstein had been.

"And so," thinks he, "the end of my virtue is likely to be that the Mohock will fall a prey to others, and that there is no earthly use in my sparing him. 'Quem deus vult'—what was that schoolmaster's adage? If I don't have him, somebody else will, that is clear. My brother has had a slice; my dear sister wants to swallow the whole of him bodily. Here have I been at home respecting his youth and innocence forsooth, declining to play beyond the value of a sixpence, and acting guardian and Mentor to him. Why, I am but a fool to fatten a goose for other people to feed off! Not many a good action have I done in this life, and here is this one, that serves to benefit whom?—other folks. Talk of remorse! By all the fires and furies, the remorse I have is for things I haven't done and might have done! Why did I spare Lucretia? She hated me ever after, and her husband went the way for which he was predestined. Why have I let this lad off?—that March and the rest, who don't want him, may pluck him! And I have a bad repute; and I am the man people point at, and call the wicked lord, and against whom women warn their sons! Pardi, I am not a penny worse, only a great deal more unlucky than my neighbours, and 'tis only my cursed weakness that has been my greatest enemy!" Here, manifestly, in setting down a speech which a gentleman only thought, a chronicler overdraws his account with the patient reader, who has a right not to accept this draft on his credulity. But have not Livy, and Thucydides, and a score more of historians, made speeches for their heroes, which we know the latter never thought of delivering? How much more may we then, knowing my Lord Castlewood's character so intimately as we do, declare what was passing in his mind, and transcribe his thoughts on this paper? What? a whole pack of the wolves are on the hunt after this lamb, and will make a meal of him presently, and one hungry old hunter is to stand by, and not have a single cutlet? Who has not admired that noble speech of my Lord Clive, when reproached on his return from India with making rather too free with jaghires, lakhs, gold mohurs, diamonds, pearls, and what not? "Upon my life," said the hero of Plassy, "when I think of my opportunities, I am surprised I took so little!"

To tell disagreeable stories of a gentleman, until one is in a manner forced to impart them, is always painful to a feeling mind. Hence, though I have known, before the very first page of this history was written, what sort of a person my Lord Castlewood was, and in what esteem he was held by his contemporaries, I have kept back much that was unpleasant about him, only allowing the candid reader to perceive that he was a nobleman who ought not to be at all of our liking. It is true that my Lord March, and other gentlemen of whom he complained, would have thought no more of betting with Mr. Warrington for his last shilling, and taking their winnings, than they would scruple to pick the bones of a chicken; that they would take any advantage of the game, or their superior skill in it, of the race, and their private knowledge of the horses engaged; in so far, they followed the practice of all gentlemen: but when they played, they played fair; and when they lost, they paid.

Now Madame Bernstein was loth to tell her Virginian nephew all she knew to his family's discredit; she was even touched by my lord's forbearance in regard to Harry on his first arrival in Europe; and pleased with his lordship's compliance with her wishes in this particular. But in the conversation which she had with her nephew Castlewood regarding Maria's designs on Harry, he had spoken his mind out with his usual cynicism, voted himself a fool for having spared a lad whom no sparing would eventually keep from ruin; pointed out Mr. Harry's undeniable extravagances and spendthrift associates, his nights at faro and hazard, and his rides to Newmarket, and asked why he alone should keep his hands from the young fellow? In vain Madame Bernstein pleaded that Harry was poor. Bah! he was heir to a principality which ought to have been his, Castlewood's, and might have set up their ruined family. (Indeed Madame Bernstein thought Mr. Warrington's Virginian property much greater than it was.) Were there not money-lenders in the town who would give him money on postobits in plenty? Castlewood knew as much to his cost: he had applied to them in his father's lifetime, and the cursed crew had eaten up two-thirds of his miserable income. He spoke with such desperate candour and ill-humour, that Madame Bernstein began to be alarmed for her favourite, and determined to caution him at the first opportunity.

That evening she began to pen a billet to Mr. Warrington: but all her life long she was slow with her pen, and disliked using it. "I never knew any good come of writing more than bon jour or business," she used to say. "What is the use of writing ill, when there are so many clever people who can do it well? and even then it were best left alone." So she sent one of her men to Mr. Harry's lodgings, bidding him come and drink a dish of tea with her next day, when she proposed to warn him.

But the next morning she was indisposed, and could not receive Mr. Harry when he came: and she kept her chamber for a couple of days, and the next day there was a great engagement, and the next day Mr. Harry was off on some expedition of his own. In the whirl of London life, what man sees his neighbour, what brother his sister, what schoolfellow his old friend? Ever so many days passed before Mr. Warrington and his aunt had that confidential conversation which the latter desired.

She began by scolding him mildly about his extravagance and madcap frolics (though, in truth, she was charmed with him for both)—he replied that young men will be young men, and that it was in dutifully waiting in attendance on his aunt, he had made the acquaintance with whom he mostly lived at present. She then with some prelude, began to warn him regarding his cousin, Lord Castlewood; on which he broke into a bitter laugh, and said the good-natured world had told him plenty about Lord Castlewood already. "To say of a man of his lordship's rank, or of any gentleman, 'Don't play with him,' is more than I like to do," continued the lady; "but..."

"Oh, you may say on, aunt!" said Harry, with something like an imprecation on his lips.

"And have you played with your cousin already?" asked the young man's worldly old monitress.

"And lost and won, madam!" answers Harry, gallantly. "It don't become me to say which. If we have a bout with a neighbour in Virginia, a bottle, or a pack of cards, or a quarrel, we don't go home and tell our mothers. I mean no offence, aunt!" And, blushing, the handsome young fellow went up and kissed the old lady. He looked very brave and brilliant, with his rich lace, his fair face and hair, his fine new suit of velvet and gold. On taking leave of his aunt he gave his usual sumptuous benefaction to her servants, who crowded round him. It was a rainy wintry day, and my gentleman, to save his fine silk stockings, must come in a chair. "To White's!" he called out to the chairmen, and away they carried him to the place where he passed a great deal of his time.

Our Virginian's friends might have wished that he had been a less sedulous frequenter of that house of entertainment; but so much may be said in favour of Mr. Warrington that, having engaged in play, he fought his battle like a hero. He was not flustered by good luck, and perfectly calm when the chances went against him. If Fortune is proverbially fickle to men at play, how many men are fickle to Fortune, run away frightened from her advances; and desert her, who, perhaps, had never thought of leaving them but for their cowardice. "By George, Mr. Warrington," said Mr. Selwyn, waking up in a rare fit of enthusiasm, "you deserve to win! You treat your luck as a gentleman should, and as long as she remains with you, behave to her with the most perfect politeness. Si celeres quatit pennas—you know the rest—no? Well, you are not much the worse off—you will call her ladyship's coach, and make her a bow at the step. Look at Lord Castlewood yonder, passing the box. Did you ever hear a fellow curse and swear so at losing five or six pieces? She must be a jade indeed, if she long give her favours to such a niggardly canaille as that!"

"We don't consider our family canaille, sir," says Mr. Warrington, "and my Lord Castlewood is one of them."

"I forgot. I forgot, and ask your pardon! And I make you my compliment upon my lord, and Mr. Will Esmond, his brother," says Harry's neighbour at the hazard-table. "The box is with me. Five's the main! Deuce Ace! my usual luck. Virtute mea me involvo!" and he sinks back in his chair.

Whether it was upon this occasion of taking the box, that Mr. Harry threw the fifteen mains mentioned in one of those other letters of Mr. Walpole's, which have not come into his present learned editor's hands, I know not; but certain it is, that on his first appearance at White's, Harry had five or six evenings of prodigious good luck, and seemed more than ever the Fortunate Youth. The five hundred pounds withdrawn from his patrimonial inheritance had multiplied into thousands. He bought fine clothes, purchased fine horses, gave grand entertainments, made handsome presents, lived as if he had been as rich as Sir James Lowther, or his Grace of Bedford, and yet the five thousand pounds never seemed to diminish. No wonder that he gave where giving was so easy; no wonder that he was generous with Fortunatus's purse in his pocket. I say no wonder that he gave, for such was his nature. Other Fortunati tie up the endless purse, drink small beer, and go to bed with a tallow candle.

During this vein of his luck, what must Mr. Harry do, but find out from Lady Maria what her ladyship's debts were, and pay them off to the last shilling. Her stepmother and half-sister, who did not love her, he treated to all sorts of magnificent presents. "Had you not better get yourself arrested, Will?" my lord sardonically said to his brother. "Although you bit him in that affair of the horse, the Mohock will certainly take you out of pawn." It was then that Mr. William felt a true remorse, although not of that humble kind which sent the repentant Prodigal to his knees. "Confound it," he groaned, "to think that I have let this fellow slip for such a little matter as forty pound! Why, he was good for a thousand at least."

As for Maria, that generous creature accepted the good fortune sent her with a grateful heart; and was ready to accept as much more as you pleased. Having paid off her debts to her various milliners, tradesmen, and purveyors, she forthwith proceeded to contract new ones. Mrs. Betty, her ladyship's maid, went round informing the tradespeople that her mistress was about to contract a matrimonial alliance with a young gentleman of immense fortune; so that they might give my lady credit to any amount. Having heard the same story twice or thrice before, the tradesfolk might not give it entire credit, but their bills were paid: even to Mrs. Pincott, of Kensington, my lady showed no rancour, and affably ordered fresh supplies from her: and when she drove about from the mercer to the toy-shop, and from the toy-shop to the jeweller in a coach, with her maid and Mr. Warrington inside, they thought her a fortunate woman indeed, to have secured the Fortunate Youth, though they might wonder at the taste of this latter in having selected so elderly a beauty. Mr. Sparks, of Tavistock Street, Covent Garden, took the liberty of waiting upon Mr. Warrington at his lodgings in Bond Street, with the pearl necklace and the gold etwee which he had bought in Lady Maria's company the day before; and asking whether he, Sparks, should leave them at his honour's lodging, or send them to her ladyship with his honour's compliments? Harry added a ring out of the stock which the jeweller happened to bring with him, to the necklace and the etwee; and sumptuously bidding that individual to send him in the bill, took a majestic leave of Mr. Sparks, who retired, bowing even to Gumbo, as he quitted his honour's presence.

Nor did his bounties end here. Ere many days the pleased young fellow drove up in his phaeton to Mr. Sparks' shop, and took a couple of trinkets for two young ladies, whose parents had been kind to him, and for whom he entertained a sincere regard. "Ah!" thought he, "how I wish I had my poor George's wit, and genius for poetry! I would send these presents with pretty verses to Hetty and Theo. I am sure, if goodwill and real regard could make a poet of me, I should have no difficulty in finding rhymes." And so he called in Parson Sampson, and they concocted a billet together.

CHAPTER XLIII. In which Harry flies High

So Mr. Harry Warrington, of Virginia, had his lodgings in Bond Street, London, England, and lived upon the fat of the land, and drank bumpers of the best wine thereof. His title of Fortunate Youth was pretty generally recognised. Being young, wealthy, good-looking, and fortunate, the fashionable world took him by the hand and made him welcome. And don't, my dear brethren, let us cry out too loudly against the selfishness of the world for being kind to the young, handsome, and fortunate, and frowning upon you and me, who may be, for argument's sake, old, ugly, and the miserablest dogs under the sun. If I have a right to choose my acquaintance, and—at the club, let us say prefer the company of a lively, handsome, well-dressed, gentleman like young man, who amuses me, to that of a slouching, ill-washed, misanthropic H-murderer, a ceaselessly prating coxcomb, or what not; has not society—the aggregate you and I—a right to the same choice? Harry was liked because he was likeable; because he was rich, handsome, jovial, well-born, well-bred, brave; because, with jolly topers, he liked a jolly song and a bottle; because, with gentlemen sportsmen, he loved any game that was a-foot or a-horseback; because, with ladies, he had a modest blushing timidity which rendered the lad interesting; because, to those humbler than himself in degree he was always magnificently liberal, and anxious to spare annoyance. Our Virginian was very grand, and high and mighty, to be sure; but, in those times, when the distinction of ranks yet obtained, to be high and distant with his inferiors, brought no unpopularity to a gentleman. Remember that, in those days, the Secretary of State always knelt when he went to the king with his despatches of a morning, and the Under-Secretary never dared to sit down in his chief's presence. If I were Secretary of State (and such there have been amongst men of letters since Addison's days) I should not like to kneel when I went in to my audience with my despatch-bog. If I were Under-Secretary, I should not like to have to stand, whilst the Right Honourable Benjamin or the Right Honourable Sir Edward looked over the papers. But there is a modus in rebus: there are certain lines which must be drawn: and I am only half pleased for my part, when Bob Bowstreet, whose connection with letters is through Policeman X and Y, and Tom Garbage, who is an esteemed contributor to the Kennel Miscellany, propose to join fellowship as brother literary men, slap me on the back, and call me old boy, or by my Christian name.

As much pleasure as the town could give in the winter season of 1756-57, Mr. Warrington had for the asking. There were operas for him, in which he took but moderate delight. (A prodigious deal of satire was brought to bear against these Italian Operas, and they were assailed for being foolish, Popish, unmanly, unmeaning; but people went, nevertheless.) There were the theatres, with Mr. Garrick and Mrs. Pritchard at one house, and Mrs. Clive at another. There were masquerades and ridottos frequented by all the fine society; there were their lordships' and ladyships' own private drums and assemblies, which began and ended with cards, and which Mr. Warrington did not like so well as White's, because the play there was neither so high nor so fair as at the club-table.

One day his kinsman, Lord Castlewood, took him to court, and presented Harry to his Majesty, who was now come to town from Kensington. But that gracious sovereign either did not like Harry's introducer, or had other reasons for being sulky. His Majesty only said, "Oh, heard of you from Lady Yarmouth. The Earl of Castlewood" (turning to his lordship, and speaking in German) "shall tell him that he plays too much!" And so saying, the Defender of the Faith turned his royal back.

Lord Castlewood shrank back quite frightened at this cold reception of his august master.

"What does he say?" asked Harry.

"His Majesty thinks they play too high at White's, and is displeased," whispered the nobleman.

"If he does not want us, we had better not come again, that is all," said Harry, simply. "I never, somehow, considered that German fellow a real King of England."

"Hush! for Heaven's sake, hold your confounded colonial tongue!" cries out my lord. "Don't you see the walls here have ears!"

"And what then?" asks Mr. Warrington. "Why, look at the people! Hang me, if it is not quite a curiosity! They were all shaking hands with me, and bowing to me, and flattering me just now; and at present they avoid me as if I were the plague!"

"Shake hands, nephew," said a broad-faced, broad-shouldered gentleman, in a scarlet-laced waistcoat, and a great old-fashioned wig. "I heard what you said. I have ears like the wall, look you. And, now, if other people show you the cold shoulder, I'll give you my hand;" and so saying, the gentleman put out a great brown hand, with which he grasped Harry's. "Something of my brother about your eyes and face. Though I suppose in your island you grow more wiry and thin like. I am thine uncle, child. My name is Sir Miles Warrington. My lord knows me well enough."

My lord looked very frightened and yellow. "Yes, my dear Harry. This is your paternal uncle, Sir Miles Warrington."

"Might as well have come to see us in Norfolk, as dangle about playing the fool at Tunbridge Wells, Mr. Warrington, or Mr. Esmond,—which do you call yourself?" said the Baronet. "The old lady calls herself Madam Esmond, don't she?"

"My mother is not ashamed of her father's name, nor am I, uncle," said Mr. Harry, rather proudly.

"Well said, lad! Come home and eat a bit of mutton with Lady Warrington, at three, in Hill Street,—that is if you can do without your White's kickshaws. You need not look frightened, my Lord Castlewood! I shall tell no tales out of school."

"I—I am sure Sir Miles Warrington will act as a gentleman!" says my lord, in much perturbation.

"Belike, he will," growled the Baronet, turning on his heel. "And thou wilt come, young man, at three; and mind, good roast mutton waits for nobody. Thou hast a great look of thy father. Lord bless us, how we used to beat each other! He was smaller than me, and in course younger; but many a time he had the best of it. Take it he was henpecked when he married, and Madam Esmond took the spirit out of him when she got him in her island. Virginia is an island. Ain't it an island?"

Harry laughed, and said "No!" And the jolly Baronet, going off, said, "Well, island or not, thou must come and tell all about it to my lady. She'll know whether 'tis an island or not."

"My dear Mr. Warrington," said my lord, with an appealing look, "I need not tell you that, in this great city, every man has enemies, and that there is a great, great deal of detraction and scandal. I never spoke to you about Sir Miles Warrington, precisely because I did know him, and because we have had differences together. Should he permit himself remarks to my disparagement, you will receive them cum grano, and remember that it is from an enemy they come." And the pair walked out of the King's apartments and into Saint James's Street. Harry found the news of his cold reception at court had already preceded him to White's. The King had turned his back upon him. The King was jealous of Harry's favour with the favourite. Harry was au mieux with Lady Yarmouth. A score of gentlemen wished him a compliment upon his conquest. Before night it was a settled matter that this was amongst the other victories of the Fortunate Youth.

Sir Miles told his wife and Harry as much, when the young man appeared at the appointed hour at the Baronet's dinner-table, and he rallied Harry in his simple rustic fashion. The lady, at first a grand and stately personage, told Harry, on their further acquaintance, that the reputation which the world had made for him was so bad, that at first she had given him but a frigid welcome. With the young ladies, Sir Miles's daughters, it was "How d'ye do, cousin?" and "No, thank you, cousin," and a number of prim curtseys to the Virginian, as they greeted him and took leave of him. The little boy, the heir of the house, dined at table, under the care of his governor; and, having his glass of port by papa after dinner, gave a loose to his innocent tongue, and asked many questions of his cousin. At last the innocent youth said, after looking hard in Harry's face, "Are you wicked, cousin Harry? You don't look very wicked!"

"My dear Master Miles!" expostulates the tutor, turning very red.

"But you know you said he was wicked!" cried the child.

"We are all miserable sinners, Miley," explains papa. "Haven't you heard the clergyman say so every Sunday?"

"Yes, but not so very wicked as cousin Harry. Is it true that you gamble, cousin, and drink all night with wicked men, and frequent the company of wicked women? You know you said so, Mr. Walker—and mamma said so, too, that Lady Yarmouth was a wicked woman."

"And you are a little pitcher," cries papa: "and my wife, nephew Harry, is a staunch Jacobite—you won't like her the worse for that. Take Miles to his sisters, Mr. Walker, and Topsham shall give thee a ride in the park, child, on thy little horse." The idea of the little horse consoled Master Miles; for, when his father ordered him away to his sisters, he had begun to cry bitterly, bawling out that he would far rather stay with his wicked cousin.

"They have made you a sad reputation among 'em, nephew!" says the jolly Baronet. "My wife, you must know, of late years, and since the death of my poor eldest son, has taken to,—to, hum!—to Tottenham Court Road and Mr. Whitfield's preaching: and we have had one Ward about the house, a friend of Mr. Walker's yonder, who has recounted sad stories about you and your brother at home."

"About me, Sir Miles, as much as he pleases," cries Harry, warm with port: "but I'll break any man's bones who dares say a word against my brother! Why, sir, that fellow was not fit to buckle my dear George's shoe; and if I find him repeating at home what he dared to say in our house in Virginia, I promise him a second caning."

"You seem to stand up for your friends, nephew Harry," says the Baronet. "Fill thy glass, lad, thou art not as bad as thou hast been painted. I always told my lady so. I drink Madam Esmond Warrington's health, of Virginia, and will have a full bumper for that toast."

Harry, as in duty bound, emptied his glass, filled again, and drank Lady Warrington and Master Miles.

"Thou wouldst be heir to four thousand acres in Norfolk, did he die, though," said the Baronet.

"God forbid, sir, and be praised that I have acres enough in Virginia of my own!" says Mr. Warrington. He went up presently and took a dish of coffee with Lady Warrington: he talked to the young ladies of the house. He was quite easy, pleasant, and natural. There was one of them somewhat like Fanny Mountain, and this young lady became his special favourite. When he went away, they all agreed their wicked cousin was not near so wicked as they had imagined him to be: at any rate, my lady had strong hopes of rescuing him from the pit. She sent him a good book that evening, whilst Mr. Harry was at White's; with a pretty note, praying that Law's Call might be of service to him: and, this despatched, she and her daughters went off to a rout at the house of a minister's lady. But Harry, before he went to White's, had driven to his friend Mr. Sparks, in Tavistock Street, and purchased more trinkets for his female cousins—"from their aunt in Virginia," he said. You see, he was full of kindness: he kindled and warmed with prosperity. There are men on whom wealth hath no such fortunate influence. It hardens base hearts: it makes those who were mean and servile, mean and proud. If it should please the gods to try me with ten thousand a year, I will, of course, meekly submit myself to their decrees, but I will pray them to give me strength enough to bear the trial. All the girls in Hill Street were delighted at getting the presents from Aunt Warrington in Virginia and addressed a collective note, which must have astonished that good lady when she received it in spring-time, when she and

Mountain and Fanny were on a visit to grim deserted Castlewood, when the snows had cleared away and a thousand peach-trees flushed with blossoms. "Poor boy!" the mother thought "This is some present he gave his cousins in my name, in the time of his prosperity—nay, of his extravagance and folly. How quickly his wealth has passed away! But he ever had a kind heart for the poor Mountain; and we must not forget him in his need. It behoves us to be more than ever careful of our own expenses, my good people!" And so, I dare say, they warmed themselves by one log, and ate of one dish, and worked by one candle. And the widow's servants, whom the good soul began to pinch more and more I fear, lied, stole, and cheated more and more: and what was saved in one way, was stole in another.

One afternoon, Mr. Harry sate in his Bond Street lodgings, arrayed in his dressing-gown, sipping his chocolate, surrounded by luxury, encased in satin, and yet enveloped in care. A few weeks previously when the luck was with him, and he was scattering his benefactions to and fro, he had royally told Parson Sampson to get together a list of his debts which he, Mr. Warrington, would pay. Accordingly Sampson had gone to work, and had got together a list, not of all his debts—no man ever does set down all,—but such a catalogue as he thought sufficient to bring in to Mr. Warrington, at whose breakfast-table the divine had humbly waited until his honour should choose to attend it.

Harry appeared at length, very pale and languid, in curl-papers, and scarce any appetite for his breakfast; and the chaplain, fumbling with his schedule in his pocket, humbly asked if his patron had had a bad night? He had been brought home from White's by two chairmen at five o'clock in the morning; had caught a confounded cold, for one of the windows of the chair would not shut, and the rain and snow came in, finally, was in such a bad humour, that all poor Sampson's quirks and jokes could scarcely extort a smile from him.

At last, to be sure, Mr. Warrington burst into a loud laugh. It was when the poor chaplain, after a sufficient discussion of muffins, eggs, tea, the news, the theatres, and so forth, pulled a paper out of his pocket and in a piteous tone said, "Here is that schedule of debts which your honour asked for—two hundred and forty-three pounds—every shilling I owe in the world, thank Heaven!—that is—ahem!—every shilling of which the payment will in the least inconvenience me—and I need not tell my dearest patron that I shall consider him my saviour and benefactor!"

It was then that Harry, taking the paper and eyeing the chaplain with rather a wicked look, burst into a laugh, which was, however, anything but jovial. Wicked execrations, moreover, accompanied this outbreak of humour, and the luckless chaplain felt that his petition had come at the wrong moment.

"Confound it, why didn't you bring it on Monday?" Harry asked.

"Confound me, why did I not bring it on Monday?" echoed the chaplain's timid soul. "It is my luck—my usual luck. Have the cards been against you, Mr. Warrington?"

"Yes: a plague on them. Monday night, and last night, have both gone against me. Don't be frightened, chaplain, there's money enough in the locker yet. But I must go into the City and get some."

"What, sell out, sir?" asks his reverence, with a voice that was reassured, though it intended to be alarmed.

"Sell out, sir? Yes! I borrowed a hundred off Mackreth in counters last night, and must pay him at dinner-time. I will do your business for you nevertheless, and never fear, my good Mr. Sampson. Come to breakfast tomorrow, and we will see and deliver your reverence from the Philistines." But though he laughed in Sampson's presence, and strove to put a good face upon the matter, Harry's head sank down on his chest when the parson quitted him, and he sate over the fire, beating the coals about with the poker, and giving utterance to many disjointed naughty words, which showed, but did not relieve, the agitation of his spirit.

In this mood, the young fellow was interrupted by the appearance of a friend, who, on any other day—even on that one when his conscience was so uneasy—was welcome to Mr. Warrington. This was no other than Mr. Lambert, in his military dress, but with a cloak over him, who had come from the country, had been to the Captain-General's levee that morning, and had come thence to visit his young friend in Bond Street.

Harry may have thought Lambert's greeting rather cold; but being occupied with his own affairs, he put away the notion. How were the ladies of Oakhurst, and Miss Hetty, who was ailing when he passed through in the autumn? Purely? Mr. Warrington was very glad. They were come to stay a while in London with their friend, Lord Wrotham? Mr. Harry was delighted—though it must be confessed his face did not exhibit any peculiar signs of pleasure when he heard the news.

"And so you live at White's, and with the great folks; and you fare sumptuously every day, and you pay your court at St. James's, and make one at my Lady Yarmouth's routs, and at all the card-parties in the Court end of the town?" asks the Colonel.

"My dear Colonel, I do what other folks do," says Harry, with rather a high manner.

"Other folks are richer folks than some folks, my dear lad."

"Sir!" says Mr. Warrington, "I would thank you to believe that I owe nothing for which I cannot pay!"

"I should never have spoken about your affairs," said the other, not noticing the young man's haughty tone, "but that you yourself confided them to me. I hear all sorts of stories about the Fortunate Youth. Only at his Royal Highness's even today, they were saying how rich you were already, and I did not undeceive them——"

"Colonel Lambert, I cannot help the world gossiping about me!" cries Mr. Warrington, more and more impatient.

"——And what prodigious sums you had won. Eighteen hundred one night—two thousand another—six or eight thousand in all! Oh! there were gentlemen from White's at the levee too, I can assure you, and the army can fling a main as well as you civilians!"

"I wish they would meddle with their own affairs," says Harry, scowling at his old friend.

"And I, too, you look as if you were going to say. Well, my boy, it is my affair and you must let Theo's father and Hetty's father, and Harry Warrington's father's old friend say how it is my affair." Here the Colonel drew a packet out of his pocket, whereof the lappets and the coat-tails and the general pocket accommodations were much more ample than in the scant military garments of present warriors. "Look you, Harry. These trinkets which you sent with the kindest heart in the world to people who love you, and would cut off their little hands to spare you needless pain, could never be bought by a young fellow with two or three hundred a year. Why, a nobleman might buy these things, or a rich City banker, and send them to his—to his daughters, let us say."

"Sir, as you say, I meant only kindness," says Harry, blushing burning-red.

"But you must not give them to my girls, my boy. Hester and Theodosia Lambert must not be dressed up with the winnings off the gaming-table, saving your presence. It goes to my heart to bring back the trinkets. Mrs. Lambert will keep her present, which is of small value, and sends you her love and a God bless you—and so say I, Harry Warrington, with all my heart." Here the good Colonel's voice was much moved, and his face grew very red, and he passed his hand over his eyes ere he held it out.

But the spirit of rebellion was strong in Mr. Warrington. He rose up from his seat, never offering to take the hand which his senior held out to him. "Give me leave to tell Colonel Lambert," he said, "that I have had somewhat too much advice from him. You are for ever volunteering it, sir, and when I don't ask it. You make it your business to inquire about my gains at play, and about the company I keep. What right have you to control my amusements or my companions? I strive to show my sense of your former kindness by little presents to your family, and you fling—you bring them back."

"I can't do otherwise, Mr. Warrington," says the Colonel, with a very sad face.

"Such a slight may mean nothing here, sir, but in our country it means war, sir!" cries Mr. Warrington. "God forbid I should talk of drawing a sword against the father of ladies who have been as mother and sister to me: but you have wounded my heart, Colonel Lambert—you have, I won't say insulted, but humiliated me, and this is a treatment I will bear from no man alive! My servants will attend you to the door, sir!" Saying which, and rustling in his brocade dressing-gown, Mr. Warrington, with much state, walked off to his bedroom.

CHAPTER XLIV. Contains what might, perhaps, have been expected

On the rejection of his peace-offerings, our warlike young American chief chose to be in great wrath not only against Colonel Lambert, but the whole of that gentleman's family. "He has humiliated me before the girls!" thought the young man. "He and Mr. Wolfe, who were forever preaching morality to me, and giving themselves airs of superiority and protection, have again been holding me up to the family as a scapegrace and prodigal. They are so virtuous that they won't shake me by the hand, forsooth; and when I want to show them a little common gratitude, they fling my presents in my face!"

"Why, sir, the things must be worth a little fortune!" says Parson Sampson, casting an eye of covetousness on the two morocco boxes, in which, on their white satin cushions, reposed Mr. Sparks's golden gewgaws.

"They cost some money, Sampson," says the young man. "Not that I would grudge ten times the amount to people who have been kind to me."

"No, faith, sir, not if I know your honour!" interjects Sampson, who never lost a chance of praising his young patron to his face.

"The repeater, they told me, was a great bargain, and worth a hundred pounds at Paris. Little Miss Hetty I remember saying that she longed to have a repeating watch."

"Oh, what a love!" cries the chaplain, "with a little circle of pearls on the back, and a diamond knob for the handle! Why, 'twould win any woman's heart, Sir!"

"There passes an apple-woman with a basket. I have a mind to fling the thing out to her!" cries Mr. Warrington, fiercely.

When Harry went out upon business, which took him to the City and the Temple, his parasite did not follow him very far into the Strand; but turned away, owning that he had a terror of Chancery Lane, its inhabitants, and precincts. Mr. Warrington went then to his broker, and they walked to the Bank together, where they did some little business, at the end of which, and after the signing of a trifling signature or two, Harry departed with a certain number of crisp bank-notes in his pocket. The broker took Mr. Warrington to one of the great dining-houses for which the City was famous then as now; and afterwards showed Mr. Warrington the Virginian walk upon 'Change, through which Harry passed rather shamefacedly. What would a certain lady in Virginia say, he thought, if she knew that he was carrying off in that bottomless gambler's pocket a great portion of his father's patrimony? Those are all Virginia merchants, thinks he, and they are all talking to one another about me, and all saying, "That is young Esmond, of Castlewood, on the Potomac, Madam Esmond's son; and he has been losing his money at play, and he has been selling out so much, and so much, and so much."

His spirits did not rise until he had passed under the traitors' heads of Temple Bar, and was fairly out of the City. From the Strand Mr. Harry walked home, looking in at St. James's Street by the way; but there was nobody there as yet, the company not coming to the Chocolate-House till a later hour.

Arrived at home, Mr. Harry pulls out his bundle of bank-notes; puts three of them into a sheet of paper, which he seals carefully, having previously written within the sheet the words, "Much good may they do you. H. E. W."

And this packet he directs to the Reverend Mr. Sampson,—leaving it on the chimney-glass, with directions to his servants to give it to that divine when he should come in.

And now his honour's phaeton is brought to the door, and he steps in, thinking to drive round the park; but the rain coming on, or the east wind blowing, or some other reason arising, his honour turns his horses' heads down St. James's Street, and is back at White's at about three o'clock. Scarce anybody has come in yet. It is the hour when folks are at dinner. There, however, is my cousin Castlewood, lounging over the Public Advertiser, having just come off from his duty at Court hard by.

Lord Castlewood is yawning over the Public Advertiser. What shall they do? Shall they have a little piquet? Harry has no objections to a little piquet. "Just for an hour," says Lord Castlewood. "I dine at Arlington Street at four." "Just for an hour," says Mr. Warrington; and they call for cards.

"Or shall we have 'em in upstairs?" says my lord. "Out of the noise?"

"Certainly, out of the noise," says Harry.

At five o'clock a half-dozen of gentlemen have come in after their dinner, and are at cards, or coffee, or talk. The folks from the ordinary have not left the table yet. There the gentlemen of White's will often sit till past midnight.

One toothpick points over the coffee-house blinds into the street. "Whose phaeton?" asks Toothpick 1 of Toothpick 2.

"The Fortunate Youth's," says No. 2.

"Not so fortunate the last three nights. Luck confoundedly against him. Lost, last night, thirteen hundred to the table. Mr. Warrington been here to-day, John?"

"Mr. Warrington is in the house now, sir. In the little tea-room with Lord Castlewood since three o'clock. They are playing at piquet," says John.

"What fun for Castlewood!" says No. 1, with a shrug.

The second gentleman growls out an execration. "Curse the fellow!" he says. "He has no right to be in this club at all. He doesn't pay if he loses. Gentlemen ought not to play with him. Sir Miles Warrington told me at court the other day, that Castlewood has owed him money on a bet these three years."

"Castlewood," says No. 1, "don't lose if he plays alone. A large company flurries him, you see—that's why he doesn't come to the table." And the facetious gentleman grins, and shows all his teeth, polished perfectly clean.

"Let's go up and stop 'em," growls No. 2.

"Why?" asks the other. "Much better look out a-window. Lamplighter going up the ladder—famous sport. Look at that old putt in the chair: did you ever see such an old quiz?"

"Who is that just gone out of the house? As I live, it's Fortunatus! He seems to have forgotten that his phaeton has been here, waiting all the time. I bet you two to one he has been losing to Castlewood."

"Jack, do you take me to be a fool?" asks the one gentleman of the other. "Pretty pair of horses the youth has got. How he is flogging 'em!" And they see Mr. Warrington galloping up the street, and scared coachmen and chairmen clearing before him: presently my Lord Castlewood is seen to enter a chair, and go his way.

Harry drives up to his own door. It was but a few yards, and those poor horses have been beating the pavement all this while in the rain. Mr. Gumbo is engaged at the door in conversation with a countrified-looking lass, who trips off with a curtsey. Mr. Gumbo is always engaged with some pretty maid or other.

"Gumbo, has Mr. Sampson been here?" asks Gumbo's master from his driving-seat.

"No, sar. Mr. Sampson have not been here!" answers Mr. Warrington's gentleman. Harry bids him to go upstairs and bring down a letter addressed to Mr. Sampson.

"Addressed to Mr. Sampson? Oh yes, sir," says Mr. Gumbo, who can't read.

"A sealed letter, stupid! on the mantelpiece, in the glass!" says Harry; and Gumbo leisurely retires to fetch that document. As soon as Harry has it, he turns his horses' heads towards St. James's Street, and the two gentlemen, still yawning out of the window at White's, behold the Fortunate Youth, in an instant, back again.

As they passed out of the little tea-room where he and Lord Castlewood had had their piquet together, Mr. Warrington had seen that several gentlemen had entered the play-room, and that there was a bank there. Some were already steadily at work, and had their gaming jackets on: they kept such coats at the club, which they put on when they had a mind to sit down to a regular night's play.

Mr. Warrington goes to the clerk's desk, pays his account of the previous night, and, sitting down at the table, calls for fresh counters. This has been decidedly an unlucky week with the Fortunate Youth, and to-night is no more fortunate than previous nights have been. He calls for more counters, and more presently. He is a little pale and silent, though very easy and polite when talked to. But he cannot win.

At last he gets up. "Hang it! stay and mend your luck!" says Lord March, who is sitting by his side with a heap of counters before him, green and white. "Take a hundred of mine, and go on!"

"I have had enough for to-night, my lord," says Harry, and rises and goes away, and eats a broiled bone in the coffee-room, and walks back to his lodgings some time about midnight. A man after a great catastrophe commonly sleeps pretty well. It is the waking in the morning which is sometimes queer and unpleasant. Last night you proposed to Miss Brown: you quarrelled over your cups with Captain Jones, and valorously pulled his nose: you played at cards with Colonel Robinson, and gave him—oh, how many I O U's! These thoughts, with a fine headache, assail you in the morning watches. What a dreary, dreary gulf between to-day and yesterday! It seems as if you are years older. Can't you leap back over that chasm again, and is it not possible that Yesterday is but a dream? There you are, in bed. No daylight in at the windows yet. Pull your nightcap over your eyes, the blankets over your nose, and sleep away Yesterday. Psha, man, it was but a dream! Oh no, no! The sleep won't come. The watchman bawls some hour—what hour? Harry minds him that he has got the repeating watch under his pillow which he had bought for Hester. Ting, ting, ting! the repeating watch sings out six times in the darkness, with a little supplementary performance indicating the half-hour. Poor dear little Hester!—so bright, so gay, so innocent! he would have liked her to have that watch. What will Maria say? (Oh, that old Maria! what a bore she is beginning to be! he thinks.) What will Madam Esmond at home say when she hears that he has lost every shilling of his ready money—of his patrimony? All his winnings, and five thousand pounds besides, in three nights. Castlewood could not have played him false? No. My lord knows piquet better than Harry does, but he would not deal unfairly with his own flesh and blood. No, no. Harry is glad his kinsman, who wanted the money, has got it. And for not one more shilling than he possessed, would he play. It was when he counted up his losses at the gaming-table, and found they would cover all the remainder of his patrimony, that he passed the box and left the table. But, O cursed bad company! O extravagance and folly! O humiliation and remorse! "Will my mother at home forgive me?" thinks the young prodigal. "Oh, that I were there, and had never left it!"

The dreary London dawn peeps at length through shutters and curtains. The housemaid enters to light his honour's fire and admit the dun morning into his windows. Her Mr. Gumbo presently follows, who warms his master's dressing-gown and sets out his shaving-plate and linen. Then arrives the hairdresser to curl and powder his honour, whilst he reads his morning's letters; and at breakfast-time comes that inevitable Parson Sampson, with eager looks and servile smiles, to wait on his patron. The parson would have returned yesterday according to mutual agreement, but some jolly fellows kept him to dinner at the St. Alban's, and, faith, they made a night of it.

"Oh, Parson!" groans Harry, "'twas the worst night you ever made in your life! Look here, sir!"

"Here is a broken envelope with the words, 'Much good may it do you,' written within," says the chaplain, glancing at the paper.

"Look on the outside, sir!" cries Mr. Warrington. "The paper was directed to you." The poor chaplain's countenance exhibited great alarm. "Has some one broke it open, sir?" he asks.

"Some one, yes. I broke it open, Sampson. Had you come here as you proposed yesterday afternoon, you would have found that envelope full of bank-notes. As it is, they were all dropped at the infernal macco-table last night."

"What, all?" says Sampson.

"Yes, all, with all the money I brought away from the city, and all the ready money I have left in the world. In the afternoon I played piquet with my cous —with a gentleman at White's—and he eased me of all the money I had about me. Remembering that there was still some money left here, unless you had fetched it, I came home and carried it back and left it at the macco-table, with every shilling besides that belongs to me—and—great heaven, Sampson, what's the matter, man?"

"It's my luck, it's my usual luck," cries out the unfortunate chaplain, and fairly burst into tears.

"What! You are not whimpering like a baby at the loss of a loan of a couple of hundred pounds?" cries out Mr. Warrington, very fierce and angry. "Leave the room, Gumbo! Confound you! why are you always poking your woolly head in at that door!"

"Some one below wants to see master with a little bill," says Mr. Gumbo.

"Tell him to go to Jericho!" roars out Mr. Warrington. "Let me see nobody! I am not at home, sir, at this hour of the morning!"

A murmur or two, a scuffle is heard on the landing-place, and silence finally ensues. Mr. Warrington's scorn and anger are not diminished by this altercation. He turns round savagely upon unhappy Sampson, who sits with his head buried in his breast.

"Hadn't you better take a bumper of brandy to keep your spirits up, Mr. Sampson?" he asks. "Hang it, man! don't be snivelling like a woman!"

"Oh, it's not me!" says Sampson, tossing his head. "I am used to it, sir."

"Not you! Who, then? Are you crying because somebody else is hurt, pray?" asks Mr. Warrington.

"Yes, sir!" says the chaplain, with some spirit; "because somebody else is hurt, and through my fault. I have lodged for many years in London with a bootmaker, a very honest man: and, a few days since, having a perfect reliance upon—upon a friend who had promised to accommodate me with a loan—I borrowed sixty pounds from my landlord which he was about to pay to his own. I can't get the money. My poor landlord's goods will be seized for rent; his wife and dear young children will be turned into the street; and this honest family will be ruined through my fault. But, as you say, Mr. Warrington, I ought not to snivel like a woman. I will remember that you helped me once, and will bid you farewell, sir."

And, taking his broad-leafed hat, Mr. Chaplain walked out of the room.

An execration and a savage laugh, I am sorry to say, burst out of Harry's lips at this sudden movement of the chaplain's. He was in such a passion with himself, with circumstances, with all people round about him, that he scarce knew where to turn, or what he said. Sampson heard the savage laughter, and then the voice of Harry calling from the stairs, "Sampson, Sampson! hang you! come back! It's a mistake! I beg your pardon!" But the chaplain was cut to the soul, and walked on. Harry heard the door of the street as the parson slammed it. It thumped on his own breast. He entered his room, and sank back on his luxurious chair there. He was Prodigal, amongst the swine—his foul remorses; they had tripped him up, and were wallowing over him. Gambling, extravagance, debauchery, dissolute life, reckless companions, dangerous women—they were all upon him in a herd, and were trampling upon the prostrate young sinner.

Prodigal was not, however, yet utterly overcome, and had some fight left in him. Dashing the filthy importunate brutes aside, and, as it were, kicking his ugly remembrances away from him, Mr. Warrington seized a great glass of that fire-water which he had recommended to poor humiliated Parson Sampson, and, flinging off his fine damask robe, rang for the trembling Gumbo, and ordered his coat. "Not that!" roars he, as Gumbo brings him a fine green coat with plated buttons and a gold cord. "A plain suit—the plainer the better! The black clothes." And Gumbo brings the mourning-coat which his master had discarded for some months past.

Mr. Harry then takes:—1, his fine new gold watch; 2, his repeater (that which he had bought for Hetty), which he puts into his other fob; 3, his necklace, which he had purchased for Theo; 4, his rings, of which my gentleman must have half a dozen at least (with the exception of his grandfather's old seal ring, which he kisses and lays down on the pincushion again); 5, his three gold snuff boxes: and 6, his purse, knitted by his mother, and containing three shillings and sixpence and a pocket-piece brought from Virginia: and, putting on his hat, issues from his door.

At the landing he is met by Mr. Ruff, his landlord, who bows and cringes and puts into his honour's hand a strip of paper a yard long. "Much obliged if Mr. Warrington will settle. Mrs. Ruff has a large account to make up to-day." Mrs. Ruff is a milliner. Mr. Ruff is one of the head-waiters and aides-de-camp of Mr. Mackreth, the proprietor of White's Club. The sight of the landlord does not add to the lodger's good-humour.

"Perhaps his honour will have the kindness to settle the little account?" asks Mr. Ruff.

"Of course I will settle the account," says Harry, glumly looking down over Mr. Ruff's head from the stair above him.

"Perhaps Mr. Warrington will settle it now?"

"No, Sir, I will not settle it now!" says Mr. Warrington, bullying forward.

"I'm very—very much in want of money, sir," pleads the voice under him. "Mrs. Ruff is——"

"Hang you, sir, get out of the way!" cries Mr. Warrington, ferociously, and driving Mr. Ruff backward to the wall, sending him almost topsy-turvy down his own landing, he tramps down the stair, and walks forth into Bond Street.

The Guards were at exercise at the King's Mews at Charing Cross, as Harry passed, and he heard their drums and fifes, and looked in at the gate, and saw them at drill. "I can shoulder a musket at any rate," thought he to himself gloomily, as he strode on. He crossed St. Martin's Lane (where he transacted some business), and so made his way into Long Acre, and to the bootmaker's house where friend Sampson lodged. The woman of the house said Mr. Sampson was not at home, but had promised to be at home at one; and, as she knew Mr. Warrington, showed him up to the parson's apartments, where he sate down, and, for want of occupation, tried to read an unfinished sermon of the chaplain's. The subject was the Prodigal Son. Mr. Harry did not take very accurate cognisance of the sermon.

Presently he heard the landlady's shrill voice on the stair, pursuing somebody who ascended, and Sampson rushed into the room, followed by the sobbing woman.

At seeing Harry, Sampson started, and the landlady stopped. Absorbed in her own domestic cares, she had doubtless forgot that a visitor was awaiting her lodger. "There's only thirteen pound in the house, and he will be here at one, I tell you!" she was bawling out, as she pursued her victim.

"Hush, hush! my good creature!" cries the gasping chaplain, pointing to Harry, who rose from the window-seat. "Don't you see Mr. Warrington? I've business with him—most important business. It will be all right, I tell you!" And he soothed and coaxed Mrs. Landlady out of the room, with the crowd of anxious little ones hanging at her coats.

"Sampson, I have come to ask your pardon again," says Mr. Warrington, rising up. "What I said to-day to you was very cruel and unjust, and unlike a gentleman."

"Not a word more, sir," says the other, coldly and sadly, bowing and scarcely pressing the hand which Harry offered him.

"I see you are still angry with me," Harry continues.

"Nay, sir, an apology is an apology. A man of my station can ask for no more from one of yours. No doubt you did not mean to give me pain. And what if you did? And you are not the only one of the family who has," he said, as he looked piteously round the room. "I wish I had never known the name of Esmond or Castlewood," he continues, "or that place yonder of which the picture hangs over my fireplace, and where I have buried myself these long, long years. My lord, your cousin, took a fancy to me, said he would make my fortune, has kept me as his dependant till fortune has passed by me, and now refuses me my due."

"How do you mean your due, Mr. Sampson?" asks Harry.

"I mean three years' salary which he owes me as chaplain of Castlewood. Seeing you could give me no money, I went to his lordship this morning and asked him. I fell on my knees, and asked him, sir. But his lordship had none. He gave me civil words, at least (saving your presence, Mr. Warrington), but no money—that is, five guineas, which he declared was all he had and which I took. But what are five guineas amongst so many Oh, those poor little children! those poor little children!"

"Lord Castlewood said he had no money?" cries out Harry. "He won eleven hundred pounds, yesterday, of me at piquet—which I paid him out of this pocket-book."

"I dare say, sir, I dare say, sir. One can't believe a word his lordship says, sir," says Mr. Sampson; "but I am thinking of execution in this house, and ruin upon these poor folks to-morrow."

"That need not happen," says Mr. Warrington. "Here are eighty guineas, Sampson. As far as they go, God help you! 'Tis all I have to give you. I wish to my heart I could give more as I promised; but you did not come at the right time, and I am a poor devil now until I get my remittances from Virginia."

The chaplain gave a wild look of surprise, and turned quite white. He flung himself down on his knees and seized Harry's hand.

"Great powers, sir!" says he, "are you a guardian angel that Heaven hath sent me? You quarrelled with my tears this morning, Mr. Warrington. I can't help them now. They burst, sir, from a grateful heart. A rock of stone would pour them forth, sir, before such goodness as yours! May Heaven eternally bless you, and give you prosperity! May my unworthy prayers be heard in your behalf, my friend, my best benefactor! May——"

"Nay, nay! get up, friend—get up, Sampson!" says Harry, whom the chaplain's adulation and fine phrases rather annoyed.

"I am glad to have been able to do you a service—sincerely glad. There—there! Don't be on your knees to me!"

"To Heaven who sent you to me, sir!" cries the chaplain. "Mrs. Weston! Mrs. Weston!"

"What is it, sir?" says the landlady, instantly, who, indeed, had been at the door the whole time. "We are saved, Mrs. Weston! We are saved!" cries the chaplain. "Kneel, kneel, woman, and thank our benefactor! Raise your innocent voices, children, and bless him!" A universal whimper arose round Harry, which the chaplain led off, whilst the young Virginian stood, simpering and well pleased, in the midst of this congregation. They would worship, do what he might. One of the children, not understanding the kneeling order, and standing up, the mother fetched her a slap on the ear, crying, "Drat it, Jane, kneel down, and bless the gentleman, I tell 'ee!"... We leave them performing this sweet benedictory service. Mr. Harry walks off from Long Acre, forgetting almost the griefs of the former four or five days, and tingling with the consciousness of having done a good action.

The young woman with whom Gumbo had been conversing on that evening when Harry drove up from White's to his lodging, was Mrs. Molly, from Oakhurst, the attendant of the ladies there. Wherever that fascinating Gumbo went, he left friends and admirers in the servants'-hall. I think we said it was on a Wednesday evening he and Mrs. Molly had fetched a walk together, and they were performing the amiable courtesies incident upon parting, when Gumbo's master came up, and put an end to their twilight whisperings and what not.

For many hours on Wednesday, on Thursday, on Friday, a pale little maiden sate at a window in Lord Wrotham's house, in Hill Street, her mother and sister wistfully watching her. She would not go out. They knew whom she was expecting. He passed the door once, and she might have thought he was coming, but he did not. He went into a neighbouring house. Papa had never told the girls of the presents which Harry had sent, and only whispered a word or two to their mother regarding his quarrel with the young Virginian.

On Saturday night there was an opera of Mr. Handel's, and papa brought home tickets for the gallery. Hetty went this evening. The change would do her good, Theo thought, and—and, perhaps there might be Somebody amongst the fine company; but Somebody was not there; and Mr. Handel's fine music fell blank upon the poor child. It might have been Signor Bononcini's, and she would have scarce known the difference.

As the children are undressing and taking off those smart new satin sacks in which they appeared at the Opera, looking so fresh and so pretty amongst all the tawdry rouged folks, Theo remarks how very sad and woebegone Mrs. Molly their maid appears. Theo is always anxious when other people seem in trouble; not so Hetty, now, who is suffering, poor thing, one of the most selfish maladies which ever visits mortals. Have you ever been amongst insane people, and remarked how they never, never think of any but themselves?

"What is the matter, Molly?" asks kind Theo: and indeed, Molly has been longing to tell her young ladies. "Oh, Miss Theo! Oh, Miss Hetty!" she says. "How ever can I tell you? Mr. Gumbo have been here, Mr. Warrington's coloured gentleman, miss; and he says Mr. Warrington have been took by two bailiffs this evening, as he comes out of Sir Miles Warrington's house three doors off."

"Silence!" cries Theo, quite sternly. Who is it that gives those three shrieks? It is Mrs. Molly, who chooses to scream, because Miss Hetty has fallen fainting from her chair.

CHAPTER XLV. In which Harry finds two Uncles

We have all of us, no doubt, had a fine experience of the world, and a vast variety of characters have passed under our eyes; but there is one sort of men not an uncommon object of satire in novels and plays—of whom I confess to have met with scarce any specimens at all in my intercourse with this sinful mankind. I mean, mere religious hypocrites, preaching for ever, and not believing a word of their own sermons; infidels in broad brims and sables, expounding, exhorting, comminating, blessing, without any faith in their own paradise, or fear about their pandemonium. Look at those candid troops of hobnails clumping to church on a Sunday evening; those rustling maid-servants in their ribbons whom the young apprentices follow; those little regiments of schoolboys; those trim young maidens and staid matrons, marching with their glistening prayer-books, as the chapel bell chinks yonder (passing Ebenezer, very likely, where the congregation of umbrellas, great bonnets, and pattens, is by this time assembled under the flaring gas-lamps). Look at those! How many of them are hypocrites, think you? Very likely the maid-servant is thinking of her sweetheart: the grocer is casting about how he can buy that parcel of sugar, and whether the County Bank will take any more of his paper: the head-schoolboy is conning Latin verses for Monday's exercise: the young scapegrace remembers that after his service and sermon, there will be papa's exposition at home, but that there will be pie for supper: the clerk who calls out the psalm has his daughter in trouble, and drones through his responses scarcely aware of their meaning: the very moment the parson hides his face on his cushion, he may be thinking of that bill which is coming due on Monday. These people are not heavenly-minded; they are of the world, worldly, and have not yet got their feet off of it; but they are not hypocrites, look you. Folks have their religion in some handy mental lock-up, as it were—a valuable medicine, to be taken in ill health; and a man administers his nostrum to his neighbour, and recommends his private cure for the other's complaint. "My dear madam, you have spasms? You will find these drops infallible!" "You have been taking too much wine, my good sir? By this pill you may defy any evil consequences from too much wine, and take your bottle of port daily." Of spiritual and bodily physic, who are more fond and eager dispensers than women? And we know that, especially a hundred years ago, every lady in the country had her still-room, and her medicine chest, her pills, powders, potions, for all the village round.

My Lady Warrington took charge of the consciences and the digestions of her husband's tenants and family. She had the faith and health of the servants'-hall in keeping. Heaven can tell whether she knew how to doctor them rightly: but, was it pill or doctrine, she administered one or the other with equal belief in her own authority, and her disciples swallowed both obediently. She believed herself to be one of the most virtuous, self-denying, wise, learned women in the world; and, dinning this opinion perpetually into the ears of all round about her, succeeded in bringing not few persons to join in her persuasion.

At Sir Miles's dinner there was so fine a sideboard of plate, and such a number of men in livery, that it required some presenter: of mind to perceive that the beer was of the smallest which the butler brought round in the splendid tankard, and that there was but one joint of mutton on the grand silver dish. When Sir Miles called the King's health, and smacked his jolly lips over his wine, he eyed it and the company as if the liquor was ambrosia. He asked Harry Warrington whether they had port like that in Virginia? He said that was nothing to the wine Harry should taste in Norfolk. He praised the wine so, that Harry almost believed that it was good, and winked into his own glass, trying to see some of the merits which his uncle perceived in the ruby nectar.

Just as we see in many a well-regulated family of this present century, the Warringtons had their two paragons. Of the two grown daughters, the one was the greatest beauty, the other the greatest genius and angel of any young lady then alive, as Lady Warrington told Harry. The eldest, the Beauty, was engaged to dear Tom Claypool, the fond mother informed her cousin Harry in confidence. But the second daughter, the Genius and Angel, was for ever set upon our young friend to improve his wits and morals. She sang to him at the harpsichord—rather out of tune for an angel, Harry thought; she was ready with advice, instruction, conversation—with almost too much instruction and advice, thought Harry, who would have far preferred the society of the little cousin who reminded him of Fanny Mountain at home. But the last-mentioned young maiden after dinner retired to her nursery commonly. Beauty went off on her own avocations; mamma had to attend to her poor or write her voluminous letters; papa dozed in his arm-chair; and the Genius remained to keep her young cousin company.

The calm of the house somehow pleased the young man, and he liked to take refuge there away from the riot and dissipation in which he ordinarily lived. Certainly no welcome could be kinder than that which he got. The doors were opened to him at all hours. If Flora was not at home, Dora was ready to receive him. Ere many days' acquaintance, he and his little cousin Miles had been to have a galloping-match in the Park, and Harry, who was kind and generous to every man alive who came near him, had in view the purchase of a little horse for his cousin, far better than that which the boy rode, when the circumstances occurred which brought all our poor Harry's coaches and horses to a sudden breakdown.

Though Sir Miles Warrington had imagined Virginia to be an island, the ladies were much better instructed in geography, and anxious to hear from Harry all about his home and his native country. He, on his part, was not averse to talk about it. He described to them the length and breadth of his estate; the rivers which it coasted; the produce which it bore. He had had with a friend a little practice of surveying in his boyhood. He made a map of his county, with some fine towns here and there, which, in truth, were but log-huts (but, for the honour of his country, he was desirous that they should wear as handsome a look as possible). Here was Potomac; here was James river; here were the wharves whence his mother's ships and tobacco were brought to the sea. In truth, the estate was as large as a county. He did not brag about the place overmuch. To see the handsome young fellow, in a fine suit of velvet and silver lace, making his draught, pointing out this hill and that forest or town, you might have imagined him a travelling prince describing the realms of the queen his mother. He almost fancied himself to be so at times. He had miles where gentlemen in England had acres. Not only Dora listened but the beauteous Flora bowed her fair head and heard him with attention. Why, what was young Tom Claypool, their brother baronet's son in Norfolk with his great boots, his great voice, and his heirdom to a poor five thousand acres, compared to this young American prince and charming stranger? Angel as she was, Dora began to lose her angelic temper, and to twit Flora for a flirt. Claypool in his red waistcoat, would sit dumb before the splendid Harry in his ruffles and laces, talking of March and Chesterfield, Selwyn and Bolingbroke, and the whole company of macaronis. Mamma began to love Harry more and more as a son. She was anxious about the spiritual welfare of those poor Indians, of those poor negroes in Virginia. What could she do to help dear Madam Esmond (a precious woman, she knew!) in the good work? She had a serious butler and housekeeper: they were delighted with the spiritual behaviour and sweet musical gifts of Gumbo.

"Ah! Harry, Harry! you have been a sad wild boy! Why did you not come sooner to us, sir, and not lose your time amongst the spendthrifts and the vain world? But 'tis not yet too late. We must reclaim thee, dear Harry! Mustn't we, Sir Miles? Mustn't we Dora? Mustn't we, Flora?"

The three ladies all look up to the ceiling. They will reclaim the dear prodigal. It is which shall reclaim him most. Dora sits by and watches Flora. As for mamma when the girls are away, she talks to him more and more seriously, more and more tenderly. She will be a mother to him in the absence of his own admirable parent. She gives him a hymn-book. She kisses him on the forehead. She is actuated by the purest love, tenderness, religious regard, towards her dear, wayward, wild, amiable nephew.

Whilst these sentimentalities were going on, it is to be presumed that Mr. Warrington kept his own counsel about his affairs out-of-doors, which we have seen were in the very worst condition. He who had been favoured by fortune for so many weeks was suddenly deserted by her, and a few days had served to kick down all his heap of winnings. Do we say that my Lord Castlewood, his own kinsman, had dealt unfairly by the young Virginian, and in the course of a couple of afternoons' closet practice had robbed him? We would insinuate nothing so disrespectful to his lordship's character; but he had won from Harry every shilling which properly belonged to him, and would have played him for his reversions, but that the young man flung up his hands when he saw himself so far beaten, and declared that he must continue the battle no more. Remembering that there still remained a spar out of the wreck, as it were—that portion which he had set aside for poor Sampson—Harry ventured it at the gaming-table; but that last resource went down along with the rest of Harry's possessions, and Fortune fluttered off in the storm, leaving the luckless adventurer almost naked on the shore.

When a man is young and generous and hearty the loss of money scarce afflicts him. Harry would sell his horses and carriages, and diminish his train of life. If he wanted immediate supplies of money, would not his Aunt Bernstein be his banker, or his kinsman who had won so much from him, or his kind Uncle Warrington and Lady Warrington who were always talking virtue and benevolence, and declaring that they loved him as a son? He would call upon these, or any one of them whom he might choose to favour, at his leisure; meanwhile, Sampson's story of his landlord's distress touched the young gentleman, and, in order to raise a hasty supply for the clergyman, he carried off all his trinkets to a certain pawnbroker's shop in St. Martin's Lane.

Now this broker was a relative or partner of that very Mr. Sparks of Tavistock Street, from whom Harry had purchased—purchased did we say?—no; taken the trinkets which he had intended to present to his Oakhurst friends; and it chanced that Mr. Sparks came to visit his brother-tradesman very soon after Mr. Warrington had disposed of his goods. Recognising immediately the little enamelled diamond-handled repeater which he had sold to the Fortunate Youth, the jeweller broke out into expressions regarding Harry which I will not mention here, being already accused of speaking much too plainly. A gentleman who is acquainted with a pawnbroker, we may be sure has a bailiff or two amongst his acquaintances; and those bailiffs have followers who, at the bidding of the impartial Law, will touch with equal hand the fiercest captain's epaulet or the finest macaroni's shoulder. The very gentlemen who had seized upon Lady Maria at Tunbridge were set upon her cousin in London. They easily learned from the garrulous Gumbo that his honour was at Sir Miles Warrington's house in Hill Street, and whilst the black was courting Mrs. Lambert's maid at the adjoining mansion, Mr. Costigan and his assistant lay in wait for poor Harry, who was enjoying the delights of intercourse with a virtuous family circle assembled round his aunt's table. Never had Uncle Miles been more cordial, never had Aunt Warrington been more gracious, gentle, and affectionate; Flora looked unusually lovely, Dora had been more than ordinarily amiable. At parting, my lady gave him both her hands, and called benedictions from the ceiling down upon him. Papa had said in his most jovial manner, "Hang it, nephew! when I was thy age I should have kissed two such fine girls as Do and Flo ere this, and my own flesh and blood too! Don't tell me! I should, my Lady Warrington! Odds-fish! 'tis the boy blushes, and not the girls! I think—I suppose they are used to it. He, he!"

"Papa!" cry the virgins.

"Sir Miles!" says the august mother at the same instant.

"There, there!" says papa. "A kiss won't do no harm, and won't tell no tales: will it, nephew Harry?" I suppose, during the utterance of the above three brief phrases, the harmless little osculatory operation has taken place, and blushing cousin Harry has touched the damask cheek of cousin Flora and cousin Dora.

As he goes downstairs with his uncle, mamma makes a speech to the girls, looking, as usual, up to the ceiling, and saying, "What precious qualities your poor dear cousin has! What shrewdness mingled with his simplicity, and what a fine genteel manner, though upon mere worldly elegance I set little store. What a dreadful pity to think that such a vessel should ever be lost! We must rescue him, my loves. We must take him away from those wicked companions, and those horrible Castlewoods—not that I would speak ill of my neighbours. But I shall hope, I shall pray, that he may be rescued from his evil courses!" And again Lady Warrington eyes the cornice in a most determined manner, as the girls wistfully look towards the door behind which their interesting cousin has just vanished.

His uncle will go downstairs with him. He calls "God bless you, my boy!" most affectionately: he presses Harry's hand, and repeats his valuable benediction at the door. As it closes, the light from the hall within having sufficiently illuminated Mr. Warrington's face and figure, two gentlemen, who have been standing on the opposite side of the way, advance rapidly, and one of them takes a strip of paper out of his pocket, and putting his hand upon Mr. Warrington's shoulder, declares him his prisoner. A hackney-coach is in attendance, and poor Harry goes to sleep in Chancery Lane.

Oh, to think that a Virginian prince's back should be slapped by a ragged bailiffs follower!—that Madam Esmond's son should be in a spunging-house in Cursitor Street! I do not envy our young prodigal his rest on that dismal night. Let us hit him now he is down, my beloved young friends. Let us imagine the stings of remorse keeping him wakeful on his dingy pillow; the horrid jollifications of other hardened inmates of the place ringing in his ears from the room hard by, where they sit boozing; the rage and shame and discomfiture. No pity on him, I say, my honest young gentlemen, for you, of course, have never indulged in extravagance or folly, or paid the reckoning of remorse.

CHAPTER XLVI. Chains and Slavery

Remorse for past misdeeds and follies Harry sincerely felt, when he found himself a prisoner in that dismal lock-up house, and wrath and annoyance at the idea of being subjected to the indignity of arrest; but the present unpleasantry he felt sure could only be momentary. He had twenty friends who would release him from his confinement: to which of them should he apply, was the question. Mr. Draper, the man of business, who had been so obsequious to him: his kind uncle the Baronet, who had offered to make his house Harry's home, who loved him as a son: his cousin Castlewood, who had won such large sums from him: his noble friends at the Chocolate-House, his good Aunt Bernstein—any one of these Harry felt sure would give him a help in his trouble, though some of the relatives, perhaps, might administer to him a little scolding for his imprudence. The main point was, that the matter should be transacted quietly, for Mr. Warrington was anxious that as few as possible of the public should know how a gentleman of his prodigious importance had been subject to such a vulgar process as an arrest. As if the public does not end by knowing everything it cares to know. As if the dinner I shall have to-day, and the hole in the stocking which I wear at this present writing, can be kept a secret from some enemy or other who has a mind to pry it out—though my boots are on, and my door was locked when I dressed myself! I mention that hole in the stocking for sake of example merely. The world can pry out everything about us which it has a mind to know. But then there is this consolation, which men will never accept in their own cases, that the world doesn't care. Consider the amount of scandal it has been forced to hear in its time, and how weary and blasé it must be of that kind of intelligence. You are taken to prison, and fancy yourself indelibly disgraced? You are bankrupt under odd circumstances? You drive a queer bargain with your friends and are found out, and imagine the world will punish you? Psha! Your shame is only vanity. Go and talk to the world as if nothing had happened, and nothing has happened. Tumble down; brush the mud off your clothes; appear with a smiling countenance, and nobody cares. Do you suppose Society is going to take out its pocket-handkerchief and be inconsolable when you die? Why should it care very much, then, whether your worship graces yourself or disgraces yourself? Whatever happens it talks, meets, jokes, yawns, has its dinner, pretty much as before. Therefore don't be so conceited about yourself as to fancy your private affairs of so much importance, mi fili. Whereas Mr. Harry Warrington chafed and fumed as though all the world was tingling with the touch of that hand which had been laid on his sublime shoulder.

"A pretty sensation my arrest must have created at the club!" thought Harry. "I suppose that Mr. Selwyn will be cutting all sorts of jokes about my misfortune, plague take him! Everybody round the table will have heard of it. March will tremble about the bet I have with him; and, faith, 'twill be difficult to pay him when I lose. They will all be setting up a whoop of congratulation at the Savage, as they call me, being taken prisoner. How shall I ever be able to appear in the world again? Whom shall I ask to come to my help? No," thought he, with his mingled acuteness and simplicity, "I will not send in the first instance to any of my relations or my noble friends at White's. I will have Sampson's counsel. He has often been in a similar predicament, and will know how to advise me." Accordingly, as soon as the light of dawn appeared, after an almost intolerable delay—for it seemed to Harry as if the sun had forgotten to visit Cursitor Street in his rounds that morning—and as soon as the inmates of the house of bondage were stirring, Mr. Warrington despatched a messenger to his friend in Long Acre, acquainting the chaplain with the calamity just befallen him, and beseeching his reverence to give him the benefit of his advice and consolation.

Mr. Warrington did not know, to be sure, that to send such a message to the parson was as if he said, "I am fallen amongst the lions. Come down, my dear friend, into the pit with me." Harry very likely thought Sampson's difficulties were over; or, more likely still, was so much engrossed with his own affairs and perplexities, as to bestow little thought upon his neighbour's. Having sent off his missive, the captive's mind was somewhat more at ease, and he condescended to call for breakfast, which was brought to him presently. The attendant who served him with his morning repast asked him whether he would order dinner, or take his meal at Mrs. Bailiff's table with some other gentlemen? No. Mr. Warrington would not order dinner. He should quit the place before dinner-time, he informed the chamberlain who waited on him in that grim tavern. The man went away, thinking no doubt that this was not the first young gentleman who had announced that he was going away ere two hours were over. "Well, if your honour does stay, there is good beef and carrot at two o'clock," says the sceptic, and closes the door on Mr. Harry and his solitary meditations.

Harry's messenger to Mr. Sampson brought back a message from that gentleman to say that he would be with his patron as soon as might be: but ten o'clock came, eleven o'clock, noon, and no Sampson. No Sampson arrived, but about twelve Gumbo with a portmanteau of his master's clothes, who flung himself, roaring with grief, at Harry's feet: and with a thousand vows of fidelity, expressed himself ready to die, to sell himself into slavery over again, to do anything to rescue his beloved Master Harry from this calamitous position. Harry was touched with the lad's expressions of affection, and told him to get up from the ground where he was grovelling on his knees, embracing his master's. "All you have to do, sir, is to give me my clothes to dress, and to hold your tongue about this business. Mind you, not a word, sir, about it to anybody!" says Mr. Warrington, severely.

"Oh no, sir, never to nobody!" says Gumbo, looking most solemnly, and proceeded to dress his master carefully, who had need of a change and a toilette after his yesterday's sudden capture, and night's dismal rest. Accordingly Gumbo flung a dash of powder in Harry's hair, and arrayed his master carefully and elegantly, so that he made Mr. Warrington look as fine and splendid as if he had been stepping into his chair to go to St. James's.

Indeed all that love and servility could do Mr. Gumbo faithfully did for his master, for whom he had an extreme regard and attachment. But there were certain things beyond Gumbo's power. He could not undo things which were done already; and he could not help lying and excusing himself when pressed upon points disagreeable to himself. The language of slaves is lies (I mean black slaves and white). The creature slinks away and hides with subterfuges, as a hunted animal runs to his covert at the sight of man, the tyrant and pursuer. Strange relics of feudality, and consequence of our ever-so-old social life! Our domestics (are they not men, too, and brethren?) are all hypocrites before us. They never speak naturally to us, or the whole truth. We should be indignant: we should say, confound their impudence: we should turn them out of doors if they did. But quo me rapis, O my unbridled hobby?

Well, the truth is, that as for swearing not to say a word about his master's arrest—such an oath as that was impossible to keep for, with a heart full of grief, indeed, but with a tongue that never could cease wagging, bragging, joking, and lying, Mr. Gumbo had announced the woeful circumstance to a prodigious number of his acquaintances already, chiefly gentlemen of the shoulder-knot and worsted lace. We have seen how he carried the news to Colonel Lambert's and Lord Wrotham's servants: he had proclaimed it at the footman's club to which he belonged, and which was frequented by the gentlemen of some of the first nobility. He had subsequently condescended to partake of a mug of ale in Sir Miles Warrington's butler's room, and there had repeated and embellished the story. Then he had gone off to Madame Bernstein's people, with some of whom he was on terms of affectionate intercourse, and had informed that domestic circle of his grief and, his master being captured, and there being no earthly call for his personal services that evening, Gumbo had stepped up to Lord Castlewood's, and informed the gentry there of the incident which had just come to pass. So when, laying his hand on his heart, and with gushing floods of tears, Gumbo says, in reply to his master's injunction, "Oh no, master! nebber to nobody!" we are in a condition to judge of the degree of credibility which ought to be given to the lad's statement.

The black had long completed his master's toilet: the dreary breakfast was over: slow as the hours went to the prisoner, still they were passing one after another, but no Sampson came in accordance with the promise sent in the morning. At length, some time after noon, there arrived, not Sampson, but a billet from him, sealed with a moist wafer, and with the ink almost yet wet.

The unlucky divine's letter ran as follows:

"Oh, sir, dear sir, I have done all that a man can at the command and in the behalf of his patron! You did not know, sir, to what you were subjecting me, did you? Else, if I was to go to prison, why did I not share yours, and why am I in a lock-up house three doors off?

"Yes. Such is the fact. As I was hastening to you, knowing full well the danger to which I was subject:—but what danger will I not affront at the call of such a benefactor as Mr. Warrington hath been to me?—I was seized by two villains who had a writ against me, and who have lodged me at Naboth's, hard by, and so close to your honour, that we could almost hear each other across the garden walls of the respective houses where we are confined.

"I had much and of importance to say, which I do not care to write down on paper regarding your affairs. May they mend! May my cursed fortunes, too, better themselves, is the prayer of—

"Your honour's afflicted Chaplain-in-Ordinary, J. S."

And now, as Mr. Sampson refuses to speak, it will be our duty to acquaint the reader with those matters whereof the poor chaplain did not care to discourse on paper.

Gumbo's loquacity had not reached so far as Long Acre, and Mr. Sampson was ignorant of the extent of his patron's calamity until he received Harry's letter and messenger from Chancery Lane. The divine was still ardent with gratitude for the service Mr. Warrington had just conferred on him, and eager to find some means to succour his distressed patron. He knew what a large sum Lord Castlewood had won from his cousin, had dined in company with his lordship on the day before, and now ran to Lord Castlewood's house, with a hope of arousing him to some pity for Mr. Warrington. Sampson made a very eloquent and touching speech to Lord Castlewood about his kinsman's misfortune, and spoke with a real kindness and sympathy, which, however, failed to touch the nobleman to whom he addressed himself.

My lord peevishly and curtly put a stop to the chaplain's passionate pleading. "Did I not tell you, two days since, when you came for money, that I was as poor as a beggar, Sampson," said his lordship, "and has anybody left me a fortune since? The little sum I won from my cousin was swallowed up by others. I not only can't help Mr. Warrington, but, as I pledge you my word, not being in the least aware of his calamity, I had positively written to him this morning to ask him to help me." And a letter to this effect did actually reach Mr. Warrington from his lodgings, whither it had been despatched by the penny post.

"I must get him money, my lord. I know he had scarcely anything left in his pocket after relieving me. Were I to pawn my cassock and bands, he must have money," cried the chaplain.

"Amen. Go and pawn your bands, your cassock, anything you please. Your enthusiasm does you credit," said my lord; and resumed the reading of his paper, whilst, in the deepest despondency, poor Sampson left him.

My Lady Maria meanwhile had heard that the chaplain was with her brother, and conjectured what might be the subject on which they had been talking. She seized upon the parson as he issued from out his fruitless interview with my lord. She drew him into the dining-room: the strongest marks of grief and sympathy were in her countenance. "Tell me, what is this has happened to Mr. Warrington?" she asked.

"Your ladyship, then, knows?" asked the chaplain.

"Have I not been in mortal anxiety ever since his servant brought the dreadful news last night?" asked my lady. "We had it as we came from the opera—from my Lady Yarmouth's box—my lord, my Lady Castlewood, and I."

"His lordship, then, did know?" continued Sampson.

"Benson told the news when we came from the playhouse to our tea," repeats Lady Maria.

The chaplain lost all patience and temper at such duplicity. "This is too bad," he said, with an oath; and he told Lady Maria of the conversation which he had just had with Lord Castlewood, and of the latter's refusal to succour his cousin, after winning great sums of money from him, and with much eloquence and feeling, of Mr. Warrington's most generous behaviour to himself.

Then my Lady Maria broke out with a series of remarks regarding her own family, which were by no means complimentary to her own kith and kin. Although not accustomed to tell truth commonly, yet, when certain families fall out, it is wonderful what a number of truths they will tell about one another. With tears, imprecations, I do not like to think how much stronger language, Lady Maria burst into a furious and impassioned tirade, in which she touched upon the history of almost all her noble family. She complimented the men and the ladies alike; she shrieked out interrogatories to Heaven, inquiring why it had made such (never mind what names she called her brothers, sisters, uncles, aunts, parents); and, emboldened with wrath, she dashed at her brother's library door, so shrill in her outcries, so furious in her demeanour, that the alarmed chaplain, fearing the scene which might ensue, made for the street.

My lord, looking up from the book or other occupation which engaged him, regarded the furious woman with some surprise, and selected a good strong oath to fling at her, as it were, and check her onset.

But, when roused, we have seen how courageous Maria could be. Afraid as she was ordinarily of her brother, she was not in a mood to be frightened now by any language of abuse or sarcasm at his command.

"So, my lord!" she called out, "you sit down with him in private to cards, and pigeon him! You get the poor boy's last shilling, and you won't give him a guinea out of his own winnings now he is penniless!"

"So that infernal chaplain has been telling tales!" says my lord.

"Dismiss him: do! Pay him his wages, and let him go,—he will be glad enough!" cries Maria.

"I keep him to marry one of my sisters, in case he is wanted," says

Castlewood, glaring at her.

"What can the women be in a family where there are such men?" says the lady.

"Effectivement!" says my lord, with a shrug of his shoulder.

"What can we be, when our fathers and brothers are what they are? We are bad enough, but what are you? I say, you neither have courage—no, nor honour, nor common feeling. As your equals won't play with you, my Lord Castlewood, you must take this poor lad out of Virginia, your own kinsman, and pigeon him! Oh, it's a shame—a shame!"

"We are all playing our own game, I suppose. Haven't you played and won one, Maria? Is it you that are squeamish of a sudden about the poor lad from Virginia? Has Mr. Harry cried off, or has your ladyship got a better offer?" cried my Lord. "If you won't have him, one of the Warrington girls will, I promise you; and the old Methodist woman in Hill Street will give him the choice of either. Are you a fool, Maria Esmond? A greater fool, I mean, than in common?"

"I should be a fool if I thought that either of my brothers could act like an honest man, Eugene!" said Maria. "I am a fool to expect that you will be other than you are; that if you find any relative in distress you will help him; that if you can meet with a victim you won't fleece him."

"Fleece him! Psha! What folly are you talking! Have you not seen, from the course which the lad has been running for months past, how he would end? If I had not won his money, some other would? I never grudged thee thy little plans regarding him. Why shouldst thou fly in a passion, because I have just put out my hand to take what he was offering to all the world? I reason with you, I don't know why, Maria. You should be old enough to understand reason, at any rate. You think this money belonged of right to Lady Maria Warrington and her children? I tell you that in three months more every shilling would have found its way to White's macco-table, and that it is much better spent in paying my debts. So much for your ladyship's anger, and tears, and menaces, and naughty language. See! I am a good brother, and repay them with reason and kind words."

"My good brother might have given a little more than kind words to the lad from whom he has just taken hundreds," interposed the sister of this affectionate brother.

"Great heavens, Maria! Don't you see that even out of this affair, unpleasant as it seems, a clever woman may make her advantage," cries my lord. Maria said she failed to comprehend.

"As thus. I name no names; I meddle in no person's business, having quite enough to do to manage my own cursed affairs. But suppose I happen to know of a case in another family which may be applicable to ours. It is this. A green young lad of tolerable expectations, comes up from the country to his friends in town—never mind from what country: never mind to what town. An elderly female relative, who has been dragging her spinsterhood about these—how many years shall we say?—extort a promise of marriage from my young gentleman, never mind on what conditions."

"My lord, do you want to insult your sister as well as to injure your cousin?" asks Maria.

"My good child, did I say a single word about fleecing or cheating, or pigeoning, or did I fly into a passion when you insulted me? I know the allowance that must be made for your temper, and the natural folly of your sex. I say I treated you with soft words—I go on with my story. The elderly relative extracts a promise of marriage from the young lad, which my gentleman is quite unwilling to keep. No, he won't keep it. He is utterly tired of his elderly relative: he will plead his mother's refusal: he will do anything to get out of his promise."

"Yes; if he was one of us Esmonds, my Lord Castlewood. But this is a man of honour we are speaking of," cried Maria, who, I suppose, admired truth in others, however little she saw it in her own family.

"I do not contradict either of my dear sister's remarks. One of us would fling the promise to the winds, especially as it does not exist in writing."

"My lord!" gasps out Maria.

"Bah! I know all. That little coup of Tunbridge was played by the Aunt Bernstein with excellent skill. The old woman is the best man of our family. While you were arrested, your boxes were searched for the Mohock's letters to you. When you were let loose, the letters had disappeared, and you said nothing, like a wise woman, as you are sometimes. You still hanker after your Cherokee. Soit. A woman of your mature experience knows the value of a husband. What is this little loss of two or three hundred pounds?"

"Not more than three hundred, my lord?" interposes Maria.

"Eh! never mind a hundred or two, more or less. What is this loss at cards? A mere bagatelle! You are playing for a principality. You want your kingdom in Virginia; and if you listen to my opinion, the little misfortune which has happened to your swain is a piece of great good-fortune to you."

"I don't understand you, my lord."

"C'est possible; but sit down, and I will explain what I mean in a manner suited to your capacity." And so Maria Esmond, who had advanced to her brother like a raging lion, now sate down at his feet like a gentle lamb.

Madame de Bernstein was not a little moved at the news of her nephew's arrest, which Mr. Gumbo brought to Clarges Street on the night of the calamity. She would have cross-examined the black, and had further particulars respecting Harry's mishap; but Mr. Gumbo, anxious to carry his intelligence to other quarters, had vanished when her ladyship sent for him. Her temper was not improved by the news, or by the sleepless night which she spent. I do not envy the dame de compagnie who played cards with her, or the servant who had to lie in her chamber. An arrest was an everyday occurrence, as she knew very well as a woman of the world. Into what difficulties had her scapegrace of a nephew fallen? How much money should she be called upon to pay to release him? And had he run through all his own? Provided he had not committed himself very deeply, she was quite disposed to aid him. She liked even his extravagances and follies. He was the only being in the world on whom, for long, long years, that weary woman had been able to bestow a little natural affection. So, on their different beds, she and Harry were lying wakeful together; and quite early in the morning the messengers which each sent forth on the same business may have crossed each other.

Madame Bernstein's messenger was despatched to the chambers of her man of business, Mr. Draper, with an order that Mr. D. should ascertain for what sums Mr. Warrington had been arrested, and forthwith repair to the Baroness. Draper's emissaries speedily found out that Mr. Warrington was locked up close beside them, and the amount of detainers against him so far. Were there other creditors, as no doubt there were, they would certainly close upon him when they were made acquainted with his imprisonment.

To Mr. Sparks, the jeweller, for those unlucky presents, so much; to the landlord in Bond Street, for board, fire, lodging, so much: these were at present the only claims against Mr. Warrington, Mr. Draper found. He was ready, at a signal from her ladyship, to settle them at a moment. The jeweller's account ought especially to be paid, for Mr. Harry had acted most imprudently in taking goods from Mr. Sparks on credit, and pledging them with a pawnbroker. He must have been under some immediate pressure for money; intended to redeem the goods immediately, meant nothing but what was honourable of course; but the affair would have an ugly look, if made public, and had better be settled out of hand. "There cannot be the least difficulty regarding a thousand pounds more or less, for a gentleman of Mr. Warrington's rank and expectations," said Madame de Bernstein. Not the least: her ladyship knew very well that there were funds belonging to Mr. Warrington, on which money could be at once raised with her ladyship's guarantee.

Should he go that instant and settle the matter with Messrs. Amos? Mr. Harry might be back to dine with her at two, and to confound the people at the clubs, "who are no doubt rejoicing over his misfortunes," said the compassionate Mr. Draper.

But the Baroness had other views. "I think, my good Mr. Draper," she said, "that my young gentleman has sown wild oats enough; and when he comes out of prison I should like him to come out clear, and without any liabilities at all. You are not aware of all his."

"No gentleman ever does tell all his debts, madam," says Mr. Draper; "no one I ever had to deal with."

"There is one which the silly boy has contracted, and from which he ought to be released, Mr. Draper. You remember a little circumstance which occurred at Tunbridge Wells in the autumn? About which I sent up my man Case to you?"

"When your ladyship pleases to recall it, I remember it—not otherwise," says Mr. Draper, with a bow. "A lawyer should be like a Popish confessor,— what is told him is a secret for ever, and for everybody." So we must not whisper Madame Bernstein's secret to Mr. Draper; but the reader may perhaps guess it from the lawyer's conduct subsequently.

The lawyer felt pretty certain that ere long he would receive a summons from the poor young prisoner in Cursitor Street, and waited for that invitation before he visited Mr. Warrington. Six-and-thirty hours passed ere the invitation came, during which period Harry passed the dreariest two days which he ever remembered to have spent.

There was no want of company in the lock-up house, the bailiff's rooms were nearly always full; but Harry preferred the dingy solitude of his own room to the society round his landlady's table, and it was only on the second day of his arrest, and when his purse was emptied by the heavy charges of the place, that he made up his mind to apply to Mr. Draper. He despatched a letter then to the lawyer at the Temple, informing him of his plight, and desiring him, in an emphatic postscript, not to say one word about the matter to his aunt, Madame de Bernstein.

He had made up his mind not to apply to the old lady except at the very last extremity. She had treated him with so much kindness that he revolted from the notion of trespassing on her bounty, and for a while tried to please himself with the idea that he might get out of durance without her even knowing that any misfortune at all had befallen him. There seemed to him something humiliating in petitioning a woman for money. No! He would apply first to his male friends, all of whom might help him if they would. It had been his intention to send Sampson to one or other of them as a negotiator, had not the poor fellow been captured on his way to succour his friend.

Sampson gone, Harry was obliged to have recourse to his own negro servant, who was kept on the trot all day between Temple Bar and the Court end of the town with letters from his unlucky master. Firstly, then, Harry sent off a most private and confidential letter to his kinsman, the Right Honourable the Earl of Castlewood, saying how he had been cast into prison, and begging Castlewood to lend him the amount of the debt. "Please to keep my application, and the cause of it, a profound secret from the dear ladies," wrote poor Harry.

"Was ever anything so unfortunate?" wrote back Lord Castlewood, in reply. "I suppose you have not got my note of yesterday? It must be lying at your lodgings, where—I hope in heaven!—you will soon be, too. My dear Mr. Warrington, thinking you were as rich as Croesus—otherwise I never should have sate down to cards with you—I wrote to you yesterday, begging you to lend me some money to appease some hungry duns whom I don't know how else to pacify. My poor fellow! every shilling of your money went to them, and but for my peer's privilege I might be hob-and-nob with you now in your dungeon. May you soon escape from it, is the prayer of your sincere CASTLEWOOD."

This was the result of application number one: and we may imagine that Mr. Harry read the reply to his petition with rather a blank face. Never mind! There was kind, jolly Uncle Warrington. Only last night his aunt had kissed him and loved him like a son. His uncle had called down blessings on his head, and professed quite a paternal regard for him. With a feeling of shyness and modesty in presence of those virtuous parents and family, Harry had never said a word about his wild doings, or his horse-racings, or his gamblings, or his extravagances. It must all out now. He must confess himself a Prodigal and a Sinner, and ask for their forgiveness and aid. So Prodigal sate down and composed a penitent letter to Uncle Warrington, and exposed his sad case, and besought him to come to the rescue. Was not that a bitter nut to crack for our haughty young Virginian? Hours of mortification and profound thought as to the pathos of the composition did Harry pass over that letter; sheet after sheet of Mr. Amos's sixpence-a-sheet letter-paper did he tear up before the missive was complete, with which poor blubbering Gumbo (much vilified by the bailiff's followers and parasites, whom he was robbing, as they conceived, of their perquisites) went his way.

At evening the faithful negro brought back a thick letter in his aunt's handwriting. Harry opened the letter with a trembling hand. He thought it was full of bank-notes. Ah me! it contained a sermon (Daniel in the Lions' Den) by Mr. Whitfield, and a letter from Lady Warrington saying that, in Sir Miles's absence from London, she was in the habit of opening his letters, and hence, perforce, was become acquainted with a fact which she deplored from her inmost soul to learn, namely, that her nephew Warrington had been extravagant and was in debt. Of course, in the absence of Sir Miles, she could not hope to have at command such a sum as that for which Mr. Warrington wrote, but she sent him her heartfelt prayers, her deepest commiseration, and a discourse by dear Mr. Whitfield, which would comfort him in his present (alas! she feared not undeserved) calamity. She added profuse references to particular Scriptural chapters which would do him good. If she might speak of things worldly, she said, at such a moment, she would hint to Mr. Warrington that his epistolary orthography was anything but correct. She would not fail for her part to comply with his express desire that his dear cousins should know nothing of this most painful circumstance, and with every wish for his welfare here and elsewhere, she subscribed herself his loving aunt, MARGARET WARRINGTON.

Poor Harry hid his face between his hands, and sate for a while with elbows on the greasy table blankly staring into the candle before him. The bailiff's servant, who was touched by his handsome face, suggested a mug of beer for his honour, but Harry could not drink, nor eat the meat that was placed before him. Gumbo, however, could, whose grief did not deprive him of appetite, and who, blubbering the while, finished all the beer, and all the bread and the meat. Meanwhile, Harry had finished another letter, with which Gumbo was commissioned to start again, and away the faithful creature ran upon his errand.

Gumbo ran as far as White's Club, to which house he was ordered in the first instance to carry the letter, and where he found the person to whom it was addressed. Even the prisoner, for whom time passed so slowly, was surprised at the celerity with which his negro had performed his errand.

At least the letter which Harry expected had not taken long to write. "My lord wrote it at the hall-porter's desk, while I stood there then with Mr Mr. Morris," said Gumbo, and the letter was to this effect:—

"DEAR SIR—I am sorry I cannot comply with your wish, I'm short of money at present, having paid large sums to you as well as to other gentlemen. —Yours obediently, MARCH AND R.

"Henry Warrington, Esq."

"Did Lord March say anything?" asked Mr. Warrington looking very pale.

"He say it was the coolest thing he ever knew. So did Mr. Morris. He showed him your letter, Master Harry. Yes, Mr. Morris say, 'Dam his imperence!'" added Gumbo.

Harry burst into such a yell of laughter that his landlord thought he had good news, and ran in in alarm lest he was about to lose his tenant. But by this time poor Harry's laughter was over, and he was flung down in his chair gazing dismally in the fire.

"I—I should like to smoke a pipe of Virginia" he groaned.

Gumbo burst into tears: he flung himself at Harry's knees. He kissed his knees and his hands. "Oh, master, my dear master, what will they say at home?" he sobbed out.

The jailor was touched at the sight of the black's grief and fidelity, and at Harry's pale face as he sank back in his chair quite overcome and beaten by his calamity.

"Your honour ain't eat anything these two days," the man said, in a voice of rough pity. "Pluck up a little, sir. You aren't the first gentleman who has been in and out of grief before this. Let me go down and get you a glass of punch and a little supper."

"My good friend," said Harry, a sickly smile playing over his white face, "you pay ready money for everything in this house, don't you? I must tell you that I haven't a shilling left to buy a dish of meat. All the money I have I want for letter-paper."

"Oh, master, my master!" roared out Gumbo. "Look here, my dear Master Harry! Here's plenty of money—here's twenty-three five-guineas. Here's gold moidore from Virginia—here—no, not that—that's keepsakes the girls gave me. Take everything—everything. I go sell myself to-morrow morning; but here's plenty for to-night, master!"

"God bless you, Gumbo!" Harry said, laying his hand on the lad's woolly head. "You are free if I am not, and Heaven forbid I should not take the offered help of such a friend as you. Bring me some supper: but the pipe too, mind—the pipe too!" And Harry ate his supper with a relish: and even the turnkeys and bailiff's followers, when Gumbo went out of the house that night, shook hands with him, and ever after treated him well.

CHAPTER XLVII. Visitors in Trouble

Mr. Gumbo's generous and feeling conduct soothed and softened the angry heart of his master, and Harry's second night in the spunging-house was passed more pleasantly than the first. Somebody at least there was to help and compassionate with him. Still, though softened in that one particular spot, Harry's heart was hard and proud towards almost all the rest of the world. They were selfish and ungenerous, he thought. His pious Aunt Warrington, his lordly friend March, his cynical cousin Castlewood,—all had been tried, and were found wanting. Not to avoid twenty years of prison would he stoop to ask a favour of one of them again. Fool that he had been, to believe in their promises, and confide in their friendship! There was no friendship in this cursed, cold, selfish country. He would leave it. He would trust no Englishman, great or small. He would go to Germany, and make a campaign with the king; or he would go home to Virginia, bury himself in the woods there, and hunt all day; become his mother's factor and land-steward; marry Polly Broadbent, or Fanny Mountain; turn regular tobacco-grower and farmer; do anything, rather than remain amongst these English fine gentlemen. So he arose with an outwardly cheerful countenance, but an angry spirit; and at an early hour in the morning the faithful Gumbo was in attendance in his master's chamber, having come from Bond Street, and brought Mr. Harry's letters thence. "I wanted to bring some more clothes," honest Gumbo said; "but Mr. Ruff, the landlord, he wouldn't let me bring no more."

Harry did not care to look at the letters: he opened one, two, three; they were all bills. He opened a fourth; it was from the landlord, to say that he would allow no more of Mr. Warrington's things to go out of the house,—that unless his bill was paid he should sell Mr. W.'s goods and pay himself: and that his black man must go and sleep elsewhere. He would hardly let Gumbo take his own clothes and portmanteau away. The black said he had found refuge elsewhere—with some friends at Lord Wrotham's house. "With Colonel Lambert's people," says Mr. Gumbo, looking very hard at his master. "And Miss Hetty she fall down in a faint, when she hear you taken up; and Mr. Lambert, he very good man, and he say to me this morning, he say, 'Gumbo, you tell your master if he want me he send to me, and I come to him.'"

Harry was touched when he heard that Hetty had been afflicted by his misfortune. He did not believe Gumbo's story about her fainting; he was accustomed to translate his black's language and to allow for exaggeration. But when Gumbo spoke of the Colonel the young Virginian's spirit was darkened again. "I send to Lambert" he thought, grinding his teeth, "the man who insulted me, and flung my presents back in my face! If I were starving I would not ask him for a crust!" And presently, being dressed, Mr. Warrington called for his breakfast, and despatched Gumbo with a brief note to Mr. Draper in the Temple, requiring that gentleman's attendance.

"The note was as haughty as if he was writing to one of his negroes, and not to a freeborn English gentleman," Draper said; whom indeed Harry had always treated with insufferable condescension. "It's all very well for a fine gentleman to give himself airs; but for a fellow in a spunging-house! Hang him!" says Draper, "I've a great mind not to go!" Nevertheless, Mr. Draper did go, and found Mr. Warrington in his misfortune even more arrogant than he had ever been in the days of his utmost prosperity. Mr. W. sat on his bed, like a lord, in a splendid gown with his hair dressed. He motioned his black man to fetch him a chair.

"Excuse me, madam, but such haughtiness and airs I ain't accustomed to!" said the outraged attorney.

"Take a chair and go on with your story, my good Mr. Draper!" said Madame de Bernstein, smiling, to whom he went to report proceedings. She was amused at the lawyer's anger. She liked her nephew for being insolent in adversity.

The course which Draper was to pursue in his interview with Harry had been arranged between the Baroness and her man of business on the previous day. Draper was an able man, and likely in most cases to do a client good service: he failed in the present instance because he was piqued and angry, or, more likely still, because he could not understand the gentleman with whom he had to deal. I presume that he who casts his eye on the present page is the most gentle of readers. Gentleman, as you unquestionably are, then, my dear sir, have you not remarked in your dealings with people who are no gentlemen, that you offend them not knowing the how or the why? So the man who is no gentleman offends you in a thousand ways of which the poor creature has no idea himself. He does or says something which provokes your scorn. He perceives that scorn (being always on the watch, and uneasy about himself, his manners and behaviour) and he rages. You speak to him naturally, and he fancies still that you are sneering at him. You have indifference towards him, but he hates you, and hates you the worse because you don't care. "Gumbo, a chair to Mr. Draper!" says Mr. Warrington, folding his brocaded dressing-gown round his legs as he sits on the dingy bed. "Sit down, if you please, and let us talk my business over. Much obliged to you for coming so soon in reply to my message. Had you heard of this piece of ill-luck before?"

Mr. Draper had heard of the circumstance. "Bad news travel quick, Mr. Warrington," he said; "and I was eager to offer my humble services as soon as ever you should require them. Your friends, your family, will be much pained that a gentleman of your rank should be in such a position."

"I have been very imprudent, Mr. Draper. I have lived beyond my means." (Mr. Draper bowed.) "I played in company with gentlemen who were much richer than myself, and a cursed run of ill-luck has carried away all my ready money, leaving me with liabilities to the amount of five hundred pounds, and more."

"Five hundred now in the office," says Mr. Draper.

"Well, this is such a trifle that I thought by sending to one or two friends, yesterday, I could have paid my debt and gone home without further to do. I have been mistaken; and will thank you to have the kindness to put me in the way of raising the money as soon as may be."

Mr. Draper said "Hm!" and pulled a very grave and long face.

"Why, sir, it can be done!" says Mr. Warrington, staring at the lawyer.

It not only could be done, but Mr. Draper had proposed to Madame Bernstein on the day before instantly to pay the money, and release Mr. Warrington. That lady had declared she intended to make the young gentleman her heir. In common with the rest of the world, Draper believed Harry's hereditary property in Virginia to be as great in money-value as in extent. He had notes in his pocket, and Madame Bernstein's order to pay them under certain conditions: nevertheless, when Harry said, "It can be done!" Draper pulled his long face, and said, "It can be done in time, sir; but it will require a considerable time. To touch the property in England which is yours on Mr. George Warrington's death, we must have the event proved, the trustees released: and who is to do either? Lady Esmond Warrington in Virginia, of course, will not allow her son to remain in prison, but we must wait six months before we hear from her. Has your Bristol agent any authority to honour your drafts?"

"He is only authorised to pay me two hundred pounds a year," says Mr. Warrington. "I suppose I have no resource, then, but to apply to my aunt, Madame de Bernstein. She will be my security."

"Her ladyship will do anything for you, sir; she has said so to me, often and often," said the lawyer; "and, if she gives the word at that moment you can walk out of this place."

"Go to her, then, from me, Mr. Draper. I did not want to have troubled my relations: but rather than continue in this horrible needless imprisonment, I must speak to her. Say where I am, and what has befallen me. Disguise nothing! And tell her, that I confide in her affection and kindness for me to release me from this—this disgrace," and Mr. Warrington's voice shook a little, and he passed his hand across his eyes.

"Sir," says Mr. Draper, eyeing the young man, "I was with her ladyship yesterday, when we talked over the whole of this here most unpleasant—I won't say as you do, disgraceful business."

"What do you mean, sir? Does Madame de Bernstein know of my misfortune?" asked Harry.

"Every circumstance, sir; the pawning the watches, and all."

Harry turned burning red. "It is an unfortunate business, the pawning them watches and things which you had never paid for," continued the lawyer. The young man started up from the bed, looking so fierce that Draper felt a little alarmed.

"It may lead to litigation and unpleasant remarks being made, in court, sir. Them barristers respect nothing; and when they get a feller in the box——"

"Great Heaven, sir, you don't suppose a gentleman of my rank can't take a watch upon credit without intending to cheat the tradesman?" cried Harry, in the greatest agitation.

"Of course you meant everything that's honourable; only, you see, the law mayn't happen to think so," says Mr. Draper, winking his eye. ("Hang the supercilious beast; I touch him there!) Your aunt says it's the most imprudent thing ever she heard of—to call it by no worse name."

"You call it by no worse name yourself, Mr. Draper?" says Harry, speaking each word very slow, and evidently trying to keep a command of himself.

Draper did not like his looks. "Heaven forbid that I should say anything as between gentleman and gentleman,—but between me and my client, it's my duty to say, 'Sir, you are in a very unpleasant scrape,' just as a doctor would have to tell his patient, 'Sir, you are very ill.'"

"And you can't help me to pay this debt off,—and you have come only to tell me that I may be accused of roguery?" says Harry.

"Of obtaining goods under false pretences? Most undoubtedly, yes. I can't help it, sir. Don't look as if you would knock me down. (Curse him, I am making him wince, though.) A young gentleman, who has only two hundred a year from his ma', orders diamonds and watches, and takes 'em to a pawnbroker. You ask me what people will think of such behaviour, and I tell you honestly. Don't be angry with me, Mr. Warrington."

"Go on, sir!" says Harry, with a groan.

The lawyer thought the day was his own. "But you ask if I can't help to pay this debt off? And I say Yes—and that here is the money in my pocket to do it now, if you like—not mine, sir, my honoured client's, your aunt, Lady Bernstein. But she has a right to impose her conditions, and I've brought 'em with me."

"Tell them, sir," says Mr. Harry.

"They are not hard. They are only for your own good: and if you say Yes, we can call a hackney-coach, and go to Clarges Street together, which I have promised to go there, whether you will or no. Mr. Warrington, I name no names, but there was a question of marriage between you and a certain party."

"Ah!" said Harry; and his countenance looked more cheerful than it had yet done.

"To that marriage my noble client, the Baroness, is most averse—having other views for you, and thinking it will be your ruin to marry a party,—of noble birth and title it is true; but, excuse me, not of first-rate character, and so much older than yourself. You had given an imprudent promise to that party."

"Yes; and she has it still," says Mr. Warrington.

"It has been recovered. She dropped it by an accident at Tunbridge," says Mr. Draper, "so my client informed me; indeed her ladyship showed it me, for the matter of that. It was wrote in bl——"

"Never mind, sir!" cries Harry, turning almost as red as the ink which he had used to write his absurd promise, of which the madness and folly had smote him with shame a thousand times over.

"At the same time letters, wrote to you, and compromising a noble family, were recovered," continues the lawyer. "You had lost 'em. It was no fault of yours. You were away when they were found again. You may say that that noble family, that you yourself, have a friend such as few young men have.

Well, sir, there's no earthly promise to bind you—only so many idle words said over a bottle, which very likely any gentleman may forget. Say you won't go on with this marriage—give me and my noble friend your word of honour. Cry off, I say, Mr. W.! Don't be such a d——fool, saving your presence, as to marry an old woman who has jilted scores of men in her time. Say the word, and I step downstairs, pay every shilling against you in the office, and put you down in my coach, either at your aunt's or at White's Club, if you like, with a couple of hundred in your pocket. Say yes; and give us your hand! There's no use in sitting grinning behind these bars all day!"

So far Mr. Draper had had the best of the talk. Harry only longed himself to be rid of the engagement from which his aunt wanted to free him. His foolish flame for Maria Esmond had died out long since. If she would release him, how thankful would he be! "Come! give us your hand, and say done!" says the lawyer, with a knowing wink. "Don't stand shilly-shallying, sir. Law bless you, Mr. W., if I had married everybody I promised, I should be like the Grand Turk, or Captain Macheath in the play!"

The lawyer's familiarity disgusted Harry, who shrank from Draper, scarcely knowing that he did so. He folded his dressing gown round him, and stepped back from the other's proffered hand. "Give me a little time to think of the matter, if you please, Mr. Draper," he said, "and have the goodness to come to me again in an hour.

"Very good, sir, very good, sir!" says the lawyer, biting his lips, and, as he seized up his hat, turning very red. "Most parties would not want an hour to consider about such an offer as I make you: but I suppose my time must be yours, and I'll come again, and see whether you are to go or to stay. Good morning, sir, good morning:" and he went his way, growling curses down the stairs. "Won't take my hand, won't he? Will tell me in an hour's time! Hang his impudence! I'll show him what an hour is!"

Mr. Draper went to his chambers in dudgeon then; bullied his clerks all round, sent off a messenger to the Baroness, to say that he had waited on the young gentleman, who had demanded a little time for consideration, which was for form's sake, as he had no doubt; the lawyer then saw clients, transacted business, went out to his dinner in the most leisurely manner; and then finally turned his steps towards the neighbouring Cursitor Street. "He'll be at home when I call, the haughty beast!" says Draper, with a sneer. "The Fortunate Youth in his room?" the lawyer asked of the sheriff's officer's aide-de-camp who came to open the double doors.

"Mr. Warrington is in his apartment," said the gentleman, "but——" and here the gentleman winked at Mr. Draper, and laid his hand on his nose.

"But what, Mr. Paddy from Cork?" said the lawyer.

"My name is Costigan; me familee is noble, and me neetive place is the Irish methrawpolis, Mr. Six-and-eightpence!" said the janitor, scowling at Draper. A rich odour of spirituous liquors filled the little space between the double doors where he held the attorney in conversation.

"Confound you, sir, let me pass!" bawled out Mr. Draper.

317

"I can hear you perfectly well, Six-and-eightpence, except your h's, which you dthrop out of your conversation. I'll thank ye not to call neems, me good friend, or me fingers and your nose will have to make an intimate hicquaintance. Walk in, sir! Be polite for the future to your shupariors in birth and manners, though they may be your infariors in temporary station. Confound the kay! Walk in, sir, I say!—Madam, I have the honour of saluting ye most respectfully!"

A lady with her face covered with a capuchin, and further hidden by her handkerchief, uttered a little exclamation as of alarm as she came down the stairs at this instant and hurried past the lawyer. He was pressing forward to look at her—for Mr. Draper was very cavalier in his manners to women—but the bailiff's follower thrust his leg between Draper and the retreating lady, crying, "Keep your own distance, if you plaise! This way, madam! I at once recognised your ladysh———" Here he closed the door on Draper's nose, and left that attorney to find his own way to his client upstairs.

At six o'clock that evening the old Baroness de Bernstein was pacing up and down her drawing-crutch, and for ever running to the window when the noise of a coach was heard passing in Clarges Street. She had delayed her dinner from hour to hour: she who scolded so fiercely, on ordinary occasions, if her cook was five minutes after his time. She had ordered two covers to be laid, plate to be set out, and some extra dishes to be prepared as if for a little fete. Four—five o'clock passed, and at six she looked from the window, and a coach actually stopped at her door.

"Mr. Draper" was announced, and entered bowing profoundly.

The old lady trembled on her stick. "Where is the boy?" she said quickly. "I told you to bring him, sir! How dare you come without him?"

"It is not my fault, madam, that Mr. Warrington refuses to come." And Draper gave his version of the interview which had just taken place between himself and the young Virginian.

CHAPTER XLVIII. An Apparition

Going off in his wrath from his morning's conversation with Harry, Mr. Draper thought he heard the young prisoner speak behind him; and, indeed, Harry had risen, and uttered a half-exclamation to call the lawyer back. But he was proud, and the other offended: Harry checked words, and Draper did not choose to stop. It wound Harry's pride to be obliged to humble himself before the lawyer, and to have to yield from mere lack and desire of money. "An hour hence will do as well," thought Harry, and lapsed sulkily on to the bed again. No, he did not care for Maria Esmond! No: he was ashamed of the way in which he had been entrapped into that engagement. A wily and experienced woman, she had cheated his boyish ardour. She had taken unfair advantage of him, as her brother had at play. They were his own flesh and blood, and they ought to have spared him. Instead, one and the other had made a prey of him, and had used him for their selfish ends. He thought how they had betrayed the rights of hospitality: how they had made a victim of the young kinsman who came confiding within their gates. His heart was sore wounded: his head sank back on his pillow: bitter tears wetted it. "Had they come to Virginia," he thought, "I had given them a different welcome!"

He was roused from this mood of despondency by Gumbo's grinning face at his door, who said a lady was come to see Master Harry, and behind the lad came the lady in the capuchin, of whom we have just made mention. Harry sat up, pale and haggard, on his bed. The lady, with a sob, and almost ere the servant-man withdrew, ran towards the young prisoner, put her arms round his neck with real emotion and a maternal tenderness, sobbed over his pale cheek and kissed it in the midst of plentiful tears, and cried out—

"Oh, my Harry! Did I ever, ever think to see thee here?"

He started back, scared as it seemed at her presence, but she sank down at the bedside, and seized his feverish hand, and embraced his knees. She had a real regard and tenderness for him. The wretched place in which she found him, his wretched look, filled her heart with a sincere love and pity.

"I—I thought none of you would come!" said poor Harry, with a groan.

More tears, more kisses of the hot young hand, more clasps and pressure with hers, were the lady's reply for a moment or two.

"Oh, my dear! my dear! I cannot bear to think of thee in misery," she sobbed out.

Hardened though it might be, that heart was not all marble—that dreary life not all desert. Harry's mother could not have been fonder, nor her tones more tender than those of his kinswoman now kneeling at his feet.

"Some of the debts, I fear, were owing to my extravagance!" she said (and this was true). "You bought trinkets and jewels in order to give me pleasure. Oh, how I hate them now! I little thought I ever could! I have brought them all with me, and more trinkets—here! and here! and all the money I have in the world!"

And she poured brooches, rings, a watch, and a score or so of guineas into Harry's lap. The sight of which strangely agitated and immensely touched the young man.

"Dearest, kindest cousin!" he sobbed out.

His lips found no more words to utter, but yet, no doubt they served to express his gratitude, his affection, his emotion.

He became quite gay presently, and smiled as he put away some of the trinkets, his presents to Maria, and told her into what danger he had fallen by selling other goods which he had purchased on credit; and how a lawyer had insulted him just now upon this very point. He would not have his dear Maria's money—he had enough, quite enough for the present: but he valued her twenty guineas as much as if they had been twenty thousand. He would never forget her love and kindness: no, by all that was sacred he would not! His mother should know of all her goodness. It had had cheered him when he was just on the point of breaking down under his disgrace and misery. Might

Heaven bless her for it! There is no need to pursue beyond this, the cousins' conversation. The dark day seemed brighter to Harry after Maria's visit: the imprisonment not so hard to bear. The world was not all selfish and cold. Here was a fond creature who really and truly loved him. Even Castlewood was not so bad as he had thought. He had expressed the deepest grief at not being able to assist his kinsman. He was hopelessly in debt. Every shilling he had won from Harry he had lost on the next day to others. Anything that lay in his power he would do. He would come soon and see Mr. Warrington: he was in waiting to-day, and as much a prisoner as Harry himself. So the pair talked on cheerfully and affectionately until the darkness began to close in, when Maria, with a sigh, bade Harry farewell.

The door scarcely closed upon her, when it opened to admit Draper.

"Your humble servant, sir," says the attorney. His voice jarred upon Harry's ear, and his presence offended the young man.

"I had expected you some hours ago, sir," he curtly said.

"A lawyer's time is not always his own, sir," said Mr. Draper, who had just been in consultation with a bottle of port at the Grecian. "Never mind, I'm at your orders now. Presume it's all right, Mr. Warrington. Packed your trunk? Why, now there you are in your bedgown still. Let me go down and settle whilst you call in your black man and titivate a bit. I've a coach at the door, and we'll be off and dine with the old lady."

"Are you going to dine with the Baroness de Bernstein, pray?"

"Not me—no such honour. Had my dinner already. It's you are a-going to dine with your aunt, I suppose?"

"Mr. Draper, you suppose a great deal more than you know," says Mr. Warrington, looking very fierce and tall, as he folds his brocade dressing-gown round him.

"Great goodness, sir, what do you mean?" asks Draper.

"I mean, sir, that I have considered, and, that having given my word to a faithful and honourable lady, it does not become me to withdraw it."

"Confound it, sir!" shrieks the lawyer, "I tell you she has lost the paper. There's nothing to bind you—nothing. Why she's old enough to be——"

"Enough, sir," says Mr. Warrington, with a stamp of his foot. "You seem to think you are talking to some other pettifogger. I take it, Mr. Draper, you are not accustomed to have dealings with men of honour."

"Pettifogger, indeed!" cries Draper in a fury. "Men of honour, indeed! I'd have you to know, Mr. Warrington, that I'm as good a man of honour as you. I don't know so many gamblers and horse-jockeys, perhaps. I haven't gambled away my patrimony, and lived as if I was a nobleman on two hundred a year. I haven't bought watches on credit, and pawned—touch me if you dare, sir," and the lawyer sprang to the door.

"That is the way out, sir. You can't go through the window, because it is barred," says Mr. Warrington.

"And the answer I take to my client is No, then!" screamed out Draper.

Harry stepped forward, with his two hands clenched. "If you utter another word," he said, "I'll———" The door was shut rapidly—the sentence was never finished, and Draper went away furious to Madame de Bernstein, from whom, though he gave her the best version of his story, he got still fiercer language than he had received from Mr. Warrington himself.

"What? Shall she trust me, and I desert her?" says Harry, stalking up and down his room in his flowing, rustling brocade. "Dear, faithful, generous woman! If I lie in prison for years, I'll be true to her."

Her lawyer dismissed after a stormy interview, the desolate old woman was fain to sit down to the meal which she had hoped to share with her nephew. The chair was before her which he was to have filled, the glasses shining by the silver. One dish after another was laid before her by the silent major-domo, and tasted and pushed away. The man pressed his mistress at last. "It is eight o'clock," he said. "You have had nothing all day. It is good for you to eat." She could not eat. She would have her coffee. Let Case go get her her coffee. The lacqueys bore the dishes off the table, leaving their mistress sitting at it before the vacant chair.

Presently the old servant re-entered the room without his lady's coffee and with a strange scared face, and said, "Mr. WARRINGTON!"

The old woman uttered an exclamation, got up from her armchair, but sank back in it trembling very much. "So you are come, sir, are you?" she said, with a fond shaking voice. "Bring back the———Ah!" here she screamed, "Gracious God, who is it?" Her eyes stared wildly: her white face looked ghastly through her rouge. She clung to the arms of her chair for support, as the visitor approached her.

A gentleman whose face and figure exactly resembled Harry Warrington and whose voice, when he spoke, had tones strangely similar, had followed the servant into the room. He bowed towards the Baroness.

"You expected my brother, madam?" he said "I am but now arrived in London. I went to his house. I met his servant at your door, who was bearing this letter for you. I thought I would bring it to your ladyship before going to him,"—and the stranger laid down a letter before Madam Bernstein.

"Are you"—gasped out the Baroness—"are you my nephew, that we supposed was———"

"Was killed—and is alive! I am George Warrington, madam and I ask his kinsfolk what have you done with my brother?"

"Look, George!" said the bewildered old lady "I expected him here to-night —that chair was set for him—I have been waiting for him, sir, till now—till I am quite faint—I don't like—I don't like being alone. Do stay an sup with me!"

"Pardon me, madam. Please God, my supper will be with Harry tonight!"

"Bring him back. Bring him back here on any conditions! It is but five hundred pounds! Here is the money, sir, if you need it!"

"I have no want, madam. I have money with me that can't be better employed than in my brother's service."

"And you will bring him to me, sir! Say you will bring him to me!"

Mr. Warrington made a very stately bow for answer, and quitted the room, passing by the amazed domestics, and calling with an air of authority to Gumbo to follow him.

Had Mr. Harry received no letters from home? Master Harry had not opened all his letters the last day or two. Had he received no letter announcing his brother's escape from the French settlements and return to Virginia? Oh no! No such letter had come, else Master Harry certainly tell Gumbo. Quick, horses! Quick by Strand to Temple Bar! Here is the house of Captivity and the Deliverer come to the rescue!

CHAPTER XLIX. Friends in Need

Quick, hackneycoach steeds, and bear George Warrington through Strand and Fleet Street to his imprisoned brother's rescue! Any one who remembers Hogarth's picture of a London hackneycoach and a London street road at that period, may fancy how weary the quick time was, and how long seemed the journey:—scarce any lights, save those carried by link-boys; badly hung coaches; bad pavements; great holes in the road, and vast quagmires of winter mud. That drive from Piccadilly to Fleet Street seemed almost as long to our young man, as the journey from Marlborough to London which he had performed in the morning.

He had written to Harry, announcing his arrival at Bristol. He had previously written to his brother, giving the great news of his existence and his return from captivity. There was war between England and France at that time; the French privateers were for ever on the look-out for British merchant-ships, and seized them often within sight of port. The letter bearing the intelligence of George's restoration must have been on board one of the many American ships of which the French took possession. The letter telling of George's arrival in England was never opened by poor Harry; it was lying at the latter's apartments, which it reached on the third morning after Harry's captivity, when the angry Mr. Ruff had refused to give up any single item more of his lodger's property.

To these apartments George first went on his arrival in London, and asked for his brother. Scared at the likeness between them, the maid-servant who opened the door screamed, and ran back to her mistress. The mistress not liking to tell the truth, or to own that poor Harry was actually a prisoner at her husband's suit, said Mr. Warrington had left his lodgings; she did not know where Mr. Warrington was. George knew that Clarges Street was close to Bond Street. Often and often had he looked over the London map. Aunt Bernstein would tell him where Harry was. He might be with her at that very moment. George had read in Harry's letters to Virginia about Aunt Bernstein's kindness to Harry. Even Madam Esmond was softened by it (and especially touched by a letter which the Baroness wrote—the letter which caused George to pack off post-haste for Europe, indeed). She heartily hoped and trusted that Madam Beatrix had found occasion to repent of her former bad ways. It was time, indeed, at her age; and Heaven knows that she had plenty to repent of! I have known a harmless, good old soul of eighty, still bepommelled and stoned by irreproachable ladies of the straitest sect of the Pharisees, for a little slip which occurred long before the present century was born, or she herself was twenty years old. Rachel Esmond never mentioned her eldest daughter: Madam Esmond Warrington never mentioned her sister. No. In spite of the order for remission of the sentence—in spite of the handwriting on the floor of the Temple—there is a crime which some folks never will pardon, and regarding which female virtue, especially, is inexorable.

I suppose the Virginians' agent at Bristol had told George fearful stories of his brother's doings. Gumbo, whom he met at his aunt's door, as soon as the lad recovered from his terror at the sudden reappearance of the master whom he supposed dead, had leisure to stammer out a word or two respecting his young master's whereabouts, and present pitiable condition; and hence Mr. George's sternness of demeanour when he presented himself to the old lady. It seemed to him a matter of course that his brother in difficulty should be rescued by his relations. Oh, George, how little you know about London and London ways! Whenever you take your walks abroad how many poor you meet—if a philanthropist were for rescuing all of them, not all the wealth of all the provinces of America would suffice him!

But the feeling and agitation displayed by the old lady touched her nephew's heart when, jolting through the dark streets towards the house of his brother's captivity, George came to think of his aunt's behaviour. "She does feel my poor Harry's misfortune," he thought to himself, "I have been too hasty in judging her." Again and again, in the course of his life, Mr. George had to rebuke himself with the same crime of being too hasty. How many of us have not? And, alas, the mischief done, there's no repentance will mend it. Quick, coachman! We are almost as slow as you are in getting from Clarges Street to the Temple. Poor Gumbo knows the way to the bailiff's house well enough. Again the bell is set ringing. The first door is opened to George and his negro; then that first door is locked warily upon them, and they find themselves in a little passage with a little Jewish janitor; then a second door is unlocked, and they enter into the house. The Jewish janitor stares, as by his flaring tallow-torch he sees a second Mr. Warrington before him. Come to see that gentleman? Yes. But wait a moment. This is Mr. Warrington's brother from America. Gumbo must go and prepare his master first. Step into this room. There's a gentleman already there about Mr. W.'s business (the porter says), and another upstairs with him now. There's no end of people have been about him.

The room into which George was introduced was a small apartment which went by the name of Mr. Amos's office, and where, by a guttering candle, and talking to the bailiff, sat a stout gentleman in a cloak and a laced hat. The young porter carried his candle, too, preceding Mr. George, so there was a sufficiency of light in the apartment.

"We are not angry any more, Harry!" says the stout gentleman, in a cheery voice, getting up and advancing with an outstretched hand to the new-comer. "Thank God, my boy! Mr. Amos here says, there will be no difficulty about James and me being your bail, and we will do your business by breakfast-time in the morning. Why... Angels and ministers of grace! who are you?" And he started back as the other had hold of his hand.

But the stranger grasped it only the more strongly. "God bless you, sir!" he said, "I know who you are. You must be Colonel Lambert, of whose kindness to him my poor Harry wrote. And I am the brother whom you have heard of, sir; and who was left for dead in Mr. Braddock's action; and came to life again after eighteen months amongst the French; and live to thank God and thank you for your kindness to my Harry," continued the lad with a faltering voice.

"James! James! Here is news!" cries Mr. Lambert to a gentleman in red, who now entered the room. "Here are the dead come alive! Here is Harry Scapegrace's brother come back, and with his scalp on his head, too!" (George had taken his hat off, and was standing by the light.) "This is my brother-bail, Mr. Warrington! This is Lieutenant-Colonel James Wolfe, at your service. You must know there has been a little difference between Harry and me, Mr. George. He is pacified, is he, James?"

"He is full of gratitude," says Mr. Wolfe, after making his bow to Mr. Warrington.

"Harry wrote home about Mr. Wolfe, too, sir," said the young man, "and I hope my brother's friends will be so kind as to be mine."

"I wish he had none other but us, Mr. Warrington. Poor Harry's fine folks have been too fine for him, and have ended by landing him here."

"Nay, your honours, I have done my best to make the young gentleman comfortable; and, knowing your honour before, when you came to bail Captain Watkins, and that your security is perfectly good,—if your honour wishes, the young gentleman can go out this very night, and I will make it all right with the lawyer in the morning," says Harry's landlord, who knew the rank and respectability of the two gentlemen who had come to offer bail for his young prisoner.

"The debt is five hundred and odd pounds, I think?" said Mr. Warrington. "With a hundred thanks to these gentlemen, I can pay the amount at this moment into the officers' hands, taking the usual acknowledgment and caution. But I can never forget, gentlemen, that you helped my brother at his need, and, for doing so, I say thank you, and God bless you, in my mother's name and mine."

Gumbo had, meanwhile, gone upstairs to his master's apartment, where Harry would probably have scolded the negro for returning that night, but that the young gentleman was very much soothed and touched by the conversation he had had with the friend who had just left him. He was sitting over his pipe of Virginia in a sad mood (for, somehow, even Maria's goodness and affection, as she had just exhibited them, had not altogether consoled him; and he had thought, with a little dismay, of certain consequences to which that very kindness and fidelity bound him), when Mr. Wolfe's homely features and eager outstretched hand came to cheer the prisoner, and he heard how Mr. Lambert was below, and the errand upon which the two officers had come. In spite of himself, Lambert would be kind to him. In spite of Harry's ill-temper, and needless suspicion and anger, the good gentleman was determined to help him if he might—to help him even against Mr. Wolfe's own advice, as the latter frankly told Harry, "For you were wrong, Mr. Warrington," said the Colonel, "and you wouldn't be set right; and you, a young man, used hard words and unkind behaviour to your senior, and what is more, one of the best gentlemen who walks God's earth. You see, sir, what his answer hath been to your wayward temper. You will bear with a friend who speaks frankly with you? Martin Lambert hath acted in this as he always doth, as the best Christian, the best friend, the most kind and generous of men. Nay, if you want another proof of his goodness, here it is: He has converted me, who, as I don't care to disguise, was angry with you for your treatment of him, and has absolutely brought me down here to be your bail. Let us both cry Peccavimus! Harry, and shake our friend by the hand! He is sitting in the room below. He would not come here till he knew how you would receive him."

"I think he is a good man!" groaned out Harry. "I was very angry and wild at the time when he and I met last, Colonel Wolfe. Nay, perhaps he was right in sending back those trinkets, hurt as I was at his doing so. Go down to him, will you be so kind, sir? and tell him I am sorry, and ask his pardon, and—and, God bless him for his generous behaviour." And here the young gentleman turned his head away, and rubbed his hand across his eyes.

"Tell him all this thyself, Harry!" cries the Colonel, taking the young fellow's hand. "No deputy will ever say it half so well. Come with me now."

"You go first, and I'll—I'll follow,—on my word I will. See! I am in my morning-gown! I will but put on a coat and come to him. Give him my message first. Just—just prepare him for me!" says poor Harry, who knew he must do it, but yet did not much like that process of eating of humble-pie.

Wolfe went out smiling—understanding the lad's scruples well enough, perhaps. As he opened the door, Mr. Gumbo entered it; almost forgetting to bow to the gentleman, profusely courteous as he was on ordinary occasions, —his eyes glaring round, his great mouth grinning—himself in a state of such high excitement and delight that his master remarked his condition.

"What, Gum? What has happened to thee? Hast thou got a new sweetheart?"

No, Gum had not got no new sweetheart, master.

"Give me my coat. What has brought thee back?"

Gum grinned prodigiously. "I have seen a ghost, mas'r!" he said.

"A ghost! and whose, and where?"

"Whar? Saw him at Madame Bernstein's house. Come with him here in the coach! He downstairs now with Colonel Lambert!" Whilst Gumbo is speaking, as he is putting on his master's coat, his eyes are rolling, his head is wagging, his hands are trembling, his lips are grinning.

"Ghost—what ghost?" says Harry, in a strange agitation. "Is anybody—is—my mother come?"

"No, sir; no, Master Harry!" Gumbo's head rolls nearly off its violent convolutions, and his master, looking oddly at him, flings the door open, and goes rapidly down the stair.

He is at the foot of it, just as a voice within the little office, of which the door is open, is saying, "and for doing so, I say thank you, and God bless you, in my mother's name and mine."

"Whose voice is that?" calls out Harry Warrington, with a strange cry in his own voice.

"It's the ghost's, mas'r!" says Gumbo, from behind; and Harry runs forward to the room,—where, if you please, we will pause a little minute before we enter. The two gentlemen who were there, turned their heads away. The lost was found again. The dead was alive. The prodigal was on his brother's heart, —his own full of love, gratitude, repentance.

"Come away, James! I think we are not wanted any more here," says the Colonel. "Good-night, boys. Some ladies in Hill Street won't be able to sleep for this strange news. Or will you go home and sup with 'em, and tell them the story?"

No, with many thanks, the boys would not go and sup to-night. They had stories of their own to tell. "Quick, Gumbo, with the trunks! Good-bye, Mr. Amos!" Harry felt almost unhappy when he went away.

CHAPTER L. Contains a Great deal of the Finest Morality

When first we had the honour to be presented to Sir Miles Warrington at the King's drawing-room, in St. James's Palace, I confess that I, for one—looking at his jolly round face, his broad round waistcoat, his hearty country manner, —expected that I had lighted upon a most eligible and agreeable acquaintance at last, and was about to become intimate with that noblest specimen of the human race, the bepraised of songs and men, the good old English country gentleman. In fact, to be a good old country gentleman is to hold a position nearest the gods, and at the summit of earthly felicity. To have a large unencumbered rent-roll, and the rents regularly paid by adoring farmers, who bless their stars at having such a landlord as his honour; to have no tenant holding back with his money, excepting just one, perhaps, who does so in order to give occasion to Good Old Country Gentleman to show his sublime charity and universal benevolence of soul; to hunt three days a week, love the sport of all things, and have perfect good health and good appetite in consequence; to have not only good appetite, but a good dinner; to sit down at church in the midst of a chorus of blessings from the villagers, the first man in the parish, the benefactor of the parish, with a consciousness of consummate desert, saying, "Have mercy upon us, miserable sinners," to be sure, but only for form's sake, because the words are written in the book, and to give other folks an example—a G. O. C. G. a miserable sinner! So healthy, so wealthy, so jolly, so much respected by the vicar, so much honoured by the tenants, so much beloved and admired by his family, amongst whom his story of grouse in the gunroom causes laughter from generation to generation;— this perfect being a miserable sinner! Allons donc! Give any man good health and temper, five thousand a year, the adoration of his parish, and the love and worship of his family, and I'll defy you to make him so heartily dissatisfied with his spiritual condition as to set himself down a miserable anything. If you were a Royal Highness, and went to church in the most perfect health and comfort, the parson waiting to begin the service until your R. H. came in, would you believe yourself to be a miserable, etc.? You might when racked with gout, in solitude, the fear of death before your eyes, the doctor having cut off your bottle of claret, and ordered arrowroot and a little sherry,—you might then be humiliated, and acknowledge your own shortcomings, and the vanity of things in general; but, in high health, sunshine, spirits, that word miserable is only a form. You can't think in your heart that you are to be pitied much for the present. If you are to be miserable, what is Colin Ploughman, with the ague, seven children, two pounds a year rent to pay for his cottage, and eight shillings a week? No: a healthy, rich, jolly, country gentleman, if miserable, has a very supportable misery: if a sinner, has very few people to tell him so.

It may be he becomes somewhat selfish; but at least he is satisfied with himself. Except my lord at the castle, there is nobody for miles and miles round so good or so great. His admirable wife ministers to him, and to the whole parish, indeed: his children bow before him: the vicar of the parish reverences him: he is respected at quarter-sessions: he causes poachers to tremble: off go all hats before him at market: and round about his great coach, in which his spotless daughters and sublime lady sit, all the country-town tradesmen cringe, bareheaded, and the farmers' women drop innumerable curtseys. From their cushions in the great coach the ladies look down beneficently, and smile on the poorer folk. They buy a yard of ribbon with affability; they condescend to purchase an ounce of salts, or a packet of flower-seeds: they deign to cheapen a goose: their drive is like a royal progress; a happy people is supposed to press round them and bless them. Tradesmen bow, farmers' wives bob, town-boys, waving their ragged hats, cheer the red-faced coachman as he drives the fat bays, and cry, "Sir Miles for ever! Throw us a halfpenny, my lady!"

But suppose the market-woman should hide her fat goose when Sir Miles's coach comes, out of terror lest my lady, spying the bird, should insist on purchasing it a bargain? Suppose no coppers ever were known to come out of the royal coach window? Suppose Sir Miles regaled his tenants with notoriously small beer, and his poor with especially thin broth? This may be our fine old English gentleman's way. There have been not a few fine English gentlemen and ladies of this sort; who patronised the poor without ever relieving them, who called out "Amen!" at church as loud as the clerk; who went through all the forms of piety, and discharged all the etiquette of old English gentlemanhood; who bought virtue a bargain, as it were, and had no doubt they were honouring her by the purchase. Poor Harry in his distress asked help from his relations: his aunt sent him a tract and her blessing; his uncle had business out of town, and could not, of course, answer the poor boy's petition. How much of this behaviour goes on daily in respectable life, think you? You can fancy Lord and Lady Macbeth concocting a murder, and coming together with some little awkwardness, perhaps, when the transaction was done and over; but my Lord and Lady Skinflint, when they consult in their bedroom about giving their luckless nephew a helping hand, and determine to refuse, and go down to family prayers, and meet their children and domestics, and discourse virtuously before them, and then remain together, and talk nose to nose,—what can they think of one another? and of the poor kinsman fallen among the thieves, and groaning for help unheeded? How can they go on with those virtuous airs? How can they dare look each other in the face?

Dare? Do you suppose they think they have done wrong? Do you suppose Skinflint is tortured with remorse at the idea of the distress which called to him in vain, and of the hunger which he sent empty away? Not he. He is indignant with Prodigal for being a fool: he is not ashamed of himself for being a curmudgeon. What? a young man with such opportunities throw them away? A fortune spent amongst gamblers and spendthrifts? Horrible, horrible! Take warning, my child, by this unfortunate young man's behaviour, and see the consequences of extravagance. According to the great and always Established Church of the Pharisees, here is an admirable opportunity for a moral discourse, and an assertion of virtue. "And to think of his deceiving us so!" cries out Lady Warrington.

"Very sad, very sad, my dear!" says Sir Miles, wagging his head.

"To think of so much extravagance in one so young!" cries Lady Warrington. "Cards, bets, feasts at taverns of the most wicked profusion, carriage and riding horses, the company of the wealthy and profligate of his own sex, and, I fear, of the most iniquitous persons of ours."

"Hush, my Lady Warrington!" cries her husband, glancing towards the spotless Dora and Flora, who held down their blushing heads, at the mention of the last naughty persons.

"No wonder my poor children hide their faces!" mamma continues. "My dears, I wish even the existence of such creatures could be kept from you!"

"They can't go to an opera, or the park, without seeing 'em, to be sure," says Sir Miles.

"To think we should have introduced such a young serpent into the bosom of our family! and have left him in the company of that guileless darling!" and she points to Master Miles.

"Who's a serpent, mamma?" inquires that youth. "First you said cousin Harry was bad: then he was good: now he is bad again. Which is he, Sir Miles?"

"He has faults, like all of us, Miley, my dear. Your cousin has been wild, and you must take warning by him."

"Was not my elder brother, who died—my naughty brother—was not he wild too? He was not kind to me when I was quite a little boy. He never gave me money, nor toys, nor rode with me, nor—why do you cry, mamma? Sure I remember how Hugh and you were always fight——"

"Silence, sir!" cry out papa and the girls in a breath. "Don't you know you are never to mention that name?"

"I know I love Harry, and I didn't love Hugh," says the sturdy little rebel. "And if cousin Harry is in prison, I'll give him my half-guinea that my godpapa gave me, and anything I have—yes, anything, except—except my little horse—and my silver waistcoat—and—and Snowball and Sweetlips at home—and—and, yes, my custard after dinner." This was in reply to a hint of sister Dora. "But I'd give him some of it," continues Miles, after a pause.

"Shut thy mouth with it, child, and then go about thy business," says papa, amused. Sir Miles Warrington had a considerable fund of easy humour.

"Who would have thought he should ever be so wild?" mamma goes on.

"Nay. Youth is the season for wild oats, my dear."

"That we should be so misled in him!" sighed the girls.

"That he should kiss us both!" cries papa.

"Sir Miles Warrington, I have no patience with that sort of vulgarity!" says the majestic matron.

"Which of you was the favourite yesterday, girls?" continues the father.

"Favourite, indeed! I told him over and over again of my engagement to dear Tom—I did, Dora—why do you sneer, if you please?" says the handsome sister.

"Nay, to do her justice, so did Dora too," said papa.

"Because Flora seemed to wish to forget her engagement with dear Tom sometimes," remarks the sister.

"I never, never, never wished to break with Tom! It's wicked of you to say so, Dora! It is you who were for ever sneering at him: it is you who are always envious because I happen—at least, because gentlemen imagine that I am not ill-looking, and prefer me to some folks, in spite of all their learning and wit!" cries Flora, tossing her head over her shoulder, and looking at the glass.

"Why are you always looking there, sister?" says the artless Miles junior. "Sure, you must know your face well enough!"

"Some people look at it just as often, child, who haven't near such good reason," says papa, gallantly.

"If you mean me, Sir Miles, I thank you," cries Dora. "My face is as Heaven made it, and my father and mother gave it me. 'Tis not my fault if I resemble my papa's family. If my head is homely, at least I have got some brains in it. I envious of Flora, indeed, because she has found favour in the sight of poor Tom Claypool! I should as soon be proud of captivating a ploughboy!"

"Pray, miss, was your Mr. Harry, of Virginia, much wiser than Tom Claypool? You would have had him for the asking!" exclaims Flora.

"And so would you, miss, and have dropped Tom Claypool into the sea!" cries Dora.

"I wouldn't."

"You would."

"I wouldn't;"—and da capo goes the conversation—the shuttlecock of wrath being briskly battled from one sister to another.

"Oh, my children! Is this the way you dwell together in unity?" exclaims their excellent female parent, laying down her embroidery. "What an example you set to this Innocent!"

"Like to see 'em fight, my lady!" cries the Innocent, rubbing his hands.

"At her, Flora! Worry her, Dora! To it again, you little rogues!" says facetious papa. "'Tis good sport, ain't it, Miley?"

"Oh, Sir Miles! Oh, my children! These disputes are unseemly. They tear a fond mother's heart," says mamma, with majestic action, though bearing the laceration of her bosom with much seeming equanimity. "What cause for thankfulness ought we to have that watchful parents have prevented any idle engagements between you and your misguided cousin. If we have been mistaken in him, is it not a mercy that we have found out our error in time? If either of you had any preference for him, your excellent good sense, my loves, will teach you to overcome, to eradicate, the vain feeling. That we cherished and were kind to him can never be a source of regret. 'Tis a proof of our good-nature. What we have to regret, I fear, is, that your cousin should have proved unworthy of our kindness, and, coming away from the society of gamblers, play-actors, and the like, should have brought contamination—pollution, I had almost said—into this pure family!"

"Oh, bother mamma's sermons!" says Flora, as my lady pursues a harangue of which we only give the commencement here, but during which papa, whistling, gently quits the room on tiptoe, whilst the artless Miles junior winds his top and pegs it under the robes of his sisters. It has done humming, and staggered and tumbled over, and expired in its usual tipsy manner, long ere Lady Warrington has finished her sermon.

"Were you listening to me, my child?" she asks, laying her hand on her darling's head.

"Yes, mother," says he, with the whipcord in his mouth, and proceeding to wind up his sportive engine. "You was a-saying that Harry was very poor now, and that we oughtn't to help him. That's what you was saying; wasn't it, madam?"

"My poor child, thou wilt understand me better when thou art older!" says mamma, turning towards that ceiling to which her eyes always have recourse.

"Get out, you little wretch!" cries one of the sisters. The artless one has pegged his top at Dora's toes, and laughs with the glee of merry boyhood at his sister's discomfiture.

But what is this? Who comes here? Why does Sir Miles return to the drawing-room, and why does Tom Claypool, who strides after the Baronet, wear a countenance so disturbed?

"Here's a pretty business, my Lady Warrington!" cries Sir Miles. "Here's a wonderful wonder of wonders, girls!"

"For goodness' sake, gentlemen, what is your intelligence?" asks the virtuous matron.

"The whole town's talking about it, my lady!" says Tom Claypool puffing for breath.

"Tom has seen him," continued Sir Miles.

"Seen both of them, my Lady Warrington. They were at Ranelagh last night, with a regular mob after 'em. And so like, that but for their different ribbons you would hardly have told one from the other. One was in blue, the other in brown; but I'm certain he has worn both the suits here."

"What suits?"

"What one,—what other?" call the girls.

"Why, your fortunate youth, to be sure."

"Our precious Virginian, and heir to the principality!" says Sir Miles.

"Is my nephew, then, released from his incarceration?" asks her ladyship. "And is he again plunged in the vortex of dissip——"

"Confound him!" roars out the Baronet, with an expression which I fear was even stronger. "What should you think, my Lady Warrington, if this precious nephew of mine should turn out to be an impostor; by George! no better than an adventurer?"

"An inward monitor whispered me as much!" cried the lady; "but I dashed from me the unworthy suspicion. Speak, Sir Miles, we burn with impatience to listen to your intelligence."

"I'll—speak, my love, when you've done," says Sir Miles. "Well, what do you think of my gentleman, who comes into my house, dines at my table, is treated as one of this family, kisses my—"

"What?" asks Tom Claypool, firing as red as his waistcoat.

"—Hem! Kisses my wife's hand, and is treated in the fondest manner, by George! What do you think of this fellow, who talks of his property and his principality, by Jupiter!—turning out to be a beggarly SECOND SON! A beggar, my Lady Warrington, by——"

"Sir Miles Warrington, no violence of language before these dear ones! I sink to the earth, confounded by this unutterable hypocrisy. And did I entrust thee to a pretender, my blessed boy? Did I leave thee with an impostor, my innocent one?" the matron cries, fondling her son.

"Who's an impostor, my lady?" asks the child.

"That confounded young scamp of a Harry Warrington!" bawls out papa; on which the little Miles, after wearing a puzzled look for a moment, and yielding to I know not what hidden emotion, bursts out crying.

His admirable mother proposes to clutch him to her heart, but he rejects the pure caress, bawling only the louder, and kicking frantically about the maternal gremium, as the butler announces "Mr. George Warrington, Mr. Henry Warrington!" Miles is dropped from his mother's lap. Sir Miles's face emulates Mr. Claypool's waistcoat. The three ladies rise up, and make three most frigid curtseys, as our two young men enter the room.

Little Miles runs towards them. He holds out a little hand. "Oh, Harry! No! which is Harry? You're my Harry," and he chooses rightly this time. "Oh, you dear Harry! I'm so glad you are come! and they've been abusing you so!"

"I am come to pay my duty to my uncle," says the dark-haired Mr. Warrington; "and to thank him for his hospitalities to my brother Henry."

"What, nephew George? My brother's face and eyes! Boys both, I am delighted to see you!" cries their uncle, grasping affectionately a hand of each, as his honest face radiates with pleasure.

"This indeed hath been a most mysterious and a most providential resuscitation," says Lady Warrington. "Only I wonder that my nephew Henry concealed the circumstance until now," she adds, with a sidelong glance at both young gentlemen.

"He knew it no more than your ladyship," says Mr. Warrington. The young ladies looked at each other with downcast eyes.

"Indeed, sir! a most singular circumstance," says mamma, with another curtsey. "We had heard of it, sir; and Mr. Claypool, our county neighbour, had just brought us the intelligence, and it even now formed the subject of my conversation with my daughters."

"Yes," cries out a little voice, "and do you know, Harry, father and mother said you was a—a imp——"

"Silence, my child! Screwby, convey Master Warrington to his own apartment! These, Mr. Warrington—or, I suppose I should say nephew George—are your cousins." Two curtseys—two cheeses are made—two hands are held out. Mr. Esmond Warrington makes a profound low bow, which embraces (and it is the only embrace which the gentleman offers) all three ladies. He lays his hat to his heart. He says, "It is my duty, madam, to pay my respects to my uncle and cousins, and to thank your ladyship for such hospitality as you have been enabled to show to my brother."

"It was not much, nephew, but it was our best. Ods bobs!" cries the hearty Sir Miles, "it was our best!"

"And I appreciate it, sir," says Mr. Warrington, looking gravely round at the family.

"Give us thy hand. Not a word more," says Sir Miles "What? do you think I'm a cannibal, and won't extend the hand of hospitality to my dear brother's son? What say you, lads? Will you eat our mutton at three? This is my neighbour, Tom Claypool, son to Sir Thomas Claypool, Baronet, and my very good friend. Hey, Tom! Thou wilt be of the party, Tom? Thou knowest our brew, hey, my boy?"

"Yes, I know it, Sir Miles," replies Tom, with no peculiar expression of rapture on his face.

"And thou shalt taste it, my boy, thou shalt taste it! What is there for dinner, my Lady Warrington? Our food is plain, but plenty, lads—plain, but plenty!"

"We cannot partake of it to-day, sir. We dine with a friend who occupies my Lord Wrotham's house, your neighbour. Colonel Lambert—Major-General

Lambert he has just been made."

"With two daughters, I think—countrified-looking girls—are they not?" asks Flora.

"I think I have remarked two little rather dowdy things," says Dora.

"They are as good girls as any in England!" breaks out Harry, to whom no one had thought of saying a single word. His reign was over, you see. He was nobody. What wonder, then, that he should not be visible?

"Oh, indeed, cousin!" says Dora, with a glance at the young man, who sate with burning cheeks, chafing at the humiliation put upon him, but not knowing how or whether he should notice it. "Oh, indeed, cousin! You are very charitable—or very lucky, I'm sure! You see angels where we only see ordinary little persons. I'm sure I could not imagine who were those odd-looking people in Lord Wrotham's coach, with his handsome liveries. But if they were three angels, I have nothing to say."

"My brother is an enthusiast," interposes George. "He is often mistaken about women."

"Oh, really!" says Dora, looking a little uneasy.

"I fear my nephew Henry has indeed met with some unfavourable specimens of our sex," the matron remarks, with a groan.

"We are so easily taken in, madam—we are both very young yet—we shall grow older and learn better."

"Most sincerely, nephew George, I trust you may. You have my best wishes, my prayers, for your brother's welfare and your own. No efforts of ours have been wanting. At a painful moment, to which I will not further allude—"

"And when my uncle Sir Miles was out of town," says George, looking towards the Baronet, who smiles at him with affectionate approval.

"—I sent your brother a work which I thought might comfort him, and I know might improve him. Nay, do not thank me; I claim no credit; I did but my duty—a humble woman's duty—for what are this world's goods, nephew, compared to the welfare of a soul? If I did good, I am thankful; if I was useful, I rejoice. If, through my means, you have been brought, Harry, to consider——"

"Oh! the sermon, is it?" breaks in downright Harry. "I hadn't time to read a single syllable of it, aunt—thank you. You see I don't care much about that kind of thing—but thank you all the same."

"The intention is everything," says Mr. Warrington, "and we are both grateful. Our dear friend, General Lambert, intended to give bail for Harry; but, happily, I had funds of Harry's with me to meet any demands upon us. But the kindness is the same, and I am grateful to the friend who hastened to my brother's rescue when he had most need of aid, and when his own relations happened—so unfortunately—to be out of town."

"Anything I could do, my dear boy, I'm sure—my brother's son—my own nephew—ods bobs! you know—that is, anything—anything, you know!" cries Sir Miles, bringing his own hand into George's with a generous smack. "You can't stay and dine with us? Put off the Colonel—the General—do, now! Or name a day. My Lady Warrington, make my nephew name a day when he will sit under his grandfather's picture, and drink some of his wine!"

"His intellectual faculties seem more developed than those of his unlucky younger brother," remarked my lady, when the young gentlemen had taken their leave. "The younger must be reckless and extravagant about money indeed, for did you remark, Sir Miles, the loss of his reversion in Virginia—the amount of which has, no doubt, been grossly exaggerated, but, nevertheless, must be something considerable—did you, I say, remark that the ruin of Harry's prospects scarcely seemed to affect him?"

"I shouldn't be at all surprised that the elder turns out to be as poor as the young one," says Dora, tossing her head.

"He! he! Did you see that cousin George had one of cousin Harry's suits of clothes on—the brown and gold—that one he wore when he went with you to the oratorio, Flora?"

"Did he take Flora to an oratorio?" asks Mr. Claypool, fiercely.

"I was ill and couldn't go, and my cousin went with her," says Dora.

"Far be it from me to object to any innocent amusement, much less to the music of Mr. Handel, dear Mr. Claypool," says mamma. "Music refines the soul, elevates the understanding, is heard in our churches, and 'tis well known was practised by King David. Your operas I shun as deleterious; your ballets I would forbid to my children as most immoral; but music, my dears! May we enjoy it, like everything else in reason—may we——"

"There's the music of the dinner-bell," says papa, rubbing his hands. "Come, girls. Screwby, go and fetch Master Miley. Tom take down my lady."

"Nay, dear Thomas, I walk but slowly. Go you with dearest Flora downstairs," says Virtue.

But Dora took care to make the evening pleasant by talking of Handel and oratorios constantly during dinner.

CHAPTER LI. Conticuere Omnes

Across the way, if the gracious reader will please to step over with us, he will find our young gentlemen at Lord Wrotham's house, which his lordship has lent to his friend the General, and that little family party assembled, with which we made acquaintance at Oakhurst and Tunbridge Wells. James Wolfe has promised to come to dinner; but James is dancing attendance upon Miss Lowther, and would rather have a glance from her eyes than the finest kickshaws dressed by Lord Wrotham's cook, or the dessert which is promised for the entertainment at which you are just going to sit down. You will make the sixth. You may take Mr. Wolfe's place. You may be sure he won't come. As for me, I will stand at the sideboard and report the conversation.

Note first, how happy the women look! When Harry Warrington was taken by those bailiffs, I had intended to tell you how the good Mrs. Lambert, hearing of the boy's mishap, had flown to her husband, and had begged, implored, insisted, that her Martin should help him. "Never mind his rebeldom of the other day; never mind about his being angry that his presents were returned—of course anybody would be angry, much more such a high-spirited lad as Harry! Never mind about our being so poor, and wanting all our spare money for the boys at college; there must be some way of getting him out of the scrape. Did you not get Charles Watkins out of the scrape two years ago; and did he not pay you back every halfpenny? Yes; and you made a whole family happy, blessed be God! and Mrs. Watkins prays for you and blesses you to this very day, and I think everything has prospered with us since. And I have no doubt it has made you a major-general—no earthly doubt," says the fond wife.

Now, as Martin Lambert requires very little persuasion to do a kind action, he in this instance lets himself be persuaded easily enough, and having made up his mind to seek for friend James Wolfe, and give bail for Harry, he takes his leave and his hat, and squeezes Theo's hand, who seems to divine his errand (or perhaps that silly mamma has blabbed it), and kisses little Hetty's flushed cheek, and away he goes out of the apartment where the girls and their mother are sitting, though he is followed out of the room by the latter.

When she is alone with him, that enthusiastic matron cannot control her feelings any longer. She flings her arms round her husband's neck, kisses him a hundred and twenty-five times in an instant—calls God to bless him—cries plentifully on his shoulder; and in this sentimental attitude is discovered by old Mrs. Quiggett, my lord's housekeeper, who is bustling about the house, and, I suppose, is quite astounded at the conjugal phenomenon.

"We have had a tiff, and we are making it up! Don't tell tales out of school, Mrs. Quiggett!" says the gentleman, walking off.

"Well, I never!" says Mrs. Quiggett, with a shrill, strident laugh, like a venerable old cockatoo—which white, hook-nosed, long-lived bird Mrs. Quiggett strongly resembles. "Well, I never!" says Quiggett, laughing and shaking her old sides till all her keys, and, as one may fancy, her old ribs clatter and jingle.

"Oh, Quiggett!" sobs out Mrs. Lambert, "what a man that is!"

"You've been a-quarrelling, have you, mum, and making it up? That's right."

"Quarrel with him? He never told a greater story. My General is an angel, Quiggett. I should like to worship him. I should like to fall down at his boots and kiss 'em, I should! There never was a man so good as my General. What have I done to have such a man? How dare I have such a good husband?"

"My dear, I think there's a pair of you," says the old cockatoo; "and what would you like for your supper?"

When Lambert comes back very late to that meal, and tells what has happened, how Harry is free, and how his brother has come to life, and rescued him, you may fancy what a commotion the whole of those people are in! If Mrs. Lambert's General was an angel before, what is he now! If she wanted to embrace his boots in the morning, pray what further office of wallowing degradation would she prefer in the evening? Little Hetty comes and nestles up to her father quite silent, and drinks a little drop out of his glass. Theo's and mamma's faces beam with happiness, like two moons of brightness.... After supper, those four at a certain signal fall down on their knees—glad homage paying in awful mirth-rejoicing, and with such pure joy as angels do, we read, for the sinner that repents. There comes a great knocking at the door whilst they are so gathered together. Who can be there? My lord is in the country miles off. It is past midnight now; so late have they been, so long have they been talking! I think Mrs. Lambert guesses who is there.

"This is George," says a young gentleman, leading in another. "We have been to Aunt Bernstein. We couldn't go to bed, Aunt Lambert, without coming to thank you too. You dear, dear, good———" There is no more speech audible. Aunt Lambert is kissing Harry, Theo has snatched up Hetty who is as pale as death, and is hugging her into life again. George Warrington stands with his hat off, and then (when Harry's transaction is concluded) goes up and kisses Mrs. Lambert's hand: the General passes his across his eyes. I protest they are all in a very tender and happy state. Generous hearts sometimes feel it, when Wrong is forgiven, when Peace is restored, when Love returns that had been thought lost.

"We came from Aunt Bernstein's; we saw lights here, you see; we couldn't go to sleep without saying good-night to you all," says Harry. "Could we, George?"

"'Tis certainly a famous nightcap you have brought us, boys," says the General. "When are you to come and dine with us? To-morrow?" No, they must go to Madame Bernstein's to-morrow.

The next day, then? Yes, they would come the next day—and that is the very day we are writing about: and this is the very dinner, at which, in the room of Lieutenant-Colonel James Wolfe, absent on private affairs, my gracious reader has just been invited to sit down.

To sit down, and why, if you please? Not to a mere Barmecide dinner—no, no—but to hear MR. GEORGE ESMOND WARRINGTON'S STATEMENT, which of course he is going to make. Here they all sit—not in my lord's grand dining-room, you know, but in the snug study or parlour in front. The cloth has been withdrawn, the General has given the King's health, the servants have left the room, the guests sit conticent, and so, after a little hemming and blushing, Mr. George proceeds:—

"I remember, at the table of our General, how the little Philadelphia agent, whose wit and shrewdness we had remarked at home, made the very objections to the conduct of the campaign of which its disastrous issue showed the justice. 'Of course,' says he, 'your Excellency's troops once before Fort Duquesne, such a weak little place will never be able to resist such a general, such an army, such artillery, as will there be found attacking it. But do you calculate, sir, on the difficulty of reaching the place? Your Excellency's march will be through woods almost untrodden, over roads which you will have to make yourself, and your line will be some four miles long. This slender line, having to make its way through the forest, will be subject to endless attacks in front, in rear, in flank, by enemies whom you will never see, and whose constant practice in war is the dexterous laying of ambuscades.'—'Psha, sir!' says the General, 'the savages may frighten your raw American militia' (Thank your Excellency for the compliment, Mr. Washington seems to say, who is sitting at the table), 'but the Indians will never make any impression on his Majesty's regular troops.'—'I heartily hope not, sir,' says Mr. Franklin, with a sigh; and of course the gentlemen of the General's family sneered at the postmaster, as at a pert civilian who had no call to be giving his opinion on matters entirely beyond his comprehension.

"We despised the Indians on our own side, and our commander made light of them and their service. Our officers disgusted the chiefs who were with us by outrageous behaviour to their women. There were not above seven or eight who remained with our force. Had we had a couple of hundred in our front on that fatal 9th of July, the event of the day must have been very different. They would have flung off the attack of the French Indians; they would have prevented the surprise and panic which ensued. 'Tis known now that the French had even got ready to give up their fort, never dreaming of the possibility of a defence, and that the French Indians themselves remonstrated against the audacity of attacking such an overwhelming force as ours.

"I was with our General with the main body of the troops when the firing began in front of us, and one aide-de-camp after another was sent forwards. At first the enemy's attack was answered briskly by our own advanced people, and our men huzzaed and cheered with good heart. But very soon our fire grew slacker, whilst from behind every tree and bush round about us came single shots, which laid man after man low. We were marching in orderly line, the skirmishers in front, the colours and two of our small guns in the centre, the baggage well guarded bringing up the rear, and were moving over a ground which was open and clear for a mile or two, and for some half mile in breadth, a thick tangled covert of brushwood and trees on either side of us. After the firing had continued for some brief time in front, it opened from both sides of the environing wood on our advancing column. The men dropped rapidly, the officers in greater number than the men. At first, as I said, these cheered and answered the enemy's fire, our guns even opening on the wood, and seeming to silence the French in ambuscade there. But the hidden rifle-firing began again. Our men halted, huddled up together, in spite of the shouts and orders of the General and officers to advance, and fired wildly into the brushwood—of course making no impression. Those in advance came running back on the main body frightened, and many of them wounded. They reported there were five thousand Frenchmen and a legion of yelling Indian devils in front, who were scalping our people as they fell. We could hear their cries from the wood around as our men dropped under their rifles. There was no inducing the people to go forward now. One aide-de-camp after another was sent forward, and never returned. At last it came to be my turn, and I was sent with a message to Captain Fraser of Halkett's in front, which he was never to receive nor I to deliver.

"I had not gone thirty yards in advance when a rifle-ball struck my leg, and I fell straightway to the ground. I recollect a rush forward of Indians and Frenchmen after that, the former crying their fiendish war-cries, the latter as fierce as their savage allies. I was amazed and mortified to see how few of the whitecoats there were. Not above a score passed me; indeed there were not fifty in the accursed action in which two of the bravest regiments of the British army were put to rout.

"One of them, who was half Indian half Frenchman, with mocassins and a white uniform coat and cockade, seeing me prostrate on the ground, turned back and ran towards me, his musket clubbed over his head to dash my brains out and plunder me as I lay. I had my little fusil which my Harry gave me when I went on the campaign; it had fallen by me and within my reach, luckily: I seized it, and down fell the Frenchman dead at six yards before me. I was saved for that time, but bleeding from my wound and very faint. I swooned almost in trying to load my piece, and it dropped from my hand, and the hand itself sank lifeless to the ground.

"I was scarcely in my senses, the yells and shots ringing dimly in my ears, when I saw an Indian before me, busied over the body of the Frenchman I had just shot, but glancing towards me as I lay on the ground bleeding. He first rifled the Frenchman, tearing open his coat, and feeling in his pockets: he then scalped him, and with his bleeding knife in his mouth advanced towards me. I saw him coming as through a film, as in a dream—I was powerless to move, or to resist him.

"He put his knee upon my chest: with one bloody hand he seized my long hair and lifted my head from the ground, and as he lifted it, he enabled me to see a French officer rapidly advancing behind him.

"Good God! It was young Florac, who was my second in the duel at Quebec. 'A moi, Florac!' I cried out. 'C'est Georges! aide moi!'

"He started; ran up to me at the cry, laid his hand on the Indian's shoulder, and called him to hold. But the savage did not understand French, or choose to understand it. He clutched my hair firmer, and waving his dripping knife round it, motioned to the French lad to leave him to his prey. I could only cry out again and piteously, 'A moi!'

"'Ah, canaille, tu veux du sang? Prends!' said Florac, with a curse; and the next moment, and with an ugh, the Indian fell over my chest dead, with Florac's sword through his body.

"My friend looked round him. 'Eh!' says he, 'la belle affaire! Where art thou wounded? in the leg?' He bound my leg tight round with his sash. 'The others will kill thee if they find thee here. Ah, tiens! Put me on this coat, and this hat with the white cockade. Call out in French if any of our people pass. They will take thee for one of us. Thou art Brunet of the Quebec Volunteers. God guard thee, Brunet! I must go forward. 'Tis a general debacle, and the whole of your redcoats are on the run, my poor boy.' Ah, what a rout it was! What a day of disgrace for England!

"Florac's rough application stopped the bleeding of my leg, and the kind creature helped me to rest against a tree, and to load my fusil, which he placed within reach of me, to protect me in case any other marauder should have a mind to attack me. And he gave me the gourd of that unlucky French soldier, who had lost his own life in the deadly game which he had just played against me, and the drink the gourd contained served greatly to refresh and invigorate me. Taking a mark of the tree against which I lay, and noting the various bearings of the country, so as to be able again to find me, the young lad hastened on to the front. 'Thou seest how much I love thee, George,' he said, 'that I stay behind in a moment like this.' I forget whether I told thee Harry, that Florac was under some obligation to me. I had won money of him at cards, at Quebec—only playing at his repeated entreaty—and there was a difficulty about paying, and I remitted his debt to me, and lighted my pipe with his note-of-hand. You see, sir, that you are not the only gambler in the family.

"At evening, when the dismal pursuit was over, the faithful fellow came back to me, with a couple of Indians, who had each reeking scalps at their belts, and whom he informed that I was a Frenchman, his brother, who had been wounded early in the day, and must be carried back to the fort. They laid me in one of their blankets, and carried me, groaning, with the trusty Florac by my side. Had he left me, they would assuredly have laid me down, plundered me, and added my hair to that of the wretches whose bleeding spoils hung at their girdles. He promised them brandy at the fort, if they brought me safely there: I have but a dim recollection of the journey: the anguish of my wound was extreme: I fainted more than once. We came to the end of our march at last. I was taken into the fort, and carried to the officer's log-house, and laid upon Florac's own bed.

"Happy for me was my insensibility. I had been brought into the fort as a wounded French soldier of the garrison. I heard afterwards, that during my delirium the few prisoners who had been made on the day of our disaster, had been brought under the walls of Duquesne by their savage captors, and there horribly burned, tortured, and butchered by the Indians, under the eyes of the garrison."

As George speaks, one may fancy a thrill of horror running through his sympathising audience. Theo takes Hetty's hand, and looks at George in a very alarmed manner. Harry strikes his fist upon the table, and cries, "The bloody, murderous, red-skinned villains! There will never be peace for us until they are all hunted down!"

"They were offering a hundred and thirty dollars apiece for Indian scalps in Pennsylvania, when I left home," says George, demurely, "and fifty for women."

"Fifty for women, my love! Do you hear that, Mrs. Lambert?" cries the Colonel, lifting up his wife's hair.

"The murderous villains!" says Harry, again. "Hunt 'em down, sir! Hunt 'em down!"

"I know not how long I lay in my fever," George resumed. "When I awoke to my senses, my dear Florac was gone. He and his company had been despatched on an enterprise against an English fort on the Pennsylvanian territory, which the French claimed, too. In Duquesne, when I came to be able to ask and understand what was said to me, there were not above thirty Europeans left. The place might have been taken over and over again, had any of our people had the courage to return after their disaster.

"My old enemy the ague-fever set in again upon me as I lay here by the river-side. 'Tis a wonder how I ever survived. But for the goodness of a half-breed woman in the fort, who took pity on me, and tended me, I never should have recovered, and my poor Harry would be what he fancied himself yesterday, our grandfather's heir, our mother's only son.

"I remembered how, when Florac laid me in his bed, he put under my pillow my money, my watch, and a trinket or two which I had. When I woke to myself these were all gone; and a surly old sergeant, the only officer left in the quarter, told me, with a curse, that I was lucky enough to be left with my life at all; that it was only my white cockade and coat had saved me from the fate which the other canaille of Rosbifs had deservedly met with.

"At the time of my recovery the fort was almost emptied of the garrison. The Indians had retired enriched with British plunder, and the chief part of the French regulars were gone upon expeditions northward. My good Florac had left me upon his service, consigning me to the care of an invalided sergeant. Monsieur de Contrecoeur had accompanied one of these expeditions, leaving an old lieutenant, Museau by name, in command at Duquesne.

"This man had long been out of France, and serving in the colonies. His character, doubtless, had been indifferent at home; and he knew that, according to the system pursued in France, where almost all promotion is given to the noblesse, he never would advance in rank. And he had made free with my guineas, I suppose, as he had with my watch, for I saw it one day on his chest when I was sitting with him in his quarter.

"Monsieur Museau and I managed to be pretty good friends. If I could be exchanged, or sent home, I told him that my mother would pay liberally for my ransom; and I suppose this idea excited the cupidity of the commandant, for a trapper coming in the winter, whilst I still lay very ill with fever, Museau consented that I should write home to my mother, but that the letter should be in French, that he should see it, and that I should say I was in the hands of the Indians, and should not be ransomed under ten thousand livres.

"In vain I said I was a prisoner to the troops of his Most Christian Majesty, that I expected the treatment of a gentleman and an officer. Museau swore that letter should go, and no other; that if I hesitated, he would fling me out of the fort, or hand me over to the tender mercies of his ruffian Indian allies. He would not let the trapper communicate with me except in his presence. Life and liberty are sweet. I resisted for a while, but I was pulled down with weakness, and shuddering with fever; I wrote such a letter as the rascal consented to let pass, and the trapper went away with my missive, which he promised, in three weeks, to deliver to my mother in Virginia.

"Three weeks, six, twelve, passed. The messenger never returned. The winter came and went, and all our little plantations round the fort, where the French soldiers had cleared corn-ground and planted gardens and peach- and apple-trees down to the Monongahela, were in full blossom. Heaven knows how I crept through the weary time! When I was pretty well, I made drawings of the soldiers of the garrison, and of the half-breed and her child (Museau's child), and of Museau himself, whom, I am ashamed to say, I flattered outrageously; and there was an old guitar left in the fort, and I sang to it, and played on it some French airs which I knew, and ingratiated myself as best I could with my gaolers; and so the weary months passed, but the messenger never returned.

"At last news arrived that he had been shot by some British Indians in Maryland: so there was an end of my hope of ransom for some months more. This made Museau very savage and surly towards me; the more so as his sergeant inflamed his rage by telling him that the Indian woman was partial to me—as I believe, poor thing, she was. I was always gentle with her, and grateful to her. My small accomplishments seemed wonders in her eyes; I was ill and unhappy, too, and these are always claims to a woman's affection.

"A captive pulled down by malady, a ferocious gaoler, and a young woman touched by the prisoner's misfortunes—sure you expect that, with these three prime characters in a piece, some pathetic tragedy is going to be enacted? You, Miss Hetty, are about to guess that the woman saved me?"

"Why, of course she did!" cries mamma.

"What else is she good for?" says Hetty.

"You, Miss Theo, have painted her already as a dark beauty—is it not so? A swift huntress—"

"Diana with a baby," says the Colonel.

"—Who scours the plain with her nymphs, who brings down the game with her unerring bow, who is queen of the forest—and I see by your looks that you think I am madly in love with her?"

"Well, I suppose she is an interesting creature, Mr. George?" says Theo, with a blush.

"What think you of a dark beauty, the colour of new mahogany with long straight black hair, which was usually dressed with a hair-oil or pomade by no means pleasant to approach, with little eyes, with high cheek-bones, with a flat nose, sometimes ornamented with a ring, with rows of glass beads round her tawny throat, her cheeks and forehead gracefully tattooed, a great love of finery, and inordinate passion for—oh! must I own it?"

"For coquetry. I know you are going to say that!" says Miss Hetty.

"For whisky, my dear Miss Hester—in which appetite my gaoler partook; so that I have often sate by, on the nights when I was in favour with Monsieur Museau, and seen him and his poor companion hob-and-nobbing together until they could scarce hold the noggin out of which they drank. In these evening entertainments, they would sing, they would dance, they would fondle, they would quarrel, and knock the cans and furniture about; and, when I was in favour, I was admitted to share their society, for Museau, jealous of his dignity, or not willing that his men should witness his behaviour, would allow none of them to be familiar with him.

"Whilst the result of the trapper's mission to my home was yet uncertain, and Museau and I myself expected the payment of my ransom, I was treated kindly enough, allowed to crawl about the fort, and even to go into the adjoining fields and gardens, always keeping my parole, and duly returning before gun-fire. And I exercised a piece of hypocrisy, for which, I hope, you will hold me excused. When my leg was sound (the ball came out in the winter, after some pain and inflammation, and the wound healed up presently), I yet chose to walk as if I was disabled and a cripple; I hobbled on two sticks, and cried Ah! and Oh! at every minute, hoping that a day might come when I might treat my limbs to a run.

"Museau was very savage when he began to give up all hopes of the first messenger. He fancied that the man might have got the ransom-money and fled with it himself. Of course he was prepared to disown any part in the transaction, should my letter be discovered. His treatment of me varied according to his hopes or fears, or even his mood for the time being. He would have me consigned to my quarters for several days at a time; then invite me to his tipsy supper-table, quarrel with me there, and abuse my nation; or again break out into maudlin sentimentalities about his native country of Normandy, where he longed to spend his old age, to buy a field or two, and to die happy.

"'Eh, Monsieur Museau!' says I, 'ten thousand livres of your money would buy a pretty field or two in your native country? You can have it for the ransom of me, if you will but let me go. In a few months you must be superseded in your command here, and then adieu the crowns and the fields in Normandy! You had better trust a gentleman and a man of honour. Let me go home, and I give you my word the ten thousand livres shall be paid to any agent you may appoint in France or in Quebec.'

"'Ah, young traitor!' roars he, 'do you wish to tamper with my honour? Do you believe an officer of France will take a bribe? I have a mind to consign thee to my black-hole, and to have thee shot in the morning.'

"'My poor body will never fetch ten thousand livres,' says I; 'and a pretty field in Normandy with a cottage...'

"'And an orchard. Ah, sacre bleu!' says Museau, whimpering, 'and a dish of tripe a la mode du pays!...'"

"This talk happened between us again and again, and Museau would order me to my quarters, and then ask me to supper the next night, and return to the subject of Normandy, and cider, and trippes a la mode de Caen. My friend is dead now—"

"He was hung, I trust?" breaks in Colonel Lambert.

"—And I need keep no secret about him. Ladies, I wish I had to offer you the account of a dreadful and tragical escape; how I slew all the sentinels of the fort; filed through the prison windows, destroyed a score or so of watchful dragons, overcame a million of dangers, and finally effected my freedom. But, in regard of that matter, I have no heroic deeds to tell of, and own that, by bribery and no other means, I am where I am."

"But you would have fought, Georgy, if need were," says Harry; "and you couldn't conquer a whole garrison, you know!" And herewith Mr. Harry blushed very much.

"See the women, how disappointed they are!" says Lambert. "Mrs. Lambert, you bloodthirsty woman, own that you are balked of a battle; and look at Hetty, quite angry because Mr. George did not shoot the commandant."

"You wished he was hung yourself, papa!" cries Miss Hetty, "and I am sure I wish anything my papa wishes."

"Nay, ladies," says George, turning a little red, "to wink at a prisoner's escape was not a very monstrous crime; and to take money? Sure other folks besides Frenchmen have condescended to a bribe before now. Although Monsieur Museau set me free, I am inclined, for my part, to forgive him. Will it please you to hear how that business was done? You see, Miss Hetty, I cannot help being alive to tell it."

"Oh, George!—that is, I mean, Mr. Warrington!—that is, I mean, I beg your pardon!" cries Hester.

"No pardon, my dear! I never was angry yet or surprised that any one should like my Harry better than me. He deserves all the liking that any man or woman can give him. See, it is his turn to blush now," says George.

"Go on, Georgy, and tell them about the escape out of Duquesne!" cries Harry, and he said to Mrs. Lambert afterwards in confidence, "You know he is always going on saying that he ought never to have come to life again, and declaring that I am better than he is. The idea of my being better than George, Mrs. Lambert! a poor, extravagant fellow like me! It's absurd!"

CHAPTER LII. Intentique Ora tenebant

"We continued for months our weary life at the fort, and the commandant and I had our quarrels and reconciliations, our greasy games at cards, our dismal duets with his asthmatic flute and my cracked guitar. The poor Fawn took her beatings and her cans of liquor as her lord and master chose to administer them; and she nursed her papoose, or her master in the gout, or her prisoner in the ague; and so matters went on until the beginning of the fall of last year, when we were visited by a hunter who had important news to deliver to the commandant, and such as set the little garrison in no little excitement. The Marquis de Montcalm had sent a considerable detachment to garrison the forts already in the French hands, and to take up further positions in the enemy's—that is, in the British—possessions. The troops had left Quebec and Montreal, and were coming up the St. Lawrence and the lakes in bateaux, with artillery and large provisions of warlike and other stores. Museau would be superseded in his command by an officer of superior rank, who might exchange me, or who might give me up to the Indians in reprisal for cruelties practised by our own people on many and many an officer and soldier of the enemy. The men of the fort were eager for the reinforcements; they would advance into Pennsylvania and New York; they would seize upon Albany and Philadelphia; they would drive the Rosbifs into the sea, and all America should be theirs from the Mississippi to Newfoundland.

"This was all very triumphant: but yet, somehow, the prospect of the French conquest did not add to Mr. Museau's satisfaction.

"'Eh, commandant!' says I, "tis fort bien, but meanwhile your farm in Normandy, the pot of cider, and the trippes a la mode de Caen, where are they?'

"'Yes; 'tis all very well, my garcon,' says he. 'But where will you be when poor old Museau is superseded? Other officers are not good companions like me. Very few men in the world have my humanity. When there is a great garrison here, will my successors give thee the indulgences which honest Museau has granted thee? Thou wilt be kept in a sty like a pig ready for killing. As sure as one of our officers falls into the hands of your brigands of frontier-men, and evil comes to him, so surely wilt thou have to pay with thy skin for his. Thou wilt be given up to our red allies—to the brethren of La Biche yonder. Didst thou see, last year, what they did to thy countrymen whom we took in the action with Braddock? Roasting was the very smallest punishment, ma foi—was it not, La Biche?'

"And he entered into a variety of jocular descriptions of tortures inflicted, eyes burned out of their sockets, teeth and nails wrenched out, limbs and bodies gashed—You turn pale, dear Miss Theo! Well, I will have pity, and will spare you the tortures which honest Museau recounted in his pleasant way as likely to befall me.

"La Biche was by no means so affected as you seem to be, ladies, by the recital of these horrors. She had witnessed them in her time. She came from the Senecas, whose villages lie near the great cataract between Ontario and Erie; her people made war for the English, and against them: they had fought with other tribes; and, in the battles between us and them, it is difficult to say whether whiteskin or redskin is most savage.

"'They may chop me into cutlets and broil me, 'tis true, commandant,' says I, coolly. 'But again, I say, you will never have the farm in Normandy.'

"'Go get the whisky-bottle, La Biche,' says Museau.

"'And it is not too late, even now. I will give the guide who takes me home a large reward. And again I say, I promise, as a man of honour, ten thousand livres to—whom shall I say? to one who shall bring me any token—who shall bring me, say, my watch and seal with my grandfather's arms—which I have seen in a chest somewhere in this fort.'

"'Ah, scelerat!' roars out the commandant, with a hoarse yell of laughter. 'Thou hast eyes, thou! All is good prize in war.'

"'Think of a house in your village, of a fine field hard by with a half-dozen of cows—of a fine orchard all covered with fruit.'

"'And Javotte at the door with her wheel, and a rascal of a child, or two, with cheeks as red as the apples! O my country! O my mother!' whimpers out the commandant. 'Quick, La Biche, the whisky!'

"All that night the commandant was deep in thought, and La Biche, too, silent and melancholy. She sate away from us, nursing her child, and whenever my eyes turned towards her I saw hers were fixed on me. The poor little infant began to cry, and was ordered away by Museau, with his usual foul language, to the building which the luckless Biche occupied with her child. When she was gone, we both of us spoke our minds freely; and I put such reasons before monsieur as his cupidity could not resist.

"'How do you know,' he asked, 'that this hunter will serve you?'

"'That is my secret,' says I. But here, if you like, as we are not on honour, I may tell it. When they come into the settlements for their bargains, the hunters often stop a day or two for rest and drink and company, and our new friend loved all these. He played at cards with the men: he set his furs against their liquor: he enjoyed himself at the fort, singing, dancing, and gambling with them. I think I said they liked to listen to my songs, and for want of better things to do, I was often singing and guitar-scraping: and we would have many a concert, the men joining in chorus, or dancing to my homely music, until it was interrupted by the drums and the retraite.

"Our guest the hunter was present at one or two of these concerts, and I thought I would try if possibly he understood English. After we had had our little stock of French songs, I said, 'My lads, I will give you an English song,' and to the tune of 'Over the hills and far away,' which my good old grandfather used to hum as a favourite air in Marlborough's camp, I made some doggerel words:—'This long, long year, a prisoner drear; Ah, me! I'm tired of lingering here: I'll give a hundred guineas gay, To be over the hills and far away.'

"'What is it?' says the hunter. 'I don't understand.'

"''Tis a girl to her lover,' I answered; but I saw by the twinkle in the man's eye that he understood me.

"The next day, when there were no men within hearing, the trapper showed that I was right in my conjecture, for as he passed me he hummed in a low tone, but in perfectly good English, 'Over the hills and far away,' the burden of my yesterday's doggerel.

"'If you are ready,' says he, 'I am ready. I know who your people are, and the way to them. Talk to the Fawn, and she will tell you what to do. What! You will not play with me?' Here he pulled out some cards, and spoke in French as two soldiers came up. 'Milor est trop grand seigneur? Bonjour, my lord!'

"And the man made me a mock bow, and walked away, shrugging up his shoulders, to offer to play and drink elsewhere.

"I knew now that the Biche was to be the agent in the affair, and that my offer to Museau was accepted. The poor Fawn performed her part very faithfully and dexterously. I had not need of a word more with Museau; the matter was understood between us. The Fawn had long been allowed free communication with me. She had tended me during my wound and in my illnesses, helped to do the work of my little chamber, my cooking, and so forth. She was free to go out of the fort, as I have said, and to the river and the fields whence the corn and garden-stuff of the little garrison were brought in.

"Having gambled away most of the money which he received for his peltries, the trapper now got together his store of flints, powder, and blankets, and took his leave. And, three days after his departure, the Fawn gave me the signal that the time was come for me to make my little trial for freedom.

"When first wounded, I had been taken by my kind Florac and placed on his bed in the officers' room. When the fort was emptied of all officers except the old lieutenant left in command, I had been allowed to remain in my quarters, sometimes being left pretty free, sometimes being locked up and fed on prisoners' rations, sometimes invited to share his mess by my tipsy gaoler.

"This officers' house, or room, was of logs like the half-dozen others within the fort, which mounted only four guns of small calibre, of which one was on the bastion behind my cabin. Looking westward over this gun, you could see a small island at the confluence of the two rivers Ohio and Monongahela whereon Duquesne is situated. On the shore opposite this island were some trees.

"'You see those trees?' my poor Biche said to me the day before, in her French jargon. 'He wait for you behind those trees.'

"In the daytime the door of my quarters was open, and the Biche free to come and go. On the day before she came in from the fields with a pick in her hand and a basketful of vegetables and potherbs for soup. She sat down on a bench at my door, the pick resting against it, and the basket at her side. I stood talking to her for a while: but I believe I was so idiotic that I never should have thought of putting the pick to any use had she actually pushed it into my open door, so that it fell into my room. 'Hide it' she said; 'want it soon.' And that afternoon it was, she pointed out the trees to me.

"On the next day, she comes, pretending to be very angry, and calls out, 'My lord! my lord! why you not come to commandant's dinner? He very bad! Entendez-vows?' And she peeps into the room as she speaks, and flings a coil of rope at me.

"'I am coming, La Biche,' says I, and hobbled after her on my crutch. As I went in to the commandant's quarters she says, 'Pour ce soir.' And then I knew the time was come.

"As for Museau, he knew nothing about the matter. Not he! He growled at me, and said the soup was cold. He looked me steadily in the face, and talked of this and that; not only whilst his servant was present, but afterwards as we smoked our pipes and played our game at piquet; whilst according to her wont, the poor Biche sate cowering in a corner.

"My friend's whisky-bottle was empty; and he said, with rather a knowing look, he must have another glass—we must both have a glass that night. And rising from the table he stumped to the inner room where he kept his firewater under lock and key, and away from the poor Biche, who could not resist that temptation.

"As he turned his back the Biche raised herself; and he was no sooner gone but she was at my feet, kissing my hand, pressing it to her heart, and bursting into tears over my knees. I confess I was so troubled by this testimony of the poor creature's silent attachment and fondness, the extent of which I scarce had suspected before, that when Museau returned, I had not recovered my equanimity, though the poor Fawn was back in her corner again and shrouded in her blanket.

"He did not appear to remark anything strange in the behaviour of either. We sate down to our game, though my thoughts were so preoccupied that I scarcely knew what cards were before me.

"'I gain everything from you to-night, milor,' says he, grimly. 'We play upon parole.'

"'And you may count upon mine,' I replied.

"'Eh! 'tis all that you have!' says he.

"'Monsieur,' says I, 'my word is good for ten thousand livres;' and we continued our game.

"At last he said he had a headache, and would go to bed, and I understood the orders too, that I was to retire. 'I wish you a good night, mon petit milor,' says he,—'stay, you will fall without your crutch,'—and his eyes twinkled at me, and his face wore a sarcastic grin. In the agitation of the moment I had quite forgotten that I was lame, and was walking away at a pace as good as a grenadier's.

"'What a vilain night!' says he, looking out. In fact there was a tempest abroad, and a great roaring, and wind. 'Bring a lanthorn, La Tulipe, and lock my lord comfortably into his quarters!' He stood a moment looking at me from his own door, and I saw a glimpse of the poor Biche behind him.

"The night was so rainy that the sentries preferred their boxes, and did not disturb me in my work. The log-house was built with upright posts, deeply fixed in the ground, and horizontal logs laid upon it. I had to dig under these, and work a hole sufficient to admit my body to pass. I began in the dark, soon after tattoo. It was some while after midnight before my work was done, when I lifted my hand up under the log and felt the rain from without falling upon it. I had to work very cautiously for two hours after that, and then crept through to the parapet and silently flung my rope over the gun; not without a little tremor of heart, lest the sentry should see me and send a charge of lead into my body.

"The wall was but twelve feet, and my fall into the ditch easy enough. I waited a while there, looking steadily under the gun, and trying to see the river and the island. I heard the sentry pacing up above and humming a tune. The darkness became more clear to me ere long, and the moon rose, and I saw the river shining before me, and the dark rocks and trees of the island rising in the waters.

"I made for this mark as swiftly as I could, and for the clump of trees to which I had been directed. Oh, what a relief I had when I heard a low voice humming there, 'Over the hills and far away'!"

When Mr. George came to this part of his narrative, Miss Theo, who was seated by a harpsichord, turned round and dashed off the tune on the instrument, whilst all the little company broke out into the merry chorus.

"Our way," the speaker went on, "lay through a level tract of forest with which my guide was familiar, upon the right bank of the Monongahela. By daylight we came to a clearer country, and my trapper asked me—Silverheels was the name by which he went—had I ever seen the spot before? It was the fatal field where Braddock had fallen, and whence I had been wonderfully rescued in the summer of the previous year. Now, the leaves were beginning to be tinted with the magnificent hues of our autumn."

"Ah, brother!" cries Harry, seizing his brother's hand. "I was gambling and making a fool of myself at the Wells and in London, when my George was flying for his life in the wilderness! Oh, what a miserable spendthrift I have been!"

"But I think thou art not unworthy to be called thy mother's son," said Mrs. Lambert, very softly, and with moistened eyes. Indeed, if Harry had erred, to mark his repentance, his love, his unselfish joy and generosity, was to feel that there was hope for the humbled and kind young sinner.

"We presently crossed the river" George resumed, "taking our course along the base of the western slopes of the Alleghanies; and through a grand forest region of oaks and maple, and enormous poplars that grow a hundred feet high without a branch. It was the Indians whom we had to avoid, besides the outlying parties of French. Always of doubtful loyalty, the savages have been specially against us, since our ill-treatment of them, and the French triumph over us two years ago.

"I was but weak still, and our journey through the wilderness lasted a fortnight or more. As we advanced, the woods became redder and redder. The frost nipped sharply of nights. We lighted fires at our feet, and slept in our blankets as best we might. At this time of year the hunters who live in the mountains get their sugar from the maples. We came upon more than one such family, camping near their trees by the mountain streams; and they welcomed us at their fires, and gave us of their venison. So we passed over the two ranges of the Laurel Hills and the Alleghanies. The last day's march of my trusty guide and myself took us down that wild, magnificent pass of Will's Creek, a valley lying between cliffs near a thousand feet high—bald, white, and broken into towers like huge fortifications, with eagles wheeling round the summits of the rocks, and watching their nests among the crags.

"And hence we descended to Cumberland, whence we had marched in the year before, and where there was now a considerable garrison of our people. Oh! you may think it was a welcome day when I saw English colours again on the banks of our native Potomac!"

CHAPTER LIII. Where we remain at the Court End of the Town

George Warrington had related the same story, which we have just heard, to Madame de Bernstein on the previous evening—a portion, that is, of the history; for the old lady nodded off to sleep many times during the narration, only waking up when George paused, saying it was most interesting, and ordering him to continue. The young gentleman hem'd and ha'd, and stuttered, and blushed, and went on, much against his will, and did not speak half so well as he did to his friendly little auditory in Hill Street, where Hetty's eyes of wonder and Theo's sympathising looks, and mamma's kind face, and papa's funny looks, were applause sufficient to cheer any modest youth who required encouragement for his eloquence. As for mamma's behaviour, the General said, 'twas as good as Mr. Addison's trunk-maker, and she would make the fortune of any tragedy by simply being engaged to cry in the front boxes. That is why we chose my Lord Wrotham's house as the theatre where George's first piece should be performed, wishing that he should speak to advantage, and not as when he was heard by that sleepy, cynical old lady, to whom he had to narrate his adventures.

"Very good and most interesting, I am sure, my dear sir," says Madame Bernstein, putting up three pretty little fingers covered with a lace mitten, to hide a convulsive movement of her mouth. "And your mother must have been delighted to see you."

George shrugged his shoulders ever so little, and made a low bow, as his aunt looked up at him for a moment with her keen old eyes.

"Have been delighted to see you" she continued drily, "and killed the fatted calf, and—and that kind of thing. Though why I say calf, I don't know, nephew George, for you never were the prodigal. I may say calf to thee, my poor Harry! Thou hast been amongst the swine sure enough. And evil companions have robbed the money out of thy pocket and the coat off thy back.

"He came to his family in England, madam," says George, with some heat, "and his friends were your ladyship's."

"He could not have come to worse advisers, nephew Warrington, and so I should have told my sister earlier, had she condescended to write to me by him, as she has done by you," said the old lady, tossing up her head. "Hey! hey!" she said, at night, as she arranged herself for the rout to which she was going, to her waiting-maid: "this young gentleman's mother is half sorry that he has come to life again, I could see that in his face. She is half sorry, and I am perfectly furious! Why didn't he lie still when he dropped there under the tree, and why did that young Florac carry him to the fort? I knew those Floracs when I was at Paris, in the time of Monsieur le Regent. They were of the Floracs of Ivry. No great house before Henri IV. His ancestor was the king's favourite. His ancestor—he! he!—his ancestress! Brett! entendez-vous?

Give me my card-purse. I don't like the grand airs of this Monsieur George; and yet he resembles, very much, his grandfather—the same look and sometimes the same tones. You have heard of Colonel Esmond when I was young? This boy has his eyes. I suppose I liked the Colonel's because he loved me."

Being engaged, then, to a card-party,—an amusement which she never missed, week-day or Sabbath, as long as she had strength to hold trumps or sit in a chair,—very soon after George had ended his narration the old lady dismissed her two nephews, giving to the elder a couple of fingers and a very stately curtsey; but to Harry two hands and a kindly pat on the cheek.

"My poor child, now thou art disinherited, thou wilt see how differently the world will use thee!" she said. "There is only, in all London, a wicked, heartless old woman who will treat thee as before. Here is a pocket-book for you, child! Do not lose it at Ranelagh to-night. That suit of yours does not become your brother half so well as it sat upon you! You will present your brother to everybody, and walk up and down the room for two hours at least, child. Were I you, I would then go to the Chocolate-House, and play as if nothing had happened. Whilst you are there, your brother may come back to me and eat a bit of chicken with me. My Lady Flint gives wretched suppers, and I want to talk his mother's letter over with him. Au revoir, gentlemen!" and she went away to her toilette. Her chairmen and flambeaux were already waiting at the door.

The gentlemen went to Ranelagh, where but a few of Mr. Harry's acquaintances chanced to be present. They paced the round, and met Mr. Tom Claypool with some of his country friends; they heard the music; they drank tea in a box; Harry was master of ceremonies, and introduced his brother to the curiosities of the place; and George was even more excited than his brother had been on his first introduction to this palace of delight. George loved music much more than Harry ever did; he heard a full orchestra for the first time, and a piece of Mr. Handel satisfactorily performed; and a not unpleasing instance of Harry's humility and regard for his elder brother was, that he could even hold George's love of music in respect at a time when fiddling was voted effeminate and unmanly in England, and Britons were, every day, called upon by the patriotic prints to sneer at the frivolous accomplishments of your Squallinis, Monsieurs, and the like. Nobody in Britain is proud of his ignorance now. There is no conceit left among us. There is no such thing as dulness. Arrogance is entirely unknown... Well, at any rate, Art has obtained her letters of naturalisation, and lives here on terms of almost equality. If Mrs. Thrale chose to marry a music-master now, I don't think her friends would shudder at the mention of her name. If she had a good fortune and kept a good cook, people would even go and dine with her in spite of the misalliance, and actually treat Mr. Piozzi with civility.

After Ranelagh, and pursuant to Madam Bernstein's advice, George returned to her ladyship's house, whilst Harry showed himself at the club, where gentlemen were accustomed to assemble at night to sup, and then to gamble. No one, of course, alluded to Mr. Warrington's little temporary absence, and Mr. Ruff, his ex-landlord, waited upon him with the utmost gravity and civility, and as if there had never been any difference between them. Mr. Warrington had caused his trunks and habiliments to be conveyed away from Bond Street in the morning, and he and his brother were now established in apartments elsewhere.

But when the supper was done, and the gentlemen, as usual, were about to seek the macco-table upstairs, Harry said he was not going to play any more. He had burned his fingers already, and could afford no more extravagance.

"Why," says Mr. Morris, in a rather flippant manner, "you must have won more than you have lost, Mr. Warrington, after all is said and done."

"And of course I don't know my own business as well as you do, Mr. Morris," says Harry sternly, who had not forgotten the other's behaviour on hearing of his arrest; "but I have another reason. A few months or days ago, I was heir to a great estate, and could afford to lose a little money. Now, thank God, I am heir to nothing." And he looked round, blushing not a little, to the knot of gentlemen, his gaming associates, who were lounging at the tables or gathered round the fire.

"How do you mean, Mr. Warrington?" cries my Lord March, "Have you lost Virginia, too? Who has won it? I always had a fancy to play you myself for that stake."

"And grow an improved breed of slaves in the colony," says another.

"The right owner has won it. You have heard me tell of my twin elder brother?"

"Who was killed in that affair of Braddock's two years ago! Yes. Gracious goodness, my dear sir, I hope in heaven he has not come to life again?"

"He arrived in London two days since. He has been a prisoner in a French fort for eighteen months; he only escaped a few months ago, and left our house in Virginia very soon after his release."

"You haven't had time to order mourning, I suppose, Mr. Warrington?" asks Mr. Selwyn very good-naturedly, and simple Harry hardly knew the meaning of his joke until his brother interpreted it to him.

"Hang me, if I don't believe the fellow is absolutely glad of the reappearance of his confounded brother!" cries my Lord March, as they continued to talk of the matter when the young Virginian had taken his leave.

"These savages practise the simple virtues of affection—they are barely civilised in America yet," yawns Selwyn.

"They love their kindred, and they scalp their enemies," simpers Mr. Walpole. "It's not Christian, but natural. Shouldn't you like to be present at a scalping-match, George, and see a fellow skinned alive?"

"A man's elder brother is his natural enemy," says Mr. Selwyn, placidly ranging his money and counters before him.

"Torture is like broiled bones and pepper. You wouldn't relish simple hanging afterwards, George!" continues Horry.

"I'm hanged if there's any man in England who would like to see his elder brother alive," says my lord.

"No, nor his father either, my lord!" cries Jack Morris.

"First time I ever knew you had one, Jack. Give me counters for five hundred."

"I say, 'tis all mighty fine about dead brothers coming to life again," continues Jack. "Who is to know that it wasn't a scheme arranged between these two fellows? Here comes a young fellow who calls himself the Fortunate Youth, who says he is a Virginian Prince and the deuce knows what, and who gets into our society———"

A great laugh ensues at Jack's phrase of "our society."

"Who is to know that it wasn't a cross?" Jack continues. "The young one is to come first. He is to marry an heiress, and, when he has got her, up is to rise the elder brother! When did this elder brother show? Why, when the younger's scheme was blown, and all was up with him! Who shall tell me that the fellow hasn't been living in Seven Dials, or in a cellar dining off tripe and cow-heel until my younger gentleman was disposed of? Dammy, as gentlemen, I think we ought to take notice of it: and that this Mr. Warrington has been taking a most outrageous liberty with the whole club."

"Who put him up? It was March, I think, put him up?" asks a bystander.

"Yes. But my lord thought he was putting up a very different person. Didn't you, March?"

"Hold your confounded tongue, and mind your game!" says the nobleman addressed: but Jack Morris's opinion found not a few supporters in the world. Many persons agreed that it was most indecorous of Mr. Harry Warrington to have ever believed in his brother's death: that there was something suspicious about the young man's first appearance and subsequent actions, and, in fine, that regarding these foreigners, adventurers, and the like, we ought to be especially cautious.

Though he was out of prison and difficulty; though he had his aunt's liberal donation of money in his pocket; though his dearest brother was restored to him, whose return to life Harry never once thought of deploring, as his friends at White's supposed he would do; though Maria had shown herself in such a favourable light by her behaviour during his misfortune: yet Harry, when alone, felt himself not particularly cheerful, and smoked his pipe of Virginia with a troubled mind. It was not that he was deposed from his principality; the loss of it never once vexed him; he knew that his brother would share with him as he would have done with his brother; but after all those struggles and doubts in his own mind, to find himself poor, and yet irrevocably bound to his elderly cousin! Yes, she was elderly, there was no doubt about it. When she came to that horrible den in Cursitor Street and the tears washed her rouge off, why, she looked as old as his mother! her face was all wrinkled and yellow, and as he thought of her he felt just such a qualm as he had when she was taken ill that day in the coach on their road to Tunbridge. What would his mother say when he brought her home, and, Lord, what battles there would be between them! He would go and live on one of the plantations—the farther from home the better—and have a few negroes, and farm as best he might, and hunt a good deal; but at Castlewood or in her own home, such as he could make it for her, what a life for poor Maria, who had been used to go to court and to cards and balls and assemblies every night! If he could be but the overseer of the estates—oh, he would be an honest factor, and try and make up for his useless life and extravagance in these past days! Five thousand pounds, all his patrimony and the accumulations of his long minority squandered in six months! He a beggar, except for dear George's kindness, with nothing in life left to him but an old wife,—a pretty beggar, dressed out in velvet and silver lace forsooth—the poor lad was arrayed in his best clothes—a pretty figure he had made in Europe, and a nice end he was come to! With all his fine friends at White's and Newmarket, with all his extravagance, had he been happy a single day since he had been in Europe? Yes, three days, four days, yesterday evening, when he had been with dear dear Mrs. Lambert, and those affectionate kind girls, and that brave good Colonel. And the Colonel was right when he rebuked him for his spendthrift follies, and he had been a brute to be angry as he had been, and God bless them all for their generous exertions in his behalf! Such were the thoughts which Harry put into his pipe, and he smoked them whilst he waited his brother's return from Madame Bernstein.

CHAPTER LIV. During which Harry sits smoking his Pipe at Home

The maternal grandfather of our Virginians, the Colonel Esmond of whom frequent mention has been made, and who had quitted England to reside in the New World, had devoted some portion of his long American leisure to the composition of the memoirs of his early life. In these volumes, Madame de Bernstein (Mrs. Beatrice Esmond was her name as a spinster) played a very considerable part; and as George had read his grandfather's manuscript many times over, he had learned to know his kinswoman long before he saw her,— to know, at least, the lady, young, beautiful, and wilful, of half a century since, with whom he now became acquainted in the decline of her days. When cheeks are faded and eyes are dim, is it sad or pleasant, I wonder, for the woman who is a beauty no more, to recall the period of her bloom! When the heart is withered, do the old love to remember how it once was fresh and beat with warm emotions? When the spirits are languid and weary, do we like to think how bright they were in other days, the hope how buoyant, the sympathies how ready, the enjoyment of life how keen and eager? So they fall —the buds of prime, the roses of beauty, the florid harvests of summer,—fall and wither, and the naked branches shiver in the winter.

"And that was a beauty once!" thinks George Warrington, as his aunt, in her rouge and diamonds, comes in from her rout, "and that ruin was a splendid palace. Crowds of lovers have sighed before those decrepit feet, and been bewildered by the brightness of those eyes." He remembered a firework at home, at Williamsburg, on the King's birthday, and afterwards looking at the skeleton-wheel and the sockets of the exploded Roman candles. The dazzle and brilliancy of Aunt Beatrice's early career passed before him, as he thought over his grandsire's journals. Honest Harry had seen them, too, but Harry was no bookman, and had not read the manuscript very carefully: nay, if he had, he would probably not have reasoned about it as his brother did, being by no means so much inclined to moralising as his melancholy senior.

Mr. Warrington thought that there was no cause why he should tell his aunt how intimate he was with her early history, and accordingly held his peace upon that point. When their meal was over, she pointed with her cane to her escritoire, and bade her attendant bring the letter which lay under the inkstand there; and George, recognising the superscription, of course knew the letter to be that of which he had been the bearer from home.

"It would appear by this letter," said the old lady, looking hard at her nephew, "that ever since your return, there have been some differences between you and my sister."

"Indeed? I did not know that Madam Esmond had alluded to them," George said.

The Baroness puts a great pair of glasses upon eyes which shot fire and kindled who knows how many passions in old days, and, after glancing over the letter, hands it to George, who reads as follows:—

"RICHMOND, VIRGINIA, December 26th, 1756.

"HONOURED MADAM! AND SISTER!—I have received, and thankfully acknowledge, your ladyship's favour, per Rose packet, of October 23 ult.; and straightway answer you at a season which should be one of goodwill and peace to all men: but in which Heaven hath nevertheless decreed we should still bear our portion of earthly sorrow and trouble. My reply will be brought to you by my eldest son, Mr. Esmond Warrington, who returned to us so miraculously out of the Valley of the Shadow of Death (as our previous letters have informed my poor Henry), and who is desirous, not without my consent to his wish, to visit Europe, though he has been amongst us so short a while. I grieve to think that my dearest Harry should have appeared at home—I mean in England—under false colours, as it were; and should have been presented to his Majesty, to our family, and his own, as his father's heir, whilst my dear son George was still alive, though dead to us. Ah, madam! During the eighteen months of his captivity, what anguish have his mother's, his brother's, hearts undergone! My Harry's is the tenderest of any man's now alive. In the joy of seeing Mr. Esmond Warrington returned to life, he will forget the worldly misfortune which befalls him. He will return to (comparative) poverty without a pang. The most generous, the most obedient of human beings, of sons, he will gladly give up to his elder brother that inheritance which had been his own but for the accident of birth, and for the providential return of my son George.

"Your beneficent intentions towards dearest Harry will be more than ever welcome, now he is reduced to a younger brother's slender portion! Many years since, an advantageous opportunity occurred of providing for him in this province, and he would by this time have been master of a noble estate and negroes, and have been enabled to make a figure with most here, could his mother's wishes have been complied with, and his father's small portion, now lying at small interest in the British funds, have been invested in this most excellent purchase. But the forms of the law, and, I grieve to own, my elder son's scruples, prevailed, and this admirable opportunity was lost to me! Harry will find the savings of his income have been carefully accumulated—long, long may he live to enjoy them! May Heaven bless you, dear sister, for what your ladyship may add to his little store! As I gather from your letter, that the sum which has been allowed to him has not been sufficient for his expenses in the fine company which he has kept (and the grandson of the Marquis of Esmond—one who had so nearly been his lordship's heir—may sure claim equality with any other nobleman in Great Britain), and having a sum by me which I had always intended for the poor child's establishment, I entrust it to my eldest son, who, to do him justice, hath a most sincere regard for his brother, to lay it out for Harry's best advantage."

"It took him out of prison yesterday, madam. I think that was the best use to which we could put it," interposed George, at this stage of his mother's letter.

"Nay, sir, I don't know any such thing! Why not have kept it to buy a pair of colours for him, or to help towards another estate and some negroes, if he has a fancy for home?" cried the old lady. "Besides, I had a fancy to pay that debt myself."

"I hope you will let his brother do that. I ask leave to be my brother's banker in this matter, and consider I have borrowed so much from my mother, to be paid back to my dear Harry."

"Do you say so, sir? Give me a glass of wine! You are an extravagant fellow! Read on, and you will see your mother thinks so. I drink to your health, nephew George! 'Tis good Burgundy. Your grandfather never loved Burgundy. He loved claret, the little he drank."

And George proceeded with the letter:

"This remittance will, I trust, amply cover any expenses which, owing to the mistake respecting his position, dearest Harry may have incurred. I wish I could trust his elder brother's prudence as confidently as my Harry's! But I fear that, even in his captivity, Mr. Esmond W. has learned little of that humility which becomes all Christians, and which I have ever endeavoured to teach to my children. Should you by chance show him these lines, when, by the blessing of Heaven on those who go down to the sea in ships, the Great Ocean divides us! he will know that a fond mother's blessing and prayers follow both her children, and that there is no act I have ever done, no desire I have ever expressed (however little he may have been inclined to obey it!) but hath been dictated by the fondest wishes for my dearest boys' welfare."

"There is a scratch with a penknife, and a great blot upon the letter there, as if water had fallen on it. Your mother writes well, George. I suppose you and she had a difference?" said George's aunt, not unkindly.

"Yes, ma'am, many," answered the young man, sadly. "The last was about a question of money—of ransom which I promised to the old lieutenant of the fort who aided me to make my escape. I told you he had a mistress, a poor Indian woman, who helped me, and was kind to me. Six weeks after my arrival at home, the poor thing made her appearance at Richmond, having found her way through the wood by pretty much the same track which I had followed, and bringing me the token which Museau had promised to send me when he connived to my flight. A commanding officer and a considerable reinforcement had arrived at Duquesne. Charges, I don't know of what peculation (for his messenger could not express herself very clearly), had been brought against this Museau. He had been put under arrest, and had tried to escape; but, less fortunate than myself, he had been shot on the rampart, and he sent the Indian woman to me, with my grandfather's watch, and a line scrawled in his prison on his deathbed, begging me to send ce que je scavais to a notary at Havre de Grace in France to be transmitted to his relatives at Caen in Normandy. My friend Silverheels, the hunter, had helped my poor Indian on her way. I don't know how she would have escaped scalping else. But at home they received the poor thing sternly. They hardly gave her a welcome. I won't say what suspicions they had regarding her and me. The poor wretch fell to drinking whenever she could find means. I ordered that she should have food and shelter, and she became the jest of our negroes, and formed the subject of the scandal and tittle-tattle of the old fools in our little town. Our Governor was, luckily, a man of sense, and I made interest with him, and procured a pass to send her back to her people. Her very grief at parting with me only served to confirm the suspicions against her. A fellow preached against me from the pulpit, I believe; I had to treat another with a cane. And I had a violent dispute with Madam Esmond—a difference which is not healed yet—because I insisted upon paying to the heirs Museau pointed out the money I had promised for my deliverance. You see that scandal flourishes at the borders of the wilderness, and in the New World as well as the Old."

"I have suffered from it myself, my dear!" said Madame Bernstein, demurely. "Fill thy glass, child! A little tass of cherry-brandy! 'Twill do thee all the good in the world."

"As for my poor Harry's marriage," Madam Esmond's letter went on, "though I know too well, from sad experience, the dangers to which youth is subject, and would keep my boy, at any price, from them, though I should wish him to marry a person of rank, as becomes his birth, yet my Lady Maria Esmond is out of the question. Her age is almost the same as mine; and I know my brother Castlewood left his daughters with the very smallest portions. My Harry is so obedient that I know a desire from me will be sufficient to cause him to give up this imprudent match. Some foolish people once supposed that I myself once thought of a second union, and with a person of rank very different from ours. No! I knew what was due to my children. As succeeding to this estate after me, Mr. Esmond W. is amply provided for. Let my task now be to save for his less fortunate younger brother: and, as I do not love to live quite alone, let him return without delay to his fond and loving mother.

"The report which your ladyship hath given of my Harry fills my heart with warmest gratitude. He is all indeed a mother may wish. A year in Europe will have given him a polish and refinement which he could not acquire in our homely Virginia. Mr. Stack, one of our invaluable ministers in Richmond, hath a letter from Mr. Ward—my darlings' tutor of early days—who knows my Lady Warrington and her excellent family, and saith that my Harry has lived much with his cousins of late. I am grateful to think that my boy has the privilege of being with his good aunt. May he follow her counsels, and listen to those around him who will guide him on the way of his best welfare! Adieu, dear madam and sister! For your kindness to my boy accept the grateful thanks of a mother's heart. Though we have been divided hitherto, may these kindly ties draw us nearer and nearer. I am thankful that you should speak of my dearest father so. He was, indeed, one of the best of men! He, too, thanks you, I know, for the love you have borne to one of his children; and his daughter subscribes herself,—With sincere thanks, your ladyship's most dutiful and grateful sister and servant, RACHEL ESMOND WN.

"P.S.—I have communicated with my Lady Maria; but there will no need to tell her and dear Harry that his mother or your ladyship hope to be able to increase his small fortune. The match is altogether unsuitable."

"As far as regards myself, madam," George said, laying down the paper, "my mother's letter conveys no news to me. I always knew that Harry was the favourite son with Madam Esmond, as he deserves indeed to be. He has a hundred good qualities which I have not the good fortune to possess. He has better looks———"

"Nay, that is not your fault," said the old lady, slily looking at him; "and, but that he is fair and you are brown, one might almost pass for the other."

Mr. George bowed, and a faint blush tinged his pale cheek.

"His disposition is bright, and mine is dark," he continued; "Harry is cheerful, and I am otherwise, perhaps. He knows how to make himself beloved by every one, and it has been my lot to find but few friends."

"My sister and you have pretty little quarrels. There were such in old days in our family," the Baroness said; "and if Madam Esmond takes after our mother ———"

"My mother has always described hers as an angel upon earth," interposed George.

"Eh! That is a common character for people when they are dead!" cried the Baroness; "and Rachel Castlewood was an angel, if you like—at least your grandfather thought so. But let me tell you, sir, that angels are sometimes not very commodes a vivre. It may be they are too good to live with us sinners, and the air down below here don't agree with them. My poor mother was so perfect that she never could forgive me for being otherwise. Ah, mon Dieu! how she used to oppress me with those angelical airs!"

George cast down his eyes, and thought of his own melancholy youth. He did not care to submit more of his family secrets to the cynical inquisition of this old worldling, who seemed, however, to understand him in spite of his reticence.

"I quite comprehend you, sir, though you hold your tongue," the Baroness continued. "A sermon in the morning: a sermon at night: and two or three of a Sunday. That is what people call being good. Every pleasure cried fie upon; all us worldly people excommunicated; a ball an abomination of desolation; a play a forbidden pastime; and a game of cards perdition! What a life! Mon Dieu, what a life!"

"We played at cards every night, if we were so inclined," said George, smiling; "and my grandfather loved Shakspeare so much, that my mother had not a word to say against her father's favourite author."

"I remember. He could say whole pages by heart; though, for my part, I like Mr. Congreve a great deal better. And then, there was that dreadful, dreary Milton, whom he and Mr. Addison pretended to admire!" cried the old lady, tapping her fan.

"If your ladyship does not like Shakspeare, you will not quarrel with my mother for being indifferent to him, too," said George. "And indeed I think, and I am sure, that you don't do her justice. Wherever there are any poor she relieves them; wherever there are any sick she——"

"She doses them with her horrible purges and boluses!" cried the Baroness. "Of course, just as my mother did!"

"She does her best to cure them! She acts for the best, and performs her duty as far as she knows it."

"I don't blame you, sir, for doing yours, and keeping your own counsel about Madam Esmond," said the old lady. "But at least there is one point upon which we all three agree—that this absurd marriage must be prevented. Do you know how old the woman is? I can tell you, though she has torn the first leaf out of the family Bible at Castlewood."

"My mother has not forgotten her cousin's age, and is shocked at the disparity between her and my poor brother. Indeed, a city-bred lady of her time of life, accustomed to London gaiety and luxury, would find but a dismal home in our Virginian plantation. Besides, the house, such as it is, is not Harry's. He is welcome there, Heaven knows; more welcome, perhaps, than I, to whom the property comes in natural reversion; but, as I told him, I doubt how his wife would—would like our colony," George said, with a blush, and a hesitation in his sentence.

The old lady laughed shrilly. "He, he! nephew Warrington!" she said, "you need not scruple to speak your mind out. I shall tell no tales to your mother: though 'tis no news to me that she has a high temper, and loves her own way. Harry has held his tongue, too; but it needed no conjurer to see who was the mistress at home, and what sort of a life my sister led you. I love my niece, my Lady Molly, so well, that I could wish her two or three years of Virginia, with your mother reigning over her. You may well look alarmed, sir! Harry has said quite enough to show me who governs the family."

"Madam," said George, smiling, "I may say as much as this, that I don't envy any woman coming into our house against my mother's will: and my poor brother knows this perfectly well."

"What? You two have talked the matter over? No doubt you have. And the foolish child considers himself bound in honour—of course he does, the gaby!"

"He says Lady Maria has behaved most nobly to him. When he was sent to prison, she brought him her trinkets and jewels, and every guinea she had in the world. This behaviour has touched him so, that he feels more deeply than ever bound to her ladyship. But I own my brother seems bound by honour rather than love—such at least is his present feeling."

"My good creature," cries Madame Bernstein, "don't you see that Maria brings a few twopenny trinkets and a half-dozen guineas to Mr. Esmond, the heir of the great estate in Virginia,—not to the second son, who is a beggar, and has just squandered away every shilling of his fortune? I swear to you, on my credit as a gentlewoman, that, knowing Harry's obstinacy, and the misery he had in store for himself, I tried to bribe Maria to give up her engagement with him, and only failed because I could not bribe high enough! When he was in prison, I sent my lawyer to him, with orders to pay his debts immediately, if he would but part from her, but Maria had been beforehand with us, and Mr. Harry chose not to go back from his stupid word. Let me tell you what has passed in the last month!" And here the old lady narrated at length the history which we know already, but in that cynical language which was common in her times, when the finest folks and the most delicate ladies called things and people by names which we never utter in good company nowadays. And so much the better on the whole. We mayn't be more virtuous, but it is something to be more decent: perhaps we are not more pure, but of a surety we are more cleanly.

Madame Bernstein talked so much, so long, and so cleverly, that she was quite pleased with herself and her listener; and when she put herself into the hands of Mrs. Brett to retire for the night, informed the waiting-maid that she had changed her opinion about her eldest nephew, and that Mr. George was handsome, that he was certainly much wittier than poor Harry (whom Heaven, it must be confessed, had not furnished with a very great supply of brains), and that he had quite the bel air—a something melancholy—a noble and distinguished je ne scais quoy—which reminded her of the Colonel. Had she ever told Brett about the Colonel? Scores of times, no doubt. And now she told Brett about the Colonel once more. Meanwhile, perhaps, her new favourite was not quite so well pleased with her as she was with him. What a strange picture of life and manners had the old lady unveiled to her nephew! How she railed at all the world round about her! How unconsciously did she paint her own family—her own self; how selfish, one and all; pursuing what mean ends; grasping and scrambling frantically for what petty prizes; ambitious for what shabby recompenses; trampling—from life's beginning to its close—through what scenes of stale dissipations and faded pleasures! "Are these the inheritors of noble blood?" thought George, as he went home quite late from his aunt's house, passing by doors whence the last guests of fashion were issuing, and where the chairmen were yawning over their expiring torches. "Are these the proud possessors of ancestral honours and ancient names, and were their forefathers, when in life, no better? We have our pedigree at home with noble coats-of-arms emblazoned all over the branches, and titles dating back before the Conquest and the Crusaders. When a knight of old found a friend in want, did he turn his back upon him, or an unprotected damsel, did he delude her and leave her? When a nobleman of the early time received a young kinsman, did he get the better of him at dice, and did the ancient chivalry cheat in horseflesh? Can it be that this wily woman of the world, as my aunt has represented, has inveigled my poor Harry into an engagement, that her tears are false, and that as soon as she finds him poor she will desert him? Had we not best pack the trunks and take a cabin in the next ship bound for home?" George reached his own door revolving these thoughts, and Gumbo came up yawning with a candle, and Harry was asleep before the extinguished fire, with the ashes of his emptied pipe on the table beside him.

He starts up; his eyes, for a moment dulled by sleep, lighten with pleasure as he sees his dear George. He puts his arm round his brother with a boyish laugh.

"There he is in flesh and blood, thank God!" he says; "I was dreaming of thee but now, George, and that Ward was hearing us our lesson! Dost thou remember the ruler, Georgy? Why, bless my soul, 'tis three o'clock! Where have you been a-gadding, Mr. George? Hast thou supped? I supped at White's, but I'm hungry again. I did not play, sir,—no, no; no more of that for younger brothers! And my Lord March paid me fifty he lost to me. I bet against his horse and on the Duke of Hamilton's! They both rode the match at Newmarket this morning, and he lost because he was under weight. And he paid me, and he was as sulky as a bear. Let us have one pipe, Georgy!—just one."

And after the smoke the young men went to bed, where I, for one, wish them a pleasant rest, for sure it is a good and pleasant thing to see brethren who love one another.

CHAPTER LV. Between Brothers

Of course our young men had had their private talk about home, and all the people and doings there, and each had imparted to the other full particulars of his history since their last meeting. How were Harry's dogs, and little Dempster, and good old Nathan, and the rest of the household? Was Mountain well, and Fanny grown to be a pretty girl? So Parson Broadbent's daughter was engaged to marry Tom Barker of Savannah, and they were to go and live in Georgia! Harry owns that at one period he was very sweet upon Parson Broadbent's daughter, and lost a great deal of pocket-money at cards, and drank a great quantity of strong-waters with the father, in order to have a pretext for being near the girl. But, Heaven help us! Madam Esmond would never have consented to his throwing himself away upon Polly Broadbent. So Colonel G. Washington's wife was a pretty woman, very good-natured and pleasant, and with a good fortune? He had brought her into Richmond, and paid a visit of state to Madam Esmond. George described, with much humour, the awful ceremonials at the interview between these two personages, and the killing politeness of his mother to Mr. Washington's young wife. "Never mind, George, my dear!" says Mrs. Mountain. "The Colonel has taken another wife, but I feel certain that at one time two young gentlemen I know of ran a very near chance of having a tall stepfather six feet two in his boots." To be sure, Mountain was for ever match-making in her mind. Two people could not play a game at cards together, or sit down to a dish of tea, but she fancied their conjunction was for life. It was she—the foolish tattler—who had set the report abroad regarding the poor Indian woman. As for Madam Esmond, she had repelled the insinuation with scorn when Parson Stack brought it to her, and said, "I should as soon fancy Mr. Esmond stealing the spoons, or marrying a negro woman out of the kitchen." But, though she disdained to find the poor Biche guilty, and even thanked her for attending her son in his illness, she treated her with such a chilling haughtiness of demeanour, that the Indian slunk away into the servants' quarters, and there tried to drown her disappointments with drink. It was not a cheerful picture that which George gave of his two months at home. "The birthright is mine, Harry," he said, "but thou art the favourite, and God help me! I think my mother almost grudges it to me. Why should I have taken the pas, and preceded your worship into the world? Had you been the elder, you would have had the best cellar, and ridden the best nag, and been the most popular man in the country, whereas I have not a word to say for myself, and frighten people by my glum face: I should have been second son, and set up as lawyer, or come to England and got my degrees, and turned parson, and said grace at your honour's table. The time is out of joint, sir. O cursed spite, that ever I was born to set it right!"

"Why, Georgy, you are talking verses, I protest you are!" says Harry.

"I think, my dear, some one else talked those verses before me," says George, with a smile.

"It's out of one of your books. You know every book that ever was wrote, that I do believe!" cries Harry, and then told his brother how he had seen the two authors at Tunbridge, and how he had taken off his hat to them. "Not that I cared much about their books, not being clever enough. But I remembered how my dear old George used to speak of 'em," says Harry, with a choke in his voice, "and that's why I liked to see them. I say, dear, it's like a dream seeing you over again. Think of that bloody Indian with his knife at my George's head! I should like to give that Monsieur de Florac something for saving you—but I haven't got much now, only my little gold knee-buckles, and they ain't worth two guineas."

"You have got the half of what I have, child, and we'll divide as soon as I have paid the Frenchman," George said.

On which Harry broke out not merely into blessings but actual imprecations, indicating his intense love and satisfaction; and he swore that there never was such a brother in the world as his brother George. Indeed, for some days after his brother's arrival his eyes followed George about: he would lay down his knife and fork, or his newspaper, when they were sitting together, and begin to laugh to himself. When he walked with George on the Mall or in Hyde Park, he would gaze round at the company, as much as to say, "Look here, gentlemen! This is he. This is my brother, that was dead and is alive again! Can any man in Christendom produce such a brother as this?"

Of course he was of opinion that George should pay to Museau's heirs the sum which he had promised for his ransom. This question had been the cause of no small unhappiness to poor George at home. Museau dead, Madam Esmond argued with much eagerness, and not a little rancour, the bargain fell to the ground, and her son was free. The man was a rogue in the first instance. She would not pay the wages of iniquity. Mr. Esmond had a small independence from his father, and might squander his patrimony if he chose. He was of age, and the money was in his power; but she would be no party to such extravagance, as giving twelve thousand livres to a parcel of peasants in Normandy with whom we were at war, and who would very likely give it all to the priests and the pope. She would not subscribe to any such wickedness. If George wanted to squander away his father's money (she must say that formerly he had not been so eager, and when Harry's benefit was in question had refused to touch a penny of it!)—if he wished to spend it now, why not give it to his own flesh and blood, to poor Harry, who was suddenly deprived of his inheritance, and not to a set of priest-ridden peasants in France? This dispute had raged between mother and son during the whole of the latter's last days in Virginia. It had never been settled. On the morning of George's departure, Madam Esmond had come to his bedside after a sleepless night, and asked him whether he still persisted in his intention to fling away his father's property?

He replied in a depth of grief and perplexity, that his word was passed, and he must do as his honour bade him. She answered that she would continue to pray that Heaven might soften his proud heart, and enable her to bear her heavy trials: and the last view George had of his mother's face was as she stood yet a moment by his bedside, pale and with tearless eyes, before she turned away and slowly left his chamber.

"Where didst thou learn the art of winning over everybody to thy side, Harry?" continued George; "and how is it that you and all the world begin by being friends? Teach me a few lessons in popularity, nay, I don't know that I will have them; and when I find and hear certain people hate me, I think I am rather pleased than angry. At first, at Richmond, Mr. Esmond Warrington, the only prisoner who had escaped from Braddock's field—the victim of so much illness and hardship—was a favourite with the town-folks, and received privately and publicly with no little kindness. The parson glorified my escape in a sermon; the neighbours came to visit the fugitive; the family coach was ordered out, and Madam Esmond and I paid our visits in return. I think some pretty little caps were set at me. But these our mother routed off, and frightened with the prodigious haughtiness of her demeanour; and my popularity was already at the decrease before the event occurred which put the last finishing stroke to it. I was not jolly enough for the officers, and didn't care for their drinking-bouts, dice-boxes, and swearing. I was too sarcastic for the ladies, and their tea and tattle stupefied me almost as much as the men's blustering and horse-talk. I cannot tell thee, Harry, how lonely I felt in that place, amidst the scandal and squabbles: I regretted my prison almost, and found myself more than once wishing for the freedom of thought, and the silent ease of Duquesne. I am very shy, I suppose: I can speak unreservedly to very few people. Before most, I sit utterly silent. When we two were at home, it was thou who used to talk at table, and get a smile now and then from our mother. When she and I were together we had no subject in common, and we scarce spoke at all until we began to dispute about law and divinity.

"So the gentlemen had determined I was supercilious, and a dull companion (and, indeed, I think their opinion was right), and the ladies thought I was cold and sarcastic,—could never make out whether I was in earnest or no, and, I think, generally voted I was a disagreeable fellow, before my character was gone quite away; and that went with the appearance of the poor Biche. Oh, a nice character they made for me, my dear!" cried George, in a transport of wrath, "and a pretty life they led me after Museau's unlucky messenger had appeared amongst us! The boys hooted the poor woman if she appeared in the street; the ladies dropped me half-curtseys, and walked over to the other side. That precious clergyman went from one tea-table to another preaching on the horrors of seduction, and the lax principles which young men learned in popish countries and brought back thence. The poor Fawn's appearance at home a few weeks after my return home, was declared to be a scheme between her and me; and the best informed agreed that she had waited on the other side of the river until I gave her the signal to come and join me in Richmond. The officers bantered me at the coffee-house, and cracked their clumsy jokes about the woman I had selected. Oh, the world is a nice charitable world! I was so enraged that I thought of going to Castlewood and living alone there,—for our mother finds the place dull, and the greatest consolation in precious Mr. Stack's ministry,—when the news arrived of your female perplexity, and I think we were all glad that I should have a pretext for coming to Europe."

"I should like to see any of the infernal scoundrels who said word against you, and break their rascally bones," roars out Harry, striding up and down the room.

"I had to do something like it for Bob Clubber."

"What! that little sneaking, backbiting, toad-eating wretch, who is always hanging about my lord at Greenway Court, and spunging on every gentleman in the country? If you whipped him, I hope you whipped him well, George?"

"We were bound over to keep the peace; and I offered to go into Maryland with him and settle our difference there, and of course the good folk said, that having made free with the seventh commandment I was inclined to break the sixth. So, by this and by that—and being as innocent of the crime imputed to me as you are—I left home, my dear Harry, with as awful a reputation as ever a young gentleman earned."

Ah, what an opportunity is there here to moralise! If the esteemed reader and his humble servant could but know—could but write down in a book—could but publish, with illustrations, a collection of the lies which have been told regarding each of us since we came to man's estate,—what a harrowing and thrilling work of fiction that romance would be! Not only is the world informed of everything about you, but of a great deal more. Not long since the kind postman brought a paper containing a valuable piece of criticism, which stated—"This author states he was born in such and such a year. It is a lie. He was born in the year so and so." The critic knew better: of course he did. Another (and both came from the country which gave MULLIGAN birth) warned some friend, saying, "Don't speak of New South Wales to him. He has a brother there, and the family never mention his name." But this subject is too vast and noble for a mere paragraph. I shall prepare a memoir, or let us have rather, par une societe de gens de lettres, a series of biographies, of lives of gentlemen, as told by their dear friends whom they don't know.

George having related his exploits as champion and martyr, of course Harry had to unbosom himself to his brother, and lay before his elder an account of his private affairs. He gave up all the family of Castlewood—my lord, not for getting the better of him at play; for Harry was a sporting man, and expected to pay when he lost, and receive when he won; but for refusing to aid the chaplain in his necessity, and dismissing him with such false and heartless pretexts. About Mr. Will he had made up his mind, after the horse-dealing matter, and freely marked his sense of the latter's conduct upon Mr. Will's eyes and nose. Respecting the Countess and Lady Fanny, Harry spoke in a manner more guarded, but not very favourable. He had heard all sorts of stories about them. The Countess was a card-playing old cat; Lady Fanny was a desperate flirt. Who told him? Well, he had heard the stories from a person who knew them both very well indeed. In fact, in those days of confidence, of which we made mention in the last volume, Maria had freely imparted to her cousin a number of anecdotes respecting her stepmother and her half-sister, which were by no means in favour of those ladies.

But in respect to Lady Maria herself, the young man was staunch and hearty. "It may be imprudent: I don't say no, George. I may be a fool: I think I am. I know there will be a dreadful piece of work at home, and that Madam and she will fight. Well! we must live apart. Our estate is big enough to live on without quarrelling, and I can go elsewhere than to Richmond or Castlewood. When you come to the property, you'll give me a bit—at any rate, Madam will let me off at an easy rent—or I'll make a famous farmer or factor. I can't and won't part from Maria. She has acted so nobly by me, that I should be a rascal to turn my back on her. Think of her bringing me every jewel she had in the world, dear brave creature! and flinging them into my lap with her last guineas, —and—and—God bless her!" Here Harry dashed his sleeve across his eyes, with a stamp of his foot, and said, "No, brother, I won't part with her—not to be made Governor of Virginia tomorrow; and my dearest old George would never advise me to do so, I know that."

"I am sent here to advise you," George replied. "I am sent to break the marriage off, if I can: and a more unhappy one I can't imagine. But I can't counsel you to break your word, my boy."

"I knew you couldn't! What's said is said, George. I have made my bed, and must lie on it," says Mr. Harry, gloomily.

Such had been the settlement between our two young worthies, when they first talked over Mr. Harry's love affair. But after George's conversation with his aunt, and the further knowledge of his family, which he acquired through the information of that keen old woman of the world, Mr. Warrington, who was naturally of a sceptical turn, began to doubt about Lady Maria, as well as regarding her brothers and sister, and looked at Harry's engagement with increased distrust and alarm. Was it for his wealth that Maria wanted Harry? Was it his handsome young person that she longed after? Were those stories true which Aunt Bernstein had told of her? Certainly he could not advise Harry to break his word; but he might cast about in his mind for some scheme for putting Maria's affection to the trial; and his ensuing conduct, which appeared not very amiable, I suppose resulted from this deliberation.

CHAPTER LVI. Ariadne

My Lord Castlewood had a house in Kensington Square spacious enough to accommodate the several members of his noble family, and convenient for their service at the palace hard by, when his Majesty dwelt there. Her ladyship had her evenings, and gave her card-parties here for such as would come; but Kensington was a long way from London a hundred years since, and George Selwyn said he for one was afraid to go, for fear of being robbed of a night,— whether by footpads with crape over their faces, or by ladies in rouge at the quadrille-table, we have no means of saying. About noon on the day after Harry had made his reappearance at White's, it chanced that all his virtuous kinsfolks partook of breakfast together, even Mr. Will being present, who was to go into waiting in the afternoon.

The ladies came first to their chocolate: them Mr. Will joined in his court suit; finally, my lord appeared, languid, in his bedgown and nightcap, having not yet assumed his wig for the day. Here was news which Will had brought home from the Star and Garter last night, when he supped in company with some men who had heard it at White's and seen it at Ranelagh!

"Heard what? seen what?" asked the head of the house, taking up his Daily Advertiser.

"Ask Maria!" says Lady Fanny. My lord turns to his elder sister, who wears a face of portentous sadness, and looks as pale as a tablecloth.

"'Tis one of Will's usual elegant and polite inventions," says Maria.

"No," swore Will, with several of his oaths; "it was no invention of his. Tom Claypool of Norfolk saw 'em both at Ranelagh; and Jack Morris came out of White's, where he heard the story from Harry Warrington's own lips. Curse him, I'm glad of it!" roars Will, slapping the table. "What do you think of your Fortunate Youth, your Virginian, whom your lordship made so much of, turning out to be a second son?"

"The elder brother not dead?" says my lord.

"No more dead than you are. Never was. It's my belief that it was a cross between the two."

"Mr. Warrington is incapable of such duplicity!" cries Maria.

"I never encouraged the fellow, I am sure you will do me justice there," says my lady. "Nor did Fanny: not we, indeed!"

"Not we, indeed!" echoes my Lady Fanny.

"The fellow is only a beggar, and, I dare say, has not paid for the clothes on his back," continues Will. "I'm glad of it, for, hang him, I hate him!"

"You don't regard him with favourable eyes; especially since he blacked yours, Will!" grins my lord. "So the poor fellow has found his brother, and lost his estate!" And here he turned towards his sister Maria, who, although she looked the picture of woe, must have suggested something ludicrous to the humourist near whom she sate; for his lordship, having gazed at her for a minute, burst into a shrill laugh, which caused the poor lady's face to flush, and presently her eyes to pour over with tears. "It's a shame! it's a shame!" she sobbed out, and hid her face in her handkerchief. Maria's stepmother and sister looked at each other. "We never quite understand your lordship's humour," the former lady remarked, gravely.

"I don't see there is the least reason why you should," said my lord, coolly. "Maria, my dear, pray excuse me if I have said—that is, done anything, to hurt your feelings."

"Done anything! You pillaged the poor lad in his prosperity, and laugh at him in his ruin!" says Maria, rising from table, and glaring round at all her family.

"Excuse me, my dear sister, I was not laughing at him," said my lord, gently.

"Oh, never mind at what or whom else, my lord! You have taken from him all he had to lose. All the world points at you as the man who feeds on his own flesh and blood. And now you have his all, you make merry over his misfortune!" And away she rustled from the room, flinging looks of defiance at all the party there assembled.

"'Tell us what has happened, or what you have heard, Will, and my sister's grief will not interrupt us." And Will told, at great length, and with immense exultation at Harry's discomfiture, the story now buzzed through all London, of George Warrington's sudden apparition. Lord Castlewood was sorry for Harry: Harry was a good, brave lad, and his kinsman liked him, as much as certain worldly folks like each other. To be sure he played Harry at cards, and took the advantage of the market upon him; but why not? The peach which other men would certainly pluck, he might as well devour. Eh! if that were all my conscience had to reproach me with, I need not be very uneasy! my lord thought. "Where does Mr. Warrington live?"

Will expressed himself ready to enter upon a state of reprobation if he knew or cared.

"He shall be invited here, and treated with every respect," said my lord.

"Including piquet, I suppose!" growls Will.

"Or will you take him to the stables, and sell him one of your bargains of horseflesh, Will?" asks Lord Castlewood. "You would have won of Harry Warrington fast enough, if you could; but you cheat so clumsily at your game that you got paid with a cudgel. I desire, once more, that every attention may be paid to our cousin Warrington."

"And that you are not to be disturbed, when you sit down to play, of course, my lord!" cries Lady Castlewood.

"Madam, I desire fair play, for Mr. Warrington, and for myself, and for every member of this amiable family," retorted Lord Castlewood, fiercely.

"Heaven help the poor gentleman if your lordship is going to be kind to him," said the stepmother, with a curtsey; and there is no knowing how far this family dispute might have been carried, had not, at this moment, a phaeton driven up to the house, in which were seated the two young Virginians.

It was the carriage which our young Prodigal had purchased in the days of his prosperity. He drove it still: George sate in it by his side; their negroes were behind them. Harry had been for meekly giving the whip and reins to his brother, and ceding the whole property to him. "What business has a poor devil like me with horses and carriages, Georgy?" Harry had humbly said. "Beyond the coat on my back, and the purse my aunt gave me, I have nothing in the world. You take the driving-seat, brother; it will ease my mind if you will take the driving-seat." George laughingly said he did not know the way, and Harry did; and that, as for the carriage, he would claim only a half of it, as he had already done with his brother's wardrobe. "But a bargain is a bargain; if I share thy coats, thou must divide my breeches' pocket, Harry; that is but fair dealing!" Again and again Harry swore there never was such a brother on earth. How he rattled his horses over the road! How pleased and proud he was to drive such a brother! They came to Kensington in famous high spirits; and Gumbo's thunder upon Lord Castlewood's door was worthy of the biggest footman in all St. James's.

Only my Lady Castlewood and her daughter Lady Fanny were in the room into which our young gentlemen were ushered. Will had no particular fancy to face Harry, my lord was not dressed, Maria had her reasons for being away, at least till her eyes were dried. When we drive up to friends' houses nowadays in our coaches-and-six, when John carries up our noble names, when, finally, we enter the drawing-room with our best hat and best Sunday smile foremost, does it ever happen that we interrupt a family row! that we come simpering and smiling in, and stepping over the delusive ashes of a still burning domestic heat? that in the interval between the hall-door and the drawing-room, Mrs., Mr., and the Misses Jones have grouped themselves in a family tableau; this girl artlessly arranging flowers in a vase, let us say; that one reclining over an illuminated work of devotion; mamma on the sofa, with the butcher's and grocer's book pushed under the cushion, some elegant work in her hand, and a pretty little foot pushed out advantageously; while honest Jones, far from saying, "Curse that Brown, he is always calling here!" holds out a kindly hand, shows a pleased face, and exclaims, "What, Brown my boy, delighted to see you! Hope you've come to lunch!" I say, does it ever happen to us to be made the victims of domestic artifices, the spectators of domestic comedies got up for our special amusement? Oh, let us be thankful, not only for faces, but for masks! not only for honest welcome, but for hypocrisy, which hides unwelcome things from us! Whilst I am talking, for instance, in this easy, chatty way, what right have you, my good sir, to know what is really passing in my mind? It may be that I am racked with gout, or that my eldest son has just sent me in a thousand pounds' worth of college-bills, or that I am writhing under an attack of the Stoke Pogis Sentinel, which has just been sent me under cover, or that there is a dreadfully scrappy dinner, the evident remains of a party to which I didn't invite you, and yet I conceal my agony, I wear a merry smile; I say, "What! come to take pot-luck with us, Brown my boy! Betsy! put a knife and fork for Mr. Brown. Eat! Welcome! Fall to! It's my best!" I say that humbug which I am performing is beautiful self-denial—that hypocrisy is true virtue. Oh, if every man spoke his mind what an intolerable society ours would be to live in!

As the young gentlemen are announced, Lady Castlewood advances towards them with perfect ease and good-humour. "We have heard, Harry," she says, looking at the latter with a special friendliness, "of this most extraordinary circumstance. My Lord Castlewood said at breakfast that he should wait on you this very day, Mr. Warrington, and, cousin Harry, we intend not to love you any the less because you are poor."

"We shall be able to show now that it is not for your acres that we like you, Harry!" says Lady Fanny, following her mamma's lead.

"And I to whom the acres have fallen?" says Mr. George, with a smile and a bow.

"Oh, cousin, we shall like you for being like Harry!" replies the arch Lady Fanny.

Ah! who that has seen the world, has not admired that astonishing ease with which fine ladies drop you and pick you up again? Both the ladies now addressed themselves almost exclusively to the younger brother. They were quite civil to Mr. George: but with Mr. Harry they were fond, they were softly familiar, they were gently kind, they were affectionately reproachful. Why had Harry not been for days and days to see them?

"Better to have had a dish of tea and a game at piquet with them than with some other folks," says Lady Castlewood. "If we had won enough to buy a paper of pins from you we should have been content; but young gentlemen don't know what is for their own good," says mamma.

"Now you have no more money to play with, you can come and play with us, cousin!" cries fond Lady Fanny, lifting up a finger, "and so your misfortune will be good fortune to us."

George was puzzled. This welcome of his brother was very different from that to which he had looked. All these compliments and attentions paid to the younger brother, though he was without a guinea! Perhaps the people were not so bad as they were painted? The Blackest of all Blacks is said not to be of quite so dark a complexion as some folks describe him.

This affectionate conversation continued for some twenty minutes, at the end of which period my Lord Castlewood made his appearance, wig on head, and sword by side. He greeted both the young men with much politeness: one not more than the other. "If you were to come to us—and I, for one, cordially rejoice to see you—what a pity it is you did not come a few months earlier! A certain evening at piquet would then most likely never have taken place. A younger son would have been more prudent."

"Yes, indeed," said Harry.

"Or a kinsman more compassionate. But I fear that love of play runs in the blood of all of us. I have it from my father, and it has made me the poorest peer in England. Those fair ladies whom you see before you are not exempt. My poor brother Will is a martyr to it; and what I, for my part, win on one day, I lose on the next. 'Tis shocking, positively, the rage for play in England. All my poor cousin's bank-notes parted company from me within twenty-four hours after I got them."

"I have played, like other gentlemen, but never to hurt myself, and never indeed caring much for the sport," remarked Mr. Warrington.

"When we heard that my lord had played with Harry, we did so scold him," cried the ladies.

"But if it had not been I, thou knowest, cousin Warrington, some other person would have had thy money. 'Tis a poor consolation, but as such Harry must please to take it, and be glad that friends won his money, who wish him well, not strangers, who cared nothing for him, and fleeced him."

"Eh! a tooth out is a tooth out, though it be your brother who pulls it, my lord!" said Mr. George, laughing. "Harry must bear the penalty of his faults, and pay his debts, like other men."

"I am sure I have never said or thought otherwise. 'Tis not like an Englishman to be sulky because he is beaten," says Harry.

"Your hand, cousin! You speak like a man!" cries my lord, with delight. The ladies smiled to each other.

"My sister, in Virginia, has known how to bring up her sons as gentlemen!"

exclaims Lady Castlewood, enthusiastically.

"I protest you must not be growing so amiable now you are poor, cousin Harry!" cries cousin Fanny. "Why, mamma, we did not know half his good qualities when he was only Fortunate Youth and Prince of Virginia! You are exactly like him, cousin George, but I vow you can't be as amiable as your brother!"

"I am the Prince of Virginia, but I fear I am not the Fortunate Youth," said George, gravely.

Harry was beginning, "By Jove, he is the best——" when the noise of a harpsichord was heard from the upper room. The lad blushed: the ladies smiled.

"'Tis Maria, above," said Lady Castlewood. "Let some of us go up to her."

The ladies rose, and made way towards the door; and Harry followed them, blushing very much. George was about to join the party, but Lord Castlewood checked him. "Nay, if all the ladies follow your brother" his lordship said, "let me at least have the benefit of your company and conversation. I long to hear the account of your captivity and rescue, cousin George!"

"Oh, we must hear that too!" cried one of the ladies, lingering.

"I am greedy, and should like it all by myself," said Lord Castlewood, looking at her very sternly; and followed the women to the door, and closed it upon them with a low bow.

"Your brother has no doubt acquainted you with the history of all that has happened to him in this house, cousin George?" asked George's kinsman.

"Yes, including the quarrel with Mr. Will and the engagement to my Lady Maria," replies George, with a bow. "I may be pardoned for saying that he hath met with but ill fortune here, my lord."

"Which no one can deplore more cordially than myself. My brother lives with horse jockeys and trainers, and the wildest bloods of the town, and between us there is very little sympathy. We should not all live together, were we not so poor. This is the house which our grandmother occupied before she went to America and married Colonel Esmond. Much of the furniture belonged to her." George looked round the wainscoted parlour with some interest. "Our house has not flourished in the last twenty years; though we had a promotion of rank a score of years since, owing to some interest we had at court, then. But the malady of play has been the ruin of us all. I am a miserable victim to it: only too proud to sell myself and title to a roturiere, as many noblemen, less scrupulous, have done. Pride is my fault, my dear cousin. I remember how I was born!" And his lordship laid his hand on his shirt-frill, turned out his toe, and looked his cousin nobly in the face.

Young George Warrington's natural disposition was to believe everything which everybody said to him. When once deceived, however, or undeceived about the character of a person, he became utterly incredulous, and he saluted this fine speech of my lord's with a sardonical, inward laughter, preserving his gravity, however, and scarce allowing any of his scorn to appear in his words.

"We have all our faults, my lord. That of play hath been condoned over and

370

over again in gentlemen of our rank. Having heartily forgiven my brother, surely I cannot presume to be your lordship's judge in the matter; and instead of playing and losing, I wish sincerely that you had both played and won!"

"So do I, with all my heart!" says my lord with a sigh. "I augur well for your goodness when you can speak in this way, and for your experience and knowledge of the world, too, cousin, of which you seem to possess a greater share than most young men of your age. Your poor Harry hath the best heart in the world; but I doubt whether his head be very strong."

"Not very strong, indeed. But he hath the art to make friends wherever he goes, and in spite of all his imprudences most people love him."

"I do—we all do, I'm sure! as if he were our brother!" cries my lord.

"He has often described in his letters his welcome at your lordship's house. My mother keeps them all, you may be sure. Harry's style is not very learned, but his heart is so good, that to read him is better than wit."

"I may be mistaken, but I fancy his brother possesses a good heart and a good wit, too!" says my lord, obstinately gracious.

"I am as Heaven made me, cousin; and perhaps some more experience and sorrow than has fallen to the lot of most young men."

"This misfortune of your poor brother—I mean this piece of good fortune, your sudden reappearance—has not quite left Harry without resources?" continued Lord Castlewood, very gently.

"With nothing but what his mother can leave him, or I, at her death, can spare him. What is the usual portion here of a younger brother, my lord?"

"Eh! a younger brother here is—you know—in fine, everybody knows what a younger brother is," said my lord, and shrugged his shoulders and looked his guest in the face.

The other went on: "We are the best of friends, but we are flesh and blood: and I don't pretend to do more for him than is usually done for younger brothers. Why give him money? That he should squander it at cards or horse-racing? My lord, we have cards and jockeys in Virginia, too; and my poor Harry hath distinguished himself in his own country already, before he came to yours. He inherits the family failing for dissipation."

"Poor fellow, poor fellow, I pity him!"

"Our estate, you see, is great, but our income is small. We have little more money than that which we get from England for our tobacco—and very little of that too—for our tobacco comes back to us in the shape of goods, clothes, leather, groceries, ironmongery, nay, wine and beer for our people and ourselves. Harry may come back and share all these: there is a nag in the stable for him, a piece of venison on the table, a little ready money to keep his pocket warm, and a coat or two every year. This will go on whilst my mother lives, unless, which is far from improbable, he gets into some quarrel with Madam Esmond. Then, whilst I live he will have the run of the house and all it contains: then, if I die leaving children, he will be less and less welcome. His future, my lord, is a dismal one, unless some strange piece of luck turn up on which we were fools to speculate. Henceforth he is doomed to dependence, and I know no worse lot than to be dependent on a self-willed woman like our mother. The means he had to make himself respected at home he hath squandered away here. He has flung his patrimony to the dogs, and poverty and subserviency are now his only portion." Mr. Warrington delivered this speech with considerable spirit and volubility, and his cousin heard him respectfully.

"You speak well, Mr. Warrington. Have you ever thought of public life?" said my lord.

"Of course I have thought of public life like every man of my station—every man, that is, who cares for something beyond a dice-box or a stable," replies George. "I hope, my lord, to be able to take my own place, and my unlucky brother must content himself with his. This I say advisedly, having heard from him of certain engagements which he has formed, and which it would be misery to all parties were he to attempt to execute now."

"Your logic is very strong," said my lord. "Shall we go up and see the ladies? There is a picture above-stairs which your grandfather is said to have executed. Before you go, my dear cousin, you will please to fix a day when our family may have the honour of receiving you. Castlewood, you know, is always your home when we are there. It is something like your Virginian Castlewood, cousin, from your account. We have beef, and mutton, and ale, and wood, in plenty; but money is woefully scarce amongst us."

They ascended to the drawing-room, where, however, they found only one of the ladies of the family. This was my Lady Maria, who came out of the embrasure of a window, where she and Harry Warrington had been engaged in talk.

George made his best bow, Maria her lowest curtsey. "You are indeed wonderfully like your brother," she said, giving him her hand. "And from what he says, cousin George, I think you are as good as he is."

At the sight of her swollen eyes and tearful face George felt a pang of remorse. "Poor thing!" he thought. "Harry has been vaunting my generosity and virtue to her, and I have beer, playing the selfish elder brother downstairs! How old she looks! How could he ever have a passion for such a woman as that?" How? Because he did not see with your eyes, Mr. George. He saw rightly too now with his own, perhaps. I never know whether to pity or congratulate a man on coming to his senses.

After the introduction a little talk took place, which for a while Lady Maria managed to carry on in an easy manner: but though ladies in this matter of social hypocrisy are, I think, far more consummate performers than men, after a sentence or two the poor lady broke out into a sob, and, motioning Harry away with her hand, fairly fled from the room.

Harry was rushing forward, but stopped—checked by that sign. My lord said his poor sister was subject to these fits of nerves, and had already been ill that morning. After this event our young gentlemen thought it was needless to prolong their visit. Lord Castlewood followed them downstairs, accompanied them to the door, admired their nags in the phaeton, and waved them a friendly farewell.

"And so we have been coaxing and cuddling in the window, and we part good friends, Harry? Is it not so?" says George to his charioteer.

"Oh, she is a good woman!" cries Harry, lashing the horses. "I know you'll think so when you come to know her."

"When you take her home to Virginia? A pretty welcome our mother will give her. She will never forgive me for not breaking the match off, nor you for making it."

"I can't help it, George! Don't you be popping your ugly head so close to my ears, Gumbo! After what has passed between us, I am bound in honour to stand by her. If she sees no objection, I must find none. I told her all. I told her that Madam would be very rusty at first; but that she was very fond of me, and must end by relenting. And when you come to the property, I told her that I knew my dearest George so well, that I might count upon sharing with him."

"The deuce you did! Let me tell you, my dear, that I have been telling my Lord Castlewood quite a different story. That as an elder brother I intend to have all my rights—there, don't flog that near horse so—and that you can but look forward to poverty and dependence."

"What! You won't help me?" cries Harry, turning quite pale.

"George, I don't believe it, though I hear it out of your own mouth! There was a minute's pause after this outbreak, during which Harry did not even look at his brother, but sate, gazing blindly before him, the picture of grief and gloom. He was driving so near to a road-post that the carriage might have been upset but for George's pulling the rein.

"You had better take the reins, sir," said Harry. "I told you you had better take them."

"Did you ever know me fail you, Harry?" George asked.

"No," said the other, "not till now"—the tears were rolling down his cheeks as he spoke.

"My dear, I think one day you will say I have done my duty."

"What have you done? asked Harry.

"I have said you were a younger brother—that you have spent all your patrimony, and that your portion at home must be very slender. Is it not true?"

"Yes, but I would not have believed it, if ten thousand men had told me," said Harry. "Whatever happened to me, I thought I could trust you, George Warrington." And in this frame of mind Harry remained during the rest of the drive.

Their dinner was served soon after their return to their lodgings, of which Harry scarce ate any, though he drank freely of the wine before him.

"That wine is a bad consoler in trouble, Harry," his brother remarked.

"I have no other, sir," said Harry, grimly; and having drunk glass after glass in silence, he presently seized his hat, and left the room.

He did not return for three hours. George, in much anxiety about his brother, had not left home meanwhile, but read his book, and smoked the pipe of patience. "It was shabby to say I would not aid him, and, God help me, it was not true. I won't leave him, though he marries a blackamoor," thought George "have I not done him harm enough already, by coming to life again? Where has he gone; has he gone to play?"

"Good God! what has happened to thee?" cried George Warrington, presently, when his brother came in, looking ghastly pale.

He came up and took his brother's hand. "I can take it now, Georgy," he said. "Perhaps what you did was right, though. I for one will never believe that you would throw your brother off in distress. I'll tell you what. At dinner, I thought suddenly, I'll go back to her and speak to her. I'll say to her, 'Maria, poor as I am, your conduct to me has been so noble, that, by heaven! I am yours to take or to leave. If you will have me, here I am: I will enlist: I will work: I will try and make a livelihood for myself somehow, and my bro—— my relations will relent, and give us enough to live on.' That's what I determined to tell her; and I did, George. I ran all the way to Kensington in the rain—look, I am splashed from head to foot,—and found them all at dinner, all except Will, that is. I spoke out that very moment to them all, sitting round the table, over their wine. 'Maria,' says I, 'a poor fellow wants to redeem his promise which he made when he fancied he was rich. Will you take him?' I found I had plenty of words, and didn't hem and stutter as I'm doing now. I spoke ever so long, and I ended by saying I would do my best and my duty by her, so help me God!

"When I had done, she came up to me quite kind. She took my hand, and kissed it before the rest. 'My dearest, best Harry!' she said (those were her words, I don't want otherwise to be praising myself), 'you are a noble heart, and I thank you with all mine. But, my dear, I have long seen it was only duty, and a foolish promise made by a young man to an old woman, that has held you to your engagement. To keep it would make you miserable, my dear. I absolve you from it, thanking you with all my heart for your fidelity, and blessing and loving my dear cousin always.' And she came up and kissed me before them all, and went out of the room quite stately, and without a single tear. They were all crying, especially my lord, who was sobbing quite loud. I didn't think he had so much feeling. And she, George? Oh, isn't she a noble creature?"

"Here's her health!" cries George, filling one of the glasses that still stood before him.

"Hip, hip, huzzay!" says Harry. He was wild with delight at being free.

CHAPTER LVII. In which Mr. Harry's Nose continues to be put out of joint

Madame de Bernstein was scarcely less pleased than her Virginian nephews at the result of Harry's final interview with Lady Maria. George informed the Baroness of what had passed, in a billet which he sent to her the same evening; and shortly afterwards her nephew Castlewood, whose visits to his aunt were very rare, came to pay his respects to her, and frankly spoke about the circumstances which had taken place; for no man knew better than my Lord Castlewood how to be frank upon occasion, and now that the business between Maria and Harry was ended what need was there of reticence or hypocrisy? The game had been played, and was over: he had no objection now to speak of its various moves, stratagems, finesses. "She is my own sister," said my lord, affectionately; "she won't have many more chances—many more such chances of marrying and establishing herself. I might not approve of the match in all respects, and I might pity your ladyship's young Virginian favourite: but of course such a piece of good fortune was not to be thrown away, and I was bound to stand by my own flesh and blood."

"Your candour does your lordship honour," says Madame de Bernstein, "and your love for your sister is quite edifying!"

"Nay, we have lost the game, and I am speaking sans rancune. It is not for you, who have won, to bear malice," says my lord, with a bow.

Madame de Bernstein protested she was never in her life in better humour. "Confess, now, Eugene, that visit of Maria to Harry at the spunging-house—that touching giving up of all his presents to her, was a stroke of thy invention?"

"Pity for the young man, and a sense of what was due from Maria to her friend—her affianced lover—in misfortune, sure these were motives sufficient to make her act as she did," replies Lord Castlewood, demurely.

"But 'twas you advised her, my good nephew?"

Castlewood, with a shrug of his shoulders, owned that he did advise his sister to see Mr. Henry Warrington. "But we should have won, in spite of your ladyship," he continued, "had not the elder brother made his appearance. And I have been trying to console my poor Maria by showing her what a piece of good fortune it is after all, that we lost."

"Suppose she had married Harry, and then cousin George had made his appearance?" remarks the Baroness.

"Effectivement," cries Eugene, taking snuff. "As the grave was to give up its dead, let us be thankful to the grave for disgorging in time! I am bound to say, that Mr. George Warrington seems to be a man of sense, and not more selfish than other elder sons and men of the world. My poor Molly fancied that he might be a—what shall I say?—a greenhorn perhaps is the term—like his younger brother. She fondly hoped that he might be inclined to go share and share alike with Twin junior; in which case, so infatuated was she about the young fellow, that I believe she would have taken him. 'Harry Warrington, with half a loaf, might do very well,' says I, 'but Harry Warrington with no bread, my dear!'"

"How no bread?" asks the Baroness.

"Well, no bread except at his brother's side-table. The elder said as much."

"What a hard-hearted wretch!" cries Madame de Bernstein.

"Ah, bah! I play with you, aunt, cartes sur table! Mr. George only did what everybody else would do; and we have no right to be angry with him, really we haven't. Molly herself acknowledged as much, after her first burst of grief was over, and I brought her to listen to reason. The silly old creature! to be so wild about a young lad at her time of life!"

"'Twas a real passion, I almost do believe," said Madame de Bernstein.

"You should have heard her take leave of him. C'etait touchant, ma parole d'honneur! I cried. Before George, I could not help myself. The young fellow with muddy stockings, and his hair about his eyes, flings himself amongst us when we were at dinner; makes his offer to Molly in a very frank and noble manner, and in good language too; and she replies. Begad, it put me in mind of Mrs. Woffington in the new Scotch play, that Lord Bute's man has wrote—Douglas—what d'ye call it? She clings round the lad: she bids him adieu in heartrending accents. She steps out of the room in a stately despair—no more chocolate, thank you. If she had made a mauvais pas no one could retire from it with more dignity. 'Twas a masterly retreat after a defeat. We were starved out of our position, but we retired with all the honours of war."

"Molly won't die of the disappointment!" said my lord's aunt, sipping her cup.

My lord snarled a grin, and showed his yellow teeth. "He, he!" he said, "she hath once or twice before had the malady very severely, and recovered perfectly. It don't kill, as your ladyship knows, at Molly's age."

How should her ladyship know? She did not marry Doctor Tusher until she was advanced in life. She did not become Madame de Bernstein until still later. Old Dido, a poet remarks, was not ignorant of misfortune, and hence learned to have compassion on the wretched.

People in the little world, as I have been told, quarrel and fight, and go on abusing each other, and are not reconciled for ever so long. But people in the great world are surely wiser in their generation. They have differences; they cease seeing each other. They make it up and come together again, and no questions are asked. A stray prodigal, or a stray puppy-dog, is thus brought in under the benefit of an amnesty, though you know he has been away in ugly company. For six months past, ever since the Castlewoods and Madame de Bernstein had been battling for possession of poor Harry Warrington, these two branches of the Esmond family had remained apart. Now, the question being settled, they were free to meet again, as though no difference ever had separated them: and Madame de Bernstein drove in her great coach to Lady Castlewood's rout, and the Esmond ladies appeared smiling at Madame de Bernstein's drums, and loved each other just as much as they previously had done.

"So, sir, I hear you have acted like a hard-hearted monster about your poor brother Harry!" says the Baroness, delighted, and menacing George with her stick.

"I acted but upon your ladyship's hint, and desired to see whether it was for himself or his reputed money that his kinsfolk wanted to have him," replies George, turning rather red.

"Nay, Maria could not marry a poor fellow who was utterly penniless, and whose elder brother said he would give him nothing!"

"I did it for the best, madam," says George, still blushing.

"And so thou didst, O thou hypocrite!" cries the old lady.

"Hypocrite, madam! and why?" asks Mr. Warrington, drawing himself up in much state.

"I know all, my infant!" says the Baroness in French. "Thou art very like thy grandfather. Come, that I embrace thee! Harry has told me all, and that thou hast divided thy little patrimony with him!"

"It was but natural, madam. We have had common hearts and purses since we were born. I but feigned hard-heartedness in order to try those people yonder," says George, with filling eyes.

"And thou wilt divide Virginia with him too?" asks the Bernstein.

"I don't say so. It were not just," replied Mr. Warrington. "The land must go to the eldest born, and Harry would not have it otherwise: and it may be I shall die, or my mother outlive the pair of us. But half of what is mine is his: and he, it must be remembered, only was extravagant because he was mistaken as to his position."

"But it is a knight of old, it is a Bayard, it is the grandfather come to life!" cried Madame de Bernstein to her attendant, as she was retiring for the night. And that evening, when the lads left her, it was to poor Harry she gave the two fingers, and to George the rouged cheek, who blushed, for his part, almost as deep as that often-dyed rose, at such a mark of his old kinswoman's favour.

Although Harry Warrington was the least envious of men, and did honour to his brother as in all respects his chief, guide, and superior, yet no wonder a certain feeling of humiliation and disappointment oppressed the young man after his deposition from his eminence as Fortunate Youth and heir to boundless Virginian territories. Our friends at Kensington might promise and vow that they would love him all the better after his fall; Harry made a low bow and professed himself very thankful; but he could not help perceiving, when he went with his brother to the state entertainment with which my Lord Castlewood regaled his new-found kinsman, that George was all in all to his cousins: had all the talk, compliments, and petits soins for himself, whilst of Harry no one took any notice save poor Maria, who followed him with wistful looks, pursued him with eyes conveying dismal reproaches, and, as it were, blamed him because she had left him. "Ah!" the eyes seemed to say, "'tis mighty well of you, Harry, to have accepted the freedom which I gave you; but I had no intention, sir, that you should be so pleased at being let off." She gave him up, but yet she did not quite forgive him for taking her at her word. She would not have him, and yet she would. Oh, my young friends, how delightful is the beginning of a love-business, and how undignified, sometimes, the end! What a romantic vista is before young Damon and young Phillis (or middle-aged ditto ditto) when, their artless loves made known to each other, they twine their arms round each other's waists and survey that charming pays du tendre which lies at their feet! Into that country, so linked together, they will wander from now until extreme old age. There may be rocks and roaring rivers, but will not Damon's strong true love enable him to carry Sweetheart over them? There may be dragons and dangers in the path, but shall not his courageous sword cut them down? Then at eve, how they will rest cuddled together, like two pretty babes in the wood, the moss their couch, the stars their canopy, their arms their mutual pillows! This is the wise plan young folks make when they set out on the love journey; and—O me!—they have not got a mile when they come to a great wall and find they must walk back again. They are squabbling with the post-boy at Barnet (the first stage on the Gretna Road, I mean), and, behold, perhaps Strephon has not got any money, or here is papa with a whacking horsewhip, who takes Miss back again, and locks her up crying in the schoolroom. The parting is heart-breaking; but, when she has married the banker and had eight children, and he has become, it may be, a prosperous barrister,—it may be, a seedy raff who has gone twice or thrice into the Gazette; when, I say, in after years Strephon and Delia meet again, is not the meeting ridiculous? Nevertheless, I hope no young man will fall in love, having any doubt in his mind as to the eternity of his passion. 'Tis when a man has had a second or third amorous attack that he begins to grow doubtful; but some women are romantic to the end, and from eighteen to eight-and-fifty (for what I know) are always expecting their hearts to break. In fine, when you have been in love and are so no more, when the King of France, with twenty thousand men, with colours flying, music playing, and all the pomp of war, having marched up the hill, then proceeds to march down again, he and you are in an absurd position.

This is what Harry Warrington, no doubt, felt when he went to Kensington and encountered the melancholy, reproachful eyes of his cousin. Yes! it is a foolish position to be in; but it is also melancholy to look into a house you have once lived in, and see black casements and emptiness where once shone the fires of welcome. Melancholy? Yes; but, ha! how bitter, how melancholy, how absurd to look up as you pass sentimentally by No. 13, and see somebody else grinning out of window, and evidently on the best terms with the landlady. I always feel hurt, even at an inn which I frequent, if I see other folks' trunks and boots at the doors of the rooms which were once mine. Have those boots lolled on the sofa which once I reclined on? I kick you from before me, you muddy, vulgar highlows!

So considering that his period of occupation was over, and Maria's rooms, if not given up to a new tenant, were, at any rate, to let, Harry did not feel very easy in his cousin's company, nor she possibly in his. He found either that he had nothing to say to her, or that what she had to say to him was rather dull and commonplace, and that the red lip of a white-necked pipe of Virginia was decidedly more agreeable to him now than Maria's softest accents and most melancholy moue. When George went to Kensington, then, Harry did not care much about going, and pleaded other engagements.

At his uncle's house in Hill Street the poor lad was no better amused, and, indeed, was treated by the virtuous people there with scarce any attention at all. The ladies did not scruple to deny themselves when he came; he could scarce have believed in such insincerity after their caresses, their welcome, their repeated vows of affection; but happening to sit with the Lamberts for an hour after he had called upon his aunt, he saw her ladyship's chairmen arrive with an empty chair, and his aunt step out and enter the vehicle, and not even blush when he made her a bow from the opposite window. To be denied by his own relations—to have that door which had opened to him so kindly, slammed in his face! He would not have believed such a thing possible, poor simple Harry said. Perhaps he thought the door-knocker had a tender heart, and was not made of brass; not more changed than the head of that knocker was my Lady Warrington's virtuous face when she passed her nephew.

"My father's own brother's wife! What have I done to offend her? Oh, Aunt Lambert, Aunt Lambert, did you ever see such cold-heartedness?" cries out Harry, with his usual impetuosity.

"Do we make any difference to you, my dear Harry?" says Aunt Lambert, with a side look at her youngest daughter. "The world may look coldly at you, but we don't belong to it: so you may come to us in safety."

"In this house you are different from other people," replies Harry. "I don't know how, but I always feel quiet and happy somehow when I come to you."

"Quis me uno vivit felicior? aut magis hac est
Optandum vita dicere quis potuit?"

calls out General Lambert. "Do you know where I got these verses, Mr. Gownsman?" and he addresses his son from college, who is come to pass an Easter holiday with his parents. "You got them out of Catullus, sir," says the scholar.

"I got them out of no such thing, sir. I got them out of my favourite Democritus Junior—out of old Burton, who has provided many indifferent scholars with learning;" and who and Montaigne, were favourite authors with the good General.

CHAPTER LVIII. Where we do what Cats may do

We have said how our Virginians, with a wisdom not uncommon in youth, had chosen to adopt strong Jacobite opinions, and to profess a prodigious affection for the exiled royal family. The banished prince had recognised Madam Esmond's father as Marquis of Esmond, and she did not choose to be very angry with an unfortunate race, that, after all, was so willing to acknowledge the merits of her family. As for any little scandal about her sister, Madame de Bernstein, and the Old Chevalier, she tossed away from her with scorn the recollection of that odious circumstance, asserting, with perfect truth, that the two first monarchs of the House of Hanover were quite as bad as any Stuarts in regard to their domestic morality. But the king de facto was the king, as well as his Majesty de jure. De Facto had been solemnly crowned and anointed at church, and had likewise utterly discomfited De Jure, when they came to battle for the kingdom together. Madam's clear opinion was, then, that her sons owed it to themselves as well as the sovereign to appear at his royal court. And if his Majesty should have been minded to confer a lucrative post, or a blue or red ribbon upon either of them, she, for her part, would not have been in the least surprised. She made no doubt but that the King knew the Virginian Esmonds as well as any other members of his nobility. The lads were specially commanded, then, to present themselves at court, and, I dare say, their mother would have been very angry had she known that George took Harry's laced coat on the day when he went to make his bow at Kensington.

A hundred years ago the King's drawing-room was open almost every day to his nobility and gentry; and loyalty—especially since the war had begun—could gratify itself a score of times in a month with the august sight of the sovereign. A wise avoidance of the enemy's ships of war, a gracious acknowledgment of the inestimable loss the British Isles would suffer by the seizure of the royal person at sea, caused the monarch to forgo those visits to his native Hanover which were so dear to his royal heart, and compelled him to remain, it must be owned, unwillingly amongst his loving Britons. A Hanoverian lady, however, whose virtues had endeared her to the prince, strove to console him for his enforced absence from Herrenhausen. And from the lips of the Countess of Walmoden (on whom the imperial beneficence had gracefully conferred a high title of British honour) the revered Defender of the Faith could hear the accents of his native home.

To this beloved Sovereign, Mr. Warrington requested his uncle, an assiduous courtier, to present him; and as Mr. Lambert had to go to court likewise, and thank his Majesty for his promotion, the two gentlemen made the journey to Kensington together, engaging a hackney-coach for the purpose, as my Lord Wrotham's carriage was now wanted by its rightful owner, who had returned to his house in town. They alighted at Kensington Palace Gate, where the sentries on duty knew and saluted the good General, and hence modestly made their way on foot to the summer residence of the sovereign. Walking under the portico of the Palace, they entered the gallery which leads to the great black marble staircase (which hath been so richly decorated and painted by Mr. Kent), and then passed through several rooms, richly hung with tapestry and adorned with pictures and bustos, until they came to the King's great drawing-room, where that famous "Venus" by Titian is, and, amongst other masterpieces, the picture of "St. Francis adoring the infant Saviour," performed by Sir Peter Paul Rubens; and here, with the rest of the visitors to the court, the gentlemen waited until his Majesty issued from his private apartments, where he was in conference with certain personages who were called in the newspaper language of that day his M-j-ty's M-n-st-rs.

George Warrington, who had never been in a palace before, had leisure to admire the place, and regard the people round him. He saw fine pictures for the first time too, and I dare say delighted in that charming piece of Sir

Athony Vandyck, representing King Charles the First, his Queen and Family, and the noble picture of "Esther before Ahasuerus," painted by Tintoret, and in which all the figures are dressed in the magnificent Venetian habit. With the contemplation of these works he was so enraptured, that he scarce heard all the remarks of his good friend the General, who was whispering into his young companion's almost heedless ear the names of some of the personages round about them.

"Yonder," says Mr. Lambert, "are two of my Lords of the Admiralty, Mr. Gilbert Elliot and Admiral Boscawen: your Boscawen, whose fleet fired the first gun in your waters two years ago. That stout gentleman all belated with gold is Mr. Fox, that was Minister, and is now content to be Paymaster with a great salary.

"He carries the auri fames on his person. Why, his waistcoat is a perfect Potosi!" says George.

"Aliena appetens—how goes the text? He loves to get money and to spend it," continues General Lambert. "Yon is my Lord Chief Justice Willes, talking to my Lord of Salisbury, Doctor Headley, who, if he serve his God as he serves his King, will be translated to some very high promotion in Heaven. He belongs to your grandfather's time, and was loved by Dick Steele and hated by the Dean. With them is my Lord of London, the learned Doctor Sherlock. My lords of the lawn sleeves have lost half their honours now. I remember when I was a boy in my mother's hand, she made me go down on my knees to the Bishop of Rochester; him who went over the water, and became Minister to somebody who shall be nameless—Perkin's Bishop. That handsome fair man is Admiral Smith. He was president of poor Byng's court-martial, and strove in vain to get him off his penalty; Tom of Ten Thousand they call him in the fleet. The French Ambassador had him broke, when he was a lieutenant, for making a French man-of-war lower topsails to him, and the King made Tom a captain the next day. That tall, haughty-looking man is my Lord George Sackville, who, now I am a Major-General myself, will treat me somewhat better than a footman. I wish my stout old Blakeney were here; he is the soldier's darling, and as kind and brave as yonder poker of a nobleman is brave and—I am your lordship's very humble servant. This is a young gentleman who is just from America, and was in Braddock's sad business two years ago."

"Oh, indeed!" says the poker of a nobleman. "I have the honour of speaking to Mr.——?"

"To Major-General Lambert, at your lordship's service, and who was in his Majesty's some time before you entered it. That, Mr. Warrington, is the first commoner in England, Mr. Speaker Onslow. Where is your uncle? I shall have to present you myself to his Majesty if Sir Miles delays much longer." As he spoke, the worthy General addressed himself entirely to his young friend, making no sort of account of his colleague, who stalked away with a scared look as if amazed at the other's audacity. A hundred years ago, a nobleman was a nobleman, and expected to be admired as such.

Sir Miles's red waistcoat appeared in sight presently, and many cordial greetings passed between him, his nephew, and General Lambert: for we have described how Sir Miles was the most affectionate of men. So the General had quitted my Lord Wrotham's house? It was time, as his lordship himself wished to occupy it? Very good; but consider what a loss for the neighbours!

"We miss you, we positively miss you, my dear General," cries Sir Miles. "My daughters were in love with those lovely young ladies—upon my word, they were; and my Lady Warrington and my girls were debating over and over again how they should find an opportunity of making the acquaintance of your charming family. We feel as if we were old friends already; indeed we do, General, if you will permit me the liberty of saying so; and we love you, if I may be allowed to speak frankly, on account of your friendship and kindness to our dear nephews: though we were a little jealous, I own a little jealous of them, because they went so often to see you. Often and often have I said to my Lady Warrington, 'My dear, why don't we make acquaintance with the General? Why don't we ask him and his ladies to come over in a family way and dine with some other plain country gentlefolks?' Carry my most sincere respects to Mrs. Lambert, I pray, sir; and thank her for her goodness to these young gentlemen. My own flesh and blood, sir; my dear, dear brother's boys!" He passed his hand across his manly eyes: he was choking almost with generous and affectionate emotion.

Whilst they were discoursing—George Warrington the while restraining his laughter with admirable gravity—the door of the King's apartments opened, and the pages entered, preceding his Majesty. He was followed by his burly son, his Royal Highness the Duke, a very corpulent Prince, with a coat and face of blazing scarlet: behind them came various gentlemen and officers of state; among whom George at once recognised the famous Mr. Secretary Pitt, by his tall stature, his eagle eye and beak, his grave and majestic presence. As I see that solemn figure passing, even a hundred years off, I protest I feel a present awe, and a desire to take my hat off. I am not frightened at George the Second; nor are my eyes dazzled by the portentous appearance of his Royal Highness the Duke of Culloden and Fontenoy; but the Great Commoner, the terrible Cornet of Horse! His figure bestrides our narrow isle of a century back like a Colossus; and I hush as he passes in his gouty shoes, his thunderbolt hand wrapped in flannel. Perhaps as we see him now, issuing with dark looks from the royal closet, angry scenes have been passing between him and his august master. He has been boring that old monarch for hours with prodigious long speeches, full of eloquence, voluble with the noblest phrases upon the commonest topics; but, it must be confessed, utterly repulsive to the little shrewd old gentleman, "at whose feet he lays himself," as the phrase is, and who has the most thorough dislike for fine boedry and for fine brose too! The sublime Minister passes solemnly through the crowd; the company ranges itself respectfully round the wall; and his Majesty walks round the circle, his royal son lagging a little behind, and engaging select individuals in conversation for his own part.

The monarch is a little, keen, fresh-coloured old man, with very protruding eyes, attired in plain, old-fashioned, snuff-coloured clothes and brown stockings, his only ornament the blue ribbon of his Order of the Garter. He speaks in a German accent, but with ease, shrewdness, and simplicity, addressing those individuals whom he has a mind to notice, or passing on with a bow. He knew Mr. Lambert well, who had served under his Majesty at Dettingen, and with his royal son in Scotland, and he congratulated him good-humouredly on his promotion.

"It is not always," his Majesty was pleased to say, "that we can do as we like; but I was glad when, for once, I could give myself that pleasure in your case, General; for my army contains no better officer as you."

The veteran blushed and bowed, deeply gratified at this speech. Meanwhile, the Best of Monarchs was looking at Sir Miles Warrington (whom his Majesty knew perfectly, as the eager recipient of all favours from all Ministers), and at the young gentleman by his side.

"Who is this?" the Defender of the Faith condescended to ask, pointing towards George Warrington, who stood before his sovereign in a respectful attitude, clad in poor Harry's best embroidered suit.

With the deepest reverence Sir Miles informed his King, that the young gentleman was his nephew, Mr. George Warrington, of Virginia, who asked leave to pay his humble duty.

"This, then, is the other brother?" the Venerated Prince deigned to observe. "He came in time, else the other brother would have spent all the money. My Lord Bishop of Salisbury, why do you come out in this bitter weather? You had much better stay at home!" and with this, the revered wielder of Britannia's sceptre passed on to other lords and gentlemen of his court. Sir Miles Warrington was deeply affected at the royal condescension. He clapped his nephew's hands. "God bless you, my boy," he cried; "I told you that you would see the greatest monarch and the finest gentleman in the world. Is he not so, my Lord Bishop?"

"That, that he is!" cried his lordship, clasping his ruffled hands, and turning his fine eyes up to the sky, "the best of princes and of men."

"That is Master Louis, my Lady Yarmouth's favourite nephew," says Lambert, pointing to a young gentleman who stood with a crowd round him; and presently the stout Duke of Cumberland came up to our little group.

His Royal Highness held out his hand to his old companion-in-arms. "Congratulate you on your promotion, Lambert," he said good-naturedly. Sir Miles Warrington's eyes were ready to burst out of his head with rapture.

"I owe it, sir, to your Royal Highness's good offices," said the grateful General.

"Not at all; not at all: ought to have had it a long time before. Always been a good officer; perhaps there'll be some employment for you soon. This is the gentleman whom James Wolfe introduced to me?"

"His brother, sir."

"Oh, the real Fortunate Youth! You were with poor Ned Braddock in

America—a prisoner, and lucky enough to escape. Come and see me, sir, in Pall Mall. Bring him to my levee, Lambert." And the broad back of the Royal Prince was turned to our friends.

"It is raining! You came on foot, General Lambert? You and George must come home in my coach. You must and shall come home with me, I say. By George, you must! I'll have no denial," cried the enthusiastic Baronet; and he drove George and the General back to Hill Street, and presented the latter to my Lady Warrington and his darlings, Flora and Dora, and insisted upon their partaking of a collation, as they must be hungry after their ride. "What, there is only cold mutton? Well, an old soldier can eat cold mutton. And a good glass of my Lady Warrington's own cordial, prepared with her own hands, will keep the cold wind out. Delicious cordial! Capital mutton! Our own, my dear General," says the hospitable Baronet, "our own from the country, six years old if a day. We keep a plain table; but all the Warringtons since the Conqueror have been remarkable for their love of mutton; and our meal may look a little scanty, and is, for we are plain people, and I am obliged to keep my rascals of servants on board-wages. Can't give them seven-year-old mutton, you know."

Sir Miles, in his nephew's presence and hearing, described to his wife and daughters George's reception at court in such flattering terms that George hardly knew himself, or the scene at which he had been present, or how to look his uncle in the face, or how to contradict him before his family in the midst of the astonishing narrative he was relating. Lambert sat by for a while with open eyes. He, too, had been at Kensington. He had seen none of the wonders which Sir Miles described.

"We are proud of you, dear George. We love you, my dear nephew—we all love you, we are all proud of you—"

"Yes; but I like Harry best," says a little voice.

"—not because you are wealthy! Screwby, take Master Miles to his governor. Go, dear child. Not because you are blest with great estates and an ancient name; but because, George, you have put to good use the talents with which Heaven has adorned you; because you have fought and bled in your country's cause, in your monarch's cause, and as such are indeed worthy of the favour of the best of sovereigns. General Lambert, you have kindly condescended to look in on a country family, and partake of our unpretending meal. I hope we may see you some day when our hospitality is a little less homely. Yes, by George, General, you must and shall name a day when you and Mrs. Lambert, and your dear girls, will dine with us. I'll take no refusal now, by George I won't," bawls the knight.

"You will accompany us, I trust, to my drawing-room?" says my lady, rising.

Mr. Lambert pleaded to be excused; but the ladies on no account would let dear George go away. No, positively, he should not go. They wanted to make acquaintance with their cousin. They must hear about that dreadful battle and escape from the Indians. Tom Claypool came in and heard some of the story. Flora was listening to it with her handkerchief to her eyes, and little Miles had just said—

"Why do you take your handkerchief, Flora? You're not crying a bit."

Being a man of great humour, Martin Lambert, when he went home, could not help entertaining his wife with an account of the new family with which he had made acquaintance. A certain cant word called humbug had lately come into vogue. Will it be believed that the General used it to designate the family of this virtuous country gentleman? He described the eager hospitalities of the father, the pompous flatteries of the mother, and the daughters' looks of admiration; the toughness and security of the mutton, and the abominable taste and odour of the cordial; and we may be sure Mrs. Lambert contrasted Lady Warrington's recent behaviour to poor Harry with her present conduct to George.

"Is this Miss Warrington really handsome?" asks Mrs Lambent.

"Yes; she is very handsome indeed, and the most astounding flirt I have ever set eyes on," replies the General.

"The hypocrite! I have no patience with such people!" cries the lady.

To which the General, strange to say, only replied by the monosyllable "Bo!"

"Why do you say 'Bo!' Martin?" asks the lady.

"I say 'Bo!' to a goose, my dear," answers the General.

And his wife vows she does not know what he means, or of what he is thinking, and the General says—

"Of course not."

CHAPTER LIX. In which we are treated to a Play

The real business of life, I fancy, can form but little portion of the novelist's budget. When he is speaking of the profession of arms, in which men can show courage or the reverse, and in treating of which the writer naturally has to deal with interesting circumstances, actions, and characters, introducing recitals of danger, devotedness, heroic deaths, and the like, the novelist may perhaps venture to deal with actual affairs of life: but otherwise, they scarcely can enter into our stories. The main part of Ficulnus's life, for instance, is spent in selling sugar, spices and cheese; of Causidicus's in poring over musty volumes of black-letter law; of Sartorius's in sitting, cross-legged, on a board after measuring gentlemen for coats and breeches. What can a story-teller say about the professional existence of these men? Would a real rustical history of hobnails and eighteenpence a day be endurable? In the days whereof we are writing, the poets of the time chose to represent a shepherd in pink breeches and a chintz waistcoat, dancing before his flocks, and playing a flageolet tied up with a blue satin ribbon. I say, in reply to some objections which have been urged by potent and friendly critics, that of the actual affairs of life the novelist cannot be expected to treat—with the almost single exception of war before named. But law, stockbroking, polemical theology, linen-drapery, apothecary-business, and the like, how can writers manage fully to develop these in their stories? All authors can do, is to depict men out of their business—in their passions, loves, laughters, amusements, hatreds, and what not—and describe these as well as they can, taking the business part for granted, and leaving it as it were for subaudition.

Thus, in talking of the present or the past world, I know I am only dangling about the theatre-lobbies, coffee-houses, ridottos, pleasure-haunts, fair-booths, and feasting- and fiddling-rooms of life; that, meanwhile, the great serious past or present world is plodding in its chambers, toiling at its humdrum looms, or jogging on its accustomed labours, and we are only seeing our characters away from their work. Corydon has to cart the litter and thresh the barley, as well as to make love to Phillis; Ancillula has to dress and wash the nursery, to wait at breakfast and on her misses, to take the children out, etc., before she can have her brief sweet interview through the area-railings with Boopis, the policeman. All day long have his heels to beat the stale pavement before he has the opportunity to snatch the hasty kiss or the furtive cold pie. It is only at moments, and away from these labours, that we can light upon one character or the other; and hence, though most of the persons of whom we are writing have doubtless their grave employments and avocations, it is only when they are disengaged and away from their work, that we can bring them and the equally disengaged reader together.

The macaronis and fine gentlemen at White's and Arthur's continued to show poor Harry Warrington such a very cold shoulder, that he sought their society less and less, and the Ring and the Mall and the gaming-table knew him no more. Madame de Bernstein was for her nephew's braving the indifference of the world, and vowed that it would be conquered, if he would but have courage to face it; but the young man was too honest to wear a smiling face when he was discontented; to disguise mortification or anger; to parry slights by adroit flatteries or cunning impudence; as many gentlemen and gentlewomen must and do who wish to succeed in society.

"You pull a long face, Harry, and complain of the world's treatment of you," the old lady said. "Fiddlededee, sir! Everybody has to put up with impertinences: and if you get a box on the ear now you are poor and cast down, you must say nothing about it, bear it with a smile, and if you can, revenge it ten years after. Moi qui vous parle, sir!—do you suppose I have had no humble-pie to eat? All of us in our turn are called upon to swallow it: and, now you are no longer the Fortunate Youth, be the Clever Youth, and win back the place you have lost by your ill luck. Go about more than ever. Go to all the routs and parties to which you are asked, and to more still. Be civil to everybody—to all women especially. Only of course take care to show your spirit, of which you have plenty. With economy, and by your brother's, I must say, admirable generosity, you can still make a genteel figure. With your handsome person, sir, you can't fail to get a rich heiress. Tenez! You should go amongst the merchants in the City, and look out there. They won't know that you are out of fashion at the Court end of the town. With a little management, there is not the least reason, sir, why you should not make a good position for yourself still. When did you go to see my Lady Yarmouth, pray? Why did you not improve that connexion? She took a great fancy to you. I desire you will be constant at her ladyship's evenings, and lose no opportunity of paying court to her."

Thus the old woman who had loved Harry so on his first appearance in England, who had been so eager for his company, and pleased with his artless conversation, was taking the side of the world, and turning against him. Instead of the smiles and kisses with which the fickle old creature used once to greet him, she received him with coldness; she became peevish and patronising; she cast gibes and scorn at him before her guests, making his honest face flush with humiliation, and awaking the keenest pangs of grief and amazement in his gentle, manly heart. Madame de Bernstein's servants, who used to treat him with such eager respect, scarcely paid him now any attention. My lady was often indisposed or engaged when he called on her; her people did not press him to wait; did not volunteer to ask whether he would stay and dine, as they used in the days when he was the Fortunate Youth and companion of the wealthy and great. Harry carried his woes to Mrs. Lambert. In a passion of sorrow he told her of his aunt's cruel behaviour to him. He was stricken down and dismayed by the fickleness and heartlessness of the world in its treatment of him. While the good lady and her daughters would move to and fro, and busy themselves with the cares of the house, our poor lad would sit glum in a window-seat, heart-sick and silent.

"I know you are the best people alive," he would say to the ladies, "and the kindest, and that I must be the dullest company in the world—yes, that I am."

"Well, you are not very lively, Harry," says Miss Hetty, who began to command him, and perhaps to ask herself, "What? Is this the gentleman whom I took to be such a hero?"

"If he is unhappy, why should he be lively?" asks Theo, gently. "He has a good heart, and is pained at his friends' desertion of him. Sure there is no harm in that?"

"I would have too much spirit to show I was hurt, though," cries Hetty, clenching her little fists. "And I would smile, though that horrible old painted woman boxed my ears. She is horrible, mamma. You think so yourself, Theo! Own, now, you think so yourself! You said so last night, and acted her coming in on her crutch, and grinning round to the company."

"I mayn't like her," said Theo, turning very red. "But there is no reason why I should call Harry's aunt names before Harry's face."

"You provoking thing; you are always right!" cries Hetty, "and that's what makes me so angry. Indeed, Harry, it was very wrong of me to make rude remarks about any of your relations."

"I don't care about the others, Hetty; but it seems hard that this one should turn upon me. I had got to be very fond of her; and you see, it makes me mad, somehow, when people I'm very fond of turn away from me, or act unkind to me."

"Suppose George were to do so?" asks Hetty. You see, it was George and

Hetty, and Theo and Harry, amongst them now.

"You are very clever and very lively, and you may suppose a number of things; but not that, Hetty, if you please," cried Harry, standing up and looking very resolute and angry. "You don't know my brother as I know him —or you wouldn't take—such a—liberty as to suppose—my brother George could do anything unkind or unworthy!" Mr. Harry was quite in a flush as he spoke.

Hetty turned very white. Then she looked up at Harry, and then she did not say a single word.

Then Harry said, in his simple way, before taking leave, "I'm very sorry, and I beg your pardon, Hetty, if I said anything rough, or that seemed unkind; but I always fight up if anybody says anything against George."

Hetty did not answer a word out of her pale lips, but gave him her hand, and dropped a prim little curtsey.

When she and Theo were together at night, making curl-paper confidences, "Oh!" said Hetty, "I thought it would be so happy to see him every day, and was so glad when papa said we were to stay in London! And now I do see him, you see, I go on offending him. I can't help offending him; and I know he is not clever, Theo. But oh! isn't he good, and kind, and brave? Didn't he look handsome when he was angry?"

"You silly little thing, you are always trying to make him look handsome," Theo replied.

It was Theo and Hetty, and Harry and George, among these young people, then; and I dare say the reason why General Lambert chose to apply the monosyllable "Bo" to the mother of his daughters, was as a rebuke to that good woman for the inveterate love of sentiment and propensity to match-making which belonged to her (and every other woman in the world whose heart is worth a fig); and as a hint that Madam Lambert was a goose if she fancied the two Virginian lads were going to fall in love with the young women of the Lambert house. Little Het might have her fancy; little girls will; but they get it over: "and you know, Molly" (which dear, soft-hearted Mrs. Lambert could not deny), "you fancied somebody else before you fancied me," says the General; but Harry had evidently not been smitten by Hetty; and now he was superseded, as it were, by having an elder brother over him, and could not even call the coat upon his back his own, Master Harry was no great catch.

"Oh yes: now he is poor we will show him the door, as all the rest of the world does, I suppose," says Mrs. Lambert.

"That is what I always do, isn't it, Molly? turn my back on my friends in distress?" asks the General.

"No, my dear! I am a goose, now, and that I own, Martin!" says the wife, having recourse to the usual pocket-handkerchief.

"Let the poor boy come to us and welcome: ours is almost the only house in this selfish place where so much can be said for him. He is unhappy, and to be with us puts him at ease; in God's name let him be with us!" says the kind-hearted officer. Accordingly, whenever poor crestfallen Hal wanted a dinner, or an evening's entertainment, Mr. Lambert's table had a corner for him. So was George welcome, too. He went among the Lamberts, not at first with the cordiality which Harry felt for these people, and inspired among them: for George was colder in his manner, and more mistrustful of himself and others than his twin-brother: but there was a goodness and friendliness about the family which touched almost all people who came into frequent contact with them; and George soon learned to love them for their own sake, as well as for their constant regard and kindness to his brother. He could not but see and own how sad Harry was, and pity his brother's depression. In his sarcastic way, George would often take himself to task before his brother for coming to life again, and say, "Dear Harry, I am George the Unlucky, though you have ceased to be Harry the Fortunate. Florac would have done much better not to pass his sword through that Indian's body, and to have left my scalp as an ornament for the fellow's belt. I say he would, sir! At White's the people would have respected you. Our mother would have wept over me, as a defunct angel, instead of being angry with me for again supplanting her favourite—you are her favourite, you deserve to be her favourite: everybody's favourite: only, if I had not come back, your favourite, Maria, would have insisted on marrying you; and that is how the gods would have revenged themselves upon you for your prosperity."

"I never know whether you are laughing at me or yourself, George" says the brother. I never know whether you are serious or jesting.

"Precisely my own case, Harry, my dear!" says George.

"But this I know, that there never was a better brother in the world; and never better people than the Lamberts."

"Never was truer word said!" cries George, taking his brother's hand.

"And if I'm unhappy, 'tis not your fault—nor their fault—nor perhaps mine, George," continues the younger. "'Tis fate, you see, 'tis the having nothing to do. I must work; and how, George? that is the question."

"We will see what our mother says. We must wait till we hear from her," says George.

"I say, George! Do you know, I don't think I should much like going back to Virginia?" says Harry, in a low, alarmed voice.

"What! in love with one of the lasses here?"

"Love 'em like sisters—with all my heart, of course, dearest, best girls! but, having come out of that business, thanks to you, I don't want to go back, you know. No! no! It is not for that I fancy staying in Europe better than going home. But, you see, I don't fancy hunting, duck-shooting, tobacco-planting, whist-playing, and going to sermon, over and over and over again, for all my life, George. And what else is there to do at home? What on earth is there for me to do at all, I say? That's what makes me miserable. It would not matter for you to be a younger son you are so clever you would make your way anywhere; but, for a poor fellow like me, what chance is there? Until I do something, George, I shall be miserable, that's what I shall!"

"Have I not always said so? Art thou not coming round to my opinion?"

"What opinion, George? You know pretty much whatever you think, I think, George!" says the dutiful junior.

"That Florac had best have left the Indian to take my scalp, my dear!"

At which Harry bursts away with an angry exclamation; and they continue to puff their pipes in friendly union.

They lived together, each going his own gait; and not much intercourse, save that of affection, was carried on between them. Harry never would venture to meddle with George's books, and would sit as dumb as a mouse at the lodgings whilst his brother was studying. They removed presently from the Court end of the town, Madame de Bernstein pishing and pshaing at their change of residence. But George took a great fancy to frequenting Sir Hans Sloane's new reading-room and museum, just set up in Montagu House, and he took cheerful lodgings in Southampton Row, Bloomsbury, looking over the delightful fields towards Hampstead, at the back of the Duke of Bedford's gardens. And Lord Wrotham's family coming to Mayfair, and Mr. Lambert having business which detained him in London, had to change his house, too, and engaged furnished apartments in Soho, not very far off from the dwelling of our young men; and it was, as we have said, with the Lamberts that Harry, night after night, took refuge.

George was with them often, too; and, as the acquaintance ripened, he frequented their house with increasing assiduity, finding their company more to his taste than that of Aunt Bernstein's polite circle of gamblers, than Sir Miles Warrington's port and mutton, or the daily noise and clatter of the coffee-houses. And as he and the Lambert ladies were alike strangers in London, they partook of its pleasures together, and, no doubt, went to Vauxhall and Ranelagh, to Marybone Gardens, and the play, and the Tower, and wherever else there was honest amusement to be had in those days. Martin Lambert loved that his children should have all the innocent pleasure which he could procure for them, and Mr. George, who was of a most generous, open-handed disposition, liked to treat his friends likewise, especially those who had been so admirably kind to his brother.

With all the passion of his heart Mr. Warrington loved a play. He had never enjoyed this amusement in Virginia, and only once or twice at Quebec, when he visited Canada; and when he came to London, where the two houses were in their full glory, I believe he thought he never could have enough of the delightful entertainment. Anything he liked himself, he naturally wished to share amongst his companions. No wonder that he was eager to take his friends to the theatre, and we may be sure our young countryfolks were not unwilling. Shall it be Drury Lane or Covent Garden, ladies? There was Garrick and Shakspeare at Drury Lane. Well, will it be believed, the ladies wanted to hear the famous new author whose piece was being played at Covent Garden?

At this time a star of genius had arisen, and was blazing with quite a dazzling brilliancy. The great Mr. John Home, of Scotland, had produced a tragedy, than which, since the days of the ancients, there had been nothing more classic and elegant. What had Mr. Garrick meant by refusing such a masterpiece for his theatre? Say what you will about Shakspeare; in the works of that undoubted great poet (who had begun to grow vastly more popular in England since Monsieur Voltaire attacked him) there were many barbarisms that could not but shock a polite auditory; whereas, Mr. Home, the modern author, knew how to be refined in the very midst of grief and passion; to represent death, not merely as awful, but graceful and pathetic; and never condescended to degrade the majesty of the Tragic Muse by the ludicrous apposition of buffoonery and familiar punning, such as the elder playwright certainly had resort to. Besides, Mr. Home's performance had been admired in quarters so high, and by personages whose taste was known to be as elevated as their rank, that all Britons could not but join in the plaudits for which august hands had given the signal. Such, it was said, was the opinion of the very best company, in the coffee-houses, and amongst the wits about town. Why, the famous Mr. Gray, of Cambridge, said there had not been for a hundred years any dramatic dialogue of such a true style; and as for the poet's native capital of Edinburgh, where the piece was first brought out, it was even said that the triumphant Scots called out from the pit (in their dialect), "Where's Wully Shakspeare noo?"

"I should like to see the man who could beat Willy Shakspeare?" says the General, laughing.

"Mere national prejudice," says Mr. Warrington.

"Beat Shakspeare, indeed!" cries Mrs. Lambert.

"Pooh, pooh! you have cried more over Mr. Sam Richardson than ever you did over Mr. Shakspeare, Molly!" remarks the General. "I think few women love to read Shakspeare: they say they love it, but they don't."

"Oh, papa!" cry three ladies, throwing up three pair of hands.

"Well, then, why do you all three prefer Douglas? And you, boys, who are such Tories, will you go see a play which is wrote by a Whig Scotchman, who was actually made prisoner at Falkirk?"

"Relicta non bene parmula," says Mr. Jack the scholar.

"Nay; it was relicta bene parmula," cried the General. "It was the Highlanders who flung their targes down, and made fierce work among us redcoats. If they had fought all their fields as well as that, and young Perkin had not turned back from Derby——"

"I know which side would be rebels, and who would be called the Young Pretender," interposed George.

"Hush! you must please to remember my cloth, Mr. Warrington," said the General, with some gravity; "and that the cockade I wear is a black, not a white one! Well, if you will not love Mr. Home for his politics, there is, I think, another reason, George, why you should like him."

"I may have Tory fancies, Mr. Lambert, but I think I know how to love and honour a good Whig," said George, with a bow to the General: "but why should I like this Mr. Home, sir?"

"Because, being a Presbyterian clergyman, he has committed the heinous crime of writing a play, and his brother-parsons have barked out an excommunication at him. They took the poor fellow's means of livelihood away from him for his performance; and he would have starved, but that the young Pretender on our side of the water has given him a pension."

"If he has been persecuted by the parsons, there is hope for him," said George, smiling. "And henceforth I declare myself ready to hear his sermons."

"Mrs. Woffington is divine in it, though not generally famous in tragedy. Barry is drawing tears from all eyes; and Garrick is wild at having refused the piece. Girls, you must bring each half a dozen handkerchiefs! As for mamma, I cannot trust her; and she positively must be left at home."

But mamma persisted she would go; and, if need were to weep, she would sit and cry her eyes out in a corner. They all went to Covent Garden, then; the most of the party duly prepared to see one of the masterpieces of the age and drama. Could they not all speak long pages of Congreve; had they not wept and kindled over Otway and Rowe? O ye past literary glories, that were to be eternal, how long have you been dead? Who knows much more now than where your graves are? Poor, neglected Muse of the bygone theatre! She pipes for us, and we will not dance; she tears her hair, and we will not weep. And the Immortals of our time, how soon shall they be dead and buried, think you? How many will survive? How long shall it be ere Nox et Domus Plutonia shall overtake them?

So away went the pleased party to Covent Garden to see the tragedy of the immortal John Home. The ladies and the General were conveyed in a glass coach, and found the young men in waiting to receive them at the theatre door. Hence they elbowed their way through a crowd of torch-boys, and a whole regiment of footmen. Little Hetty fell to Harry's arm in this expedition, and the blushing Miss Theo was handed to the box by Mr. George. Gumbo had kept the places until his masters arrived, when he retired, with many bows, to take his own seat in the footman's gallery. They had good places in a front box, and there was luckily a pillar behind which mamma could weep in comfort. And opposite them they had the honour to see the august hope of the empire, his Royal Highness George Prince of Wales, with the Princess Dowager his mother, whom the people greeted with loyal, but not very enthusiastic, plaudits. That handsome man standing behind his Royal Highness was my Lord Bute, the Prince's Groom of the Stole, the patron of the poet whose performance they had come to see, and over whose work the Royal party had already wept more than once.

How can we help it, if during the course of the performance, Mr. Lambert would make his jokes and mar the solemnity of the scene? At first, as the reader of the tragedy well knows, the characters are occupied in making a number of explanations. Lady Randolph explains how it is that she is so melancholy. Married to Lord Randolph somewhat late in life, she owns, and his lordship perceives, that a dead lover yet occupies all her heart; and her husband is fain to put up with this dismal, second-hand regard, which is all that my lady can bestow. Hence, an invasion of Scotland by the Danes is rather a cause of excitement than disgust to my lord, who rushes to meet the foe, and forgets the dreariness of his domestic circumstances. Welcome, Vikings and Norsemen! Blow, northern blasts, the invaders' keels to Scotland's shore! Randolph and other heroes will be on the beach to give the foemen a welcome! His lordship has no sooner disappeared behind the trees of the forest, but Lady Randolph begins to explain to her confidante the circumstances of her early life. The fact was, she had made a private marriage, and what would the confidante say, if, in early youth, she, Lady Randolph, had lost a husband? In the cold bosom of the earth was lodged the husband of her youth, and in some cavern of the ocean lies her child and his!

Up to this the General behaved with as great gravity as any of his young companions to the play; but when Lady Randolph proceeded to say, "Alas! Hereditary evil was the cause of my misfortunes," he nudged George Warrington, and looked so droll, that the young man burst out laughing.

The magic of the scene was destroyed after that. These two gentlemen went on cracking jokes during the whole of the subsequent performance, to their own amusement, but the indignation of their company, and perhaps of the people in the adjacent boxes. Young Douglas, in those days, used to wear a white satin "shape" slashed at the legs and body, and when Mr. Barry appeared in this droll costume, the General vowed it was the exact dress of the Highlanders in the late war. The Chevalier's Guard, he declared, had all white satin slashed breeches, and red boots—"only they left them at home, my dear," adds this wag. Not one pennyworth of sublimity would he or George allow henceforth to Mr. Home's performance. As for Harry, he sate in very deep meditation over the scene; and when Mrs. Lambert offered him a penny for his thoughts, he said, "That he thought, Young Norval, Douglas, What-d'ye-call-'em, the fellow in white satin—who looked as old as his mother—was very lucky to be able to distinguish himself so soon. I wish I could get a chance, Aunt Lambert," says he, drumming on his hat; on which mamma sighed, and Theo, smiling, said, "We must wait, and perhaps the Danes will land."

"How do you mean?" asks simple Harry.

"Oh, the Danes always land, pour qui scait attendre!" says kind Theo, who had hold of her sister's little hand, and, I dare say, felt its pressure.

She did not behave unkindly—that was not in Miss Theo's nature—but somewhat coldly to Mr. George, on whom she turned her back, addressing remarks, from time to time, to Harry. In spite of the gentlemen's scorn, the women chose to be affected. A mother and son, meeting in love and parting in tears, will always awaken emotion in female hearts.

"Look, papa! there is an answer to all your jokes!" says Theo, pointing towards the stage.

At a part of the dialogue between Lady Randolph and her son, one of the grenadiers on guard on each side of the stage, as the custom of those days was, could not restrain his tears, and was visibly weeping before the side-box.

"You are right, my dear," says papa.

"Didn't I tell you she always is?" interposes Hetty.

"Yonder sentry is a better critic than we are, and a touch of nature masters us all."

"Tamen usque recurrit!" cries the young student from college.

George felt abashed somehow, and interested too. He had been sneering, and Theo sympathising. Her kindness was better—nay, wiser—than his scepticism, perhaps. Nevertheless, when, at the beginning of the fifth act of the play, young Douglas, drawing his sword and looking up at the gallery, bawled out—

"Ye glorious stars! high heaven's resplendent host!
To whom I oft have of my lot complained,
Hear and record my soul's unaltered wish
Living or dead, let me but be renowned!
May Heaven inspire some fierce gigantic Dane
To give a bold defiance to our host!
Before he speaks it out, I will accept,
Like Douglas conquer, or like Douglas die!"—

The gods, to whom Mr. Barry appealed, saluted this heroic wish with immense applause, and the General clapped his hands prodigiously. His daughter was rather disconcerted.

"This Douglas is not only brave, but he is modest!" says papa.

"I own I think he need not have asked for a gigantic Dane," says Theo, smiling, as Lady Randolph entered in the midst of the gallery thunder.

When the applause had subsided, Lady Randolph is made to say—

"My son, I heard a voice!"

"I think she did hear a voice!" cries papa. "Why, the fellow was bellowing like a bull of Bashan." And the General would scarcely behave himself from thenceforth to the end of the performance. He said he was heartily glad that the young gentleman was put to death behind the scenes. When Lady Randolph's friend described how her mistress had "flown like lightning up the hill, and plunged herself into the empty air," Mr. Lambert said he was delighted to be rid of her. "And as for that story of her early marriage," says he, "I have my very strongest doubts about it."

"Nonsense, Martin! Look, children! their Royal Highnesses are moving."

The tragedy over, the Princess Dowager and the Prince were, in fact, retiring; though, I dare say, the latter, who was always fond of a farce, would have been far better pleased with that which followed than he had been with Mr. Home's dreary tragic masterpiece.

CHAPTER LX. Which treats of Macbeth, a Supper, and a Pretty Kettle of
Fish

When the performances were concluded, our friends took coach for Mr.

Warrington's lodging, where the Virginians had provided an elegant supper. Mr. Warrington was eager to treat them in the handsomest manner, and the General and his wife accepted the invitation of the two bachelors, pleased to think that they could give their young friends pleasure. General and Mrs. Lambert, their son from college, their two blooming daughters, and Mr. Spencer of the Temple, a new friend whom George had met at the coffee-house, formed the party, and partook with cheerfulness of the landlady's fare. The order of their sitting I have not been able exactly to ascertain; but, somehow, Miss Theo had a place next to the chickens and Mr. George Warrington, whilst Miss Hetty and a ham divided the attentions of Mr. Harry. Mrs. Lambert must have been on George's right hand, so that we have but to settle the three places of the General, his son, and the Templar.

Mr. Spencer had been at the other theatre, where, on a former day, he had actually introduced George to the greenroom. The conversation about the play was resumed, and some of the party persisted in being delighted with it.

"As for what our gentlemen say, sir," cries Mrs. Lambert to Mr. Spencer, "you must not believe a word of it. 'Tis a delightful piece, and my husband and Mr. George behaved as ill as possible."

"We laughed in the wrong place, and when we ought to have cried," the General owned, "that's the truth."

"You caused all the people in the boxes about us to look round and cry 'Hush!' You made the pit folks say, 'Silence in the boxes, yonder!' Such behaviour I never knew, and quite blushed for you, Mr. Lambert!"

"Mamma thought it was a tragedy, and we thought it was a piece of fun," says the General. "George and I behaved perfectly well, didn't we, Theo?"

"Not when I was looking your way, papa!" Theo replies. At which the General asks, "Was there ever such a saucy baggage seen?"

"You know, sir, I didn't speak till I was bid," Theo continues, modestly. "I own I was very much moved by the play, and the beauty and acting of Mrs. Woffington. I was sorry that the poor mother should find her child, and lose him. I am sorry, too, papa, if I oughtn't to have been sorry!" adds the young lady, with a smile.

"Women are not so clever as men, you know, Theo," cries Hetty from her end of the table, with a sly look at Harry. "The next time we go to the play, please, brother Jack, pinch us when we ought to cry, or give us a nudge when it is right to laugh."

"I wish we could have had the fight," said General Lambert, "the fight between little Norval and the gigantic Norwegian—that would have been rare sport: and you should write, Jack, and suggest it to Mr. Rich, the manager."

"I have not seen that: but I saw Slack and Broughton at Marybone Gardens!" says Harry, gravely; and wondered if he had said something witty, as all the company laughed so? "It would require no giant," he added, "to knock over yonder little fellow in the red boots. I, for one, could throw him over my shoulder."

"Mr. Garrick is a little man. But there are times when he looks a giant," says

Mr. Spencer. "How grand he was in Macbeth, Mr. Warrington! How awful that dagger-scene was! You should have seen our host, ladies! I presented Mr. Warrington, in the greenroom, to Mr. Garrick and Mrs. Pritchard, and Lady Macbeth did him the honour to take a pinch out of his box."

"Did the wife of the Thane of Cawdor sneeze?" asked the General, in an awful voice.

"She thanked Mr. Warrington, in tones so hollow and tragic, that he started back, and must have upset some of his rappee, for Macbeth sneezed thrice."

"Macbeth, Macbeth, Macbeth!" cries the General.

"And the great philosopher who was standing by Mr. Johnson, says, 'You must mind, Davy, lest thy sneeze should awaken Duncan!' who, by the way, was talking with the three witches as they sat against the wall."

"What! Have you been behind the scenes at the play? Oh, I would give worlds to go behind the scenes!" cries Theo.

"And see the ropes pulled, and smell the tallow-candles, and look at the pasteboard gold, and the tinsel jewels, and the painted old women, Theo? No. Do not look too close," says the sceptical young host, demurely drinking a glass of hock. "You were angry with your papa and me."

"Nay, George!" cries the girl.

"Nay? I say, yes! You were angry with us because we laughed when you were disposed to be crying. If I may speak for you, sir, as well as myself," says George (with a bow to his guest, General Lambert), "I think we were not inclined to weep, like the ladies, because we stood behind the author's scenes of the play, as it were. Looking close up to the young hero, we saw how much of him was rant and tinsel; and as for the pale, tragical mother, that her pallor was white chalk, and her grief her pocket-handkerchief. Own now, Theo, you thought me very unfeeling?"

"If you find it out, sir, without my owning it,—what is the good of my confessing?" says Theo.

"Suppose I were to die?" goes on George, "and you saw Harry in grief, you would be seeing a genuine affliction, a real tragedy; you would grieve too. But you wouldn't be affected if you saw the undertaker in weepers and a black cloak!"

"Indeed, but I should, sir!" says Mrs. Lambert; "and so, I promise you, would any daughter of mine."

"Perhaps we might find weepers of our own, Mr. Warrington," says Theo, "in such a case."

"Would you?" cries George, and his cheeks and Theo's simultaneously flushed up with red; I suppose because they both saw Hetty's bright young eyes watching them.

"The elder writers understood but little of the pathetic," remarked Mr. Spencer, the Temple wit.

"What do you think of Sophocles and Antigone?" calls out Mr. John Lambert.

"Faith, our wits trouble themselves little about him, unless an Oxford gentleman comes to remind us of him! I did not mean to go back farther than Mr. Shakspeare, who, as you will all agree, does not understand the elegant and pathetic as well as the moderns. Has he ever approached Belvidera, or Monimia, or Jane Shore; or can you find in his comic female characters the elegance of Congreve?" and the Templar offered snuff to the right and left.

"I think Mr. Spencer himself must have tried his hand?" asks some one.

"Many gentlemen of leisure have. Mr. Garrick, I own, has had a piece of mine and returned it."

"And I confess that I have four acts of a play in one of my boxes," says George.

"I'll be bound to say it's as good as any of 'em," whispers Harry to his neighbour.

"Is it a tragedy or a comedy?" asks Mrs. Lambert.

"Oh, a tragedy, and two or three dreadful murders at least!" George replies.

"Let us play it, and let the audience look to their eyes! Yet my chief humour is for a tyrant," says the General.

"The tragedy, the tragedy! Go and fetch the tragedy this moment, Gumbo!" calls Mrs. Lambert to the black. Gumbo makes a low bow and says, "Tragedy? yes, madam."

"In the great cowskin trunk, Gumbo," George says, gravely.

Gumbo bows and says, "Yes, sir," with still superior gravity.

"But my tragedy is at the bottom of I don't know how much linen, packages, books, and boots, Hetty."

"Never mind, let us have it, and fling the linen out of window!" cries Miss Hetty.

"And the great cowskin trunk is at our agent's at Bristol: so Gumbo must get post-horses, and we can keep it up till he returns the day after to-morrow," says George.

The ladies groaned a comical "Oh!" and papa, perhaps more seriously, said, "Let us be thankful for the escape. Let us be thinking of going home too. Our young gentlemen have treated us nobly, and we will all drink a parting bumper to Madam Esmond Warrington of Castlewood, in Virginia. Suppose, boys, you were to find a tall, handsome stepfather when you got home? Ladies as old as she have been known to marry before now."

"To Madam Esmond Warrington, my old schoolfellow!" cries Mrs. Lambert. "I shall write and tell her what a pretty supper her sons have given us: and, Mr. George, I won't say how ill you behaved at the play!" And, with this last toast, the company took leave; the General's coach and servant, with a flambeau, being in waiting to carry his family home.

After such an entertainment as that which Mr. Warrington had given, what could be more natural or proper than a visit from him to his guests, to inquire how they had reached home and rested? Why, their coach might have taken the open country behind Montague House, in the direction of Oxford Road, and been waylaid by footpads in the fields. The ladies might have caught cold or slept ill after the excitement of the tragedy. In a word, there was no reason why he should make any excuse at all to himself or them for visiting his kind friends; and he shut his books early at the Sloane Museum, and perhaps thought, as he walked away thence, that he remembered very little about what he had been reading.

Pray what is the meaning of this eagerness, this hesitation, this pshaing and shilly-shallying, these doubts, this tremor as he knocks at the door of Mr. Lambert's lodgings in Dean Street, and survey the footman who comes to his summons? Does any young man read? does any old one remember? does any wearied, worn, disappointed pulseless heart recall the time of its full beat and early throbbing? It is ever so many hundred years since some of us were young; and we forget, but do not all forget. No, madam, we remember with advantages, as Shakspeare's Harry promised his soldiers they should do if they survived Agincourt and that day of St. Crispin. Worn old chargers turned out to grass, if the trumpet sounds over the hedge, may we not kick up our old heels, and gallop a minute or so about the paddock, till we are brought up roaring? I do not care for clown and pantaloon now, and think the fairy ugly, and her verses insufferable: but I like to see children at a pantomime. I do not dance, or eat supper any more; but I like to watch Eugenio and Flirtilla twirling round in a pretty waltz, or Lucinda and Ardentio pulling a cracker. Burn your little fingers, children! Blaze out little kindly flames from each other's eyes! And then draw close together and read the motto (that old namby-pamby motto, so stale and so new!)—I say, let her lips read it, and his construe it; and so divide the sweetmeat, young people, and crunch it between you. I have no teeth. Bitter almonds and sugar disagree with me, I tell you; but, for all that, shall not bonbons melt in the mouth?

We follow John upstairs to the General's apartments, and enter with Mr. George Esmond Warrington, who makes a prodigious fine bow. There is only one lady in the room, seated near a window: there is not often much sunshine in Dean Street: the young lady in the window is no especial beauty: but it is spring-time, and she is blooming vernally. A bunch of fresh roses is flushing in her honest cheek. I suppose her eyes are violets. If we lived a hundred years ago, and wrote in the Gentleman's or the London Magazine, we should tell Mr. Sylvanus Urban that her neck was the lily, and her shape the nymph's: we should write an acrostic about her, and celebrate our Lambertella in an elegant poem, still to be read between a neat new engraved plan of the city of Prague and the King of Prussia's camp, and a map of Maryland and the Delaware counties.

Here is Miss Theo blushing like a rose. What could mamma have meant an hour since by insisting that she was very pale and tired, and had best not come out to-day with the rest of the party? They were gone to pay their compliments to my Lord Wrotham's ladies, and thank them for the house in their absence; and papa was at the Horse Guards. He is in great spirits. I believe he expects some command, though mamma is in a sad tremor lest he should again be ordered abroad.

"Your brother and mine are gone to see our little brother at his school at the

Chartreux. My brothers are both to be clergymen, I think," Miss Theo continues. She is assiduously hemming at some article of boyish wearing apparel as she talks. A hundred years ago, young ladies were not afraid either to make shirts, or to name them. Mind, I don't say they were the worse or the better for that plain stitching or plain speaking: and have not the least desire, my dear young lady, that you should make puddings or I should black boots.

So Harry has been with them? "He often comes, almost every day," Theo says, looking up in George's face. "Poor fellow! He likes us better than the fine folks, who don't care for him now—now he is no longer a fine folk himself," adds the girl, smiling. "Why have you not set up for the fashion, and frequented the chocolate-houses and the racecourses, Mr. Warrington?"

"Has my brother got so much good out of his gay haunts or his grand friends, that I should imitate him?"

"You might at least go to Sir Miles Warrington; sure his arms are open to receive you. Her ladyship was here this morning in her chair, and to hear her praises of you! She declares you are in a certain way to preferment. She says his Royal Highness the Duke made much of you at court. When you are a great man will you forget us, Mr. Warrington?"

"Yes, when I am a great man I will, Miss Lambert."

"Well! Mr. George, then———"

"—Mr. George!"

"When papa and mamma are here, I suppose there need be no mistering," says Theo, looking out of the window, ever so little frightened. "And what have you been doing, sir? Reading books, or writing more of your tragedy? Is it going to be a tragedy to make us cry, as we like them, or only to frighten us, as you like them?"

"There is plenty of killing, but, I fear, not much crying. I have not met many women. I have not been very intimate with those. I daresay what I have written is only taken out of books or parodied from poems which I have read and imitated like other young men. Women do not speak to me, generally; I am said to have a sarcastic way which displeases them."

"Perhaps you never cared to please them?" inquires Miss Theo, with a blush.

"I displeased you last night; you know I did?"

"Yes; only it can't be called displeasure, and afterwards thought I was wrong."

"Did you think about me at all when I was away, Theo?"

"Yes, George—that is, Mr.—well, George! I thought you and papa were right about the play; and, as you said, that it was no real sorrow, only affectation, which was moving us. I wonder whether it is good or ill fortune to see so clearly? Hetty and I agreed that we would be very careful, for the future, how we allowed ourselves to enjoy a tragedy. So, be careful when yours comes! What is the name of it?"

"He is not christened. Will you be the godmother? The name of the chief character is———" But at this very moment mamma and Miss Hetty arrived from their walk; and mamma straightway began protesting that she never expected to see Mr. Warrington at all that day—that is, she thought he might come—that is, it was very good of him to come, and the play and the supper of yesterday were all charming, except that Theo had a little headache this morning.

"I dare say it is better now, mamma," says Miss Hetty.

"Indeed, my dear, it never was of any consequence; and I told mamma so," says Miss Theo, with a toss of her head.

Then they fell to talking about Harry. He was very low. He must have something to do. He was always going to the Military Coffee-House, and perpetually poring over the King of Prussia's campaigns. It was not fair upon him, to bid him remain in London, after his deposition, as it were. He said nothing, but you could see how he regretted his previous useless life, and felt his present dependence, by the manner in which he avoided his former haunts and associates. Passing by the guard at St. James's, with John Lambert, he had said to brother Jack, "Why mayn't I be a soldier too? I am as tall as yonder fellow, and can kill with a fowling-piece as well as any man I know. But I can't earn so much as sixpence a day. I have squandered my own bread, and now I am eating half my brother's. He is the best of brothers, but so much the more shame that I should live upon him. Don't tell my brother, Jack Lambert." "And my boy promised he wouldn't tell," says Mrs. Lambert. No doubt. The girls were both out of the room when their mother made this speech to George Warrington. He, for his part, said he had written home to his mother —that half his little patrimony, the other half likewise, if wanted, were at Harry's disposal, for purchasing a commission, or for any other project which might bring him occupation or advancement.

"He has got a good brother, that is sure. Let us hope for good times for him," sighs the lady.

"The Danes always come pour qui scait attendre," George said, in a low voice.

"What, you heard that? Ah, George! my Theo is an——Ah! never mind what she is, George Warrington," cried the pleased mother, with brimful eyes. "Bah! I am going to make a gaby of myself, as I did at the tragedy."

Now Mr. George had been revolving a fine private scheme, which he thought might turn to his brother's advantage. After George's presentation to his Royal Highness at Kensington, more persons than one, his friend General Lambert included, had told him that the Duke had inquired regarding him, and had asked why the young man did not come to his levee. Importunity so august could not but be satisfied. A day was appointed between Mr. Lambert and his young friend, and they went to pay their duty to his Royal Highness at his house in Pall Mall.

When it came to George's turn to make a bow, the Prince was especially gracious; he spoke to Mr. Warrington at some length about Braddock and the war, and was apparently pleased with the modesty and intelligence of the young gentleman's answers. George ascribed the failure of the expedition to the panic and surprise certainly, but more especially to the delays occasioned by the rapacity, selfishness, and unfair dealing of the people of the colonies towards the King's troops who were come to defend them. "Could we have moved, sir, a month sooner, the fort was certainly ours, and the little army had never been defeated," Mr. Warrington said; in which observation his Royal Highness entirely concurred.

"I am told you saved yourself, sir, mainly by your knowledge of the French language," the Royal Duke then affably observed. Mr. Warrington modestly mentioned how he had been in the French colonies in his youth, and had opportunities of acquiring that tongue.

The Prince (who had a great urbanity when well pleased, and the finest sense of humour) condescended to ask who had taught Mr. Warrington the language; and to express his opinion, that, for the pronunciation, the French ladies were by far the best teachers.

The young Virginian gentleman made a low bow, and said it was not for him to gainsay his Royal Highness; upon which the Duke was good enough to say (in a jocose manner) that Mr. Warrington was a sly dog.

Mr. W. remaining respectfully silent, the Prince continued, most kindly: "I take the field immediately against the French, who, as you know, are threatening his Majesty's Electoral dominions, If you have a mind to make the campaign with me, your skill in the language may be useful, and I hope we shall be more fortunate than poor Braddock!" Every eye was fixed on a young man to whom so great a Prince offered so signal a favour.

And now it was that Mr. George thought he would make his very cleverest speech. "Sir," he said, "your Royal Highness's most kind proposal does me infinite honour, but——"

"But what, sir?" says the Prince, staring at him.

"But I have entered myself of the Temple, to study our laws, and to fit myself for my duties at home. If my having been wounded in the service of my country be any claim on your kindness, I would humbly ask that my brother, who knows the French language as well as myself, and has far more strength, courage, and military genius, might be allowed to serve your Royal Highness; in the place of——"

"Enough, enough, sir!" cried out the justly irritated son of the monarch. "What? I offer you a favour, and you hand it over to your brother? Wait, sir, till I offer you another!" And with this the Prince turned his back upon Mr. Warrington, just as abruptly as he turned it on the French a few months afterwards.

"Oh, George! oh, George! Here's a pretty kettle of fish!" groaned General Lambert, as he and his young friend walked home together.

CHAPTER LXI. In which the Prince marches up the Hill and down again

We understand the respectful indignation of all loyal Britons when they come to read of Mr. George Warrington's conduct towards a gallant and gracious Prince, the beloved son of the best of monarchs, and the Captain-General of the British army. What an inestimable favour has not the young man slighted! What a chance of promotion had he not thrown away! Will Esmond, whose language was always rich in blasphemies, employed his very strongest curses in speaking of his cousin's behaviour, and expressed his delight that the confounded young Mohock was cutting his own throat. Cousin Castlewood said that a savage gentleman had a right to scalp himself if he liked; or perhaps, he added charitably, our cousin Mr. Warrington heard enough of the war-whoop in Braddock's affair, and has no more stomach for fighting. Mr. Will rejoiced that the younger brother had gone to the deuce, and he rejoiced to think that the elder was following him. The first time he met the fellow, Will said, he should take care to let Mr. George know what he thought of him.

"If you intend to insult George, at least you had best take care that his brother Harry is out of hearing!" cried Lady Maria—on which we may fancy more curses uttered by Mr. Will, with regard to his twin kinsfolk.

"Ta, ta, ta!" says my lord. "No more of this squabbling! We can't be all warriors in the family!"

"I never heard your lordship laid claim to be one!" says Maria.

"Never, my dear; quite the contrary! Will is our champion, and one is quite enough in the house. So I dare say with the two Mohocks;—George is the student, and Harry is the fighting man. When you intended to quarrel, Will, what a pity it was you had not George, instead of t'other, to your hand!"

"Your lordship's hand is famous—at piquet," says Will's mother.

"It is a pretty one," says my lord, surveying his fingers, with a simper. "My Lord Hervey's glove and mine were of a size. Yes, my hand, as you say, is more fitted for cards than for war. Yours, my Lady Castlewood, is pretty dexterous, too. How I bless the day when you bestowed it on my lamented father!" In this play of sarcasm, as in some other games of skill, his lordship was not sorry to engage, having a cool head, and being able to beat his family all round.

Madame de Bernstein, when she heard of Mr. Warrington's bevue, was exceedingly angry, stormed, and scolded her immediate household; and would have scolded George but she was growing old, and had not the courage of her early days. Moreover, she was a little afraid of her nephew, and respectful in her behaviour to him. "You will never make your fortune at court, nephew!" she groaned, when, soon after his discomfiture, the young gentleman went to wait upon her.

"It was never my wish, madam," said Mr. George, in a very stately manner.

"Your wish was to help Harry? You might hereafter have been of service to your brother, had you accepted the Duke's offer. Princes do not love to have their favours refused, and I don't wonder that his Royal Highness was offended."

"General Lambert said the same thing," George confessed, turning rather red; "and I see now that I was wrong. But you must please remember that I had never seen a court before, and I suppose I am scarce likely to shine in one."

"I think possibly not, my good nephew," says the aunt, taking snuff.

"And what then?" asked George. "I never had ambition for that kind of glory, and can make myself quite easy without it. When his Royal Highness spoke to me—most kindly, as I own—my thought was, I shall make a very bad soldier, and my brother would be a very good one. He has a hundred good qualities for the profession, in which I am deficient; and would have served a Commanding Officer far better than I ever could. Say the Duke is in battle, and his horse is shot, as my poor chief's was at home, would he not be better for a beast that had courage and strength to bear him anywhere, than with one that could not carry his weight?"

"Au fait. His Royal Highness's charger must be a strong one, my dear!" says the old lady.

"Expende Hannibalem," mutters George, with a shrug. "Our Hannibal weighs no trifle."

"I don't quite follow you, sir, and your Hannibal," the Baroness remarks.

"When Mr. Wolfe and Mr. Lambert remonstrated with me as you have done, madam," George rejoins, with a laugh, "I made this same defence which I am making to you. I said I offered to the Prince the best soldier in the family, and the two gentlemen allowed that my blunder at least had some excuse. Who knows but that they may set me right with his Royal Highness? The taste I have had of battles has shown me how little my genius inclines that way. We saw the Scotch play which everybody is talking about t'other night. And when the hero, young Norval, said how he longed to follow to the field some warlike lord, I thought to myself, 'how like my Harry is to him, except that he doth not brag.' Harry is pining now for a red coat, and if we don't mind, will take the shilling. He has the map of Germany for ever under his eyes, and follows the King of Prussia everywhere. He is not afraid of men or gods. As for me, I love my books and quiet best, and to read about battles in Homer or Lucan."

"Then what made a soldier of you at all, my dear? And why did you not send Harry with Mr. Braddock, instead of going yourself?" asked Madame de Bernstein.

"My mother loved her younger son the best," said George, darkly. "Besides, with the enemy invading our country, it was my duty, as the head of our family, to go on the campaign. Had I been a Scotchman twelve years ago, I should have been a———"

"Hush, sir! or I shall be more angry than ever!" said the old lady, with a perfectly pleased face.

George's explanation might thus appease Madame de Bernstein, an old woman whose principles we fear were but loose: but to the loyal heart of Sir Miles Warrington and his lady, the young man's conduct gave a severe blow indeed! "I should have thought," her ladyship said, "from my sister Esmond Warrington's letter, that my brother's widow was a woman of good sense and judgment, and that she had educated her sons in a becoming manner. But what, Sir Miles, what, my dear Thomas Claypool, can we think of an education which has resulted so lamentably for both these young men?"

"The elder seems to know a power of Latin, though, and speaks the French and the German too. I heard him with the Hanover Envoy, at the Baroness's rout," says Mr. Claypool. "The French he jabbered quite easy: and when he was at a loss for the High Dutch, he and the Envoy began in Latin, and talked away till all the room stared."

"It is not language, but principles, Thomas Claypool!" exclaims the virtuous matron. "What must Mr. Warrington's principles be, when he could reject an offer made him by his Prince? Can he speak the High Dutch? So much the more ought he to have accepted his Royal Highness's condescension, and made himself useful in the campaign! Look at our son, look at Miles!"

"Hold up thy head, Miley, my boy!" says papa.

"I trust, Sir Miles, that, as a member of the House of Commons, as an English gentleman, you will attend his Royal Highness's levee to-morrow, and say, if such an offer had been made to us for that child, we would have taken it, though our boy is but ten years of age."

"Faith, Miley, thou wouldst make a good little drummer or fifer!" says papa. "Shouldst like to be a little soldier, Miley?"

"Anything, sir, anything! a Warrington ought to be ready at any moment to have himself cut in pieces for his sovereign!" cries the matron, pointing to the boy; who, as soon as he comprehended his mother's proposal, protested against it by a loud roar, in the midst of which he was removed by Screwby. In obedience to the conjugal orders, Sir Miles went to his Royal Highness's levee the next day, and made a protest of his love and duty, which the Prince deigned to accept, saying:

"Nobody ever supposed that Sir Miles Warrington would ever refuse any place offered to him."

A compliment gracious indeed, and repeated everywhere by Lady Warrington, as showing how implicitly the august family on the throne could rely on the loyalty of the Warringtons.

Accordingly, when this worthy couple saw George, they received him with a ghastly commiseration, such as our dear relatives or friends will sometimes extend to us when we have done something fatal or clumsy in life; when we have come badly out of our lawsuit; when we enter the room just as the company has been abusing us; when our banker has broke; or we for our sad part have had to figure in the commercial columns of the London Gazette;—when, in a word, we are guilty of some notorious fault, or blunder, or misfortune. Who does not know that face of pity? Whose dear relations have not so deplored him, not dead, but living? Not yours? Then, sir, if you have never been in scrapes; if you have never sowed a handful of wild oats or two; if you have always been fortunate, and good, and careful, and butter has never melted in your mouth, and an imprudent word has never come out of it; if you have never sinned and repented, and been a fool and been sorry—then, sir, you are a wiseacre who won't waste your time over an idle novel, and it is not de te that the fable is narrated at all.

Not that it was just on Sir Miles's part to turn upon George, and be angry with his nephew for refusing the offer of promotion made by his Royal Highness, for Sir Miles himself had agreed in George's view of pursuing quite other than a military career, and it was in respect to this plan of her son's that Madam Esmond had written from Virginia to Sir Miles Warrington. George had announced to her his intention of entering at the Temple, and qualifying himself for the magisterial and civil duties which, in the course of nature, he would be called to fulfil; nor could any one applaud his resolution more cordially than his uncle Sir Miles, who introduced George to a lawyer of reputation, under whose guidance we may fancy the young gentleman reading leisurely. Madam Esmond from home signified her approval of her son's course, fully agreeing with Sir Miles (to whom and his lady she begged to send her grateful remembrances) that the British Constitution was the envy of the world, and the proper object of every English gentleman's admiring study. The chief point to which George's mother objected was the notion that Mr. Warrington should have to sit down in the Temple dinner-ball, and cut at a shoulder of mutton, and drink small-beer out of tin pannikins, by the side of rough students who wore gowns like the parish-clerk. George's loyal younger brother shared too this repugnance. Anything was good enough for him, Harry said; he was a younger son, and prepared to rough it; but George, in a gown, and dining in a mess with three nobody's sons off dirty pewter platters! Harry never could relish this condescension on his brother's part, or fancy George in his proper place at any except the high table; and was sorry that a plan Madam Esmond hinted at in her letters was not feasible—viz., that an application should be made to the Master of the Temple, who should be informed that Mr. George Warrington was a gentleman of most noble birth, and of great property in America, and ought only to sit with the very best company in the Hall. Rather to Harry's discomfiture, when he communicated his own and his mother's ideas to the gentlemen's new coffee-house friend, Mr. Spencer, Mr. Spencer received the proposal with roars of laughter; and I cannot learn, from the Warrington papers, that any application was made to the Master of the Temple on this subject. Besides his literary and historical pursuits, which were those he most especially loved, Mr. Warrington studied the laws of his country, attended the courts at Westminster, where he heard a Henley, a Pratt, a Murray, and those other great famous schools of eloquence and patriotism, the two houses of parliament.

Gradually Mr. Warrington made acquaintance with some of the members of the House and the Bar; who, when they came to know him, spoke of him as a young gentleman of good parts and good breeding, and in terms so generally complimentary, that his good uncle's heart relented towards him, and Dora and Flora began once more to smile upon him. This reconciliation dated from the time when his Royal Highness the Duke, after having been defeated by the French, in the affair of Hastenbeck, concluded the famous capitulation with the French, which his Majesty George II. refused to ratify. His Royal Highness, as 'tis well known, flung up his commissions after this disgrace, laid down his commander's baton—which, it must be confessed, he had not wielded with much luck or dexterity—and never again appeared at the head of armies or in public life. The stout warrior would not allow a word of complaint against his father and sovereign to escape his lips; but, as he retired with his wounded honour, and as he would have no interest or authority more, nor any places to give, it may be supposed that Sir Miles Warrington's anger against his nephew diminished as his respect for his Royal Highness diminished.

As our two gentlemen were walking in St. James's Park, one day, with their friend Mr. Lambert, they met his Royal Highness in plain clothes and without a star, and made profound bows to the Prince, who was pleased to stop and speak to them.

He asked Mr. Lambert how he liked my Lord Ligonier, his new chief at the Horse Guards, and the new duties there in which he was engaged? And, recognising the young men, with that fidelity of memory for which his Royal race hath ever been remarkable, he said to Mr. Warrington:

"You did well, sir, not to come with me when I asked you in the spring."

"I was sorry, then, sir," Mr. Warrington said, making a very low reverence, "but I am more sorry now."

On which the Prince said, "Thank you, sir," and, touching his hat, walked away. And the circumstances of this interview, and the discourse which passed at it, being related to Mrs. Esmond Warrington in a letter from her younger son, created so deep an impression in that lady's mind, that she narrated the anecdote many hundreds of times until all her friends and acquaintances knew and, perhaps, were tired of it.

Our gentlemen went through the Park, and so towards the Strand, where they had business. And Mr. Lambert, pointing to the lion on the top of the Earl of Northumberland's house at Charing Cross, says:

"Harry Warrington! your brother is like yonder lion."

"Because he is as brave as one," says Harry.

"Because I respect virgins!" says George, laughing.

"Because you are a stupid lion. Because you turn your back on the East, and absolutely salute the setting sun. Why, child, what earthly good can you get by being civil to a man in hopeless dudgeon and disgrace? Your uncle will be more angry with you than ever—and so am I, sir." But Mr. Lambert was always laughing in his waggish way, and, indeed, he did not look the least angry.

CHAPTER LXII. Arma Virumque

Indeed, if Harry Warrington had a passion for military pursuits and studies, there was enough of war stirring in Europe, and enough talk in all societies which he frequented in London, to excite and inflame him. Though our own gracious Prince of the house of Hanover had been beaten, the Protestant Hero, the King of Prussia, was filling the world with his glory, and winning those astonishing victories in which I deem it fortunate on my own account that my poor Harry took no part; for then his veracious biographer would have had to narrate battles the description whereof has been undertaken by another pen. I am glad, I say, that Harry Warrington was not at Rossbach on that famous Gunpowder Fete-day, on the 5th of November, in the year 1757; nor at that tremendous slaughtering-match of Leuthen, which the Prussian king played a month afterwards; for these prodigious actions will presently be narrated in other volumes, which I and all the world are eager to behold. Would you have this history compete with yonder book? Could my jaunty, yellow park-phaeton run counter to that grim chariot of thundering war? Could my meek little jog-trot Pegasus meet the shock of yon steed of foaming bit and flaming nostril? Dear, kind reader (with whom I love to talk from time to time, stepping down from the stage where our figures are performing, attired in the habits and using the parlance of past ages),—my kind, patient reader! it is a mercy for both of us that Harry Warrington did not follow the King of the Borussians, as he was minded to do, for then I should have had to describe battles which Carlyle is going to paint; and I don't wish you should make odious comparisons between me and that master.

Harry Warrington not only did not join the King of the Borussians, but he pined and chafed at not going. He led a sulky useless life, that is the fact. He dangled about the military coffee-houses. He did not care for reading anything save a newspaper. His turn was not literary. He even thought novels were stupid; and, as for the ladies crying their eyes out over Mr. Richardson, he could not imagine how they could be moved by any such nonsense. He used to laugh in a very hearty jolly way, but a little late, and some time after the joke was over. Pray, why should all gentlemen have a literary turn? And do we like some of our friends the worse because they never turned a couplet in their lives? Ruined, perforce idle, dependent on his brother for supplies, if he read a book falling asleep over it, with no fitting work for his great strong hands to do—how lucky it is that he did not get into more trouble! Why, in the case of Achilles himself, when he was sent by his mamma to the court of King What-d'ye-call-'em in order to be put out of harm's reach, what happened to him amongst a parcel of women with whom he was made to idle his life away? And how did Pyrrhus come into the world? A powerful mettlesome young Achilles ought not to be leading-stringed by women too much; is out of his place dawdling by distaffs or handing coffee-cups; and when he is not fighting, depend on it, is likely to fall into much worse mischief.

Those soft-hearted women, the two elder ladies of the Lambert family, with whom he mainly consorted, had an untiring pity and kindness for Harry, such as women only—and only a few of those—can give. If a man is in grief, who cheers him; in trouble, who consoles him; in wrath, who soothes him; in joy, who makes him doubly happy; in prosperity, who rejoices; in disgrace, who backs him against the world, and dresses with gentle unguents and warm poultices the rankling wounds made by the slings and arrows of outrageous Fortune? Who but woman, if you please? You who are ill and sore from the buffets of Fate, have you one or two of these sweet physicians? Return thanks to the gods that they have left you so much of consolation. What gentleman is not more or less a Prometheus? Who has not his rock (ai, ai), his chain (ea, ea), and his liver in a deuce of a condition? But the sea-nymphs come—the gentle, the sympathising; they kiss our writhing feet; they moisten our parched lips with their tears; they do their blessed best to console us Titans; they don't turn their backs upon us after our overthrow.

Now Theo and her mother were full of pity for Harry; but Hetty's heart was rather hard and seemingly savage towards him. She chafed that his position was not more glorious; she was angry that he was still dependent and idle. The whole world was in arms, and could he not carry a musket? It was harvest-time, and hundreds of thousands of reapers were out with their flashing sickles; could he not use his, and cut down his sheaf or two of glory?

"Why, how savage the little thing is with him!" says papa, after a scene in which, according to her wont, Miss Hetty had been firing little shots into that quivering target which came and set itself up in Mrs. Lambert's drawing-room every day.

"Her conduct is perfectly abominable!" cries mamma; "she deserves to be whipped, and sent to bed."

"Perhaps, mother, it is because she likes him better than any of us do," says Theo, "and it is for his sake that Hetty is angry. If I were fond of—of some one, I should like to be able to admire and respect him always—to think everything he did right—and my gentleman better than all the gentlemen in the world."

"The truth is, my dear," answers Mrs. Lambert, "that your father is so much better than all the world, he has spoiled us. Did you ever see any one to compare with him?"

"Very few, indeed," owns Theo, with a blush.

"Very few. Who is so good-tempered?"

"I think nobody, mamma," Theo acknowledges.

"Or so brave?"

"Why, I dare say Mr. Wolfe, or Harry, or Mr. George, are very brave."

"Or so learned and witty?"

"I am sure Mr. George seems very learned, and witty too, in his way," says Theo; "and his manners are very fine—you own they are. Madame de Bernstein says they are, and she hath seen the world. Indeed, Mr. George has a lofty way with him, which I don't see in other people; and, in reading books, I find he chooses the fine noble things always, and loves them in spite of all his satire. He certainly is of a satirical turn, but then he is only bitter against mean things and people. No gentleman hath a more tender heart I am sure; and but yesterday, after he had been talking so bitterly as you said, I happened to look out of window, and saw him stop and treat a whole crowd of little children to apples at the stall at the corner. And the day before yesterday, when he was coming and brought me the Moliere, he stopped and gave money to a beggar, and how charmingly, sure, he reads the French! I agree with him though about Tartuffe, though 'tis so wonderfully clever and lively, that a mere villain and hypocrite is a figure too mean to be made the chief of a great piece. Iago, Mr. George said, is near as great a villain; but then he is not the first character of the tragedy, which is Othello, with his noble weakness. But what fine ladies and gentlemen Moliere represents—so Mr. George thinks—and—but oh, I don't dare to repeat the verses after him."

"But you know them by heart, my dear?" asks Mrs. Lambert.

And Theo replies, "Oh yes, mamma! I know them by... Nonsense!"

I here fancy osculations, palpitations, and exit Miss Theo, blushing like a rose. Why had she stopped in her sentence? Because mamma was looking at her so oddly. And why was mamma looking at her so oddly? And why had she looked after Mr. George when he was going away, and looked for him when he was coming? Ah, and why do cheeks blush, and why do roses bloom? Old Time is still a-flying. Old spring and bud time; old summer and bloom time; old autumn and seed time; old winter time, when the cracking, shivering old tree-tops are bald or covered with snow.

A few minutes after George arrived, Theo would come downstairs with a fluttering heart, may be, and a sweet nosegay in her cheeks, just culled, as it were, fresh in his honour; and I suppose she must have been constantly at that window which commanded the street, and whence she could espy his generosity to the sweep, or his purchases from the apple-woman. But if it was Harry who knocked, she remained in her own apartment with her work or her books, sending her sister to receive the young gentleman, or her brothers when the elder was at home from college, or Doctor Crusius from the Chartreux gave the younger leave to go home. And what good eyes Theo must have had—and often in the evening, too—to note the difference between Harry's yellow hair and George's dark locks—and between their figures, though they were so like that people continually were mistaking one for the other brother. Now it is certain that Theo never mistook one or t'other; and that Hetty, for her part, was not in the least excited, or rude, or pert, when she found the black-haired gentleman in her mother's drawing-room.

Our friends could come when they liked to Mr. Lambert's house, and stay as long as they chose; and, one day, he of the golden locks was sitting on a couch there, in an attitude of more than ordinary idleness and despondency, when who should come down to him but Miss Hetty? I say it was a most curious thing (though the girls would have gone to the rack rather than own any collusion), that when Harry called, Hetty appeared; when George arrived, Theo somehow came; and so, according to the usual dispensation, it was Miss Lambert, junior, who now arrived to entertain the younger Virginian.

After usual ceremonies and compliments we may imagine that the lady says to the gentleman:

"And pray, sir, what makes your honour look so glum this morning?"

"Ah, Hetty!" says he, "I have nothing else to do but to look glum. I remember when we were boys—and I a rare idle one, you may be sure—I would always be asking my tutor for a holiday, which I would pass very likely swinging on a gate, or making ducks and drakes over the pond, and those do-nothing days were always the most melancholy. What have I got to do now from morning till night?"

"Breakfast, walk—dinner, walk—tea, supper, I suppose; and a pipe of your Virginia," says Miss Hetty, tossing her head.

"I tell you what, when I went back with Charley to the Chartreux, t'other night, I had a mind to say to the master, 'Teach me, sir. Here's a boy knows a deal more Latin and Greek, at thirteen, than I do, who am ten years older. I have nothing to do from morning till night, and I might as well go to my books again, and see if I can repair my idleness as a boy.' Why do you laugh, Hetty?"

"I laugh to fancy you at the head of a class, and called up by the master!" cries Hetty.

"I shouldn't be at the head of the class," Harry says, humbly. "George might be at the head of any class, but I am not a bookman, you see; and when I was young neglected myself, and was very idle. We would not let our tutors cane us much at home, but, if we had, it might have done me good."

Hetty drubbed with her little foot, and looked at the young man sitting before her—strong, idle, melancholy.

"Upon my word, it might do you good now!" she was minded to say. "What does Tom say about the caning at school? Does his account of it set you longing for it, pray?" she asked.

"His account of his school," Harry answered simply, "makes me see that I have been idle when I ought to have worked, and that I have not a genius for books, and for what am I good? Only to spend my patrimony when I come abroad, or to lounge at coffee-houses or racecourses, or to gallop behind dogs when I am at home. I am good for nothing, I am."

"What, such a great, brave, strong fellow as you good for nothing?" cries Het. "I would not confess as much to any woman, if I were twice as good for nothing!"

"What am I to do? I ask for leave to go into the army, and Madam Esmond does not answer me. 'Tis the only thing I am fit for. I have no money to buy. Having spent all my own, and so much of my brother's, I cannot and won't ask for more. If my mother would but send me to the army, you know I would jump to go."

"Eh! A gentleman of spirit does not want a woman to buckle his sword on for him or to clean his firelock! What was that our papa told us of the young gentleman at court yesterday?—Sir John Armytage——"

"Sir John Armytage? I used to know him when I frequented White's and the club-houses—a fine, noble young gentleman, of a great estate in the North."

"And engaged to be married to a famous beauty, too—Miss Howe, my Lord Howe's sister—but that, I suppose, is not an obstacle to gentlemen?"

"An obstacle to what?" asks the gentleman.

"An obstacle to glory!" says Miss Hetty. "I think no woman of spirit would say 'Stay!' though she adored her lover ever so much, when his country said 'Go!' Sir John had volunteered for the expedition which is preparing, and being at court yesterday his Majesty asked him when he would be ready to go? 'Tomorrow, please your Majesty,' replies Sir John, and the king said, that was a soldier's answer. My father himself is longing to go, though he has mamma and all us brats at home. Oh dear, oh dear! Why wasn't I a man myself? Both my brothers are for the Church; but, as for me, I know I should have made a famous little soldier!" And, so speaking, this young person strode about the room, wearing a most courageous military aspect, and looking as bold as Joan of Arc.

Harry beheld her with a tender admiration. "I think," says he, "I would hardly like to see a musket on that little shoulder, nor a wound on that pretty face, Hetty."

"Wounds! who fears wounds?" cries the little maid. "Muskets? If I could carry one, I would use it. You men fancy that we women are good for nothing but to make puddings or stitch samplers. Why wasn't I a man, I say? George was reading to us yesterday out of Tasso—look, here it is, and I thought the verses applied to me. See! Here is the book, with the mark in it where we left off."

"With the mark in it?" says Harry dutifully.

"Yes! it is about a woman who is disappointed because—because her brother does not go to war, and she says of herself—

"'Alas! why did not Heaven these members frail
With lively force and vigour strengthen, so
That I this silken gown...'"

"Silken gown?" says downright Harry, with a look of inquiry.

"Well, sir, I know 'tis but Calimanco;—but so it is in the book—

"'... this silken gown and slender veil
Might for a breastplate and a helm forgo;
Then should not heat, nor cold, nor rain, nor hail,
Nor storms that fall, nor blust'ring winds that blow,
Withhold me; but I would, both day and night,
In pitched field or private combat, fight—'

"Fight? Yes, that I would! Why are both my brothers to be parsons, I say? One of my papa's children ought to be a soldier!"

Harry laughed, a very gentle, kind laugh, as he looked at her. He felt that he would not like much to hit such a tender little warrior as that.

"Why," says he, holding a finger out, "I think here is a finger nigh as big as your arm. How would you stand up before a great, strong man? I should like to see a man try and injure you, though; I should just like to see him! You little, delicate, tender creature! Do you suppose any scoundrel would dare to do anything unkind to you?" And, excited by this flight of his imagination, Harry fell to walking up and down the room, too, chafing at the idea of any rogue of a Frenchman daring to be rude to Miss Hester Lambert.

It was a belief in this silent courage of his which subjugated Hetty, and this quality which she supposed him to possess, which caused her specially to admire him. Miss Hetty was no more bold, in reality, than Madam Erminia, whose speech she had been reading out of the book, and about whom Mr. Harry Warrington never heard one single word. He may have been in the room when brother George was reading his poetry out to the ladies, but his thoughts were busy with his own affairs, and he was entirely bewildered with your Clotildas and Erminias, and giants, and enchanters, and nonsense. No, Miss Hetty, I say and believe, had nothing of the virago in her composition; else, no doubt, she would have taken a fancy to a soft young fellow with a literary turn, or a genius for playing the flute, according to the laws of contrast and nature provided in those cases; and who has not heard how great, strong men have an affinity for frail, tender little women; how tender little women are attracted by great, honest, strong men; and how your burly heroes and champions of war are constantly henpecked? If Mr. Harry Warrington falls in love with a woman who is like Miss Lambert in disposition, and if he marries her—without being conjurers, I think we may all see what the end will be.

So, whilst Hetty was firing her little sarcasms into Harry, he for a while scarcely felt that they were stinging him, and let her shoot on without so much as taking the trouble to shake the little arrows out of his hide. Did she mean by her sneers and innuendoes to rouse him into action? He was too magnanimous to understand such small hints. Did she mean to shame him by saying that she, a weak woman, would don the casque and breastplate? The simple fellow either melted at the idea of her being in danger, or at the notion of her fighting fell a-laughing.

"Pray what is the use of having a strong hand if you only use it to hold a skein of silk for my mother?" cries Miss Hester; "and what is the good of being ever so strong in a drawing-room? Nobody wants you to throw anybody out of window, Harry! A strong man, indeed! I suppose there's a stronger at Bartholomew Fair. James Wolfe is not a strong man. He seems quite weakly and ill. When he was here last he was coughing the whole time, and as pale as if he had seen a ghost."

"I never could understand why a man should be frightened at a ghost," says Harry.

"Pray, have you seen one, sir?" asks the pert young lady.

"No. I thought I did once at home—when we were boys; but it was only Nathan in his night-shirt; but I wasn't frightened when I thought he was a ghost. I believe there's no such things. Our nurses tell a pack of lies about 'em," says Harry, gravely. "George was a little frightened; but then he's——" Here he paused.

"Then George is what?" asked Hetty.

"George is different from me, that's all. Our mother's a bold woman as ever you saw, but she screams at seeing a mouse—always does—can't help it. It's her nature. So, you see, perhaps my brother can't bear ghosts. I don't mind 'em."

"George always says you would have made a better soldier than he."

"So I think I should, if I had been allowed to try. But he can do a thousand things better than me, or anybody else in the world. Why didn't he let me volunteer on Braddock's expedition? I might have got knocked on the head, and then I should have been pretty much as useful as I am now, and then I shouldn't have ruined myself, and brought people to point at me and say that I had disgraced the name of Warrington. Why mayn't I go on this expedition, and volunteer like Sir John Armytage? Oh, Hetty! I'm a miserable fellow—that's what I am," and the miserable fellow paced the room at double quick time. "I wish I had never come to Europe," he groaned out.

"What a compliment to us! Thank you, Harry!" But presently, on an appealing look from the gentleman, she added, "Are you—are you thinking of going home?"

"And have all Virginia jeering at me! There's not a gentleman there that wouldn't, except one, and him my mother doesn't like. I should be ashamed to go home now, I think. You don't know my mother, Hetty. I ain't afraid of most things; but, somehow, I am of her. What shall I say to her, when she says, 'Harry, where's your patrimony?' 'Spent, mother,' I shall have to say. 'What have you done with it?' 'Wasted it, mother, and went to prison after.' 'Who took you out of prison?' 'Brother George, ma'am, he took me out of prison; and now I'm come back, having done no good for myself, with no profession, no prospects, no nothing—only to look after negroes, and be scolded at home; or to go to sleep at sermons; or to play at cards, and drink, and fight cocks at the taverns about.' How can I look the gentlemen of the country in the face? I'm ashamed to go home in this way, I say. I must and will do something! What shall I do, Hetty? Ah! what shall I do?"

"Do? What did Mr. Wolfe do at Louisbourg? Ill as he was, and in love as we knew him to be, he didn't stop to be nursed by his mother, Harry, or to dawdle with his sweetheart. He went on the King's service, and hath come back covered with honour. If there is to be another great campaign in America, papa says he is sure of a great command."

"I wish he would take me with him, and that a ball would knock me on the head and finish me," groaned Harry. "You speak to me, Hetty, as though it were my fault that I am not in the army, when you know I would give—give, forsooth, what have I to give?—yes! my life to go on service!"

"Life indeed!" says Miss Hetty, with a shrug of her shoulders.

"You don't seem to think that of much value, Hetty," remarked Harry, sadly. "No more it is—to anybody. I'm a poor useless fellow. I'm not even free to throw it away as I would like, being under orders here and at home."

"Orders indeed! Why under orders?" cries Miss Hetty. "Aren't you tall enough, and old enough, to act for yourself, and must you have George for a master here, and your mother for a schoolmistress at home? If I were a man, I would do something famous before I was two-and-twenty years old, that I would! I would have the world speak of me. I wouldn't dawdle at apron-strings. I wouldn't curse my fortune—I'd make it. I vow and declare I would!"

Now, for the first time, Harry began to wince at the words of his young lecturer.

"No negro on our estate is more a slave than I am, Hetty," he said, turning very red as he addressed her; "but then, Miss Lambert, we don't reproach the poor fellow for not being free. That isn't generous. At least, that isn't the way I understand honour. Perhaps with women it's different, or I may be wrong, and have no right to be hurt at a young girl telling me what my faults are. Perhaps my faults are not my faults—only my cursed luck. You have been talking ever so long about this gentleman volunteering, and that man winning glory, and cracking up their courage as if I had none of my own. I suppose, for the matter of that, I'm as well provided as other gentlemen. I don't brag but I'm not afraid of Mr. Wolfe, nor of Sir John Armytage, nor of anybody else that ever I saw. How can I buy a commission when I've spent my last shilling, or ask my brother for more who has already halved with me? A gentleman of my rank can't go a common soldier—else, by Jupiter, I would! And if a ball finished me, I suppose Miss Hetty Lambert wouldn't be very sorry. It isn't kind, Hetty—I didn't think it of you."

"What is it I have said?" asks the young lady. "I have only said Sir John Armytage has volunteered, and Mr. Wolfe has covered himself with honour, and you begin to scold me! How can I help it if Mr. Wolfe is brave and famous? Is that any reason you should be angry, pray?"

"I didn't say angry," said Harry, gravely. "I said I was hurt."

"Oh, indeed! I thought such a little creature as I am couldn't hurt anybody! I'm sure 'tis mighty complimentary to me to say that a young lady whose arm is no bigger than your little finger can hurt such a great strong man as you!"

"I scarce thought you would try, Hetty," the young man said. "You see, I'm not used to this kind of welcome in this house."

"What is it, my poor boy?" asks kind Mrs. Lambert, looking in at the door at this juncture, and finding the youth with a very woeworn countenance.

"Oh, we have heard the story before, mamma!" says Hetty, hurriedly. "Harry is making his old complaint of having nothing to do. And he is quite unhappy; and he is telling us so over and over again, that's all."

"So are you hungry over and over again, my dear! Is that a reason why your papa and I should leave off giving you dinner?" cries mamma, with some emotion. "Will you stay and have ours, Harry? 'Tis just three o'clock!" Harry agreed to stay, after a few faint negations. "My husband dines abroad. We are but three women, so you will have a dull dinner," remarks Mrs. Lambert.

"We shall have a gentleman to enliven us, mamma, I dare say!" says Madam Pert, and then looked in mamma's face with that admirable gaze of blank innocence which Madam Pert knows how to assume when she has been specially and successfully wicked.

When the dinner appeared. Miss Hetty came downstairs, and was exceedingly chatty, lively, and entertaining. Theo did not know that any little difference had occurred (such, alas, my Christian friends, will happen in the most charming families), did not know, I say, that anything had happened until Hetty's uncommon sprightliness and gaiety roused her suspicions. Hetty would start a dozen subjects of conversation—the King of Prussia, and the news from America; the last masquerade, and the highwayman shot near Barnet; and when her sister, admiring this volubility, inquired the reason of it, with her eyes,—

"Oh, my dear, you need not nod and wink at me!" cries Hetty. "Mamma asked Harry on purpose to enliven us, and I am talking until he begins, just like the fiddles at the playhouse, you know, Theo! First the fiddles. Then the play. Pray begin, Harry!"

"Hester!" cries mamma.

"I merely asked Harry to entertain us. You said yourself, mother, that we were only three women, and the dinner would be dull for a gentleman; unless, indeed, he chose to be very lively."

"I'm not that on most days—and, Heaven knows, on this day less than most," says poor Harry.

"Why on this day less than another? Tuesday is as good a day to be lively as Wednesday. The only day when we mustn't be lively is Sunday. Well, you know it is, ma'am! We mustn't sing, nor dance, nor do anything on Sunday."

And in this naughty way the young woman went on for the rest of the evening, and was complimented by her mother and sister when poor Harry took his leave. He was not ready of wit, and could not fling back the taunts which Hetty cast against him. Nay, had he been able to retort, he would have been silent. He was too generous to engage in that small war, and chose to take all Hester's sarcasms without an attempt to parry or evade them. Very likely the young lady watched and admired that magnanimity, while she tried it so cruelly. And after one of her fits of ill-behaviour, her parents and friends had not the least need to scold her, as she candidly told them, because she suffered a great deal more than they would ever have had her, and her conscience punished her a great deal more severely than her kind elders would have thought of doing. I suppose she lies awake all that night, and tosses and tumbles in her bed. I suppose she wets her pillow with tears, and should not mind about her sobbing: unless it kept her sister awake; unless she was unwell the next day, and the doctor had to be fetched; unless the whole family is to be put to discomfort; mother to choke over her dinner in flurry and indignation; father to eat his roast-beef in silence and with bitter sauce; everybody to look at the door each time it opens, with a vague hope that Harry is coming in. If Harry does not come, why at least does not George come? thinks Miss Theo.

Some time in the course of the evening comes a billet from George Warrington, with a large nosegay of lilacs, per Mr. Gumbo. "'I send my best duty and regards to Mrs. Lambert and the ladies,'" George says, "'and humbly beg to present to Miss Theo this nosegay of lilacs, which she says she loves in the early spring. You must not thank me for them, please, but the gardener of Bedford House, with whom I have made great friends by presenting him with some dried specimens of a Virginian plant which some ladies don't think as fragrant as lilacs.

"'I have been in the garden almost all the day. It is alive with sunshine and spring; and I have been composing two scenes of you know what, and polishing the verses which the Page sings in the fourth act, under Sybilla's window, which she cannot hear, poor thing, because she has just had her head off.'"

"Provoking! I wish he would not always sneer and laugh! The verses are beautiful," says Theo.

"You really think so, my dear? How very odd!" remarks papa.

Little Het looks up from her dismal corner with a faint smile of humour. Theo's secret is a secret for nobody in the house, it seems. Can any young people guess what it is? Our young lady continues to read:

"'Spencer has asked the famous Mr. Johnson to breakfast to-morrow, who condescends to hear the play, and who won't, I hope, be too angry because my heroine undergoes the fate of his in Irene. I have heard he came up to London himself as a young man with only his tragedy in his wallet. Shall I ever be able to get mine played? Can you fancy the catcall music beginning, and the pit hissing at that perilous part of the fourth act, where my executioner comes out from the closet with his great sword, at the awful moment when he is called upon to amputate? They say Mr. Fielding, when the pit hissed at a part of one of his pieces, about which Mr. Garrick had warned him, said, 'Hang them, they have found it out, have they?' and finished his punch in tranquillity. I suppose his wife was not in the boxes. There are some women to whom I would be very unwilling to give pain, and there are some to whom I would give the best I have.'"

"Whom can he mean? The letter is to you, my dear. I protest he is making love to your mother before my face!" cries papa to Hetty, who only gives a little sigh, puts her hand in her father's hand, and then withdraws it.

"'To whom I would give the best I have. To-day it is only a bunch of lilacs. To-morrow it may be what?—a branch of rue—a sprig of bays, perhaps—anything, so it be my best and my all.

"'I have had a fine long day, and all to myself. What do you think of Harry playing truant?'" (Here we may imagine, what they call in France, or what they used to call, when men dared to speak or citizens to hear, sensation dans l'auditoire.)

"'I suppose Carpezan wearied the poor fellow's existence out. Certain it is he has been miserable for weeks past; and a change of air and scene may do him good. This morning, quite early, he came to my room, and told me he had taken a seat in the Portsmouth machine, and proposed to go to the Isle of Wight, to the army there.'"

The army! Hetty looks very pale at this announcement, and her mother continues:

"'And a little portion of it, namely, the thirty-second regiment, is commanded by Lieutenant-Colonel Richmond Webb—the nephew of the famous old General under whom my grandfather Esmond served in the great wars of Marlborough. Mr. Webb met us at our uncle's, accosting us very politely, and giving us an invitation to visit him at his regiment. Let my poor brother go and listen to his darling music of fife and drum! He bade me tell the ladies that they should hear from him. I kiss their hands, and go to dress for dinner, at the Star and Garter, in Pall Mall. We are to have Mr. Soame Jenyns, Mr. Cambridge, Mr. Walpole, possibly, if he is not too fine to dine in a tavern; a young Irishman, a Mr. Bourke, who they say is a wonder of eloquence and learning—in fine, all the wits of Mr. Dodsley's shop. Quick, Gumbo, a coach, and my French grey suit! And if gentlemen ask me, 'Who gave you that sprig of lilac you wear on your heart-side?' I shall call a bumper, and give Lilac for a toast.'"

I fear there is no more rest for Hetty on this night than on the previous one, when she had behaved so mutinously to poor Harry Warrington. Some secret resolution must have inspired that gentleman, for, after leaving Mr. Lambert's table, he paced the streets for a while, and appeared at a late hour in the evening at Madame de Bernstein's house in Clarges Street. Her ladyship's health had been somewhat ailing of late, so that even her favourite routs were denied her, and she was sitting over a quiet game of ecarte, with a divine of whom our last news were from a lock-up house hard by that in which Harry Warrington had been himself confined. George, at Harry's request, had paid the little debt under which Mr. Sampson had suffered temporarily. He had been at his living for a year. He may have paid and contracted ever so many debts, have been in and out of jail many times since we saw him. For some time past he had been back in London stout and hearty as usual, and ready for any invitation to cards or claret. Madame de Bernstein did not care to have her game interrupted by her nephew, whose conversation had little interest now for the fickle old woman. Next to the very young, I suppose the very old are the most selfish. Alas, the heart hardens as the blood ceases to run. The cold snow strikes down from the head, and checks the glow of feeling. Who wants to survive into old age after abdicating all his faculties one by one, and be sans teeth, sans eyes, sans memory, sans hope, sans sympathy? How fared it with those patriarchs of old who lived for their nine centuries, and when were life's conditions so changed that, after threescore years and ten, it became but a vexation and a burden?

Getting no reply but Yes and No to his brief speeches, poor Harry sat a while on a couch opposite his aunt, who shrugged her shoulders, had her back to her nephew, and continued her game with the chaplain. Sampson sat opposite Mr. Warrington, and could see that something disturbed him. His face was very pale, and his countenance disturbed and full of gloom. "Something has happened to him, ma'am," he whispered to the Baroness.

"Bah!" She shrugged her shoulders again, and continued to deal her cards. "What is the matter with you, sir," she at last said, at a pause in the game, "that you have such a dismal countenance? Chaplain, that last game makes us even, I think!"

Harry got up from his place. "I am going on a journey: I am come to bid you good-bye, aunt," he said, in a very tragical voice.

"On a journey! Are you going home to America? I mark the king, Chaplain, and play him."

No, Harry said: he was not going to America yet going to the Isle of Wight for the present.

"Indeed!—a lovely spot!" says the Baroness. "Bon jour, mon ami, et bon voyage!" And she kissed a hand to her nephew.

"I mayn't come back for some time, aunt," he groaned out.

"Indeed! We shall be inconsolable without you! Unless you have a spade, Mr. Sampson, the game is mine. Good-bye, my child! No more about your journey at present: tell us about it when you come back!" And she gaily bade him farewell. He looked for a moment piteously at her, and was gone.

"Something grave has happened, madam," says the chaplain.

"Oh! The boy is always getting into scrapes! I suppose he has been falling in love with one of those country girls—what are their names, Lamberts?—with whom he is ever dawdling about. He has been doing no good here for some time. I am disappointed in him, really quite grieved about him—I will take two cards, if you please—again?—quite grieved. What do you think they say of his cousin—the Miss Warrington who made eyes at him when she thought he was a prize—they say the King has remarked her, and the Yarmouth is creving with rage. He, he!—those methodistical Warringtons! They are not a bit less worldly than their neighbours; and, old as he is, if the Grand Seignior throws his pocket-handkerchief, they will jump to catch it!"

"Ah, madam; how your ladyship knows the world!" sighs the chaplain. "I propose, if you please!"

"I have lived long enough in it, Mr. Sampson, to know something of it. 'Tis sadly selfish, my dear sir, sadly selfish; and everybody is struggling to pass his neighbour! No, I can't give you any more cards. You haven't the king? I play queen, knave, and a ten,—a sadly selfish world, indeed. And here comes my chocolate!"

The more immediate interest of the cards entirely absorbs the old woman. The door shuts out her nephew and his cares. Under his hat, he bears them into the street, and paces the dark town for a while.

"Good God!" he thinks, "what a miserable fellow I am, and what a spendthrift of my life I have been! I sit silent with George and his friends. I am not clever and witty as he is. I am only a burthen to him; and, if I would help him ever so much, don't know how. My dear Aunt Lambert's kindness never tires, but I begin to be ashamed of trying it. Why, even Hetty can't help turning on me; and when she tells me I am idle and should be doing something, ought I to be angry? The rest have left me. There's my cousins and uncle and my lady my aunt, they have shown me the cold shoulder this long time. They didn't even ask me to Norfolk when they went down to the country, and offer me so much as a day's partridge-shooting. I can't go to Castlewood—after what has happened; I should break that scoundrel William's bones; and, faith, am well out of the place altogether."

He laughs a fierce laugh as he recalls his adventures since he has been in Europe. Money, friends, pleasure, all have passed away, and he feels the past like a dream. He strolls into White's Chocolate-House, where the waiters have scarce seen him for a year. The parliament is up. Gentlemen are away; there is not even any play going on:—not that he would join it, if there were.

He has but a few pieces in his pocket; George's drawer is open, and he may take what money he likes thence; but very, very sparingly will he avail himself of his brother's repeated invitation. He sits and drinks his glass in moody silence. Two or three officers of the Guards enter from St. James's. He knew them in former days, and the young men, who have been already dining and drinking on guard, insist on more drink at the club. The other battalion of their regiment is at Winchester: it is going on this great expedition, no one knows whither, which everybody is talking about. Cursed fate that they do not belong to the other battalion; and must stay and do duty in London and at Kensington! There is Webb, who was of their regiment: he did well to exchange his company in the Coldstreams for the lieutenant-colonelcy of the thirty-second. He will be of the expedition. Why, everybody is going; and the young gentlemen mention a score of names of men of the first birth and fashion who have volunteered. "It ain't Hanoverians this time, commanded by the big Prince," says one young gentleman (whose relatives may have been Tories forty years ago)—"it's Englishmen, with the Guards at the head of 'em, and a Marlborough for a leader! Will the Frenchmen ever stand against them? No, by George, they are irresistible." And a fresh bowl is called, and loud toasts are drunk to the success of the expedition.

Mr. Warrington, who is a cup too low, the young Guardsmen say, walks away when they are not steady enough to be able to follow him, thinks over the matter on his way to his lodgings, and lies thinking of it all through the night.

"What is it, my boy?" asks George Warrington of his brother, when the latter enters his chamber very early on a blushing May morning.

"I want a little money out of the drawer," says Harry, looking at his brother. "I am sick and tired of London."

"Good heavens! Can anybody be tired of London?" George asks, who has reasons for thinking it the most delightful place in the world.

"I am for one. I am sick and ill," says Harry.

"You and Hetty have been quarrelling?"

"She don't care a penny-piece about me, nor I for her neither," says Harry, nodding his head. "But I am ill, and a little country air will do me good," and he mentions how he thinks of going to visit Mr. Webb in the Isle of Wight, and how a Portsmouth coach starts from Holborn.

"There's the till, Harry," says George, pointing from his bed. "Put your hand in, and take what you will. What a lovely morning, and how fresh the Bedford House garden looks!"

"God bless you, brother!" Harry says.

"Have a good time, Harry!" and down goes George's head on the pillow again, and he takes his pencil and notebook from under his bolster, and falls to polishing his verses, as Harry, with his cloak over his shoulder and a little valise in his hand, walks to the inn in Holborn whence the Portsmouth machine starts.

CHAPTER LXIII. Melpomene

George Warrington by no means allowed his legal studies to obstruct his comfort and pleasures, or interfere with his precious health. Madam Esmond had pointed out to him in her letters that though he wore a student's gown, and sate down with a crowd of nameless people to hall-commons, he had himself a name, and a very ancient one, to support, and could take rank with the first persons at home or in his own country; and desired that he would study as a gentleman, not a mere professional drudge. With this injunction the young man complied obediently enough: so that he may be said not to have belonged to the rank and file of the law, but may be considered to have been a volunteer in her service, like some young gentlemen of whom we have just heard. Though not so exacting as she since has become—though she allowed her disciples much more leisure, much more pleasure, much more punch, much more frequenting of coffee-houses and holiday-making, than she admits nowadays, when she scarce gives her votaries time for amusement, recreation, instruction, sleep, or dinner—the law a hundred years ago was still a jealous mistress, and demanded a pretty exclusive attention. Murray, we are told, might have been an Ovid, but he preferred to be Lord Chief Justice, and to wear ermine instead of bays. Perhaps Mr. Warrington might have risen to a peerage and the woolsack, had he studied very long and assiduously,—had he been a dexterous courtier, and a favourite of attorneys: had he been other than he was, in a word. He behaved to Themis with a very decent respect and attention; but he loved letters more than law always; and the black-letter of Chaucer was infinitely more agreeable to him than the Gothic pages of Hale and Coke.

Letters were loved indeed in those quaint times, and authors were actually authorities. Gentlemen appealed to Virgil or Lucan in the Courts or the House of Commons. What said Statius, Juvenal—let alone Tully or Tacitus—on such and such a point? Their reign is over now, the good old Heathens: the worship of Jupiter and Juno is not more out of mode than the cultivation of Pagan poetry or ethics. The age of economists and calculators has succeeded, and Tooke's Pantheon is deserted and ridiculous. Now and then, perhaps, a Stanley kills a kid, a Gladstone bangs up a wreath, a Lytton burns incense, in honour of the Olympians. But what do they care at Lambeth, Birmingham, the Tower Hamlets, for the ancient rites, divinities, worship? Who the plague are the Muses, and what is the use of all that Greek and Latin rubbish? What is Elicon, and who cares? Who was Thalia, pray, and what is the length of her i? Is Melpomene's name in three syllables or four? And do you know from whose design I stole that figure of Tragedy which adorns the initial G of this chapter?

Now, it has been said how Mr. George in his youth, and in the long leisure which he enjoyed at home, and during his imprisonment in the French fort on the banks of Monongahela, had whiled away his idleness by paying court to Melpomene; and the result of their union was a tragedy, which has been omitted in Bell's Theatre, though I dare say it is no worse than some of the pieces printed there. Most young men pay their respects to the Tragic Muse first, as they fall in love with women who are a great deal older than themselves. Let the candid reader own, if ever he had a literary turn, that his ambition was of the very highest, and that however, in his riper age, he might come down in his pretensions, and think that to translate an ode of Horace, or to turn a song of Waller or Prior into decent alcaics or sapphics, was about the utmost of his capability, tragedy and epic only did his green unknowing youth engage, and no prize but the highest was fit for him.

George Warrington, then, on coming to London, attended the theatrical performances at both houses, frequented the theatrical coffee-houses, and heard the opinions of the critics, and might be seen at the Bedford between the plays, or supping at the Cecil along with the wits and actors when the performances were over. Here he gradually became acquainted with the players and such of the writers and poets as were known to the public. The tough old Macklin, the frolicsome Foote, the vivacious Hippisley, the sprightly Mr. Garrick himself, might occasionally be seen at these houses of entertainment; and our gentleman, by his wit and modesty, as well, perhaps, as for the high character for wealth which he possessed, came to be very much liked in the coffee-house circles, and found that the actors would drink a bowl of punch with him, and the critics sup at his expense with great affability. To be on terms of intimacy with an author or an actor has been an object of delight to many a young man; actually to hob and nob with Bobadil or Henry the Fifth or Alexander the Great, to accept a pinch out of Aristarchus's own box, to put Juliet into her coach, or hand Monimia to her chair, are privileges which would delight most young men of a poetic turn; and no wonder George Warrington loved the theatre. Then he had the satisfaction of thinking that his mother only half approved of plays and playhouses, and of feasting on fruit forbidden at home. He gave more than one elegant entertainment to the players, and it was even said that one or two distinguished geniuses had condescended to borrow money of him.

And as he polished and added new beauties to his masterpiece, we may be sure that he took advice of certain friends of his, and that they gave him applause and counsel. Mr. Spencer, his new acquaintance, of the Temple, gave a breakfast at his chambers in Fig Tree Court, when Mr. Warrington read part of his play, and the gentlemen present pronounced that it had uncommon merit. Even the learned Mr. Johnson, who was invited, was good enough to say that the piece had showed talent. It warred against the unities, to be sure; but these had been violated by other authors, and Mr. Warrington might sacrifice them as well as another. There was in Mr. W.'s tragedy a something which reminded him both of Coriolanus and Othello. "And two very good things too, sir!" the author pleaded. "Well, well, there was no doubt on that point; and 'tis certain your catastrophe is terrible, just, and being in part true, is not the less awful," remarks Mr. Spencer.

Now the plot of Mr. Warrington's tragedy was quite full indeed of battle and murder. A favourite book of his grandfather had been the life of old George Frundsberg of Mindelheim, a colonel of foot-folk in the Imperial service at Pavia fight, and during the wars of the Constable Bourbon: and one of Frundsberg's military companions was a certain Carpzow, or Carpezan, whom our friend selected as his tragedy hero. His first act, as it at present stands in Sir George Warrington's manuscript, is supposed to take place before a convent on the Rhine, which the Lutherans, under Carpezan, are besieging. A godless gang these Lutherans are. They have pulled the beards of Roman friars, and torn the veils of hundreds of religious women. A score of these are trembling within the walls of the convent yonder, of which the garrison, unless the expected succours arrive before midday, has promised to surrender. Meanwhile there is armistice, and the sentries within look on with hungry eyes, as the soldiers and camp people gamble on the grass before the gate. Twelve o'clock, ding, ding, dong! it sounds upon the convent bell. No succours have arrived. Open gates, warder! and give admission to the famous Protestant hero, the terror of Turks on the Danube, and Papists in the Lombard plains—Colonel Carpezan! See, here he comes, clad in complete steel, his hammer of battle over his shoulder, with which he has battered so many infidel sconces, his flags displayed, his trumpets blowing. "No rudeness, my men," says Carpezan; "the wine is yours, and the convent larder and cellar are good: the church plate shall be melted: any of the garrison who choose to take service with Gaspar Carpezan are welcome, and shall have good pay. No insult to the religious ladies! I have promised them a safe-conduct, and he who lays a finger on them, hangs! Mind that Provost Marshal!" The Provost Marshal, a huge fellow in a red doublet, nods his head.

"We shall see more of that Provost Marshal, or executioner," Mr. Spencer explains to his guests.

"A very agreeable acquaintance, I am sure,—shall be delighted to meet the gentleman again!" says Mr. Johnson, wagging his head over his tea. "This scene of the mercenaries, the camp followers, and their wild sports, is novel and stirring, Mr. Warrington, and I make you my compliments on it. The Colonel has gone into the convent, I think? Now let us hear what he is going to do there."

The Abbess, and one or two of her oldest ladies, make their appearance before the conqueror. Conqueror as he is, they heard him in their sacred halls. They have heard of his violent behaviour in conventual establishments before. That hammer, which he always carries in action, has smashed many sacred images in religious houses. Pounds and pounds of convent plate is he known to have melted, the sacrilegious plunderer! No wonder the Abbess-Princess of St. Mary's, a lady of violent prejudices, free language, and noble birth, has a dislike to the lowborn heretic who lords it in her convent, and tells Carpezan a bit of her mind, as the phrase is. This scene, in which the lady gets somewhat better of the Colonel, was liked not a little by Mr. Warrington's audience at the Temple. Terrible as he might be in war, Carpezan was shaken at first by the Abbess's brisk opening charge of words; and, conqueror as he was, seemed at first to be conquered by his actual prisoner. But such an old soldier was not to be beaten ultimately by any woman. "Pray, madam," says he, "how many ladies are there in your convent, for whom my people shall provide conveyance?" The Abbess, with a look of much trouble and anger, says that, "besides herself, the noble sisters of Saint Mary's House are twenty—twenty-three." She was going to say twenty-four, and now says twenty-three? "Ha! why this hesitation?" asks Captain Ulric, one of Carpezan's gayest officers.

The dark chief pulls a letter from his pocket. "I require from you, madam," he says sternly to the Lady Abbess, "the body of the noble lady Sybilla of Hoya. Her brother was my favourite captain, slain by my side, in the Milanese. By his death, she becomes heiress of his lands. 'Tis said a greedy uncle brought her hither; and fast immured the lady against her will. The damsel shall herself pronounce her fate—to stay a cloistered sister of Saint Mary's, or to return to home and liberty, as Lady Sybil, Baroness of ———." Ha! The Abbess was greatly disturbed by this question. She says, haughtily: "There is no Lady Sybil in this house: of which every inmate is under your protection, and sworn to go free. The Sister Agnes was a nun professed, and what was her land and wealth revert to this Order."

"Give me straightway the body of the Lady Sybil of Hoya!" roars Carpezan, in great wrath. "If not, I make a signal to my Reiters, and give you and your convent up to war."

"Faith, if I lead the storm, and have my right, 'tis not my Lady Abbess that I'll choose," says Captain Ulric, "but rather some plump, smiling, red-lipped maid like—like———" Here, as he, the sly fellow, is looking under the veils of the two attendant nuns, the stern Abbess cries, "Silence, fellow, with thy ribald talk! The lady, warrior, whom you ask of me is passed away from sin, temptation, vanity, and three days since our Sister Agnes—died."

At this announcement Carpezan is immensely agitated. The Abbess calls upon the chaplain to confirm her statement. Ghastly and pale, the old man has to own that three days since the wretched Sister Agnes was buried.

This is too much! In the pocket of his coat of mail Carpezan has a letter from Sister Agnes herself, in which she announces that she is going to be buried indeed, but in an oubliette of the convent, where she may either be kept on water and bread, or die starved outright. He seizes the unflinching Abbess by the arm, whilst Captain Ulric lays hold of the chaplain by the throat. The Colonel blows a blast upon his horn: in rush his furious Lanzknechts from without. Crash, bang! They knock the convent walls about. And in the midst of flames, screams, and slaughter, who is presently brought in by Carpezan himself, and fainting on his shoulder, but Sybilla herself? A little sister nun (that gay one with the red lips) had pointed out to the Colonel and Ulric the way to Sister Agnes's dungeon, and, indeed, had been the means of making her situation known to the Lutheran chief.

"The convent is suppressed with a vengeance," says Mr. Warrington. "We end our first act with the burning of the place, the roars of triumph of the soldiery, and the outcries of the nuns. They had best go change their dresses immediately, for they will have to be court ladies in the next act—as you will see." Here the gentlemen talked the matter over. If the piece were to be done at Drury Lane, Mrs. Pritchard would hardly like to be Lady Abbess, as she doth but appear in the first act. Miss Pritchard might make a pretty Sybilla, and Miss Gates the attendant nun. Mr. Garrick was scarce tall enough for Carpezan—though, when he is excited, nobody ever thinks of him but as big as a grenadier. Mr. Johnson owns Woodward will be a good Ulric, as he plays the Mercutio parts very gaily; and so, by one and t'other, the audience fancies the play already on the boards, and casts the characters.

In act the second, Carpezan has married Sybilla. He has enriched himself in the wars, has been ennobled by the Emperor, and lives at his castle on the Danube in state and splendour.

But, truth to say, though married, rich, and ennobled, the Lord Carpezan was not happy. It may be that in his wild life, as leader of condottieri on both sides, he had committed crimes which agitated his mind with remorse. It may be that his rough soldier-manners consorted ill with his imperious highborn bride. She led him such a life—I am narrating as it were the Warrington manuscript, which is too long to print in entire—taunting him with his low birth, his vulgar companions, whom the old soldier loved to see about him, and so forth—that there were times when he rather wished that he had never rescued this lovely, quarrelsome, wayward vixen from the oubliette out of which he fished her. After the bustle of the first act this is a quiet one, and passed chiefly in quarrelling between the Baron and Baroness Carpezan, until horns blow, and it is announced that the young King of Bohemia and Hungary is coming hunting that way.

Act III. is passed at Prague, whither his Majesty has invited Lord Carpezan and his wife, with noble offers of preferment to the latter. From Baron he shall be promoted to be Count, from Colonel he shall be General-in-Chief. His wife is the most brilliant and fascinating of all the ladies of the court—and as for Carpzoff——

"Oh, stay—I have it—I know your story, sir, now," says Mr. Johnson. "'Tis in 'Meteranus,' in the Theatrum Universum. I read it in Oxford as a boy—Carpezanus or Carpzoff——"

"That is the fourth act," says Mr. Warrington. In the fourth act the young King's attentions towards Sybilla grow more and more marked; but her husband, battling against his jealousy, long refuses to yield to it, until his wife's criminality is put beyond a doubt—and here he read the act, which closes with the terrible tragedy which actually happened. Being convinced of his wife's guilt, Carpezan caused the executioner who followed his regiment to slay her in her own palace. And the curtain of the act falls just after the dreadful deed is done, in a side-chamber illuminated by the moon shining through a great oriel window, under which the King comes with his lute, and plays the song which was to be the signal between him and his guilty victim.

This song (writ in the ancient style, and repeated in the piece, being sung in the third act previously at a great festival given by the King and Queen) was pronounced by Mr. Johnson to be a happy imitation of Mr. Waller's manner, and its gay repetition at the moment of guilt, murder, and horror, very much deepened the tragic gloom of the scene.

"But whatever came afterwards?" he asked. "I remember in the Theatrum, Carpezan is said to have been taken into favour again by Count Mansfield, and doubtless to have murdered other folks on the reformed side."

Here our poet has departed from historic truth. In the fifth act of Carpezan King Louis of Hungary and Bohemia (sufficiently terror-stricken, no doubt, by the sanguinary termination of his intrigue) has received word that the Emperor Solyman is invading his Hungarian dominions. Enter two noblemen who relate how, in the council which the King held upon the news, the injured Carpezan rushed infuriated into the royal presence, broke his sword, and flung it at the King's feet—along with a glove which he dared him to wear, and which he swore he would one day claim. After that wild challenge the rebel fled from Prague, and had not since been heard of; but it was reported that he had joined the Turkish invader, assumed the turban, and was now in the camp of the Sultan, whose white tents glance across the river yonder, and against whom the King was now on his march. Then the King comes to his tent with his generals, prepares his order of battle; and dismisses them to their posts, keeping by his side an aged and faithful knight, his master of the horse, to whom he expresses his repentance for his past crimes, his esteem for his good and injured Queen, and his determination to meet the day's battle like a man.

"What is this field called?"

"Mohacz, my liege!" says the old warrior, adding the remark that "Ere set of sun, Mohacz will see a battle bravely won."

Trumpets and alarms now sound; they are the cymbals and barbaric music of the Janissaries: we are in the Turkish camp, and yonder, surrounded by turbaned chiefs, walks the Sultan Solyman's friend, the conqueror of Rhodes, the redoubted Grand Vizier.

Who is that warrior in an Eastern habit, but with a glove in his cap? 'Tis Carpezan. Even Solyman knew his courage and ferocity as a soldier. He knows; the ordnance of the Hungarian host; in what arms King Louis is weakest: how his cavalry, of which the shock is tremendous, should be received, and inveigled into yonder morass, where certain death may await them—he prays for a command in the front, and as near as possible to the place where the traitor King Louis will engage. "'Tis well," says the grim Vizier, "our invincible Emperor surveys the battle from yonder tower. At the end of the day, he will know how to reward your valour." The signal-guns fire —the trumpets blow—the Turkish captains retire, vowing death to the infidel, and eternal fidelity to the Sultan.

And now the battle begins in earnest, and with those various incidents which the lover of the theatre knoweth. Christian knights and Turkish warriors clash and skirmish over the stage. Continued alarms are sounded. Troops on both sides advance and retreat. Carpezan, with his glove in his cap, and his dreadful hammer smashing all before him, rages about the field, calling for King Louis. The renegade is about to slay a warrior who faces him, but recognising young Ulric, his ex-captain, he drops the uplifted hammer, and bids him fly, and think of Carpezan. He is softened at seeing his young friend, and thinking of former times when they fought and conquered together in the cause of Protestantism. Ulric bids him to return, but of course that is now out of the question. They fight. Ulric will have it, and down he goes under the hammer. The renegade melts in sight of his wounded comrade, when who appears but King Louis, his plumes torn, his sword hacked, his shield dented with a thousand blows which he has received and delivered during the day's battle. Ha! who is this? The guilty monarch would turn away (perhaps Macbeth may have done so before), but Carpezan is on him. All his softness is gone. He rages like a fury. "An equal fight!" he roars. "A traitor against a traitor! Stand, King Louis! False King, false knight, false friend—by this glove in my helmet, I challenge you!" And he tears the guilty token out of his cap, and flings it at the King.

Of course they set to, and the monarch falls under the terrible arm of the man whom he has injured. He dies, uttering a few incoherent words of repentance, and Carpezan, leaning upon his murderous mace, utters a heartbroken soliloquy over the royal corpse. The Turkish warriors have gathered meanwhile: the dreadful day is their own. Yonder stands the dark Vizier, surrounded by his Janissaries, whose bows and swords are tired of drinking death. He surveys the renegade standing over the corpse of the King.

"Christian renegade!" he says, "Allah has given us a great victory. The arms of the Sublime Emperor are everywhere triumphant. The Christian King is slain by you."

"Peace to his soul! He died like a good knight," gasps Ulric, himself dying on the field.

"In this day's battle," the grim Vizier continues, "no man hath comported himself more bravely than you. You are made Bassa of Transylvania! Advance bowmen—Fire!"

An arrow quivers in the breast of Carpezan.

"Bassa of Transylvania, you were a traitor to your King, who lies murdered by your hand!" continues grim Vizier. "You contributed more than any soldier to this day's great victory. 'Tis thus my sublime Emperor meetly rewards you. Sound trumpets! We march for Vienna to-night!"

And the curtain drops as Carpezan, crawling towards his dying comrade, kisses his hands, and gasps—

"Forgive me, Ulric!"

When Mr. Warrington has finished reading his tragedy, he turns round to Mr. Johnson, modestly, and asks,—

"What say you, sir? Is there any chance for me?"

But the opinion of this most eminent critic is scarce to be given, for Mr. Johnson had been asleep for some time, and frankly owned that he had lost the latter part of the play.

The little auditory begins to hum and stir as the noise of the speaker ceased. George may have been very nervous when he first commenced to read; but everybody allows that he read the last two acts uncommonly well, and makes him a compliment upon his matter and manner. Perhaps everybody is in good-humour because the piece has come to an end. Mr. Spencer's servant hands about refreshing drinks. The Templars speak out their various opinions whilst they sip the negus. They are a choice band of critics, familiar with the pit of the theatre, and they treat Mr. Warrington's play with the gravity which such a subject demands.

Mr. Fountain suggests that the Vizier should not say "Fire!" when he bids the archers kill Carpezan, as you certainly don't fire with a bow and arrows. A note is taken of the objection.

Mr. Figtree, who is of a sentimental turn, regrets that Ulric could not be saved, and married to the comic heroine.

"Nay, sir, there was an utter annihilation of the Hungarian army at Mohacz," says Mr. Johnson, "and Ulric must take his knock on the head with the rest. He could only be saved by flight, and you wouldn't have a hero run away! Pronounce sentence of death against Captain Ulric, but kill him with honours of war."

Messrs. Essex and Tanfield wonder to one another who is this queer-looking pert whom Spencer has invited, and who contradicts everybody; and suggest a boat up the river and a little fresh air after the fatigues of the tragedy.

The general opinion is decidedly favourable to Mr. Warrington's performance; and Mr. Johnson's opinion, on which he sets a special value, is the most favourable of all. Perhaps Mr. Johnson is not sorry to compliment a young gentleman of fashion and figure like Mr. W. "Up to the death of the heroine," he says, "I am frankly with you, sir. And I may speak, as a playwright who have killed my own heroine, and had my share of the plausus in the atro. To hear your own lines nobly delivered to an applauding house, is indeed a noble excitement. I like to see a young man of good name and lineage who condescends to think that the Tragic Muse is not below his advances. It was to a sordid roof that I invited her, and I asked her to rescue me from poverty and squalor. Happy you, sir, who can meet her upon equal terms, and can afford to marry her without a portion!"

"I doubt whether the greatest genius is not debased who has to make a bargain with Poetry," remarks Mr. Spencer.

"Nay, sir," Mr. Johnson answered, "I doubt if many a great genius would work at all without bribes and necessities; and so a man had better marry a poor Muse for good and all, for better or worse, than dally with a rich one. I make you my compliment to your play, Mr. Warrington, and if you want an introduction to the stage, shall be very happy if I can induce my friend Mr. Garrick to present you."

"Mr. Garrick shall be his sponsor," cried the florid Mr. Figtree. "Melpomene shall be his godmother, and he shall have the witches' caldron in Macbeth for a christening font."

"Sir, I neither said font nor godmother!"—remarks the man of letters. "I would have no play contrary to morals or religion nor, as I conceive, is Mr. Warrington's piece otherwise than friendly to them. Vice is chastised, as it should be, even in kings, though perhaps we judge of their temptations too lightly. Revenge is punished—as not to be lightly exercised by our limited notion of justice. It may have been Carpezan's wife who perverted the King, and not the King who led the woman astray. At any rate, Louis is rightly humiliated for his crime, and the Renegade most justly executed for his. I wish you a good afternoon, gentlemen!" And with these remarks, the great author took his leave of the company.

Towards the close of the reading, General Lambert had made his appearance at Mr. Spencer's chambers, and had listened to the latter part of the tragedy. The performance over, he and George took their way to the latter's lodgings in the first place, and subsequently to the General's own house, where the young author was expected, in order to recount the reception which his play had met from his Temple critics.

At Mr. Warrington's apartments in Southampton Row, they found a letter awaiting George, which the latter placed in his pocket unread, so that he might proceed immediately with his companion to Soho. We may be sure the ladies there were eager to know about the Carpezan's fate in the morning's small rehearsal.

Hetty said George was so shy, that perhaps it would be better for all parties if some other person had read the play. Theo, on the contrary, cried out:

"Read it, indeed! Who can read a poem better than the author who feels it in his heart? And George had his whole heart in the piece!"

Mr. Lambert very likely thought that somebody else's whole heart was in the piece too, but did not utter this opinion to Miss Theo.

"I think Harry would look very well in your figure of a Prince," says the General. "That scene where he takes leave of his wife before departing for the wars reminds me of your brother's manner not a little."

"Oh, papa! surely Mr. Warrington himself would act the Prince's part best!" cries Miss Theo.

"And be deservedly slain in battle at the end?" asks the father of the house.

"I did not say that,—only that Mr. George would make a very good Prince, papa!" cries Miss Theo.

"In which case he would find a suitable Princess, I have no doubt. What news of your brother Harry?"

George, who had been thinking about theatrical triumphs; about monumentum aere perennius; about lilacs; about love whispered and tenderly accepted, remembers that he has a letter from Harry in his pocket, and gaily produces it.

"Let us hear what Mr. Truant says for himself, Aunt Lambert!" cries George, breaking the seal.

Why is he so disturbed, as he reads the contents of his letter? Why do the women look at him with alarmed eyes? And why, above all, is Hetty so pale?

"Here is the letter," says George, and begins to read it:

"RYDE, June 1, 1758.

"I did not tell my dearest George what I hoped and intended, when I left home on Wednesday. 'Twas to see Mr. Webb at Portsmouth or the Isle of Wight, wherever his Regiment was, and if need was to go down on my knees to him to take me as volunteer on the Expedition. I took boat from Portsmouth, where I learned that he was with our regiment incampt at the village of Ryde. Was received by him most kindly, and my petition granted out of hand. That is why I say our regiment. We are eight gentlemen volunteers with Mr. Webb, all men of birth, and good fortunes except poor me, who don't deserve one. We are to mess with the officers; we take the right of the collumn, and have always the right to be in front, and in an hour we embark on board his Majesty's Ship the Rochester of 60 guns, while our Commodore's, Mr. Howe's, is the Essex, 70. His squadron is about 20 ships, and I should think 100 transports at least. Though 'tis a secret expedition, we make no doubt France is our destination—where I hope to see my friends the Monsieurs once more, and win my colours, a la point de mon epee, as we used to say in Canada. Perhaps my service as interpreter may be useful; I speaking the language not so well as some one I know, but better than most here.

"I scarce venture to write to our mother to tell her of this step. Will you, who have a coxing tongue will wheadle any one, write to her as soon as you have finisht the famous tradgedy? Will you give my affectionate respects to dear General Lambert and ladies? and if any accident should happen, I know you will take care of poor Gumbo as belonging to my dearest best George's most affectionate brother, HENRY E. WARRINGTON.

"P.S.—Love to all at home when you write, including Dempster, Mountain, and Fanny M. and all the people, and duty to my honoured mother, wishing I had pleased her better. And if I said anything unkind to dear Miss Hester Lambert, I know she will forgive me, and pray God bless all.—H. E. W."

"To G. Esmond Warrington, Esq., at Mr. Scrace's House in Southampton Row, Opposite Bedford House Gardens, London."

He has not read the last words with a very steady voice. Mr. Lambert sits silent, though not a little moved. Theo and her mother look at one another; but Hetty remains with a cold face and a stricken heart. She thinks, "He is gone to danger, perhaps to death, and it was I sent him!"

CHAPTER LXIV. In which Harry lives to fight another Day

The trusty Gumbo could not console himself for the departure of his beloved master: at least, to judge from his tears and howls on first hearing the news of Mr. Harry's enlistment, you would have thought the negro's heart must break at the separation. No wonder he went for sympathy to the maid-servants at Mr. Lambert's lodgings. Wherever that dusky youth was, he sought comfort in the society of females. Their fair and tender bosoms knew how to feel pity for the poor African, and the darkness of Gumbo's complexion was no more repulsive to them than Othello's to Desdemona. I believe Europe has never been so squeamish in regard to Africa, as a certain other respected Quarter. Nay, some Africans—witness the Chevalier de St. Georges, for instance—have been notorious favourites with the fair sex.

So, in his humbler walk, was Mr. Gumbo. The Lambert servants wept freely in his company; the maids kindly considered him not only as Mr. Harry's man, but their brother. Hetty could not help laughing when she found Gumbo roaring because his master had gone a volumteer, as he called it, and had not taken him. He was ready to save Master Harry's life any day, and would have done it and had himself cut in twenty thousand hundred pieces for Master Harry, that he would! Meanwhile, Nature must be supported, and he condescended to fortify her by large supplies of beer and cold meat in the kitchen. That he was greedy, idle, and told lies, is certain; but yet Hetty gave him half a crown, and was especially kind to him. Her tongue, that was wont to wag so pertly, was so gentle now, that you might fancy it had never made a joke. She moved about the house mum and meek. She was humble to mamma; thankful to John and Betty when they waited at dinner; patient to Polly when the latter pulled her hair in combing it; long-suffering when Charley from school trod on her toes, or deranged her workbox; silent in papa's company,—oh, such a transmogrified little Hetty! If papa had ordered her to roast the leg of mutton, or walk to church arm-in-arm with Gumbo, she would have made a curtsey, and said, "Yes, if you please, dear papa!" Leg of mutton! What sort of meal were some poor volunteers having, with the cannon-balls flying about their heads? Church! When it comes to the prayer in time of war, oh, how her knees smite together as she kneels, and hides her head in the pew! She holds down her head when the parson reads out, "Thou shalt do no murder," from the communion-rail, and fancies he must be looking at her. How she thinks of all travellers by land or by water! How she sickens as she runs to the paper to read if there is news of the Expedition! How she watches papa when he comes home from his Ordnance Office, and looks in his face to see if there is good news or bad! Is he well? Is he made a General yet? Is he wounded and made a prisoner? ah me! or, perhaps, are both his legs taken off by one shot, like that pensioner they saw in Chelsea Garden t'other day? She would go on wooden legs all her life, if his can but bring him safe home; at least, she ought never to get up off her knees until he is returned. "Haven't you heard of people, Theo," says she, "whose hair has grown grey in a single night? I shouldn't wonder if mine did,—shouldn't wonder in the least." And she looks in the glass to ascertain that phenomenon.

"Hetty dear, you used not to be so nervous when papa was away in Minorca," remarks Theo.

"Ah, Theo! one may very well see that George is not with the army, but safe at home," rejoins Hetty; whereat the elder sister blushes, and looks very pensive. Au fait, if Mr. George had been in the army, that, you see, would have been another pair of boots. Meanwhile, we don't intend to harrow anybody's kind feelings any longer, but may as well state that Harry is, for the present, as safe as any officer of the Life Guards at Regent's Park Barracks.

The first expedition in which our gallant volunteer was engaged may be called successful, but certainly was not glorious. The British Lion, or any other lion, cannot always have a worthy enemy to combat, or a battle-royal to deliver. Suppose he goes forth in quest of a tiger who won't come, and lays his paws on a goose, and gobbles him up? Lions, we know, must live like any other animals. But suppose, advancing into the forest in search of the tiger aforesaid, and bellowing his challenge of war, he espies not one but six tigers coming towards him? This manifestly is not his game at all. He puts his tail between his royal legs, and retreats into his own snug den as quickly as he may. Were he to attempt to go and fight six tigers, you might write that Lion down an Ass.

Now, Harry Warrington's first feat of war was in this wise. He and about 13,000 other fighting men embarked in various ships and transports on the 1st of June, from the Isle of Wight, and at daybreak on the 5th the fleet stood in to the Bay of Cancale in Brittany. For a while he and the gentlemen volunteers had the pleasure of examining the French coast from their ships, whilst the Commander-in-Chief and the Commodore reconnoitred the bay in a cutter. Cattle were seen, and some dragoons, who trotted off into the distance; and a little fort with a couple of guns had the audacity to fire at his Grace of Marlborough and the Commodore in the cutter. By two o'clock the whole British fleet was at anchor, and signal was made for all the grenadier companies of eleven regiments to embark on board flat-bottomed boats and assemble round the Commodore's ship, the Essex. Meanwhile, Mr. Howe, hoisting his broad pennant on board the Success frigate, went in as near as possible to shore, followed by the other frigates, to protect the landing of the troops; and, now, with Lord George Sackville and General Dury in command, the gentlemen volunteers, the grenadier companies, and three battalions of guards pulled to shore.

The gentlemen volunteers could not do any heroic deed upon this occasion, because the French, who should have stayed to fight them, ran away, and the frigates having silenced the fire of the little fort which had disturbed the reconnaissance of the Commander-in-Chief, the army presently assaulted it, taking the whole garrison prisoner, and shooting him in the leg. Indeed, he was but one old gentleman, who gallantly had fired his two guns, and who told his conquerors, "If every Frenchman had acted like me, you would not have landed at Cancale at all."

The advanced detachment of invaders took possession of the village of Cancale, where they lay upon their arms all night; and our volunteer was joked by his comrades about his eagerness to go out upon the war-path, and bring in two or three scalps of Frenchmen. None such, however, fell under his tomahawk; the only person slain on the whole day being a French gentleman, who was riding with his servant, and was surprised by volunteer Lord Downe, marching in the front with a company of Kingsley's. My Lord Downe offered the gentleman quarter, which he foolishly refused, whereupon he, his servant, and the two horses, were straightway shot.

Next day the whole force was landed, and advanced from Cancale to St. Malo. All the villages were emptied through which the troops passed, and the roads were so narrow in many places that the men had to march single file, and might have been shot down from behind the tall leafy hedges had there been any enemy to disturb them.

At nightfall the army arrived before St. Malo, and were saluted by a fire of artillery from that town, which did little damage in the darkness. Under cover of this, the British set fire to the ships, wooden buildings, pitch and tar magazines in the harbour, and made a prodigious conflagration that lasted the whole night.

This feat was achieved without any attempt on the part of the French to molest the British force: but, as it was confidently asserted that there was a considerable French force in the town of St. Malo, though they wouldn't come out, his Grace the Duke of Marlborough and my Lord George Sackville determined not to disturb the garrison, marched back to Cancale again, and—and so got on board their ships.

If this were not a veracious history, don't you see that it would have been easy to send our Virginian on a more glorious campaign? Exactly four weeks after his departure from England, Mr. Warrington found himself at Portsmouth again, and addressed a letter to his brother George, with which the latter ran off to Dean Street so soon as ever he received it.

"Glorious news, ladies!" cries he, finding the Lambert family all at breakfast. "Our champion has come back. He has undergone all sorts of dangers, but has survived them all. He has seen dragons—upon my word, he says so."

"Dragons! What do you mean, Mr. Warrington?"

"But not killed any—he says so, as you shall hear. He writes:

"'DEAREST BROTHER—I think you will be glad to hear that I am returned, without any commission as yet; without any wounds or glory; but,—at any rate, alive and harty. On board our ship, we were almost as crowded as poor Mr. Holwell and his friends in their Black Hole at Calicutta. We had rough weather, and some of the gentlemen volunteers, who prefer smooth water, grumbled not a little. My gentlemen's stomachs are dainty; and after Braund's cookery and White's kick-shaws, they don't like plain sailor's rum and bisket. But I, who have been at sea before, took my rations and can of flip very contentedly: being determined to put a good face on everything before our fine English macaronis, and show that a Virginia gentleman is as good as the best of 'em. I wish, for the honour of old Virginia, that I had more to brag about. But all I can say in truth is, that we have been to France and come back again. Why, I don't think even your tragick pen could make anything of such a campaign as ours has been. We landed on the 6 at Cancalle Bay, we saw a few dragons on a hill...'

"There! Did I not tell you there were dragons?" asks George, laughing.

"Mercy! What can he mean by dragons?" cries Hetty.

"Immense, long-tailed monsters, with steel scales on their backs, who vomit fire, and gobble up a virgin a day. Haven't you read about them in The Seven Champions?" says papa. "Seeing St. George's flag, I suppose, they slunk off."

"I have read of 'em," says the little boy from Chartreux, solemnly. "They like to eat women. One was going to eat Andromeda, you know, papa; and Jason killed another, who was guarding the apple-tree."

"... A few dragons on a hill," George resumes, "who rode away from us without engaging. We slept under canvass. We marched to St. Malo, and burned ever so many privateers there. And we went on board shipp again, without ever crossing swords with an enemy or meeting any except a few poor devils whom the troops plundered. Better luck next time! This hasn't been very much nor particular glorious: but I have liked it for my part. I have smelt powder, besides a good deal of rosn and pitch we burned. I've seen the enemy; have sleppt under canvass, and been dredful crowdid and sick at sea. I like it. My best compliments to dear Aunt Lambert, and tell Miss Hetty I wasn't very much fritened when I saw the French horse.—Your most affectionate brother, H. E. WARRINGTON."

We hope Miss Hetty's qualms of conscience were allayed by Harry's announcement that his expedition was over, and that he had so far taken no hurt. Far otherwise. Mr. Lambert, in the course of his official duties, had occasion to visit the troops at Portsmouth and the Isle of Wight, and George Warrington bore him company. They found Harry vastly improved in spirits and health from the excitement produced by the little campaign, quite eager and pleased to learn his new military duties, active, cheerful, and healthy, and altogether a different person from the listless moping lad who had dawdled in London coffee-houses and Mrs. Lambert's drawing-room. The troops were under canvas; the weather was glorious, and George found his brother a ready pupil in a fine brisk open-air school of war. Not a little amused, the elder brother, arm-in-arm with the young volunteer, paced the streets of the warlike city, recalled his own brief military experiences of two years back, and saw here a much greater army than that ill-fated one of which he had shared the disasters. The expedition, such as we have seen it, was certainly not glorious, and yet the troops and the nation were in high spirits with it. We were said to have humiliated the proud Gaul. We should have vanquished as well as humbled him had he dared to appear. What valour, after all, is like British valour? I dare say some such expressions have been heard in later times. Not that I would hint that our people brag much more than any other, or more now than formerly. Have not these eyes beheld the battle-grounds of Leipzig, Jena, Dresden, Waterloo, Blenheim, Bunker's Hill, New Orleans? What heroic nation has not fought, has not conquered, has not run away, has not bragged in its turn? Well, the British nation was much excited by the glorious victory of St. Malo. Captured treasures were sent home and exhibited in London. The people were so excited, that more laurels and more victories were demanded, and the enthusiastic army went forth to seek some.

With this new expedition went a volunteer so distinguished, that we must give him precedence of all other amateur soldiers or sailors. This was our sailor Prince, H.R.H. Prince Edward, who was conveyed on board the Essex in the ship's twelve-oared barge, the standard of England flying in the bow of the boat, the Admiral with his flag and boat following the Prince's, and all the captains following in seniority.

Away sails the fleet, Harry, in high health and spirits, waving his hat to his friends as they cheer from the shore. He must and will have his commission before long. There can be no difficulty about that, George thinks. There is plenty of money in his little store to buy his brother's ensigncy; but if he can win it without purchase by gallantry and good conduct, that were best. The colonel of the regiment reports highly of his recruit; men and officers like him. It is easy to see that he is a young fellow of good promise and spirit.

Hip, hip, huzzay! What famous news are these which arrive ten days after the expedition has sailed? On the 7th and 8th of August his Majesty's troops had effected a landing in the Bay des Marais, two leagues westward of Cherbourg, in the face of a large body of the enemy. Awed by the appearance of British valour, that large body of the enemy has disappeared. Cherbourg has surrendered at discretion; and the English colours are hoisted on the three outlying forts. Seven-and-twenty ships have been burned in the harbours, and a prodigious number of fine brass cannon taken. As for your common iron guns, we have destroyed 'em, likewise the basin (about which the mounseers bragged so), and the two piers at the entrance to the harbour.

There is no end of jubilation in London; just as Mr. Howe's guns arrive from Cherbourg, come Mr. Wolfe's colours captured at Louisbourg. The colours are taken from Kensington to St Paul's, escorted by fourscore life-guards and fourscore horse-grenadiers with officers in proportion, their standards, kettle-drums, and trumpets. At St. Paul's they are received by the Dean and Chapter at the West Gate, and at that minute—bang, bong, bung—the Tower and Park guns salute them! Next day is the turn of the Cherbourg cannon and mortars. These are the guns we took. Look at them with their carving and flaunting emblems—their lilies, and crowns, and mottoes! Here they are, the Teneraire, the Malfaisant, the Vainqueur (the Vainqueur, indeed! a pretty vainqueur of Britons!), and ever so many more. How the people shout as the pieces are trailed through the streets in procession! As for Hetty and Mrs. Lambert, I believe they are of opinion that Harry took every one of the guns himself, dragging them out of the batteries, and destroying the artillerymen. He has immensely risen in the general estimation in the last few days. Madame de Bernstein has asked about him. Lady Maria has begged her dear cousin George to see her, and, if possible, give her news of his brother. George, who was quite the head of the family a couple of months since, finds himself deposed, and of scarce any account, in Miss Hetty's eyes at least. Your wit, and your learning, and your tragedies, may be all very well; but what are these in comparison to victories and brass cannon? George takes his deposition very meekly. They are fifteen thousand Britons. Why should they not march and take Paris itself? Nothing more probable, think some of the ladies. They embrace; they congratulate each other; they are in a high state of excitement. For once, they long that Sir Miles and Lady Warrington were in town, so that they might pay her ladyship a visit, and ask, "What do you say to your nephew now, pray? Has he not taken twenty-one finest brass cannon; flung a hundred and twenty iron guns into the water, seized twenty-seven ships in the harbour, and destroyed the basin and the two piers at the entrance?" As the whole town rejoices and illuminates, so these worthy folks display brilliant red hangings in their cheeks, and light up candles of joy in their eyes, in honour of their champion and conqueror.

But now, I grieve to say, comes a cloudy day after the fair weather. The appetite of our commanders, growing by what it fed on, led them to think they had not feasted enough on the plunder of St. Malo; and thither, after staying a brief time at Portsmouth and the Wight, the conquerors of Cherbourg returned. They were landed in the Bay of St. Lunar, at a distance of a few miles from the place, and marched towards it, intending to destroy it this time. Meanwhile the harbour of St. Lunar was found insecure, and the fleet moved up to St. Cas, keeping up its communication with the invading army.

Now the British Lion found that the town of St. Malo—which he had proposed to swallow at a single mouthful—was guarded by an army of French, which the Governor of Brittany had brought to the succour of his good town, and the meditated coup-de-main being thus impossible, our leaders marched for their ships again, which lay duly awaiting our warriors in the Bay of St. Cas.

Hide, blushing glory, hide St. Cas's day! As our troops were marching down to their ships they became aware of an army following them, which the French governor of the province had sent from Brest. Two-thirds of the troops, and all the artillery, were already embarked, when the Frenchmen came down upon the remainder. Four companies of the first regiment of guards and the grenadier companies of the army, faced about on the beach to await the enemy, whilst the remaining troops were carried off in the boats. As the French descended from the heights round the bay, these guards and grenadiers marched out to attack them, leaving an excellent position which they had occupied—a great dyke raised on the shore, and behind which they might have resisted to advantage. And now, eleven hundred men were engaged with six—nay, ten times their number; and, after a while, broke and made for the boats with a sauve qui peut! Seven hundred out of the eleven were killed, drowned, or taken prisoners—the General himself was killed—and, ah! where were the volunteers?

A man of peace myself, and little intelligent of the practice or the details of war, I own I think less of the engaged troops than of the people they leave behind. Jack the Guardsman and La Tulipe of the Royal Bretagne are face to face, and striving to knock each other's brains out. Bon! It is their nature to—

like the bears and lions—and we will not say Heaven, but some power or other has made them so to do. But the girl of Tower Hill, who hung on Jack's neck before he departed; and the lass at Quimper, who gave the Frenchman his brule-gueule and tobacco-box before he departed on the noir trajet? What have you done, poor little tender hearts, that you should grieve so? My business is not with the army, but with the people left behind. What a fine state Miss Hetty Lambert must be in, when she hears of the disaster to the troops and the slaughter of the grenadier companies! What grief and doubt are in George Warrington's breast; what commiseration in Martin Lambert's, as he looks into his little girl's face and reads her piteous story there! Howe, the brave Commodore, rowing in his barge under the enemy's fire, has rescued with his boats scores and scores of our flying people. More are drowned; hundreds are prisoners, or shot on the beach. Among these, where is our Virginian?

CHAPTER LXV. Soldier's Return

Great Powers! will the vainglory of men, especially of Frenchmen, never cease? Will it be believed, that after the action of St. Cas—a mere affair of cutting off a rearguard, as you are aware—they were so unfeeling as to fire away I don't know how much powder at the Invalides at Paris, and brag and bluster over our misfortune? Is there any magnanimity in hallooing and huzzaying because five or six hundred brave fellows have been caught by ten thousand on a seashore, and that fate has overtaken them which is said to befall the hindmost? I had a mind to design an authentic picture of the rejoicings at London upon our glorious success at St. Malo. I fancied the polished guns dragged in procession by our gallant tars; the stout horse-grenadiers prancing by; the mob waving hats, roaring cheers, picking pockets, and our friends in a balcony in Fleet Street looking on and blessing this scene of British triumph. But now that the French Invalides have been so vulgar as to imitate the Tower, and set up their St. Cas against our St. Malo, I scorn to allude to the stale subject. I say Nolo, not Malo: content, for my part, if Harry has returned from one expedition and t'other with a whole skin. And have I ever said he was so much as bruised? Have I not, for fear of exciting my fair young reader, said that he was as well as ever he had been in his life? The sea air had browned his cheek, and the ball whistling by his side-curl had spared it. The ocean had wet his gaiters and other garments, without swallowing up his body. He had, it is true, shown the lapels of his coat to the enemy; but for as short a time as possible, withdrawing out of their sight as quick as might be. And what, pray, are lapels but reverses? Coats have them, as well as men; and our duty is to wear them with courage and good-humour.

"I can tell you," said Harry, "we all had to run for it; and when our line broke, it was he who could get to the boats who was most lucky. The French horse and foot pursued us down to the sea, and were mingled among us, cutting our men down, and bayoneting them on the ground. Poor Armytage was shot in advance of me, and fell; and I took him up and staggered through the surf to a boat. It was lucky that the sailors in our boat weren't afraid; for the shot were whistling about their ears, breaking the blades of their oars, and riddling their flag with shot; but the officer in command was as cool as if he had been drinking a bowl of punch at Portsmouth, which we had one on landing, I can promise you. Poor Sir John was less lucky than me. He never lived to reach the ship, and the service has lost a fine soldier, and Miss Howe a true gentleman to her husband. There must be these casualties, you see; and his brother gets the promotion—the baronetcy."

"It is of the poor lady I am thinking," says Miss Hetty (to whom haply our volunteer is telling his story); "and the King. Why did the King encourage Sir John Armytage to go? A gentleman could not refuse a command from such a quarter. And now the poor gentleman is dead! Oh, what a state his Majesty must be in!"

"I have no doubt his Majesty will be in a deep state of grief," says papa, wagging his head.

"Now you are laughing! Do you mean, sir, that when a gentleman dies in his service, almost at his feet, the King of England won't feel for him?" Hetty asks. "If I thought that, I vow I would be for the Pretender!"

"The sauce-box would make a pretty little head for Temple Bar," says the General, who could see Miss Hetty's meaning behind her words, and was aware in what a tumult of remorse, of consternation, of gratitude that the danger was over, the little heart was beating. "No," says he, "my dear. Were kings to weep for every soldier, what a life you would make for them! I think better of his Majesty than to suppose him so weak; and, if Miss Hester Lambert got her Pretender, I doubt whether she would be any the happier. That family was never famous for too much feeling."

"But if the King sent Harry—I mean Sir John Armytage—actually to the war in which he lost his life, oughtn't his Majesty to repent very much?" asks the young lady.

"If Harry had fallen, no doubt the court would have gone into mourning: as it is, gentlemen and ladies were in coloured clothes yesterday," remarks the General.

"Why should we not make bonfires for a defeat, and put on sackcloth and ashes after a victory?" asks George. "I protest I don't want to thank Heaven for helping us to burn the ships at Cherbourg."

"Yes you do, George! Not that I have a right to speak, and you ain't ever so much cleverer. But when your country wins you're glad—I know I am. When I run away before Frenchmen I'm ashamed—I can't help it, though I done it," says Harry. "It don't seem to me right somehow that Englishmen should have to do it," he added, gravely. And George smiled; but did not choose to ask his brother what, on the other hand, was the Frenchman's opinion.

"'Tis a bad business," continued Harry, gravely; "but 'tis lucky 'twas no worse. The story about the French is, that their Governor, the Duke of Aiguillon, was rather what you call a moistened chicken. Our whole retreat might have been cut off, only, to be sure, we ourselves were in a mighty hurry to move. The French local militia behaved famous, I am happy to say; and there was ever so many gentlemen volunteers with 'em, who showed, as they ought to do, in the front. They say the Chevalier of Tour d'Auvergne engaged in spite of the Duke of Aiguillon's orders. Officers told us, who came off with a list of our prisoners and wounded to General Bligh and Lord Howe. He is a lord now, since the news came of his brother's death to home, George. He is a brave fellow, whether lord or commoner."

"And his sister, who was to have married poor Sir John Armytage, think what her state must be!" sighs Miss Hetty, who has grown of late so sentimental.

"And his mother!" cries Mrs. Lambert. "Have you seen her ladyship's address in the papers to the electors of Nottingham? 'Lord Howe being now absent upon the publick service, and Lieutenant-Colonel Howe with his regiment at Louisbourg, it rests upon me to beg the favour of your votes and interests that Lieutenant-Colonel Howe may supply the place of his late brother as your representative in Parliament.' Isn't this a gallant woman?"

"A Laconic woman," says George.

"How can sons help being brave who have been nursed by such a mother as that?" asks the General.

Our two young men looked at each other.

"If one of us were to fall in defence of his country, we have a mother in Sparta who would think and write so too," says George.

"If Sparta is anywhere Virginia way, I reckon we have," remarks Mr. Harry. "And to think that we should both of us have met the enemy, and both of us been whipped by him, brother!" he adds pensively.

Hetty looks at him, and thinks of him only as he was the other day, tottering through the water towards the boats, his comrade bleeding on his shoulder, the enemy in pursuit, the shot flying round. And it was she who drove him into the danger! Her words provoked him. He never rebukes her now he is returned. Except when asked, he scarcely speaks about his adventures at all. He is very grave and courteous with Hetty; with the rest of the family especially frank and tender. But those taunts of hers wounded him. "Little hand!" his looks and demeanour seem to say, "thou shouldst not have been lifted against me! It is ill to scorn any one, much more one who has been so devoted to you and all yours. I may not be over quick of wit, but in as far as the heart goes, I am the equal of the best, and the best of my heart your family has had."

Harry's wrong, and his magnanimous endurance of it, served him to regain in Miss Hetty's esteem that place which he had lost during the previous months' inglorious idleness. The respect which the fair pay to the brave she gave him. She was no longer pert in her answers, or sarcastic in her observations regarding his conduct. In a word, she was a humiliated, an altered, an improved Miss Hetty.

And all the world seemed to change towards Harry, as he towards the world.

He was no longer sulky and indolent: he no more desponded about himself, or defied his neighbours. The colonel of his regiment reported his behaviour as exemplary, and recommended him for one of the commissions vacated by the casualties during the expedition. Unlucky as its termination was, it at least was fortunate to him. His brother-volunteers, when they came back to St. James's Street, reported highly of his behaviour. These volunteers and their actions were the theme of everybody's praise. Had he been a general commanding, and slain in the moment of victory, Sir John Armytage could scarce have had more sympathy than that which the nation showed him. The papers teemed with letters about him, and men of wit and sensibility vied with each other in composing epitaphs in his honour. The fate of his affianced bride was bewailed. She was, as we have said, the sister of the brave Commodore who had just returned from this unfortunate expedition, and succeeded to the title of his elder brother, an officer as gallant as himself, who had just fallen in America.

My Lord Howe was heard to speak in special praise of Mr. Warrington, and so he had a handsome share of the fashion and favour which the town now bestowed on the volunteers. Doubtless there were thousands of men employed who were as good as they but the English ever love their gentlemen, and love that they should distinguish themselves; and these volunteers were voted Paladins and heroes by common accord. As our young noblemen will, they accepted their popularity very affably. White's and Almack's illuminated when they returned, and St. James's embraced its young knights. Harry was restored to full favour amongst them. Their hands were held out eagerly to him again. Even his relations congratulated him; and there came a letter from Castlewood, whither Aunt Bernstein had by this time betaken herself, containing praises of his valour, and a pretty little bank-bill, as a token of his affectionate aunt's approbation. This was under my Lord Castlewood's frank, who sent his regards to both his kinsmen, and an offer of the hospitality of his country-house, if they were minded to come to him. And besides this, there came to him a private letter through the post—not very well spelt, but in a handwriting which Harry smiled to see again, in which his affeetionate cousin, Maria Esmond, told him she always loved to hear his praises (which were in everybody's mouth now), and sympathised in his good or evil fortune; and that, whatever occurred to him, she begged to keep a little place in his heart. Parson Sampson, she wrote, had preached a beautiful sermon about the horrors of war, and the noble actions of men who volunteered to face battle and danger in the service of their country. Indeed, the chaplain wrote himself, presently, a letter full of enthusiasm, in which he saluted Mr. Harry as his friend, his benefactor, his glorious hero. Even Sir Miles Warrington despatched a basket of game from Norfolk: and one bird (shot sitting), with love to my cousin, had a string and paper round the leg, and was sent as the first victim of young Miles's fowling-piece.

And presently, with joy beaming in his countenance, Mr. Lambert came to visit his young friends at their lodgings in Southampton Row, and announced to them that Mr. Henry Warrington was forthwith to be gazetted as Ensign in the Second Battalion of Kingsley's, the 20th Regiment, which had been engaged in the campaign, and which now at this time was formed into a separate regiment, the 67th. Its colonel was not with his regiment during its expedition to Brittany. He was away at Cape Breton, and was engaged in capturing those guns at Louisbourg, of which the arrival in England had caused such exultation.

CHAPTER LXVI. In which we go a-courting

Some of my amiable readers no doubt are in the custom of visiting that famous garden in the Regent's Park, in which so many of our finned, feathered, four-footed fellow-creatures are accommodated with board and lodging, in return for which they exhibit themselves for our instruction and amusement: and there, as a man's business and private thoughts follow him everywhere, and mix themselves with all life and nature round about him, I found myself, whilst looking at some fish in the aquarium, still actually thinking of our friends the Virginians.

One of the most beautiful motion-masters I ever beheld, sweeping through his green bath in harmonious curves, now turning his black glistening back to me, now exhibiting his fair white chest, in every movement active and graceful, turned out to be our old homely friend the flounder, whom we have all gobbled up out of his bath of water souchy at Greenwich, without having the slightest idea that he was a beauty.

As is the race of man, so is the race of flounders. If you can but see the latter in his right element, you may view him agile, healthy, and comely: put him out of his place, and behold his beauty is gone, his motions are disgraceful: he flaps the unfeeling ground ridiculously with his tail, and will presently gasp his feeble life out. Take him up tenderly, ere it be too late, and cast him into his native Thames again——But stop: I believe there is a certain proverb about fish out of water, and that other profound naturalists have remarked on them before me. Now Harry Warrington had been floundering for ever so long a time past, and out of his proper element. As soon as he found it, health, strength, spirits, energy, returned to him, and with the tap of the epaulet on his shoulder he sprang up an altered being. He delighted in his new profession; he engaged in all its details, and mastered them with eager quickness. Had I the skill of my friend Lorrequer, I would follow the other Harry into camp, and see him on the march, at the mess, on the parade-ground; I would have many a carouse with him and his companions; I would cheerfully live with him under the tents; I would knowingly explain all the manoeuvres of war, and all the details of the life military. As it is, the reader must please, out of his experience and imagination, to fill in the colours of the picture of which I can give but meagre hints and outlines, and, above all, fancy Mr. Harry Warrington in his new red coat and yellow facings, very happy to bear the King's colours, and pleased to learn and perform all the duties of his new profession.

As each young man delighted in the excellence of the other, and cordially recognised his brother's superior qualities, George, we may be sure, was proud of Harry's success, and rejoiced in his returning good fortune. He wrote an affectionate letter to his mother in Virginia, recounting all the praises which he had heard of Harry, and which his brother's modesty, George knew, would never allow him to repeat. He described how Harry had won his own first step in the army, and how he, George, would ask his mother leave to share with her the expense of purchasing a higher rank for him.

Nothing, said George, would give him a greater delight, than to be able to help his brother, and the more so, as, by his sudden return into life, as it were, he had deprived Harry of an inheritance which he had legitimately considered as his own. Labouring under that misconception, Harry had indulged in greater expenses than he ever would have thought of incurring as a younger brother; and George thought it was but fair, and as it were, as a thank-offering for his own deliverance, that he should contribute liberally to any scheme for his brother's advantage.

And now, having concluded his statement respecting Harry's affairs, George took occasion to speak of his own, and addressed his honoured mother on a point which very deeply concerned himself. She was aware that the best friends he and his brother had found in England were the good Mr. and Mrs. Lambert, the latter Madam Esmond's schoolfellow of earlier years. Where their own blood relations had been worldly and unfeeling, these true friends had ever been generous and kind. The General was respected by the whole army, and beloved by all who knew him. No mother's affection could have been more touching than Mrs. Lambert's for both Madam Esmond's children; and now, wrote Mr. George, he himself had formed an attachment for the elder Miss Lambert, on which he thought the happiness of his life depended, and which he besought his honoured mother to approve. He had made no precise offers to the young lady or her parents; but he was bound to say that he had made little disguise of his sentiments, and that the young lady, as well as her parents, seemed favourable to him. She had been so admirable and exemplary a daughter to her own mother, that he felt sure she would do her duty by his. In a word, Mr. Warrington described the young lady as a model of perfection, and expressed his firm belief that the happiness or misery of his own future life depended upon possessing or losing her. Why do you not produce this letter? haply asks some sentimental reader, of the present Editor, who has said how he has the whole Warrington correspondence in his hands. Why not? Because 'tis cruel to babble the secrets of a young man's love; to overhear his incoherent vows and wild raptures, and to note, in cold blood, the secrets—it may be, the follies—of his passion. Shall we play eavesdropper at twilight embrasures, count sighs and hand-shakes, bottle hot tears: lay our stethoscope on delicate young breasts, and feel their heart-throbs? I protest, for one, love is sacred. Wherever I see it (as one sometimes may in this world) shooting suddenly out of two pair of eyes; or glancing sadly even from one pair; or looking down from the mother to the baby in her lap; or from papa at his girl's happiness as she is whirling round the room with the captain; or from John Anderson, as his old wife comes into the room—the bonne vieille, the ever peerless among women; wherever we see that signal, I say, let us salute it. It is not only wrong to kiss and tell, but to tell about kisses. Everybody who has been admitted to the mystery,—hush about it. Down with him qui Deae sacrum vulgarit arcanae. Beware how you dine with him, he will print your private talk: as sure as you sail with him, he will throw you over.

Whilst Harry's love of battle has led him to smell powder—to rush upon reluctantes dracones, and to carry wounded comrades out of fire, George has been pursuing an amusement much more peaceful and delightful to him; penning sonnets to his mistress's eyebrow, mayhap; pacing in the darkness under her window, and watching the little lamp which shone upon her in her chamber; finding all sorts of pretexts for sending little notes which don't seem to require little answers, but get them; culling bits out of his favourite poets, and flowers out of Covent Garden for somebody's special adornment and pleasure; walking to St. James's Church, singing very likely out of the same Prayer-book, and never hearing one word of the sermon, so much do other thoughts engross him; being prodigiously affectionate to all Miss Theo's relations—to her little brother and sister at school; to the elder at college; to Miss Hetty, with whom he engages in gay passages of wit; and to mamma, who is half in love with him herself, Martin Lambert says; for if fathers are sometimes sulky at the appearance of the destined son-in-law, is it not a fact that mothers become sentimental and, as it were, love their own loves over again?

Gumbo and Sady are for ever on the trot between Southampton Row and Dean Street. In the summer months all sorts of junketings and pleasure-parties are devised; and there are countless proposals to go to Ranelagh, to Hampstead, to Vauxhall, to Marylebone Gardens, and what not. George wants the famous tragedy copied out fair for the stage, and who can write such a beautiful Italian hand as Miss Theo? As the sheets pass to and fro they are accompanied by little notes of thanks, of interrogation, of admiration, always. See, here is the packet, marked in Warrington's neat hand, "T's letters, 1758-9." Shall we open them and reveal their tender secrets to the public gaze? Those virgin words were whispered for one ear alone. Years after they were written, the husband read, no doubt, with sweet pangs of remembrance, the fond lines addressed to the lover. It were a sacrilege to show the pair to public eyes: only let kind readers be pleased to take our word that the young lady's letters are modest and pure, the gentleman's most respectful and tender. In fine, you see, we have said very little about it; but, in these few last months, Mr. George Warrington has made up his mind that he has found the woman of women. She mayn't be the most beautiful. Why, there is Cousin Flora, there is Coelia, and Ardelia, and a hundred more, who are ever so much more handsome: but her sweet face pleases him better than any other in the world. She mayn't be the most clever, but her voice is the dearest and pleasantest to hear; and in her company he is so clever himself; he has such fine thoughts; he uses such eloquent words; he is so generous, noble, witty, that no wonder he delights in it. And, in regard to the young lady,—as thank Heaven I never thought so ill of women as to suppose them to be just, we may be sure that there is no amount of wit, of wisdom, of beauty, of valour, of virtue with which she does not endow her young hero.

When George's letter reached home, we may fancy that it created no small excitement in the little circle round Madam Esmond's fireside. So he was in love, and wished to marry! It was but natural, and would keep him out of harm's way. If he proposed to unite himself with a well-bred Christian young woman, Madam saw no harm.

"I knew they would be setting their caps at him," says Mountain. "They fancy that his wealth is as great as his estate. He does not say whether the young lady has money. I fear otherwise."

"People would set their caps at him here, I dare say," says Madam Esmond, grimly looking at her dependant, "and try and catch Mr. Esmond Warrington for their own daughters, who are no richer than Miss Lambert may be."

"I suppose your ladyship means me!" says Mountain. "My Fanny is poor, as you say; and 'tis kind of you to remind me of her poverty!"

"I said people would set their caps at him. If the cap fits you, tant pis! as my papa used to say."

"You think, madam, I am scheming to keep George for my daughter? I thank you, on my word! A good opinion you seem to have of us after the years we have lived together!"

"My dear Mountain, I know you much better than to suppose you could ever fancy your daughter would be a suitable match for a gentleman of Mr. Esmond's rank and station," says Madam, with much dignity.

"Fanny Parker was as good as Molly Benson at school, and Mr. Mountain's daughter is as good as Mr. Lambert's!" Mrs. Mountain cries out.

"Then you did think of marrying her to my son! I shall write to Mr. Esmond Warrington, and say how sorry I am that you should be disappointed!" says the mistress of Castlewood. And we, for our parts, may suppose that Mrs. Mountain was disappointed, and had some ambitious views respecting her daughter—else, why should she have been so angry at the notion of Mr. Warrington's marriage?

In reply to her son, Madam Esmond wrote back that she was pleased with the fraternal love George exhibited; that it was indeed but right in some measure to compensate Harry, whose expectations had led him to adopt a more costly mode of life than he would have entered on had he known he was only a younger son. And with respect to purchasing his promotion, she would gladly halve the expense with Harry's elder brother, being thankful to think his own gallantry had won him his first step. This bestowal of George's money, Madam Esmond added, was at least much more satisfactory than some other extravagances to which she would not advert.

The other extravagance to which Madam alluded was the payment of the ransom to the French captain's family, to which tax George's mother never would choose to submit. She had a determined spirit of her own, which her son inherited. His persistence she called pride and obstinacy. What she thought of her own pertinacity, her biographer, who lives so far from her time, does not pretend to say. Only I dare say people a hundred years ago pretty much resembled their grandchildren of the present date, and loved to have their own way, and to make others follow it.

Now, after paying his own ransom, his brother's debts, and half the price for his promotion, George calculated that no inconsiderable portion of his private patrimony would be swallowed up: nevertheless he made the sacrifice with a perfect good heart. His good mother always enjoined him in her letters to remember who his grandfather was, and to support the dignity of his family accordingly. She gave him various commissions to purchase goods in England, and though she as yet had sent him very trifling remittances, she alluded so constantly to the exalted rank of the Esmonds, to her desire that he should do nothing unworthy of that illustrious family; she advised him so peremptorily and frequently to appear in the first society of the country, to frequent the court where his ancestors had been accustomed to move, and to appear always in the world in a manner worthy of his name, that George made no doubt his mother's money would be forthcoming when his own ran short, and generously obeyed her injunctions as to his style of life. I find in the Esmond papers of this period, bills for genteel entertainments, tailors' bills for court suits supplied, and liveries for his honour's negro servants and chairmen, horse-dealers' receipts, and so forth; and am thus led to believe that the elder of our Virginians was also after a while living at a considerable expense.

He was not wild or extravagant like his brother. There was no talk of gambling or racehorses against Mr. George; his table was liberal, his equipages handsome, his purse always full, the estate to which he was heir was known to be immense. I mention these circumstances because they may probably have influenced the conduct both of George and his friends in that very matter concerning which, as I have said, he and his mother had been just corresponding. The young heir of Virginia was travelling for his pleasure and improvement in foreign kingdoms. The queen, his mother, was in daily correspondence with his Highness, and constantly enjoined him to act as became his lofty station. There could be no doubt from her letters that she desired he should live liberally and magnificently. He was perpetually making purchases at his parent's order. She had not settled as yet; on the contrary, she had wrote out by the last mail for twelve new sets of waggon harness, and an organ that should play fourteen specified psalm-tunes: which articles George dutifully ordered. She had not paid as yet, and might not to-day or to-morrow, but eventually, of course, she would: and Mr. Warrington never thought of troubling his friends about these calculations, or discussing with them his mother's domestic affairs. They, on their side, took for granted that he was in a state of competence and ease, and, without being mercenary folks, Mr. and

Mrs. Lambert were no doubt pleased to see an attachment growing up between their daughter and a young gentleman of such good principles, talents, family, and expectations. There was honesty in all Mr. Esmond Warrington's words and actions, and in his behaviour to the world a certain grandeur and simplicity, which showed him to be a true gentleman. Somewhat cold and haughty in his demeanour to strangers, especially towards the great, he was not in the least supercilious: he was perfectly courteous towards women, and with those people whom he loved, especially kind, amiable, lively, and tender.

No wonder that one young woman we know of got to think him the best man in all the world—alas! not even excepting papa. A great love felt by a man towards a woman makes him better, as regards her, than all other men. We have said that George used to wonder himself when he found how witty, how eloquent, how wise he was, when he talked with the fair young creature whose heart had become all his…. I say we will not again listen to their love whispers. Those soft words do not bear being written down. If you please—good sir, or madam, who are sentimentally inclined—lay down the book and think over certain things for yourself. You may be ever so old now; but you remember. It may be all dead and buried; but in a moment, up it springs out of its grave, and looks, and smiles, and whispers as of yore when it clung to your arm, and dropped fresh tears on your heart. It is here, and alive, did I say? O far, far away! O lonely hearth and cold ashes! Here is the vase, but the roses are gone; here is the shore, and yonder the ship was moored; but the anchors are up, and it has sailed away for ever.

Et cetera, et cetera, et cetera. This, however, is mere sentimentality; and as regards George and Theo, is neither here nor there. What I mean to say is, that the young lady's family were perfectly satisfied with the state of affairs between her and Mr. Warrington; and though he had not as yet asked the decisive question, everybody else knew what the answer would be when it came.

Mamma perhaps thought the question was a long time coming.

"Psha! my dear!" says the General. "There is time enough in all conscience. Theo is not much more than seventeen; George, if I mistake not, is under forty; and, besides, he must have time to write to Virginia, and ask mamma."

"But suppose she refuses?"

"That will be a bad day for old and young," says the General, "Let us rather say, suppose she consents, my love?—I can't fancy anybody in the world refusing Theo anything she has set her heart on," adds the father: "and I am sure 'tis bent upon this match."

So they all waited with the utmost anxiety until an answer from Madam Esmond should arrive; and trembled lest the French privateers should take the packet-ship by which the precious letter was conveyed.

CHAPTER LXVII. In which a Tragedy is acted, and two more are begun

James Wolfe, Harry's new Colonel, came back from America a few weeks after our Virginian had joined his regiment. Wolfe had previously been Lieutenant-Colonel of Kingsley's, and a second battalion of the regiment had been formed and given to him in reward for his distinguished gallantry and services at Cape Breton. Harry went with quite unfeigned respect and cordiality to pay his duty to his new commander, on whom the eyes of the world began to be turned now,—the common opinion being that he was likely to become a great general. In the late affairs in France, several officers of great previous repute had been tried and found lamentably wanting. The Duke of Marlborough had shown himself no worthy descendant of his great ancestor. About my Lord George Sackville's military genius there were doubts, even before his unhappy behaviour at Minden prevented a great victory. The nation was longing for military glory, and the Minister was anxious to find a general who might gratify the eager desire of the people. Mr. Wolfe's and Mr. Lambert's business keeping them both in London, the friendly intercourse between those officers was renewed, no one being more delighted than Lambert at his younger friend's good fortune.

Harry, when he was away from his duty, was never tired of hearing Mr. Wolfe's details of the military operations of the last year, about which Wolfe talked very freely and openly. Whatever thought was in his mind, he appears to have spoken it out generously. He had that heroic simplicity which distinguished Nelson afterwards: he talked frankly of his actions. Some of the fine gentlemen at St. James's might wonder and sneer at him; but amongst our little circle of friends we may be sure he found admiring listeners. The young General had the romance of a boy on many matters. He delighted in music and poetry. On the last day of his life he said he would rather have written Gray's Elegy than have won a battle. We may be sure that with a gentleman of such literary tastes our friend George would become familiar; and as they were both in love, and both accepted lovers, and both eager for happiness, no doubt they must have had many sentimental conversations together which would be very interesting to report could we only have accurate accounts of them. In one of his later letters, Warrington writes:

"I had the honour of knowing the famous General Wolfe, and seeing much of him during his last stay in London. We had a subject of conversation then which was of unfailing interest to both of us, and I could not but admire Mr. Wolfe's simplicity, his frankness, and a sort of glorious bravery which characterised him. He was much in love, and he wanted heaps and heaps of laurels to take to his mistress. 'If it be a sin to covet honour,' he used to say with Harry the Fifth (he was passionately fond of plays and poetry), 'I am the most offending soul alive.' Surely on his last day he had a feast which was enough to satisfy the greediest appetite for glory. He hungered after it. He seemed to me not merely like a soldier going resolutely to do his duty, but rather like a knight in quest of dragons and giants. My own country has furnished of late a chief of a very different order, and quite an opposite genius. I scarce know which to admire most. The Briton's chivalrous ardour, or the more than Roman constancy of our great Virginian."

As Mr. Lambert's official duties detained him in London, his family remained contentedly with him, and I suppose Mr. Warrington was so satisfied with the rural quiet of Southampton Row and the beautiful flowers and trees of Bedford Gardens, that he did not care to quit London for any long period. He made his pilgrimage to Castlewood, and passed a few days there, occupying the chamber of which he had often heard his grandfather talk, and which Colonel Esmond had occupied as a boy and he was received kindly enough by such members of the family as happened to be at home. But no doubt he loved better to be in London by the side of a young person in whose society he found greater pleasure than any which my Lord Castlewood's circle could afford him, though all the ladies were civil, and Lady Maria especially gracious, and enchanted with the tragedy which George and Parson Sampson read out to the ladies. The chaplain was enthusiastic in its praises, and indeed it was through his interest and not through Mr. Johnson's after all, that Mr. Warrington's piece ever came on the stage. Mr. Johnson, it is true, pressed the play on his friend Mr. Garrick for Drury Lane, but Garrick had just made an arrangement with the famous Mr. Home for a tragedy from the pen of the author of Douglas. Accordingly, Carpezan was carried to Mr. Rich at Covent Garden, and accepted by that manager.

On the night of the production of the piece, Mr. Warrington gave an elegant entertainment to his friends at the Bedford Head, in Covent Garden, whence they adjourned in a body to the theatre; leaving only one or two with our young author, who remained at the coffee-house, where friends from time to time came to him with an account of the performance. The part of Carpezan was filled by Barry, Shuter was the old nobleman, Reddish, I need scarcely say, made an excellent Ulric, and the King of Bohemia was by a young actor from Dublin, Mr. Geoghegan, or Hagan as he was called on the stage, and who looked and performed the part to admiration. Mrs. Woffington looked too old in the first act as the heroine, but her murder in the fourth act, about which great doubts were expressed, went off to the terror and delight of the audience. Miss Wayn sang the ballad which is supposed to be sung by the king's page, just at the moment of the unhappy wife's execution, and all agreed that Barry was very terrible and pathetic as Carpezan, especially in the execution scene. The grace and elegance of the young actor, Hagan, won general applause. The piece was put very elegantly on the stage by Mr. Rich, though there was some doubt whether, in the march of Janissaries in the last, the manager was correct in introducing a favourite elephant, which had figured in various pantomimes, and by which one of Mr. Warrington's black servants marched in a Turkish habit. The other sate in the footman's gallery, and uproariously wept and applauded at the proper intervals.

The execution of Sybilla was the turning-point of the piece. Her head off, George's friends breathed freely, and one messenger after another came to him at the coffee-house, to announce the complete success of the tragedy. Mr. Barry, amidst general applause, announced the play for repetition, and that it was the work of a young gentleman of Virginia, his first attempt in the dramatic style.

We should like to have been in the box where all our friends were seated during the performance, to have watched Theo's flutter and anxiety whilst the success of the play seemed dubious, and have beheld the blushes and the sparkles in her eyes, when the victory was assured. Harry, during the little trouble in the fourth act, was deadly pale—whiter, Mrs. Lambert said, than Barry, with all his chalk. But if Briareus could have clapped hands, he could scarcely have made more noise than Harry at the end of the piece. Mr. Wolfe and General Lambert huzzayed enthusiastically. Mrs. Lambert, of course, cried: and though Hetty said, "Why do you cry, mamma? I you don't want any of them alive again; you know it serves them all right"—the girl was really as much delighted as any person present, including little Charley from the Chartreux, who had leave from Dr. Crusius for that evening, and Miss Lucy, who had been brought from boarding-school on purpose to be present on the great occasion. My Lord Castlewood and his sister, Lady Maria, were present; and his lordship went from his box and complimented Mr. Barry and the other actors on the stage; and Parson Sampson was invaluable in the pit, where he led the applause, having, I believe, given previous instructions to Gumbo to keep an eye upon him from the gallery, and do as he did.

Be sure there was a very jolly supper of Mr. Warrington's friends that night —much more jolly than Mr. Garrick's, for example, who made but a very poor success with his Agis and its dreary choruses, and who must have again felt that he had missed a good chance, in preferring Mr. Home's tragedy to our young author's. A jolly supper, did we say?—Many jolly suppers. Mr. Gumbo gave an entertainment to several gentlemen of the shoulder-knot, who had concurred in supporting his master's masterpiece: Mr. Henry Warrington gave a supper at the Star and Garter, in Pall Mall, to ten officers of his new regiment, who had come up for the express purpose of backing Carpezan; and finally, Mr. Warrington received the three principal actors of the tragedy, our family party from the side box, Mr. Johnson and his ingenious friend, Mr. Reynolds the painter, my Lord Castlewood and his sister, and one or two more. My Lady Maria happened to sit next to the young actor who had performed the part of the King. Mr. Warrington somehow had Miss Theo for a neighbour, and no doubt passed a pleasant evening beside her. The greatest animation and cordiality prevailed, and when toasts were called, Lady Maria gaily gave "The King of Hungary" for hers. That gentleman, who had plenty of eloquence and fire, and excellent manners, on as well as off the stage, protested that he had already suffered death in the course of the evening, hoped that he should die a hundred times more on the same field; but, dead or living, vowed he knew whose humble servant he ever should be. Ah, if he had but a real crown in place of his diadem of pasteboard and tinsel, with what joy would he lay it at her ladyship's feet! Neither my lord nor Mr.

Esmond were over well pleased with the gentleman's exceeding gallantry—a part of which they attributed, no doubt justly, to the wine and punch, of which he had been partaking very freely. Theo and her sister, who were quite new to the world, were a little frightened by the exceeding energy of Mr. Hagan's manner—but Lady Maria, much more experienced, took it in perfectly good part. At a late hour coaches were called, to which the gentlemen attended the ladies, after whose departure some of them returned to the supper-room, and the end was that Carpezan had to be carried away in a chair, and that the King of Hungary had a severe headache; and that the Poet, though he remembered making a great number of speeches, was quite astounded when half a dozen of his guests appeared at his house the next day, whom he had invited overnight to come and sup with him once more.

As he put Mrs. Lambert and her daughters into their coach on the night previous, all the ladies were flurried, delighted, excited; and you may be sure our gentleman was with them the next day, to talk of the play and the audience, and the actors, and the beauties of the piece, over and over again. Mrs. Lambert had heard that the ladies of the theatre were dangerous company for young men. She hoped George would have a care, and not frequent the greenroom too much.

George smiled, and said he had a preventive against all greenroom temptations, of which he was not in the least afraid; and as he spoke he looked in Theo's face, as if in those eyes lay the amulet which was to preserve him from all danger.

"Why should he be afraid, mamma?" asks the maiden simply. She had no idea of danger or of guile.

"No, my darling, I don't think he need be afraid," says the mother, kissing her.

"You don't suppose Mr. George would fall in love with that painted old creature who performed the chief part?" asks Miss Hetty, with a toss of her head. "She must be old enough to be his mother."

"Pray, do you suppose that at our age nobody can care for us, or that we have no hearts left?" asks mamma, very tartly. "I believe, or I may say, I hope and trust, your father thinks otherwise. He is, I imagine, perfectly satisfied, miss. He does not sneer at age, whatever little girls out of the schoolroom may do. And they had much better be back there, and they had much better remember what the fifth commandment is—that they had, Hetty!"

"I didn't think I was breaking it by saying that an actress was as old as George's mother," pleaded Hetty.

"George's mother is as old as I am, miss!—at least she was when we were at school. And Fanny Parker—Mrs. Mountain who now is—was seven months older, and we were in the French class together; and I have no idea that our age is to be made the subject of remarks and ridicule by our children, and I will thank you to spare it, if you please! Do you consider your mother too old, George?"

"I am glad my mother is of your age, Aunt Lambert," says George, in the most sentimental manner.

Strange infatuation of passion—singular perversity of reason! At some period before his marriage, it not unfrequently happens that a man actually is fond of his mother-in-law! At this time our good General vowed, and with some reason, that he was jealous. Mrs. Lambert made much more of George than of any other person in the family. She dressed up Theo to the utmost advantage in order to meet him; she was for ever caressing her, and appealing to her when he spoke. It was, "Don't you think he looks well?"—"Don't you think he looks pale, Theo, to-day?"—"Don't you think he has been sitting up over his books too much at night?" and so forth. If he had a cold, she would have liked to make gruel for him and see his feet in hot water. She sent him recipes of her own for his health. When he was away, she never ceased talking about him to her daughter. I dare say Miss Theo liked the subject well enough. When he came, she was sure to be wanted in some other part of the house, and would bid Theo take care of him till she returned. Why, before she returned to the room, could you hear her talking outside the door to her youngest innocent children, to her servants in the upper regions, and so forth? When she reappeared, was not Mr. George always standing or sitting at a considerable distance from Miss Theo—except, to be sure, on that one day when she had just happened to drop her scissors, and he had naturally stooped down to pick them up? Why was she blushing? Were not youthful cheeks made to blush, and roses to bloom in the spring? Not that mamma ever noted the blushes, but began quite an artless conversation about this or that, as she sate down brimful of happiness to her worktable.

And at last there came a letter from Virginia in Madam Esmond's neat, well-known hand, and over which George trembled and blushed before he broke the seal. It was in answer to the letter which he had sent home, respecting his brother's commission and his own attachment to Miss Lambert. Of his intentions respecting Harry, Madam Esmond fully approved. As for his marriage, she was not against early marriages. She would take his picture of Miss Lambert with the allowance that was to be made for lovers' portraits, and hope, for his sake, that the young lady was all he described her to be. With money, as Madam Esmond gathered from her son's letter, she did not appear to be provided at all, which was a pity, as, though wealthy in land, their family had but little ready-money. However, by Heaven's blessing, there was plenty at home for children and children's children, and the wives of her sons should share all she had. When she heard more at length from Mr. and Mrs. Lambert, she would reply for her part more fully. She did not pretend to say that she had not greater hopes for her son, as a gentleman of his name and prospects might pretend to the hand of the first lady of the land; but as Heaven had willed that her son's choice should fall upon her old friend's daughter, she acquiesced, and would welcome George's wife as her own child. This letter was brought by Mr. Van den Bosch of Albany, who had lately bought a very large estate in Virginia, and who was bound for England to put his granddaughter to a boarding-school. She, Madam Esmond, was not mercenary, nor was it because this young lady was heiress of a very great fortune that she desired her sons to pay Mr. Van d. B. every attention. Their properties lay close together, and could Harry find in the young lady those qualities of person and mind suitable for a companion for life, at least she would have the satisfaction of seeing both her children near her in her declining years. Madam Esmond concluded by sending her affectionate compliments to Mrs. Lambert, from whom she begged to hear further, and her blessing to the young lady who was to be her daughter-in-law.

The letter was not cordial, and the writer evidently but half satisfied; but, such as it was, her consent was here formally announced. How eagerly George ran away to Soho with the long-desired news in his pocket! I suppose our worthy friends there must have read his news in his countenance—else why should Mrs. Lambert take her daughter's hand and kiss her with such uncommon warmth, when George announced that he had received letters from home? Then, with a break in his voice, a pallid face, and a considerable tremor, turning to Mr. Lambert, he said: "Madam Esmond's letter, sir, is in reply to one of mine, in which I acquainted her that I had formed an attachment in England, for which I asked my mother's approval. She gives her consent, I am grateful to say, and I have to pray my dear friends to be equally kind to me."

"God bless thee, my dear boy!" says the good General, laying a hand on the young man's head. "I am glad to have thee for a son, George. There, there, don't go down on your knees, young folks! George may, to be sure, and thank God for giving him the best little wife in all England. Yes, my dear, except when you were ill, you never caused me a heartache—and happy is the man, I say, who wins thee!"

I have no doubt the young people knelt before their parents, as was the fashion in those days; and am perfectly certain that Mrs. Lambert kissed both of them, and likewise bedewed her pocket-handkerchief in the most plentiful manner. Hetty was not present at this sentimental scene, and when she heard of it, spoke with considerable asperity, and a laugh that was by no means pleasant, saying: "Is this all the news you have to give me? Why, I have known it these months past. Do you think I have no eyes to see, and no ears to hear, indeed?" But in private she was much more gentle. She flung herself on her sister's neck, embracing her passionately, and vowing that never, never would Theo find any one to love her like her sister. With Theo she became entirely mild and humble. She could not abstain from her jokes and satire with George, but he was too happy to heed her much, and too generous not to see the cause of her jealousy.

When all parties concerned came to read Madam Esmond's letter, that document, it is true, appeared rather vague. It contained only a promise that she would receive the young people at her house, and no sort of proposal for a settlement. The General shook his head over the letter—he did not think of examining it until some days after the engagement had been made between George and his daughter: but now he read Madam Esmond's words, they gave him but small encouragement.

"Bah!" says George. "I shall have three hundred pounds for my tragedy. I can easily write a play a year; and if the worst comes to the worst, we can live on that."

"On that and your patrimony," says Theo's father.

George now had to explain, with some hesitation, that what with paying bills for his mother, and Harry's commission and debts, and his own ransom—George's patrimony proper was well-nigh spent.

Mr. Lambert's countenance looked graver still at this announcement, but he saw his girl's eyes turned towards him with an alarm so tender, that he took her in his arms and vowed that, let the worst come to the worst, his darling should not be balked of her wish.

About the going back to Virginia, George frankly owned that he little liked the notion of returning to be entirely dependent on his mother. He gave General Lambert an idea of his life at home, and explained how little to his taste that slavery was. No. Why should he not stay in England, write more tragedies, study for the bar, get a place, perhaps? Why, indeed? He straightway began to form a plan for another tragedy. He brought portions of his work, from time to time, to Miss Theo and her sister: Hetty yawned over the work, but Theo pronounced it to be still more beautiful and admirable than the last, which was perfect.

The engagement of our young friends was made known to the members of their respective families, and announced to Sir Miles Warrington, in a ceremonious letter from his nephew. For a while Sir Miles saw no particular objection to the marriage; though, to be sure, considering his name and prospects, Mr. Warrington might have looked higher. The truth was, that Sir Miles imagined that Madam Esmond had made some considerable settlement on her son, and that his circumstances were more than easy. But when he heard that George was entirely dependent on his mother, and that his own small patrimony was dissipated, as Harry's had been before, Sir Miles's indignation at his nephew's imprudence knew no bounds; he could not find words to express his horror and anger at the want of principle exhibited by both these unhappy young men: he thought it his duty to speak his mind about them, and wrote his opinion to his sister Esmond in Virginia. As for General and Mrs. Lambert, who passed for respectable persons, was it to be borne that such people should inveigle a penniless young man into a marriage with their penniless daughter? Regarding them, and George's behaviour, Sir Miles fully explained his views to Madam Esmond, gave half a finger to George whenever his nephew called on him in town, and did not even invite him to partake of the famous family small-beer. Towards Harry his uncle somewhat unbent; Harry had done his duty in the campaign, and was mentioned with praise in high quarters. He had sown his wild oats,—he at least was endeavouring to amend; but George was a young prodigal, fast careering to ruin, and his name was only mentioned in the family with a groan. Are there any poor fellows nowadays, I wonder, whose polite families fall on them and persecute them; groan over them and stone them, and hand stones to their neighbours that they may do likewise? All the patrimony spent! Gracious heavens! Sir Miles turned pale when he saw his nephew coming. Lady Warrington prayed for him as a dangerous reprobate; and, in the meantime, George was walking the town, quite unconscious that he was occasioning so much wrath and so much devotion. He took little Miley to the play and brought him back again. He sent tickets to his aunt and cousins which they could not refuse, you know; it would look too marked were they to break altogether. So they not only took the tickets, but whenever country constituents came to town they asked for more, taking care to give the very worst motives to George's intimacy with the theatre, and to suppose that he and the actresses were on terms of the most disgraceful intimacy. An august personage having been to the theatre, and expressed his approbation of Mr. Warrington's drama to Sir Miles, when he attended his R-y-l H-ghn-ss's levee at Saville House, Sir Miles, to be sure, modified his opinion regarding the piece, and spoke henceforth more respectfully of it. Meanwhile, as we have said, George was passing his life entirely careless of the opinion of all the uncles, aunts, and cousins in the world.

Most of the Esmond cousins were at least more polite and cordial than George's kinsfolk of the Warrington side. In spite of his behaviour over the cards, Lord Castlewood, George always maintained, had a liking for our Virginians, and George was pleased enough to be in his company. He was a far abler man than many who succeeded in life. He had a good name, and somehow only stained it; a considerable wit, and nobody trusted it; and a very shrewd experience and knowledge of mankind, which made him mistrust them, and himself most of all, and which perhaps was the bar to his own advancement. My Lady Castlewood, a woman of the world, wore always a bland mask, and received Mr. George with perfect civility, and welcomed him to lose as many guineas as he liked at her ladyship's card-tables. Between Mr. William and the Virginian brothers there never was any love lost; but, as for Lady Maria, though her love affair was over, she had no rancour; she professed for her cousins a very great regard and affection, a part of which the young gentlemen very gratefully returned. She was charmed to hear of Harry's valour in the campaign; she was delighted with George's success at the theatre; she was for ever going to the play, and had all the favourite passages of Carpezan by heart. One day, as Mr. George and Miss Theo were taking a sentimental walk in Kensington Gardens, whom should they light upon but their cousin Maria in company with a gentleman in a smart suit and handsome laced hat, and who should the gentleman be but his Majesty King Louis of Hungary, Mr. Hagan? He saluted the party, and left them presently. Lady Maria had only just happened to meet him. Mr. Hagan came sometimes, he said, for quiet, to study his parts in Kensington Gardens, and George and the two ladies walked together to Lord Castlewood's door in Kensington Square, Lady Maria uttering a thousand compliments to Theo upon her good looks, upon her virtue, upon her future happiness, upon her papa and mamma, upon her destined husband, upon her paduasoy cloak and dear little feet and shoe-buckles.

Harry happened to come to London that evening, and slept at his accustomed quarters. When George appeared at breakfast, the Captain was already in the room (the custom of that day was to call all army gentlemen Captains), and looking at the letters on the breakfast-table.

"Why, George," he cries, "there is a letter from Maria!"

"Little boy bring it from Common Garden last night—Master George asleep," says Gumbo.

"What can it be about?" asks Harry, as George peruses his letter with a queer expression of face.

"About my play, to be sure," George answers, tearing up the paper, and still wearing his queer look.

"What, she is not writing love-letters to you, is she, Georgy?"

"No, certainly not to me," replies the other. But he spoke no word more about the letter; and when at dinner in Dean Street Mrs. Lambert said, "So you met somebody walking with the King of Hungary yesterday in Kensington Gardens?"

"What little tell-tale told you? A mere casual rencontre—the King goes there to study his parts, and Lady Maria happened to be crossing the garden to visit some of the other King's servants at Kensington Palace." And so there was an end to that matter for the time being.

Other events were at hand fraught with interest to our Virginians. One evening after Christmas, the two gentlemen, with a few more friends, were met round General Lambert's supper-table; and among the company was Harry's new Colonel of the 67th, Major-General Wolfe. The young General was more than ordinarily grave. The conversation all related to the war. Events of great importance were pending. The great minister now in power was determined to carry on the war on a much more extended scale than had been attempted hitherto: an army was ordered to Germany to help Prince Ferdinand, another great expedition was preparing for America, and here, says Mr. Lambert, "I will give you the health of the Commander—a glorious campaign, and a happy return to him!"

"Why do you not drink the toast, General James!" asked the hostess of her guest.

"He must not drink his own toast," says General Lambert; "it is we must do that!"

What? was James appointed?—All the ladies must drink such a toast as that, and they mingled their kind voices with the applause of the rest of the company.

Why did he look so melancholy? the ladies asked of one another when they withdrew. In after days they remembered his pale face.

"Perhaps he has been parting from his sweetheart," suggests tender-hearted Mrs. Lambert. And at this sentimental notion, no doubt all the ladies looked sad.

The gentlemen, meanwhile, continued their talk about the war and its chances. Mr. Wolfe did not contradict the speakers when they said that the expedition was to be directed against Canada.

"Ah, sir," says Harry, "I wish your regiment was going with you, and that I might pay another visit to my old friends at Quebec."

What, had Harry been there? Yes. He described his visit to the place five years before, and knew the city, and the neighbourhood, well. He lays a number of bits of biscuit on the table before him, and makes a couple of rivulets of punch on each side. "This fork is the Isle d'Orleans," says he, "with the north and south branches of St. Lawrence on each side. Here's the Low Town, with a battery—how many guns was mounted there in our time, brother?—but at long shots from the St. Joseph shore you might play the same game. Here's what they call the little river, the St. Charles, and a bridge of boats with a tete du pont over to the place of arms. Here's the citadel, and here's convents—ever so many convents—and the cathedral; and here, outside the lines to the west and south, is what they call the Plains of Abraham—where a certain little affair took place, do you remember, brother? He and a young officer of the Rousillon regiment ca ca'd at each other for twenty minutes, and George pinked him, and then they jure'd each other an amitie eternelle. Well it was for George: for his second saved his life on that awful day of Braddock's defeat. He was a fine little fellow, and I give his toast: Je bois a la sante du Chevalier de Florac!"

"What, can you speak French, too, Harry?" asks Mr. Wolfe. The young man looked at the General with eager eyes.

"Yes," says he, "I can speak, but not so well as George."

"But he remembers the city, and can place the batteries, you see, and knows the ground a thousand times better than I do!" cries the elder brother.

The two elder officers exchanged looks with one another; Mr. Lambert smiled and nodded, as if in reply to the mute queries of his comrade: on which the other spoke. "Mr. Harry," he said, "if you have had enough of fine folks, and White's, and horse-racing——"

"Oh, sir!" says the young man, turning very red.

"And if you have a mind to a sea voyage at a short notice, come and see me at my lodgings to-morrow."

What was that sudden uproar of cheers which the ladies heard in their drawing-room? It was the hurrah which Harry Warrington gave when he leaped up at hearing the General's invitation.

The women saw no more of the gentlemen that night. General Lambert had to be away upon his business early next morning, before seeing any of his family; nor had he mentioned a word of Harry's outbreak on the previous evening. But when he rejoined his folks at dinner, a look at Miss Hetty's face informed the worthy gentleman that she knew what had passed on the night previous, and what was about to happen to the young Virginian. After dinner Mrs. Lambert sat demurely at her work, Miss Theo took her book of Italian Poetry. Neither of the General's customary guests happened to be present that evening.

He took little Hetty's hand in his, and began to talk with her. He did not allude to the subject which he knew was uppermost in her mind, except that by a more than ordinary gentleness and kindness he perhaps caused her to understand that her thoughts were known to him.

"I have breakfasted," says he, "with James Wolfe this morning, and our friend Harry was of the party. When he and the other guests were gone, I remained and talked with James about the great expedition on which he is going to sail. Would that his brave father had lived a few months longer to see him come back covered with honours from Louisbourg, and knowing that all England was looking to him to achieve still greater glory! James is dreadfully ill in body—so ill that I am frightened for him—and not a little depressed in mind at having to part from the young lady whom he has loved so long. A little rest, he thinks, might have set his shattered frame up; and to call her his has been the object of his life. But, great as his love is (and he is as romantic as one of you young folks of seventeen), honour and duty are greater, and he leaves home, and wife, and ease, and health, at their bidding. Every man of honour would do the like; every woman who loves him truly would buckle on his armour for him. James goes to take leave of his mother to-night; and though she loves him devotedly, and is one of the tenderest women in the world, I am sure she will show no sign of weakness at his going away."

"When does he sail, papa?" the girl asked.

"He will be on board in five days." And Hetty knew quite well who sailed with him.

CHAPTER LXVIII. In which Harry goes westward

Our tender hearts are averse to all ideas and descriptions of parting; and I shall therefore say nothing of Harry Warrington's feelings at taking leave of his brother and friends. Were not thousands of men in the same plight? Had not Mr. Wolfe his mother to kiss (his brave father had quitted life during his son's absence on the glorious Louisbourg campaign), and his sweetheart to clasp in a farewell embrace? Had not stout Admiral Holmes, before sailing westward with his squadron, The Somerset, The Terrible, The Northumberland, The Royal William, The Trident, The Diana, The Seahorse —his own flag being hoisted on board The Dublin—to take leave of Mrs. and the Misses Holmes? Was Admiral Saunders, who sailed the day after him, exempt from human feeling? Away go William and his crew of jovial sailors, ploughing through the tumbling waves, and poor Black-eyed Susan on shore watches the ship as it dwindles in the sunset.

It dwindles in the West. The night falls darkling over the ocean. They are gone: but their hearts are at home yet a while. In silence, with a heart inexpressibly soft and tender, how each man thinks of those he has left! What a chorus of pitiful prayer rises up to the Father, at sea and on shore, on that parting night at home by the vacant bedside, where the wife kneels in tears;

round the fire, where the mother and children together pour out their supplications: or on deck, where the seafarer looks up to the stars of heaven, as the ship cleaves through the roaring midnight waters! To-morrow the sun rises upon our common life again, and we commence our daily task of toil and duty.

George accompanies his brother, and stays a while with him at Portsmouth whilst they are waiting for a wind. He shakes Mr. Wolfe's hand, looks at his pale face for the last time, and sees the vessels depart amid the clangour of bells, and the thunder of cannon from the shore. Next day he is back at his home, and at that business which is sure one of the most selfish and absorbing of the world's occupations, to which almost every man who is thirty years old has served ere this his apprenticeship. He has a pang of sadness, as he looks in at the lodgings to the little room which Harry used to occupy, and sees his half-burned papers still in the grate. In a few minutes he is on his way to Dean Street again, and whispering by the fitful firelight in the ear of the clinging sweetheart. She is very happy—oh, so happy! at his return. She is ashamed of being so. Is it not heartless to be so, when poor Hetty is so melancholy? Poor little Hetty! Indeed, it is selfish to be glad when she is in such a sad way. It makes one quite wretched to see her. "Don't, sir! Well, I ought to be wretched, and it's very, very wicked of me if I'm not," says Theo; and one can understand her soft-hearted repentance. What she means by "Don't" who can tell? I have said the room was dark, and the fire burned fitfully—and "Don't" is no doubt uttered in one of the dark fits. Enter servants with supper and lights. The family arrives; the conversation becomes general. The destination of the fleet is known everywhere now. The force on board is sufficient to beat all the French in Canada; and, under such an officer as Wolfe, to repair the blunders and disasters of previous campaigns. He looked dreadfully ill, indeed. But he has a great soul in a feeble body. The ministers, the country hope the utmost from him. After supper, according to custom, Mr. Lambert assembles his modest household, of whom George Warrington may be said quite to form a part; and as he prays for all travellers by land and water, Theo and her sister are kneeling together. And so, as the ship speeds farther and farther into the West, the fond thoughts pursue it; and the night passes, and the sun rises.

A day or two more, and everybody is at his books or his usual work. As for George Warrington, that celebrated dramatist is busy about another composition. When the tragedy of Carpezan had run some thirty or twoscore nights, other persons of genius took possession of the theatre.

There may have been persons who wondered how the town could be so fickle as ever to tire of such a masterpiece as the Tragedy—who could not bear to see the actors dressed in other habits, reciting other men's verses; but George, of a sceptical turn of mind, took the fate of his Tragedy very philosophically, and pocketed the proceeds with much quiet satisfaction. From Mr. Dodsley, the bookseller, he had the usual complement of a hundred pounds; from the manager of the theatre two hundred or more; and such praises from the critics and his friends, that he set to work to prepare another piece, with which he hoped to achieve even greater successes than by his first performance.

Over these studies, and the other charming business which occupies him, months pass away. Happy business! Happiest time of youth and life, when love is first spoken and returned; when the dearest eyes are daily shining welcome, and the fondest lips never tire of whispering their sweet secrets; when the parting look that accompanies "Good night!" gives delightful warning of to-morrow; when the heart is so overflowing with love and happiness, that it has to spare for all the world; when the day closes with glad prayers, and opens with joyful hopes; when doubt seems cowardice, misfortune impossible, poverty only a sweet trial of constancy! Theo's elders, thankfully remembering their own prime, sit softly by and witness this pretty comedy performed by their young people. And in one of his later letters, dutifully written to his wife during a temporary absence from home, George Warrington records how he had been to look up at the windows of the dear old house in Dean Street, and wondered who was sitting in the chamber where he and Theo had been so happy.

Meanwhile we can learn how the time passes, and our friends are engaged, by some extracts from George's letters to his brother.

"From the old window opposite Bedford Gardens, this 20th August 1759.

"Why are you gone back to rugged rocks, bleak shores, burning summers, nipping winters, at home, when you might have been cropping ever so many laurels in Germany? Kingsley's are coming back as covered with 'em as Jack-a-Green on May-day. Our six regiments did wonders; and our horse would have done if my Lord George Sackville only had let them. But when Prince Ferdinand said 'Charge!' his lordship could not hear, or could not translate the German word for 'Forward;' and so we only beat the French, without utterly annihilating them, as we might, had Lord Granby or Mr. Warrington had the command. My lord is come back to town, and is shouting for a Court-Martial. He held his head high enough in prosperity: in misfortune he shows such a constancy of arrogance that one almost admires him. He looks as if he rather envied poor Mr. Byng, and the not shooting him were a manque d'egards towards him.

"The Duke has had notice to get himself in readiness for departing from this world of grandeurs and victories, and downfalls and disappointments. An attack of palsy has visited his Royal Highness; and pallida mors has just peeped in at his door, as it were, and said, 'I will call again.' Tyrant as he was, this prince has been noble in disgrace; and no king has ever had a truer servant than ours has found in his son. Why do I like the losing side always, and am I disposed to revolt against the winners? Your famous Mr. P——, your chief's patron and discoverer, I have been to hear in the House of Commons twice or thrice. I revolt against his magniloquence. I wish some little David would topple over that swelling giant. His thoughts and his language are always attitudinising. I like Barry's manner best, though the other is the more awful actor.

"Pocahontas gets on apace. Barry likes his part of Captain Smith; and, though he will have him wear a red coat and blue facings and an epaulet, I have a fancy to dress him exactly like one of the pictures of Queen Elizabeth's gentlemen at Hampton Court: with a ruff and a square beard and square shoes. 'And Pocahontas—would you like her to be tattooed?' asks Uncle Lambert. Hagan's part as the warrior who is in love with her, and, seeing her partiality for the captain, nobly rescues him from death, I trust will prove a hit. A strange fish is this Hagan: his mouth full of stage-plays and rant, but good, honest, and brave, if I don't err. He is angry at having been cast lately for Sir O'Brallaghan, in Mr. Macklin's new farce of Love A-la-mode. He says that he does not keer to disgreece his tongue with imiteetions of that rascal brogue. As if there was any call for imiteetions, when he has such an admirable twang of his own!

"Shall I tell you? Shall I hide the circumstance? Shall I hurt your feelings? Shall I set you in a rage of jealousy, and cause you to ask for leave to return to Europe? Know, then, that though Carpezan is long since dead, cousin Maria is for ever coming to the playhouse. Tom Spencer has spied her out night after night in the gallery, and she comes on the nights when Hagan performs. Quick, Burroughs, Mr. Warrington's boots and portmanteau! Order a chaise and four for Portsmouth immediately! The letter which I burned one morning when we were at breakfast (I may let the cat out of the bag, now puss has such a prodigious way to run) was from cousin M., hinting that she wished me to tell no tales about her: but I can't help just whispering to you that Maria at this moment is busy consoling herself as fast as possible. Shall I spoil sport? Shall I tell her brother? Is the affair any business of mine? What have the Esmonds done for you and me but win our money at cards? Yet I like our noble cousin. It seems to me that he would be good if he could—or rather, he would have been once. He has been set on a wrong way of life, from which 'tis now probably too late to rescue him. O beati agricolae! Our Virginia was dull, but let us thank Heaven we were bred there. We were made little slaves, but not slaves to wickedness, gambling, bad male and female company. It was not until my poor Harry left home that he fell among thieves. I mean thieves en grand, such as waylaid him and stripped him on English highroads. I consider you none the worse because you were the unlucky one, and had to deliver your purse up. And now you are going to retrieve, and make a good name for yourself; and kill more 'French dragons,' and become a great commander. And our mother will talk of her son the Captain, the Colonel, the General, and have his picture painted with all his stars and epaulets, when poor I shall be but a dawdling poetaster, or, if we may hope for the best, a snug placeman, with a little box at Richmond or Kew, and a half-score of little picaninnies, that will come and bob curtseys at the garden-gate when their uncle the General rides up on his great charger, with his aide-de-camp's pockets filled with gingerbread for the nephews and nieces. 'Tis for you to brandish the sword of Mars. As for me, I look forward to a quiet life: a quiet little home, a quiet little library full of books, and a little Some one dulce ridentem, dulce loquentem, on t'other side of the fire, as I scribble away at my papers. I am so pleased with this prospect, so utterly contented and happy, that I feel afraid as I think of it, lest it should escape me; and, even to my dearest Hal, am shy of speaking of my happiness. What is ambition to me, with this certainty? What do I care for wars, with this beatific peace smiling near?

"Our mother's friend, Mynheer Van den Bosch, has been away on a tour to discover his family in Holland, and, strange to say, has found one. Miss (who was intended by maternal solicitude to be a wife for your worship) has had six months at Kensington School, and is coming out with a hundred pretty accomplishments, which are to complete her a perfect fine lady. Her papa brought her to make a curtsey in Dean Street, and a mighty elegant curtsey she made. Though she is scarce seventeen, no dowager of sixty can be more at her ease. She conversed with Aunt Lambert on an equal footing; she treated the girls as chits—to Hetty's wrath and Theo's amusement. She talked politics with the General, and the last routs, dresses, operas, fashions, scandal, with such perfect ease that, but for a blunder or two, you might have fancied Miss Lydia was born in Mayfair. At the Court end of the town she will live, she says; and has no patience with her father, who has a lodging in Monument Yard. For those who love a brown beauty, a prettier little mignonne creature cannot be seen. But my taste, you know, dearest brother, and..."

Here follows a page of raptures and quotations of verse, which, out of a regard for the reader, and the writer's memory, the editor of the present pages declines to reprint. Gentlemen and ladies of a certain age may remember the time when they indulged in these rapturous follies on their own accounts; when the praises of the charmer were for ever warbling from their lips or trickling from their pens; when the flowers of life were in full bloom, and all the birds of spring were singing. The twigs are now bare, perhaps, and the leaves have fallen; but, for all that, shall we not,—remember the vernal time? As for you, young people, whose May (or April, is it?) has not commenced yet, you need not be detained over other folks' love-rhapsodies; depend on it, when your spring-season arrives, kindly Nature will warm all your flowers into bloom, and rouse your glad bosoms to pour out their full song.

CHAPTER LXIX. A Little Innocent

George Warrington has mentioned in the letter just quoted, that in spite of my Lord Castlewood's previous play transactions with Harry, my lord and George remained friends, and met on terms of good kinsmanship. Did George want franks, or an introduction at court, or a place in the House of Lords to hear a debate, his cousin was always ready to serve him, was a pleasant and witty companion, and would do anything which might promote his relative's interests, provided his own were not prejudiced.

Now he even went so far as to promise that he would do his best with the people in power to provide a place for Mr. George Warrington, who daily showed a greater disinclination to return to his native country, and place himself once more under the maternal servitude. George had not merely a sentimental motive for remaining in England: the pursuits and society of London pleased him infinitely better than any which he could have at home. A planter's life of idleness might have suited him, could he have enjoyed independence with it. But in Virginia he was only the first, and, as he thought, the worst treated, of his mother's subjects. He dreaded to think of returning with his young bride to his home, and of the life which she would be destined to lead there. Better freedom and poverty in England, with congenial society, and a hope perchance of future distinction, than the wearisome routine of home life, the tedious subordination, the frequent bickerings, the certain jealousies and differences of opinion, to which he must subject his wife so soon as they turned their faces homeward.

So Lord Castlewood's promise to provide for George was very eagerly accepted by the Virginian. My lord had not provided very well for his own brother to be sure, and his own position, peer as he was, was anything but enviable; but we believe what we wish to believe, and George Warrington chose to put great stress upon his kinsman's offer of patronage. Unlike the Warrington family, Lord Castlewood was quite gracious when he was made acquainted with George's engagement to Miss Lambert; came to wait upon her parents; praised George to them and the young lady to George, and made himself so prodigiously agreeable in their company that these charitable folk forgot his bad reputation, and thought it must be a very wicked and scandalous world which maligned him. He said, indeed, that he was improved in their society, as every man must be who came into it. Among them he was witty, lively, good for the time being. He left his wickedness and worldliness with his cloak in the hall, and only put them on again when he stepped into his chair. What worldling on life's voyage does not know of some such harbour of rest and calm, some haven where he puts in out of the storm? Very likely Lord Castlewood was actually better whilst he stayed with those good people, and for the time being at least no hypocrite.

And, I dare say, the Lambert elders thought no worse of his lordship for openly proclaiming his admiration for Miss Theo. It was quite genuine, and he did not profess it was very deep.

"It don't affect my sleep, and I am not going to break my heart because Miss Lambert prefers somebody else," he remarked. "Only I wish when I was a young man, madam, I had had the good fortune to meet with somebody so innocent and good as your daughter. I might have been kept out of a deal of harm's way: but innocent and good young women did not fall into mine, or they would have made me better than I am."

"Sure, my lord, it is not too late!" says Mrs. Lambert, very softly.

Castlewood started back, misunderstanding her.

"Not too late, madam?" he inquired.

She blushed. "It is too late to court my dear daughter, my lord, but not too late to repent. We read, 'tis never too late to do that. If others have been received at the eleventh hour, is there any reason why you should give up hope?"

"Perhaps I know my own heart better than you," he says in a plaintive tone. "I can speak French and German very well, and why? because I was taught both in the nursery. A man who learns them late can never get the practice of them on his tongue. And so 'tis the case with goodness, I can't learn it at my age. I can only see others practise it, and admire them. When I am on—on the side opposite to Lazarus, will Miss Theo give me a drop of water? Don't frown! I know I shall be there, Mrs. Lambert. Some folks are doomed so; and I think some of our family are amongst these. Some people are vacillating, and one hardly knows which way the scale will turn. Whereas some are predestined angels, and fly Heavenwards naturally, and do what they will."

"Oh, my lord, and why should you not be of the predestined? Whilst there is a day left—whilst there is an hour—there is hope!" says the fond matron.

"I know what is passing in your mind, my dear madam—nay, I read your prayers in your looks; but how can they avail?" Lord Castlewood asked sadly. "You don't know all, my good lady. You don't know what a life ours is of the world; how early it began; how selfish Nature, and then necessity and education, have made us. It is Fate holds the reins of the chariot, and we can't escape our doom. I know better: I see better people: I go my own way. My own? No, not mine—Fate's: and it is not altogether without pity for us, since it allows us, from time to time, to see such people as you." And he took her hand and looked her full in the face, and bowed with a melancholy grace. Every word he said was true. No greater error than to suppose that weak and bad men are strangers to good feelings, or deficient of sensibility. Only the good feeling does not last—nay, the tears are a kind of debauch of sentiment, as old libertines are said to find that the tears and grief of their victims add a zest to their pleasure. But Mrs. Lambert knew little of what was passing in this man's mind (how should she?), and so prayed for him with the fond persistence of woman. He was much better—yes, much better than he was supposed to be. He was a most interesting man. There were hopes, why should there not be the most precious hopes for him still?

It remains to be seen which of the two speakers formed the correct estimate of my lord's character. Meanwhile, if the gentleman was right, the lady was mollified, and her kind wishes and prayers for this experienced sinner's repentance, if they were of no avail for his amendment, at least could do him no harm. Kind-souled doctors (and what good woman is not of the faculty?) look after a reprobate as physicians after a perilous case. When the patient is converted to health their interest ceases in him, and they drive to feel pulses and prescribe medicines elsewhere.

But, while the malady was under treatment, our kind lady could not see too much of her sick man. Quite an intimacy sprung up between my Lord Castlewood and the Lamberts. I am not sure that some worldly views might not suit even with good Mrs. Lambert's spiritual plans (for who knows into what pure Eden, though guarded by flaming-sworded angels, worldliness will not creep?). Her son was about to take orders. My Lord Castlewood feared very much that his present chaplain's, Mr. Sampson's, careless life and heterodox conversations might lead him to give up his chaplaincy: in which case, my lord hinted the little modest cure would be vacant, and at the service of some young divine of good principles and good manners, who would be content with a small stipend, and a small but friendly congregation.

Thus an acquaintance was established between the two families, and the ladies of Castlewood, always on their good behaviour, came more than once to make their curtseys in Mrs. Lambert's drawing-room. They were civil to the parents and the young ladies. My Lady Castlewood's card assemblies were open to Mrs. Lambert and her family. There was play, certainly—all the world played—his Majesty, the Bishops, every Peer and Peeress in the land. But nobody need play who did not like; and surely nobody need have scruples regarding the practice, when such august and venerable personages were daily found to abet it. More than once Mrs. Lambert made her appearance at her ladyship's routs, and was grateful for the welcome which she received, and pleased with the admiration which her daughters excited.

Mention has been made, in a foregoing page and letter, of an American family of Dutch extraction, who had come to England very strongly recommended by Madam Esmond, their Virginian neighbour, to her sons in Europe. The views expressed in Madam Esmond's letter were so clear, that that arch match-maker, Mrs. Lambert, could not but understand them. As for George, he was engaged already; as for poor Hetty's flame, Harry, he was gone on service, for which circumstance Hetty's mother was not very sorry perhaps. She laughingly told George that he ought to obey his mamma's injunctions, break off his engagement with Theo, and make up to Miss Lydia, who was ten times—ten times! a hundred times as rich as her poor girl, and certainly much handsomer. "Yes, indeed," says George, "that I own: she is handsomer, and she is richer, and perhaps even cleverer." (All which praises Mrs. Lambert but half liked.) "But say she is all these? So is Mr. Johnson much cleverer than I am: so is, whom shall we say?—so is Mr. Hagan the actor much taller and handsomer: so is Sir James Lowther much richer: yet pray, ma'am, do you suppose I am going to be jealous of any one of these three, or think my Theo would jilt me for their sakes? Why should I not allow that Miss Lydia is handsomer, then? and richer, and clever, too, and lively, and well bred, if you insist on it, and an angel if you will have it so? Theo is not afraid: art thou, child?"

"No, George," says Theo, with such an honest look of the eyes as would convince any scepticism, or shame any jealousy. And if, after this pair of speeches, mamma takes occasion to leave the room for a minute to fetch her scissors, or her thimble, or a bootjack and slippers, or the cross and ball on the top of St. Paul's, or her pocket-handkerchief which she has forgotten in the parlour—if, I say, Mrs. Lambert quits the room on any errand or pretext, natural or preposterous, I shall not be in the least surprised, if, at her return in a couple of minutes, she finds George in near proximity to Theo, who has a heightened colour, and whose hand George is just dropping—I shall not have the least idea of what they have been doing. Have you, madam? Have you any remembrance of what used to happen when Mr. Grundy came a-courting? Are you, who, after all, were not in the room with our young people, going to cry out fie and for shame? Then fie and for shame upon you, Mrs. Grundy!

Well, Harry being away, and Theo and George irrevocably engaged, so that there was no possibility of bringing Madam Esmond's little plans to bear, why should not Mrs. Lambert have plans of her own; and if a rich, handsome, beautiful little wife should fall in his way, why should not Jack Lambert from Oxford have her? So thinks mamma, who was always thinking of marrying and giving in marriage, and so she prattles to General Lambert, who, as usual, calls her a goose for her pains. At any rate, Mrs. Lambert says beauty and riches are no objection; at any rate, Madam Esmond desired that this family should be hospitably entertained, and it was not her fault that Harry was gone away to Canada. Would the General wish him to come back; leave the army and his reputation, perhaps; yes, and come to England and marry this American, and break poor Hetty's heart—would her father wish that? Let us spare further arguments, and not be so rude as to hint that Mr. Lambert was in the right in calling a fond wife by the name of that absurd splay-footed bird, annually sacrificed at the Feast of St. Michael.

In those early days, there were vast distinctions of rank drawn between the court and city people: and Mr. Van den Bosch, when he first came to London, scarcely associated with any but the latter sort. He had a lodging near his agent's in the city. When his pretty girl came from school for a holiday, he took her an airing to Islington or Highgate, or an occasional promenade in the Artillery Ground in Bunhill Fields. They went to that Baptist meeting-house in Finsbury Fields, and on the sly to see Mr. Garrick once or twice, or that funny rogue Mr. Foote, at the Little Theatre. To go to a Lord Mayor's feast was a treat to the gentleman of the highest order: and to dance with a young mercer at Hampstead Assembly gave the utmost delight to the young lady. When George first went to wait upon his mother's friends, he found our old acquaintance, Mr. Draper, of the Temple, sedulous in his attentions to her; and the lawyer, who was married, told Mr. Warrington to look out, as the young lady had a plumb to her fortune. Mr. Drabshaw, a young Quaker gentleman, and nephew of Mr. Trail, Madam Esmond's Bristol agent, was also in constant attendance upon the young lady, and in dreadful alarm and suspicion when Mr. Warrington first made his appearance. Wishing to do honour to his mother's neighbours, Mr. Warrington invited them to an entertainment at his own apartments; and who should so naturally meet them as his friends from Soho? Not one of them but was forced to own little Miss Lydia's beauty. She had the foot of a fairy: the arms, neck, flashing eyes of a little brown huntress of Diana. She had brought a little plaintive accent from home with her—of which I, moi qui vous parle, have heard a hundred gross Cockney imitations, and watched as many absurd disguises, and which I say (in moderation) is charming in the mouth of a charming woman. Who sets up to say No, forsooth? You dear Miss Whittington, with whose h's fate has dealt so unkindly?—you lovely Miss Nicol Jarvie, with your northern burr?—you beautiful Miss Molony, with your Dame Street warble? All accents are pretty from pretty lips, and who shall set the standard up? Shall it be a rose, or a thistle, or a shamrock, or a star and stripe? As for Miss Lydia's accent, I have no doubt it was not odious even from the first day when she set foot on these polite shores, otherwise Mr. Warrington, as a man of taste, had certainly disapproved of her manner of talking, and her schoolmistress at Kensington had not done her duty by her pupil.

After the six months were over, during which, according to her father's calculation, she was to learn all the accomplishments procurable at the Kensington Academy, Miss Lydia returned nothing loth to her grandfather, and took her place in the world. A narrow world at first it was to her; but she was a resolute little person, and resolved to enlarge her sphere in society; and whither she chose to lead the way, the obedient grandfather followed her. He had been thwarted himself in early life, he said, and little good came of the severity he underwent. He had thwarted his own son, who had turned out but ill. As for little Lyddy, he was determined she should have as pleasant a life as was possible. Did not Mr. George think he was right? 'Twas said in Virginia—he did not know with what reason—that the young gentlemen of Castlewood had been happier if Madam Esmond had allowed them a little of their own way. George could not gainsay this public rumour, or think of inducing the benevolent old gentleman to alter his plans respecting his granddaughter. As for the Lambert family, how could they do otherwise than welcome the kind old man, the parent so tender and liberal, Madam Esmond's good friend?

When Miss came from school, grandpapa removed from Monument Yard to an elegant house in Bloomsbury; whither they were followed at first by their city friends. There were merchants from Virginia Walk; there were worthy tradesmen, with whom the worthy old merchant had dealings; there were their ladies and daughters and sons, who were all highly gracious to Miss Lyddy. It would be a long task to describe how these disappeared one by one—how there were no more junketings at Belsize, or trips to Highgate, or Saturday jaunts to Deputy Higgs' villa, Highbury, or country-dances at honest Mr. Lutestring's house at Hackney. Even the Sunday practice was changed; and, oh, abomination of abominations! Mr. Van den Bosch left Bethesda Chapel in Bunhill Row, and actually took a pew in Queen Square Church!

Queen Square Church, and Mr. George Warrington lived hard by in Southampton Row! 'Twas easy to see at whom Miss Lyddy was setting her cap, and Mr. Draper, who had been full of her and her grandfather's praises before, now took occasion to warn Mr. George, and gave him very different reports regarding Mr. Van den Bosch to those which had first been current. Mr. Van d. B., for all he bragged so of his Dutch parentage, came from Albany, and was nobody's son at all. He had made his money by land speculation, or by privateering (which was uncommonly like piracy), and by the Guinea trade. His son had married—if marriage it could be called, which was very doubtful—an assigned servant, and had been cut off by his father, and had taken to bad courses, and had died, luckily for himself, in his own bed.

"Mr. Draper has told you bad tales about me," said the placid old gentleman to George. "Very likely we are all sinners, and some evil may be truly said of all of us, with a great deal more that is untrue. Did he tell you that my son was unhappy with me? I told you so too. Did he bring you wicked stories about my family? He liked it so well that he wanted to marry my Lyddy to his brother. Heaven bless her! I have had a many offers for her. And you are the young gentleman I should have chose for her, and I like you none the worse because you prefer somebody else; though what you can see in your Miss, as compared to my Lyddy, begging your honour's pardon, I am at a loss to understand."

"There is no accounting for tastes, my good sir," said Mr. George, with his most superb air.

"No, sir; 'tis a wonder of nature, and daily happens. When I kept store to Albany, there was one of your tiptop gentry there that might have married my dear daughter that was alive then, and with a pretty piece of money, whereby —for her father and I had quarrelled—Miss Lyddy would have been a pauper, you see: and in place of my beautiful Bella, my gentleman chooses a little homely creature, no prettier than your Miss, and without a dollar to her fortune. The more fool he, saving your presence, Mr. George."

"Pray don't save my presence, my good sir," says George, laughing. "I suppose the gentleman's word was given to the other lady, and he had seen her first, and hence was indifferent to your charming daughter."

"I suppose when a young fellow gives his word to perform a cursed piece of folly, he always sticks to it, my dear sir, begging your pardon. But Lord, Lord, what am I speaking of? I am aspeaking of twenty year ago. I was well-to-do then, but I may say Heaven has blessed my store, and I am three times as well off now. Ask my agents how much they will give for Joseph Van den Bosch's bill at six months on New York—or at sight may be for forty thousand pound? I warrant they will discount the paper."

"Happy he who has the bill, sir!" says George, with a bow, not a little amused with the candour of the old gentleman.

"Lord, Lord, how mercenary you young men are!" cries the elder, simply. "Always thinking about money nowadays! Happy he who has the girl, I should say—the money ain't the question, my dear sir, when it goes along with such a lovely young thing as that—though I humbly say it, who oughtn't, and who am her fond silly old grandfather. We were talking about you, Lyddy darling— come, give me a kiss, my blessing! We were talking about you, and Mr. George said he wouldn't take you with all the money your poor old grandfather can give you."

"Nay, sir," says George.

"Well, you are right to say nay, for I didn't say all, that's the truth. My

466

Blessing will have a deal more than that trifle I spoke of, when it shall please Heaven to remove me out of this world to a better—when poor old Gappy is gone, Lyddy will be a rich little Lyddy, that she will. But she don't wish me to go yet, does she?"

"Oh, you darling dear grandpapa!" says Lyddy.

"This young gentleman won't have you." (Lyddy looks an arch "Thank you, sir," from her brown eyes.) "But at any rate he is honest, and that is more than we can say of some folks in this wicked London. Oh, Lord, Lord, how mercenary they are! Do you know that yonder, in Monument Yard, they were all at my poor little Blessing for her money? There was Tom Lutestring; there was Mr. Draper, your precious lawyer; there was actually Mr. Tubbs, of Bethesda Chapel; and they must all come buzzing like flies round the honey-pot. That is why we came out of the quarter where my brother-tradesmen live."

"To avoid the flies,—to be sure!" says Miss Lydia, tossing up her little head.

"Where my brother-tradesmen live," continues the old gentleman. "Else who am I to think of consorting with your grandees and fine folk? I don't care for the fashions, Mr. George; I don't care for plays and poetry, begging your honour's pardon; I never went to a play in my life, but to please this little minx."

"Oh, sir, 'twas lovely! and I cried so, didn't I, grandpapa?" says the child.

"At what, my dear?"

"At—at Mr. Warrington's play, grandpapa."

"Did you, my dear? I dare say; I dare say! It was mail day: and my letters had come in: and my ship the Lovely Lyddy had just come into Falmouth; and Captain Joyce reported how he had mercifully escaped a French privateer; and my head was so full of thanks for that escape, which saved me a deal of money, Mr. George—for the rate at which ships is underwrote this war-time is so scandalous that I often prefer to venture than to insure—that I confess I didn't listen much to the play, sir, and only went to please this little Lyddy."

"And you did please me, dearest Gappy!" cries the young lady.

"Bless you! then it's all I want. What does a man want more here below than to please his children, Mr. George? especially me, who knew what was to be unhappy when I was young, and to repent of having treated this darling's father too hard."

"Oh, grandpapa!" cries the child, with more caresses.

"Yes, I was too hard with him, dear; and that's why I spoil my little Lydkin so!"

More kisses ensue between Lyddy and Gappy. The little creature flings the pretty polished arms round the old man's neck, presses the dark red lips on his withered cheek, surrounds the venerable head with a halo of powder beaten out of his wig by her caresses; and eyes Mr. George the while, as much as to say, There, sir! should you not like me to do as much for you?

We confess;—but do we confess all? George certainly told the story of his interview with Lyddy and Gappy, and the old man's news regarding his granddaughter's wealth; but I don't think he told everything; else Theo would scarce have been so much interested, or so entirely amused and good-humoured with Lyddy when next the two young ladies met.

They met now pretty frequently, especially after the old American gentleman took up his residence in Bloomsbury. Mr. Van den Bosch was in the city for the most part of the day, attending to his affairs, and appearing at his place upon 'Change. During his absence Lyddy had the command of the house, and received her guests there like a lady, or rode abroad in a fine coach, which she ordered her grandpapa to keep for her, and into which he could very seldom be induced to set his foot. Before long Miss Lyddy was as easy in the coach as if she had ridden in one all her life. She ordered the domestics here and there; she drove to the mercer's and the jeweller's, and she called upon her friends with the utmost stateliness, or rode abroad with them to take the air. Theo and Hetty were both greatly diverted with her: but would the elder have been quite as well pleased had she known all Miss Lyddy's doings? Not that Theo was of a jealous disposition,—far otherwise; but there are cases when a lady has a right to a little jealousy, as I maintain, whatever my fair readers may say to the contrary.

It was because she knew he was engaged, very likely, that Miss Lyddy permitted herself to speak so frankly in Mr. George's praise. When they were alone—and this blessed chance occurred pretty often at Mr. Van den Bosch's house, for we have said he was constantly absent on one errand or the other—it was wonderful how artlessly the little creature would show her enthusiasm, asking him all sorts of simple questions about himself, his genius, his way of life at home and in London, his projects of marriage, and so forth.

"I am glad you are going to be married, oh, so glad!" she would say, heaving the most piteous sigh the while; "for I can talk to you frankly, quite frankly as a brother, and not be afraid of that odious politeness about which they were always scolding me at boarding-school. I may speak to you frankly; and if I like you, I may say so, mayn't I, Mr. George?"

"Pray, say so," says George, with a bow and a smile. "That is a kind of talk which most men delight to hear, especially from such pretty lips as Miss Lydia's."

"What do you know about my lips?" says the girl, with a pout and an innocent look into his face.

"What, indeed?" asks George. "Perhaps I should like to know a great deal more."

"They don't tell nothin' but truth, anyhow!" says the girl; "that's why some people don't like them! If I have anything on my mind, it must come out. I am a country-bred girl, I am—with my heart in my mouth—all honesty and simplicity; not like your English girls, who have learned I don't know what at their boarding-schools, and from the men afterwards."

"Our girls are monstrous little hypocrites, indeed!" cries George.

"You are thinking of Miss Lamberts? and I might have thought of them; but I declare I did not then. They have been at boarding-school; they have been in the world a great deal—so much the greater pity for them, for be certain they learned no good there. And now I have said so, of course you will go and tell Miss Theo, won't you, sir?"

"That she has learned no good in the world? She has scarce spoken to men at all, except her father, her brother, and me. Which of us would teach her any wrong, think you?"

"Oh, not you! Though I can understand its being very dangerous to be with you!" says the girl, with a sigh.

"Indeed there is no danger, and I don't bite!" says George, laughing.

"I didn't say bite," says the girl, softly. "There's other things dangerous besides biting, I should think. Aren't you very witty? Yes, and sarcastic, and clever, and always laughing at people? Haven't you a coaxing tongue? If you was to look at me in that kind of way, I don't know what would come to me. Was your brother like you, as I was to have married? Was he as clever and witty as you? I have heard he was like you: but he hadn't your coaxing tongue. Heigho! 'Tis well you are engaged, Master George, that is all. Do you think if you had seen me first, you would have liked Miss Theo best?"

"They say marriages were made in Heaven, my dear, and let us trust that mine has been arranged there," says George.

"I suppose there was no such thing never known, as a man having two sweethearts?" asks the artless little maiden. "Guess it's a pity. O me! What nonsense I'm a-talking; there now! I'm like the little girl who cried for the moon; and I can't have it. 'Tis too high for me—too high and splendid and shining: can't reach up to it nohow. Well, what a foolish, wayward, little spoilt thing I am now! But one thing you promise.-on your word and your honour, now, Mr. George?"

"And what is that?"

"That you won't tell Miss Theo, else she'll hate me."

"Why should she hate you?"

"Because I hate her, and wish she was dead!" breaks out the young lady. And the eyes that were looking so gentle and lachrymose but now, flame with sudden wrath, and her cheeks flush up. "For shame!" she adds, after a pause. "I'm a little fool to speak! But whatever is in my heart must come out. I am a girl of the woods, I am. I was bred where the sun is hotter than in this foggy climate. And I am not like your cold English girls; who, before they speak, or think, or feel, must wait for mamma to give leave. There, there! I may be a little fool for saying what I have. I know you'll go and tell Miss Lambert. Well, do!"

But, as we have said, George didn't tell Miss Lambert. Even from the beloved person there must be some things kept secret; even to himself, perhaps, he did not quite acknowledge what was the meaning of the little girl's confession; or, if he acknowledged it, did not act on it; except in so far as this, perhaps, that my gentleman, in Miss Lydia's presence, was particularly courteous and tender; and in her absence thought of her very kindly, and always with a certain pleasure. It were hard, indeed, if a man might not repay by a little kindness and gratitude the artless affection of such a warm young heart.

What was that story meanwhile which came round to our friends, of young Mr. Lutestring and young Mr. Drabshaw the Quaker having a boxing-match at a tavern in the city, and all about this young lady? They fell out over their cups, and fought probably. Why did Mr. Draper, who had praised her so at first, tell such stories now against her grandfather? "I suspect," says Madame de Bernstein, "that he wants the girl for some client or relation of his own; and that he tells these tales in order to frighten all suitors from her. When she and her grandfather came to me, she behaved perfectly well; and I confess, sir, I thought it was a great pity that you should prefer yonder red-cheeked countrified little chit, without a halfpenny, to this pretty, wild, artless girl, with such a fortune as I hear she has."

"Oh, she has been with you, has she, aunt?" asks George of his relative.

"Of course she has been with me," the other replies, curtly. "Unless your brother has been so silly as to fall in love with that other little Lambert girl——"

"Indeed, ma'am, I think I can say he has not," George remarks.

"Why, then, when he comes back with Mr. Wolfe, should he not take a fancy to this little person, as his mamma wishes—only, to do us justice, we Esmonds care very little for what our mammas wish—and marry her, and set up beside you in Virginia? She is to have a great fortune, which you won't touch. Pray, why should it go out of the family?"

George now learned that Mr. Van den Bosch and his granddaughter had been often at Madame de Bernstein's house. Taking his favourite walk with his favourite companion to Kensington Gardens, he saw Mr. Van den Bosch's chariot turning into Kensington Square. The Americans were going to visit Lady Castlewood, then? He found, on some little inquiry, that they had been more than once with her ladyship. It was, perhaps, strange that they should have said nothing of their visits to George; but, being little curious of other people's affairs, and having no intrigues or mysteries of his own, George was quite slow to imagine them in other people. What mattered to him how often Kensington entertained Bloomsbury, or Bloomsbury made its bow at Kensington?

A number of things were happening at both places, of which our Virginian had not the slightest idea. Indeed, do not things happen under our eyes, and we not see them? Are not comedies and tragedies daily performed before us of which we understand neither the fun nor the pathos? Very likely George goes home thinking to himself, "I have made an impression on the heart of this young creature. She has almost confessed as much. Poor artless little maiden! I wonder what there is in me that she should like me?" Can he be angry with her for this unlucky preference? Was ever a man angry at such a reason? He would not have been so well pleased, perhaps, had he known all; and that he was only one of the performers in the comedy, not the principal character by any means; Rosencrantz and Guildenstern in the Tragedy, the part of Hamlet by a gentleman unknown. How often are our little vanities shocked in this way, and subjected to wholesome humiliation! Have you not fancied that Lucinda's eyes beamed on you with a special tenderness, and presently become aware that she ogles your neighbour with the very same killing glances? Have you not exchanged exquisite whispers with Lalage at the dinner-table (sweet murmurs heard through the hum of the guests, and clatter of the banquet!) and then overheard her whispering the very same delicious phrases to old Surdus in the drawing-room? The sun shines for everybody; the flowers smell sweet for all noses; and the nightingale and Lalage warble for all ears—not your long ones only, good Brother!

CHAPTER LXX. In which Cupid plays a Considerable Part

We must now, however, and before we proceed with the history of Miss Lydia and her doings, perform the duty of explaining that sentence in Mr. Warrington's letter to his brother which refers to Lady Maria Esmond, and which, to some simple readers, may be still mysterious. For how, indeed, could well-regulated persons divine such a secret? How could innocent and respectable young people suppose that a woman of noble birth, of ancient family, of mature experience,—a woman whom we have seen exceedingly in love only a score of months ago,—should so far forget herself as (oh, my very finger-tips blush as I write the sentence!)—as not only to fall in love with a person of low origin, and very many years her junior, but actually to marry him in the face of the world? That is, not exactly in the face, but behind the back of the world, so to speak; for Parson Sampson privily tied the indissoluble knot for the pair at his chapel in Mayfair.

Now stop before you condemn her utterly. Because Lady Maria had had, and overcome, a foolish partiality for her young cousin, was that any reason why she should never fall in love with anybody else? Are men to have the sole privilege of change, and are women to be rebuked for availing themselves now and again of their little chance of consolation? No invectives can be more rude, gross, and unphilosophical than, for instance, Hamlet's to his mother about her second marriage. The truth, very likely, is, that that tender, parasitic creature wanted a something to cling to, and, Hamlet senior out of the way, twined herself round Claudius. Nay, we have known females so bent on attaching themselves, that they can twine round two gentlemen at once. Why, forsooth, shall there not be marriage-tables after funeral baked-meats? If you said grace for your feast yesterday, is that any reason why you shall not be hungry to-day? Your natural fine appetite and relish for this evening's feast, shows that to-morrow evening at eight o'clock you will most probably be in want of your dinner. I, for my part, when Flirtilla or Jiltissa were partial to me (the kind reader will please to fancy that I am alluding here to persons of the most ravishing beauty and lofty rank), always used to bear in mind that a time would come when they would be fond of somebody else. We are served a la Russe, and gobbled up a dish at a time, like the folks in Polyphemus's cave.

'Tis hodie mihi, cras tibi: there are some Anthropophagi who devour dozens of us, the old, the young, the tender, the tough, the plump, the lean, the ugly, the beautiful: there's no escape, and one after another, as our fate is, we disappear down their omnivorous maws. Look at Lady Ogresham! We all remember, last year, how she served poor Tom Kydd: seized upon him, devoured him, picked his bones, and flung them away. Now it is Ned Suckling she has got into her den. He lies under her great eyes, quivering and fascinated. Look at the poor little trepid creature, panting and helpless under the great eyes! She trails towards him nearer and nearer; he draws to her, closer and closer. Presently there will be one or two feeble squeaks for pity, and—hobblegobble—he will disappear! Ah me! it is pity, too. I knew, for instance, that Maria Esmond had lost her heart ever so many times before Harry Warrington found it; but I like to fancy that he was going to keep it; that, bewailing mischance and times out of joint, she would yet have preserved her love, and fondled it in decorous celibacy. If, in some paroxysm of senile folly, I should fall in love to-morrow, I shall still try and think I have acquired the fee-simple of my charmer's heart;—not that I am only a tenant, on a short lease, of an old battered furnished apartment, where the dingy old wine-glasses have been clouded by scores of pairs of lips, and the tumbled old sofas are muddy with the last lodger's boots. Dear, dear nymph! Being beloved and beautiful! Suppose I had a little passing passion for Glycera (and her complexion really was as pure as splendent Parian marble); suppose you had a fancy for Telephus, and his low collars and absurd neck;—those follies are all over now, aren't they? We love each other for good now, don't we? Yes, for ever; and Glycera may go to Bath, and Telephus take his cervicem roseam to Jack Ketch, n'est-ce pas?

No. We never think of changing, my dear. However winds blow, or time flies, or spoons stir, our potage, which is now so piping hot, will never get cold. Passing fancies we may have allowed ourselves in former days; and really your infatuation for Telephus (don't frown so, my darling creature! and make the wrinkles in your forehead worse)—I say, really it was the talk of the whole town; and as for Glycera, she behaved confoundedly ill to me. Well, well, now that we understand each other, it is for ever that our hearts are united, and we can look at Sir Cresswell Cresswell, and snap our fingers at his wig. But this Maria of the last century was a woman of an ill-regulated mind. You, my love, who know the world, know that in the course of this lady's career a great deal must have passed that would not bear the light, or edify in the telling. You know (not, my dear creature, that I mean you have any experience; but you have heard people say—you have heard your mother say) that an old flirt, when she has done playing the fool with one passion, will play the fool with another; that flirting is like drinking; and the brandy being drunk up, you—no, not you—Glycera—the brandy being drunk up, Glycera, who has taken to drinking, will fall upon the gin. So, if Maria Esmond has found a successor for Harry Warrington, and set up a new sultan in the precious empire of her heart, what, after all, could you expect from her? That territory was like the

Low Countries, accustomed to being conquered, and for ever open to invasion.

And Maria's present enslaver was no other than Mr. Geoghegan or Hagan, the young actor who had performed in George's tragedy. His tones were so thrilling, his eye so bright, his mien so noble, he looked so beautiful in his gilt leather armour and large buckled periwig, giving utterance to the poet's glowing verses, that the lady's heart was yielded up to him, even as Ariadne's to Bacchus when her affair with Theseus was over. The young Irishman was not a little touched and elated by the highborn damsel's partiality for him. He might have preferred a Lady Maria Hagan more tender in years, but one more tender in disposition it were difficult to discover. She clung to him closely, indeed. She retired to his humble lodgings in Westminster with him, when it became necessary to disclose their marriage, and when her furious relatives disowned her.

General Lambert brought the news home from his office in Whitehall one day, and made merry over it with his family. In those homely times a joke was none the worse for being a little broad; and a fine lady would laugh at a jolly page of Fielding, and weep over a letter of Clarissa, which would make your present ladyship's eyes start out of your head with horror. He uttered all sorts of waggeries, did the merry General, upon the subject of this marriage; upon George's share in bringing it about; upon Barry's jealousy when he should hear of it, He vowed it was cruel that cousin Hagan had not selected George as groomsman; that the first child should be called Carpezan or Sybilla, after the tragedy, and so forth. They would not quite be able to keep a coach, but they might get a chariot and pasteboard dragons from Mr. Rich's theatre. The baby might be christened in Macbeth's caldron; and Harry and harlequin ought certainly to be godfathers.

"Why shouldn't she marry him if she likes him?" asked little Hetty. "Why should he not love her because she is a little old? Mamma is a little old, and you love her none the worse. When you married my mamma, sir, I have heard you say you were very poor; and yet you were very happy, and nobody laughed at you!" Thus this impudent little person spoke by reason of her tender age, not being aware of Lady Maria Esmond's previous follies.

So her family has deserted her? George described what wrath they were in; how Lady Castlewood had gone into mourning; how Mr. Will swore he would have the rascal's ears; how furious Madame de Bernstein was, the most angry of all. "It is an insult to the family," says haughty little Miss Hett; "and I can fancy how ladies of that rank must be indignant at their relative's marriage with a person of Mr. Hagan's condition; but to desert her is a very different matter."

"Indeed, my dear child," cries mamma, "you are talking of what you don't understand. After my Lady Maria's conduct, no respectable person can go to see her."

"What conduct, mamma?"

"Never mind," cries mamma. "Little girls can't be expected to know, and ought not to be too curious to inquire, what Lady Maria's conduct has been! Suffice it, miss, that I am shocked her ladyship should ever have been here; and I say again, no honest person should associate with her!"

"Then, Aunt Lambert, I must be whipped and sent to bed," says George, with mock gravity. "I own to you (though I did not confess sooner, seeing that the affair was not mine) that I have been to see my cousin the player, and her ladyship his wife. I found them in very dirty lodgings in Westminster, where the wretch has the shabbiness to keep not only his wife, but his old mother, and a little brother, whom he puts to school. I found Mr. Hagan, and came away with a liking, and almost a respect for him, although I own he has made a very improvident marriage. But how improvident some folks are about marriage, aren't they, Theo?"

"Improvident, if they marry such spendthrifts as you," says the General. "Master George found his relations, and I'll be bound to say he left his purse behind him."

"No, not the purse, sir," says George, smiling very tenderly. "Theo made that. But I am bound to own it came empty away. Mr. Rich is in great dudgeon. He says he hardly dares have Hagan on his stage, and is afraid of a riot, such as Mr. Garrick had about the foreign dancers. This is to be a fine gentleman's riot. The macaronis are furious, and vow they will pelt Mr. Hagan, and have him cudgelled afterwards. My cousin Will, at Arthur's, has taken his oath he will have the actor's ears. Meanwhile, as the poor man does not play, they have cut off his salary; and without his salary, this luckless pair of lovers have no means to buy bread and cheese."

"And you took it to them, sir? It was like you, George!" says Theo, worshipping him with her eyes.

"It was your purse took it, dear Theo!" replies George.

"Mamma, I hope you will go and see them to-morrow!" prays Theo.

"If she doesn't, I shall get a divorce, my dear!" cries papa. "Come and kiss me, you little wench—that is, avec la bonne permission de monsieur mon beau-fils."

"Monsieur mon beau fiddlestick, papa!" says Miss Lambert, and I have no doubt complies with the paternal orders. And this was the first time George Esmond Warrington, Esquire, was ever called a fiddlestick.

Any man, even in our time, who makes an imprudent marriage, knows how he has to run the gauntlet of the family, and undergo the abuse, the scorn, the wrath, the pity of his relations. If your respectable family cry out because you marry the curate's daughter, one in ten, let us say, of his charming children; or because you engage yourself to the young barrister whose only present pecuniary resources come from the court which he reports, and who will have to pay his Oxford bills out of your slender little fortune;—if your friends cry out for making such engagements as these, fancy the feelings of Lady Maria Hagan's friends, and even those of Mr. Hagan's, on the announcement of this marriage.

There is old Mrs. Hagan, in the first instance. Her son has kept her dutifully and in tolerable comfort, ever since he left Trinity College at his father's death, and appeared as Romeo at Crow Street Theatre. His salary has sufficed of late years to keep the brother at school, to help the sister who has gone out as companion, and to provide fire, clothing, tea, dinner, and comfort for the old clergyman's widow. And now, forsooth, a fine lady, with all sorts of extravagant habits, must come and take possession of the humble home, and share the scanty loaf and mutton! Were Hagan not a high-spirited fellow, and the old mother very much afraid of him, I doubt whether my lady's life at the Westminster lodgings would be very comfortable. It was very selfish perhaps to take a place at that small table, and in poor Hagan's narrow bed. But Love in some passionate and romantic dispositions never regards consequences, or measures accommodation. Who has not experienced that frame of mind; what thrifty wife has not seen and lamented her husband in that condition; when, with rather a heightened colour and a deuce-may-care smile on his face, he comes home and announces that he has asked twenty people to dinner next Saturday? He doesn't know whom exactly; and he does know the dining-room will only hold sixteen. Never mind! Two of the prettiest girls can sit upon young gentlemen's knees: others won't come: there's sure to be plenty! In the intoxication of love people venture upon this dangerous sort of housekeeping; they don't calculate the resources of their dining-table, or those inevitable butchers' and fishmongers' bills which will be brought to the ghastly housekeeper at the beginning of the month.

Yes: it was rather selfish of my Lady Maria to seat herself at Hagan's table and take the cream off the milk, and the wings of the chickens, and the best half of everything where there was only enough before; and no wonder the poor old mamma-in-law was disposed to grumble. But what was her outcry compared to the clamour at Kensington among Lady Maria's noble family? Think of the talk and scandal all over the town! Think of the titters and whispers of the ladies in attendance at the Princess's court, where Lady Fanny had a place; of the jokes of Mr. Will's brother-officers at the usher's table; of the waggeries in the daily prints and magazines; of the comments of outraged prudes; of the laughter of the clubs and the sneers of the ungodly! At the receipt of the news Madame Bernstein had fits and ran off to the solitude of her dear rocks at Tunbridge Wells, where she did not see above forty people of a night at cards. My lord refused to see his sister; and the Countess in mourning, as we have said, waited upon one of her patronesses, a gracious Princess, who was pleased to condole with her upon the disgrace and calamity which had befallen her house. For one, two, three whole days the town was excited and amused by the scandal; then there came other news—a victory in Germany; doubtful accounts from America; a general officer coming home to take his trial; an exquisite new soprano singer from Italy; and the public forgot Lady Maria in her garret, eating the hard-earned meal of the actor's family.

This is an extract from Mr. George Warrington's letter to his brother, in which he describes other personal matters, as well as a visit he had paid to the newly married pair:—

"My dearest little Theo," he writes, "was eager to accompany her mamma upon this errand of charity; but I thought Aunt Lambert's visit would be best under the circumstances, and without the attendance of her little spinster aide-de-camp. Cousin Hagan was out when we called; we found her ladyship in a loose undress, and with her hair in not the neatest papers, playing at cribbage with a neighbour from the second floor, while good Mrs. Hagan sate on the other side of the fire with a glass of punch, and the Whole Duty of Man.

"Maria, your Maria once, cried a little when she saw us; and Aunt Lambert, you may be sure, was ready with her sympathy. While she bestowed it on Lady Maria, I paid the best compliments I could invent to the old lady. When the conversation between Aunt L. and the bride began to flag, I turned to the latter, and between us we did our best to make a dreary interview pleasant. Our talk was about you, about Wolfe, about war; you must be engaged face to face with the Frenchmen by this time, and God send my dearest brother safe and victorious out of the battle! Be sure we follow your steps anxiously—we fancy you at Cape Breton. We have plans of Quebec, and charts of the St. Lawrence. Shall I ever forget your face of joy that day when you saw me return safe and sound from the little combat with the little Frenchman? So will my Harry, I know, return from his battle. I feel quite assured of it; elated somehow with the prospect of your certain success and safety. And I have made all here share my cheerfulness. We talk of the campaign as over, and Captain Warrington's promotion as secure. Pray Heaven, all our hopes may be fulfilled one day ere long.

"How strange it is that you who are the mettlesome fellow (you know you are) should escape quarrels hitherto, and I, who am a peaceful youth, wishing no harm to anybody, should have battles thrust upon me! What do you think actually of my having had another affair upon my wicked hands, and with whom, think you? With no less a personage than your old enemy, our kinsman, Mr. Will.

"What or who set him to quarrel with me, I cannot think. Spencer (who acted as second for me, for matters actually have gone this length;—don't be frightened; it is all over, and nobody is a scratch the worse) thinks some one set Will on me, but who, I say? His conduct has been most singular; his behaviour quite unbearable. We have met pretty frequently lately at the house of good Mr. Van den Bosch, whose pretty granddaughter was consigned to both of us by our good mother. Oh, dear mother! did you know that the little thing was to be such a causa belli, and to cause swords to be drawn, and precious lives to be menaced? But so it has been. To show his own spirit, I suppose, or having some reasonable doubt about mine, whenever Will and I have met at Mynheer's house—and he is for ever going there—he has shown such downright rudeness to me, that I have required more than ordinary patience to keep my temper. He has contradicted me once, twice, thrice in the presence of the family, and out of sheer spite and rage, as it appeared to me. Is he paying his addresses to Miss Lydia, and her father's ships, negroes, and forty thousand pounds? I should guess so. The old gentleman is for ever talking about his money, and adores his granddaughter, and as she is a beautiful little creature, numbers of folk here are ready to adore her too. Was Will rascal enough to fancy that I would give up my Theo for a million of guineas, and negroes, and Venus to boot? Could the thought of such baseness enter into the man's mind? I don't know that he has accused me of stealing Van den Bosch's spoons and tankards when we dine there, or of robbing on the highway. But for one reason or the other he has chosen to be jealous of me, and as I have parried his impertinences with little sarcastic speeches (though perfectly civil before company), perhaps I have once or twice made him angry. Our little Miss Lydia has unwittingly added fuel to the fire on more than one occasion, especially yesterday, when there was talk about your worship.

"'Ah!' says the heedless little thing, as we sat over our dessert, "tis lucky for you, Mr. Esmond, that Captain Harry is not here.'

"'Why, miss?' asks he, with one of his usual conversational ornaments. He must have offended some fairy in his youth, who has caused him to drop curses for ever out of his mouth, as she did the girl to spit out toads and serpents. (I know some one from whose gentle lips there only fall pure pearls and diamonds.) 'Why?' says Will, with a cannonade of oaths.

"'O fie!' says she, putting up the prettiest little fingers to the prettiest little rosy ears in the world. 'O fie, sir! to use such naughty words. 'Tis lucky the Captain is not here, because he might quarrel with you; and Mr. George is so peaceable and quiet, that he won't. Have you heard from the Captain, Mr. George?'

"'From Cape Breton,' says I. 'He is very well, thank you; that is——' I couldn't finish the sentence, for I was in such a rage that I scarce could contain myself.

"'From the Captain, as you call him, Miss Lyddy,' says Will. 'He'll distinguish himself as he did at Saint Cas! Ho, ho!'

"'So I apprehend he did, sir,' says Will's brother.

"'Did he?' says our dear cousin; 'always thought he ran away; took to his legs; got a ducking, and ran away as if a bailiff was after him.'

"'La!' says Miss, 'did the Captain ever have a bailiff after him?'

"'Didn't he? Ho, ho!' laughs Mr. Will.

"I suppose I must have looked very savage, for Spencer, who was dining with us, trod on my foot under the table. 'Don't laugh so loud, cousin,' I said, very gently; 'you may wake good old Mr. Van den Bosch.' The good old gentleman was asleep in his arm-chair, to which he commonly retires for a nap after dinner.

"'Oh, indeed, cousin,' says Will, and he turns and winks at a friend of his, Captain Deuceace, whose own and whose wife's reputation I dare say you heard of when you frequented the clubs, and whom Will has introduced into this simple family as a man of the highest fashion. 'Don't be afraid, miss,' says Mr. Will, 'nor my cousin needn't be.'

"'Oh, what a comfort!' cries Miss Lyddy. 'Keep quite quiet, gentlemen, and don't quarrel, and come up to me when I send to say the tea is ready.' And with this she makes a sweet little curtsey, and disappears.

"'Hang it, Jack, pass the bottle, and don't wake the old gentleman!' continues Mr. Will. 'Won't you help yourself, cousin?' he continues; being particularly facetious in the tone of that word cousin.

"'I am going to help myself,' I said; 'but I am not going to drink the glass; and I'll tell you what I am going to do with it, if you will be quite quiet, cousin.' (Desperate kicks from Spencer all this time.)

"'And what the deuce do I care what you are going to do with it?' asks Will, looking rather white.

"'I am going to fling it into your face, cousin,' says I, very rapidly performing that feat.

"'By Jove, and no mistake!' cries Mr. Deuceace; and as he and William roared out an oath together, good old Van den Bosch woke up, and, taking the pocket-handkerchief off his face, asked what was the matter.

"I remarked it was only a glass of wine gone the wrong way and the old man said; 'Well, well, there is more where that came from! Let the butler bring you what you please, young gentlemen!' and he sank back in his great chair, and began to sleep again.

"'From the back of Montagu House Gardens there is a beautiful view of Hampstead at six o'clock in the morning; and the statue of the King on St. George's Church is reckoned elegant, cousin!' says I, resuming the conversation.

"'D—— the statue!' begins Will; but I said, 'Don't, cousin! or you will wake up the old gentleman. Had we not best go upstairs to Miss Lyddy's tea-table?'

"We arranged a little meeting for the next morning; and a coroner might have been sitting upon one or other, or both, of our bodies this afternoon; but, would you believe it? just as our engagement was about to take place, we were interrupted by three of Sir John Fielding's men, and carried to Bow Street, and ignominiously bound over to keep the peace.

"Who gave the information? Not I, or Spencer, I can vow. Though I own I was pleased when the constables came running to us; bludgeon in hand: for I had no wish to take Will's blood, or sacrifice my own to such a rascal. Now, sir, have you such a battle as this to describe to me?—a battle of powder and no shot?—a battle of swords as bloody as any on the stage? I have filled my paper, without finishing the story of Maria and her Hagan. You must have it by the next ship. You see, the quarrel with Will took place yesterday, very soon after I had written the first sentence or two of my letter. I had been dawdling till dinner-time (I looked at the paper last night, when I was grimly making certain little accounts up, and wondered shall I ever finish this letter?), and now the quarrel has been so much more interesting to me than poor Molly's love-adventures, that behold my paper is full to the brim! Wherever my dearest Harry reads it, I know that there will be a heart full of love for—His loving brother,

"G. E. W."

CHAPTER LXXI. White Favours

The little quarrel between George and his cousin caused the former to discontinue his visits to Bloomsbury in a great measure; for Mr. Will was more than ever assiduous in his attentions; and, now that both were bound over to peace, so outrageous in his behaviour, that George found the greatest difficulty in keeping his hands from his cousin. The artless little Lydia had certainly a queer way of receiving her friends. But six weeks before madly jealous of George's preference for another, she now took occasion repeatedly to compliment Theo in her conversation. Miss Theo was such a quiet, gentle creature, Lyddy was sure George was just the husband for her. How fortunate that horrible quarrel had been prevented! The constables had come up just in time; and it was quite ridiculous to hear Mr. Esmond cursing and swearing, and the rage he was in at being disappointed of his duel! "But the arrival of the constables saved your valuable life, dear Mr. George, and I am sure Miss Theo ought to bless them forever," says Lyddy, with a soft smile. "You won't stop and meet Mr. Esmond at dinner to-day? You don't like being in his company? He can't do you any harm; and I am sure you will do him none." Kind speeches like these addressed by a little girl to a gentleman, and spoken by a strange inadvertency in company, and when other gentlemen and ladies were present, were not likely to render Mr. Warrington very eager for the society of the young American lady.

George's meeting with Mr. Will was not known for some days in Dean Street, for he did not wish to disturb those kind folks with his quarrel; but when the ladies were made aware of it, you may be sure there was a great flurry and to-do. "You were actually going to take a fellow-creature's life, and you came to see us, and said not a word! Oh, George, it was shocking!" said Theo.

"My dear, he had insulted me and my brother," pleaded George. "Could I let him call us both cowards, and sit by and say, Thank you?"

The General sate by and looked very grave.

"You know you think, papa, it is a wicked and un-Christian practice; and have often said you wished gentlemen would have the courage to refuse!"

"To refuse? Yes," says Mr. Lambert, still very glum.

"It must require a prodigious strength of mind to refuse," says Jack Lambert, looking as gloomy as his father; "and I think if any man were to call me a coward, I should be apt to forget my orders."

"You see brother Jack is with me!" cries George.

"I must not be against you, Mr. Warrington," says Jack Lambert.

"Mr. Warrington!" cries George, turning very red.

"Would you, a clergyman, have George break the Commandments, and commit murder, John?" asks Theo, aghast.

"I am a soldier's son, sister," says the young divine, drily. "Besides, Mr.

Warrington has committed no murder at all. We must soon be hearing from Canada, father. The great question of the supremacy of the two races must be tried there ere long!" He turned his back on George as he spoke, and the latter eyed him with wonder.

Hetty, looking rather pale at this original remark of brother Jack, is called out of the room by some artful pretext of her sister. George started up and followed the retreating girls to the door.

"Great powers, gentlemen!" says he, coming back, "I believe, on my honour, you are giving me the credit of shirking this affair with Mr. Esmond!" The clergyman and his father looked at one another.

"A man's nearest and dearest are always the first to insult him," says George, flashing out.

"You mean to say, 'Not guilty?' God bless thee, my boy!" cries the General. "I told thee so, Jack." And he rubbed his hand across his eyes, and blushed, and wrung George's hand with all his might.

"Not guilty of what, in heaven's name?" asks Mr. Warrington.

"Nay," said the General, "Mr. Jack, here, brought the story. Let him tell it. I believe 'tis a ———— lie, with all my heart." And uttering this wicked expression, the General fairly walked out of the room.

The Rev. J. Lambert looked uncommonly foolish.

"And what is this—this d————d lie, sir, that somebody has been telling of me?" asked George, grinning at the young clergyman.

"To question the courage of any man is always an offence to him," says Mr. Lambert, "and I rejoice that yours has been belied."

"Who told the falsehood, sir, which you repeated?" bawls out Mr. Warrington. "I insist on the man's name!"

"You forget you are bound over to keep the peace," says Jack.

"Curse the peace, sir! We can go and fight in Holland. Tell me the man's name, I say!"

"Fair and softly, Mr. Warrington!" cries the young parson; "my hearing is perfectly good. It was not a man who told me the story which, I confess, I imparted to my father."

"What?" asks George, the truth suddenly occurring. "Was it that artful, wicked little vixen in Bloomsbury Square?"

"Vixen is not the word to apply to any young lady, George Warrington!" exclaims Lambert, "much less to the charming Miss Lydia. She artful—the most innocent of Heaven's creatures! She wicked—that angel! With unfeigned delight that the quarrel should be over—with devout gratitude to think that blood consanguineous should not be shed—she spoke in terms of the highest praise of you for declining this quarrel, and of the deepest sympathy with you for taking the painful but only method of averting it."

"What method?" demands George, stamping his foot.

"Why, of laying an information, to be sure!" says Mr. Jack; on which George burst forth into language much too violent for us to repeat here, and highly uncomplimentary to Miss Lydia.

"Don't utter such words, sir!" cried the parson, who, as it seemed, now took his turn to be angry. "Do not insult, in my hearing, the most charming, the most innocent of her sex! If she has been mistaken in her information regarding you, and doubted your willingness to commit what, after all, is a crime—for a crime homicide is, and of the most awful description—you, sir, have no right to blacken that angel's character with foul words: and, innocent yourself, should respect the most innocent as she is the most lovely of women! Oh, George, are you to be my brother?"

"I hope to have that honour," answered George, smiling. He began to perceive the other's drift.

"What, then, what—though 'tis too much bliss to be hoped for by sinful man—what, if she should one day be your sister? Who could see her charms without being subjugated by them? I own that I am a slave. I own that those Latin Sapphics in the September number of the Gentleman's Magazine, beginning Lydicae quondam cecinit venustae (with an English version by my friend Hickson of Corpus), were mine. I have told my mother what hath passed between us, and Mrs. Lambert also thinks that the most lovely of her sex has deigned to look favourably on me. I have composed a letter—she another. She proposes to wait on Miss Lydia's grandpapa this very day, and to bring me the answer, which shall make me the happiest or the most wretched of men! It was in the unrestrained intercourse of family conversation that I chanced to impart to my father the sentiments which my dear girl had uttered. Perhaps I spoke slightingly of your courage, which I don't doubt—by Heaven, I don't doubt: it may be, she has erred, too, regarding you. It may be that the fiend jealousy has been gnawing at my bosom, and—horrible suspicion!—that I thought my sister's lover found too much favour with her I would have all my own. Ah, dear George, who knows his faults? I am as one distracted with passion. Confound it, sir! What right have you to laugh at me? I would have you to know that risu inepto."

"What, have you two boys made it up?" cries the General, entering at this moment, in the midst of a roar of laughter from George.

"I was giving my opinion to Mr. Warrington upon laughter, and upon his laughter in particular," says Jack Lambert, in a fume.

"George is bound over to keep the peace, Jack! Thou canst not fight him for two years; and between now and then, let us trust you will have made up your quarrel. Here is dinner, boys! We will drink absent friends, and an end to the war, and no fighting out of the profession!"

George pleaded an engagement, as a reason for running away early from his dinner; and Jack must have speedily followed him, for when the former, after transacting some brief business at his own lodgings, came to Mr. Van den Bosch's door, in Bloomsbury Square, he found the young parson already in parley with a servant there. "His master and mistress had left town yesterday," the servant said.

"Poor Jack! And you had the decisive letter in your pocket?" George asked of his future brother-in-law.

"Well, yes,"—Jack owned he had the document—"and my mother has ordered a chair, and was coming to wait on Miss Lyddy," he whispered piteously, as the young men lingered on the steps.

George had a note, too, in his pocket for the young lady, which he had not cared to mention to Jack. In truth, his business at home had been to write a smart note to Miss Lyddy, with a message for the gentleman who had brought her that funny story of his giving information regarding the duel! The family being absent, George, too, did not choose to leave his note. "If cousin Will has been the slander-bearer, I will go and make him recant," thought George. "Will the family soon be back?" he blandly asked.

"They are gone to visit the quality," the servant replied. "Here is the address on this paper;" and George read, in Miss Lydia's hand, "The box from Madam Hocquet's to be sent by the Farnham Flying Coach; addressed to Miss Van den Bosch, at the Right Honourable the Earl of Castlewood's, Castlewood, Hants."

"Where?" cried poor Jack, aghast.

"His lordship and their ladyships have been here often," the servant said, with much importance. "The families is quite intimate."

This was very strange; for, in the course of their conversation, Lyddy had owned but to one single visit from Lady Castlewood.

"And they must be a-going to stay there some time, for Miss have took a power of boxes and gowns with her!" the man added. And the young men walked away, each crumpling his letter in his pocket.

"What was that remark you made?" asks George of Jack, at some exclamation of the latter. "I think you said——"

"Distraction! I am beside myself, George! I—I scarce know what I am saying," groans the clergyman. "She is gone to Hampshire, and Mr. Esmond is gone with her!"

"Othello could not have spoken better! and she has a pretty scoundrel in her company!" says Mr. George. "Ha! here is your mother's chair!" Indeed, at this moment poor Aunt Lambert came swinging down Great Russell Street, preceded by her footman. "'Tis no use going farther, Aunt Lambert!" cries George. "Our little bird has flown."

"What little bird?"

"The bird Jack wished to pair with:—the Lyddy bird, aunt. Why, Jack, I protest you are swearing again! This morning 'twas the Sixth Commandment you wanted to break; and now——"

"Confound it! leave me alone, Mr. Warrington, do you hear?" growls Jack, looking very savage; and away he strides far out of the reach of his mother's bearers.

"What is the matter, George?" asks the lady.

George, who has not been very well pleased with brother Jack's behaviour all day, says: "Brother Jack has not a fine temper, Aunt Lambert. He informs you all that I am a coward, and remonstrates with me for being angry. He finds his mistress gone to the country, and he bawls, and stamps, and swears.

O fie! Oh, Aunt Lambert, beware of jealousy! Did the General ever make you jealous?"

"You will make me very angry if you speak to me in this way," says poor Aunt Lambert from her chair.

"I am respectfully dumb. I make my bow. I withdraw," says George, with a low bow, and turns towards Holborn. His soul was wrath within him. He was bent on quarrelling with somebody. Had he met cousin Will that night, it had gone ill with his sureties.

He sought Will at all his haunts, at Arthur's, at his own house. There Lady Castlewood's servants informed him that they believed Mr. Esmond had gone to join the family in Hants. He wrote a letter to his cousin:

"My dear, kind cousin William," he said, "you know I am bound over, and would not quarrel with any one, much less with a dear, truth-telling, affectionate kinsman, whom my brother insulted by caning. But if you can find any one who says that I prevented a meeting the other day by giving information, will you tell your informant that I think it is not I but somebody else is the coward? And I write to Mr. Van den Bosch by the same post, to inform him and Miss Lyddy that I find some rascal has been telling them lies to my discredit, and to beg them to have a care of such persons." And, these neat letters being despatched, Mr. Warrington dressed himself, showed himself at the play, and took supper cheerfully at the Bedford.

In a few days George found a letter on his breakfast-table franked "Castlewood," and, indeed, written by that nobleman.

"Dear Cousin," my lord wrote, "there has been so much annoyance in our family of late, that I am sure 'tis time our quarrels should cease. Two days since my brother William brought me a very angry letter, signed G. Warrington, and at the same time, to my great grief and pain, acquainted me with a quarrel that had taken place between you, in which, to say the least, your conduct was violent. 'Tis an ill use to put good wine to—that to which you applied good Mr. Van den Bosch's. Sure, before an old man, young ones should be more respectful. I do not deny that Wm.'s language and behaviour are often irritating. I know he has often tried my temper, and that within the 24 hours.

"Ah! why should we not all live happily together? You know, cousin, I have ever professed a sincere regard for you—that I am a sincere admirer of the admirable young lady to whom you are engaged, and to whom I offer my most cordial compliments and remembrances. I would live in harmony with all my family where 'tis possible—the more because I hope to introduce to it a Countess of Castlewood.

"At my mature age, 'tis not uncommon for a man to choose a young wife. My Lydia (you will divine that I am happy in being able to call mine the elegant Miss Van den Bosch) will naturally survive me. After soothing my declining years, I shall not be jealous if at their close she should select some happy man to succeed me; though I shall envy him the possession of so much perfection and beauty. Though of a noble Dutch family, her rank, the dear girl declares, is not equal to mine, which she confesses that she is pleased to share. I, on the other hand, shall not be sorry to see descendants to my house, and to have it, through my Lady Castlewood's means, restored to something of the splendour which it knew before two or three improvident predecessors impaired it. My Lydia, who is by my side, sends you and the charming Lambert family her warmest remembrances.

"The marriage will take place very speedily here. May I hope to see you at church? My brother will not be present to quarrel with you. When I and dear Lydia announced the match to him yesterday, he took the intelligence in bad part, uttered language that I know he will one day regret, and is at present on a visit to some neighbours. The Dowager Lady Castlewood retains the house at Kensington; we having our own establishment, where you will ever be welcomed, dear cousin, by your affectionate humble servant, CASTLEWOOD."

From the London Magazine of November 1759:

"Saturday, October 13th, married, at his seat, Castlewood, Hants, the Right Honourable Eugene, Earl of Castlewood, to the beautiful Miss Van den Bosch, of Virginia. 70,000 pounds."

CHAPTER LXXII. (From the Warrington MS.) In which My Lady is on the Top

of the Ladder

Looking across the fire, towards her accustomed chair, who has been the beloved partner of my hearth during the last half of my life, I often ask (for middle aged gentlemen have the privilege of repeating their jokes, their questions, their stories) whether two young people ever were more foolish and imprudent than we were when we married, as we did, in the year of the old King's death? My son, who has taken some prodigious leaps in the heat of his fox-hunting, says he surveys the gaps and rivers which he crossed so safely over with terror afterwards, and astonishment at his own foolhardiness in making such desperate ventures; and yet there is no more eager sportsman in the two counties than Miles. He loves his amusement so much that he cares for no other. He has broken his collar-bone, and had a hundred tumbles (to his mother's terror); but so has his father (thinking, perhaps, of a copy of verse, or his speech at Quarter Sessions) been thrown over his old mare's head, who has slipped on a stone as they were both dreaming along a park road at four miles an hour; and Miles's reckless sport has been the delight of his life, as my marriage has been the blessing of mine; and I never think of it but to thank Heaven. Mind, I don't set up my worship as an example. I don't say to all young folks, "Go and marry upon twopence a year;" or people would look very black at me at our vestry-meetings; but my wife is known to be a desperate match-maker; and when Hodge and Susan appear in my justice-room with a talk of allowance, we urge them to spend their half-crown a week at home, add a little contribution of our own, and send for the vicar.

Now, when I ask a question of my dear oracle, I know what the answer will be; and hence, no doubt, the reason why I so often consult her. I have but to wear a particular expression of face and my Diana takes her reflection from it. Suppose I say, "My dear, don't you think the moon was made of cream cheese to-night?" She will say, "Well, papa, it did look very like cream cheese, indeed—there's nobody like you for droll similes." Or, suppose I say, "My love, Mr. Pitt's speech was very fine, but I don't think he is equal to what I remember his father." "Nobody was equal to my Lord Chatham," says my wife. And then one of the girls cries, "Why, I have often heard our papa say Lord Chatham was a charlatan!" On which mamma says, "How like she is to her Aunt Hetty!"

As for Miles, Tros Tyriusve is all one to him. He only reads the sporting announcements in the Norwich paper. So long as there is good scent, he does not care about the state of the country. I believe the rascal has never read my poems, much more my tragedies (for I mentioned Pocahontas to him the other day, and the dunce thought she was a river in Virginia); and with respect to my Latin verses, how can he understand them when I know he can't construe Corderius? Why, this notebook lies publicly on the little table at my corner of the fireside, and any one may read in it who will take the trouble of lifting my spectacles off the cover: but Miles never hath. I insert in the loose pages caricatures of Miles: jokes against him: but he never knows nor heeds them. Only once, in place of a neat drawing of mine, in China-ink, representing Miles asleep after dinner, and which my friend Bunbury would not disown, I found a rude picture of myself going over my mare Sultana's head, and entitled "The Squire on Horseback, or Fish out of Water." And the fellow to roar with laughter, and all the girls to titter, when I came upon the page! My wife said she never was in such a fright as when I went to my book: but I can bear a joke against myself, and have heard many, though (strange to say, for one who has lived among some of the chief wits of the age) I never heard a good one in my life. Never mind, Miles, though thou art not a wit, I love thee none the worse (there never was any love lost between two wits in a family); though thou hast no great beauty, thy mother thinks thee as handsome as Apollo, or his Royal Highness the Prince of Wales, who was born in the very same year with thee. Indeed, she always think Coates's picture of the Prince is very like her eldest boy, and has the print in her dressing-room to this very day.

[Note, in a female hand: "My son is not a spendthrift, nor a breaker of women's hearts, as some gentlemen are; but that he was exceeding like H.R.H. when they were both babies, is most certain, the Duchess of Aneaster having herself remarked him in St. James's Park, where Gumbo and my poor Molly used often to take him for an airing. Th. W."]

In that same year, with what different prospects! my Lord Esmond, Lord Castlewood's son, likewise appeared to adorn the world. My Lord C. and his humble servant had already come to a coolness at that time, and, heaven knows! my honest Miles's godmother, at his entrance into life, brought no gold pap-boats to his christening! Matters have mended since, laus Deo—laus

Deo, indeed! for I suspect neither Miles nor his father would ever have been able to do much for themselves, and by their own wits.

Castlewood House has quite a different face now from that venerable one which it wore in the days of my youth, when it was covered with the wrinkles of time, the scars of old wars, the cracks and blemishes which years had marked on its hoary features. I love best to remember it in its old shape, as I saw it when young Mr. George Warrington went down at the owner's invitation, to be present at his lordship's marriage with Miss Lydia Van den Bosch—"an American lady of noble family of Holland," as the county paper announced her ladyship to be. Then the towers stood as Warrington's grandfather the Colonel (the Marquis, as Madam Esmond would like to call her father) had seen them. The woods (thinned not a little to be sure) stood, nay, some of the self-same rooks may have cawed over them, which the Colonel had seen threescore years back. His picture hung in the hall which might have been his, had he not preferred love and gratitude to wealth and worldly honour; and Mr. George Esmond Warrington (that is, Egomet Ipse who write this page down), as he walked the old place, pacing the long corridors, the smooth dew-spangled terraces and cool darkling avenues, felt a while as if he was one of Mr. Walpole's cavaliers with ruff, rapier, buff-coat, and gorget, and as if an Old Pretender, or a Jesuit emissary in disguise, might appear from behind any tall tree-trunk round about the mansion, or antique carved cupboard within it. I had the strangest, saddest, pleasantest, old-world fancies as I walked the place; I imagined tragedies, intrigues, serenades, escaladoes, Oliver's Roundheads battering the towers, or bluff Hal's Beefeaters pricking over the plain before the castle. I was then courting a certain young lady (madam, your ladyship's eyes had no need of spectacles then, and on the brow above them there was never a wrinkle or a silver hair), and I remember I wrote a ream of romantic description, under my Lord Castlewood's franks, to the lady who never tired of reading my letters then. She says I only send her three lines now, when I am away in London or elsewhere. 'Tis that I may not fatigue your old eyes, my dear!

Mr. Warrington thought himself authorised to order a genteel new suit of clothes for my lord's marriage, and with Mons. Gumbo in attendance, made his appearance at Castlewood a few days before the ceremony. I may mention that it had been found expedient to send my faithful Sady home on board a Virginia ship. A great inflammation attacking the throat and lungs, and proving fatal in very many cases, in that year of Wolfe's expedition, had seized and well-nigh killed my poor lad, for whom his native air was pronounced to be the best cure. We parted with an abundance of tears, and Gumbo shed as many when his master went to Quebec: but he had attractions in this country and none for the military life, so he remained attached to my service. We found Castlewood House full of friends, relations, and visitors. Lady Fanny was there upon compulsion, a sulky bridesmaid. Some of the virgins of the neighbourhood also attended the young Countess. A bishop's widow herself, the Baroness Beatrix brought a holy brother-in-law of the bench from

London to tie the holy knot of matrimony between Eugene Earl of Castlewood and Lydia Van den Bosch, spinster; and for some time before and after the nuptials the old house in Hampshire wore an appearance of gaiety to which it had long been unaccustomed. The country families came gladly to pay their compliments to the newly married couple. The lady's wealth was the subject of everybody's talk, and no doubt did not decrease in the telling. Those naughty stories which were rife in town, and spread by her disappointed suitors there, took some little time to travel into Hampshire; and when they reached the country found it disposed to treat Lord Castlewood's wife with civility, and not inclined to be too curious about her behaviour in town. Suppose she had jilted this man, and laughed at the other? It was her money they were anxious about, and she was no more mercenary than they. The Hampshire folks were determined that it was a great benefit to the country to have Castlewood House once more open, with beer in the cellars, horses in the stables, and spits turning before the kitchen fires. The new lady took her place with great dignity, and 'twas certain she had uncommon accomplishments and wit. Was it not written, in the marriage advertisements, that her ladyship brought her noble husband seventy thousand pounds? On a beaucoup d'esprit with seventy thousand pounds. The Hampshire people said this was only a small portion of her wealth. When the grandfather should fall, ever so many plums would be found on that old tree.

That quiet old man, and keen reckoner, began quickly to put the dilapidated Castlewood accounts in order, of which long neglect, poverty, and improvidence had hastened the ruin. The business of the old gentleman's life now, and for some time henceforth, was to advance, improve, mend my lord's finances; to screw the rents up where practicable, to pare the expenses of the establishment down. He could, somehow, look to every yard of worsted lace on the footmen's coats, and every pound of beef that went to their dinner. A watchful old eye noted every flagon of beer which was fetched from the buttery, and marked that no waste occurred in the larder. The people were fewer, but more regularly paid; the liveries were not so ragged, and yet the tailor had no need to dun for his money; the gardeners and grooms grumbled, though their wages were no longer overdue: but the horses fattened on less corn, and the fruit and vegetables were ever so much more plentiful—so keenly did my lady's old grandfather keep a watch over the household affairs, from his lonely little chamber in the turret.

These improvements, though here told in a paragraph or two, were the affairs of months and years at Castlewood; where, with thrift, order, and judicious outlay of money (however, upon some pressing occasions, my lord might say he had none), the estate and household increased in prosperity. That it was a flourishing and economical household no one could deny: not even the dowager lady and her two children, who now seldom entered within Castlewood gates, my lady considering them in the light of enemies—for who, indeed, would like a stepmother-in-law? The little reigning Countess gave the dowager battle, and routed her utterly and speedily. Though educated in the colonies, and ignorant of polite life during her early years, the Countess Lydia had a power of language and a strength of will that all had to acknowledge who quarrelled with her. The dowager and my Lady Fanny were no match for the young American: they fled from before her to their jointure house in Kensington, and no wonder their absence was not regretted by my lord, who was in the habit of regretting no one whose back was turned. Could cousin Warrington, whose hand his lordship pressed so affectionately on coming and parting, with whom cousin Eugene was so gay and frank and pleasant when they were together, expect or hope that his lordship would grieve at his departure, at his death, at any misfortune which could happen to him, or any souls alive? Cousin Warrington knew better. Always of a sceptical turn, Mr. W. took a grim delight in watching the peculiarities of his neighbours, and could like this one even though he had no courage and no heart. Courage? Heart? What are these to you and me in the world? A man may have private virtues as he may have half a million in the funds. What we du monde expect is, that he should be lively, agreeable, keep a decent figure, and pay his way. Colonel Esmond Warrington's grandfather (in whose history and dwelling-place Mr. W. took an extraordinary interest), might once have been owner of this house of Castlewood, and of the titles which belonged to its possessor. The gentleman often looked at the Colonel's grave picture as it still hung in the saloon, a copy or replica of which piece Mr. Warrington fondly remembered in Virginia.

"He must have been a little touched here," my lord said, tapping his own tall, placid forehead.

There are certain actions, simple and common with some men, which others cannot understand, and deny as utter lies, or deride as acts of madness.

"I do you the justice to think, cousin," says Mr. Warrington to his lordship, "that you would not give up any advantage for any friend in the world."

"Eh! I am selfish: but am I more selfish than the rest of the world?" asks my lord, with a French shrug of his shoulders, and a pinch out of his box. Once, in their walks in the fields, his lordship happening to wear a fine scarlet coat, a cow ran towards him; and the ordinarily languid nobleman sprang over a stile with the agility of a schoolboy. He did not conceal his tremor, or his natural want of courage. "I dare say you respect me no more than I respect myself, George," he would say, in his candid way, and begin a very pleasant sardonical discourse upon the fall of man, and his faults, and shortcomings; and wonder why Heaven had not made us all brave and tall, and handsome and rich? As for Mr. Warrington, who very likely loved to be king of his company (as some people do), he could not help liking this kinsman of his, so witty, graceful, polished, high-placed in the world—so utterly his inferior. Like the animal in Mr. Sterne's famous book, "Do not beat me," his lordship's look seemed to say, "but, if you will, you may." No man, save a bully and coward himself, deals hardly with a creature so spiritless.

CHAPTER LXXIII. We keep Christmas at Castlewood. 1759

We know, my dear children, from our favourite fairy story-books, how at all christenings and marriages some one is invariably disappointed, and vows vengeance; and so need not wonder that good cousin Will should curse and rage energetically at the news of his brother's engagement with the colonial heiress. At first, Will fled the house, in his wrath, swearing he would never return. But nobody, including the swearer, believed much in Master Will's oaths; and this unrepentant prodigal, after a day or two, came back to the paternal house. The fumes of the marriage-feast allured him: he could not afford to resign his knife and fork at Castlewood table. He returned, and drank and ate there in token of revenge. He pledged the young bride in a bumper, and drank perdition to her under his breath. He made responses of smothered maledictions as her father gave her away in the chapel, and my lord vowed to love, honour and cherish her. He was not the only grumbler respecting that marriage, as Mr. Warrington knew: he heard, then and afterwards, no end of abuse of my lady and her grandfather. The old gentleman's City friends, his legal adviser, the Dissenting clergyman at whose chapel they attended on their first arrival in England, and poor Jack Lambert, the orthodox young divine, whose eloquence he had fondly hoped had been exerted over her in private, were bitter against the little lady's treachery, and each had a story to tell of his having been enslaved, encouraged, jilted, by the young American. The lawyer, who had had such an accurate list of all her properties, estates, moneys, slaves, ships, expectations, was ready to vow and swear that he believed the whole account was false; that there was no such place as New York or Virginia; or at any rate, that Mr. Van den Bosch had no land there; that there was no such thing as a Guinea trade, and that the negroes were so many black falsehoods invented by the wily old planter. The Dissenting pastor moaned over his stray lambling—if such a little, wily, mischievous monster could be called a lamb at all. Poor Jack Lambert ruefully acknowledged to his mamma the possession of a lock of black hair, which he bedewed with tears and apostrophised in quite unclerical language: and, as for Mr. William Esmond, he, with the shrieks and curses in which he always freely indulged, even at Castlewood, under his sister-in-law's own pretty little nose, when under any strong emotion, called Acheron to witness, that out of that region there did not exist such an artful young devil as Miss Lydia. He swore that she was an infernal female Cerberus, and called down all the wrath of this world and the next upon his swindling rascal of a brother, who had cajoled him with fair words, and filched his prize from him.

"Why," says Mr. Warrington (when Will expatiated on these matters with him), "if the girl is such a she-devil as you describe her, you are all the better for losing her. If she intends to deceive her husband, and to give him a dose of poison, as you say, how lucky for you, you are not the man! You ought to thank the gods, Will, instead of cursing them, for robbing you of such a fury, and can't be better revenged on Castlewood than by allowing him her sole possession."

"All this was very well," Will Esmond said; but—not unjustly, perhaps,—remarked that his brother was not the less a scoundrel for having cheated him out of the fortune which he expected to get, and which he had risked his life to win, too.

George Warrington was at a loss to know how his cousin had been made so to risk his precious existence (for which, perhaps, a rope's end had been a fitting termination), on which Will Esmond, with the utmost candour, told his kinsman how the little Cerbera had actually caused the meeting between them, which was interrupted somehow by Sir John Fielding's men; how she was always saying that George Warrington was a coward for ever sneering at Mr. Will, and the latter doubly a poltroon for not taking notice of his kinsman's taunts; how George had run away and nearly died of fright in Braddock's expedition; and "Deuce take me," says Will, "I never was more surprised, cousin, than when you stood to your ground so coolly in Tottenham Court Fields yonder, for me and my second offered to wager that you would never come!"

Mr. Warrington laughed, and thanked Mr. Will for this opinion of him.

"Though," says he, "cousin, 'twas lucky for me the constables came up, or you would have whipped your sword through my body in another minute. Didn't you see how clumsy I was as I stood before you? And you actually turned white and shook with anger!"

"Yes, curse me," says Mr. Will (who turned very red this time), "that's my way of showing my rage; and I was confoundedly angry with you, cousin! But now 'tis my brother I hate, and that little devil of a Countess—a countess! a pretty countess, indeed!" And with another rumbling cannonade of oaths, Will saluted the reigning member of his family.

"Well, cousin," says George, looking him queerly in the face, "you let me off easily, and I dare say I owe my life to you, or at any rate a whole waistcoat, and I admire your forbearance and spirit. What a pity that a courage like yours should be wasted as a mere court usher! You are a loss to his Majesty's army. You positively are!"

"I never know whether you are joking or serious, Mr. Warrington," growls Will.

"I should think very few gentlemen would dare to joke with you, cousin, if they had a regard for their own lives or ears! cries Mr. Warrington, who loved this grave way of dealing with his noble kinsman, and used to watch, with a droll interest, the other choking his curses, grinding his teeth because afraid to bite, and smothering his cowardly anger.

"And you should moderate your expressions, cousin, regarding the dear Countess and my lord your brother," Mr. Warrington resumed. "Of you they always speak most tenderly. Her ladyship has told me everything."

"What everything?" cries Will, aghast.

"As much as women ever do tell, cousin. She owned that she thought you had been a little epris with her. What woman can help liking a man who has admired her?"

"Why, she hates you, and says you were wild about her, Mr. Warrington!" says Mr. Esmond.

"Spretae injuria formae, cousin!"

"For me—what's for me?" asks the other.

"I never did care for her, and hence, perhaps, she does not love me. Don't you remember that case of the wife of the Captain of the Guard?"

"Which Guard?" asks Will.

"My Lord Potiphar," says Mr. Warrington.

"Lord Who? My Lord Falmouth is Captain of the Yeomen of the Guard, and my Lord Berkeley of the Pensioners. My Lord Hobart had 'em before. Suppose you haven't been long enough in England to know who's who, cousin!" remarks Mr. William.

But Mr. Warrington explained that he was speaking of a Captain of the Guard of the King of Egypt, whose wife had persecuted one Joseph for not returning her affection for him. On which Will said that, as for Egypt, he believed it was a confounded long way off; and that if Lord What-d'ye-call's wife told lies about him, it was like her sex, who he supposed were the same everywhere.

Now the truth is, that when he paid his marriage-visit to Castlewood, Mr. Warrington had heard from the little Countess her version of the story of differences between Will Esmond and herself. And this tale differed, in some respects, though he is far from saying it is more authentic than the ingenuous narrative of Mr. Will. The lady was grieved to think how she had been deceived in her brother-in-law. She feared that his life about the court and town had injured those high principles which all the Esmonds are known to be born with; that Mr. Will's words were not altogether to be trusted; that a loose life and pecuniary difficulties had made him mercenary, blunted his honour, perhaps even impaired the high chivalrous courage "which we Esmonds, cousin," the little lady said, tossing her head, "which we Esmonds must always possess—leastways, you and me, and my lord, and my cousin Harry have it, I know!" says the Countess. "Oh, cousin George! and must I confess that I was led to doubt of yours, without which a man of ancient and noble family like ours isn't worthy to be called a man! I shall try, George, as a Christian lady, and the head of one of the first families in this kingdom and the whole world, to forgive my brother William for having spoke ill of a member of our family, though a younger branch and by the female side, and made me for a moment doubt of you. He did so. Perhaps he told me ever so many bad things you had said of me."

"I, my dear lady!" cries Mr. Warrington.

"Which he said you said of me, cousin, and I hope you didn't, and heartily pray you didn't; and I can afford to despise 'em. And he paid me his court, that's a fact; and so have others, and that I'm used to; and he might have prospered better than he did perhaps (for I did not know my dear lord, nor come to vally his great and eminent qualities, as I do out of the fulness of this grateful heart now!), but, oh! I found William was deficient in courage, and no man as wants that can ever have the esteem of Lydia, Countess of Castlewood, no more he can! He said 'twas you that wanted for spirit, cousin, and angered me by telling me that you was always abusing of me. But I forgive you, George, that I do! And when I tell you that it was he was afraid—the mean skunk!—and actually sent for them constables to prevent the match between you and he, you won't wonder I wouldn't vally a feller like that—no, not that much!" and her ladyship snapped her little fingers. "I say, noblesse oblige, and a man of our family who hasn't got courage, I don't care not this pinch of snuff for him—there, now, I don't! Look at our ancestors, George, round these walls! Haven't the Esmonds always fought for their country and king? Is there one of us that, when the moment arrives, ain't ready to show that he's an Esmond and a nobleman? If my eldest son was to show the white feather, 'My Lord Esmond!' I would say to him (for that's the second title in our family), 'I disown your lordship!'" And so saying, the intrepid little woman looked round at her ancestors, whose effigies, depicted by Lely and Kneller, figured round the walls of her drawing-room at Castlewood.

Over that apartment, and the whole house, domain, and village, the new Countess speedily began to rule with an unlimited sway. It was surprising how quickly she learned the ways of command; and, if she did not adopt those methods of precedence usual in England among great ladies, invented regulations for herself, and promulgated them, and made others submit. Having been bred a Dissenter, and not being over-familiar with the Established Church service, Mr. Warrington remarked that she made a blunder or two during the office (not knowing, for example, when she was to turn her face towards the east, a custom not adopted, I believe, in other Reforming churches besides the English); but between Warrington's first bridal visit to Castlewood and his second, my lady had got to be quite perfect in that part of her duty, and sailed into chapel on her cousin's arm, her two footmen bearing her ladyship's great Prayer-book behind her, as demurely as that delightful old devotee with her lackey, in Mr. Hogarth's famous picture of "Morning," and as if my Lady Lydia had been accustomed to have a chaplain all her life. She seemed to patronise not only the new chaplain, but the service and the church itself, as if she had never in her own country heard a Ranter in a barn. She made the oldest established families in the country—grave baronets and their wives—worthy squires of twenty descents, who rode over to Castlewood to pay the bride and bridegroom honour—know their distance, as the phrase is, and give her the pas. She got an old heraldry book; and a surprising old maiden lady from Winton, learned in politeness and genealogies, from whom she learned the court etiquette (as the old Winton lady had known it in Queen Anne's time); and ere long she jabbered gules and sables, bends and saltires, not with correctness always, but with a wonderful volubility and perseverance. She made little progresses to the neighbouring towns in her gilt coach-and-six, or to the village in her chair, and asserted a quasi-regal right of homage from her tenants and other clodpoles. She lectured the parson on his divinity; the bailiff on his farming; instructed the astonished housekeeper how to preserve and pickle; would have taught the great London footmen to jump behind the carriage, only it was too high for her little ladyship to mount; gave the village gossips instructions how to nurse and take care of their children long before she had one herself; and as for physic, Madam Esmond in Virginia was not more resolute about her pills and draughts than Miss Lydia, the earl's new bride. Do you remember the story of the Fisherman and the Genie, in the Arabian Nights? So one wondered with regard to this lady, how such a prodigious genius could have been corked down into such a little bottle as her body. When Mr. Warrington returned to London after his first nuptial visit, she brought him a little present for her young friends in Dean Street, as she called them (Theo being older, and Hetty scarce younger than herself), and sent a trinket to one and a book to the other —G. Warrington always vowing that Theo's present was a doll, while Hetty's share was a nursery-book with words of one syllable. As for Mr. Will, her younger brother-in-law, she treated him with a maternal gravity and tenderness, and was in the habit of speaking of and to him with a protecting air, which was infinitely diverting to Warrington, although Will's usual curses and blasphemies were sorely increased by her behaviour.

As for old age, my Lady Lydia had little respect for that accident in the life of some gentlemen and gentlewomen; and, once the settlements were made in her behalf, treated the ancient Van den Bosch and his large periwig with no more ceremony than Dinah her black attendant, whose great ears she would pinch, and whose woolly pate she would pull without scruple, upon offence given—so at least Dinah told Gumbo, who told his master. All the household trembled before my lady the Countess: the housekeeper, of whom even my lord and the dowager had been in awe; the pampered London footmen, who used to quarrel if they were disturbed at their cards, and grumbled as they swilled the endless beer, now stepped nimbly about their business when they heard her ladyship's call; even old Lockwood, who had been gate-porter for half a century or more, tried to rally his poor old wandering wits when she came into his lodge to open his window, inspect his wood-closet, and turn his old dogs out of doors. Lockwood bared his old bald head before his new mistress, turned an appealing look towards his niece, and vaguely trembled before her little ladyship's authority. Gumbo, dressing his master for dinner, talked about Elisha (of whom he had heard the chaplain read in the morning), "and his bald head and de boys who call um names, and de bars eat em up, and serve um right," says Gumbo. But as for my lady, when discoursing with her cousin about the old porter, "Pooh, pooh! Stupid old man!" says she; "past his work, he and his dirty old dogs! They are as old and ugly as those old fish in the pond!" (Here she pointed to two old monsters of carp that had been in a pond in Castlewood gardens for centuries, according to tradition, and had their backs all covered with a hideous grey mould.) "Lockwood must pack off; the workhouse is the place for him; and I shall have a smart, good-looking, tall fellow in the lodge that will do credit to our livery."

"He was my grandfather's man, and served him in the wars of Queen Anne," interposed Mr. Warrington. On which my lady cried, petulantly, "O Lord! Queen Anne's dead, I suppose, and we ain't a-going into mourning for her."

This matter of Lockwood was discussed at the family dinner, when her ladyship announced her intention of getting rid of the old man.

"I am told," demurely remarks Mr. Van den Bosch, "that, by the laws, poor servants and poor folks of all kinds are admirably provided in their old age here in England. I am sure I wish we had such an asylum for our folks at home, and that we were eased of the expense of keeping our old hands."

"If a man can't work he ought to go!" cries her ladyship.

"Yes, indeed, and that's a fact!" says grandpapa.

"What! an old servant?" asks my lord.

"Mr. Van den Bosch possibly was independent of servants when he was young," remarks Mr. Warrington.

"Greased my own boots, opened my own shutters, sanded and watered my own———"

"Sugar, sir?" says my lord.

"No; floor, son-in-law!" says the old man, with a laugh; "though there is such tricks, in grocery stores, saving your ladyship's presence."

"La, pa! what should I know about stores and groceries?" cries her ladyship.

"He! Remember stealing the sugar, and what came on it, my dear ladyship?" says grandpapa.

"At any rate, a handsome, well-grown man in our livery will look better than that shrivelled old porter creature!" cries my lady.

"No livery is so becoming as old age, madam, and no lace as handsome as silver hairs," says Mr. Warrington. "What will the county say if you banish old Lockwood?"

"Oh! if you plead for him, sir, I suppose he must stay. Hadn't I better order a couch for him out of my drawing-room, and send him some of the best wine from the cellar?"

"Indeed your ladyship couldn't do better," Mr. Warrington remarked, very gravely.

And my lord said, yawning, "Cousin George is perfectly right, my dear. To turn away such an old servant as Lockwood would have an ill look."

"You see those mouldy old carps are, after all, a curiosity, and attract visitors," continues Mr. Warrington, gravely. "Your ladyship must allow this old wretch to remain. It won't be for long. And you may then engage the tall porter. It is very hard on us, Mr. Van den Bosch, that we are obliged to keep our old negroes when they are past work. I shall sell that rascal Gumbo in eight or ten years."

"Don't tink you will, master!" says Gumbo, grinning.

"Hold your tongue, sir! He doesn't know English ways, you see, and perhaps thinks an old servant has a claim on his master's kindness," says Mr. Warrington.

The next day, to Warrington's surprise, my lady absolutely did send a basket of good wine to Lockwood, and a cushion for his armchair.

"I thought of what you said, yesterday, at night when I went to bed; and guess you know the world better than I do, cousin; and that it's best to keep the old man, as you say."

And so this affair of the porter's lodge ended, Mr. Warrington wondering within himself at this strange little character out of the West, with her naivete and simplicities, and a heartlessness would have done credit to the most battered old dowager who ever turned trumps in St. James's.

"You tell me to respect old people. Why? I don't see nothin' to respect in the old people, I know," she said to Warrington. "They ain't so funny, and I'm sure they ain't so handsome. Look at grandfather; look at Aunt Bernstein. They say she was a beauty once! That picture painted from her! I don't believe it, nohow. No one shall tell me that I shall ever be as bad as that! When they come to that, people oughtn't to live. No, that they oughtn't."

Now, at Christmas, Aunt Bernstein came to pay her nephew and niece a visit, in company with Mr. Warrington. They travelled at their leisure in the Baroness's own landau; the old lady being in particular good health and spirits, the weather delightfully fresh and not too cold; and, as they approached her paternal home, Aunt Beatrice told her companion a hundred stories regarding it and old days. Though often lethargic, and not seldom, it must be confessed, out of temper, the old lady would light up at times, when her conversation became wonderfully lively, her wit and malice were brilliant, and her memory supplied her with a hundred anecdotes of a bygone age and society. Sure, 'tis hard with respect to Beauty, that its possessor should not have even a life-enjoyment of it, but be compelled to resign it after, at the most, some forty years' lease. As the old woman prattled of her former lovers and admirers (her auditor having much more information regarding her past career than her ladyship knew of), I would look in her face, and, out of the ruins, try to build up in my fancy a notion of her beauty in its prime. What a homily I read there! How the courts were grown with grass, the towers broken, the doors ajar, the fine gilt saloons tarnished, and the tapestries cobwebbed and torn! Yonder dilapidated palace was all alive once with splendour and music, and those dim windows were dazzling and blazing with light! What balls and feasts were once here, what splendour and laughter! I could see lovers in waiting, crowds in admiration, rivals furious. I could imagine twilight assignations, and detect intrigues, though the curtains were close and drawn. I was often minded to say to the old woman as she talked, "Madam, I know the story was not as you tell it, but so and so"—(I had read at home the history of her life, as my dear old grandfather had wrote it): and my fancy wandered about in her, amused and solitary, as I had walked about our father's house at Castlewood, meditating on departed glories, and imagining ancient times.

When Aunt Bernstein came to Castlewood, her relatives there, more, I think, on account of her own force of character, imperiousness, and sarcastic wit, than from their desire to possess her money, were accustomed to pay her a great deal of respect and deference, which she accepted as her due. She expected the same treatment from the new Countess, whom she was prepared to greet with special good-humour. The match had been of her making. "As you, you silly creature, would not have the heiress," she said, "I was determined she should not go out of the family," and she laughingly told of many little schemes for bringing the marriage about. She had given the girl a coronet and her nephew a hundred thousand pounds. Of course she should be welcome to both of them. She was delighted with the little Countess's courage and spirit in routing the Dowager and Lady Fanny. Almost always pleased with pretty people on her first introduction to them, Madame Bernstein raffled of her niece Lydia's bright eyes and lovely little figure. The marriage was altogether desirable. The old man was an obstacle, to be sure, and his talk and appearance somewhat too homely. But he will be got rid of. He is old and in delicate health. "He will want to go to America, or perhaps farther," says the Baroness, with a shrug. "As for the child, she had great fire and liveliness, and a Cherokee manner which is not without its charm," said the pleased old Baroness. "Your brother had it—so have you, Master George! Nous la formerons, cette petite. Eugene wants character and vigour, but he is a finished gentleman, and between us we shall make the little savage perfectly presentable." In this way we discoursed on the second afternoon as we journeyed towards Castlewood. We lay at the King's Arms at Bagshot the first night, where the Baroness was always received with profound respect, and thence drove post to Hexton, where she had written to have my lord's horses in waiting for her; but these were not forthcoming at the inn, and after a couple of hours we were obliged to proceed with our Bagshot horses to Castlewood.

During this last stage of the journey, I am bound to say the old aunt's testy humour returned, and she scarce spoke a single word for three hours. As for her companion; being prodigiously in love at the time, no doubt he did not press his aunt for conversation, but thought unceasingly about his Dulcinea, until the coach actually reached Castlewood Common, and rolled over the bridge before the house.

The housekeeper was ready to conduct her ladyship to her apartments. My lord and lady were both absent. She did not know what had kept them, the housekeeper said, heading the way.

"Not that door, my lady!" cries the woman, as Madame de Bernstein put her hand upon the door of the room which she had always occupied. "That's her ladyship's room now. This way," and our aunt followed, by no means in increased good-humour. I do not envy her maids when their mistress was displeased. But she had cleared her brow before she joined the family, and appeared in the drawing-room before supper-time with a countenance of tolerable serenity.

"How d'ye do, aunt?" was the Countess's salutation. "I declare now, I was taking a nap when your ladyship arrived! Hope you found your room fixed to your liking!"

Having addressed three brief sentences to the astonished old lady, the Countess now turned to her other guests, and directed her conversation to them. Mr. Warrington was not a little diverted by her behaviour, and by the appearance of surprise and wrath which began to gather over Madame Bernstein's face. "La petite," whom the Baroness proposed to "form," was rather a rebellious subject, apparently, and proposed to take a form of her own. Looking once or twice rather anxiously towards his wife, my lord tried to atone for her pertness towards his aunt by profuse civility on his own part; indeed, when he so wished, no man could be more courteous or pleasing. He found a score of agreeable things to say to Madame Bernstein. He warmly congratulated Mr. Warrington on the glorious news which had come from America, and on his brother's safety. He drank a toast at supper to Captain Warrington. "Our family is distinguishing itself, cousin," he said; and added, looking with fond significance towards his Countess, "I hope the happiest days are in store for us all."

"Yes, George!" says the little lady. "You'll write and tell Harry that we are all very much pleased with him. This action at Quebec is a most glorious action; and now we have turned the French king out of the country, shouldn't be at all surprised if we set up for ourselves in America."

"My love, you are talking treason!" cries Lord Castlewood.

"I am talking reason, anyhow, my lord. I've no notion of folks being kept down, and treated as children for ever!"

George! Harry! I protest I was almost as much astonished as amused. "When my brother hears that your ladyship is satisfied with his conduct, his happiness will be complete," I said gravely.

Next day, when talking beside her sofa, where she chose to lie in state, the little Countess no longer called her cousin "George," but "Mr. George," as before; on which Mr. George laughingly said she had changed her language since the previous day.

"Guess I did it to tease old Madam Buzwig," says her ladyship. "She wants to treat me as a child, and do the grandmother over me. I don't want no grandmothers, I don't. I'm the head of this house, and I intend to let her know it. And I've brought her all the way from London in order to tell it her, too! La! how she did look when I called you George! I might have called you George—only you had seen that little Theo first, and liked her best, I suppose."

"Yes, I suppose I like her best," says Mr. George.

"Well, I like you because you tell the truth. Because you was the only one of 'em in London who didn't seem to care for my money, though I was downright mad and angry with you once, and with myself too, and with that little sweetheart of yours, who ain't to be compared to me, I know she ain't."

"Don't let us make the comparison, then!" I said, laughing.

"I suppose people must lie on their beds as they make 'em," says she, with a little sigh. "Dare say Miss Theo is very good, and you'll marry her and go to Virginia, and be as dull as we are here. We were talking of Miss Lambert, my lord, and I was wishing my cousin joy. How is old Goody to-day? What a supper she did eat last night, and drink!—drink like a dragoon! No wonder she has got a headache, and keeps her room. Guess it takes her ever so long to dress herself."

"You, too, may be feeble when you are old, and require rest and wine to warm you!" says Mr. Warrington.

"Hope I shan't be like her when I'm old, anyhow!" says the lady. "Can't see why I am to respect an old woman, because she hobbles on a stick, and has shaky hands, and false teeth!" And the little heathen sank back on her couch, and showed twenty-four pearls of her own.

"Law!" she adds, after gazing at both her hearers through the curled lashes of her brilliant dark eyes. "How frightened you both look! My lord has already given me ever so many sermons about old Goody. You are both afraid of her: and I ain't, that's all. Don't look so scared at one another! I ain't a-going to bite her head off. We shall have a battle, and I intend to win. How did I serve the Dowager, if you please, and my Lady Fanny, with their high and mighty airs, when they tried to put down the Countess of Castlewood in her own house, and laugh at the poor American girl? We had a fight, and which got the best of it, pray? Me and Goody will have another, and when it is over, you will see that we shall both be perfect friends!"

When at this point of our conversation the door opened, and Madame Beatrix, elaborately dressed according to her wont, actually made her appearance, I, for my part, am not ashamed to own that I felt as great a panic as ever coward experienced. My lord, with his profoundest bows and blandest courtesies, greeted his aunt and led her to the fire, by which my lady (who was already hoping for an heir to Castlewood) lay reclining on her sofa. She did not attempt to rise, but smiled a greeting to her venerable guest. And then, after a brief talk, in which she showed a perfect self-possession, while the two gentlemen blundered and hesitated with the most dastardly tremor, my lord said:

"If we are to look for those pheasants, cousin, we had better go now."

"And I and aunt will have a cosy afternoon. And you will tell me about Castlewood in the old times, won't you, Baroness?" says the new mistress of the mansion.

O les laches que les hommes! I was so frightened, that I scarce saw anything, but vaguely felt that Lady Castlewood's dark eyes were following me. My lord gripped my arm in the corridor, we quickened our paces till our retreat became a disgraceful run. We did not breathe freely till we were in the open air in the courtyard, where the keepers and the dogs were waiting.

And what happened? I protest, children, I don't know. But this is certain: if your mother had been a woman of the least spirit, or had known how to scold for five minutes during as many consecutive days of her early married life, there would have been no more humble, henpecked wretch in Christendom than your father. When Parson Blake comes to dinner, don't you see how at a glance from his little wife he puts his glass down and says, "No, thank you, Mr.

Gumbo," when old Gum brings him wine? Blake wore a red coat before he took to black, and walked up Breeds Hill with a thousand bullets whistling round his ears, before ever he saw our Bunker Hill in Suffolk. And the fire-eater of the 43rd now dare not face a glass of old port wine! 'Tis his wife has subdued his courage. The women can master us, and did they know their own strength, were invincible.

Well, then, what happened I know not on that disgraceful day of panic when your father fled the field, nor dared to see the heroines engage; but when we returned from our shooting, the battle was over. America had revolted, and conquered the mother country.

CHAPTER LXXIV. News from Canada

Our Castlewood relatives kept us with them till the commencement of the new year, and after a fortnight's absence (which seemed like an age to the absurd and infatuated young man) he returned to the side of his charmer. Madame de Bernstein was not sorry to leave the home of her father. She began to talk more freely as we got away from the place. What passed during that interview in which the battle-royal between her and her niece occurred, she never revealed. But the old lady talked no more of forming cette petite, and, indeed, when she alluded to her, spoke in a nervous, laughing way, but without any hostility towards the young Countess. Her nephew Eugene, she said, was doomed to be henpecked for the rest of his days that she saw clearly. A little order brought into the house would do it all the good possible. The little old vulgar American gentleman seemed to be a shrewd person, and would act advantageously as a steward. The Countess's mother was a convict, she had heard, sent out from England, where no doubt she had beaten hemp in most of the gaols; but this news need not be carried to the town-crier; and, after all, in respect to certain kind of people, what mattered what their birth was? The young woman would be honest for her own sake now: was shrewd enough, and would learn English presently; and the name to which she had a right was great enough to get her into any society. A grocer, a smuggler, a slave-dealer, what mattered Mr. Van den Bosch's pursuit or previous profession? The Countess of Castlewood could afford to be anybody's daughter, and as soon as my nephew produced her, says the old lady, it is our duty to stand by her.

The ties of relationship binding Madame de Bernstein strongly to her nephew, Mr. Warrington hoped that she would be disposed to be equally affectionate to her niece; and spoke of his visit to Mr. Hagan and his wife, for whom he entreated her aunt's favour. But the old lady was obdurate regarding Lady Maria; begged that her name might never be mentioned, and immediately went on for two hours talking about no one else. She related a series of anecdotes regarding her niece, which, as this book lies open virginibus puerisque, to all the young people of the family, I shall not choose to record. But this I will say of the kind creature, that if she sinned, she was not the only sinner of the family, and if she repented, that others will do well to follow her example. Hagan, 'tis known, after he left the stage, led an exemplary life, and was remarkable for elegance and eloquence in the pulpit. His lady adopted extreme views, but was greatly respected in the sect which she joined; and when I saw her last, talked to me of possessing a peculiar spiritual illumination, which I strongly suspected at the time to be occasioned by the too free use of liquor: but I remember when she and her husband were good to me and mine, at a period when sympathy was needful, and many a Pharisee turned away.

I have told how easy it was to rise and fall in my fickle aunt's favour, and how each of us brothers, by turns, was embraced and neglected. My turn of glory had been after the success of my play. I was introduced to the town-wits; held my place in their company tolerably well; was pronounced to be pretty well bred by the macaronis and people of fashion, and might have run a career amongst them had my purse been long enough; had I chose to follow that life; had I not loved at that time a pair of kind eyes better than the brightest orbs of the Gunnings or Chudleighs, or all the painted beauties of the Ranelagh ring. Because I was fond of your mother, will it be believed, children, that my tastes were said to be low, and deplored by my genteel family? So it was, and I know that my godly Lady Warrington and my worldly Madame Bernstein both laid their elderly heads together and lamented my way of life. "Why, with his name, he might marry anybody," says meek Religion, who had ever one eye on Heaven and one on the main chance. "I meddle with no man's affairs, and admire genius," says uncle, "but it is a pity you consort with those poets and authors, and that sort of people, and that, when you might have had a lovely creature, with a hundred thousand pounds, you let her slip and make up to a country girl without a penny-piece."

"But if I had promised her, uncle?" says I.

"Promise, promise! these things are matters of arrangement and prudence, and demand a careful look-out. When you first committed yourself with little Miss Lambert, you had not seen the lovely American lady whom your mother wished you to marry, as a good mother naturally would. And your duty to your mother, nephew,—your duty to the Fifth Commandment, would have warranted your breaking with Miss L., and fulfilling your excellent mother's intentions regarding Miss—What was the Countess's Dutch name? Never mind. A name is nothing; but a plumb, Master George, is something to look at! Why, I have my dear little Miley at a dancing-school with Miss Barwell, Nabob Barwell's daughter, and I don't disguise my wish that the children may contract an attachment which may endure through their lives! I tell the Nabob so. We went from the House of Commons one dancing-day and saw them. 'Twas beautiful to see the young things walking a minuet together! It brought tears into my eyes, for I have a feeling heart, George, and I love my boy!"

"But if I prefer Miss Lambert, uncle, with twopence to her fortune, to the Countess, with her hundred thousand pounds?"

"Why then, sir, you have a singular taste, that's all," says the old gentleman, turning on his heel and leaving me. And I could perfectly understand his vexation at my not being able to see the world as he viewed it.

Nor did my Aunt Bernstein much like the engagement which I had made, or the family with which I passed so much of my time. Their simple ways wearied, and perhaps annoyed, the old woman of the world, and she no more relished their company than a certain person (who is not so black as he is painted) likes holy water. The old lady chafed at my for ever dangling at my sweetheart's lap. Having risen mightily in her favour, I began to fall again: and once more Harry was the favourite, and his brother, Heaven knows, not jealous.

He was now our family hero. He wrote us brief letters from the seat of war where he was engaged; Madame Bernstein caring little at first about the letters or the writer, for they were simple, and the facts he narrated not over interesting. We had early learned in London the news of the action on the glorious first of August at Minden, where Wolfe's old regiment was one of the British six which helped to achieve the victory on that famous day. At the same hour, the young General lay in his bed, in sight of Quebec, stricken down by fever, and perhaps rage and disappointment at the check which his troops had just received.

Arriving in the St. Lawrence in June, the fleet which brought Wolfe and his army had landed them on the last day of the month on the Island of Orleans, opposite which rises the great cliff of Quebec. After the great action in which his General fell, the dear brother who accompanied the chief, wrote home to me one of his simple letters, describing his modest share in that glorious day, but added nothing to the many descriptions already wrote of the action of the 13th of September, save only I remember he wrote, from the testimony of a brother aide-de-camp who was by his side, that the General never spoke at all after receiving his death-wound, so that the phrase which has been put into the mouth of the dying hero may be considered as no more authentic than an oration of Livy or Thucydides.

From his position on the island, which lies in the great channel of the river to the north of the town, the General was ever hungrily on the look-out for a chance to meet and attack his enemy. Above the city and below it he landed,— now here and now there; he was bent upon attacking wherever he saw an opening. 'Twas surely a prodigious fault on the part of the Marquis of Montcalm, to accept a battle from Wolfe on equal terms, for the British General had no artillery, and when we had made our famous scalade of the heights, and were on the Plains of Abraham, we were a little nearer the city, certainly, but as far off as ever from being within it.

The game that was played between the brave chiefs of those two gallant little armies, and which lasted from July until Mr. Wolfe won the crowning hazard in September, must have been as interesting a match as ever eager players engaged in. On the very first night after the landing (as my brother has narrated it) the sport began. At midnight the French sent a flaming squadron of fireships down upon the British ships which were discharging their stores at Orleans. Our seamen thought it was good sport to tow the fireships clear of the fleet, and ground them on the shore, where they burned out.

As soon as the French commander heard that our ships had entered the river, he marched to Beauport in advance of the city and there took up a strong position. When our stores and hospitals were established, our General crossed over from his island to the left shore, and drew nearer to his enemy. He had the ships in the river behind him, but the whole country in face of him was in arms. The Indians in the forest seized our advanced parties as they strove to clear it, and murdered them with horrible tortures. The French were as savage as their Indian friends. The Montmorenci River rushed between Wolfe and the enemy. He could neither attack these nor the city behind them.

Bent on seeing whether there was no other point at which his foe might be assailable, the General passed round the town of Quebec and skirted the left shore beyond. Everywhere it was guarded, as well as in his immediate front, and having run the gauntlet of the batteries up and down the river, he returned to his post at Montmorenci. On the right of the French position, across the Montmorenci River, which was fordable at low tide, was a redoubt of the enemy. He would have that. Perhaps, to defend it the French chief would be forced out from his lines, and a battle be brought on. Wolfe determined to play these odds. He would fetch over the body of his army from the Island of Orleans, and attack from the St. Lawrence. He would time his attack, so that, at shallow water, his lieutenants, Murray and Townsend, might cross the Montmorenci, and, at the last day of July, he played this desperate game.

He first, and General Monckton, his second in command (setting out from Point Levi, which he occupied), crossed over the St. Lawrence from their respective stations, being received with a storm of shot and artillery as they rowed to the shore. No sooner were the troops landed than they rushed at the French redoubt without order, were shot down before it in great numbers, and were obliged to fall back. At the preconcerted signal the troops on the other side of the Montmorenci avanced across the river in perfect order. The enemy even evacuated the redoubt and fell back to their lines; but from these the assailants were received with so severe a fire that an impression on them was hopeless, and the General had to retreat.

The battle of Montmorenci (which my brother Harry and I have fought again many a time over our wine) formed the dismal burthen of the first despatch from Mr. Wolfe which reached England and plunged us all in gloom. What more might one expect of a commander so rash? What disasters might one not foretell? Was ever scheme so wild as to bring three great bodies of men, across broad rivers, in the face of murderous batteries, merely on the chance of inducing an enemy, strongly entrenched and guarded, to leave his position and come out and engage us? 'Twas the talk of the town. No wonder grave people shook their heads, and prophesied fresh disaster. The General, who took to his bed after this failure, shuddering with fever, was to live barely six weeks longer, and die immortal! How is it, and by what, and whom, that

Greatness is achieved? Is Merit—is Madness the patron? Is it Frolic or Fortune? Is it Fate that awards successes and defeats? Is it the Just Cause that ever wins? How did the French gain Canada from the savage, and we from the French, and after which of the conquests was the right time to sing Te Deum? We are always for implicating Heaven in our quarrels, and causing the gods to intervene whatever the nodus may be. Does Broughton, after pummelling and beating Slack, lift up a black eye to Jove and thank him for the victory? And if ten thousand boxers are to be so heard, why not one? And if Broughton is to be grateful, what is Slack to be?

"By the list of disabled officers (many of whom are of rank) you may perceive, sir, that the army is much weakened. By the nature of this river the most formidable part of the armament is deprived of the power of acting, yet we have almost the whole force of Canada to oppose. In this situation there is such a choice of difficulties, that I own myself at a loss how to determine. The affairs of Great Britain, I know, require the most vigorous measures; but then the courage of a handful of brave men should be exerted only where there is some hope of a favourable event. The admiral and I have examined the town with a view to a general assault: and he would readily join in this or any other measure for the public service; but I cannot propose to him an undertaking of so dangerous a nature, and promising so little success.... I found myself so ill, and am still so weak, that I begged the general officers to consult together for the public utility. They are of opinion that they should try by conveying up a corps of 4000 or 5000 men (which is nearly the whole strength of the army, after the points of Levi and Orleans are put in a proper state of defence) to draw the enemy from their present position, and bring them to an action. I have acquiesced in their proposal, and we are preparing to put it into execution."

So wrote the General (of whose noble letters it is clear our dear scribe was not the author or secretary) from his headquarters at Montmorenci Falls on 2nd day of September; and on the 14th of October following, the Rodney cutter arrived with the sad news in England. The attack had failed, the chief was sick, the army dwindling, the menaced city so strong that assault was almost impossible; "the only chance was to fight the Marquis of Montcalm upon terms of less disadvantage than attacking his entrenchments, and, if possible, to draw him from his present position." Would the French chief, whose great military genius was known in Europe, fall into such a snare? No wonder there were pale looks in the City at the news, and doubt and gloom wheresoever it was known.

Three days after this first melancholy intelligence, came the famous letters announcing that wonderful consummation of fortune with which Mr. Wolfe's wonderful career ended. If no man is to be styled happy till his death, what shall we say of this one? His end was so glorious, that I protest not even his mother nor his mistress ought to have deplored it, or at any rate have wished him alive again. I know it is a hero we speak of; and yet I vow I scarce know whether in the last act of his life I admire the result of genius, invention, and daring, or the boldness of a gambler winning surprising odds. Suppose his ascent discovered a half-hour sooner, and his people, as they would have been assuredly, beaten back? Suppose the Marquis of Montcalm not to quit his entrenched lines to accept that strange challenge? Suppose these points—and none of them depend upon Mr. Wolfe at all—and what becomes of the glory of the young hero, of the great minister who discovered him, of the intoxicated nation which rose up frantic with self-gratulation at the victory? I say, what fate is it that shapes our ends, or those of nations? In the many hazardous games which my Lord Chatham played, he won this prodigious one. And as the greedy British hand seized the Canadas, it let fall the United States out of its grasp.

To be sure this wisdom d'apres coup is easy. We wonder at this man's rashness now the deed is done, and marvel at the other's fault. What generals some of us are upon paper! what repartees come to our mind when the talk is finished! and, the game over, how well we see how it should have been played! Writing of an event at a distance of thirty years, 'tis not difficult now to criticise and find fault. But at the time when we first heard of Wolfe's glorious deeds upon the Plains of Abraham—of that army marshalled in darkness and carried silently up the midnight river—of those rocks scaled by the intrepid leader and his troops—of that miraculous security of the enemy, of his present acceptance of our challenge to battle, and of his defeat on the open plain by the sheer valour of his conqueror—we were all intoxicated in England by the news. The whole nation rose up and felt itself the stronger for Wolfe's victory. Not merely all men engaged in the battle, but those at home who had condemned its rashness, felt themselves heroes. Our spirit rose as that of our enemy faltered. Friends embraced each other when they met. Coffee-houses and public places were thronged with people eager to talk the news. Courtiers rushed to the King and the great Minister by whose wisdom the campaign had been decreed. When he showed himself, the people followed him with shouts and blessings. People did not deplore the dead warrior, but admired his euthanasia. Should James Wolfe's friends weep and wear mourning, because a chariot had come from the skies to fetch him away? Let them watch with wonder, and see him departing, radiant; rising above us superior. To have a friend who had been near or about him was to be distinguished. Every soldier who fought with him was a hero. In our fond little circle I know 'twas a distinction to be Harry's brother. We should not in the least wonder but that he, from his previous knowledge of the place, had found the way up the heights which the British army took, and pointed it out to his General. His promotion would follow as a matter of course. Why, even our Uncle Warrington wrote letters to bless Heaven and congratulate me and himself upon the share Harry had had in the glorious achievement. Our Aunt Beatrix opened her house and received company upon the strength of the victory. I became a hero from my likeness to my brother. As for Parson Sampson, he preached such a sermon that his auditors (some of whom had been warned by his reverence of the coming discourse) were with difficulty restrained from huzzaing the orator, and were mobbed as they left the chapel. "Don't talk to me, madam, about grief," says General Lambert to his wife, who, dear soul, was for allowing herself some small indulgence of her favourite sorrow on the day when Wolfe's remains were gloriously buried at Greenwich. "If our boys could come by such deaths as James's, you know you wouldn't prevent them from being shot, but would scale the Abraham heights to see the thing done! Wouldst thou mind dying in the arms of victory, Charley?" he asks of the little hero from the Chartreux. "That I wouldn't," says the little man; "and the doctor gave us a holiday, too."

Our Harry's promotion was insured after his share in the famous battle, and our aunt announced her intention of purchasing a company for him.

CHAPTER LXXV. The Course of True Love

Had your father, young folks, possessed the commonest share of prudence, not only would this chapter of his history never have been written, but you yourselves would never have appeared in the world to plague him in a hundred ways to shout and laugh in the passages when he wants to be quiet at his books; to wake him when he is dozing after dinner, as a healthy country gentleman should: to mislay his spectacles for him, and steal away his newspaper when he wants to read it; to ruin him with tailors' bills, mantua-makers' bills, tutors' bills, as you all of you do: to break his rest of nights when you have the impudence to fall ill, and when he would sleep undisturbed but that your silly mother will never be quiet for half an hour; and when Joan can't sleep, what use, pray, is there in Darby putting on his nightcap? Every trifling ailment that any one of you has had, has scared her so that I protest I have never been tranquil; and, were I not the most long-suffering creature in the world, would have liked to be rid of the whole pack of you. And now, forsooth, that you have grown out of childhood, long petticoats, chicken-pox, small-pox, whooping-cough, scarlet fever, and the other delectable accidents of puerile life, what must that unconscionable woman propose but to arrange the south rooms as a nursery for possible grandchildren, and set up the Captain with a wife, and make him marry early because we did! He is too fond, she says, of Brookes's and Goosetree's when he is in London. She has the perversity to hint that, though an entree to Carlton House may be very pleasant, 'tis very dangerous for a young gentleman: and she would have Miles live away from temptation, and sow his wild oats, and marry, as we did. Marry! my dear creature, we had no business to marry at all! By the laws of common prudence and duty, I ought to have backed out of my little engagement with Miss Theo (who would have married somebody else), and taken a rich wife. Your Uncle John was a parson and couldn't fight, poor Charley was a boy at school, and your grandfather was too old a man to call me to account with sword and pistol. I repeat there never was a more foolish match in the world than ours, and our relations were perfectly right in being angry with us. What are relations made for, indeed, but to be angry and find fault? When Hester marries, do you mind, Master George, to quarrel with her if she does not take a husband of your selecting. When George has got his living, after being senior wrangler and fellow of his college, Miss Hester, do you toss up your little nose at the young lady he shall fancy. As for you, my little Theo, I can't part with you. You must not quit your old father; for he likes you to play Haydn to him, and peel his walnuts after dinner.

[On the blank leaf opposite this paragraph is written, in a large, girlish hand: "I never intend to go.—THEODOSIA."
"Nor I.—HESTER."

They both married, as I see by the note in the family Bible—Miss Theodosia Warrington to Joseph Clinton, son of the Rev. Joseph Blake, and himself subsequently Master of Rodwell Regis Grammar School; and Miss Hester Mary, in 1804, to Captain F. Handyman, R.N.—ED.]

Whilst they had the blessing (forsooth!) of meeting, and billing and cooing every day, the two young people, your parents, went on in a fool's paradise, little heeding the world round about them, and all its tattling and meddling. Rinaldo was as brave a warrior as ever slew Turk, but you know he loved dangling in Armida's garden. Pray, my Lady Armida, what did you mean by flinging your spells over me in youth, so that not glory, not fashion, not gaming-tables, not the society of men of wit in whose way I fell, could keep me long from your apron-strings, or out of reach of your dear simple prattle? Pray, my dear, what used we to say to each other during those endless hours of meeting? I never went to sleep after dinner then. Which of us was so witty? Was it I or you? And how came it our conversations were so delightful? I remember that year I did not even care to go and see my Lord Ferrers tried and hung, when all the world was running after his lordship. The King of Prussia's capital was taken; had the Austrians and Russians been encamped round the Tower there could scarce have been more stir in London: yet Miss Theo and her young gentleman felt no inordinate emotion of pity or indignation. What to us was the fate of Leipzig or Berlin? The truth is, that dear old house in Dean Street was an enchanted garden of delights. I have been as idle since, but never as happy. Shall we order the postchaise, my dear, leave the children to keep house; and drive up to London and see if the old lodgings are still to be let? And you shall sit at your old place in the window, and wave a little handkerchief as I walk up the street. Say what we did was imprudent. Would we not do it over again? My good folks, if Venus had walked into the room and challenged the apple, I was so infatuated, I would have given it your mother. And had she had the choice, she would have preferred her humble servant in a threadbare coat to my Lord Clive with all his diamonds.

Once, to be sure, and for a brief time in that year, I had a notion of going on the highway in order to be caught and hung as my Lord Ferrers: or of joining the King of Prussia, and requesting some of his Majesty's enemies to knock my brains out; or of enlisting for the India service, and performing some desperate exploit which should end in my bodily destruction. Ah me!

that was indeed a dreadful time! Your mother scarce dares speak of it now, save in a whisper of terror; or think of it—it was such cruel pain. She was unhappy years after on the anniversary of the day, until one of you was born on it. Suppose we had been parted: what had come to us? What had my lot been without her? As I think of that possibility, the whole world is a blank. I do not say were we parted now. It has pleased God to give us thirty years of union. We have reached the autumn season. Our successors are appointed and ready; and that one of us who is first called away, knows the survivor will follow ere long. But we were actually parted in our youth; and I tremble to think what might have been, had not a dearest friend brought us together.

Unknown to myself, and very likely meaning only my advantage, my relatives in England had chosen to write to Madam Esmond in Virginia, and represent what they were pleased to call the folly of the engagement I had contracted. Every one of them sang the same song: and I saw the letters, and burned the whole cursed pack of them years afterwards when my mother showed them to me at home in Virginia. Aunt Bernstein was forward with her advice. A young person, with no wonderful good looks, of no family, with no money;—was ever such an imprudent connexion, and ought it not for dear George's sake to be broken off? She had several eligible matches in view for me. With my name and prospects, 'twas a shame I should throw myself away on this young lady; her sister ought to interpose—and so forth.

My Lady Warrington must write, too, and in her peculiar manner. Her ladyship's letter was garnished with scripture texts.

She dressed her worldliness out in phylacteries. She pointed out how I was living in an unworthy society of player-folks, and the like people, who she could not say were absolutely without religion (Heaven forbid!), but who were deplorably worldly. She would not say an artful woman had inveigled me for her daughter, having in vain tried to captivate my younger brother. She was far from saying any harm of the young woman I had selected; but at least this was certain, Miss L. had no fortune or expectations, and her parents might naturally be anxious to compromise me. She had taken counsel, etc. etc. She had sought for guidance where it was, etc. Feeling what her duty was, she had determined to speak. Sir Miles, a man of excellent judgment in the affairs of this world (though he knew and sought a better), fully agreed with her in opinion, nay, desired her to write, and entreat her sister to interfere, that the ill-advised match should not take place.

And who besides must put a little finger into the pie but the new Countess of Castlewood? She wrote a majestic letter to Madam Esmond, and stated, that having been placed by Providence at the head of the Esmond family, it was her duty to communicate with her kinswoman and warn her to break off this marriage. I believe the three women laid their heads together previously; and, packet after packet, sent off their warnings to the Virginian lady.

One raw April morning, as Corydon goes to pay his usual duty to Phillis, he finds, not his charmer with her dear smile as usual ready to welcome him, but Mrs. Lambert, with very red eyes, and the General as pale as death. "Read this,

George Warrington!" says he, as his wife's head drops between her hands; and he puts a letter before me, of which I recognised the handwriting. I can hear now the sobs of the good Aunt Lambert, and to this day the noise of fire-irons stirring a fire in a room overhead gives me a tremor. I heard such a noise that day in the girls' room where the sisters were together. Poor, gentle child! Poor Theo!

"What can I do after this, George, my poor boy?" asks the General, pacing the room with desperation in his face.

I did not quite read the whole of Madam Esmond's letter, for a kind of sickness and faintness came over me; but I fear I could say some of it now by heart. Its style was good, and its actual words temperate enough, though they only implied that Mr. and Mrs. Lambert had inveigled me into the marriage; that they knew such an union was unworthy of me; that (as Madam E. understood) they had desired a similar union for her younger son, which project, not unluckily for him, perhaps, was given up when it was found that Mr. Henry Warrington was not the inheritor of the Virginian property. If Mr. Lambert was a man of spirit and honour, as he was represented to be, Madam Esmond scarcely supposed that, after her representations, he would persist in desiring this match. She would not lay commands upon her son, whose temper she knew; but for the sake of Miss Lambert's own reputation and comfort, she urged that the dissolution of the engagement should come from her family, and not from the just unwillingness of Rachel Esmond Warrington of Virginia.

"God help us, George!" the General said, "and give us all strength to bear this grief, and these charges which it has pleased your mother to bring! They are hard, but they don't matter now. What is of most importance, is to spare as much sorrow as we can to my poor girl. I know you love her so well, that you will help me and her mother to make the blow as tolerable as we may to that poor gentle heart. Since she was born she has never given pain to a soul alive, and 'tis cruel that she should be made to suffer." And as he spoke he passed his hand across his dry eyes.

"It was my fault, Martin! It was my fault!" weeps the poor mother.

"Your mother spoke us fair, and gave her promise," said the father.

"And do you think I will withdraw mine?" cried I; and protested, with a thousand frantic vows, what they knew full well, that I was bound to Theo before Heaven, and that nothing should part me from her.

"She herself will demand the parting. She is a good girl, God help me! and a dutiful. She will not have her father and mother called schemers, and treated with scorn. Your mother knew not, very likely, what she was doing, but 'tis done. You may see the child, and she will tell you as much. Is Theo dressed, Molly? I brought the letter home from my office last evening after you were gone. The women have had a bad night. She knew at once by my face that there was bad news from America. She read the letter quite firmly. She said she would like to see you and say good-bye. Of course, George, you will give me your word of honour not to try and see her afterwards. As soon as my business will let me we will get away from this, but mother and I think we are best all together. 'Tis you, perhaps, had best go. But give me your word, at any rate, that you will not try and see her. We must spare her pain, sir! We must spare her pain!" And the good man sate down in such deep anguish himself that I, who was not yet under the full pressure of my own grief, actually felt his, and pitied it. It could not be that the dear lips I had kissed yesterday were to speak to me only once more. We were all here together; loving each other, sitting in the room where we met every day; my drawing on the table by her little workbox; she was in the chamber upstairs; she must come down presently.

Who is this opens the door? I see her sweet face. It was like our little Mary's when we thought she would die of the fever. There was even a smile upon her lips. She comes up and kisses me. "Good-bye, dear George!" she says. Great Heaven! An old man sitting in this room,—with my wife's workbox opposite, and she but five minutes away, my eyes grow so dim and full that I can't see the book before me. I am three-and-twenty years old again. I go through every stage of that agony. I once had it sitting in my own postchaise, with my wife actually by my side. Who dared to sully her sweet love with suspicion? Who had a right to stab such a soft bosom? Don't you see my ladies getting their knives ready, and the poor child baring it? My wife comes in. She has been serving out tea or tobacco to some of her pensioners. "What is it makes you look so angry, papa?" she says. "My love!" I say, "it is the thirteenth of April." A pang of pain shoots across her face, followed by a tender smile. She has undergone the martyrdom, and in the midst of the pang comes a halo of forgiveness. I can't forgive; not until my days of dotage come, and I cease remembering anything. "Hal will be home for Easter; he will bring two or three of his friends with him from Cambridge," she says. And straightway she falls to devising schemes for amusing the boys. When is she ever occupied, but with plans for making others happy?

A gentleman sitting in spectacles before an old ledger, and writing down pitiful remembrances of his own condition, is a quaint and ridiculous object. My corns hurt me, I know, but I suspect my neighbour's shoes pinch him too. I am not going to howl much over my own grief, or enlarge at any great length on this one. Many another man, I dare say, has had the light of his day suddenly put out, the joy of his life extinguished, and has been left to darkness and vague torture. I have a book I tried to read at this time of grief—Howel's Letters—and when I come to the part about Prince Charles in Spain, up starts the whole tragedy alive again. I went to Brighthelmstone, and there, at the inn, had a room facing the east, and saw the sun get up ever so many mornings, after blank nights of wakefulness, and smoked my pipe of Virginia in his face. When I am in that place by chance, and see the sun rising now, I shake my fist at him, thinking, O orient Phoebus, what horrible grief and savage wrath have you not seen me suffer! Though my wife is mine ever so long, I say I am angry just the same. Who dared, I want to know, to make us suffer so? I was forbidden to see her. I kept my promise, and remained away from the house:

that is, after that horrible meeting and parting. But at night I would go and look at her window, and watch the lamp burning there; I would go to the Chartreux (where I knew another boy), and call for her brother, and gorge him with cakes and half-crowns. I would meanly have her elder brother to dine, and almost kiss him when he went away. I used to breakfast at a coffee-house in Whitehall, in order to see Lambert go to his office; and we would salute each other sadly, and pass on without speaking. Why did not the women come out? They never did. They were practising on her, and persuading her to try and forget me. Oh, the weary, weary days! Oh, the maddening time! At last a doctor's chariot used to draw up before the General's house every day. Was she ill? I fear I was rather glad she was ill. My own suffering was so infernal, that I greedily wanted her to share my pain. And would she not? What grief of mine has it not felt, that gentlest and most compassionate of hearts? What pain would it not suffer to spare mine a pang?

I sought that doctor out. I had an interview with him. I told my story, and laid bare my heart to him, with an outburst of passionate sincerity, which won his sympathy. My confession enabled him to understand his young patient's malady; for which his drugs had no remedy or anodyne. I had promised not to see her, or to go to her: I had kept my promise. I had promised to leave London: I had gone away. Twice, thrice I went back and told my sufferings to him. He would take my fee now and again, and always receive me kindly, and let me speak. Ah, how I clung to him! I suspect he must have been unhappy once in his own life, he knew so well and gently how to succour the miserable.

He did not tell me how dangerously, though he did not disguise from me how gravely and seriously, my dearest girl had been ill. I told him everything—that I would marry her and brave every chance and danger; that, without her, I was a man utterly wrecked and ruined, and cared not what became of me. My mother had once consented, and had now chosen to withdraw her consent, when the tie between us had been, as I held, drawn so closely together, as to be paramount to all filial duty.

"I think, sir, if your mother heard you, and saw Miss Lambert, she would relent," said the doctor. Who was my mother to hold me in bondage; to claim a right of misery over me; and to take this angel out of my arms?

"He could not," he said, "be a message-carrier between young ladies who were pining and young lovers on whom the sweethearts' gates were shut: but so much he would venture to say, that he had seen me, and was prescribing for me, too." Yes, he must have been unhappy once, himself. I saw him, you may be sure, on the very day when he had kept his promise to me. He said she seemed to be comforted by hearing news of me.

"She bears her suffering with an angelical sweetness. I prescribe Jesuit's bark, which she takes; but I am not sure the hearing of you has not done more good than the medicine." The women owned afterwards that they had never told the General of the doctor's new patient.

I know not what wild expressions of gratitude I poured out to the good doctor for the comfort he brought me. His treatment was curing two unhappy sick persons. 'Twas but a drop of water, to be sure; but then a drop of water to a man raging in torment. I loved the ground he trod upon, blessed the hand that took mine, and had felt her pulse. I had a ring with a pretty cameo head of a Hercules on it. 'Twas too small for his finger, nor did the good old man wear such ornaments. I made him hang it to his watch-chain, in hopes that she might see it, and recognise that the token came from me. How I fastened upon Spencer at this time (my friend of the Temple who also had an unfortunate love-match), and walked with him from my apartments to the Temple, and he back with me to Bedford Gardens, and our talk was for ever about our women! I dare say I told everybody my grief. My good landlady and Betty the housemaid pitied me. My son Miles, who, for a wonder, has been reading in my MS., says, "By Jove, sir, I didn't know you and my mother were took in this kind of way. The year I joined, I was hit very bad myself. An infernal little jilt that threw me over for Sir Craven Oaks of our regiment. I thought I should have gone crazy." And he gives a melancholy whistle, and walks away.

The General had to leave London presently on one of his military inspections, as the doctor casually told me; but, having given my word that I would not seek to present myself at his house, I kept it, availing myself, however, as you may be sure, of the good physician's leave to visit him, and have news of his dear patient. His accounts of her were, far from encouraging. "She does not rally," he said. "We must get her back to Kent again, or to the sea." I did not know then that the poor child had begged and prayed so piteously not to be moved, that her parents, divining, perhaps, the reason of her desire to linger in London, and feeling that it might be dangerous not to humour her, had yielded to her entreaty, and consented to remain in town.

At last one morning I came, pretty much as usual, and took my place in my doctor's front parlour, whence his patients were called in their turn to his consulting-room. Here I remained, looking heedlessly over the books on the table and taking no notice of any person in the room, which speedily emptied itself of all, save me and one lady who sate with her veil down. I used to stay till the last, for Osborn, the doctor's man, knew my business, and that it was not my own illness I came for.

When the room was empty of all save me and the lady, she puts out two little hands, cries in a voice which made me start "Don't you know me, George?" And the next minute I have my arms round her, and kissed her as heartily as ever I kissed in my life, and gave way to a passionate outgush of emotion the most refreshing, for my parched soul had been in rage and torture for six weeks past, and this was a glimpse of Heaven.

Who was it, children? You think it was your mother whom the doctor had brought to me? No. It was Hetty.

CHAPTER LXXVI. Informs us how Mr. Warrington jumped into a Landau

The emotion at the first surprise and greeting over, the little maiden began at once.

"So you are come at last to ask after Theo, and you feel sorry that your neglect has made her so ill? For six weeks she has been unwell, and you have never asked a word about her! Very kind of you, Mr. George, I'm sure!"

"Kind!" gasps out Mr. Warrington.

"I suppose you call it kind to be with her every day and all day for a year, and then to leave her without a word?"

"My dear, you know my promise to your father?" I reply.

"Promise!" says Miss Hetty, shrugging her shoulders. "A very fine promise, indeed, to make my darling ill, and then suddenly, one fine day, to say, 'Good-bye, Theo,' and walk away for ever. I suppose gentlemen make these promises, because they wish to keep 'em. I wouldn't trifle with a poor child's heart, and leave her afterwards, if I were a man. What has she ever done to you, but be a fool and too fond of you? Pray, sir, by what right do you take her away from all of us, and then desert her, because an old woman in America don't approve of her? She was happy with us before you came. She loved her sister—there never was such a sister—until she saw you. And now, because your mamma thinks her young gentleman might do better, you must leave her forsooth!"

"Great powers, child!" I cried, exasperated at this wrongheadedness. "Was it I that drew back? Is it not I that am forbidden your house? and did not your father require, on my honour, that I should not see her?"

"Honour! And you are the men who pretend to be our superiors; and it is we who are to respect you and admire you! I declare, George Warrington, you ought to go back to your schoolroom in Virginia again; have your black nurse to tuck you up in bed, and ask leave from your mamma when you might walk out. Oh, George! I little thought that my sister was giving her heart away to a man who hadn't the spirit to stand by her; but, at the first difficulty, left her! When Doctor Heberden said he was attending you, I determined to come and see you, and you do look very ill, that I am glad to see; and I suppose it's your mother you are frightened of. But I shan't tell Theo that you are unwell. She hasn't left off caring for you. She can't walk out of a room, break her solemn engagements, and go into the world the next day as if nothing had happened! That is left for men, our superiors in courage and wisdom; and to desert an angel—yes, an angel ten thousand times too good for you; an angel who used to love me till she saw you, and who was the blessing of life and of all of us —is what you call honour? Don't tell me, sir! I despise you all! You are our betters, are you? We are to worship and wait on you, I suppose? I don't care about your wit, and your tragedies, and your verses; and I think they are often very stupid. I won't set up of nights copying your manuscripts, nor watch hour after hour at a window wasting my time and neglecting everybody because I want to see your worship walk down the street with your hat cocked!

If you are going away, and welcome, give me back my sister, I say! Give me back my darling of old days, who loved every one of us, till she saw you. And you leave her because your mamma thinks she can find somebody richer for you! Oh, you brave gentleman! Go and marry the person your mother chooses, and let my dear die here deserted!"

"Great heavens, Hetty!" I cry, amazed at the logic of the little woman. "Is it I who wish to leave your sister? Did I not offer to keep my promise, and was it not your father who refused me, and made me promise never to try and see her again? What have I but my word, and my honour?"

"Honour, indeed! You keep your word to him, and you break it to her! Pretty honour! If I were a man, I would soon let you know what I thought of your honour! Only I forgot—you are bound to keep the peace and mustn't... Oh, George, George! Don't you see the grief I am in? I am distracted, and scarce know what I say. You must not leave my darling. They don't know it at home. They don't think so but I know her best of all, and she will die if you leave her. Say you won't! Have pity upon me, Mr. Warrington, and give me my dearest back!" Thus the warm-hearted, distracted creature ran from anger to entreaty, from scorn to tears. Was my little doctor right in thus speaking of the case of her dear patient? Was there no other remedy than that which Hetty cried for? Have not others felt the same cruel pain of amputation, undergone the same exhaustion and fever afterwards, lain hopeless of anything save death, and yet recovered after all, and limped through life subsequently? Why, but that love is selfish, and does not heed other people's griefs and passions, or that ours was so intense and special that we deemed no other lovers could suffer like ourselves;—here in the passionate young pleader for her sister, we might have shown an instance that a fond heart could be stricken with the love malady and silently suffer it, live under it, recover from it. What had happened in Hetty's own case? Her sister and I, in our easy triumph and fond confidential prattle, had many a time talked over that matter, and, egotists as we were, perhaps drawn a secret zest and security out of her less fortunate attachment. 'Twas like sitting by the fireside and hearing the winter howling without; 'twas like walking by the maxi magno, and seeing the ship tossing at sea. We clung to each other only the more closely, and, wrapped in our own happiness, viewed others' misfortunes with complacent pity. Be the truth as it may. Grant that we might have been sundered, and after a while survived the separation, so much my sceptical old age may be disposed to admit. Yet, at that time, I was eager enough to share my ardent little Hetty's terrors and apprehensions, and willingly chose to believe that the life dearest to me in the world would be sacrificed if separated from mine. Was I wrong? I would not say as much now. I may doubt about myself (or not doubt, I know), but of her, never; and Hetty found in her quite a willing sharer in her alarms and terrors. I was for imparting some of these to our doctor; but the good gentleman shut my mouth. "Hush," says he, with a comical look of fright. "I must hear none of this. If two people who happen to know each other chance to meet and talk in my patients' room, I cannot help myself; but as for match-making and love-making, I am your humble servant! What will the General do when he comes back to town? He will have me behind Montagu House as sure as I am a live doctor, and alive I wish to remain, my good sir!" and he skips into his carriage, and leaves me there meditating. "And you and Miss Hetty must have no meetings here again, mind you that," he had said previously.

Oh no! Of course we would have none! We are gentlemen of honour, and so forth, and our word is our word. Besides, to have seen Hetty, was not that an inestimable boon, and would we not be for ever grateful? I am so refreshed with that drop of water I have had, that I think I can hold out for ever so long a time now. I walk away with Hetty to Soho, and never once thought of arranging a new meeting with her. But the little emissary was more thoughtful, and she asks me whether I go to the Museum now to read? And I say, "Oh yes, sometimes, my dear; but I am too wretched for reading now; I cannot see what is on the paper. I do not care about my books. Even Pocahontas is wearisome to me. I..." I might have continued ever so much further, when, "Nonsense!" she says, stamping her little foot. "Why, I declare, George, you are more stupid than Harry!"

"How do you mean, my dear child?" I asked.

"When do you go? You go away at three o'clock. You strike across on the road to Tottenham Court. You walk through the village, and return by the Green Lane that leads back towards the new hospital. You know you do! If you walk for a week there, it can't do you any harm. Good morning, sir! You'll please not follow me any farther." And she drops me a curtsey, and walks away with a veil over her face.

That Green Lane, which lay to the north of the new hospital, is built all over with houses now. In my time, when good old George II. was yet king, 'twas a shabby rural outlet of London; so dangerous, that the City folks who went to their villas and junketing houses at Hampstead and the outlying villages, would return in parties of nights, and escorted by waiters with lanthorns, to defend them from the footpads who prowled about the town outskirts. Hampstead and Highgate churches, each crowning its hill, filled up the background of the view which you saw as you turned your back to London; and one, two, three days Mr. George Warrington had the pleasure of looking upon this landscape, and walking back in the direction of the new hospital.

Along the lane were sundry small houses of entertainment; and I remember at one place, where they sold cakes and beer, at the sign of the Protestant Hero, a decent woman smiling at me on the third or fourth day, and curtseying in her clean apron, as she says, "It appears the lady don't come, sir! Your honour had best step in, and take a can of my cool beer."

At length, as I am coming back through Tottenham Road, on the 25th of May—O day to be marked with the whitest stone!—a little way beyond Mr. Whitefield's Tabernacle, I see a landau before me, and on the box-seat by the driver is my young friend Charley, who waves his hat to me and calls out, "George! George!" I ran up to the carriage, my knees knocking together so that I thought I should fall by the wheel; and inside I see Hetty, and by her my dearest Theo, propped with a pillow. How thin the little hand had become since last it was laid in mine! The cheeks were flushed and wasted, the eyes strangely bright, and the thrill of the voice when she spoke a word or two, smote me with a pang, I know not of grief or joy was it, so intimately were they blended.

"I am taking her an airing to Hampstead," says Hetty, demurely. "The doctor says the air will do her good."

"I have been ill, but I am better now, George," says Theo. There came a great burst of music from the people in the chapel hard by, as she was speaking. I held her hand in mine. Her eyes were looking into mine once more. It seemed as if we had never been parted.

I can never forget the tune of that psalm. I have heard it all through my life. My wife has touched it on her harpsichord, and her little ones have warbled it. Now, do you understand, young people, why I love it so? Because 'twas the music played at our amoris redintegratio. Because it sang hope to me, at the period of my existence the most miserable. Yes, the most miserable: for that dreary confinement of Duquesne had its tendernesses and kindly associations connected with it; and many a time in after days I have thought with fondness of the poor Biche and my tipsy jailor, and the reveille of the forest birds and the military music of my prison.

Master Charley looks down from his box-seat upon his sister and me engaged in beatific contemplation, and Hetty listening too, to the music. "I think I should like to go and hear it. And that famous Mr. Whitfield, perhaps he is going to preach this very day! Come in with me, Charley—and George can drive for half an hour with dear Theo towards Hampstead and back."

Charley did not seem to have any very strong desire for witnessing the devotional exercises of good Mr. Whitfield and his congregation, and proposed that George Warrington should take Hetty in; but Het was not to be denied. "I will never help you in another exercise as long as you live, sir," cries Miss Hetty, "if you don't come on,"—while the youth clambered down from his box-seat, and they entered the temple together.

Can any moralist, bearing my previous promises in mind, excuse me for jumping into the carriage and sitting down once more by my dearest Theo? Suppose I did break 'em? Will he blame me much? Reverend sir, you are welcome. I broke my promise; and if you would not do as much, good friend, you are welcome to your virtue. Not that I for a moment suspect my own children will ever be so bold as to think of having hearts of their own, and bestowing them according to their liking. No, my young people, you will let papa choose for you; be hungry when he tells you; be thirsty when he orders; and settle your children's marriages afterwards.

And now of course you are anxious to hear what took place when papa jumped into the landau by the side of poor little mamma, propped up by her pillows. "I am come to your part of the story, my dear," says I, looking over to my wife as she is plying her needles.

"To what, pray?" says my lady. "You should skip all that part, and come to the grand battles, and your heroic defence of——"

"Of Fort Fiddlededee in the year 1778, when I pulled off Mr. Washington's epaulet, gouged General Gates's eye, cut off Charles Lee's head, and pasted it on again!"

"Let us hear all about the fighting," say the boys. Even the Captain condescends to own he will listen to any military details, though only from a militia officer.

"Fair and softly, young people! Everything in its turn. I am not yet arrived at the war. I am only a young gentleman, just stepping into a landau, by the side of a young lady whom I promised to avoid. I am taking her hand, which, after a little ado, she leaves in mine. Do you remember how hot it was, the little thing, how it trembled, and how it throbbed and jumped a hundred and twenty in a minute? And as we trot on towards Hampstead, I address Miss Lambert in the following terms——"

"Ah, ah, ah!" say the girls in a chorus with mademoiselle, their French governess, who cries, "Nous ecoutons maintenant. La parole est a vous, Monsieur le Chevalier!"

Here we have them all in a circle: mamma is at her side of the fire, papa at his; Mademoiselle Eleonore, at whom the Captain looks rather sweetly (eyes off, Captain!); the two girls, listening like—like nymphas discentes to Apollo, let us say; and John and Tummas (with obtuse ears), who are bringing in the tea-trays and urns.

"Very good," says the Squire, pulling out the MS., and waving it before him. "We are going to tell your mother's secrets and mine."

"I am sure you may, papa," cries the house matron. "There's nothing to be ashamed of." And a blush rises over her kind face.

"But before I begin, young folks, permit me two or three questions."

"Allons, toujours des questions!" says mademoiselle, with a shrug of her pretty shoulders. (Florac has recommended her to us, and I suspect the little Chevalier has himself an eye upon this pretty Mademoiselle de Blois.)

To the questions, then.

CHAPTER LXXVII. And how everybody got out again

"You, Captain Miles Warrington, have the honour of winning the good graces of a lady—of ever so many ladies—of the Duchess of Devonshire, let us say, of Mrs. Crew, of Mrs. Fitzherbert, of the Queen of Prussia, of the Goddess Venus, of Mademoiselle Hillisberg of the Opera—never mind of whom, in fine. If you win a lady's good graces, do you always go to the mess and tell what happened?"

"Not such a fool, Squire!" says the Captain, surveying his side curl in the glass.

"Have you, Miss Theo, told your mother every word you said to Mr. Joe Blake, junior, in the shrubbery this morning?"

"Joe Blake, indeed!" cries Theo junior.

"And you, mademoiselle? That scented billet which came to you under Sir Thomas's frank, have you told us all the letter contains? Look how she blushes! As red as the curtain, on my word! No, mademoiselle, we all have our secrets" (says the Squire, here making his best French bow). "No, Theo, there was nothing in the shrubbery—only nuts, my child! No, Miles, my son, we don't tell all, even to the most indulgent of fathers—and if I tell what happened in a landau on the Hampstead Road, on the 25th of May, 1760, may the Chevalier Ruspini pull out every tooth in my head!"

"Pray tell, papa!" cries mamma: "or, as Jobson, who drove us, is in your service now, perhaps you will have him in from the stables! I insist upon your telling!"

"What is, then, this mystery?" asks mademoiselle, in her pretty French accent, of my wife.

"Eh, ma fille!" whispers the lady. "Thou wouldst ask me what I said? I said 'Yes!'—behold all I said." And so 'tis my wife has peached, and not I; and this was the sum of our conversation, as the carriage, all too swiftly as I thought, galloped towards Hampstead, and flew back again. Theo had not agreed to fly in the face of her honoured parents—no such thing. But we would marry no other person; no, not if we lived to be as old as Methuselah; no, not the Prince of Wales himself would she take. Her heart she had given away with her papa's consent—nay, order—it was not hers to resume. So kind a father must relent one of these days; and, if George would keep his promise—were it now, or were it in twenty years, or were it in another world, she knew she should never break hers.

Hetty's face beamed with delight when, my little interview over, she saw Theo's countenance wearing a sweet tranquillity. All the doctor's medicine has not done her so much good, the fond sister said. The girls went home after their act of disobedience. I gave up the place which I had held during a brief period of happiness by my dear invalid's side. Hetty skipped back into her seat, and Charley on to his box. He told me in after days, that it was a very dull, stupid sermon he had heard. The little chap was too orthodox to love dissenting preachers' sermons.

Hetty was not the only one of the family who remarked her sister's altered countenance and improved spirits. I am told that on the girls' return home their mother embraced both of them, especially the invalid, with more than common ardour of affection. "There was nothing like a country ride," Aunt Lambert said, "for doing her dear Theo good. She had been on the road to Hampstead, had she? She must have another ride to-morrow. Heaven be blessed, my Lord Wrotham's horses were at their orders three or four times a week, and the sweet child might have the advantage of them!" As for the idea that Mr. Warrington might have happened to meet the children on their drive, Aunt Lambert never once entertained it,—at least spoke of it. I leave anybody who is interested in the matter to guess whether Mrs. Lambert could by any possibility have supposed that her daughter and her sweetheart could ever have come together again. Do women help each other in love perplexities? Do women scheme, intrigue, make little plans, tell little fibs, provide little amorous opportunities, hang up the rope-ladder, coax, wheedle, mystify the guardian or Abigail, and turn their attention away while Strephon and Chloe are billing and cooing in the twilight, or whisking off in the postchaise to Gretna Green? My dear young folks, some people there are of this nature; and some kind souls who have loved tenderly and truly in their own time, continue ever after to be kindly and tenderly disposed towards their young successors, when they begin to play the same pretty game.

Miss Prim doesn't. If she hears of two young persons attached to each other, it is to snarl at them for fools, or to imagine of them all conceivable evil. Because she has a hump-back herself, she is for biting everybody else's. I believe if she saw a pair of turtles cooing in a wood, she would turn her eyes down, or fling a stone to frighten them; but I am speaking, you see, young ladies, of your grandmother, Aunt Lambert, who was one great syllabub of human kindness; and, besides, about the affair at present under discussion, how am I ever to tell whether she knew anything regarding it or not?

So, all she says to Theo on her return home is, "My child, the country air has done you all the good in the world, and I hope you will take another drive to-morrow, and another, and another, and so on."

"Don't you think, papa, the ride has done the child most wonderful good, and must not she be made to go out in the air?" Aunt Lambert asks of the General, when he comes in for supper.

"Yes, sure, if a coach-and-six will do his little Theo good, she shall have it," Lambert says, "or he will drag the landau up Hampstead Hill himself, if there are no horses;" and so the good man would have spent, freely, his guineas, or his breath, or his blood, to give his child pleasure. He was charmed at his girl's altered countenance; she picked a bit of chicken with appetite: she drank a little negus, which he made for her: indeed it did seem to be better than the kind doctor's best medicine, which hitherto, God wot, had been of little benefit. Mamma was gracious and happy. Hetty was radiant and rident. It was quite like an evening at home at Oakhurst. Never for months past, never since that fatal, cruel day, that no one spoke of, had they spent an evening so delightful.

But, if the other women chose to coax and cajole the good, simple father, Theo herself was too honest to continue for long even that sweet and fond delusion. When, for the third or fourth time, he comes back to the delightful theme of his daughter's improved health, and asks, "What has done it? Is it the country air? is it the Jesuit's bark? is it the new medicine?"

"Can't you think, dear, what it is?" she says, laying a hand upon her father's, with a tremor in her voice, perhaps, but eyes that are quite open and bright.

"And what is it, my child?" asks the General.

"It is because I have seen him again, papa!" she says.

The other two women turned pale, and Theo's heart too begins to palpitate, and her cheek to whiten, as she continues to look in her father's scared face.

"It was not wrong to see him," she continues, more quickly; "it would have been wrong not to tell you."

"Great God!" groans the father, drawing his hand back, and with such a dreadful grief in his countenance, that Hetty runs to her almost swooning sister, clasps her to her heart, and cries out, rapidly, "Theo knew nothing of it, sir! It was my doing—it was all my doing!"

Theo lies on her sister's neck, and kisses it twenty, fifty times.

"Women, women! are you playing with my honour?" cries the father, bursting out with a fierce exclamation.

Aunt Lambert sobs, wildly, "Martin! Martin! Don't say a word to her!" again calls out Hetty, and falls back herself staggering towards the wall, for Theo has fainted on her shoulder.

I was taking my breakfast next morning, with what appetite I might, when my door opens, and my faithful black announces, "General Lambert." At once I saw, by the General's face, that the yesterday's transaction was known to him. "Your accomplices did not confess," the General said, as soon as my servant had left us, "but sided with you against their father—a proof how desirable clandestine meetings are. It was from Theo herself I heard that she had seen you."

"Accomplices, sir!" I said (perhaps not unwilling to turn the conversation from the real point at issue). "You know how fondly and dutifully your young people regard their father. If they side against you in this instance, it must be because justice is against you. A man like you is not going to set up sic volo sic jubeo as the sole law in his family!"

"Psha, George!" cries the General. "For though we are parted, God forbid I should desire that we should cease to love each other. I had your promise that you would not seek to see her."

"Nor did I go to her, sir," I said, turning red, no doubt; for though this was truth, I own it was untrue.

"You mean she was brought to you?" says Theo's father, in great agitation. "Is it behind Hester's petticoat that you will shelter yourself? What a fine defence for a gentleman!"

"Well, I won't screen myself behind the poor child," I replied. "To speak as I did was to make an attempt at evasion, and I am ill-accustomed to dissemble. I did not infringe the letter of my agreement, but I acted against the spirit of it. From this moment I annul it altogether."

"You break your word given to me!" cries Mr. Lambert.

"I recall a hasty promise made on a sudden at a moment of extreme excitement and perturbation. No man can be for ever bound by words uttered at such a time; and, what is more, no man of honour or humanity, Mr. Lambert, would try to bind him."

"Dishonour to me! sir," exclaims the General.

"Yes, if the phrase is to be shuttlecocked between us!" I answered, hotly. "There can be no question about love, or mutual regard, or difference of age, when that word is used: and were you my own father—and I love you better than a father, Uncle Lambert,—I would not bear it! What have I done? I have seen the woman whom I consider my wife before God and man, and if she calls me I will see her again. If she comes to me, here is my home for her, and the half of the little I have. 'Tis you, who have no right, having made me the gift, to resume it. Because my mother taunts you unjustly, are you to visit Mrs. Esmond's wrong upon this tender, innocent creature? You profess to love your daughter, and you can't bear a little wounded pride for her sake. Better she should perish away in misery, than an old woman in Virginia should say that Mr. Lambert had schemed to marry one of his daughters. Say that to satisfy what you call honour and I call selfishness, we part, we break our hearts well nigh, we rally, we try to forget each other, we marry elsewhere? Can any man be to my dear as I have been? God forbid! Can any woman be to me what she is? You shall marry her to the Prince of Wales to-morrow, and it is a cowardice and treason. How can we, how can you, undo the promises we have made to each other before Heaven? You may part us: and she will die as surely as if she were Jephthah's daughter. Have you made any vow to Heaven to compass her murder? Kill her if you conceive your promise so binds you: but this I swear, that I am glad you have come, so that I may here formally recall a hasty pledge which I gave, and that, call me when she will, I will come to her!"

No doubt this speech was made with the flurry and agitation belonging to Mr. Warrington's youth, and with the firm conviction that death would infallibly carry off one or both of the parties, in case their worldly separation was inevitably decreed. Who does not believe his first passion eternal? Having watched the world since, and seen the rise, progress, and—alas, that I must say it!—decay of other amours, I may smile now as I think of my own youthful errors and ardours; but, if it be a superstition, I had rather hold it; I had rather think that neither of us could have lived with any other mate, and that, of all its innumerable creatures, Heaven decreed these special two should be joined together.

"We must come, then, to what I had fain have spared myself," says the General, in reply to my outbreak; "to an unfriendly separation. When I meet you, Mr. Warrington, I must know you no more. I must order—and they will not do other than obey me—my family and children not to recognise you when they see you, since you will not recognise in your intercourse with me the respect due to my age, the courtesy of gentlemen. I had hoped so far from your sense of honour, and the idea I had formed of you, that, in my present great grief and perplexity, I should have found you willing to soothe and help me as far as you might—for, God knows, I have need of everybody's sympathy. But, instead of help, you fling obstacles in my way. Instead of a friend—a gracious Heaven pardon me!—I find in you an enemy! An enemy to the peace of my home and the honour of my children, sir! And as such I shall treat you, and know how to deal with you, when you molest me!"

And, waving his hand to me, and putting on his hat, Mr. Lambert hastily quitted my apartment.

I was confounded, and believed, indeed, there was war between us. The brief happiness of yesterday was clouded over and gone, and I thought that never since the day of the first separation had I felt so exquisitely unhappy as now, when the bitterness of quarrel was added to the pangs of parting, and I stood not only alone but friendless. In the course of one year's constant intimacy I had come to regard Lambert with a reverence and affection which I had never before felt for any mortal man except my dearest Harry. That his face should be turned from me in anger was as if the sun had gone out of my sphere, and all was dark around me. And yet I felt sure that in withdrawing the hasty promise I had made not to see Theo, I was acting rightly—that my fidelity to her, as hers now to me, was paramount to all other ties of duty or obedience, and that, ceremony or none, I was hers, first and before all. Promises were passed between us, from which no parent could absolve either; and all the priests in Christendom could no more than attest and confirm the sacred contract which had tacitly been ratified between us.

I saw Jack Lambert by chance that day, as I went mechanically to my not unusual haunt, the library of the new Museum; and with the impetuousness of youth, and eager to impart my sorrow to some one, I took him out of the room and led him about the gardens, and poured out my grief to him. I did not much care for Jack (who in truth was somewhat of a prig, and not a little pompous and wearisome with his Latin quotations) except in the time of my own sorrow, when I would fasten upon him or any one; and having suffered himself in his affair with the little American, being haud ignarus mali (as I knew he would say), I found the college gentleman ready to compassionate another's misery. I told him, what has here been represented at greater length, of my yesterday's meeting with his sister; of my interview with his father in the morning; of my determination at all hazards never to part with Theo. When I found from the various quotations from the Greek and Latin authors which he uttered that he leaned to my side in the dispute, I thought him a man of great sense, clung eagerly to his elbow, and bestowed upon him much more affection than he was accustomed at other times to have from me. I walked with him up to his father's lodgings in Dean Street; saw him enter at the dear door; surveyed the house from without with a sickening desire to know from its exterior appearance how my beloved fared within; and called for a bottle at the coffee-house where I waited Jack's return. I called him Brother when I sent him away. I fondled him as the condemned wretch at Newgate hangs about the jailor or the parson, or any one who is kind to him in his misery. I drank a whole bottle of wine at the coffee-house—by the way, Jack's Coffee-House was its name—called another. I thought Jack would never come back.

He appeared at length with rather a scared face; and, coming to my box, poured out for himself two or three bumpers from my second bottle, and then fell to his story, which, to me at least, was not a little interesting. My poor Theo was keeping her room, it appeared, being much agitated by the occurrences of yesterday; and Jack had come home in time to find dinner on table; after which his good father held forth upon the occurrences of the morning, being anxious and able to speak more freely, he said, because his eldest son was present and Theodosia was not in the room. The General stated what had happened at my lodgings between me and him. He bade Hester be silent, who indeed was as dumb as a mouse, poor thing! he told Aunt Lambert (who was indulging in that madefaction of pocket-handkerchiefs which I have before described), and with something like an imprecation, that the women were all against him, and pimps (he called them) for one another; and frantically turning round to Jack, asked what was his view in the matter?

To his father's surprise and his mother's and sister's delight, Jack made a speech on my side. He ruled with me (citing what ancient authorities I don't know), that the matter had gone out of the hands of the parents on either side; that having given their consent, some months previously, the elders had put themselves out of court. Though he did not hold with a great, a respectable, he might say a host of divines, those sacramental views of the marriage-ceremony—for which there was a great deal to be said—yet he held it, if possible, even more sacredly than they; conceiving that though marriages were made before the civil magistrate, and without the priest, yet they were, before Heaven, binding and indissoluble.

"It is not merely, sir," says Jack, turning to his father, "those whom I, John Lambert, Priest, have joined, let no man put asunder; it is those whom God has joined let no man separate." (Here he took off his hat, as he told the story to me.) "My views are clear upon the point, and surely these young people were joined, or permitted to plight themselves to each other by the consent of you, the priest of your own family. My views, I say, are clear, and I will lay them down at length in a series of two or three discourses which, no doubt, will satisfy you. Upon which," says Jack, "my father said, 'I am satisfied already, my dear boy,' and my lively little Het (who has much archness) whispers to me, 'Jack, mother and I will make you a dozen shirts, as sure as eggs is eggs.'"

"Whilst we were talking," Mr. Lambert resumed, "my sister Theodosia made her appearance, I must say very much agitated and pale, kissed our father, and sate down at his side, and took a sippet of toast—(my dear George, this port is excellent, and I drink your health)—and took a sippet of toast and dipped it in his negus.

"'You should have been here to hear Jack's sermon!' says Hester. 'He has been preaching most beautifully.'

"'Has he?' asks Theodosia, who is too languid and weak, poor thing, much to care for the exercises of eloquence, or the display of authorities, such as I must own," says Jack, "it was given to me this afternoon to bring forward.

"'He has talked for three quarters of an hour by Shrewsbury clock,' says my father, though I certainly had not talked so long or half so long by my own watch. 'And his discourse has been you, my dear,' says papa, playing with Theodosia's hand.

"'Me, papa?'

"'You and—and Mr. Warrington—and—and George, my love,' says papa. Upon which" (says Mr. Jack). "my sister came closer to the General, and laid her head upon him, and wept upon his shoulder.

"'This is different, sir,' says I, 'to a passage I remember in Pausanias.'

"'In Pausanias? Indeed!' said the General. 'And pray who was he?'

"I smiled at my father's simplicity in exposing his ignorance before his children. 'When Ulysses was taking away Penelope from her father, the king hastened after his daughter and bridegroom, and besought his darling to return. Whereupon, it is related, Ulysses offered her her choice,—whether she would return, or go on with him? Upon which the daughter of Icarius covered her face with her veil. For want of a veil my sister has taken refuge in your waistcoat, sir,' I said, and we all laughed; though my mother vowed that if such a proposal had been made to her, or Penelope had been a girl of spirit, she would have gone home with her father that instant.

"'But I am not a girl of any spirit, dear mother!' says Theodosia, still in gremio patris. I do not remember that this habit of caressing was frequent in my own youth," continues Jack. "But after some more discourse, Brother Warrington! bethought me of you, and left my parents insisting upon Theodosia returning to bed. The late transactions have, it appears, weakened and agitated her much. I myself have experienced, in my own case, how full of solliciti timoris is a certain passion; how it racks the spirits; and I make no doubt, if carried far enough, or indulged to the extent to which women who have little philosophy will permit it to go—I make no doubt, I say, is ultimately injurious to the health. My service to you, brother!"

From grief to hope, how rapid the change was! What a flood of happiness poured into my soul, and glowed in my whole being! Landlord, more port! Would honest Jack have drunk a binful I would have treated him; and, to say truth, Jack's sympathy was large in this case, and it had been generous all day. I decline to score the bottles of port: and place to the fabulous computations of interested waiters, the amount scored against me in the reckoning. Jack was my dearest, best of brothers. My friendship for him I swore should be eternal. If I could do him any service, were it a bishopric, by George! he should have it. He says I was interrupted by the watchman rhapsodising verses beneath the loved one's window. I know not. I know I awoke joyfully and rapturously, in spite of a racking headache the next morning.

Nor did I know the extent of my happiness quite, or the entire conversion of my dear noble enemy of the previous morning. It must have been galling to the pride of an elder man to have to yield to representations and objections couched in language so little dutiful as that I had used towards Mr. Lambert. But the true Christian gentleman, retiring from his talk with me, mortified and wounded by my asperity of remonstrance, as well as by the pain which he saw his beloved daughter suffer, went thoughtfully and sadly to his business, as he subsequently told me, and in the afternoon (as his custom not unfrequently was) into a church which was open for prayers. And it was here, on his knees, submitting his case in the quarter whither he frequently, though privately, came for guidance and comfort, that it seemed to him that his child was right in her persistent fidelity to me, and himself wrong in demanding her utter submission. Hence Jack's cause was won almost before he began to plead it; and the brave, gentle heart, which could bear no rancour, which bled at inflicting pain on those it loved, which even shrank from asserting authority or demanding submission, was only too glad to return to its natural pulses of love and affection.

CHAPTER LXXVIII. Pyramus and Thisbe

In examining the old papers at home, years afterwards, I found, docketed and labelled with my mother's well-known neat handwriting, "From London, April, 1760. My son's dreadful letter." When it came to be mine I burnt the document, not choosing that that story of domestic grief and disunion should remain amongst our family annals for future Warringtons to gaze on, mayhap, and disobedient sons to hold up as examples of foregone domestic rebellions. For similar reasons, I have destroyed the paper which my mother despatched to me at this time of tyranny, revolt, annoyance, and irritation.

Maddened by the pangs of separation from my mistress, and not unrightly considering that Mrs. Esmond was the prime cause of the greatest grief and misery which had ever befallen me in the world, I wrote home to Virginia a letter, which might have been more temperate, it is true, but in which I endeavoured to maintain the extremest respect and reticence. I said I did not know by what motives she had been influenced, but that I held her answerable for the misery of my future life, which she had chosen wilfully to mar and render wretched. She had occasioned a separation between me and a virtuous and innocent young creature, whose own hopes, health, and happiness were cast down for ever by Mrs. Esmond's interference. The deed was done, as I feared, and I would offer no comment upon the conduct of the perpetrator, who was answerable to God alone; but I did not disguise from my mother that the injury which she had done me was so dreadful and mortal, that her life or mine could never repair it; that the tie of my allegiance was broken towards her, and that I never could be, as heretofore, her dutiful and respectful son.

Madam Esmond replied to me in a letter of very great dignity (her style and correspondence were extraordinarily elegant and fine). She uttered not a single reproach or hard word, but coldly gave me to understand that it was before that awful tribunal of God she had referred the case between us, and asked for counsel; that, in respect of her own conduct, as a mother, she was ready, in all humility, to face it. Might I, as a son, be equally able to answer for myself, and to show, when the Great Judge demanded the question of me, whether I had done my own duty, and honoured my father and mother! O popoi! My grandfather has quoted in his memoir a line of Homer, showing how in our troubles and griefs the gods are always called in question. When our pride, our avarice, our interest, our desire to domineer, are worked upon, are we not for ever pestering Heaven to decide in their favour? In our great American quarrel, did we not on both sides appeal to the skies as to the justice of our causes, sing Te Deum for victory, and boldly express our confidence that the right should prevail? Was America right because she was victorious? Then I suppose Poland was wrong because she was defeated?—How am I wandering into this digression about Poland, America, and what not, and all the while thinking of a little woman now no more, who appealed to Heaven and confronted it with a thousand texts out of its own book, because her son wanted to make a marriage not of her liking? We appeal, we imprecate, we go down on our knees, we demand blessings, we shriek out for sentence according to law; the great course of the great world moves on; we pant, and strive, and struggle; we hate; we rage; we weep passionate tears; we reconcile; we race and win; we race and lose; we pass away, and other little strugglers succeed; our days are spent; our night comes, and another morning rises, which shines on us no more.

My letter to Madam Esmond, announcing my revolt and disobedience (perhaps I myself was a little proud of the composition of that document), I showed in duplicate to Mr. Lambert, because I wished him to understand what my relations to my mother were, and how I was determined, whatever of threats or quarrels the future might bring, never for my own part to consider my separation from Theo as other than a forced one. Whenever I could see her again I would. My word given to her was in secula seculorum, or binding at least as long as my life should endure. I implied that the girl was similarly bound to me, and her poor father knew indeed as much. He might separate us; as he might give her a dose of poison, and the gentle, obedient creature would take it and die; but the death or separation would be his doing: let him answer them. Now he was tender about his children to weakness, and could not have the heart to submit any one of them—this one especially—to torture. We had tried to part: we could not. He had endeavoured to separate us: it was more than was in his power. The bars were up, but the young couple —the maid within and the knight without—were loving each other all the same. The wall was built, but Pyramus and Thisbe were whispering on either side. In the midst of all his grief and perplexity, Uncle Lambert had plenty of humour, and could not but see that his role was rather a sorry one. Light was beginning to show through that lime and rough plaster of the wall: the lovers were getting their hands through, then their heads through—indeed, it was wall's best business to retire.

I forget what happened stage by stage and day by day; nor, for the instruction of future ages, does it much matter. When my descendants have love scrapes of their own, they will find their own means of getting out of them. I believe I did not go back to Dean Street, but that practice of driving in the open air was considered most healthful for Miss Lambert. I got a fine horse, and rode by the side of her carriage. The old woman at Tottenham Court came to know both of us quite well, and nod and wink in the most friendly manner when we passed by. I fancy the old goody was not unaccustomed to interest herself in young couples, and has dispensed the hospitality of her roadside cottage to more than one pair.

The doctor and the country air effected a prodigious cure upon Miss

Lambert. Hetty always attended as duenna, and sometimes of his holiday, Master Charley rode my horse when I got into the carriage. What a deal of love-making Miss Hetty heard!—with what exemplary patience she listened to it! I do not say she went to hear the Methodist sermons any more, but 'tis certain that when we had a closed carriage she would very kindly and considerately look out of the window. Then, what heaps of letters there were! —what running to and fro! Gumbo's bandy legs were for ever on the trot from my quarters to Dean Street; and, on my account or her own, Mrs. Molly, the girl's maid, was for ever bringing back answers to Bloomsbury. By the time when the autumn leaves began to turn pale, Miss Theo's roses were in full bloom again, and my good Doctor Heberden's cure was pronounced to be complete. What else happened during this blessed period? Mr. Warrington completed his great tragedy of Pocahontas, which was not only accepted by Mr. Garrick this time (his friend Dr. Johnson having spoken not unfavourably of the work), but my friend and cousin, Hagan, was engaged by the manager to perform the part of the hero, Captain Smith. Hagan's engagement was not made before it was wanted. I had helped him and his family with means disproportioned, perhaps, to my power, especially considering my feud with Madam Esmond, whose answer to my angry missive of April came to me towards autumn, and who wrote back from Virginia with war for war, controlment for controlment. These menaces, however, frightened me little: my poor mother's thunder could not reach me; and my conscience, or casuistry, supplied me with other interpretations for her texts of Scripture, so that her oracles had not the least weight with me in frightening me from my purpose. How my new loves speeded I neither informed her, nor any other members of my maternal or paternal family, who, on both sides, had been bitter against my marriage. Of what use wrangling with them? It was better to carpere diem and its sweet loves and pleasures, and to leave the railers to grumble, or the seniors to advise, at their ease.

Besides Madam Esmond I had, it must be owned, in the frantic rage of my temporary separation, addressed notes of wondrous sarcasm to my Uncle Warrington, to my Aunt Madame de Bernstein, and to my Lord or Lady of Castlewood (I forget to which individually), thanking them for the trouble which they had taken in preventing the dearest happiness of my life, and promising them a corresponding gratitude from their obliged relative. Business brought the jovial Baronet and his family to London somewhat earlier than usual, and Madame de Bernstein was never sorry to get back to Clarges Street and her cards. I saw them. They found me perfectly well. They concluded the match was broken off, and I did not choose to undeceive them. The Baroness took heart at seeing how cheerful I was, and made many sly jokes about my philosophy, and my prudent behaviour as a man of the world. She was, as ever, bent upon finding a rich match for me: and I fear I paid many compliments at her house to a rich young soap-boiler's daughter from Mile End, whom the worthy Baroness wished to place in my arms.

"You court her with infinite wit and esprit, my dear," says my pleased kinswoman, "but she does not understand half you say, and the other half, I think, frightens her. This ton de persiflage is very well in our society, but you must be sparing of it, my dear nephew, amongst these roturiers."

Miss Badge married a young gentleman of royal dignity, though shattered fortunes, from a neighbouring island; and I trust Mrs. Mackshane has ere this pardoned my levity. There was another person besides Miss at my aunt's house, who did not understand my persiflage much better than Miss herself; and that was a lady who had seen James the Second's reign, and who was alive and as worldly as ever in King George's. I loved to be with her: but that my little folks have access to this volume, I could put down a hundred stories of the great old folks whom she had known in the great old days—of George the First and his ladies, of St. John and Marlborough, of his reigning Majesty and the late Prince of Wales, and the causes of the quarrel between them— but my modest muse pipes for boys and virgins. Son Miles does not care about court stories, or if he doth, has a fresh budget from Carlton House, quite as bad as the worst of our old Baroness. No, my dear wife, thou hast no need to shake thy powdered locks at me! Papa is not going to scandalise his nursery with old-world gossip, nor bring a blush over our chaste bread-and-butter.

But this piece of scandal I cannot help. My aunt used to tell it with infinite gusto; for, to do her justice, she hated your would-be good people, and sniggered over the faults of the self-styled righteous with uncommon satisfaction. In her later days she had no hypocrisy, at least; and in so far was better than some whitewashed... Well, to the story. My Lady Warrington, one of the tallest and the most virtuous of her sex, who had goodness for ever on her lips and "Heaven in her eye," like the woman in Mr. Addison's tedious tragedy (which has kept the stage, from which some others, which shall be nameless, have disappeared), had the world in her other eye, and an exceedingly shrewd desire of pushing herself in it. What does she do, when my marriage with your ladyship yonder was supposed to be broken off, but attempt to play off on me those arts which she had tried on my poor Harry with such signal ill success, and which failed with me likewise! It was not the Beauty—Miss Flora was for my master—(and what a master! I protest I take off my hat at the idea of such an illustrious connexion!)—it was Dora, the Muse, was set upon me to languish at me and to pity me, and to read even my godless tragedy, and applaud me and console me. Meanwhile, how was the Beauty occupied? Will it be believed that my severe aunt gave a great entertainment to my Lady Yarmouth, presented her boy to her, and placed poor little Miles under her ladyship's august protection? That, so far, is certain; but can it be that she sent her daughter to stay at my lady's house, which our gracious lord and master daily visited, and with the views which old Aunt Bernstein attributed to her? "But for that fit of apoplexy, my dear," Bernstein said, "that aunt of yours intended there should have been a Countess in her own right in the Warrington family!" [Compare Walpole's letters in Mr. Cunningham's excellent new edition. See the story of the supper at N. House, to show what great noblemen would do for a king's mistress, and the pleasant account of the waiting for the Prince of Wales before Holland House.- EDITOR.] My neighbour and kinswoman, my Lady Claypole, is dead and buried. Grow white, ye daisies, upon Flora's tomb! I can see my pretty Miles, in a gay little uniform of the Norfolk Militia, led up by his parent to the lady whom the King delighted to honour, and the good-natured old Jezebel laying her hand upon the boy's curly pate. I am accused of being but a lukewarm royalist; but sure I can contrast those times with ours, and acknowledge the difference between the late sovereign and the present, who, born a Briton, has given to every family in the empire an example of decorum and virtuous life. [The Warrington MS. is dated 1793.-ED.]

Thus my life sped in the pleasantest of all occupation; and, being so happy myself, I could afford to be reconciled to those who, after all, had done me no injury, but rather added to the zest of my happiness by the brief obstacle which they had placed in my way. No specific plans were formed, but Theo and I knew that a day would come when we need say Farewell no more. Should the day befall a year hence—ten years hence—we were ready to wait. Day after day we discussed our little plans, with Hetty for our confidante. On our drives we spied out pretty cottages that we thought might suit young people of small means; we devised all sorts of delightful schemes and childish economies. We were Strephon and Chloe to be sure. A cot and a brown loaf should content us! Gumbo and Molly should wait upon us (as indeed they have done from that day until this). At twenty, who is afraid of being poor? Our trials would only confirm our attachment. The "sweet sorrow" of every day's parting but made the morrow's meeting more delightful; and when we separated we ran home and wrote each other those precious letters which we and other young gentlemen and ladies write under such circumstances; but though my wife has them all in a great tin sugar-box in the closet in her bedroom, and, I own, I myself have looked at them once, and even thought some of them pretty,—I hereby desire my heirs and executors to burn them all, unread, at our demise; specially desiring my son the Captain (to whom I know the perusal of MSS. is not pleasant) to perform this duty. Those secrets whispered to the penny-post, or delivered between Molly and Gumbo, were intended for us alone, and no ears of our descendants shall overhear them.

We heard in successive brief letters how our dear Harry continued with the army, as Mr. General Amherst's aide-de-camp, after the death of his own glorious general. By the middle of October there came news of the Capitulation of Montreal and the whole of Canada, and a brief postscript in which Hal said he would ask for leave now, and must go and see the old lady at home, who wrote as sulky as a bare, Captain Warrington remarked. I could guess why, though the claws could not reach me. I had written pretty fully to my brother how affairs were standing with me in England.

Then, on the 25th October, comes the news that his Majesty has fallen down dead at Kensington, and that George III. reigned over us. I fear we grieved but little. What do those care for the Atridae whose hearts are strung only to erota mounon? A modest, handsome, brave new Prince, we gladly accept the common report that he is endowed with every virtue; and we cry huzzay with the loyal crowd that hails his accession: it could make little difference to us, as we thought, simple young sweethearts, whispering our little love-stories in our corner.

But who can say how great events affect him? Did not our little Charley, at the Chartreux, wish impiously for a new king immediately, because on his gracious Majesty's accession Doctor Crusius gave his boys a holiday? He and I, and Hetty, and Theo (Miss Theo was strong enough to walk many a delightful mile now), heard the Heralds proclaim his new Majesty before Savile House in Leicester Fields, and a pickpocket got the watch and chain of a gentleman hard by us, and was caught and carried to Bridewell, all on account of his Majesty's accession. Had the king not died, the gentleman would not have been in the crowd; the chain would not have been seized; the thief would not have been caught and soundly whipped: in this way many of us, more or less remotely, were implicated in the great change which ensued, and even we humble folks were affected by it presently.

As thus. My Lord Wrotham was a great friend of the august family of Savile House, who knew and esteemed his many virtues. Now, of all living men, my Lord Wrotham knew and loved best his neighbour and old fellow-soldier, Martin Lambert, declaring that the world contained few better gentlemen. And my Lord Bute, being all potent, at first, with his Majesty, and a nobleman, as I believe, very eager at the commencement of his brief and luckless tenure of power, to patronise merit wherever he could find it, was strongly prejudiced in Mr. Lambert's favour by the latter's old and constant friend.

My (and Harry's) old friend Parson Sampson, who had been in and out of gaol I don't know how many times of late years, and retained an ever-enduring hatred for the Esmonds of Castlewood, and as lasting a regard for me and my brother, was occupying poor Hal's vacant bed at my lodgings at this time (being, in truth, hunted out of his own by the bailiffs). I liked to have Sampson near me, for a more amusing Jack-friar never walked in cassock; and, besides, he entered into all my rhapsodies about Miss Theo; was never tired (so he vowed) of hearing me talk of her; admired Pocahontas and Carpezan with, I do believe, an honest enthusiasm; and could repeat whole passages of those tragedies with an emphasis and effect that Barry or cousin Hagan himself could not surpass. Sampson was the go-between between Lady Maria and such of her relations as had not disowned her; and, always in debt himself, was never more happy than in drinking a pot, or mingling his tears with his friends in similar poverty. His acquaintance with pawnbrokers' shops was prodigious. He could procure more money, he boasted, on an article than any gentleman of his cloth. He never paid his own debts, to be sure, but he was ready to forgive his debtors. Poor as he was, he always found means to love and help his needy little sister, and a more prodigal, kindly, amiable rogue never probably grinned behind bars. They say that I love to have parasites about me. I own to have had a great liking for Sampson, and to have esteemed him much better than probably much better men.

When he heard how my Lord Bute was admitted into the cabinet, Sampson vowed and declared that his lordship—a great lover of the drama, who had been to see Carpezan, who had admired it, and who would act the part of the king very finely in it—he vowed, by George! that my lord must give me a place worthy of my birth and merits. He insisted upon it that I should attend his lordship's levee. I wouldn't? The Esmonds were all as proud as Lucifer; and, to be sure, my birth was as good as that of any man in Europe. Demmy! Where was my lord himself when the Esmonds were lords of great counties, warriors, and Crusaders? Where were they? Beggarly Scotchmen, without a rag to their backs—by George! tearing raw fish in their islands. But now the times were changed. The Scotchmen were in luck. Mum's the word! "I don't envy him," says Sampson, "but he shall provide for you and my dearest, noblest, heroic captain! He SHALL, by George!" would my worthy parson roar out. And when, in the month after his accession, his Majesty ordered the play of Richard III. at Drury Lane, my chaplain cursed, vowed, swore, but he would have him to Covent Garden to see Carpezan too. And now, one morning, he bursts into my apartment, where I happened to lie rather late, waving the newspaper in his hand, and singing "Huzza!" with all his might.

"What is it, Sampson?" says I. "Has my brother got his promotion?"

"No, in truth: but some one else has. Huzzay! huzzay! His Majesty has appointed Major-General Martin Lambert to be Governor and Commander-in-Chief of the Island of Jamaica."

I started up. Here was news, indeed! Mr. Lambert would go to his government: and who would go with him? I had been supping with some genteel young fellows at the Cocoa-Tree. The rascal Gumbo had a note for me from my dear mistress on the night previous, conveying the same news to me, and had delayed to deliver it. Theo begged me to see her at the old place at midday the next day without fail. [In the Warrington MS. there is not a word to say what the "old place" was. Perhaps some obliging reader of Notes and Queries will be able to inform me, and who Mrs. Goodison was.-ED.]

There was no little trepidation in our little council when we reached our place of meeting. Papa had announced his acceptance of the appointment, and his speedy departure. He would have a frigate given him, and take his family with him. Merciful powers! and were we to be parted? My Theo's old deathly paleness returned to her. Aunt Lambert thought she would have swooned; one of Mrs. Goodison's girls had a bottle of salts, and ran up with it from the workroom. "Going away? Going away in a frigate, Aunt Lambert? Going to tear her away from me? Great God! Aunt Lambert, I shall die!" She was better when mamma came up from the workroom with the young lady's bottle of salts. You see the women used to meet me: knowing dear Theo's delicate state, how could they refrain from compassionating her! But the General was so busy with his levees and his waiting on Ministers, and his outfit, and the settlement of his affairs at home, that they never happened to tell him about our little walks and meetings; and even when orders for the outfit of the ladies were given, Mrs. Goodison, who had known and worked for Miss Molly Benson as a schoolgirl (she remembered Miss Esmond of Virginia perfectly, the worthy lady told me, and a dress she made for the young lady to be presented at her Majesty's Ball)—"even when the outfit was ordered for the three ladies," says Mrs. Goodison, demurely, "why, I thought I could do no harm in completing the order."

Now I need not say in what perturbation of mind Mr. Warrington went home in the evening to his lodgings, after the discussion with the ladies of the above news. No, or at least a very few, more walks; no more rides to dear, dear Hampstead or beloved Islington; no more fetching and carrying of letters for Gumbo and Molly! The former blubbered so, that Mr. Warrington was quite touched by his fidelity, and gave him a crown-piece to go to supper with the poor girl, who turned out to be his sweetheart. What, you too unhappy, Gumbo, and torn from the maid you love? I was ready to mingle with him tear for tear.

What a solemn conference I had with Sampson that evening! He knew my affairs, my expectations, my mother's anger. Psha! that was far off, and he knew some excellent liberal people (of the order of Melchizedek) who would discount the other. The General would not give his consent? Sampson shrugged his broad shoulders and swore a great roaring oath. My mother would not relent? What then? A man was a man, and to make his own way in the world? he supposed. He is only a churl who won't play for such a stake as that, and lose or win, by George! shouts the chaplain, over a bottle of Burgundy at the Bedford Head, where he dined. I need not put down our conversation. We were two of us, and I think there was only one mind between us. Our talk was of a Saturday night....

I did not tell Theo, nor any relative of hers, what was being done. But when the dear child faltered and talked, trembling, of the coming departure, I bade her bear up, and vowed all would be well, so confidently, that she, who ever has taken her alarms and joys from my face (I wish, my dear, it were sometimes not so gloomy), could not but feel confidence; and placed (with many fond words that need not here be repeated) her entire trust in me—murmuring those sweet words of Ruth that must have comforted myriads of tender hearts in my dearest maiden's plight; that whither I would go she would go, and that my people should be hers. At last, one day, the General's preparations being made, the trunks encumbering the passages of the dear old Dean Street lodging, which I shall love as long as I shall remember at all—one day, almost the last of his stay, when the good man (his Excellency we called him now) came home to his dinner—a comfortless meal enough it was in the present condition of the family—he looked round the table at the place where I had used to sit in happy old days, and sighed out: "I wish, Molly, George was here."

"Do you, Martin?" says Aunt Lambert, flinging into his arms.

"Yes, I do; but I don't wish you to choke me, Molly," he says. "I love him dearly. I may go away and never see him again, and take his foolish little sweetheart along with me. I suppose you will write to each other, children? I can't prevent that, you know; and until he changes his mind, I suppose Miss Theo won't obey papa's orders, and get him out of her foolish little head. Wilt thou, Theo?"

"No, dearest, dearest, best papa!"

"What! more embraces and kisses! What does all this mean?"

"It means that—that George is in the drawing-room," says mamma.

"Is he! My dearest boy!" cries the General. "Come to me—come in!" And when I entered he held me to his heart, and kissed me.

I confess at this I was so overcome that I fell down on my knees before the dear, good man, and sobbed on his own.

"God bless you, my dearest boy!" he mutters hurriedly. "Always loved you as a son—haven't I, Molly? Broke my heart nearly when I quarrelled with you about this little—What!—odds marrowbones!—all down on your knees! Mrs. Lambert, pray what is the meaning of all this?"

"Dearest, dearest papa! I will go with you all the same!" whimpers one of the kneeling party. "And I will wait—oh!—as long as ever my dearest father wants me!"

"In Heaven's name!" roars the General, "tell me what has happened?"

What had happened was, that George Esmond Warrington and Theodosia Lambert had been married in Southwark that morning, their banns having been duly called in the church of a certain friend of the Reverend Mr. Sampson.

CHAPTER LXXIX. Containing both Comedy and Tragedy

We, who had been active in the guilty scene of the morning, felt trebly guilty when we saw the effect which our conduct had produced upon him, who, of all others, we loved and respected. The shock to the good man was strange, and pitiful to us to witness who had administered it. The child of his heart had deceived and disobeyed him—I declare I think, my dear, now, we would not or could not do it over again; his whole family had entered into a league against him. Dear, kind friend and father! We know thou hast pardoned our wrong—in the Heaven where thou dwellest amongst purified spirits who learned on earth how to love and pardon! To love and forgive were easy duties with that man. Beneficence was natural to him, and a sweet, smiling humility; and to wound either was to be savage and brutal, as to torture a child, or strike blows at a nursing woman. The deed done, all we guilty ones grovelled in the earth, before the man we had injured. I pass over the scenes of forgiveness, of reconciliation, of common worship together, of final separation when the good man departed to his government, and the ship sailed away before us, leaving me and Theo on the shore. We stood there hand in hand, horribly abashed, silent, and guilty. My wife did not come to me till her father went: in the interval between the ceremony of our marriage and his departure, she had remained at home, occupying her old place by her father, and bed by her sister's side: he as kind as ever, but the women almost speechless among themselves; Aunt Lambert, for once, unkind and fretful in her temper; and little Hetty feverish and strange, and saying, "I wish we were gone. I wish we were gone." Though admitted to the house, and forgiven, I slunk away during those last days, and only saw my wife for a minute or two in the street, or with her family. She was not mine till they were gone. We went to Winchester and Hampton for what may be called our wedding. It was but a dismal business. For a while we felt utterly lonely: and of our dear father as if we had buried him, or drove him to the grave by our undutifulness.

I made Sampson announce our marriage in the papers. (My wife used to hang down her head before the poor fellow afterwards.) I took Mrs. Warrington back to my old lodgings in Bloomsbury, where there was plenty of room for us, and our modest married life began. I wrote home a letter to my mother in Virginia, informing her of no particulars, but only that Mr. Lambert being about to depart for his government, I considered myself bound in honour to fulfil my promise towards his dearest daughter; and stated that I intended to carry out my intention of completing my studies for the Bar, and qualifying myself for employment at home, or in our own or any other colony. My good Mrs. Mountain answered this letter, by desire of Madam Esmond, she said, who thought that for the sake of peace my communications had best be conducted that way. I found my relatives in a fury which was perfectly amusing to witness. The butler's face, as he said, "Not at home," at my uncle's house in Hill Street, was a blank tragedy that might have been studied by Garrick when he sees Banque. My poor little wife was on my arm, and we were tripping away, laughing at the fellow's accueil, when we came upon my lady in a street stoppage in her chair. I took off my hat and made her the lowest possible bow. I affectionately asked after my dear cousins. "I—I wonder you dare look me in the face!" Lady Warrington gasped out. "Nay, don't deprive me of that precious privilege!" says I. "Move on, Peter," she screams to her chairman. "Your ladyship would not impale your own husband's flesh and blood!" says I. She rattles up the glass of her chair in a fury. I kiss my hand, take off my hat, and perform another of my very finest bows.

Walking shortly afterwards in Hyde Park with my dearest companion, I met my little cousin exercising on horseback with a groom behind him. As soon as he sees us, he gallops up to us, the groom powdering afterwards and bawling out, "Stop, Master Miles, stop!"

"I am not to speak to my cousin," says Miles, "but telling you to send my love to Harry is not speaking to you, is it? Is that my new cousin? I'm not told not to speak to her. I'm Miles, cousin, Sir Miles Warrington Baronet's son, and you are very pretty!" "Now, duee now, Master Miles," says the groom, touching his hat to us; and the boy trots away laughing and looking at us over his shoulder. "You see how my relations have determined to treat me," I say to my partner. "As if I married you for your relations!" says Theo, her eyes beaming joy and love into mine. Ah, how happy we were! how brisk and pleasant the winter! How snug the kettle by the fire (where the abashed Sampson sometimes came and made the punch); how delightful the night at the theatre, for which our friends brought us tickets of admission, and where we daily expected our new play of Pocahontas would rival the successes of all former tragedies.

The fickle old aunt of Clarges Street, who received me, on my first coming to London with my wife, with a burst of scorn, mollified presently, and as soon as she came to know Theo (who she had pronounced to be an insignificant little country-faced chit), fell utterly in love with her, and would have her to tea and supper every day when there was no other company. "As for company, my dears," she would say, "I don't ask you. You are no longer du monde. Your marriage has put that entirely out of the question." So she would have had us come to amuse her, and go in and out by the back-stairs. My wife was fine lady enough to feel only amused at this reception; and, I must do the Baroness's domestics the justice to say that, had we been duke and duchess, we could not have been received with more respect. Madame de Bernstein was very much tickled and amused with my story of Lady Warrington and the chair. I acted it for her, and gave her anecdotes of the pious Baronet's lady and her daughters, which pleased the mischievous, lively old woman.

The Dowager Countess of Castlewood, now established in her house at Kensington, gave us that kind of welcome which genteel ladies extend to their poorer relatives. We went once or twice to her ladyship's drums at Kensington; but, losing more money at cards, and spending more money in coach-hire than I liked to afford, we speedily gave up those entertainments, and, I dare say, were no more missed or regretted than other people in the fashionable world, who are carried by death, debt, or other accident out of the polite sphere. My Theo did not in the least regret this exclusion. She had made her appearance at one of these drums, attired in some little ornaments which her mother left behind her, and by which the good lady set some store; but I thought her own white neck was a great deal prettier than these poor twinkling stones; and there were dowagers, whose wrinkled old bones blazed with rubies and diamonds, which, I am sure, they would gladly have exchanged for her modest parure of beauty and freshness. Not a soul spoke to her—except, to be sure, Beau Lothair, a friend of Mr. Will's, who prowled about Bloomsbury afterwards, and even sent my wife a billet. I met him in Covent Garden shortly after, and promised to break his ugly face if ever I saw it in the neighbourhood of my lodgings, and Madam Theo was molested no further.

The only one of our relatives who came to see us (Madame de Bernstein never came; she sent her coach for us sometimes, or made inquiries regarding us by her woman or her major-domo) was our poor Maria, who, with her husband, Mr. Hagan, often took a share of our homely dinner. Then we had friend Spencer from the Temple, who admired our Arcadian felicity, and gently asked our sympathy for his less fortunate loves; and twice or thrice the famous Doctor Johnson came in for a dish of Theo's tea. A dish? a pailful!

"And a pail the best thing to feed him, sar!" says Mr. Gumbo, indignantly: for the Doctor's appearance was not pleasant, nor his linen particularly white. He snorted, he grew red, and sputtered in feeding; he flung his meat about, and bawled out in contradicting people: and annoyed my Theo, whom he professed to admire greatly, by saying, every time he saw her, "Madam, you do not love me; I see by your manner you do not love me; though I admire you, and come here for your sake. Here is my friend Mr. Reynolds that shall paint you: he has no ceruse in his paint-box that is as brilliant as your complexion." And so Mr. Reynolds, a most perfect and agreeable gentleman, would have painted my wife; but I knew what his price was, and did not choose to incur that expense. I wish I had now, for the sake of the children, that they might see what yonder face was like some five-and-thirty years ago. To me, madam, 'tis the same now as ever; and your ladyship is always young!

What annoyed Mrs. Warrington with Dr. Johnson more than his contradictions, his sputterings, and his dirty nails, was, I think, an unfavourable opinion which he formed of my new tragedy. Hagan once proposed that he should read some scenes from it after tea.

"Nay, sir, conversation is better," says the Doctor. "I can read for myself, or hear you at the theatre. I had rather hear Mrs. Warrington's artless prattle than your declamation of Mr. Warrington's decasyllables. Tell us about your household affairs, madam, and whether his Excellency your father is well, and whether you made the pudden and the butter sauce. The butter sauce was delicious!" (He loved it so well that he had kept a large quantity in the bosom of a very dingy shirt.) "You made it as though you loved me. You helped me as though you loved me, though you don't."

"Faith, sir, you are taking some of the present away with you in your waistcoat," says Hagan, with much spirit.

"Sir, you are rude!" bawls the Doctor. "You are unacquainted with the first principles of politeness, which is courtesy before ladies. Having received an university education, I am surprised that you have not learned the rudiments of politeness. I respect Mrs. Warrington. I should never think of making personal remarks about her guests before her!"

"Then, sir," says Hagan, fiercely, "why did you speak of my theatre?"

"Sir, you are saucy!" roars the Doctor.

"De te fabula," says the actor. "I think it is your waistcoat that is saucy. Madam, shall I make some punch in the way we make it in Ireland?"

The Doctor, puffing, and purple in the face, was wiping the dingy shirt with a still more dubious pocket-handkerchief, which he then applied to his forehead. After this exercise, he blew a hyperborean whistle, as if to blow his wrath away. "It is de me, sir—though, as a young man, perhaps you need not have told me so."

"I drop my point, sir! If you have been wrong, I am sure I am bound to ask your pardon for setting you so!" says Mr. Hagan, with a fine bow.

"Doesn't he look like a god?" says Maria, clutching my wife's hand: and indeed Mr. Hagan did look like a handsome young gentleman. His colour had risen; he had put his hand to his breast with a noble air: Chamont or Castalio could not present himself better.

"Let me make you some lemonade, sir; my papa has sent us a box of fresh limes. May we send you some to the Temple?"

"Madam, if they stay in your house, they will lose their quality and turn sweet," says the Doctor. "Mr. Hagan, you are a young sauce-box, that's what you are! Ho! ho! It is I have been wrong."

"Oh, my lord, my Polidore!" bleats Lady Maria, when she was alone in my wife's drawing-room:

"'Oh, I could hear thee talk for ever thus,
Eternally admiring,—fix and gaze
On those dear eyes, for every glance they send
Darts through my soul, and fills my heart with rapture!'

"Thou knowest not, my Theo, what a pearl and paragon of a man my Castalio is; my Chamont, my—oh, dear me, child, what a pity it is that in your husband's tragedy he should have to take the horrid name of Captain Smith!"

Upon this tragedy not only my literary hopes, but much of my financial prospects were founded. My brother's debts discharged, my mother's drafts from home duly honoured, my own expenses paid, which, though moderate, were not inconsiderable,—pretty nearly the whole of my patrimony had been spent, and this auspicious moment I must choose for my marriage! I could raise money on my inheritance: that was not impossible, though certainly costly. My mother could not leave her eldest son without a maintenance, whatever our quarrels might be. I had health, strength, good wits, some friends, and reputation—above all, my famous tragedy, which the manager had promised to perform, and upon the proceeds of this I counted for my present support. What becomes of the arithmetic of youth? How do we then calculate that a hundred pounds is a maintenance, and a thousand a fortune? How did I dare play against Fortune with such odds? I succeeded, I remember, in convincing my dear General, and he left home convinced that his son-in-law had for the present necessity at least a score of hundred pounds at his command. He and his dear Molly had begun life with less, and the ravens had somehow always fed them. As for the women, the question of poverty was one of pleasure to those sentimental souls, and Aunt Lambert, for her part, declared it would be wicked and irreligious to doubt of a provision being made for her children. Was the righteous ever forsaken? Did the just man ever have to beg his bread? She knew better than that! "No, no, my dears! I am not going to be afraid on that account, I warrant you! Look at me and my General!"

Theo believed all I said and wished to believe myself. So we actually began life upon a capital of Five Acts, and about three hundred pounds of ready money in hand!

Well, the time of the appearance of the famous tragedy drew near, and my friends canvassed the town to get a body of supporters for the opening night. I am ill at asking favours from the great; but when my Lord Wrotham came to

London, I went, with Theo in my hand, to wait on his lordship, who received us kindly, out of regard for his old friend, her father—though he good-naturedly shook a finger at me (at which my little wife hung down her head), for having stole a march on the good General. However, he would do his best for her father's daughter; hoped for a success; said he had heard great things of the piece; and engaged a number of places for himself and his friends. But this patron secured, I had no other. "Mon cher, at my age," says the Baroness, "I should bore myself to death at a tragedy: but I will do my best; and I will certainly send my people to the boxes. Yes! Case in his best black looks like a nobleman; and Brett in one of my gowns has a faux air de moi which is quite distinguished. Put down my name for two in the front boxes. Good-bye, my dear. Bonne chance!" The Dowager Countess presented compliments (on the back of the nine of clubs), had a card-party that night, and was quite sorry she and Fanny could not go to my tragedy. As for my uncle and Lady Warrington, they were out of the question. After the affair of the sedan-chair I might as well have asked Queen Elizabeth to go to Drury Lane. These were all my friends—that host of aristocratic connexions about whom poor Sampson had bragged; and on the strength of whom, the manager, as he said, had given Mr. Hagan his engagement! "Where was my Lord Bute? Had I not promised his lordship should come?" he asks, snappishly, taking snuff (how different from the brisk, and engaging, and obsequious little manager of six months ago!) —"I promised Lord Bute should come?"

"Yes," says Mr. Garrick, "and her Royal Highness the Princess of Wales, and his Majesty too."

Poor Sampson owned that he, buoyed up by vain hopes, had promised the appearance of these august personages.

The next day, at rehearsal, matters were worse still, and the manager in a fury.

"Great heavens, sir!" says he, "into what a pretty guet-a-pens have you led me! Look at that letter, sir!—read that letter!" And he hands me one:

"MY DEAR SIR" (said the letter)—"I have seen his lordship, and conveyed to him Mr. Warrington's request that he would honour the tragedy of Pocahontas by his presence. His lordship is a patron of the drama, and a magnificent friend of all the liberal arts; but he desires me to say that he cannot think of attending himself, much less of asking his Gracious Master to witness the performance of a play, a principal part in which is given to an actor who has made a clandestine marriage with a daughter of one of his Majesty's nobility.—Your well-wisher, SAUNDERS MCDUFF."

"Mr. D. Garrick, at the Theatre Royal in Drury Lane."

My poor Theo had a nice dinner waiting for me after the rehearsal. I pleaded fatigue as the reason for looking so pale: I did not dare to convey to her this dreadful news.

CHAPTER LXXX. Pocahontas

The English public not being so well acquainted with the history of Pocahontas as we of Virginia, who still love the memory of that simple and kindly creature, Mr. Warrington, at the suggestion of his friends, made a little ballad about this Indian princess, which was printed in the magazines a few days before the appearance of the tragedy. This proceeding Sampson and I considered to be very artful and ingenious. "It is like ground-bait, sir," says the enthusiastic parson, "and you will see the fish rise in multitudes, on the great day!" He and Spencer declared that the poem was discussed and admired at several coffee-houses in their hearing, and that it had been attributed to Mr. Mason, Mr. Cowper of the Temple, and even to the famous Mr. Gray. I believe poor Sam had himself set abroad these reports; and, if Shakspeare had been named as the author of the tragedy, would have declared Pocahontas to be one of the poet's best performances. I made acquaintance with brave Captain Smith, as a boy in my grandfather's library at home, where I remember how I would sit at the good old man's knees, with my favourite volume on my own, spelling out the exploits of our Virginian hero. I loved to read of Smith's travels, sufferings, captivities, escapes, not only in America but Europe. I become a child again almost as I take from the shelf before me in England the familiar volume, and all sorts of recollections of my early home come crowding over my mind. The old grandfather would make pictures for me of Smith doing battle with the Turks on the Danube, or led out by our Indian savages to death. Ah, what a terrific fight was that in which he was engaged with the three Turkish champions, and how I used to delight over the story of his combat with Bonny Molgro, the last and most dreadful of the three! What a name Bonny Molgro was, and with what a prodigious turban, scimitar, and whiskers we represented him! Having slain and taken off the heads of his first two enemies, Smith and Bonny Molgro met, falling to (says my favourite old book) "with their battle-axes, whose piercing bills made sometimes the one, sometimes the other, to have scarce sense to keep their saddles: especially the Christian received such a wound that he lost his battle-axe, whereat the supposed conquering Turke had a great shout from the rampires. Yet, by the readinesse of his horse, and his great judgment and dexteritie, he not only avoided the Turke's blows, but, having drawn his falchion, so pierced the Turke under the cutlets, through back and body, that though hee alighted from his horse, he stood not long ere hee lost his head as the rest had done. In reward for which deed, Duke Segismundus gave him 3 Turke's head in a shield for armes and 300 Duckats yeerely for a pension." Disdaining time and place (with that daring which is the privilege of poets) in my tragedy, Smith is made to perform similar exploits on the banks of our Potomac and James's river. Our "ground-bait" verses, ran thus:—

"POCAHONTAS

"Wearied arm and broken sword
Wage in vain the desperate fight

Round him press the countless horde,
  He is but a single knight.
Hark! a cry of triumph shrill
  Through the wilderness resounds,
  As, with twenty bleeding wounds,
Sinks the warrior, fighting still.

"Now they heap the fatal pyre,
  And the torch of death they light
Ah! 'tis hard to die of fire!
  Who will shield the captive knight?
Round the stake with fiendish cry
  Wheel and dance the savage crowd,
  Cold the victim's mien and proud,
And his breast is bared to die.

"Who will shield the fearless heart?
  Who avert the murderous blade?
From the throng, with sudden start,
  See, there springs an Indian maid.
Quick she stands before the knight,
  'Loose the chain, unbind the ring,
  I am daughter of the king,
And I claim the Indian right!'

"Dauntlessly aside she flings
  Lifted axe and thirsty knife;
Fondly to his heart she clings,
  And her bosom guards his life!
In the woods of Powhattan,
  Still 'tis told, by Indian fires,
  How a daughter of their sires
Saved the captive Englishman."

I need not describe at length the plot of my tragedy, as my children can take it down from the shelves any day and peruse it for themselves. Nor shall I, let me add, be in a hurry to offer to read it again to my young folks, since Captain Miles and the parson both chose to fall asleep last Christmas, when, at mamma's request, I read aloud a couple of acts. But any person having a moderate acquaintance with plays and novels can soon, out of the above sketch, fill out a picture to his liking. An Indian king; a loving princess, and her attendant, in love with the British captain's servant; a traitor in the English fort; a brave Indian warrior, himself entertaining an unhappy passion for Pocahontas; a medicine-man and priest of the Indians (very well played by Palmer), capable of every treason, stratagem, and crime, and bent upon the torture and death of the English prisoner;—these, with the accidents of the wilderness, the war-dances and cries (which Gumbo had learned to mimic very accurately from the red people at home), and the arrival of the English fleet, with allusions to the late glorious victories in Canada, and the determination of Britons ever to rule and conquer in America, some of us not unnaturally thought might contribute to the success of our tragedy.

But I have mentioned the ill omens which preceded the day: the difficulties which a peevish, and jealous, and timid management threw in the way of the piece, and the violent prejudice which was felt against it in certain high quarters. What wonder then, I ask, that Pocahontas should have turned out not to be a victory? I laugh to scorn the malignity of the critics who found fault with the performance. Pretty critics, forsooth, who said that Carpezan was a masterpiece, whilst a far superior and more elaborate work received only their sneers! I insist on it that Hagan acted his part so admirably that a certain actor and manager of the theatre might well be jealous of him; and that, but for the cabal made outside, the piece would have succeeded. The order had been given that the play should not succeed; so at least Sampson declared to me. "The house swarmed with Macs, by George, and they should have the galleries washed with brimstone," the honest fellow swore, and always vowed that Mr. Garrick himself would not have had the piece succeed for the world; and was never in such a rage as during that grand scene in the second act, where Smith (poor Hagan) being bound to the stake, Pocahontas comes and saves him, and when the whole house was thrilling with applause and sympathy.

Anybody who has curiosity sufficient, may refer to the published tragedy (in the octavo form, or in the subsequent splendid quarto edition of my Collected Works, and Poems Original and Translated), and say whether the scene is without merit, whether the verses are not elegant, the language rich and noble? One of the causes of the failure was my actual fidelity to history. I had copied myself at the Museum, and tinted neatly, a figure of Sir Walter Raleigh in a frill and beard; and (my dear Theo giving some of her mother's best lace for the ruff) we dressed Hagan accurately after this drawing, and no man could look better. Miss Pritchard as Pocahontas, I dressed too as a Red Indian, having seen enough of that costume in my own experience at home. Will it be believed the house tittered when she first appeared? They got used to her, however, but just at the moment when she rushes into the prisoner's arms, and a number of people were actually in tears, a fellow in the pit bawls out, "Bedad! here's the Belle Savage kissing the Saracen's Head;" on which an impertinent roar of laughter sprang up in the pit, breaking out with fitful explosions during the remainder of the performance. As the wag in Mr. Sheridan's amusing Critic admirably says about the morning guns, the playwrights were not content with one of them, but must fire two or three; so with this wretched pothouse joke of the Belle Savage (the ignorant people not knowing that Pocahontas herself was the very Belle Sauvage from whom the tavern took its name!). My friend of the pit repeated it ad nauseam during the performance, and as each new character appeared, saluted him by the name of some tavern—for instance, the English governor (with a long beard) he called the Goat and Boots; his lieutenant (Barker), whose face certainly was broad, the Bull and Mouth, and so on! And the curtain descended amidst a shrill storm of whistles and hisses, which especially assailed poor Hagan every time he opened his lips. Sampson saw Master Will in the green boxes, with some pretty acquaintances of his, and has no doubt that the treacherous scoundrel was one of the ringleaders in the conspiracy. "I would have flung him over into the pit," the faithful fellow said (and Sampson was man enough to execute his threat), "but I saw a couple of Mr. Nadab's followers prowling about the lobby, and was obliged to sheer off." And so the eggs we had counted on selling at market were broken, and our poor hopes lay shattered before us!

I looked in at the house from the stage before the curtain was lifted, and saw it pretty well filled, especially remarking Mr. Johnson in the front boxes, in a laced waistcoat, having his friend Mr. Reynolds by his side; the latter could not hear, and the former could not see, and so they came good-naturedly A deux to form an opinion of my poor tragedy. I could see Lady Maria (I knew the hood she wore) in the lower gallery, where she once more had the opportunity of sitting and looking at her beloved actor performing a principal character in a piece. As for Theo, she fairly owned that, unless I ordered her, she had rather not be present, nor had I any such command to give, for, if things went wrong, I knew that to see her suffer would be intolerable pain to myself, and so acquiesced in her desire to keep away.

Being of a pretty equanimous disposition, and, as I flatter myself, able to bear good or evil fortune without disturbance, I myself, after taking a light dinner at the Bedford, went to the theatre a short while before the commencement of the play, and proposed to remain there, until the defeat or victory was decided. I own now, I could not help seeing which way the fate of the day was likely to turn. There was something gloomy and disastrous in the general aspect of all things around. Miss Pritchard had the headache: the barber who brought home Hagan's wig had powdered it like a wretch: amongst the gentlemen and ladies in the greenroom, I saw none but doubtful faces: and the manager (a very flippant, not to say impertinent gentleman, in my opinion, and who himself on that night looked as dismal as a mute at a funeral) had the insolence to say to me, "For Heaven's sake, Mr. Warrington, go and get a glass of punch at the Bedford, and don't frighten us all here by your dismal countenance!"

"Sir," says I, "I have a right, for five shillings, to comment upon your face, but I never gave you any authority to make remarks upon mine." "Sir," says he in a pet, "I most heartily wish I had never seen your face at all!" "Yours, sir!" said I, "has often amused me greatly; and when painted for Abel Drugger is exceedingly comic"—and indeed I have always done Mr. G. the justice to think that in low comedy he was unrivalled. I made him a bow, and walked off to the coffee-house, and for five years after never spoke a word to the gentleman, when he apologised to me, at a nobleman's house where we chanced to meet. I said I had utterly forgotten the circumstance to which he alluded, and that, on the first night of a play, no doubt author and manager were flurried alike. And added, "After all, there is no shame in not being made for the theatre. Mr. Garrick—you were." A compliment with which he appeared to be as well pleased as I intended he should.

Fidus Achates ran over to me at the end of the first act to say that all things were going pretty well; though he confessed to the titter in the house upon Miss Pritchard's first appearance, dressed exactly like an Indian princess.

"I cannot help it, Sampson," said I (filling him a bumper of good punch), "if Indians are dressed so."

"Why," says he, "would you have had Caractacus painted blue like an ancient Briton, or Bonduca with nothing but a cow-skin?" And indeed it may be that the fidelity to history was the cause of the ridicule cast on my tragedy, in which case I, for one, am not ashamed of its defeat.

After the second act, my aide-de-camp came from the field with dismal news indeed. I don't know how it is that, nervous before action, in disaster I become pretty cool and cheerful. [The writer seems to contradict himself here, having just boasted of possessing a pretty equanimous disposition. He was probably mistaken in his own estimate of himself, as other folks have been besides.-ED.] "Are things going ill?" says I. I call for my reckoning, put on my hat, and march to the theatre as calmly as if I was going to dine at the Temple; fidus Achates walking by my side, pressing my elbow, kicking the link-boys out of the way, and crying, "By George, Mr. Warrington, you are a man of spirit—a Trojan, sir!" So, there were men of spirit in Troy; but alas! fate was too strong for them.

At any rate, no man can say that I did not bear my misfortune with calmness: I could no more help the clamour and noise of the audience than a captain can help the howling and hissing of the storm in which his ship goes down. But I was determined that the rushing waves and broken masts should impavidum ferient, and flatter myself that I bore my calamity without flinching. "Not Regulus, my dear madam, could step into his barrel more coolly," Sampson said to my wife. 'Tis unjust to say of men of the parasitic nature that they are unfaithful in misfortune. Whether I was prosperous or poor, the wild parson was equally true and friendly, and shared our crust as eagerly as ever he had partaken of our better fortune.

I took my place on the stage, whence I could see the actors of my poor piece, and a portion of the audience who condemned me. I suppose the performers gave me a wide berth out of pity for me. I must say that I think I was as little moved as any spectator; and that no one would have judged from my mien that I was the unlucky hero of the night.

But my dearest Theo, when I went home, looked so pale and white, that I saw from the dear creature's countenance that the knowledge of my disaster had preceded my return. Spencer, Sampson, cousin Hagan, and Lady Maria were to come after the play, and congratulate the author, God wot! (Poor Miss Pritchard was engaged to us likewise, but sent word that I must understand that she was a great deal too unwell to sup that night.) My friend the gardener of Bedford House had given my wife his best flowers to decorate her little table. There they were; the poor little painted standards—and the battle lost! I had borne the defeat well enough, but as I looked at the sweet pale face of the wife across the table, and those artless trophies of welcome which she had set up for her hero, I confess my courage gave way, and my heart felt a pang almost as keen as any that ever has smitten it.

Our meal, it may be imagined, was dismal enough, nor was it rendered much gayer by the talk we strove to carry on. Old Mrs. Hagan was, luckily, very ill at this time; and her disease, and the incidents connected with it, a great blessing to us. Then we had his Majesty's approaching marriage, about which there was a talk. (How well I remember the most futile incidents of the day down to a tune which a carpenter was whistling by my side at the playhouse, just before the dreary curtain fell!) Then we talked about the death of good Mr. Richardson, the author of Pamela and Clarissa, whose works we all admired exceedingly. And as we talked about Clarissa, my wife took on herself to wipe her eyes once or twice, and say, faintly, "You know, my love, mamma and I could never help crying over that dear book. Oh, my dearest, dearest mother" (she adds), "how I wish she could be with me now!" This was an occasion for more open tears, for of course a young lady may naturally weep for her absent mother. And then we mixed a gloomy bowl with Jamaica limes, and drank to the health of his Excellency the Governor: and then, for a second toast, I filled a bumper, and, with a smiling face, drank to "our better fortune!"

This was too much. The two women flung themselves into each other's arms, and irrigated each other's neck-handkerchiefs with tears. "Oh, Maria! Is not—is not my George good and kind?" sobs Theo. "Look at my Hagan—how great, how godlike he was in his part!" gasps Maria. "It was a beastly cabal which threw him over—and I could plunge this knife into Mr. Garrick's black heart—the odious little wretch!" and she grasps a weapon at her side. But throwing it presently down, the enthusiastic creature rushes up to her lord and master, flings her arms round him, and embraces him in the presence of the little company.

I am not sure whether some one else did not do likewise. We were all in a state of extreme excitement and enthusiasm. In the midst of grief, Love the consoler appears amongst us, and soothes us with such fond blandishments and tender caresses, that one scarce wishes the calamity away. Two or three days afterwards, on our birthday, a letter was brought me in my study, which contained the following lines:—

"FROM POCAHONTAS

"Returning from the cruel fight
How pale and faint appears my knight!
He sees me anxious at his side;
'Why seek, my love, your wounds to hide?
Or deem your English girl afraid

To emulate the Indian maid?'

> "Be mine my husband's grief to cheer,
> In peril to be ever near;
> Whate'er of ill or woe betide,
> To bear it clinging at his side;
> The poisoned stroke of fate to ward,
> His bosom with my own to guard;
> Ah! could it spare a pang to his,
> It could not know a purer bliss!
> 'Twould gladden as it felt the smart,
> And thank the hand that flung the dart!"

I do not say the verses are very good, but that I like them as well as if they were—and that the face of the writer (whose sweet young voice I fancy I can hear as I hum the lines), when I went into her drawing-room after getting the letter, and when I saw her blushing and blessing me—seemed to me more beautiful than any I can fancy out of Heaven.

CHAPTER LXXXI. Res Angusta Domi

I have already described my present feelings as an elderly gentleman, regarding that rash jump into matrimony, which I persuaded my dear partner to take with me when we were both scarce out of our teens. As a man and a father—with a due sense of the necessity of mutton chops, and the importance of paying the baker—with a pack of rash children round about us who might be running off to Scotland to-morrow, and pleading papa's and mamma's example for their impertinence,—I know that I ought to be very cautious in narrating this early part of the married life of George Warrington, Esquire, and Theodosia his wife—to call out mea culpa, and put on a demure air, and, sitting in my comfortable easy-chair here, profess to be in a white sheet and on the stool of repentance, offering myself up as a warning to imprudent and hot-headed youth.

But, truth to say, that married life, regarding which my dear relatives prophesied so gloomily, has disappointed all those prudent and respectable people. It has had its trials; but I can remember them without bitterness—its passionate griefs, of which time, by God's kind ordinance, has been the benign consoler—its days of poverty, which we bore, who endured it, to the wonder of our sympathising relatives looking on—its precious rewards and blessings, so great that I scarce dare to whisper them to this page; to speak of them, save with awful respect and to One Ear, to which are offered up the prayers and thanks of all men. To marry without a competence is wrong and dangerous, no doubt, and a crime against our social codes; but do not scores of thousands of our fellow-beings commit the crime every year with no other trust but in, Heaven, health, and their labour? Are young people entering into the married life not to take hope into account, nor dare to begin their housekeeping until the cottage is completely furnished, the cellar and larder stocked, the cupboard full of plate, and the strong-box of money? The increase and multiplication of the world would stop, were the laws which regulate the genteel part of it to be made universal. Our gentlefolks tremble at the brink in their silk stockings and pumps, and wait for whole years, until they find a bridge or a gilt barge to carry them across; our poor do not fear to wet their bare feet, plant them in the brook, and trust to fate and strength to bear them over. Who would like to consign his daughter to poverty? Who would counsel his son to undergo the countless risks of poor married life, to remove the beloved girl from comfort and competence, and subject her to debt, misery, privation, friendlessness, sickness, and the hundred gloomy consequences of the res angusta domi? I look at my own wife and ask her pardon for having imposed a task so fraught with pain and danger upon one so gentle. I think of the trials she endured, and am thankful for them and for that unfailing love and constancy with which God blessed her and strengthened her to bear them all. On this question of marriage, I am not a fair judge: my own was so imprudent—and has been so happy, that I must not dare to give young people counsel. I have endured poverty, but scarcely ever found it otherwise than tolerable: had I not undergone it, I never could have known the kindness of friends, the delight of gratitude, the surprising joys and consolations which sometimes accompany the scanty meal and narrow fire, and cheer the long day's labour. This at least is certain, in respect of the lot of the decent poor, that a great deal of superfluous pity is often thrown away upon it. Good-natured fine folks, who sometimes stepped out of the sunshine of their riches into a narrow obscurity, were blinded as it were, whilst we could see quite cheerfully and clearly: they stumbled over obstacles which were none to us: they were surprised at the resignation with which we drank small beer, and that we could heartily say grace over such very cold mutton.

 The good General, my father-in-law, had married his Molly, when he was a subaltern of a foot regiment, and had a purse scarce better filled than my own. They had had their ups and downs of fortune. I think (though my wife will never confess to this point) they had married, as people could do in their young time, without previously asking papa's and mamma's leave. [The Editor has looked through Burn's Registers of Fleet Marriages without finding the names of Martin Lambert and Mary Benson.] At all events, they were so well pleased with their own good luck in matrimony, that they did not grudge their children's, and were by no means frightened at the idea of any little hardships which we in the course of our married life might be called upon to undergo. And I suppose when I made my own pecuniary statements to Mr. Lambert, I was anxious to deceive both of us. Believing me to be master of a couple of thousand pounds, he went to Jamaica quite easy in his mind as to his darling daughter's comfort and maintenance, at least for some years to come. After paying the expenses of his family's outfit, the worthy man went away not much richer than his son-in-law; and a few trinkets, and some lace of Aunt Lambert's, with twenty new guineas in a purse which her mother and sisters made for her, were my Theo's marriage portion. But in valuing my stock, I chose to count as a good debt a sum which my honoured mother never could be got to acknowledge up to the day when the resolute old lady was called to pay the last debt of all. The sums I had disbursed for her, she argued, were spent for the improvement and maintenance of the estate which was to be mine at her decease. What money she could spare was to be for my poor brother, who had nothing, who would never have spent his own means had he not imagined himself to be sole heir of the Virginian property, as he would have been—the good lady took care to emphasise this point in many of her letters—but for a half-hour's accident of birth. He was now distinguishing himself in the service of his king and country. To purchase his promotion was his mother's, she should suppose his brother's duty! When I had finished my bar-studies and my dramatic amusements, Madam Esmond informed me that I was welcome to return home and take that place in our colony to which my birth entitled me. This statement she communicated to me more than once through Mountain, and before the news of my marriage had reached her.

There is no need to recall her expressions of maternal indignation when she was informed of the step I had taken. On the pacification of Canada, my dear Harry asked for leave of absence, and dutifully paid a visit to Virginia. He wrote, describing his reception at home, and the splendid entertainments which my mother made in honour of her son. Castlewood, which she had not inhabited since our departure for Europe, was thrown open again to our friends of the colony; and the friend of Wolfe, and the soldier of Quebec, was received by all our acquaintance with every becoming honour. Some dismal quarrels, to be sure, ensued, because my brother persisted in maintaining his friendship with Colonel Washington, of Mount Vernon, whose praises Harry never was tired of singing. Indeed I allow the gentleman every virtue; and in the struggles which terminated so fatally for England a few years since, I can admire as well as his warmest friends, General Washington's glorious constancy and success.

If these battles between Harry and our mother were frequent, as, in his letters, he described them to be, I wondered, for my part, why he should continue at home? One reason naturally suggested itself to my mind, which I scarcely liked to communicate to Mrs. Warrington; for we had both talked over our dear little Hetty's romantic attachment for my brother, and wondered that he had never discovered it. I need not say, I suppose, that my gentleman had found some young lady at home more to his taste than our dear Hester, and hence accounted for his prolonged stay in Virginia.

Presently there came, in a letter from him, not a full confession but an admission of this interesting fact. A person was described, not named—a Being all beauty and perfection, like other young ladies under similar circumstances. My wife asked to see the letter: I could not help showing it, and handed it to her, with a very sad face. To my surprise she read it, without exhibiting any corresponding sorrow of her own.

"I have thought of this before, my love," I said. "I feel with you for your disappointment regarding poor Hetty."

"Ah! poor Hetty," says Theo, looking down at the carpet.

"It would never have done," says I.

"No—they would not have been happy," sighs Theo.

"How strange he never should have found out her secret!" I continued.

She looked me full in the face with an odd expression. "Pray, what does that look mean?" I asked.

"Nothing, my dear—nothing! only I am not surprised!" says Theo, blushing.

"What," I ask, "can there be another?"

"I am sure I never said so, George," says the lady, hurriedly. "But if Hetty has overcome her childish folly, ought we not all to be glad? Do you gentlemen suppose that you only are to fall in love and grow tired, indeed?"

"What!" I say, with a strange commotion of my mind. "Do you mean to tell me, Theo, that you ever cared for any one but me?"

"Oh, George," she whimpers, "when I was at school, there was—there was one of the boys of Doctor Backhouse's school, who sate in the loft next to us; and I thought he had lovely eyes, and I was so shocked when I recognised him behind the counter at Mr. Grigg's the mercer's, when I went to buy a cloak for baby, and I wanted to tell you, my dear, and I didn't know how!"

I went to see this creature with the lovely eyes, having made my wife describe the fellow's dress to me, and I saw a little bandy-legged wretch in a blue camlet coat, with his red hair tied with a dirty ribbon, about whom I forbore generously even to reproach my wife; nor will she ever know that I have looked at the fellow, until she reads the confession in this page. If our wives saw us as we are, I thought, would they love us as they do? Are we as much mistaken in them, as they in us? I look into one candid face at least, and think it never has deceived me.

Lest I should encourage my young people to an imitation of my own imprudence, I will not tell them with how small a capital Mrs. Theo and I commenced life. The unfortunate tragedy brought us nothing; though the reviewers, since its publication of late, have spoken not unfavourably as to its merits, and Mr. Kemble himself has done me the honour to commend it. Our kind friend Lord Wrotham was for having the piece published by subscription, and sent me a bank-note, with a request that I would let him have a hundred copies for his friends; but I was always averse to that method of levying money, and, preferring my poverty sine dote, locked up my manuscript, with my poor girl's verses inserted at the first page. I know not why the piece should have given such offence at court, except for the fact that an actor who had run off with an earl's daughter, performed a principal part in the play; but I was told that sentiments which I had put into the mouths of some of the Indian characters (who were made to declaim against ambition, the British desire of rule, and so forth), were pronounced dangerous and unconstitutional; so that the little hope of royal favour, which I might have had, was quite taken away from me.

What was to be done? A few months after the failure of the tragedy, as I counted up the remains of my fortune (the calculation was not long or difficult), I came to the conclusion that I must beat a retreat out of my pretty apartments in Bloomsbury, and so gave warning to our good landlady, informing her that my wife's health required that we should have lodgings in the country. But we went no farther than Lambeth, our faithful Gumbo and Molly following us; and here, though as poor as might be, we were waited on by a maid and a lackey in livery, like any folks of condition. You may be sure kind relatives cried out against our extravagance; indeed, are they not the people who find our faults out for us, and proclaim them to the rest of the world?

Returning home from London one day, whither I had been on a visit to some booksellers, I recognised the family arms and livery on a grand gilt chariot which stood before a public-house near to our lodgings. A few loitering inhabitants were gathered round the splendid vehicle, and looking with awe at the footmen, resplendent in the sun, and quaffing blazing pots of beer. I found my Lady Castlewood seated opposite to my wife in our little apartment (whence we had a very bright, pleasant prospect of the river, covered with barges and wherries, and the ancient towers and trees of the Archbishop's palace and gardens), and Mrs. Theo, who has a very droll way of describing persons and scenes, narrated to me all the particulars of her ladyship's conversation, when she took her leave.

"I have been here this ever-so-long," says the Countess, "gossiping with cousin Theo, while you have been away at the coffee-house, I dare say, making merry with your friends, and drinking your punch and coffee. Guess she must find it rather lonely here, with nothing to do but work them little caps and hem them frocks. Never mind, dear; reckon you'll soon have a companion who will amuse you when cousin George is away at his coffee-house! What a nice lodging you have got here, I do declare! Our new house which we have took is twenty times as big, and covered with gold from top to bottom; but I like this quite as well. Bless you being rich is no better than being poor. When we lived to Albany, and I did most all the work myself, scoured the rooms, biled the kettle, helped the wash, and all, I was just as happy as I am now. We only had one old negro to keep the store. Why don't you sell Gumbo, cousin George? He ain't no use here idling and dawdling about, and making love to the servant-girl. Fogh! guess they ain't particular, these English people!" So she talked, rattling on with perfect good-humour, until her hour for departure came; when she produced a fine repeating watch, and said it was time for her to pay a call upon her Majesty at Buckingham House. "And mind you come to us, George," says her ladyship, waving a little parting hand out of the gilt coach. "Theo and I have settled all about it."

"Here, at least," said I, when the laced footmen had clambered up behind the carriage, and our magnificent little patroness had left us;—"here is one who is not afraid of our poverty, nor ashamed to remember her own."

"Ashamed!" said Theo, resuming her lilliputian needlework. "To do her justice, she would make herself at home in any kitchen or palace in the world.

She has given me and Molly twenty lessons in housekeeping. She says, when she was at home to Albany, she roasted, baked, swept the house, and milked the cow." (Madam Theo pronounced the word cow archly in our American way, and imitated her ladyship's accent very divertingly.)

"And she has no pride," I added. "It was good-natured of her to ask us to dine with her and my lord. When will Uncle Warrington ever think of offering us a crust again, or a glass of his famous beer?"

"Yes, it was not ill-natured to invite us," says Theo, slily. "But, my dear, you don't know all the conditions!" And then my wife, still imitating the Countess's manner, laughingly informed me what these conditions were. "She took out her pocket-book, and told me," says Theo, "what days she was engaged abroad and at home. On Monday she received a Duke and a Duchess, with several other members of my lord's house, and their ladies. On Tuesday came more earls, two bishops, and an ambassador. 'Of course you won't come on them days?' says the Countess. 'Now you are so poor, you know, that fine company ain't no good for you. Lord bless you! father never dines on our company days! he don't like it; he takes a bit of cold meat anyways.' On which," says Theo, laughing, "I told her that Mr. Warrington did not care for any but the best of company, and proposed that she should ask us on some day when the Archbishop of Canterbury dined with her, and his Grace must give us a lift home in his coach to Lambeth. And she is an economical little person, too," continues Theo. "'I thought of bringing with me some of my baby's caps and things, which his lordship has outgrown 'em, but they may be wanted again, you know, my dear.' And so we lose that addition to our wardrobe," says Theo, smiling, "and Molly and I must do our best without her ladyship's charity. 'When people are poor, they are poor,' the Countess said, with her usual outspokenness, 'and must get on the best they can. What we shall do for that poor Maria, goodness only knows! we can't ask her to see us as we can you, though you are so poor: but an earl's daughter to marry a play-actor! La, my dear, it's dreadful: his Majesty and the Princess have both spoken of it! Every other noble family in this kingdom as has ever heard of it pities us; though I have a plan for helping those poor unhappy people, and have sent down Simons, my groom of the chambers, to tell them on it.' This plan was, that Hagan, who had kept almost all his terms at Dublin College, should return thither and take his degree, and enter into holy orders, 'when we will provide him with a chaplaincy at home, you know,' Lady Castlewood added." And I may mention here, that this benevolent plan was executed a score of months later; when I was enabled myself to be of service to Mr. Hagan, who was one of the kindest and best of our friends during our own time of want and distress. Castlewood then executed his promise loyally enough, got orders and a colonial appointment for Hagan, who distinguished himself both as soldier and preacher, as we shall presently hear; but not a guinea did his lordship spare to aid either his sister or his kinsman in their trouble. I never asked him, thank Heaven, to assist me in my own; though, to do him justice, no man could express himself more amiably, and with a joy which I believe was quite genuine, when my days of poverty were ended.

As for my Uncle Warrington, and his virtuous wife and daughters, let me do them justice likewise, and declare that throughout my period of trial, their sorrow at my poverty was consistent and unvarying. I still had a few acquaintances who saw them, and of course (as friends will) brought me a report of their opinions and conversation; and I never could hear that my relatives had uttered one single good word about me or my wife. They spoke even of my tragedy as a crime—I was accustomed to hear that sufficiently maligned—of the author as a miserable reprobate, for ever reeling about Grub Street, in rags and squalor. They held me out no hand of help. My poor wife might cry in her pain, but they had no twopence to bestow upon her. They went to church a half-dozen times in the week. They subscribed to many public charities. Their tribe was known eighteen hundred years ago, and will flourish as long as men endure. They will still thank Heaven that they are not as other folks are; and leave the wounded and miserable to other succour.

I don't care to recall the dreadful doubts and anxieties which began to beset me; the plan after plan which I tried, and in which I failed, for procuring work and adding to our dwindling stock of money. I bethought me of my friend Mr. Johnson, and when I think of the eager kindness with which he received me, am ashamed of some pert speeches which I own to have made regarding his manners and behaviour. I told my story and difficulties to him, the circumstance of my marriage, and the prospects before me. He would not for a moment admit they were gloomy, or, si male nunc, that they would continue to be so. I had before me the chances, certainly very slender, of a place in England; the inheritance which must be mine in the course of nature, or at any rate would fall to the heir I was expecting. I had a small stock of money for present actual necessity—a possibility, "though, to be free with you, sir" (says he), "after the performance of your tragedy, I doubt whether nature has endowed you with those peculiar qualities which are necessary for achieving a remarkable literary success"—and finally a submission to the maternal rule, and a return to Virginia, where plenty and a home were always ready for me. "Why, sir!" he cried, "such a sum as you mention would have been a fortune to me when I began the world, and my friend Mr. Goldsmith would set up a coach-and-six on it. With youth, hope, to-day, and a couple of hundred pounds in cash—no young fellow need despair. Think, sir, you have a year at least before you, and who knows what may chance between now and then. Why, sir, your relatives here may provide for you, or you may succeed to your Virginian property, or you may come into a fortune!" I did not in the course of that year, but he did. My Lord Bute gave Mr. Johnson a pension, which set all Grub Street in a fury against the recipient, who, to be sure, had published his own not very flattering opinion upon pensions and pensioners.

Nevertheless, he did not altogether discourage my literary projects, promised to procure me work from the booksellers, and faithfully performed that kind promise. "But," says he, "sir, you must not appear amongst them in forma pauperis.—Have you never a friend's coach, in which we can ride to see them?

You must put on your best laced hat and waistcoat; and we must appear, sir, as if we were doing them a favour." This stratagem answered, and procured me respect enough at the first visit or two; but when the booksellers knew that I wanted to be paid for my work, their backs refused to bend any more, and they treated me with a familiarity which I could ill stomach. I overheard one of them, who had been a footman, say, "Oh, it's Pocahontas, is it? let him wait." And he told his boy to say as much to me. "Wait, sir?" says I, fuming with rage and putting my head into his parlour, "I'm not accustomed to waiting, but I have heard you are." And I strode out of the shop into Pall Mall in a mighty fluster.

And yet Mr. D. was in the right. I came to him, if not to ask a favour, at any rate to propose a bargain, and surely it was my business to wait his time and convenience. In more fortunate days I asked the gentleman's pardon, and the kind author of the Muse in Livery was instantly appeased.

I was more prudent, or Mr. Johnson more fortunate, in an application elsewhere, and Mr. Johnson procured me a little work from the booksellers in translating from foreign languages, of which I happen to know two or three. By a hard day's labour I could earn a few shillings; so few that a week's work would hardly bring me a guinea: and that was flung to me with insolent patronage by the low hucksters who employed me. I can put my finger upon two or three magazine articles written at this period, and paid for with a few wretched shillings, which papers as I read them awaken in me the keenest pangs of bitter remembrance. [Mr. George Warrington, of the Upper Temple, says he remembers a book, containing his grandfather's book-plate, in which were pasted various extracts from reviews and newspapers in an old type, and lettered outside Les Chains de l'Esclavage. These were no doubt the contributions above mentioned; but the volume has not been found, either in the town-house or in the library at Warrington Manor. The Editor, by the way, is not answerable for a certain inconsistency, which may be remarked in the narrative. The writer says earlier, that he speaks without bitterness of past times, and presently falls into a fury with them. The same manner of forgiving our enemies is not uncommon in the present century.] I recall the doubts and fears which agitated me, see the dear wife nursing her infant and looking up into my face with hypocritical smiles that vainly try to mask her alarm: the struggles of pride are fought over again: the wounds under which I smarted re-open. There are some acts of injustice committed against me which I don't know how to forgive; and which, whenever I think of them, awaken in me the same feelings of revolt and indignation. The gloom and darkness gather over me—till they are relieved by a reminiscence of that love and tenderness which through all gloom and darkness have been my light and consolation.

CHAPTER LXXXII. Miles's Moidore

Little Miles made his appearance in this world within a few days of the gracious Prince who commands his regiment. Illuminations and cannonading saluted the Royal George's birth, multitudes were admitted to see him as he lay behind a gilt railing at the Palace with noble nurses watching over him. Few nurses guarded the cradle of our little Prince; no courtiers, no faithful retainers saluted it, except our trusty Gumbo and kind Molly, who to be sure loved and admired the little heir of my poverty as loyally as our hearts could desire. Why was our boy not named George like the other paragon just mentioned, and like his father? I gave him the name of a little scapegrace of my family, a name which many generations of Warringtons had borne likewise; but my poor little Miles's love and kindness touched me at a time when kindness and love were rare from those of my own blood, and Theo and I agreed that our child should be called after that single little friend of my paternal race.

We wrote to acquaint our royal parents with the auspicious event, and bravely inserted the child's birth in the Daily Advertiser, and the place, Church Street, Lambeth, where he was born. "My dear," says Aunt Bernstein, writing to me in reply to my announcement, "how could you point out to all the world that you live in such a trou as that in which you have buried yourself? I kiss the little mamma, and send a remembrance for the child." This remembrance was a fine silk coverlid, with a lace edging fit for a prince. It was not very useful: the price of the lace would have served us much better, but Theo and Molly were delighted with the present, and my eldest son's cradle had a cover as fine as any nobleman's.

Good Dr. Heberden came over several times to visit my wife, and see that all things went well. He knew and recommended to us a surgeon in the vicinage, who took charge of her; luckily, my dear patient needed little care, beyond that which our landlady and her own trusty attendant could readily afford her. Again our humble precinct was adorned with the gilded apparition of Lady Castlewood's chariot wheels; she brought a pot of jelly, which she thought Theo might like, and which, no doubt, had been served at one of her ladyship's banquets on a previous day. And she told us of all the ceremonies at court, and of the splendour and festivities attending the birth of the august heir to the crown; Our good Mr. Johnson happened to pay me a visit on one of those days when my lady countess's carriage flamed up to our little gate. He was not a little struck by her magnificence, and made her some bows, which were more respectful than graceful. She called me cousin very affably, and helped to transfer the present of jelly from her silver dish into our crockery pan with much benignity. The Doctor tasted the sweetmeat, and pronounced it to be excellent. "The great, sir," says he, "are fortunate in every way. They can engage the most skilful practitioners of the culinary art, as they can assemble the most amiable wits round their table. If, as you think, sir, and, from the appearance of the dish, your suggestion at least is plausible, this sweetmeat may have appeared already at his lordship's table, it has been there in good company. It has quivered under the eyes of celebrated beauties, it has been tasted by ruby lips, it has divided the attention of the distinguished company, with fruits, tarts, and creams, which I make no doubt were like itself delicious." And so saying, the good Doctor absorbed a considerable portion of Lady Castlewood's benefaction; though as regards the epithet delicious I am bound to say, that my poor wife, after tasting the jelly, put it away from her as not to her liking; and Molly, flinging up her head, declared it was mouldy.

My boy enjoyed at least the privilege of having an earl's daughter for his godmother; for this office was performed by his cousin, our poor Lady Maria, whose kindness and attention to the mother and the infant were beyond all praise; and who, having lost her own solitary chance for maternal happiness, yearned over our child in a manner not a little touching to behold. Captain Miles is a mighty fine gentleman, and his uniforms of the Prince's Hussars as splendid as any that ever bedizened a soldier of fashion; but he hath too good a heart, and is too true a gentleman, let us trust, not to be thankful when he remembers that his own infant limbs were dressed in some of the little garments which had been prepared for the poor player's child. Sampson christened him in that very chapel in Southwark, where our marriage ceremony had been performed. Never were the words of the Prayer-book more beautifully and impressively read than by the celebrant of the service; except at its end, when his voice failed him, and he and the rest of the little congregation were fain to wipe their eyes. "Mr. Garrick himself, sir," says Hagan, "could not have read those words so nobly. I am sure little innocent never entered the world accompanied by wishes and benedictions more tender and sincere."

And now I have not told how it chanced that the Captain came by his name of Miles. A couple of days before his christening, when as yet I believe it was intended that our firstborn should bear his father's name, a little patter of horse's hoofs comes galloping up to our gate; and who should pull at the bell but young Miles, our cousin? I fear he had disobeyed his parents when he galloped away on that undutiful journey.

"You know," says he, "cousin Harry gave me my little horse; and I can't help liking you, because you are so like Harry, and because they're always saying things of you at home, and it's a shame; and I have brought my whistle and coral that my godmamma Lady Suckling gave me, for your little boy; and if you're so poor, cousin George, here's my gold moidore, and it's worth ever so much, and it's no use to me, because I mayn't spend it, you know."

We took the boy up to Theo in her room (he mounted the stair in his little tramping boots, of which he was very proud); and Theo kissed him, and thanked him; and his moidore has been in her purse from that day.

My mother, writing through her ambassador as usual, informed me of her royal surprise and displeasure on learning that my son had been christened Miles—a name not known, at least in the Esmond family. I did not care to tell the reason at the time; but when, in after years, I told Madam Esmond how my boy came by his name, I saw a tear roll down her wrinkled cheek, and I heard afterwards that she had asked Gumbo many questions about the boy who gave his name to our Miles—our Miles Gloriosus of Pall Mall, Valenciennes, Almack's, Brighton.

CHAPTER LXXXIII. Troubles and Consolations

In our early days at home, when Harry and I used to be so undutiful to our tutor, who would have thought that Mr. Esmond Warrington of Virginia would turn Bearleader himself? My mother (when we came together again) never could be got to speak directly of this period of my life; but would allude to it as "that terrible time, my love, which I can't bear to think of," "those dreadful years when there was difference between us," and so forth; and though my pupil, a worthy and grateful man, sent me out to Jamestown several barrels of that liquor by which his great fortune was made, Madam Esmond spoke of him as "your friend in England," "your wealthy Lambeth friend," etc., but never by his name; nor did she ever taste a drop of his beer. We brew our own too at Warrington Manor, but our good Mr. Foker never fails to ship to Ipswich every year a couple of butts of his entire. His son is a young sprig of fashion, and has married an earl's daughter; the father is a very worthy and kind gentleman, and it is to the luck of making his acquaintance that I owe the receipt of some of the most welcome guineas that ever I received in my life.

It was not so much the sum, as the occupation and hope given me by the office of Governor, which I took on myself, which were then so precious to me. Mr. F.'s Brewery (the site has since been changed) then stood near to Pedlar's Acre in Lambeth and the surgeon who attended my wife in her confinement, likewise took care of the wealthy brewer's family. He was a Bavarian, originally named Voelker. Mr. Lance, the surgeon, I suppose, made him acquainted with my name and history. The worthy doctor would smoke many a pipe of Virginia in my garden, and had conceived an attachment for me and my family. He brought his patron to my house; and when Mr. F. found that I had a smattering of his language, and could sing "Prinz Eugen the noble Ritter" (a song that my grandfather had brought home from the Marlborough wars), the German conceived a great friendship for me: his lady put her chair and her chariot at Mrs. Warrington's service: his little daughter took a prodigious fancy to our baby (and to do him justice, the Captain, who is as ugly a fellow now as ever wore a queue, was beautiful as an infant) [The very image of the Squire at 30, everybody says so. M. W. (Note in the MS.)]: and his son and heir, Master Foker, being much maltreated at Westminster School because of his father's profession of brewer, the parents asked if I would take charge of him; and paid me a not insufficient sum for superintending his education.

Mr. F. was a shrewd man of business, and as he and his family really interested themselves in me and mine, I laid all my pecuniary affairs pretty unreservedly before him; and my statement, he was pleased to say, augmented the respect and regard which he felt for me. He laughed at our stories of the aid which my noble relatives had given me—my aunt's coverlid, my Lady

Castlewood's mouldy jelly, Lady Warrington's contemptuous treatment of us. But he wept many tears over the story of little Miles's moidore; and as for Sampson and Hagan, "I wow," says he, "dey shall have so much beer als ever dey can drink." He sent his wife to call upon Lady Maria, and treated her with the utmost respect and obsequiousness, whenever she came to visit him. It was with Mr. Foker that Lady Maria stayed when Hagan went to Dublin to complete his college terms; and the good brewer's purse also ministered to our friend's wants and supplied his outfit.

When Mr. Foker came fully to know my own affairs and position, he was pleased to speak of me with terms of enthusiasm, and as if my conduct showed some extraordinary virtue. I have said how my mother saved money for Harry, and how the two were in my debt. But when Harry spent money, he spent it fancying it to be his; Madam Esmond never could be made to understand she was dealing hardly with me—the money was paid and gone, and there was an end of it. Now, at the end of '62, I remember Harry sent over a considerable remittance for the purchase of his promotion, begging me at the same time to remember that he was in my debt, and to draw on his agents if I had any need. He did not know how great the need was, or how my little capital had been swallowed.

Well, to take my brother's money would delay his promotion, and I naturally did not draw on him, though I own I was tempted; nor, knowing my dear General Lambert's small means, did I care to impoverish him by asking for supplies. These simple acts of forbearance my worthy brewer must choose to consider as instances of exalted virtue. And what does my gentleman do but write privately to my brother in America, lauding me and my wife as the most admirable of human beings, and call upon Madame de Bernstein, who never told me of his visit indeed, but who, I perceived, about this time treated us with singular respect and gentleness, that surprised me in one whom I could not but consider as selfish and worldly. In after days I remember asking him how he had gained admission to the Baroness? He laughed: "De Baroness!" says he. "I knew de Baron when he was a walet at Munich, and I was a brewer-apprentice." I think our family had best not be too curious about our uncle the Baron.

Thus, the part of my life which ought to have been most melancholy was in truth made pleasant by many friends, happy circumstances, and strokes of lucky fortune. The bear I led was a docile little cub, and danced to my piping very readily. Better to lead him about, than to hang round booksellers' doors, or wait the pleasure or caprice of managers! My wife and I, during our exile, as we may call it, spent very many pleasant evenings with these kind friends and benefactors. Nor were we without intellectual enjoyments; Mrs. Foker and Mrs. Warrington sang finely together; and sometimes when I was in the mood, I read my own play of Pocahontas, to this friendly audience, in a manner better than Hagan's own, Mr. Foker was pleased to say.

After that little escapade of Miles Warrington, junior, I saw nothing of him, and heard of my paternal relatives but rarely. Sir Miles was assiduous at court (as I believe he would have been at Nero's), and I laughed one day when Mr. Foker told me that he had heard on 'Change "that they were going to make my uncle a Beer."—"A Beer?" says I in wonder. "Can't you understand de vort, ven I say it?" says the testy old gentleman. "Vell, veil, a Lort!" Sir, Miles indeed was the obedient humble servant of the Minister, whoever he might be. I am surprised he did not speak English with a Scotch accent during the first favourite's brief reign. I saw him and his wife coming from court, when Mrs. Claypool was presented to her Majesty on her marriage. I had my little boy on my shoulder. My uncle and aunt stared resolutely at me from their gilt coach window. The footmen looked blank over their nosegays. Had I worn the Fairy's cap and been invisible, my father's brother could not have passed me with less notice.

We did not avail ourselves much, or often, of that queer invitation of Lady Castlewood, to go and drink tea and sup with her ladyship when there was no other company. Old Van den Bosch, however shrewd his intellect, and great his skill in making a fortune, was not amusing in conversation, except to his daughter, who talked household and City matters, bulling and bearing, raising and selling farming-stock, and so forth, quite as keenly and shrewdly as her father. Nor was my Lord Castlewood often at home, or much missed by his wife when absent, or very much at ease in the old father's company. The Countess told all this to my wife in her simple way. "Guess," says she, "my lord and father don't pull well together nohow. Guess my lord is always wanting money, and father keeps the key of the box and quite right, too. If he could have the fingering of all our money, my lord would soon make away with it, and then what's to become of our noble family? We pay everything, my dear (except play-debts, and them we won't have nohow). We pay cooks, horses, wine-merchants, tailors, and everybody—and lucky for them too—reckon my lord wouldn't pay 'em! And we always take care that he has a guinea in his pocket, and goes out like a real nobleman. What that man do owe to us: what he did before we come—gracious goodness only knows! Me and father does our best to make him respectable: but it's no easy job, my dear. Law! he'd melt the plate, only father keeps the key of the strong-room; and when we go to Castlewood, my father travels with me, and papa is armed too, as well as the people."

"Gracious heavens!" cries my wife, "your ladyship does not mean to say you suspect your own husband of a desire to———"

"To what?—Oh no, nothing, of course! And I would trust our brother Will with untold money, wouldn't I? As much as I'd trust the cat with the cream-pan! I tell you, my dear, it's not all pleasure being a woman of rank and fashion: and if I have bought a countess's coronet, I have paid a good price for it—that I have!"

And so had my Lord Castlewood paid a large price for having his estate freed from incumbrances, his houses and stables furnished, and his debts discharged. He was the slave of the little wife and her father. No wonder the old man's society was not pleasant to the poor victim, and that he gladly slunk away from his own fine house, to feast at the club when he had money, or at least to any society save that which he found at home. To lead a bear, as I did, was no very pleasant business, to be sure: to wait in a bookseller's anteroom until it should please his honour to finish his dinner and give me audience, was sometimes a hard task for a man of my name and with my pride; but would I have exchanged my poverty against Castlewood's ignominy, or preferred his miserable dependence to my own? At least I earned my wage, such as it was; and no man can say that I ever flattered my patrons, or was servile to them; or indeed, in my dealings with them, was otherwise than sulky, overbearing, and, in a word, intolerable.

Now there was a certain person with whom Fate had thrown me into a life-partnership, who bore her poverty with such a smiling sweetness and easy grace, that niggard Fortune relented before her, and, like some savage Ogre in the fairy tales, melted at the constant goodness and cheerfulness of that uncomplaining, artless, innocent creature. However poor she was, all who knew her saw that here was a fine lady; and the little tradesmen and humble folks round about us treated her with as much respect as the richest of our neighbours. "I think, my dear," says good-natured Mrs. Foker, when they rode out in the latter's chariot, "you look like the mistress of the carriage, and I only as your maid." Our landladies adored her; the tradesfolk executed her little orders as eagerly as if a duchess gave them, or they were to make a fortune by waiting on her. I have thought often of the lady in Comus, and how, through all the rout and rabble, she moves, entirely serene and pure.

Several times, as often as we chose indeed, the good-natured parents of my young bear lent us their chariot to drive abroad or to call on the few friends we had. If I must tell the truth, we drove once to the Protestant Hero and had a syllabub in the garden there: and the hostess would insist upon calling my wife her ladyship during the whole afternoon. We also visited Mr. Johnson, and took tea with him (the ingenious Mr. Goldsmith was of the company); the Doctor waited upon my wife to her coach. But our most frequent visits were to Aunt Bernstein, and I promise you I was not at all jealous because my aunt presently professed to have a wonderful liking for Theo.

This liking grew so that she would have her most days in the week, or to stay altogether with her, and thought that Theo's child and husband were only plagues to be sure, and hated us in the most amusing way for keeping her favourite from her. Not that my wife was unworthy of anybody's favour; but her many forced absences, and the constant difficulty of intercourse with her, raised my aunt's liking for a while to a sort of passion. She poured in notes like love-letters; and her people were ever about our kitchen. If my wife did not go to her, she wrote heartrending appeals, and scolded me severely when I saw her; and, the child being ill once (it hath pleased Fate to spare our Captain to be a prodigious trouble to us, and a wholesome trial for our tempers), Madame Bernstein came three days running to Lambeth; vowed there was nothing the matter with the baby;—nothing at all;—and that we only pretended his illness, in order to vex her.

The reigning Countess of Castlewood was just as easy and affable with her old aunt, as with other folks great and small. "What air you all about, scraping and bowing to that old woman, I can't tell, noways!" her ladyship would say. "She a fine lady! Nonsense! She ain't no more fine than any other lady: and I guess I'm as good as any of 'em with their high heels and their grand airs! She a beauty once! Take away her wig, and her rouge, and her teeth; and what becomes of your beauty, I'd like to know? Guess you'd put it all in a bandbox, and there would be nothing left but a shrivelled old woman!" And indeed the little homilist only spoke too truly. All beauty must at last come to this complexion; and decay, either underground or on the tree. Here was old age, I fear, without reverence. Here were grey hairs, that were hidden or painted. The world was still here, and she tottering on it, and clinging to it with her crutch. For fourscore years she had moved on it, and eaten of the tree, forbidden and permitted. She had had beauty, pleasure, flattery: but what secret rages, disappointments, defeats, humiliations! what thorns under the roses! what stinging bees in the fruit! "You are not a beauty, my dear," she would say to my wife: "and may thank your stars that you are not." (If she contradicted herself in her talk, I suppose the rest of us occasionally do the like.) "Don't tell me that your husband is pleased with your face, and you want no one else's admiration! We all do. Every woman would rather be beautiful than be anything else in the world—ever so rich, or ever so good, or have all the gifts of the fairies! Look at that picture, though I know 'tis but a bad one, and that stupid vapouring Kneller could not paint my eyes, nor my hair, nor my complexion. What a shape I had then—and look at me now, and this wrinkled old neck! Why have we such a short time of our beauty? I remember Mademoiselle de l'Enclos at a much greater age than mine, quite fresh and well-conserved. We can't hide our ages. They are wrote in Mr. Collins's books for us. I was born in the last year of King James's reign. I am not old yet. I am but seventy-six. But what a wreck, my dear: and isn't it cruel that our time should be so short?"

Here my wife has to state the incontrovertible proposition, that the time of all of us is short here below.

"Ha!" cries the Baroness. "Did not Adam live near a thousand years, and was not Eve beautiful all the time? I used to perplex Mr. Tusher with that—poor creature! What have we done since, that our lives are so much lessened, I say?"

"Has your life been so happy that you would prolong it ever so much more?" asks the Baroness's auditor. "Have you, who love wit, never read Dean Swift's famous description of the deathless people in Gulliver? My papa and my husband say 'tis one of the finest and most awful sermons ever wrote. It were better not to live at all, than to live without love; and I'm sure," says my wife, putting her handkerchief to her eyes, "should anything happen to my dearest George, I would wish to go to Heaven that moment."

"Who loves me in Heaven? I am quite alone, child—that is why I had rather stay here," says the Baroness, in a frightened and rather piteous tone. "You are kind to me, God bless your sweet face! Though I scold, and have a frightful temper, my servants will do anything to make me comfortable, and get up at any hour of the night, and never say a cross word in answer. I like my cards still. Indeed, life would be a blank without 'em. Almost everything is gone except that. I can't eat my dinner now, since I lost those last two teeth. Everything goes away from us in old age. But I still have my cards—thank Heaven, I still have my cards!" And here she would begin to doze: waking up, however, if my wife stirred or rose, and imagining that Theo was about to leave her. "Don't go away, I can't bear to be alone. I don't want you to talk. But I like to see your face, my dear! It is much pleasanter than that horrid old Brett's, that I have had scowling about my bedroom these ever so long years."

"Well, Baroness! still at your cribbage?" (We may fancy a noble Countess interrupting a game at cards between Theo and Aunt Bernstein.) "Me and my Lord Esmond have come to see you! Go and shake hands with grandaunt, Esmond! and tell her ladyship that your lordship's a good boy!"

"My lordship's a good boy," says the child. (Madam Theo used to act these scenes for me in a very lively way.)

"And if he is, I guess he don't take after his father," shrieks out Lady Castlewood. She chose to fancy that Aunt Bernstein was deaf, and always bawled at the old lady.

"Your ladyship chose my nephew for better or for worse," says Aunt Bernstein, who was now always very much flurried in the presence of the young Countess.

"But he is a precious deal worse than ever I thought he was. I am speaking of your Pa, Ezzy. If it wasn't for your mother, my son, Lord knows what would become of you! We are a-going to see his little Royal Highness. Sorry to see your ladyship not looking quite so well to-day. We can't always remain young and law! how we do change as we grow old! Go up and kiss that lady, Ezzy. She has got a little boy, too. Why, bless us! have you got the child downstairs?" Indeed, Master Miles was down below, for special reasons accompanying his mother on her visits to Aunt Bernstein sometimes; and our aunt desired the mother's company so much, that she was actually fain to put up with the child. "So you have got the child here? Oh, you slyboots!" says the Countess. "Guess you come after the old lady's money! Law bless you! Don't look so frightened. She can't hear a single word I say. Come, Ezzy. Good-bye, aunt!" And my lady Countess rustles out of the room.

Did Aunt Bernstein hear her or not? Where was the wit for which the old lady had been long famous? and was that fire put out, as well as the brilliancy of her eyes? With other people—she was still ready enough, and unsparing of her sarcasms. When the Dowager of Castlewood and Lady Fanny visited her (these exalted ladies treated my wife with perfect indifference and charming good breeding),—the Baroness, in their society, was stately, easy, and even commanding. She would mischievously caress Mrs. Warrington before them; in her absence, vaunt my wife's good breeding; say that her nephew had made a foolish match, perhaps, but that I certainly had taken a charming wife. "In a word, I praise you so to them, my dear," says she, "that I think they would like

559

to tear your eyes out." But, before the little American, 'tis certain that she was uneasy and trembled. She was so afraid, that she actually did not dare to deny her door; and, the Countess's back turned, did not even abuse her. However much they might dislike her, my ladies did not tear out Theo's eyes. Once—they drove to our cottage at Lambeth, where my wife happened to be sitting at the open window, holding her child on her knee, and in full view of her visitors. A gigantic footman strutted through our little garden, and delivered their ladyships' visiting tickets at our door. Their hatred hurt us no more than their visit pleased us. When next we had the loan of our friend the Brewer's carriage Mrs. Warrington drove to Kensington, and Gumbo handed over to the giant our cards in return for those which his noble mistresses had bestowed on us.

The Baroness had a coach, but seldom thought of giving it to us: and would let Theo and her maid and baby start from Clarges Street in the rain, with a faint excuse that she was afraid to ask her coachman to take his horses out. But, twice on her return home, my wife was frightened by rude fellows on the other side of Westminster Bridge; and I fairly told my aunt that I should forbid Mrs. Warrington to go to her, unless she could be brought home in safety; so grumbling Jehu had to drive his horses through the darkness. He grumbled at my shillings: he did not know how few I had. Our poverty wore a pretty decent face. My relatives never thought of relieving it, nor I of complaining before them. I don't know how Sampson got a windfall of guineas; but, I remember, he brought me six once; and they were more welcome than any money I ever had in my life. He had been looking into Mr. Miles's crib, as the child lay asleep; and, when the parson went away, I found the money in the baby's little rosy hand. Yes, Love is best of all. I have many such benefactions registered in my heart—precious welcome fountains springing up in desert places, kind, friendly lights cheering our despondency and gloom.

This worthy divine was willing enough to give as much of his company as she chose to Madame de Bernstein, whether for cards or theology. Having known her ladyship for many years now, Sampson could see, and averred to us, that she was breaking fast; and as he spoke of her evidently increasing infirmities, and of the probability of their fatal termination, Mr. S. would discourse to us in a very feeling manner of the necessity for preparing for a future world; of the vanities of this, and of the hope that in another there might be happiness for all repentant sinners.

"I have been a sinner for one," says the chaplain, bowing his head. "God knoweth, and I pray Him to pardon me. I fear, sir, your aunt, the Lady Baroness, is not in such a state of mind as will fit her very well for the change which is imminent. I am but a poor weak wretch, and no prisoner in Newgate could confess that more humbly and heartily. Once or twice of late, I have sought to speak on this matter with her ladyship, but she has received me very roughly. 'Parson,' says she, 'if you come for cards, 'tis mighty well, but I will thank you to spare me your sermons.' What can I do, sir? I have called more than once of late, and Mr. Case hath told me his lady was unable to see me." In fact Madame Bernstein told my wife, whom she never refused, as I said, that the poor chaplain's ton was unendurable, and as for his theology, "Haven't I been a Bishop's wife?" says she, "and do I want this creature to teach me?"

The old lady was as impatient of doctors as of divines; pretending that my wife was ailing, and that it was more convenient for our good Doctor Heberden to visit her in Clarges Street than to travel all the way to our Lambeth lodgings, we got Dr. H. to see Theo at our aunt's house, and prayed him if possible to offer his advice to the Baroness: we made Mrs. Brett, her woman, describe her ailments, and the doctor confirmed our opinion that they were most serious, and might speedily end. She would rally briskly enough of some evenings, and entertain a little company; but of late she scarcely went abroad at all. A somnolence, which we had remarked in her, was attributable in part to opiates which she was in the habit of taking; and she used these narcotics to smother habitual pain. One night, as we two sat with her (Mr. Miles was weaned by this time, and his mother could leave him to the charge of our faithful Molly), she fell asleep over her cards. We hushed the servants who came to lay out the supper-table (she would always have this luxurious, nor could any injunction of ours or the Doctor's teach her abstinence), and we sat a while as we had often done before, waiting in silence till she should arouse from her doze.

When she awoke, she looked fixedly at me for a while, fumbled with the cards, and dropt them again in her lap, and said, "Henry, have I been long asleep?" I thought at first that it was for my brother she mistook me; but she went on quickly, and with eyes fixed as upon some very far distant object, and said, "My dear, 'tis of no use, I am not good enough for you. I love cards, and play, and court; and oh, Harry, you don't know all!" Here her voice changed, and she flung her head up. "His father married Anne Hyde, and sure the Esmond blood is as good as any that's not royal. Mamma, you must please to treat me with more respect. Vos sermons me fatiguent; entendez-vous?—faites place a mon Altesse royale: mesdames, me connaissez-vous? je suis la ———" Here she broke out into frightful hysterical shrieks and laughter, and as we ran up to her, alarmed, "Oui, Henri," she says, "il a jure de m'epouser et les princes tiennent parole—n'est-ce pas? O oui! ils tiennent parole; si non, tu le tueras, cousin; tu le—ah! que je suis folle!" And the pitiful shrieks and laughter recommenced. Ere her frightened people had come up to her summons, the poor thing had passed out of this mood into another; but always labouring under the same delusion—that I was the Henry of past times, who had loved her and had been forsaken by her, whose bones were lying far away by the banks of the Potomac.

My wife and the women put the poor lady to bed as I ran myself for medical aid. She rambled, still talking wildly, through the night, with her nurses and the surgeon sitting by her. Then she fell into a sleep, brought on by more opiate. When she awoke, her mind did not actually wander; but her speech was changed, and one arm and side were paralysed.

'Tis needless to relate the progress and termination of her malady, or watch that expiring flame of life as it gasps and flickers. Her senses would remain with her for a while (and then she was never satisfied unless Theo was by her bedside), or again her mind would wander, and the poor decrepit creature, lying upon her bed, would imagine herself young again, and speak incoherently of the scenes and incidents of her early days. Then she would address me as Henry again, and call upon me to revenge some insult or slight, of which (whatever my suspicions might be) the only record lay in her insane memory. "They have always been so," she would murmur: "they never loved man or woman but they forsook them. Je me vengerai, O oui, je me vengerai! I know them all: I know them all: and I will go to my Lord Stair with the list. Don't tell me! His religion can't be the right one. I will go back to my mother's though she does not love me. She never did. Why don't you, mother? Is it because I am too wicked? Ah! Pitie, pitie. O mon pere! I will make my confession"—and here the unhappy paralysed lady made as if she would move in her bed.

Let us draw the curtain round it. I think with awe still, of those rapid words, uttered in the shadow of the canopy, as my pallid wife sits by her, her Prayer-book on her knee; as the attendants move to and fro noiselessly; as the clock ticks without, and strikes the fleeting hours; as the sun falls upon the Kneller picture of Beatrix in her beauty, with the blushing cheeks, the smiling lips, the waving auburn tresses, and the eyes which seem to look towards the dim figure moaning in the bed. I could not for a while understand why our aunt's attendants were so anxious that we should quit it. But towards evening, a servant stole in, and whispered her woman; and then Brett, looking rather disturbed, begged us to go downstairs, as the—as the Doctor was come to visit the Baroness. I did not tell my wife, at the time, who "the Doctor" was; but as the gentleman slid by us, and passed upstairs, I saw at once that he was a Catholic ecclesiastic. When Theo next saw our poor lady, she was speechless; she never recognised any one about her, and so passed unconsciously out of life. During her illness her relatives had called assiduously enough, though she would see none of them save us. But when she was gone, and we descended to the lower rooms after all was over, we found Castlewood with his white face, and my lady from Kensington, and Mr. Will already assembled in the parlour. They looked greedily at us as we appeared. They were hungry for the prey.

When our aunt's will was opened, we found it dated five years back, and everything she had was left to her dear nephew, Henry Esmond Warrington, of Castlewood, in Virginia, "in affectionate love and remembrance of the name which he bore." The property was not great. Her revenue had been derived from pensions from the Crown as it appeared (for what services I cannot say), but the pension of course died with her, and there were only a few hundred pounds, besides jewels, trinkets, and the furniture of the house in Clarges Street, of which all London came to the sale. Mr. Walpole bid for her portrait, but I made free with Harry's money so far as to buy the picture in: and it now hangs over the mantelpiece of the chamber in which I write. What with jewels, laces, trinkets, and old china which she had gathered—Harry became possessed of more than four thousand pounds by his aunt's legacy. I made so free as to lay my hand upon a hundred, which came, just as my stock was reduced to twenty pounds; and I procured bills for the remainder, which I forwarded to Captain Henry Esmond in Virginia. Nor should I have scrupled to take more (for my brother was indebted to me in a much greater sum), but he wrote me there was another wonderful opportunity for buying an estate and negroes in our neighbourhood at home; and Theo and I were only too glad to forgo our little claim, so as to establish our brother's fortune. As to mine, poor Harry at this time did not know the state of it. My mother had never informed him that she had ceased remitting to me. She helped him with a considerable sum, the result of her savings, for the purchase of his new estate; and Theo and I were most heartily thankful at his prosperity.

And how strange ours was! By what curious good fortune, as our purse was emptied, was it filled again! I had actually come to the end of our stock, when poor Sampson brought me his six pieces—and with these I was enabled to carry on, until my half-year's salary, as young Mr. Foker's Governor, was due: then Harry's hundred, on which I laid main basse, helped us over three months (we were behindhand with our rent, or the money would have lasted six good weeks longer): and when this was pretty near expended, what should arrive but a bill of exchange for a couple of hundred pounds from Jamaica, with ten thousand blessings, from the dear friends there, and fond scolding from the General that we had not sooner told him of our necessity—of which he had only heard through our friend, Mr. Foker, who spoke in such terms of Theo and myself as to make our parents more than ever proud of their children. Was my quarrel with my mother irreparable? Let me go to Jamaica. There was plenty there for all, and employment which his Excellency as Governor would immediately procure for me. "Come to us!" writes Hetty. "Come to us!" writes Aunt Lambert. "Have my children been suffering poverty, and we rolling in our Excellency's coach, with guards to turn out whenever we pass? Has Charley been home to you for ever so many holidays, from the Chartreux, and had ever so many of my poor George's half-crowns in his pocket, I dare say?" (this was indeed the truth, for where was he to go for holidays but to his sister? and was there any use in telling the child how scarce half-crowns were with us?). "And you always treating him with such goodness, as his letters tell me, which are brimful of love for George and little Miles! Oh, how we long to see Miles!" wrote Hetty and her mother; "and as for his godfather" (writes Het), "who has been good to my dearest and her child, I promise him a kiss whenever I see him!"

Our young benefactor was never to hear of our family's love and gratitude to him. That glimpse of his bright face over the railings before our house at Lambeth, as he rode away on his little horse, was the last we ever were to have of him. At Christmas a basket comes to us, containing a great turkey, and three brace of partridges, with a card, and "shot by M. W." wrote on one of them. And on receipt of this present, we wrote to thank the child and gave him our sister's message.

To this letter, there came a reply from Lady Warrington, who said she was bound to inform me, that in visiting me her child had been guilty of disobedience, and that she learned his visit to me now for the first time. Knowing my views regarding duty to my parents (which I had exemplified in my marriage), she could not wish her son to adopt them. And fervently hoping that I might be brought to see the errors of my present course, she took leave of this most unpleasant subject, subscribing herself, etc. etc. And we got this pretty missive as sauce for poor Miles's turkey, which was our family feast for New Year's Day. My Lady Warrington's letter choked our meal, though Sampson and Charley rejoiced over it.

Ah me! Ere the month was over, our little friend was gone from amongst us. Going out shooting, and dragging his gun through a hedge after him, the trigger caught in a bush, and the poor little man was brought home to his father's house, only to live a few days and expire in pain and torture. Under the yew-trees yonder, I can see the vault which covers him, and where my bones one day no doubt will be laid. And over our pew at church, my children have often wistfully spelt the touching epitaph in which Miles's heartbroken father has inscribed his grief and love for his only son.

CHAPTER LXXXIV. In which Harry submits to the Common Lot

Hard times were now over with me, and I had to battle with poverty no more. My little kinsman's death made a vast difference in my worldly prospects. I became next heir to a good estate. My uncle and his wife were not likely to have more children. "The woman is capable of committing any crime to disappoint you," Sampson vowed; but, in truth, my Lady Warrington was guilty of no such treachery. Cruelly smitten by the stroke which fell upon them, Lady Warrington was taught by her religious advisers to consider it as a chastisement of Heaven, and submit to the Divine Will. "Whilst your son lived, your heart was turned away from the better world" (her clergyman told her), "and your ladyship thought too much of this. For your son's advantage you desired rank and title. You asked and might have obtained an earthly coronet. Of what avail is it now, to one who has but a few years to pass upon earth—of what importance compared to the heavenly crown, for which you are an assured candidate?" The accident caused no little sensation. In the chapels of that enthusiastic sect, towards which, after her son's death, she now more than ever inclined, many sermons were preached bearing reference to the event. Far be it from me to question the course which the bereaved mother pursued, or to regard with other than respect and sympathy any unhappy soul seeking that refuge whither sin and grief and disappointment fly for consolation. Lady Warrington even tried a reconciliation with myself. A year after her loss, being in London, she signified that she would see me, and I waited on her; and she gave me, in her usual didactic way, a homily upon my position and her own. She marvelled at the decree of Heaven, which had permitted, and how dreadfully punished! her poor child's disobedience to her —a disobedience by which I was to profit. (It appeared my poor little man had disobeyed orders, and gone out with his gun, unknown to his mother.) She hoped that, should I ever succeed to the property, though the Warringtons were, thank Heaven, a long-lived family, except in my own father's case, whose life had been curtailed by the excesses of a very ill-regulated youth,—but should I ever succeed to the family estate and honours, she hoped, she prayed, that my present course of life might be altered; that I should part from my unworthy associates; that I should discontinue all connexion with the horrid theatre and its licentious frequenters; that I should turn to that quarter where only peace was to be had; and to those sacred duties which she feared—she very much feared that I had neglected. She filled her exhortation with Scripture language, which I do not care to imitate. When I took my leave she gave me a packet of sermons for Mrs. Warrington, and a little book of hymns by Miss Dora, who has been eminent in that society of which she and her mother became avowed professors subsequently, and who, after the dowager's death, at Bath, three years since, married young Mr. Juffles, a celebrated preacher. The poor lady forgave me then, but she could not bear the sight of our boy. We lost our second child, and then my aunt and her daughter came eagerly enough to the poor suffering mother, and even invited us hither. But my uncle was now almost every day in our house. He would sit for hours looking at our boy. He brought him endless toys and sweetmeats. He begged that the child might call him Godpapa. When we felt our own grief (which at times still, and after the lapse of five-and-twenty years, strikes me as keenly as on the day when we first lost our little one)—when I felt my own grief, I knew how to commiserate his. But my wife could pity him before she knew what it was to lose a child of her own. The mother's anxious heart had already divined the pang which was felt by the sorrow-stricken father; mine, more selfish, has only learned pity from experience, and I was reconciled to my uncle by my little baby's coffin.

The poor man sent his coach to follow the humble funeral, and afterwards took out little Miles, who prattled to him unceasingly, and forgot any grief he might have felt in the delights of his new black clothes, and the pleasures of the airing. How the innocent talk of the child stabbed the mother's heart! Would we ever wish that it should heal of that wound? I know her face so well that, to this day, I can tell when, sometimes, she is thinking of the loss of that little one. It is not a grief for a parting so long ago; it is a communion with a soul we love in Heaven.

We came back to our bright lodgings in Bloomsbury soon afterwards, and my young bear, whom I could no longer lead, and who had taken a prodigious friendship for Charley, went to the Chartreux School, where his friend took care that he had no more beating than was good for him, and where (in consequence of the excellence of his private tutor, no doubt) he took and kept a good place. And he liked the school so much, that he says, if ever he has a son, he shall be sent to that seminary.

Now, I could no longer lead my bear, for this reason, that I had other business to follow. Being fully reconciled to us, I do believe, for Mr. Miles's sake, my uncle (who was such an obsequious supporter of Government, that I wonder the Minister ever gave him anything, being perfectly sure of his vote) used his influence in behalf of his nephew and heir; and I had the honour to be gazetted as one of his Majesty's Commissioners for licensing hackney-coaches, a post I filled, I trust, with credit, until a quarrel with the Minister (to be mentioned in its proper place) deprived me of that one. I took my degree also at the Temple, and appeared in Westminster Hall in my gown and wig. And, this year, my good friend, Mr. Foker, having business at Paris, I had the pleasure of accompanying him thither, where I was received a bras ouverts by my dear American preserver, Monsieur de Florac, who introduced me to his noble family, and to even more of the polite society of the capital than I had leisure to frequent; for I had too much spirit to desert my kind patron Foker, whose acquaintance lay chiefly amongst the bourgeoisie, especially with Monsieur Santerre, a great brewer of Paris, a scoundrel who hath since distinguished himself in blood and not beer. Mr. F. had need of my services as interpreter, and I was too glad that he should command them, and to be able to pay back some of the kindness which he had rendered to me. Our ladies, meanwhile, were residing at Mr. Foker's new villa at Wimbledon, and were pleased to say that they were amused with the "Parisian letters" which I sent to them, through my distinguished friend Mr. Hume, then of the Embassy, and which subsequently have been published in a neat volume.

Whilst I was tranquilly discharging my small official duties in London, those troubles were commencing which were to end in the great separation between our colonies and the mother country. When Mr. Grenville proposed his stamp-duties, I said to my wife that the bill would create a mighty discontent at home, for we were ever anxious to get as much as we could from England, and pay back as little; but assuredly I never anticipated the prodigious anger which the scheme created. It was with us as with families or individuals. A pretext is given for a quarrel: the real cause lies in long bickerings and previous animosities. Many foolish exactions and petty tyrannies, the habitual insolence of Englishmen towards all foreigners, all colonists, all folk who dare to think their rivers as good as our Abana and Pharpar, the natural spirit of men outraged by our imperious domineering spirit, set Britain and her colonies to quarrel; and the astonishing blunders of the system adopted in England brought the quarrel to an issue, which I, for one, am not going to deplore. Had I been in Virginia instead of London, 'tis very possible I should have taken the provincial side, if out of mere opposition to that resolute mistress of Castlewood, who might have driven me into revolt, as England did the colonies. Was the Stamp Act the cause of the revolution?—a tax no greater than that cheerfully paid in England. Ten years earlier, when the French were within our territory, and we were imploring succour from home, would the colonies have rebelled at the payment of this tax? Do not most people consider the tax-gatherer the natural enemy? Against the British in America there were arrayed thousands and thousands of the high-spirited and brave, but there were thousands more who found their profit in the quarrel, or had their private reasons for engaging in it. I protest I don't know now whether mine were selfish or patriotic, or which side was in the right, or whether both were not. I am sure we in England had nothing to do but to fight the battle out; and, having lost the game, I do vow and believe that, after the first natural soreness, the loser felt no rancour.

What made brother Hal write home from Virginia, which he seemed exceedingly loth to quit, such flaming patriotic letters? My kind, best brother was always led by somebody; by me when we were together (he had such an idea of my wit and wisdom, that if I said the day was fine, he would ponder over the observation as though it was one of the sayings of the Seven Sages), by some other wiseacre when I was away. Who inspired these flaming letters, this boisterous patriotism, which he sent to us in London? "He is rebelling against Madam Esmond," said I. "He is led by some colonial person—by that lady, perhaps," hinted my wife. Who "that lady" was Hal never had told us; and, indeed, besought me never to allude to the delicate subject in my letters to him; "for Madam wishes to see 'em all, and I wish to say nothing about you know what until the proper moment," he wrote. No affection could be greater than that which his letters showed. When he heard (from the informant whom I have mentioned) that in the midst of my own extreme straits I had retained no more than a hundred pounds out of his aunt's legacy, he was for mortgaging the estate which he had just bought; and had more than one quarrel with his mother in my behalf, and spoke his mind with a great deal more frankness than I should ever have ventured to show. Until her angry recriminations (when she charged him with ingratitude, after having toiled and saved so much and so long for him), the poor fellow did not know that our mother had cut off my supplies to advance his interests; and by the time this news came to him his bargains were made, and I was fortunately quite out of want.

Every scrap of paper which we ever wrote, our thrifty parent at Castlewood taped and docketed and put away. We boys were more careless about our letters to one another: I especially, who perhaps chose rather to look down upon my younger brother's literary performances; but my wife is not so supercilious, and hath kept no small number of Harry's letters, as well as those of the angelic being whom we were presently to call sister.

"To think whom he has chosen, and whom he might have had! Oh, 'tis cruel!" cries my wife, when we got that notable letter in which Harry first made us acquainted with the name of his charmer.

"She was a very pretty little maid when I left home, she may be a perfect beauty now," I remarked, as I read over the longest letter Harry ever wrote on private affairs.

"But is she to compare to my Hetty?" says Mrs. Warrington.

"We agreed that Hetty and Harry were not to be happy together, my love," say I.

Theo gives her husband a kiss. "My dear, I wish they had tried," she says with a sigh. "I was afraid lest—lest Hetty should have led him, you see; and I think she hath the better head. But, from reading this, it appears that the new lady has taken command of poor Harry," and she hands me the letter:—

"My dearest George hath been prepared by previous letters to understand how a certain lady has made a conquest of my heart, which I have given away in exchange for something infinitely more valuable, namely, her own. She is at my side as I write this letter, and if there is no bad spelling, such as you often used to laugh at, 'tis because I have my pretty dictionary at hand, which makes no faults in the longest word, nor in anything else I know of: being of opinion that she is perfection.

"As Madam Esmond saw all your letters, I writ you not to give any hint of a certain delicate matter—but now 'tis no secret, and is known to all the country. Mr. George is not the only one of our family who has made a secret marriage, and been scolded by his mother. As a dutiful younger brother I have followed his example; and now I may tell you how this mighty event came about.

"I had not been at home long before I saw my fate was accomplisht. I will not tell you how beautiful Miss Fanny Mountain had grown since I had been away in Europe. She saith, 'You never will think so,' and I am glad, as she is the only thing in life I would grudge to my dearest brother.

"That neither Madam Esmond nor my other mother (as Mountain is now) should have seen our mutual attachment, is a wonder—only to be accounted for by supposing that love makes other folks blind. Mine for my Fanny was increased by seeing what the treatment was she had from Madam Esmond, who indeed was very rough and haughty with her, which my love bore with a sweetness perfectly angelic (this I will say, though she will order me not to write any such nonsense). She was scarce better treated than a servant of the house—indeed our negroes can talk much more free before Madam Esmond than ever my Fanny could.

"And yet my Fanny says she doth not regret Madam's unkindness, as without it I possibly never should have been what I am to her. Oh, dear brother! when I remember how great your goodness hath been, how, in my own want, you paid my debts, and rescued me out of prison; how you have been living in poverty which never need have occurred but for my fault; how you might have paid yourself back my just debt to you and would not, preferring my advantage to your own comfort, indeed I am lost at the thought of such goodness; and ought I not to be thankful to Heaven that hath given me such a wife and such a brother?

"When I writ to you requesting you to send me my aunt's legacy money, for which indeed I had the most profitable and urgent occasion, I had no idea that you were yourself suffering poverty. That you, the head of our family, should condescend to be governor to a brewer's son!—that you should have to write for booksellers (except in so far as your own genius might prompt you), never once entered my mind, until Mr. Foker's letter came to us, and this would never have been shown—for Madam kept it secret—had it not been for the difference which sprang up between us.

"Poor Tom Diggle's estate and negroes being for sale, owing to Tom's losses and extravagance at play, and his father's debts before him—Madam Esmond saw here was a great opportunity of making a provision for me, and that with six thousand pounds for the farm and stock, I should be put in possession of as pretty a property as falls to most younger sons in this country. It lies handy enough to Richmond, between Kent and Hanover Court House—the mansion nothing for elegance compared to ours at Castlewood, but the land excellent and the people extraordinary healthy.

"Here was a second opportunity, Madam Esmond said, such as never might again befall. By the sale of my commissions and her own savings I might pay more than half of the price of the property, and get the rest of the money on mortgage; though here, where money is scarce to procure, it would have been difficult and dear. At this juncture, with our new relative, Mr. Van den Bosch, bidding against us (his agent is wild that we should have bought the property over him), my aunt's legacy most opportunely fell in. And now I am owner of a good house and negroes in my native country, shall be called, no doubt, to our House of Burgesses, and hope to see my dearest brother and family under my own roof-tree. To sit at my own fireside, to ride my own horses to my own hounds, is better than going a-soldiering, now war is over, and there are no French to fight. Indeed, Madam Esmond made a condition that I should leave the army, and live at home, when she brought me her 1750 pounds of savings. She had lost one son, she said, who chose to write play-books, and live in England—let the other stay with her at home.

"But, after the purchase of the estate was made, and my papers for selling out were sent home, my mother would have had me marry a person of her choosing, but by no means of mine. You remember Miss Betsy Pitts at Williamsburgh? She is in no wise improved by having had her face dreadfully scarred with small-pock, and though Madam Esmond saith the young lady hath every virtue, I own her virtues did not suit me. Her eyes do not look straight; she hath one leg shorter than another; and oh, brother! didst thou never remark Fanny's ankles when we were boys? Neater I never saw at the Opera.

"Now, when 'twas agreed that I should leave the army, a certain dear girl (canst thou guess her name?) one day, when we were private, burst into tears of such happiness, that I could not but feel immensely touched by her sympathy.

"'Ah!' says she, 'do you think, sir, that the idea of the son of my revered benefactress going to battle doth not inspire me with terror? Ah, Mr. Henry! do you imagine I have no heart? When Mr. George was with Braddock, do you fancy we did not pray for him? And when you were with Mr. Wolfe—oh!'

"Here the dear creature hid her eyes in her handkerchief, and had hard work to prevent her mama, who came in, from seeing that she was crying. But my dear Mountain declares that, though she might have fancied, might have prayed in secret for such a thing (she owns to that now), she never imagined it for one moment. Nor, indeed, did my good mother, who supposed that Sam Lintot, the apothecary's lad at Richmond, was Fanny's flame—an absurd fellow that I near kicked into James River.

"But when the commission was sold, and the estate bought, what does Fanny do but fall into a deep melancholy? I found her crying one day, in her mother's room, where the two ladies had been at work trimming hats for my negroes.

"'What! crying, miss?' says I. 'Has my mother been scolding you?'

"'No,' says the dear creature. 'Madam Esmond has been kind to-day.'

"And her tears drop down on a cockade which she is sewing on to a hat for Sady, who is to be head-groom.

"'Then, why, miss, are those dear eyes so red?' say I.

"'Because I have the toothache,' she says, 'or because—because I am a fool.' Here she fairly bursts out. 'Oh, Mr. Harry! oh, Mr. Warrington! You are going to leave us, and 'tis as well. You will take your place in your country, as becomes you. You will leave us poor women in our solitude and dependence. You will come to visit us from time to time. And when you are happy and honoured, and among your gay companions, you will remember your——'

"Here she could say no more, and hid her face with one hand as I, I confess, seized the other.

"'Dearest, sweetest Miss Mountain!' says I. 'Oh, could I think that the parting from me has brought tears to those lovely eyes! Indeed, I fear, I should be almost happy! Let them look upon your——'

"'Oh, sir!' cries my charmer. 'Oh, Mr. Warrington! consider who I am, sir, and who you are! Remember the difference between us! Release my hand, sir! What would Madam Esmond say if—if——'

"If what, I don't know, for here our mother was in the room.

"'What would Madam Esmond say?' she cries out. 'She would say that you are an ungrateful, artful, false, little——'

"'Madam!' says I.

"'Yes, an ungrateful, artful, false, little wretch!' cries out my mother. 'For shame, miss! What would Mr. Lintot say if he saw you making eyes at the Captain? And for you, Harry, I will have you bring none of your garrison manners hither. This is a Christian family, sir, and you will please to know that my house is not intended for captains and their misses!'

"'Misses, mother!' says I. 'Gracious powers, do you ever venture for to call Miss Mountain by such a name? Miss Mountain, the purest of her sex!'

"'The purest of her sex! Can I trust my own ears?' asks Madam, turning very pale.

"'I mean that if a man would question her honour, I would fling him out of window,' says I.

"'You mean that you—your mother's son—are actually paying honourable attention to this young person?'

"'He would never dare to offer any other,' cries my Fanny; 'nor any woman but you, madam, to think so!'

"'Oh, I didn't know, miss!' says mother, dropping her a fine curtsey, 'I didn't know the honour you were doing our family! You propose to marry with us, do you? Do I understand Captain Warrington aright, that he intends to offer me Miss Mountain as a daughter-in-law?'

"''Tis to be seen, madam, that I have no protector, or you would not insult me so!' cries my poor victim.

"'I should think the apothecary protection sufficient!' says our mother.

"'I don't, mother!' I bawl out, for I was very angry; 'and if Lintot offers her any liberty, I'll brain him with his own pestle!'

"'Oh! if Lintot has withdrawn, sir, I suppose I must be silent. But I did not know of the circumstance. He came hither, as I supposed, to pay court to Miss: and we all thought the match equal, and I encouraged it.'

"'He came because I had the toothache!' cries my darling (and indeed she had a dreadful bad tooth. And he took it out for her, and there is no end to the suspicions and calumnies of women).

"'What more natural than that he should marry my housekeeper's daughter—'twas a very suitable match!' continues Madam, taking snuff. 'But I confess,' she adds, going on, 'I was not aware that you intended to jilt the apothecary for my son!'

"'Peace, for Heaven's sake, peace, Mr. Warrington!' cries my angel.

"'Pray, sir, before you fully make up your mind, had you not better look round the rest of my family?' says Madam. 'Dinah is a fine tall girl, and not very black; Cleopatra is promised to Ajax the blacksmith, to be sure; but then we could break the marriage, you know. If with an apothecary, why not with a blacksmith? Martha's husband has run away, and——'

"Here, dear brother, I own I broke out a-swearing. I can't help it; but at times, when a man is angry, it do relieve him immensely. I'm blest, but I should have gone wild, if it hadn't been for them oaths.

"'Curses, blasphemy, ingratitude, disobedience,' says mother, leaning now on her tortoiseshell stick, and then waving it—something like a queen in a play. 'These are my rewards!' says she. 'O Heaven, what have I done, that I should merit this awful punishment? and does it please you to visit the sins of my fathers upon me? Where do my children inherit their pride? When I was young, had I any? When my papa bade me marry, did I refuse? Did I ever think of disobeying? No, sir. My fault hath been, and I own it, that my love was centred upon you, perhaps to the neglect of your elder brother.' (Indeed, brother, there was some truth in what Madam said.) 'I turned from Esau, and I clung to Jacob. And now I have my reward, I have my reward! I fixed my vain thoughts on this world, and its distinctions. To see my son advanced in worldly rank was my ambition. I toiled, and spared, that I might bring him worldly wealth. I took unjustly from my eldest son's portion, that my younger might profit. And oh! that I should see him seducing the daughter of my own housekeeper under my own roof, and replying to my just anger with oaths and blasphemies!'

"'I try to seduce no one, madam,' I cried out. 'If I utter oaths and blasphemies, I beg your pardon; but you are enough to provoke a saint to speak 'em. I won't have this young lady's character assailed—no, not by own mother nor any mortal alive. No, dear Miss Mountain! If Madam Esmond chooses to say that my designs on you are dishonourable,—let this undeceive her!' And, as I spoke, I went down on my knees, seizing my adorable Fanny's hand. 'And if you will accept this heart and hand, miss,' says I, 'they are yours for ever.'

"'You, at least, I knew, sir,' says Fanny, with a noble curtsey, 'never said a word that was disrespectful to me, or entertained any doubt of my honour. And I trust it is only Madam Esmond, in the world, who can have such an opinion of me. After what your ladyship hath said of me, of course I can stay no longer in your house.'

"'Of course, madam, I never intended you should; and the sooner you leave it the better,' cries our mother.

"'If you are driven from my mother's house, mine, miss, is at your service,' says I, making her a low bow. 'It is nearly ready now. If you will take it and stay in it for ever, it is yours! And as Madam Esmond insulted your honour, at least let me do all in my power to make a reparation!' I don't know what more I exactly said, for you may fancy I was not a little flustered and excited by the scene. But here Mountain came in, and my dearest Fanny, flinging herself into her mother's arms, wept upon her shoulder; whilst Madam Esmond, sitting down in her chair, looked at us as pale as a stone. Whilst I was telling my story to Mountain (who, poor thing, had not the least idea, not she, that Miss Fanny and I had the slightest inclination for one another), I could hear our mother once or twice still saying, 'I am punished for my crime!'

"Now, what our mother meant by her crime I did not know at first, or indeed take much heed of what she said; for you know her way, and how, when she is angry, she always talks sermons. But Mountain told me afterwards, when we had some talk together, as we did at the tavern, whither the ladies presently removed with their bag and baggage—for not only would they not stay at Madam's house after the language she used, but my mother determined to go away likewise. She called her servants together, and announced her intention of going home instantly to Castlewood; and I own to you 'twas with a horrible pain I saw the family coach roll by, with six horses, and ever so many of the servants on mules and on horseback, as I and Fanny looked through the blinds of the Tavern.

"After the words Madam used to my spotless Fanny, 'twas impossible that the poor child or her mother should remain in our house: and indeed M. said that she would go back to her relations in England: and a ship bound homewards lying in James River, she went and bargained with the captain about a passage, so bent was she upon quitting the country, and so little did she think of making a match between me and my angel. But the cabin was mercifully engaged by a North Carolina gentleman and his family, and before the next ship sailed (which bears this letter to my dearest George) they have agreed to stop with me. Almost all the ladies in this neighbourhood have waited on them. When the marriage takes place, I hope Madam Esmond will be reconciled. My Fanny's father was a British officer; and sure, ours was no more. Some day, please Heaven, we shall visit Europe, and the places where my wild oats were sown, and where I committed so many extravagances from which my dear brother rescued me.

"The ladies send you their affection and duty, and to my sister. We hear his Excellency General Lambert is much beloved in Jamaica: and I shall write to our dear friends there announcing my happiness. My dearest brother will participate in it, and I am ever his grateful and affectionate H. E. W.

"P.S.—Till Mountain told me, I had no more notion than the ded that Madam E. had actially stopt your allowances; besides making you pay for ever so much—near upon 1000 pounds Mountain says—for goods, etc., provided for the Virginian proparty. Then there was all the charges of me out of prison, which I. O. U. with all my hart. Draw upon me, please, dearest brother —to any amount—adressing me to care of Messrs. Horn and Sandon, Williamsburg, privit; who remitt by present occasion a bill for 225 pounds, payable by their London agents on demand. Please don't acknolledge this in answering; as there's no good in bothering women with accounts—and with the extra 5 pounds by a capp or what she likes for my dear sister, and a toy for my nephew from Uncle Hal."

The conclusion to which we came on the perusal of this document was, that the ladies had superintended the style and spelling of my poor Hal's letter, but that the postscript was added without their knowledge. And I am afraid we argued that the Virginian Squire was under female domination—as Hercules, Samson, and fortes multi had been before him.

CHAPTER LXXXV. Inveni Portum

When my mother heard of my acceptance of a place at home, I think she was scarcely well pleased. She may have withdrawn her supplies, in order to starve me into a surrender, and force me to return with my family to Virginia, and to dependence under her. We never, up to her dying day, had any explanation on the pecuniary dispute between us. She cut off my allowances: I uttered not a word; but managed to live without her aid. I never heard that she repented of her injustice, or acknowledged it, except from Harry's private communication to me. In after days, when we met, by a great gentleness in her behaviour, and an uncommon respect and affection shown to my wife, Madam Esmond may have intended I should understand her tacit admission that she had been wrong; but she made no apology, nor did I ask one. Harry being provided for (whose welfare I could not grudge), all my mother's savings and economical schemes went to my advantage, who was her heir. Time was when a few guineas would have been more useful to me than hundreds which might come to me when I had no need; but when Madam Esmond and I met, the period of necessity was long passed away; I had no need to scheme ignoble savings, or to grudge the doctor his fee: I had plenty, and she could but bring me more. No doubt she suffered in her own mind to think that my children had been hungry, and she had offered them no food; and that strangers had relieved the necessity from which her proud heart had caused her to turn aside. Proud? Was she prouder than I? A soft word of explanation between us might have brought about a reconciliation years before it came but I would never speak, nor did she. When I commit a wrong, and know it subsequently, I love to ask pardon; but 'tis as a satisfaction to my own pride, and to myself I am apologising for having been wanting to myself. And hence, I think (out of regard to that personage of ego), I scarce ever could degrade myself to do a meanness. How do men feel whose whole lives (and many men's lives are) are lies, schemes, and subterfuges? What sort of company do they keep when they are alone? Daily in life I watch men whose every smile is an artifice, and every wink is an hypocrisy. Doth such a fellow wear a mask in his own privacy, and to his own conscience? If I choose to pass over an injury, I fear 'tis not from a Christian and forgiving spirit: 'tis because I can afford to remit the debt, and disdain to ask a settlement of it. One or two sweet souls I have known in my life (and perhaps tried) to whom forgiveness is no trouble—a plant that grows naturally, as it were, in the soil. I know how to remit, I say, not forgive. I wonder are we proud men proud of being proud?

So I showed not the least sign of submission towards my parent in Virginia yonder, and we continued for years to live in estrangement, with occasionally a brief word or two (such as the announcement of the birth of a child, or what not) passing between my wife and her. After our first troubles in America about the Stamp Act, troubles fell on me in London likewise. Though I have been on the Tory side in our quarrel (as indeed upon the losing side in most controversies), having no doubt that the Imperial Government had a full right to levy taxes in the colonies, yet at the time of the dispute I must publish a pert letter to a member of the House of Burgesses in Virginia, in which the question of the habitual insolence of the mother country to the colonies was so freely handled, and sentiments were uttered so disagreeable to persons in power, that I was deprived of my place as hackney-coach licenser, to the terror and horror of my uncle, who never could be brought to love people in disgrace. He had grown to have an extreme affection for my wife as well as my little boy; but towards myself, personally, entertained a kind of pitying contempt which always infinitely amused me. He had a natural scorn and dislike for poverty, and a corresponding love for success and good fortune. Any opinion departing at all from the regular track shocked and frightened him, and all truth-telling made him turn pale. He must have had originally some warmth of heart and genuine love of kindred: for, spite of the dreadful shocks I gave him, he continued to see Theo and the child (and me too, giving me a mournful recognition when we met); and though broken-hearted by my free-spokenness, he did not refuse to speak to me as he had done at the time of our first differences, but looked upon me as a melancholy lost creature, who was past all worldly help or hope. Never mind, I must cast about for some new scheme of life; and the repayment of Harry's debt to me at this juncture enabled me to live at least for some months even, or years to come. O strange fatuity of youth! I often say. How was it that we dared to be so poor and so little cast down?

At this time his Majesty's royal uncle of Cumberland fell down and perished in a fit; and, strange to say, his death occasioned a remarkable change in my fortune. My poor Sir Miles Warrington never missed any court ceremony to which he could introduce himself. He was at all the drawing-rooms, christenings, balls, funerals of the court. If ever a prince or princess was ailing, his coach was at their door: Leicester Fields, Carlton House, Gunnersbury, were all the same to him, and nothing must satisfy him now but going to the stout duke's funeral. He caught a great cold and an inflammation of the throat from standing bareheaded at this funeral in the rain; and one morning, before almost I had heard of his illness, a lawyer waits upon me at my lodgings in Bloomsbury, and salutes me by the name of Sir George Warrington.

Party and fear of the future were over now. We laid the poor gentleman by the side of his little son, in the family churchyard where so many of his race repose. Little Miles and I were the chief mourners. An obsequious tenantry bowed and curtseyed before us, and did their utmost to conciliate my honour and my worship. The dowager and her daughter withdrew to Bath presently; and I and my family took possession of the house, of which I have been master for thirty years. Be not too eager, O my son! Have but a little patience, and I too shall sleep under yonder yew-trees, and the people will be tossing up their caps for Sir Miles.

The records of a prosperous country life are easily and briefly told. The steward's books show what rents were paid and forgiven, what crops were raised, and in what rotation. What visitors came to us, and how long they stayed: what pensioners my wife had, and how they were doctored and relieved, and how they died: what year I was sheriff, and how often the hounds met near us; all these are narrated in our house journals, which any of my heirs may read who choose to take the trouble. We could not afford the fine mansion in Hill Street, which my predecessor had occupied; but we took a smaller house, in which, however, we spent more money. We made not half the show (with liveries, equipages, and plate) for which my uncle had been famous; but our beer was stronger, and my wife's charities were perhaps more costly than those of the Dowager Lady Warrington. No doubt she thought there was no harm in spoiling the Philistines; for she made us pay unconscionably for the goods she left behind her in our country-house, and I submitted to most of her extortions with unutterable good-humour. What a value she imagined the potted plants in her greenhouses bore! What a price she set upon that horrible old spinet she left in her drawing-room! and the framed pieces of worsted-work, performed by the accomplished Dora and the lovely Flora, had they been masterpieces of Titian or Vandyck, to be sure my lady dowager could hardly have valued them at a higher price. But though we paid so generously, though we were, I may say without boast, far kinder to our poor than ever she had been, for a while we had the very worst reputation in the county, where all sorts of stories had been told to my discredit. I thought I might perhaps succeed to my uncle's seat in Parliament, as well as to his landed property; but I found, I knew not how, that I was voted to be a person of very dangerous opinions. I would not bribe: I would not coerce my own tenants to vote for me in the election of '68. A gentleman came down from Whitehall with a pocket-book full of bank-notes; and I found that I had no chance against my competitor.

Bon Dieu! Now that we were at ease in respect of worldly means,—now that obedient tenants bowed and curtseyed as we went to church; that we drove to visit our friends, or to the neighbouring towns, in the great family coach with the four fat horses; did we not often regret poverty, and the dear little cottage at Lambeth, where Want was ever prowling at the door? Did I not long to be bear-leading again, and vow that translating for booksellers was not such very hard drudgery? When we went to London, we made sentimental pilgrimages to all our old haunts. I dare say my wife embraced all her landladies. You may be sure we asked all the friends of those old times to share the comforts of our new home with us. The Reverend Mr. Hagan and his lady visited us more than once. His appearance in the pulpit at B——— (where he preached very finely, as we thought) caused an awful scandal there. Sampson came too, another unlucky Levite, and was welcome as long as he would stay among us. Mr. Johnson talked of coming, but he put us off once or twice. I suppose our house was dull. I know that I myself would be silent for days, and fear that my moodiness must often have tried the sweetest-tempered woman in the world who lived with me. I did not care for field sports. The killing one partridge was so like killing another, that I wondered how men could pass days after days in the pursuit of that kind of slaughter. Their fox-hunting stories would begin at four o'clock, when the tablecloth was removed, and last till supper-time. I sate silent, and listened: day after day I fell asleep: no wonder I was not popular with my company.

What admission is this I am making? Here was the storm over, the rocks avoided, the ship in port and the sailor not overcontented? Was Susan I had been sighing for during the voyage, not the beauty I expected to find her? In the first place, Susan and all the family can look in her William's logbook, and so, madam, I am not going to put my secrets down there. No, Susan, I never had secrets from thee. I never cared for another woman. I have seen more beautiful, but none that suited me as well as your ladyship. I have met Mrs. Carter and Miss Mulso, and Mrs. Thrale and Madam Kaufmann, and the angelical Gunnings, and her Grace of Devonshire, and a host of beauties who were not angelic, by any means: and I was not dazzled by them. Nay, young folks, I may have led your mother a weary life, and been a very Bluebeard over her, but then I had no other heads in the closet. Only, the first pleasure of taking possession of our kingdom over, I own I began to be quickly tired of the crown. When the captain wears it his Majesty will be a very different Prince. He can ride a-hunting five days in the week, and find the sport amusing. I believe he would hear the same sermon at church fifty times, and not yawn more than I do at the first delivery. But sweet Joan, beloved Baucis! being thy faithful husband and true lover always, thy Darby is rather ashamed of having been testy so often! and, being arrived at the consummation of happiness, Philemon asks pardon for falling asleep so frequently after dinner. There came a period of my life, when having reached the summit of felicity I was quite tired of the prospect I had there: I yawned in Eden, and said, "Is this all? What, no lions to bite? no rain to fall? no thorns to prick you in the rose-bush when you sit down?—only Eve, for ever sweet and tender, and figs for breakfast, dinner, supper, from week's end to week's end!" Shall I make my confessions? Hearken! Well, then, if I must make a clean breast of it.

* * * * * *

Here three pages are torn out of Sir George Warrington's MS. book, for which the editor is sincerely sorry.

I know the theory and practice of the Roman Church; but, being bred of another persuasion (and sceptical and heterodox regarding that), I can't help doubting the other, too, and wondering whether Catholics, in their confessions, confess all? Do we Protestants ever do so; and has education rendered those other fellow-men so different from us? At least, amongst us, we are not accustomed to suppose Catholic priests or laymen more frank and open than ourselves. Which brings me back to my question,—does any man confess all? Does yonder dear creature know all my life, who has been the partner of it for thirty years; who, whenever I have told her a sorrow, has been ready with the best of her gentle power to soothe it; who has watched when I did not speak, and when I was silent has been silent herself, or with the charming hypocrisy of woman has worn smiles and an easy appearance so as to make me imagine she felt no care, or would not even ask to disturb her lord's secret when he seemed to indicate a desire to keep it private? Oh, the dear hypocrite! Have I not watched her hiding the boys' peccadilloes from papa's anger? Have I not known her cheat out of her housekeeping to pay off their little extravagances; and talk to me with an artless face, as if she did not know that our revered captain had had dealings with the gentlemen of Duke's Place, and our learned collegian, at the end of his terms, had very pressing reasons for sporting his oak (as the phrase is) against some of the University tradesmen? Why, from the very earliest days, thou wise woman, thou wert for ever concealing something from me,—this one stealing jam from the cupboard; that one getting into disgrace at school; that naughty rebel (put on the caps, young folks, according to the fit) flinging an inkstand at mamma in a rage, whilst I was told the gown and the carpet were spoiled by accident. We all hide from one another. We have all secrets. We are all alone. We sin by ourselves, and, let us trust, repent too. Yonder dear woman would give her foot to spare mine a twinge of the gout; but, when I have the fit, the pain is in my slipper. At the end of the novel or the play, the hero and heroine marry or die, and so there is an end of them as far as the poet is concerned, who huzzas for his young couple till the postchaise turns the corner; or fetches the hearse and plumes, and shovels them underground. But when Mr. Random and Mr. Thomas Jones are married, is all over? Are there no quarrels at home? Are there no Lady Bellastons abroad? are there no constables to be outrun? no temptations to conquer us, or be conquered by us? The Sirens sang after Ulysses long after his marriage, and the suitors whispered in Penelope's ear, and he and she had many a weary day of doubt and care, and so have we all. As regards money I was put out of trouble by the inheritance I made: but does not Atra Cura sit behind baronets as well as equites? My friends in London used to congratulate me on my happiness. Who would not like to be master of a good house and a good estate? But can Gumbo shut the hall-door upon blue devils, or lay them always in a red sea of claret? Does a man sleep the better who has four-and-twenty hours to doze in? Do his intellects brighten after a sermon from the dull old vicar; a ten minutes' cackle and flattery from the village apothecary; or the conversation of Sir John and Sir Thomas with their ladies, who come ten moonlight muddy miles to eat a haunch, and play a rubber? 'Tis all very well to have tradesmen bowing to your carriage-door, room made for you at quarter-sessions, and my lady wife taken down the second or the third to dinner: but these pleasures fade—nay, have their inconveniences. In our part of the country, for seven years after we came to Warrington Manor, our two what they called best neighbours were my Lord Tutbury and Sir John Mudbrook. We are of an older date than the Mudbrooks; consequently, my Lady Tutbury always fell to my lot, when we dined together, who was deaf and fell asleep after dinner; or if I had Lady Mudbrook, she chattered with a folly so incessant and intense, that even my wife could hardly keep her complacency (consummate hypocrite as her ladyship is), knowing the rage with which I was fuming at the other's clatter. I come to London. I show my tongue to Dr. Heberden. I pour out my catalogue of complaints. "Psha, my dear Sir George!" says the unfeeling physician. "Headaches, languor, bad sleep, bad temper—" ("Not bad temper: Sir George has the sweetest temper in the world, only he is sometimes a little melancholy," says my wife.) "—Bad sleep, bad temper," continues the implacable doctor. "My dear lady, his inheritance has been his ruin, and a little poverty and a great deal of occupation would do him all the good in life."

No, my brother Harry ought to have been the squire, with remainder to my son Miles, of course. Harry's letters were full of gaiety and good spirits. His estate prospered: his negroes multiplied; his crops were large; he was a member of our House of Burgesses; he adored his wife; could he but have a child his happiness would be complete. Had Hal been master of Warrington Manor-house, in my place, he would have been beloved through the whole country; he would have been steward at all the races, the gayest of all the jolly huntsmen, the bien venu at all the mansions round about, where people scarce cared to perform the ceremony of welcome at sight of my glum face. As for my wife, all the world liked her, and agreed in pitying her. I don't know how the report got abroad, but 'twas generally agreed that I treated her with awful cruelty, and that for jealousy I was a perfect Bluebeard. Ah me! And so it is true that I have had many dark hours; that I pass days in long silence; that the conversation of fools and whipper-snappers makes me rebellious and peevish, and that, when I feel contempt, I sometimes don't know how to conceal it, or I should say did not. I hope as I grow older I grow more charitable. Because I do not love bawling and galloping after a fox, like the captain yonder, I am not his superior; but, in this respect, humbly own that he is mine. He has perceptions which are denied me; enjoyments which I cannot understand. Because I am blind the world is not dark. I try now and listen with respect when Squire Codgers talks of the day's run. I do my best to laugh when Captain Rattleton tells his garrison stories. I step up to the harpsichord with old Miss Humby (our neighbour from Beccles) and try and listen as she warbles her ancient ditties. I play whist laboriously. Am I not trying to do the duties of life? and I have a right to be garrulous and egotistical, because I have been reading Montaigne all the morning.

I was not surprised, knowing by what influences my brother was led, to find his name in the list of Virginia burgesses who declared that the sole right of imposing taxes on the inhabitants of this colony is now, and ever hath been, legally and constitutionally vested in the House of Burgesses, and called upon the other colonies to pray for the Royal interposition in favour of the violated rights of America. And it was now, after we had been some three years settled in our English home, that a correspondence between us and Madam Esmond began to take place. It was my wife who (upon some pretext such as women always know how to find) re-established the relations between us. Mr. Miles must need have the small-pox, from which he miraculously recovered without losing any portion of his beauty; and on his recovery the mother writes her prettiest little wheedling letter to the grandmother of the fortunate babe. She coaxes her with all sorts of modest phrases and humble offerings of respect and goodwill. She narrates anecdotes of the precocious genius of the lad (what hath subsequently happened, I wonder, to stop the growth of that gallant young officer's brains?), and she must have sent over to his grandmother a lock of the darling boy's hair, for the old lady, in her reply, acknowledged the receipt of some such present. I wonder, as it came from England, they allowed it to pass our custom-house at Williamsburg. In return for these peace-offerings and smuggled tokens of submission, comes a tolerably gracious letter from my Lady of Castlewood. She inveighs against the dangerous spirit pervading the colony: she laments to think that her unhappy son is consorting with people who, she fears, will be no better than rebels and traitors. She does not wonder, considering who his friends and advisers are. How can a wife taken from an almost menial situation be expected to sympathise with persons of rank and dignity who have the honour of the Crown at heart? If evil times were coming for the monarchy (for the folks in America appeared to be disinclined to pay taxes, and required that everything should be done for them without cost), she remembered how to monarchs in misfortune, the Esmonds—her father the Marquis especially —had ever been faithful. She knew not what opinions (though she might judge from my newfangled Lord Chatham) were in fashion in England. She prayed, at least, she might hear that one of her sons was not on the side of rebellion. When we came, in after days, to look over old family papers in Virginia, we found "Letters from my daughter Lady Warrington," neatly tied up with a ribbon. My Lady Theo insisted I should not open them; and the truth, I believe, is, that they were so full of praises of her husband that she thought my vanity would suffer from reading them.

When Madam began to write, she gave us brief notices of Harry and his wife. "The two women," she wrote, "still govern everything with my poor boy at Fannystown (as he chooses to call his house). They must save money there, for I hear but a shabby account of their manner of entertaining. The Mount Vernon gentleman continues to be his great friend, and he votes in the House of Burgesses very much as his guide advises him. Why he should be so sparing of his money I cannot understand: I heard, of five negroes who went with his equipages to my Lord Bottetourt's, only two had shoes to their feet. I had reasons to save, having sons for whom I wished to provide, but he hath no children, wherein he certainly is spared from much grief, though, no doubt, Heaven in its wisdom means our good by the trials which, through our children, it causes us to endure. His mother-in-law," she added in one of her letters, "has been ailing. Ever since his marriage, my poor Henry has been the creature of these two artful women, and they rule him entirely. Nothing, my dear daughter, is more contrary to common sense and to Holy Scripture than this. Are we not told, Wives, be obedient to your husbands? Had Mr. Warrington lived, I should have endeavoured to follow up that sacred precept, holding that nothing so becomes a woman as humility and obedience."

Presently we had a letter sealed with black, and announcing the death of our dear good Mountain, for whom I had a hearty regret and affection, remembering her sincere love for us as children. Harry deplored the event in his honest way, and with tears which actually blotted his paper. And Madam Esmond, alluding to the circumstance, said: "My late housekeeper, Mrs. Mountain, as soon as she found her illness was fatal, sent to me requesting a last interview on her deathbed, intending, doubtless, to pray my forgiveness for her treachery towards me. I sent her word that I could forgive her as a Christian, and heartily hope (though I confess I doubt it) that she had a due sense of her crime towards me. But our meeting, I considered, was of no use, and could only occasion unpleasantness between us. If she repented, though at the eleventh hour, it was not too late, and I sincerely trusted that she was now doing so. And, would you believe her lamentable and hardened condition? she sent me word through Dinah, my woman, whom I dispatched to her with medicines for her soul's and her body's health, that she had nothing to repent of as far as regarded her conduct to me, and she wanted to be left alone! Poor Dinah distributed the medicine to my negroes, and our people took it eagerly—whilst Mrs. Mountain, left to herself, succumbed to the fever. Oh, the perversity of human kind! This poor creature was too proud to take my remedies, and is now beyond the reach of cure and physicians. You tell me your little Miles is subject to fits of cholic. My remedy, and I will beg you to let me know if effectual, is," etc. etc.—and here followed the prescription, which thou didst not take, O my son, my heir, and my pride! because thy fond mother had her mother's favourite powder, on which in his infantine troubles our firstborn was dutifully nurtured. Did words not exactly consonant with truth pass between the ladies in their correspondence? I fear my Lady Theo was not altogether candid: else how to account for a phrase in one of Madam Esmond's letters, who said: "I am glad to hear the powders have done the dear child good. They are, if not on a first, on a second or third application, almost infallible, and have been the blessed means of relieving many persons round me, both infants and adults, white and coloured. I send my grandson an Indian bow and arrows. Shall these old eyes never behold him at Castlewood, I wonder, and is Sir George so busy with his books and his politics that he can't afford a few months to his mother in Virginia? I am much alone now. My son's chamber is just as he left it: the same books are in the presses: his little hanger and fowling-piece over the bed, and my father's picture over the mantelpiece. I never allow anything to be altered in his room or his brother's. I fancy the children playing near me sometimes, and that I can see my dear father's head as he dozes in his chair. Mine is growing almost as white as my father's. Am I never to behold my children ere I go hence? The Lord's will be done."

CHAPTER LXXXVI. At Home

Such an appeal as this of our mother would have softened hearts much less obdurate than ours; and we talked of a speedy visit to Virginia, and of hiring all the Young Rachel's cabin accommodation. But our child must fall ill, for whom the voyage would be dangerous, and from whom the mother of course could not part; and the Young Rachel made her voyage without us that year. Another year there was another difficulty, in my worship's first attack of the gout (which occupied me a good deal, and afterwards certainly cleared my wits and enlivened my spirits); and now came another much sadder cause for delay in the sad news we received from Jamaica. Some two years after our establishment at the Manor, our dear General returned from his government, a little richer in the world's goods than when he went away, but having undergone a loss for which no wealth could console him, and after which, indeed, he did not care to remain in the West Indies. My Theo's poor mother —the most tender and affectionate friend (save one) I have ever had—died abroad of the fever. Her last regret was that she should not be allowed to live to see our children and ourselves in prosperity.

"She sees us, though we do not see her; and she thanks you, George, for having been good to her children," her husband said.

He, we thought, would not be long ere he joined her. His love for her had been the happiness and business of his whole life. To be away from her seemed living no more. It was pitiable to watch the good man as he sate with us. My wife, in her air and in many tones and gestures, constantly recalled her mother to the bereaved widower's heart. What cheer we could give him in his calamity we offered; but, especially, little Hetty was now, under Heaven, his chief support and consolation. She had refused more than one advantageous match in the Island, the General told us; and on her return to England, my Lord Wrotham's heir laid himself at her feet. But she loved best to stay with her father, Hetty said. As long as he was not tired of her she cared for no husband.

"Nay," said we, when this last great match was proposed, "let the General stay six months with us at the Manor here, and you can have him at Oakhurst for the other six."

But Hetty declared her father never could bear Oakhurst again now that her mother was gone; and she would marry no man for his coronet and money—not she! The General, when we talked this matter over, said gravely that the child had no desire for marrying, owing possibly to some disappointment in early life, of which she never spoke; and we, respecting her feelings, were for our parts equally silent. My brother Lambert had by this time a college living near to Winchester, and a wife of course to adorn his parsonage. We professed but a moderate degree of liking for this lady, though we made her welcome when she came to us. Her idea regarding our poor Hetty's determined celibacy was different to that which I had. This Mrs. Jack was a chatterbox of a woman, in the habit of speaking her mind very freely, and of priding herself excessively on her skill in giving pain to her friends.

"My dear Sir George," she was pleased to say, "I have often and often told our dear Theo that I wouldn't have a pretty sister in my house to make tea for Jack when I was upstairs, and always to be at hand when I was wanted in the kitchen or nursery, and always to be dressed neat and in her best when I was very likely making pies or puddings or looking to the children. I have every confidence in Jack, of course. I should like to see him look at another woman, indeed! And so I have in Jemima but they don't come together in my house when I'm upstairs—that I promise you! And so I told my sister Warrington."

"Am I to understand," says the General, "that you have done my Lady Warrington the favour to warn her against her sister, my daughter Miss Hester?"

"Yes, pa, of course I have. A duty is a duty, and a woman is a woman, and a man's a man, as I know very well. Don't tell me! He is a man. Every man is a man, with all his sanctified airs!"

"You yourself have a married sister, with whom you were staying when my son Jack first had the happiness of making your acquaintance?" remarks the General.

"Yes, of course I have a married sister; every one knows that and I have been as good as a mother to her children, that I have!"

"And am I to gather from your conversation that your attractions proved a powerful temptation for your sister's husband?"

"Law, General! I don't know how you can go for to say I ever said any such a thing!" cries Mrs. Jack, red and voluble.

"Don't you perceive, my dear madam, that it is you who have insinuated as much, not only regarding yourself, but regarding my own two daughters?"

"Never, never, never, as I'm a Christian woman! And it's most cruel of you to say so, sir. And I do say a sister is best out of the house, that I do! And as Theo's time is coming, I warn her, that's all."

"Have you discovered, my good madam, whether my poor Hetty has stolen any of the spoons? When I came to breakfast this morning, my daughter was alone, and there must have been a score of pieces of silver on the table."

"Law, sir! who ever said a word about spoons? Did I ever accuse the poor dear? If I did, may I drop down dead at this moment on this hearth-rug! And I ain't used to be spoke to in this way. And me and Jack have both remarked it; and I've done my duty, that I have." And here Mrs. Jack flounces out of the room, in tears.

"And has the woman had the impudence to tell you this, my child?" asks the General, when Theo (who is a little delicate) comes to the tea-table.

"She has told me every day since she has been here. She comes into my dressing-room to tell me. She comes to my nursery, and says, 'Ah, I wouldn't have a sister prowling about my nursery, that I wouldn't.' Ah, how pleasant it is to have amiable and well-bred relatives, say I."

"Thy poor mother has been spared this woman," groans the General.

"Our mother would have made her better, papa," says Theo, kissing him.

"Yes, dear." And I see that both of them are at their prayers.

But this must be owned, that to love one's relatives is not always an easy task; to live with one's neighbours is sometimes not amusing. From Jack Lambert's demeanour next day, I could see that his wife had given him her version of the conversation. Jack was sulky, but not dignified. He was angry, but his anger did not prevent his appetite. He preached a sermon for us which was entirely stupid. And little Miles, once more in sables, sate at his grandfather's side, his little hand placed in that of the kind old man.

Would he stay and keep house for us during our Virginian trip? The housekeeper should be put under the full domination of Hetty. The butler's keys should be handed over to him; for Gumbo, not I thought with an over good grace, was to come with us to Virginia: having, it must be premised, united himself with Mrs. Molly in the bonds of matrimony, and peopled a cottage in my park with sundry tawny Gumbos. Under the care of our good General and his daughter we left our house, then; we travelled to London, and thence to Bristol, and our obsequious agent there had the opportunity of declaring that he should offer up prayers for our prosperity, and of vowing that children so beautiful as ours (we had an infant by this time to accompany Miles) were never seen on any ship before. We made a voyage without accident. How strange the feeling was as we landed from our boat at Richmond! A coach and a host of negroes were there in waiting to receive us; and hard by a gentleman on horseback, with negroes in our livery, too, who sprang from his horse and rushed up to embrace us. Not a little charmed were both of us to see our dearest Hal. He rode with us to our mother's door. Yonder she stood on the steps to welcome us; and Theo knelt down to ask her blessing.

Harry rode in the coach with us as far as our mother's house; but would not, as he said, spoil sport by entering with us. "She sees me," he owned, "and we are pretty good friends; but Fanny and she are best apart; and there is no love lost between 'em, I can promise you. Come over to me at the Tavern, George, when thou art free. And to-morrow I shall have the honour to present her sister to Theo. 'Twas only from happening to be in town yesterday that I heard the ship was signalled, and waited to see you. I have sent a negro boy home to my wife, and she'll be here to pay her respects to my Lady Warrington." And Harry, after this brief greeting, jumped out of the carriage, and left us to meet our mother alone.

Since I parted from her I had seen a great deal of fine company, and Theo and I had paid our respects to the King and Queen at St. James's; but we had seen no more stately person than this who welcomed us, and raising my wife from her knee, embraced her and led her into the house. 'Twas a plain, wood-built place, with a gallery round, as our Virginian houses are; but if it had been a palace, with a little empress inside, our reception could not have been more courteous. There was old Nathan, still the major-domo, a score of kind black faces of blacks, grinning welcome. Some whose names I remembered as children were grown out of remembrance, to be sure, to be buxom lads and lasses; and some I had left with black pates were grizzling now with snowy polls: and some who were born since my time were peering at doorways with their great eyes and little naked feet. It was, "I'm little Sip, Master George!" and "I'm Dinah, Sir George!" and "I'm Master Miles's boy!" says a little chap in a new livery and boots of nature's blacking. Ere the day was over the whole household had found a pretext for passing before us, and grinning and bowing and making us welcome. I don't know how many repasts were served to us. In the evening my Lady Warrington had to receive all the gentry of the little town, which she did with perfect grace and good-humour, and I had to shake hands with a few old acquaintances—old enemies I was going to say; but I had come into a fortune and was no longer a naughty prodigal. Why, a drove of fatted calves was killed in my honour! My poor Hal was of the entertainment, but gloomy and crestfallen. His mother spoke to him, but it was as a queen to a rebellious prince, her son who was not yet forgiven. We two slipped away from the company, and went up to the rooms assigned to me: but there, as we began a free conversation, our mother, taper in hand, appeared with her pale face. Did I want anything? Was everything quite as I wished it? She had peeped in at the dearest children, who were sleeping like cherubs. How she did caress them, and delight over them! How she was charmed with Miles's dominating airs, and the little Theo's smiles and dimples! "Supper is just coming on the table, Sir George. If you like our cookery better than the tavern, Henry, I beg you to stay." What a different welcome there was in the words and tone addressed to each of us! Hal hung down his head, and followed to the lower room. A clergyman begged a blessing on the meal. He touched with not a little art and eloquence upon our arrival at home, upon our safe passage across the stormy waters, upon the love and forgiveness which awaited us in the mansions of the Heavenly Parent when the storms of life were over.

Here was a new clergyman, quite unlike some whom I remembered about us in earlier days, and I praised him, but Madam Esmond shook her head. She was afraid his principles were very dangerous: she was afraid others had adopted those dangerous principles. Had I not seen the paper signed by the burgesses and merchants at Williamsburg the year before—the Lees, Randolphs, Bassets, Washingtons, and the like, and oh, my dear, that I should have to say it, our name, that is, your brother's (by what influence I do not like to say), and this unhappy Mr. Belman's who begged a blessing last night?

If there had been quarrels in our little colonial society when I left home, what were these to the feuds I found raging on my return? We had sent the Stamp Act to America, and been forced to repeal it. Then we must try a new set of duties on glass, paper, and what not, and repeal that Act too, with the exception of a duty on tea. From Boston to Charleston the tea was confiscated. Even my mother, loyal as she was, gave up her favourite drink; and my poor wife would have had to forgo hers, but we had brought a quantity for our private drinking on board ship, which had paid four times as much duty at home. Not that I for my part would have hesitated about paying duty. The home Government must have some means of revenue, or its pretensions to authority were idle. They say the colonies were tried and tyrannised over; I say the home Government was tried and tyrannised over. ('Tis but an affair of argument and history, now; we tried the question, and were beat; and the matter is settled as completely as the conquest of Britain by the Normans.) And all along, from conviction I trust, I own to have taken the British side of the quarrel. In that brief and unfortunate experience of war which I had had in my early life, the universal cry of the army and well-affected persons was, that Mr. Braddock's expedition had failed, and defeat and disaster had fallen upon us in consequence of the remissness, the selfishness, and the rapacity of many of the very people for whose defence against the French arms had been taken up. The colonists were for having all done for them, and for doing nothing, They made extortionate bargains with the champions who came to defend them; they failed in contracts; they furnished niggardly supplies; they multiplied delays until the hour for beneficial action was past, and until the catastrophe came which never need have occurred but for their ill-will. What shouts of joy were there, and what ovations for the great British Minister who had devised and effected the conquest of Canada! Monsieur de Vaudreuil said justly that that conquest was the signal for the defection of the North American colonies from their allegiance to Great Britain; and my Lord Chatham, having done his best to achieve the first part of the scheme, contributed more than any man in England towards the completion of it. The colonies were insurgent, and he applauded their rebellion. What scores of thousands of waverers must he have encouraged into resistance! It was a general who says to an army in revolt, "God save the king! My men, you have a right to mutiny!" No wonder they set up his statue in this town, and his picture in t'other; whilst here and there they hanged Ministers and Governors in effigy. To our Virginian town of Williamsburg, some wiseacres must subscribe to bring over a portrait of my lord, in the habit of a Roman orator speaking in the Forum, to be sure, and pointing to the palace of Whitehall, and the special window out of which Charles I. was beheaded! Here was a neat allegory, and a pretty compliment to a British statesman! I hear, however, that my lord's head was painted from a bust, and so was taken off without his knowledge.

Now my country is England, not America or Virginia; and I take, or rather took, the English side of the dispute. My sympathies had always been with home, where I was now a squire and a citizen: but had my lot been to plant tobacco, and live on the banks of James River or Potomac, no doubt my opinions had been altered. When, for instance, I visited my brother at his new house and plantation, I found him and his wife as staunch Americans as we were British. We had some words upon the matter in dispute,—who had not in those troublesome times?—but our argument was carried on without rancour; even my new sister could not bring us to that, though she did her best when we were together, and in the curtain lectures which I have no doubt she inflicted on her spouse, like a notable housewife as she was. But we trusted in each other so entirely that even Harry's duty towards his wife would not make him quarrel with his brother. He loved me from old times, when my word was law with him; he still protested that he and every Virginian gentleman of his side was loyal to the Crown. War was not declared as yet, and gentlemen of different opinions were courteous enough to one another. Nay, at our public dinners and festivals, the health of the King was still ostentatiously drunk; and the assembly of every colony, though preparing for Congress, though resisting all attempts at taxation on the part of the home authorities, was loud in its expressions of regard for the King our Father, and pathetic in its appeals to that paternal sovereign to put away evil counsellors from him, and listen to the voice of moderation and reason. Up to the last, our Virginian gentry were a grave, orderly, aristocratic folk, with the strongest sense of their own dignity and station. In later days, and nearer home, we have heard of fraternisation and equality. Amongst the great folks of our Old World I have never seen a gentleman standing more on his dignity and maintaining it better than Mr. Washington: no—not the King against whom he took arms. In the eyes of all the gentry of the French court, who gaily joined in the crusade against us, and so took their revenge for Canada, the great American chief always appeared as anax andron, and they allowed that his better could not be seen in Versailles itself. Though they were quarrelling with the Governor, the gentlemen of the House of Burgesses still maintained amicable relations with him, and exchanged dignified courtesies. When my Lord Bottetourt arrived, and held his court at Williamsburg in no small splendour and state, all the gentry waited upon him, Madam Esmond included. And at his death, Lord Dunmore, who succeeded him, and brought a fine family with him, was treated with the utmost respect by our gentry privately, though publicly the House of Assembly and the Governor were at war.

Their quarrels are a matter of history, and concern me personally only so far as this, that our burgesses being convened for the 1st of March in the year after my arrival in Virginia, it was agreed that we should all pay a visit to our capital, and our duty to the Governor. Since Harry's unfortunate marriage Madam Esmond had not performed this duty, though always previously accustomed to pay it; but now that her eldest son was arrived in the colony, my mother opined that we must certainly wait upon his Excellency the Governor, nor were we sorry, perhaps, to get away from our little Richmond to enjoy the gaieties of the provincial capital. Madam engaged, and at a great price, the best house to be had at Richmond for herself and her family. Now I was rich, her generosity was curious. I had more than once to interpose (her old servants likewise wondering at her new way of life), and beg her not to be so lavish. But she gently said, in former days she had occasion to save, which now existed no more. Harry had enough, sure, with such a wife as he had taken out of the housekeeper's room. If she chose to be a little extravagant now, why should she hesitate? She had not her dearest daughter and grandchildren with her every day (she fell in love with all three of them, and spoiled them as much as they were capable of being spoiled). Besides, in former days I could not accuse her of too much extravagance, and this I think was almost the only allusion she made to the pecuniary differences between us. So she had her people dressed in their best, and her best wines, plate, and furniture from Castlewood by sea at no small charge, and her dress in which she had been married in George II.'s reign, and we all flattered ourselves that our coach made the greatest figure of any except his Excellency's, and we engaged Signor Formicalo, his Excellency's major-domo, to superintend the series of feasts that were given in my honour; and more fleshpots were set a-stewing in our kitchens in one month, our servants said, than had been known in the family since the young gentlemen went away. So great was Theo's influence over my mother, that she actually persuaded her, that year, to receive our sister Fanny, Hal's wife, who would have stayed upon the plantation rather than face Madam Esmond. But, trusting to Theo's promise of amnesty, Fanny (to whose house we had paid more than one visit) came up to town, and made her curtsey to Madam Esmond, and was forgiven. And rather than be forgiven in that way, I own, for my part, that I would prefer perdition or utter persecution.

"You know these, my dear?" says Madam Esmond, pointing to her fine silver sconces. "Fanny hath often cleaned them when she was with me at Castlewood. And this dress, too, Fanny knows, I dare say? Her poor mother had the care of it. I always had the greatest confidence in her."

Here there is wrath flashing from Fanny's eyes, which our mother, who has forgiven her, does not perceive—not she!

"Oh, she was a treasure to me!" Madam resumes. "I never should have nursed my boys through their illnesses but for your mother's admirable care of them. Colonel Lee, permit me to present you to my daughter, my Lady Warrington. Her ladyship is a neighbour of your relatives the Bunburys at home. Here comes his Excellency. Welcome, my lord!"

And our princess performs before his lordship one of those curtseys of which she was not a little proud; and I fancy I see some of the company venturing to smile.

"By George! madam," says Mr. Lee, "since Count Borulawski, I have not seen a bow so elegant as your ladyship's."

"And pray, sir, who was Count Borulawski?" asks Madam.

"He was a nobleman high in favour with his Polish Majesty," replies Mr. Lee. "May I ask you, madam, to present me to your distinguished son?"

"This is Sir George Warrington," says my mother, pointing to me.

"Pardon me, madam. I meant Captain Warrington, who was by Mr. Wolfe's side when he died. I had been contented to share his fate, so I had been near him."

And the ardent Lee swaggers up to Harry, and takes his hand with respect, and pays him a compliment or two, which makes me, at least, pardon him for his late impertinence; for my dearest Hal walks gloomily through his mother's rooms in his old uniform of the famous corps which he has quitted.

We had had many meetings, which the stern mother could not interrupt, and in which that instinctive love which bound us to one another, and which nothing could destroy, had opportunity to speak. Entirely unlike each other in our pursuits, our tastes, our opinions—his life being one of eager exercise, active sport, and all the amusements of the field, while mine is to dawdle over books and spend my time in languid self-contemplation—we have, nevertheless, had such a sympathy as almost passes the love of women. My poor Hal confessed as much to me, for his part, in his artless manner, when we went away without wives or womankind, except a few negroes left in the place, and passed a week at Castlewood together.

The ladies did not love each other. I know enough of my Lady Theo, to see after a very few glances whether or not she takes a liking to another of her amiable sex. All my powers of persuasion or command fail to change the stubborn creature's opinion. Had she ever said a word against Mrs. This or Miss That? Not she! Has she been otherwise than civil? No, assuredly! My Lady Theo is polite to a beggar-woman, treats her kitchenmaids like duchesses, and murmurs a compliment to the dentist for his elegant manner of pulling her tooth out. She would black my boots, or clean the grate, if I ordained it (always looking like a duchess the while); but as soon as I say to her, "My dear creature, be fond of this lady, or t'other!" all obedience ceases; she executes the most refined curtseys; smiles and kisses even to order; but performs that mysterious undefinable freemasonic signal, which passes between women, by which each knows that the other hates her. So, with regard to Fanny, we had met at her house, and at others. I remembered her affectionately from old days, I fully credited poor Hal's violent protests and tearful oaths, that, by George, it was our mother's persecution which made him marry her. He couldn't stand by and see a poor thing tortured as she was, without coming to her rescue; no, by heavens, he couldn't! I say I believed all this; and had for my sister-in-law a genuine compassion, as well as an early regard; and yet I had no love to give her; and, in reply to Hal's passionate outbreaks in praise of her beauty and worth, and eager queries to me whether I did not think her a perfect paragon? I could only answer with faint compliments or vague approval, feeling all the while that I was disappointing my poor ardent fellow, and cursing inwardly that revolt against flattery and falsehood into which I sometimes frantically rush. Why should I not say, "Yes dear Hal, thy wife is a paragon; her singing is delightful, her hair and shape are beautiful;" as I might have said by a little common stretch of politeness? Why could I not cajole this or that stupid neighbour or relative, as I have heard Theo do a thousand times, finding all sorts of lively prattle to amuse them, whilst I sit before them dumb and gloomy? I say it was a sin not to have more words to say in praise of Fanny. We ought to have praised her, we ought to have liked her. My Lady Warrington certainly ought to have liked her, for she can play the hypocrite, and I cannot. And there was this young creature—pretty, graceful, shaped like a nymph, with beautiful black eyes—and we cared for them no more than for two gooseberries! At Warrington my wife and I, when we pretended to compare notes, elaborately complimented each other on our new sister's beauty. What lovely eyes!—Oh yes! What a sweet little dimple on her chin!—Ah oui! What wonderful little feet!—Perfectly Chinese! where should we in London get slippers small enough for her? And, these compliments exhausted, we knew that we did not like Fanny the value of one penny-piece; we knew that we disliked her; we knew that we ha... Well, what hypocrites women are! We heard from many quarters how eagerly my brother had taken up the new anti-English opinion, and what a champion he was of so-called American rights and freedom. "It is her doing, my dear," says I to my wife. "If I had said so much, I am sure you would have scolded me," says my Lady Warrington, laughing: and I did straightway begin to scold her, and say it was most cruel of her to suspect our new sister; and what earthly right had we to do so? But I say again, I know Madam Theo so well, that when once she has got a prejudice against a person in her little head, not all the king's horses nor all the king's men will get it out again. I vow nothing would induce her to believe that Harry was not henpecked—nothing.

Well, we went to Castlewood together without the women, and stayed at the dreary, dear old place, where we had been so happy, and I, at least, so gloomy. It was winter, and duck-time, and Harry went away to the river, and shot dozens and scores and bushels of canvasbacks, whilst I remained in my grandfather's library amongst the old mouldering books which I loved in my childhood—which I see in a dim vision still resting on a little boy's lap, as he sits by an old white-headed gentleman's knee. I read my books; I slept in my own bed and room—religiously kept, as my mother told me, and left as on the day when I went to Europe. Hal's cheery voice would wake me, as of old. Like all men who love to go a-field, he was an early riser: he would come and wake me, and sit on the foot of the bed and perfume the air with his morning pipe, as the house negroes laid great logs on the fire. It was a happy time! Old Nathan had told me of cunning crypts where ancestral rum and claret were deposited. We had had cares, struggles, battles, bitter griefs, and disappointments; we were boys again as we sat there together. I am a boy now even as I think of the time.

That unlucky tea-tax, which alone of the taxes lately imposed upon the colonies, the home Government was determined to retain, was met with defiance throughout America. 'Tis true we paid a shilling in the pound at home, and asked only threepence from Boston or Charleston; but as a question of principle, the impost was refused by the provinces, which indeed ever showed a most spirited determination to pay as little as they could help. In Charleston the tea-ships were unloaded, and the cargoes stored in cellars. From New York and Philadelphia, the vessels were turned back to London. In Boston (where there was an armed force, whom the inhabitants were perpetually mobbing), certain patriots, painted and disguised as Indians, boarded the ships, and flung the obnoxious cargoes into the water. The wrath of our white Father was kindled against this city of Mohocks in masquerade. The notable Boston Port Bill was brought forward in the British House of Commons; the port was closed, and the Custom House removed to Salem. The Massachusetts Charter was annulled; and,—in just apprehension that riots might ensue, in dealing with the perpetrators of which the colonial courts might be led to act partially,—Parliament decreed that persons indicted for acts of violence and armed resistance, might be sent home, or to another colony, for trial. If such acts set all America in a flame, they certainly drove all wellwisbers of our country into a fury. I might have sentenced Master Miles Warrington, at five years old, to a whipping, and he would have cried, taken down his little small-clothes and submitted: but suppose I offered (and he richly deserving it) to chastise Captain Miles of the Prince's Dragoons? He would whirl my paternal cane out of my hand, box my hair-powder out of my ears. Lord a-mercy! I tremble at the very idea of the controversy? He would assert his independence in a word; and if, I say, I think the home Parliament had a right to levy taxes in the colonies, I own that we took means most captious, most insolent, most irritating, and, above all, most impotent, to assert our claim.

My Lord Dunmore, our Governor of Virginia, upon Lord Bottetourt's death, received me into some intimacy soon after my arrival in the colony, being willing to live on good terms with all our gentry. My mother's severe loyalty was no secret to him; indeed, she waved the king's banner in all companies, and talked so loudly and resolutely, that Randolph and Patrick Henry himself were struck dumb before her. It was Madam Esmond's celebrated reputation for loyalty (his Excellency laughingly told me) which induced him to receive her eldest son to grace.

"I have had the worst character of you from home," his lordship said. "Little birds whisper to me, Sir George, that you are a man of the most dangerous principles. You are a friend of Mr. Wilkes and Alderman Beckford. I am not sure you have not been at Medmenham Abbey. You have lived with players, poets, and all sorts of wild people. I have been warned against you, sir, and I find you——"

"Not so black as I have been painted," I interrupted his lordship, with a smile.

"Faith," says my lord, "if I tell Sir George Warrington that he seems to me a very harmless, quiet gentleman, and that 'tis a great relief to me to talk to him amidst these loud politicians; these lawyers with their perpetual noise about Greece and Rome; these Virginian squires who are for ever professing their loyalty and respect, whilst they are shaking their fists in my face—I hope nobody overhears us," says my lord, with an arch smile, "and nobody will carry my opinions home."

His lordship's ill opinion having been removed by a better knowledge of me, our acquaintance daily grew more intimate; and, especially between the ladies of his family and my own, a close friendship arose—between them and my wife at least. Hal's wife, received kindly at the little provincial court, as all ladies were, made herself by no means popular there by the hot and eager political tone which she adopted. She assailed all the Government measures with indiscriminating acrimony. Were they lenient? She said the perfidious British Government was only preparing a snare, and biding its time until it could forge heavier chains for unhappy America. Were they angry? Why did not every American citizen rise, assert his rights as a freeman, and serve every British governor, officer, soldier, as they had treated the East India Company's tea? My mother, on the other hand, was pleased to express her opinions with equal frankness, and, indeed, to press her advice upon his Excellency with a volubility which may have fatigued that representative of the Sovereign. Call out the militia; send for fresh troops from New York, from home, from anywhere; lock up the Capitol! (this advice was followed, it must be owned) and send every one of the ringleaders amongst those wicked burgesses to prison! was Madam Esmond's daily counsel to the Governor by word and letter. And if not only the burgesses, but the burgesses' wives could have been led off to punishment and captivity, I think this Brutus of a woman would scarce have appealed against the sentence.

CHAPTER LXXXVII. The Last of God Save the King

What perverse law of Fate is it that ever places me in a minority? Should a law be proposed to hand over this realm to the Pretender of Rome, or the Grand Turk, and submit it to the new sovereign's religion, it might pass, as I should certainly be voting against it. At home in Virginia, I found myself disagreeing with everybody as usual. By the Patriots I was voted (as indeed I professed myself to be) a Tory; by the Tories I was presently declared to be a dangerous Republican. The time was utterly out of joint. O cursed spite! Ere I had been a year in Virginia, how I wished myself back by the banks of the Waveney! But the aspect of affairs was so troublous, that I could not leave my mother, a lone lady, to face possible war and disaster, nor would she quit the country at such a juncture, nor should a man of spirit leave it. At his Excellency's table, and over his Excellency's plentiful claret, that point was agreed on by numbers of the well-affected, that vow was vowed over countless brimming bumpers. No: it was statue signum, signifer! We Cavaliers would all rally round it; and at these times, our Governor talked like the bravest of the brave.

Now, I will say, of all my Virginian acquaintance, Madam Esmond was the most consistent. Our gentlefolks had come in numbers to Williamsburg; and a great number of them proposed to treat her Excellency, the Governor's lady, to a ball, when the news reached us of the Boston Port Bill. Straightway the House of Burgesses adopts an indignant protest against this measure of the British Parliament, and decrees a solemn day of fast and humiliation throughout the country, and of solemn prayer to Heaven to avert the calamity of Civil War. Meanwhile, the invitation to my Lady Dunmore having been already given and accepted, the gentlemen agreed that their ball should take place on the appointed evening, and then sackcloth and ashes should be assumed some days afterwards.

"A ball!" says Madam Esmond. "I go to a ball which is given by a set of rebels who are going publicly to insult his Majesty a week afterwards! I will die sooner!" And she wrote to the gentlemen who were stewards for the occasion to say, that viewing the dangerous state of the country, she, for her part, could not think of attending a ball.

What was her surprise then, the next time she went abroad in her chair, to be cheered by a hundred persons, white and black, and shouts of "Huzzah, Madam!" "Heaven bless your ladyship!" They evidently thought her patriotism had caused her determination not to go to the ball.

Madam, that there should be no mistake, puts her head out of the chair, and cries out "God save the King" as loud as she can. The people cried "God save the King," too. Everybody cried "God save the King" in those days. On the night of that entertainment, my poor Harry, as a Burgess of the House, and one of the givers of the feast, donned his uniform red coat of Wolfe's (which he so soon was to exchange for another colour), and went off with Madam Fanny to the ball. My Lady Warrington and her humble servant, as being strangers in the country, and English people as it were, were permitted by

Madam to attend the assembly from which she of course absented herself. I had the honour to dance a country-dance with the lady of Mount Vernon, whom I found a most lively, pretty, and amiable partner; but am bound to say that my wife's praises of her were received with a very grim acceptance by my mother, when Lady Warrington came to recount the events of the evening. Could not Sir George Warrington have danced with my Lady Dunmore or her daughters, or with anybody but Mrs. Washington; to be sure the Colonel thought so well of himself and his wife, that no doubt he considered her the grandest lady in the room; and she who remembered him a road-surveyor at a guinea a day! Well, indeed! there was no measuring the pride of these provincial upstarts, and as for this gentleman, my Lord Dunmore's partiality for him had evidently turned his head. I do not know about Mr. Washington's pride, I know that my good mother never could be got to love him or anything that was his.

She was no better pleased with him for going to the ball, than with his conduct three days afterwards, when the day of fast and humiliation was appointed, and when he attended the service which our new clergyman performed. She invited Mr. Belman to dinner that day, and sundry colonial authorities. The clergyman excused himself. Madam Esmond tossed up her head, and said he might do as he liked. She made a parade of a dinner; she lighted her house up at night, when all the rest of the city was in darkness and gloom; she begged Mr. Hardy, one of his Excellency's aides-de-camp, to sing "God save the King," to which the people in the street outside listened, thinking that it might be a part of some religious service which Madam was celebrating; but then she called for "Britons, strike home!" which the simple young gentleman just from Europe began to perform, when a great yell arose in the street, and a large stone, flung from some rebellious hand, plumped into the punch-bowl before me, and scattered it and its contents about our dining-room.

My mother went to the window nothing daunted. I can see her rigid little figure now, as she stands with a tossed-up head, outstretched frilled arms, and the twinkling stars for a background, and sings in chorus, "Britons, strike home! strike home!" The crowd in front of the palings shout and roar, "Silence! for shame! go back!" but she will not go back, not she. "Fling more stones, if you dare!" says the brave little lady; and more might have come, but some gentlemen issuing out of the Raley Tavern interpose with the crowd. "You mustn't insult a lady," says a voice I think I know. "Huzza, Colonel! Hurrah, Captain! God bless your honour!" say the people in the street. And thus the enemies are pacified.

My mother, protesting that the whole disturbance was over, would have had Mr. Hardy sing another song, but he gave a sickly grin, and said, "he really did not like to sing to such accompaniments," and the concert for that evening was ended; though I am bound to say that some scoundrels returned at night, frightened my poor wife almost out of wits, and broke every single window in the front of our tenement. "Britons, strike home!" was a little too much;

Madam should have contented herself with "God save the King." Militia was drilled, bullets were cast, supplies of ammunition got ready, cunning plans for disappointing the royal ordinances devised and carried out; but, to be sure, "God save the King" was the cry everywhere, and in reply to my objections to the gentlemen-patriots, "Why, you are scheming for a separation; you are bringing down upon you the inevitable wrath of the greatest power in the world!"—the answer to me always was, "We mean no separation at all; we yield to no men in loyalty; we glory in the name of Britons," and so forth, and so forth. The powder-barrels were heaped in the cellar, the train was laid, but Mr. Fawkes was persistent in his dutiful petitions to King and Parliament and meant no harm, not he! 'Tis true when I spoke of the power of our country, I imagined she would exert it; that she would not expect to overcome three millions of fellow-Britons on their own soil with a few battalions, a half-dozen generals from Bond Street, and a few thousand bravos hired out of Germany. As if we wanted to insult the thirteen colonies as well as to subdue them, we must set upon them these hordes of Hessians, and the murderers out of the Indian wigwams. Was our great quarrel not to be fought without tali auxilio and istis defensoribus? Ah! 'tis easy, now we are worsted, to look over the map of the great empire wrested from us, and show how we ought not to have lost it. Long Island ought to have exterminated Washington's army; he ought never to have come out of Valley Forge except as a prisoner. The South was ours after the battle of Camden, but for the inconceivable meddling of the Commander-in-Chief at New York, who paralysed the exertions of the only capable British General who appeared during the war, and sent him into that miserable cul-de-sac at York Town, whence he could only issue defeated and a prisoner. Oh, for a week more! a day more, an hour more of darkness or light! In reading over our American campaigns from their unhappy commencement to their inglorious end, now that we are able to see the enemy's movements and conditions as well as our own, I fancy we can see how an advance, a march, might have put enemies into our power who had no means to withstand it, and changed the entire issue of the struggle. But it was ordained by Heaven, and for the good, as we can now have no doubt, of both empires, that the great Western Republic should separate from us: and the gallant soldiers who fought on her side, their indomitable and heroic Chief above all, had the glory of facing and overcoming, not only veteran soldiers amply provided and inured to war, but wretchedness, cold, hunger, dissensions, treason within their own camp, where all must have gone to rack, but for the pure unquenchable flame of patriotism that was for ever burning in the bosom of the heroic leader. What a constancy, what a magnanimity, what a surprising persistence against fortune! Washington before the enemy was no better nor braver than hundreds that fought with him or against him (who has not heard the repeated sneers against "Fabius" in which his factious captains were accustomed to indulge?), but Washington the Chief of a nation in arms, doing battle with distracted parties; calm in the midst of conspiracy; serene against the open foe before him and the darker enemies at his back;

Washington inspiring order and spirit into troops hungry and in rags; stung by ingratitude, but betraying no anger, and ever ready to forgive; in defeat invincible, magnanimous in conquest, and never so sublime as on that day when he laid down his victorious sword and sought his noble retirement:— here indeed is a character to admire and revere; a life without a stain, a fame without a flaw. Quando invenies parem? In that more extensive work, which I have planned and partly written on the subject of this great war, I hope I have done justice to the character of its greatest leader. [And I trust that in the opinions I have recorded regarding him, I have shown that I also can be just and magnanimous towards those who view me personally with no favour. For my brother Hal being at Mount Vernon, and always eager to bring me and his beloved Chief on good terms, showed his Excellency some of the early sheets of my History. General Washington (who read but few books, and had not the slightest pretensions to literary taste) remarked, "If you will have my opinion, my dear General, I think Sir George's projected work, from the specimen I have of it, is certain to offend both parties."—G. E. W.]. And this from the sheer force of respect which his eminent virtues extorted. With the young Mr. Washington of my own early days I had not the honour to enjoy much sympathy: though my brother, whose character is much more frank and affectionate than mine, was always his fast friend in early times, when they were equals, as in latter days when the General, as I do own and think, was all mankind's superior.

I have mentioned that contrariety in my disposition, and, perhaps, in my brother's, which somehow placed us on wrong sides in the quarrel which ensued, and which from this time forth raged for five years, until the mother country was fain to acknowledge her defeat. Harry should have been the Tory, and I the Whig. Theoretically my opinions were very much more liberal than those of my brother, who, especially after his marriage, became what our Indian nabobs call a Bahadoor—a person ceremonious, stately, and exacting respect. When my Lord Dunmore, for instance, talked about liberating the negroes, so as to induce them to join the King's standard, Hal was for hanging the Governor and the Black Guards (as he called them) whom his Excellency had crimped. "If you, gentlemen are fighting for freedom," says I, "sure the negroes may fight, too." On which Harry roars out, shaking his fist, "Infernal villains, if I meet any of 'em, they shall die by this hand!" And my mother agreed that this idea of a negro insurrection was the most abominable and parricidal notion which had ever sprung up in her unhappy country. She at least was more consistent than brother Hal. She would have black and white obedient to the powers that be: whereas Hal only could admit that freedom was the right of the latter colour.

As a proof of her argument, Madam Esmond and Harry too would point to an instance in our own family in the person of Mr. Gumbo. Having got his freedom from me, as a reward for his admirable love and fidelity to me when times were hard, Gumbo, on his return to Virginia, was scarce a welcome guest in his old quarters, amongst my mother's servants. He was free, and they were not: he was, as it were, a centre of insurrection. He gave himself no small airs of protection and consequence amongst them; bragging of his friends in Europe ("at home," as he called it), and his doings there; and for a while bringing the household round about him to listen to him and admire him, like the monkey who had seen the world. Now, Sady, Hal's boy, who went to America of his own desire, was not free. Hence jealousies between him and Mr. Gum; and battles, in which they both practised the noble art of boxing and butting, which they had learned at Marybone Gardens and Hockley-in-the-Hole. Nor was Sady the only jealous person: almost all my mother's servants hated Signor Gumbo for the airs which he gave himself; and I am sorry to say, that our faithful Molly, his wife, was as jealous as his old fellow-servants. The blacks could not pardon her for having demeaned herself so far as to marry one of their kind. She met with no respect, could exercise no authority, came to her mistress with ceaseless complaints of the idleness, knavery, lies, stealing of the black people; and finally with a story of jealousy against a certain Dinah, or Diana, who, I heartily trust, was as innocent as her namesake the moonlight visitant of Endymion. Now, on the article of morality Madam Esmond was a very Draconess; and a person accused was a person guilty. She made charges against Mr. Gumbo to which he replied with asperity. Forgetting that he was a free gentleman, my mother now ordered Gumbo to be whipped, on which Molly flew at her ladyship, all her wrath at her husband's infidelity vanishing at the idea of the indignity put upon him; there was a rebellion in our house at Castlewood. A quarrel took place between me and my mother, as I took my man's side. Hal and Fanny sided with her, on the contrary; and in so far the difference did good, as it brought about some little intimacy between Madam and her younger children. This little difference was speedily healed; but it was clear that the Standard of Insurrection must be removed out of our house; and we determined that Mr. Gumbo and his lady should return to Europe.

My wife and I would willingly have gone with them, God wot, for our boy sickened and lost his strength, and caught the fever in our swampy country; but at this time she was expecting to lie in (of our son Henry), and she knew, too, that I had promised to stay in Virginia. It was agreed that we should send the two back; but when I offered Theo to go, she said her place was with her husband;—her father and Hetty at home would take care of our children; and she scarce would allow me to see a tear in her eyes whilst she was making her preparations for the departure of her little ones. Dost thou remember the time, madam, and the silence round the worktables, as the piles of little shirts are made ready for the voyage? and the stealthy visits to the children's chambers whilst they are asleep and yet with you? and the terrible time of parting, as our barge with the servants and children rows to the ship, and you stand on the shore? Had the Prince of Wales been going on that voyage, he could not have been better provided. Where, sirrah, is the Tompion watch your grandmother gave you? and how did you survive the boxes of cakes which the good lady stowed away in your cabin?

The ship which took out my poor Theo's children, returned with the Reverend Mr. Hagan and my Lady Maria on board, who meekly chose to resign her rank, and was known in the colony (which was not to be a colony very long) only as Mrs. Hagan. At the time when I was in favour with my Lord Dunmore, a living falling vacant in Westmoreland county, he gave it to our kinsman, who arrived in Virginia time enough to christen our boy Henry, and to preach some sermons on the then gloomy state of affairs, which Madam Esmond pronounced to be prodigious fine. I think my Lady Maria won Madam's heart by insisting on going out of the room after her. "My father, your brother, was an earl, 'tis true," says she, "but you know your ladyship is a marquis's daughter, and I never can think of taking precedence of you!" So fond did Madam become of her niece, that she even allowed Hagan to read plays—my own humble compositions amongst others—and was fairly forced to own that there was merit in the tragedy of Pocahontas, which our parson delivered with uncommon energy and fire.

Hal and his wife came but rarely to Castlewood and Richmond when the chaplain and his lady were with us. Fanny was very curt and rude with Maria, used to giggle and laugh strangely in her company, and repeatedly remind her of her age, to our mother's astonishment, who would often ask, was there any cause of quarrel between her niece and her daughter-in-law? I kept my own counsel on these occasions, and was often not a little touched by the meekness with which the elder lady bore her persecutions. Fanny loved to torture her in her husband's presence (who, poor fellow, was also in happy ignorance about his wife's early history), and the other bore her agony, wincing as little as might be. I sometimes would remonstrate with Madam Harry, and ask her was she a Red Indian, that she tortured her victims so? "Have not I had torture enough in my time?" says the young lady, and looked as though she was determined to pay back the injuries inflicted on her.

"Nay," says I, "you were bred in our wigwam, and I don't remember anything but kindness!"

"Kindness!" cries she. "No slave was ever treated as I was. The blows which wound most, often are those which never are aimed. The people who hate us are not those we have injured."

I thought of little Fanny in our early days, silent, smiling, willing to run and do all our biddings for us, and I grieved for my poor brother, who had taken this sly creature into his bosom.

CHAPTER LXXXVIII. Yankee Doodle comes to Town

One of the uses to which we put America in the days of our British dominion was to make it a refuge for our sinners. Besides convicts and assigned servants whom we transported to our colonies, we discharged on their shores scapegraces and younger sons, for whom dissipation, despair, and bailiffs made the old country uninhabitable. And as Mr. Cook, in his voyages, made his newly discovered islanders presents of English animals (and other specimens of European civilisation), we used to take care to send samples of our black sheep over to the colonies, there to browse as best they might, and propagate their precious breed. I myself was perhaps a little guilty in this matter, in busying myself to find a living in America for the worthy Hagan, husband of my kinswoman,—at least was guilty in so far as this, that as we could get him no employment in England, we were glad to ship him to Virginia, and give him a colonial pulpit-cushion to thump. He demeaned himself there as a brave honest gentleman, to be sure; he did his duty thoroughly by his congregation, and his king too; and in so far did credit to my small patronage. Madam Theo used to urge this when I confided to her my scruples of conscience on this subject, and show, as her custom was and is, that my conduct in this, as in all other matters, was dictated by the highest principle of morality and honour. But would I have given Hagan our living at home, and selected him and his wife to minister to our parish? I fear not. I never had a doubt of our cousin's sincere repentance; but I think I was secretly glad when she went to work it out in the wilderness. And I say this, acknowledging my pride and my error. Twice, when I wanted them most, this kind Maria aided me with her sympathy and friendship. She bore her own distresses courageously, and soothed those of others with admirable affection and devotion. And yet I, and some of mine (not Theo), would look down upon her. Oh, for shame, for shame on our pride!

My poor Lady Maria was not the only one of our family who was to be sent out of the way to American wildernesses. Having borrowed, stolen, cheated at home, until he could cheat, borrow, and steal no more, the Honourable William Esmond, Esquire, was accommodated with a place at New York; and his noble brother and royal master heartily desired that they might see him no more. When the troubles began, we heard of the fellow and his doings in his new habitation. Lies and mischief were his avant-couriers wherever he travelled. My Lord Dunmore informed me that Mr. Will declared publicly, that our estate of Castlewood was only ours during his brother's pleasure; that his father, out of consideration for Madam Esmond, his lordship's half-sister, had given her the place for life, and that he, William, was in negotiation with his brother, the present Lord Castlewood, for the purchase of the reversion of the estate! We had the deed of gift in our strongroom at Castlewood, and it was furthermore registered in due form at Williamsburg; so that we were easy on that score. But the intention was everything; and Hal and I promised, as soon as ever we met Mr. William, to get from him a confirmation of this pretty story. What Madam Esmond's feelings and expressions were when she heard it, I need scarcely here particularise. "What! my father, the Marquis of Esmond, was a liar, and I am a cheat, am I?" cries my mother. "He will take my son's property at my death, will he?" And she was for writing, not only to Lord Castlewood in England, but to his Majesty himself at St. James's, and was only prevented by my assurance that Mr. Will's lies were notorious amongst all his acquaintance, and that we could not expect, in our own case, that he should be so inconsistent as to tell the truth. We heard of him presently as one of the loudest amongst the Loyalists in New York, as Captain, and presently Major of a corps of volunteers who were sending their addresses to the well-disposed in all the other colonies, and announcing their perfect readiness to die for the mother country.

We could not lie in a house without a whole window, and closing the shutters of that unlucky mansion we had hired at Williamsburg, Madam Esmond left our little capital, and my family returned to Richmond, which also was deserted by the members of the (dissolved) Assembly. Captain Hal and his wife returned pretty early to their plantation; and I, not a little annoyed at the course which events were taking, divided my time pretty much between my own family and that of our Governor, who professed himself very eager to have my advice and company. There were the strongest political differences, but as yet no actual personal quarrel. Even after the dissolution of our House of Assembly (the members of which adjourned to a tavern, and there held that famous meeting where, I believe, the idea of a congress of all the colonies was first proposed), the gentlemen who were strongest in opposition remained good friends with his Excellency, partook of his hospitality, and joined him in excursions of pleasure. The session over, the gentry went home and had meetings in their respective counties; and the Assemblies in most of the other provinces having been also abruptly dissolved, it was agreed everywhere that a general congress should be held. Philadelphia, as the largest and most important city on our continent, was selected as the place of meeting; and those celebrated conferences began, which were but the angry preface of war. We were still at God save the King; we were still presenting our humble petitions to the throne; but when I went to visit my brother Harry at Fanny's Mount (his new plantation lay not far from ours, but with Rappahannock between us, and towards Mattaponey River), he rode out on business one morning, and I in the afternoon happened to ride too, and was told by one of the grooms that master was gone towards Willis's Ordinary; in which direction, thinking no harm, I followed. And upon a clear place not far from Willis's, as I advance out of the wood, I come on Captain Hal on horseback, with three- or four-and-thirty countrymen round about him, armed with every sort of weapon, pike, scythe, fowling-piece, and musket; and the Captain, with two or three likely young fellows as officers under him, putting the men through their exercise. As I rode up a queer expression comes over Hal's face. "Present arms!" says he (and the army tries to perform the salute as well they could). "Captain Cade, this is my brother, Sir George Warrington."

"As a relation of yours, Colonel," says the individual addressed as captain, "the gentleman is welcome," and he holds out a hand accordingly.

"And—and a true friend to Virginia," says Hal, with a reddening face.

"Yes, please God! gentlemen," say I, on which the regiment gives a hearty huzzay for the Colonel and his brother. The drill over, the officers, and the men too, were for adjourning to Willis's and taking some refreshment, but Colonel Hal said he could not drink with them that afternoon, and we trotted homewards together.

"So, Hal, the cat's out of the bag!" I said.

He gave me a hard look. "I guess there's wilder cats in it. It must come to this, George. I say, you mustn't tell Madam," he adds.

"Good God!" I cried, "do you mean that with fellows such as those I saw yonder, you and your friends are going to make fight against the greatest nation and the best army in the world?"

"I guess we shall get an awful whipping," says Hal, "and that's the fact. But then, George," he added, with his sweet kind smile, "we are young, and a whipping or two may do us good. Won't it do us good, Dolly, you old slut?" and he gives a playful touch with his whip to an old dog of all trades, that was running by him.

I did not try to urge upon him (I had done so in vain many times previously) our British side of the question, the side which appears to me to be the best. He was accustomed to put off my reasons by saying, "All mighty well, brother, you speak as an Englishman, and have cast in your lot with your country, as I have with mine." To this argument I own there is no answer, and all that remains for the disputants is to fight the matter out, when the strongest is in the right. Which had the right in the wars of the last century? The king or the parliament? The side that was uppermost was the right, and on the whole much more humane in their victory than the Cavaliers would have been had they won. Nay, suppose we Tories had won the day in America; how frightful and bloody that triumph would have been! What ropes and scaffolds one imagines, what noble heads laid low! A strange feeling this, I own; I was on the Loyalist side, and yet wanted the Whigs to win. My brother Hal, on the other hand, who distinguished himself greatly with his regiment, never allowed a word of disrespect against the enemy whom he opposed. "The officers of the British army," he used to say, "are gentlemen: at least, I have not heard that they are very much changed since my time. There may be scoundrels and ruffians amongst the enemy's troops; I dare say we could find some such amongst our own. Our business is to beat his Majesty's forces, not call them names;—any rascal can do that." And from a name which Mr. Lee gave my brother, and many of his rough horsemen did not understand, Harry was often called "Chevaleer Baird" in the Continental army. He was a knight, indeed, without fear and without reproach.

As for the argument, "What could such people as those you were drilling do against the British army?" Hal had as confident answer.

"They can beat them," says he, "Mr. George, that's what they can do."

"Great heavens!" I cry, "do you mean with your company of Wolfe's you would hesitate to attack five hundred such?"

"With my company of the 67th, I would go anywhere. And, agreed with you, that at this present moment I know more of soldiering than they;—but place me on that open ground where you found us, armed as you please, and half a dozen of my friends, with rifles, in the woods round about me; which would get the better? You know best, Mr. Braddock's aide-de-camp!"

There was no arguing with such a determination as this. "Thou knowest my way of thinking, Hal," I said; "and having surprised you at your work, I must tell my lord what I have seen."

"Tell him, of course. You have seen our county militia exercising. You will see as much in every colony from here to the Saint Lawrence or Georgia. As I am an old soldier, they have elected me colonel. What more natural? Come, brother, let us trot on; dinner will be ready, and Mrs. Fan does not like me to keep it waiting." And so we made for his house, which was open like all the houses of our Virginian gentlemen, and where not only every friend and neighbour, but every stranger and traveller, was sure to find a welcome.

"So, Mrs. Fan," I said, "I have found out what game my brother has been playing."

"I trust the Colonel will have plenty of sport ere long," says she, with a toss of her head.

My wife thought Harry had been hunting, and I did not care to undeceive her, though what I had seen and he had told me, made me naturally very anxious.

CHAPTER LXXXIX. A Colonel without a Regiment

When my visit to my brother was concluded, and my wife and young child had returned to our maternal house at Richmond, I made it my business to go over to our Governor, then at his country house, near Williamsburg, and confer with him regarding these open preparations for war, which were being made not only in our own province, but in every one of the colonies as far as we could learn. Gentlemen, with whose names history has since made all the world familiar, were appointed from Virginia as Delegates to the General Congress about to be held in Philadelphia. In Massachusetts the people and the Royal troops were facing each other almost in open hostility: in Maryland and Pennsylvania we flattered ourselves that a much more loyal spirit was prevalent: in the Carolinas and Georgia the mother country could reckon upon staunch adherents, and a great majority of the inhabitants: and it never was to be supposed that our own Virginia would forgo its ancient loyalty. We had but few troops in the province, but its gentry were proud of their descent from the Cavaliers of the old times: and round about our Governor were swarms of loud and confident Loyalists who were only eager for the moment when they might draw the sword, and scatter the rascally rebels before them. Of course, in these meetings I was forced to hear many a hard word against my poor Harry. His wife, all agreed (and not without good reason, perhaps), had led him to adopt these extreme anti-British opinions which he had of late declared; and he was infatuated by his attachment to the gentleman of Mount Vernon, it was farther said, whose opinions my brother always followed, and who, day by day, was committing himself farther in the dreadful and desperate course of resistance. "This is your friend," the people about his Excellency said, "this is the man you favoured, who has had your special confidence, and who has repeatedly shared your hospitality!" It could not but be owned much of this was true: though what some of our eager Loyalists called treachery was indeed rather a proof of the longing desire Mr. Washington and other gentlemen had, not to withdraw from their allegiance to the Crown, but to remain faithful, and exhaust the very last chance of reconciliation, before they risked the other terrible alternative of revolt and separation. Let traitors arm, and villains draw the parricidal sword! We at least would remain faithful; the unconquerable power of England would be exerted, and the misguided and ungrateful provinces punished and brought back to their obedience. With what cheers we drank his Majesty's health after our banquets! We would die in defence of his rights; we would have a Prince of his Royal house to come and govern his ancient dominions! In consideration of my own and my excellent mother's loyalty, my brother's benighted conduct should be forgiven. Was it yet too late to secure him by offering him a good command? Would I not intercede with him, who, it was known, had a great influence over him? In our Williamsburg councils we were alternately in every state of exaltation and triumph, of hope, of fury against the rebels, of anxious expectancy of home succour, of doubt, distrust, and gloom.

I promised to intercede with my brother; and wrote to him, I own, with but little hope of success, repeating, and trying to strengthen the arguments which I had many a time used in our conversations. My mother, too, used her authority; but from this, I own, I expected little advantage. She assailed him, as her habit was, with such texts of Scripture as she thought bore out her own opinion, and threatened punishment to him. She menaced him with the penalties which must fall upon those who were disobedient to the powers that be. She pointed to his elder brother's example; and hinted, I fear, at his subjection to his wife, the very worst argument she could use in such a controversy. She did not show me her own letter to him; possibly she knew I might find fault with the energy of some of the expressions she thought proper to employ; but she showed me his answer, from which I gathered what the style and tenor of her argument had been. And if Madam Esmond brought Scripture to her aid, Mr. Hal, to my surprise, brought scores of texts to bear upon her in reply, and addressed her in a very neat, temperate, and even elegant composition, which I thought his wife herself was scarcely capable of penning. Indeed, I found he had enlisted the services of Mr. Belman, the New Richmond clergyman, who had taken up strong opinions on the Whig side, and who preached and printed sermons against Hagan (who, as I have said, was of our faction), in which I fear Belman had the best of the dispute.

My exhortations to Hal had no more success than our mother's. He did not answer my letters. Being still farther pressed by the friends of the Government, I wrote over most imprudently to say I would visit him at the end of the week at Fanny's Mount; but on arriving, I only found my sister, who received me with perfect cordiality, but informed me that Hal was gone into the country, ever so far towards the Blue Mountains to look at some horses, and was to be away—she did not know how long he was to be away!

I knew then there was no hope. "My dear," I said, "as far as I can judge from the signs of the times, the train that has been laid these years must have a match put to it before long. Harry is riding away. God knows to what end."

"The Lord prosper the righteous cause, Sir George," says she.

"Amen, with all my heart. You and he speak as Americans; I as an Englishman. Tell him from me, that when anything in the course of nature shall happen to our mother, I have enough for me and mine in England, and shall resign all our land here in Virginia to him."

"You don't mean that, George?" she cries, with brightening eyes. "Well, to be sure, it is but right and fair," she presently added. "Why should you, who are the eldest but by an hour, have everything? a palace and lands in England—the plantation here—the title—and children—and my poor Harry none? But 'tis generous of you all the same—leastways handsome and proper, and I didn't expect it of you; and you don't take after your mother in this, Sir George, that you don't, nohow. Give my love to sister Theo!" And she offers me a cheek to kiss, ere I ride away from her door. With such a woman as Fanny to guide him, how could I hope to make a convert of my brother?

Having met with this poor success in my enterprise, I rode back to our Governor, with whom I agreed that it was time to arm in earnest, and prepare ourselves against the shock that certainly was at hand. He and his whole Court of Officials were not a little agitated and excited; needlessly savage, I thought, in their abuse of the wicked Whigs, and loud in their shouts of Old England for ever; but they were all eager for the day when the contending parties could meet hand to hand, and they could have an opportunity of riding those wicked Whigs down. And I left my lord, having received the thanks of his Excellency in Council, and engaged to do my best endeavours to raise a body of men in defence of the Crown. Hence the corps, called afterwards the Westmoreland Defenders, had its rise, of which I had the honour to be appointed Colonel, and which I was to command when it appeared in the field. And that fortunate event must straightway take place, so soon as the county knew that a gentleman of my station and name would take the command of the force. The announcement was duly made in the Government Gazette, and we filled in our officers readily enough; but the recruits, it must be owned, were slow to come in, and quick to disappear. Nevertheless, friend Hagan eagerly came forward to offer himself as chaplain. Madam Esmond gave us our colours, and progressed about the country engaging volunteers; but the most eager recruiter of all was my good old tutor, little Mr. Dempster, who had been out as a boy on the Jacobite side in Scotland, and who went specially into the Carolinas, among the children of his banished old comrades, who had worn the white cockade of Prince Charles, and who most of all showed themselves in this contest still loyal to the Crown.

Hal's expedition in search of horses led him not only so far as the Blue Mountains in our colony, but thence on a long journey to Annapolis and

Baltimore; and from Baltimore to Philadelphia, to be sure; where a second General Congress was now sitting, attended by our Virginian gentlemen of the last year. Meanwhile, all the almanacs tell what had happened. Lexington had happened, and the first shots were fired in the war which was to end in the independence of our native country. We still protested of our loyalty to his Majesty; but we stated our determination to die or be free; and some twenty thousand of our loyal petitioners assembled round about Boston with arms in their hands and cannon, to which they had helped themselves out of the Government stores. Mr. Arnold had begun that career which was to end so brilliantly, by the daring and burglarious capture of two forts, of which he forced the doors. Three generals from Bond Street, with a large reinforcement, were on their way to help Mr. Gage out of his ugly position at Boston. Presently the armies were actually engaged; and our British generals commenced their career of conquest and pacification in the colonies by the glorious blunder of Breed's Hill. Here they fortified themselves, feeling themselves not strong enough for the moment to win any more glorious victories over the rebels; and the two armies lay watching each other whilst Congress was deliberating at Philadelphia who should command the forces of the confederated colonies.

We all know on whom the most fortunate choice of the nation fell. Of the Virginian regiment which marched to join the new General-in-Chief, one was commanded by Henry Esmond Warrington, Esq., late a Captain in his Majesty's service; and by his side rode his little wife, of whose bravery we often subsequently heard. I was glad, for one, that she had quitted Virginia; for, had she remained after her husband's departure, our mother would infallibly have gone over to give her battle; and I was thankful, at least, that that terrific incident of civil war was spared to our family and history.

The rush of our farmers and country-folk was almost all directed towards the new northern army; and our people were not a little flattered at the selection of a Virginian gentleman for the principal command. With a thrill of wrath and fury the provinces heard of the blood drawn at Lexington; and men yelled denunciations against the cruelty and wantonness of the bloody British invader. The invader was but doing his duty, and was met and resisted by men in arms, who wished to prevent him from helping himself to his own; but people do not stay to weigh their words when they mean to be angry; the colonists had taken their side; and, with what I own to be a natural spirit and ardour, were determined to have a trial of strength with the braggart domineering mother country. Breed's Hill became a mountain, as it were, which all men of the American Continent might behold, with Liberty, Victory, Glory, on its flaming summit. These dreaded troops could be withstood, then, by farmers and ploughmen. These famous officers could be outgeneralled by doctors, lawyers, and civilians! Granted that Britons could conquer all the world;—here were their children who could match and conquer Britons! Indeed, I don't know which of the two deserves the palm, either for bravery or vainglory. We are in the habit of laughing at our French neighbours for boasting, gasconading, and so forth; but for a steady self-esteem and indomitable confidence in our own courage, greatness, magnanimity;—who can compare with Britons, except their children across the Atlantic?

The people round about us took the people's side for the most part in the struggle, and, truth to say, Sir George Warrington found his regiment of Westmoreland Defenders but very thinly manned at the commencement, and woefully diminished in numbers presently, not only after the news of battle from the north, but in consequence of the behaviour of my Lord our Governor, whose conduct enraged no one more than his own immediate partisans, and the loyal adherents of the Crown throughout the colony. That he would plant the King's standard, and summon all loyal gentlemen to rally round it, had been a measure agreed in countless meetings, and applauded over thousands of bumpers. I have a pretty good memory, and could mention the name of many a gentleman, now a smug officer of the United States Government, whom I have heard hiccup out a prayer that he might be allowed to perish under the folds of his country's flag; or roar a challenge to the bloody traitors absent with the rebel army. But let bygones be bygones. This, however, is matter of public history, that his lordship, our Governor, a peer of Scotland, the Sovereign's representative in his Old Dominion, who so loudly invited all the lieges to join the King's standard, was the first to put it in his pocket, and fly to his ships out of reach of danger. He would not leave them, save as a pirate at midnight to burn and destroy. Meanwhile, we loyal gentry remained on shore, committed to our cause, and only subject to greater danger in consequence of the weakness and cruelty of him who ought to have been our leader. It was the beginning of June, our orchards and gardens were all blooming with plenty and summer; a week before I had been over at Williamsburg, exchanging compliments with his Excellency, devising plans for future movements by which we should be able to make good head against rebellion, shaking hands heartily at parting, and vincere aut mori the very last words upon all our lips. Our little family was gathered at Richmond, talking over, as we did daily, the prospect of affairs in the north, the quarrels between our own Assembly and his Excellency, by whom they had been afresh convened, when our ghostly Hagan rushes into our parlour, and asks, "Have we heard the news of the Governor?"

"Has he dissolved the Assembly again, and put that scoundrel Patrick Henry in irons?" asks Madam Esmond.

"No such thing! His lordship with his lady and family have left their palace privately at night. They are on board a man-of-war off York, whence my lord has sent a despatch to the Assembly, begging them to continue their sitting, and announcing that he himself had only quitted his Government House out of fear of the fury of the people."

What was to become of the sheep, now the shepherd had run away? No entreaties could be more pathetic than those of the gentlemen of the House of Assembly, who guaranteed their Governor security if he would but land, and implored him to appear amongst them, if but to pass bills and transact the necessary business. No: the man-of-war was his seat of government, and my lord desired his House of Commons to wait upon him there. This was erecting the King's standard with a vengeance. Our Governor had left us; our Assembly perforce ruled in his stead; a rabble of people followed the fugitive Viceroy on board his ships. A mob of negroes deserted out of the plantations to join this other deserter. He and his black allies landed here and there in darkness, and emulated the most lawless of our opponents in their alacrity at seizing and burning. He not only invited runaway negroes, but he sent an ambassador to Indians with entreaties to join his standard. When he came on shore it was to burn and destroy: when the people resisted, as at Norfolk and Hampton, he retreated and betook himself to his ships again.

Even my mother, after that miserable flight of our chief, was scared at the aspect of affairs, and doubted of the speedy putting down of the rebellion. The arming of the negroes was, in her opinion, the most cowardly blow of all. The loyal gentry were ruined, and robbed, many of them, of their only property. A score of our worst hands deserted from Richmond and Castlewood, and fled to our courageous Governor's fleet; not all of them, though some of them, were slain, and a couple hung by the enemy for plunder and robbery perpetrated whilst with his lordship's precious army. Because her property was wantonly injured, and his Majesty's chief officer an imbecile, would Madam Esmond desert the cause of Royalty and Honour? My good mother was never so prodigiously dignified, and loudly and enthusiastically loyal, as after she heard of our Governor's lamentable defection. The people round about her, though most of them of quite a different way of thinking, listened to her speeches without unkindness. Her oddities were known far and wide through our province; where, I am afraid, many of the wags amongst our young men were accustomed to smoke her, as the phrase then was, and draw out her stories about the Marquis her father, about the splendour of her family, and so forth. But along with her oddities, her charities and kindness were remembered, and many a rebel, as she called them, had a sneaking regard for the pompous little Tory lady.

As for the Colonel of the Westmoreland Defenders, though that gentleman's command dwindled utterly away after the outrageous conduct of his chief, yet I escaped from some very serious danger which might have befallen me and mine in consequence of some disputes which I was known to have had with my Lord Dunmore. Going on board his ship after he had burned the stores at Hampton, and issued the proclamation calling the negroes to his standard, I made so free as to remonstrate with him in regard to both measures; I implored him to return to Williamsburg, where hundreds of us, thousands, I hoped, would be ready to defend him to the last extremity; and in my remonstrance used terms so free, or rather, as I suspect, indicated my contempt for his conduct so clearly by my behaviour, that his lordship flew into a rage, said I was a rebel like all the rest of them, and ordered me under arrest there on board his own ship. In my quality of militia officer (since the breaking out of the troubles I commonly used a red coat, to show that I wore the King's colour) I begged for a court-martial immediately; and turning round to two officers who had been present during our altercation, desired them to remember all that had passed between his lordship and me. These gentlemen were no doubt of my way of thinking as to the chief's behaviour, and our interview ended in my going ashore unaccompanied by a guard. The story got wind amongst the Whig gentry, and was improved in the telling. I had spoken out my mind manfully to the Governor; no Whig could have uttered sentiments more liberal. When riots took place in Richmond, and of the Loyalists remaining there, many were in peril of life and betook themselves to the ships, my mother's property and house were never endangered, nor her family insulted. We were still at the stage when a reconciliation was fondly thought possible. "Ah! if all the Tories were like you," a distinguished Whig has said to me, "we and the people at home should soon come together again." This, of course, was before the famous Fourth of July, and that Declaration which rendered reconcilement impossible. Afterwards, when parties grew more rancorous, motives much less creditable were assigned for my conduct, and it was said I chose to be a Liberal Tory because I was a cunning fox, and wished to keep my estate whatever way things went. And this, I am bound to say, is the opinion regarding my humble self which has obtained in very high quarters at home, where a profound regard for my own interest has been supposed not uncommonly to have occasioned my conduct during the late unhappy troubles.

There were two or three persons in the world (for I had not told my mother how I was resolved to cede to my brother all my life-interest in our American property) who knew that I had no mercenary motives in regard to the conduct I pursued. It was not worth while to undeceive others; what were life worth, if a man were forced to feel himself a la piste of all the calumnies uttered against him? And I do not quite know to this present day, how it happened that my mother, that notorious Loyalist, was left for several years quite undisturbed in her house at Castlewood, a stray troop or company of Continentals being occasionally quartered upon her. I do not know for certain, I say, how this piece of good fortune happened, though I can give a pretty shrewd guess as to the cause of it. Madam Fanny, after a campaign before Boston, came back to Fanny's Mount, leaving her Colonel. My modest Hal, until the conclusion of the war, would accept no higher rank, believing that in command of a regiment he could be more useful than in charge of a division. Madam Fanny, I say, came back, and it was remarkable after her return how her old asperity towards my mother seemed to be removed, and what an affection she showed for her and all the property. She was great friends with the Governor and some of the most influential gentlemen of the new Assembly:—Madam Esmond was harmless, and for her son's sake, who was bravely battling for his country, her errors should be lightly visited:—I know not how it was, but for years she remained unharmed, except in respect of heavy Government requisitions, which of course she had to pay, and it was not until the redcoats appeared about our house, that much serious evil came to it.

CHAPTER XC
In which we both fight and run away

What was the use of a Colonel without a regiment? The Governor and Council who had made such a parade of thanks in endowing me with mine, were away out of sight, skulking on board ships, with an occasional piracy and arson on shore. My Lord Dunmore's black allies frightened away those of his own blood; and besides these negroes whom he had summoned round him in arms, we heard that he had sent an envoy among the Indians of the South, and that they were to come down in numbers and tomahawk our people into good behaviour. "And these are to be our allies!" I say to my mother, exchanging ominous looks with her, and remembering, with a ghastly distinctness, that savage whose face glared over mine, and whose knife was at my throat when Florac struck him down on Braddock's Field. We put our house of Castlewood into as good a state of defence as we could devise; but, in truth, it was more of the red men and the blacks than of the rebels we were afraid. I never saw my mother lose courage but once, and then when she was recounting to us the particulars of our father's death in a foray of Indians more than forty years ago. Seeing some figures one night moving in front of our house, nothing could persuade the good lady but that they were savages, and she sank on her knees crying out, "The Lord have mercy upon us! The Indians—the Indians!"

My lord's negro allies vanished on board his ships, or where they could find pay and plunder; but the painted heroes from the South never made their appearance, though I own to have looked at my mother's grey head, my wife's brown hair, and our little one's golden ringlets, with a horrible pang of doubt lest these should fall the victims of ruffian war. And it was we who fought with such weapons, and enlisted these allies! But that I dare not (so to speak) be setting myself up as interpreter of Providence, and pointing out the special finger of Heaven (as many people are wont to do), I would say our employment of these Indians, and of the German mercenaries, brought their own retribution with them in this war. In the field, where the mercenaries were attacked by the Provincials, they yielded, and it was triumphing over them that so raised the spirit of the Continental army; and the murder of one woman (Miss McCrea) by a half-dozen drunken Indians, did more harm to the Royal cause than the loss of a battle or the destruction of regiments.

Now, the Indian panic over, Madam Esmond's courage returned: and she began to be seriously and not unjustly uneasy at the danger which I ran myself, and which I brought upon others, by remaining in Virginia.

"What harm can they do me," says she, "a poor woman? If I have one son a colonel without a regiment, I have another with a couple of hundred Continentals behind him in Mr. Washington's camp. If the Royalists come, they will let me off for your sake; if the rebels appear, I shall have Harry's passport. I don't wish, sir, I don't like that your delicate wife and this dear little baby should be here, and only increase the risk of all of us! We must have them away to Boston or New York. Don't talk about defending me! Who will think of hurting a poor, harmless, old woman? If the rebels come, I shall shelter behind Mrs. Fanny's petticoats, and shall be much safer without you in the house than in it." This she said in part, perhaps, because 'twas reasonable; more so because she would have me and my family out of the danger; and danger or not, for her part felt that she was determined to remain in the land where her father was buried, and she was born. She was living backwards, so to speak. She had seen the new generation, and blessed them, and bade them farewell. She belonged to the past, and old days and memories.

While we were debating about the Boston scheme, comes the news that the British have evacuated that luckless city altogether, never having ventured to attack Mr. Washington in his camp at Cambridge (though he lay there for many months without powder at our mercy); but waiting until he procured ammunition, and seized and fortified Dorchester heights, which commanded the town, out of which the whole British army and colony was obliged to beat a retreat. That the King's troops won the battle at Bunker's Hill, there is no more doubt than that they beat the French at Blenheim; but through the war their chiefs seem constantly to have been afraid of assaulting entrenched Continentals afterwards; else why, from July to March, hesitate to strike an almost defenceless enemy? Why the hesitation at Long Island, when the Continental army was in our hand? Why that astonishing timorousness—of Howe before Valley Forge, where the relics of a force starving, sickening, and in rags, could scarcely man the lines, which they held before a great, victorious, and perfectly appointed army?

As the hopes and fears of the contending parties rose and fell, it was curious to mark the altered tone of the partisans of either. When the news came to us in the country of the evacuation of Boston, every little Whig in the neighbourhood made his bow to Madam, and advised her to a speedy submission. She did not carry her loyalty quite so openly as heretofore, and flaunt her flag in the faces of the public, but she never swerved. Every night and morning in private poor Hagan prayed for the Royal Family in our own household, and on Sundays any neighbours were welcome to attend the service, where my mother acted as a very emphatic clerk, and the prayer for the High Court of Parliament under our most religious and gracious King was very stoutly delivered. The brave Hagan was a parson without a living, as I was a Militia Colonel without a regiment. Hagan had continued to pray stoutly for King George in Williamsburg, long after his Excellency our Governor had run away: but on coming to church one Sunday to perform his duty, he found a corporal's guard at the church-door, who told him that the Committee of Safety had put another divine in his place, and he was requested to keep a quiet tongue in his head. He told the men to "lead him before their chiefs" (our honest friend always loved tall words and tragic attitudes); and accordingly was marched through the streets to the Capitol, with a chorus of white and coloured blackguards at the skirts of his gown; and had an interview with Messrs. Henry and the new State officers, and confronted the robbers, as he said, in their den. Of course he was for making an heroic speech before these gentlemen (and was one of many men who perhaps would have no objection to be made martyrs, so that they might be roasted coram populo, or tortured in a full house), but Mr. Henry was determined to give him no such chance. After keeping Hagan three or four hours waiting in an anteroom in the company of negroes, when the worthy divine entered the new chief magistrate's room with an undaunted mien, and began a prepared speech with—"Sir, by what authority am I, a minister of the——" "Mr. Hagan," says the other, interrupting him, "I am too busy to listen to speeches. And as for King George, he has henceforth no more authority in this country than King Nebuchadnezzar. Mind you that, and hold your tongue, if you please! Stick to King John, sir, and King Macbeth; and if you will send round your benefit-tickets, all the Assembly shall come and hear you. Did you ever see Mr. Hagan on the boards, when you was in London, General?" And, so saying, Henry turns round upon Mr. Washington's second in command, General Lee, who was now come into Virginia upon State affairs, and our shamefaced good Hagan was bustled out of the room, reddening, and almost crying with shame. After this event we thought that Hagan's ministrations were best confined to us in the country, and removed the worthy pastor from his restive lambs in the city.

The selection of Virginians to the very highest civil and military appointments of the new government bribed and flattered many of our leading people, who, otherwise, and but for the outrageous conduct of our government, might have remained faithful to the Crown, and made good head against the rising rebellion. But, although we Loyalists were gagged and muzzled, though the Capitol was in the hands of the Whigs, and our vaunted levies of loyal recruits so many Falstaff's regiments for the most part, the faithful still kept intelligences with one another in the colony, and with our neighbours; and though we did not rise, and though we ran away, and though, in examination before committees, justices, and so forth, some of our frightened people gave themselves Republican airs, and vowed perdition to kings and nobles; yet we knew each other pretty well, and—according as the chances were more or less favourable to us, the master more or less hard—we concealed our colours, showed our colours, half showed our colours, or downright apostatised for the nonce, and cried, "Down with King George!" Our negroes bore about, from house to house, all sorts of messages and tokens. Endless underhand plots and schemes were engaged in by those who could not afford the light. The battle over, the neutrals come and join the winning side, and shout as loudly as the patriots. The runaways are not counted. Will any man tell me that the signers and ardent well-wishers of the Declaration of Independence were not in a minority of the nation, and that the minority did not win? We knew that apart of the defeated army of Massachusetts was about to make an important expedition southward, upon the success of which the very greatest hopes were founded; and I, for one, being anxious to make a movement as soon as there was any chance of activity, had put myself in communication with the ex-Governor Martin, of North Carolina, whom I proposed to join, with three or four of our Virginian gentlemen, officers of that notable corps of which we only wanted privates. We made no particular mystery about our departure from Castlewood; the affairs of Congress were not going so well yet that the new government could afford to lay any particular stress or tyranny upon persons of a doubtful way of thinking. Gentlemen's houses were still open; and in our southern fashion we would visit our friends for months at a time. My wife and I, with our infant and a fitting suite of servants, took leave of Madam Esmond on a visit to a neighbouring plantation. We went thence to another friend's house, and then to another, till finally we reached Wilmington, in North Carolina, which was the point at which we expected to stretch a hand to the succours which were coming to meet us.

Ere our arrival, our brother Carolinian Royalists had shown themselves in some force. Their encounters with the Whigs had been unlucky. The poor Highlanders had been no more fortunate in their present contest in favour of King George, than when they had drawn their swords against him in their own country. We did not reach Wilmington until the end of May, by which time we found Admiral Parker's squadron there, with General Clinton and five British regiments on board, whose object was a descent upon Charleston.

The General, to whom I immediately made myself known, seeing that my regiment consisted of Lady Warrington, our infant, whom she was nursing, and three negro servants, received us at first with a very grim welcome. But Captain Horner of the Sphinx frigate, who had been on the Jamaica station, and received, like all the rest of the world, many kindnesses from our dear Governor there, when he heard that my wife was General Lambert's daughter, eagerly received her on board, and gave up his best cabin to our service; and so we were refugees, too, like my Lord Dunmore, having waved our flag, to be sure, and pocketed it, and slipped out at the back door. From Wilmington we bore away quickly to Charleston, and in the course of the voyage and our delay in the river, previous to our assault on the place, I made some acquaintance with Mr. Clinton, which increased to a further intimacy. It was the King's birthday when we appeared in the river: we determined it was a glorious day for the commencement of the expedition.

It did not take place for some days after, and I leave out, purposely, all descriptions of my Penelope parting from her Hector, going forth on this expedition. In the first place, Hector is perfectly well (though a little gouty), nor has any rascal of a Pyrrhus made a prize of his widow: and in times of war and commotion, are not such scenes of woe and terror, and parting, occurring every hour? I can see the gentle face yet over the bulwark, as we descend the ship's side into the boats, and the smile of the infant on her arm. What old stories, to be sure! Captain Miles, having no natural taste for poetry, you have forgot the verses, no doubt, in Mr. Pope's Homer, in which you are described as parting with your heroic father; but your mother often read them to you as a boy, and keeps the gorget I wore on that day somewhere amongst her dressing-boxes now.

My second venture at fighting was no more lucky than my first. We came back to our ships that evening thoroughly beaten. The madcap Lee, whom Clinton had faced at Boston, now met him at Charleston. Lee, and the gallant garrison there, made a brilliant and most successful resistance. The fort on Sullivan's Island, which we attacked, was a nut we could not crack. The fire of all our frigates was not strong enough to pound its shell; the passage by which we moved up to the assault of the place was not fordable, as those officers found—Sir Henry at the head of them, who was always the first to charge—who attempted to wade it. Death by shot, by drowning, by catching my death of cold, I had braved before I returned to my wife; and our frigate being aground for a time and got off with difficulty, was agreeably cannonaded by the enemy until she got off her bank.

A small incident in the midst of this unlucky struggle was the occasion of a subsequent intimacy which arose between me and Sir Harry Clinton, and bound me to that most gallant officer during the Period in which it was my fortune to follow the war. Of his qualifications as a leader there may be many opinions: I fear to say, regarding a man I heartily respect and admire, there ought only to be one. Of his personal bearing and his courage there can be no doubt; he was always eager to show it; and whether at the final charge on Breed's Hill, when at the head of the rallied troops he carried the Continental lines, or here before Sullivan's Fort, or a year later at Fort Washington, when, standard in hand, he swept up the height, and entered the fort at the head of the storming column, Clinton was always foremost in the race of battle, and the King's service knew no more admirable soldier.

We were taking to the water from our boats, with the intention of forcing a column to the fort, through a way which our own guns had rendered practicable, when a shot struck a boat alongside of us, so well aimed, as actually to put three-fourths of the boat's crew hors de combat, and knock down the officer steering, and the flag behind him. I could not help crying out, "Bravo! well aimed!" for no ninepins ever went down more helplessly than these poor fellows before the round shot. Then the General, turning round to me, says, rather grimly, "Sir, the behaviour of the enemy seems to please you!" "I am pleased, sir," says I, "that my countrymen, yonder, should fight as becomes our nation." We floundered on towards the fort in the midst of the same amiable attentions from small arms and great, until we found the water was up to our breasts and deepening at every step, when we were fain to take to our boats again and pull out of harm's way. Sir Henry waited upon my Lady Warrington on board the Sphinx after this, and was very gracious to her, and mighty facetious regarding the character of the humble writer of the present memoir, whom his Excellency always described as a rebel at heart. I pray my children may live to see or engage in no great revolutions,—such as that, for instance, raging in the country of our miserable French neighbours.

Save a very, very few indeed, the actors in those great tragedies do not bear to be scanned too closely; the chiefs are often no better than ranting quacks; the heroes ignoble puppets; the heroines anything but pure. The prize is not always to the brave. In our revolution it certainly did fall, for once and for a wonder, to the most deserving: but who knows his enemies now? His great and surprising triumphs were not in those rare engagements with the enemy where he obtained a trifling mastery; but over Congress; over hunger and disease; over lukewarm friends, or smiling foes in his own camp, whom his great spirit had to meet and master. When the struggle was over, and our important chiefs who had conducted it began to squabble and accuse each other in their own defence before the nation—what charges and counter-charges were brought; what pretexts of delay were urged; what piteous excuses were put forward that this fleet arrived too late; that that regiment mistook its orders; that these cannon-balls would not fit those guns; and so to the end of the chapter! Here was a general who beat us with no shot at times, and no powder, and no money; and he never thought of a convention; his courage never capitulated! Through all the doubt and darkness, the danger and long tempest of the war, I think it was only the American leader's indomitable soul that remained entirely steady.

Of course our Charleston expedition was made the most of, and pronounced a prodigious victory by the enemy, who had learnt (from their parents, perhaps) to cry victory if a corporal's guard were surprised, as loud as if we had won a pitched battle. Mr. Lee rushed back to New York, the conqueror of conquerors, trumpeting his glory, and by no man received with more eager delight than by the Commander-in-Chief of the American Army. It was my dear Lee and my dear General between them, then; and it hath always touched me in the history of our early Revolution to note that simple confidence and admiration with which the General-in-Chief was wont to regard officers under him, who had happened previously to serve with the King's army. So the Mexicans of old looked and wondered when they first saw an armed Spanish horseman! And this mad, flashy braggart (and another Continental general, whose name and whose luck afterwards were sufficiently notorious) you may be sure took advantage of the modesty of the Commander-in-Chief, and advised, and blustered, and sneered, and disobeyed orders; daily presenting fresh obstacles (as if he had not enough otherwise!) in the path over which only Mr. Washington's astonishing endurance could have enabled him to march.

Whilst we were away on our South Carolina expedition, the famous Fourth of July had taken place, and we and the thirteen United States were parted for ever. My own native state of Virginia had also distinguished itself by announcing that all men are equally free; that all power is vested in the people, who have an inalienable right to alter, reform, or abolish their form of government at pleasure, and that the idea of an hereditary first magistrate is unnatural and absurd! Our General presented me with this document fresh from Williamsburg, as we were sailing northward by the Virginia capes, and, amidst not a little amusement and laughter, pointed out to me the faith to which, from the Fourth inst. inclusive, I was bound. There was no help for it; I was a Virginian—my godfathers had promised and vowed, in my name, that all men were equally free (including, of course, the race of poor Gumbo), that the idea of a monarchy is absurd, and that I had the right to alter my form of government at pleasure. I thought of Madam Esmond at home, and how she would look when these articles of faith were brought her to subscribe; how would Hagan receive them? He demolished them in a sermon, in which all the logic was on his side, but the U.S. Government has not, somehow, been affected by the discourse; and when he came to touch upon the point that all men being free, therefore Gumbo and Sady, and Nathan, had assuredly a right to go to Congress: "Tut, tut! my good Mr. Hagan," says my mother, "let us hear no more of this nonsense; but leave such wickedness and folly to the rebels!"

By the middle of August we were before New York, whither Mr. Howe had brought his army that had betaken itself to Halifax after its inglorious expulsion from Boston. The American Commander-in-Chief was at New York, and a great battle inevitable; and I looked forward to it with an inexpressible feeling of doubt and anxiety, knowing that my dearest brother and his regiment formed part of the troops whom we must attack, and could not but overpower. Almost the whole of the American army came over to fight on a small island, where every officer on both sides knew that they were to be beaten, and whence they had not a chance of escape. Two frigates, out of a hundred we had placed so as to command the enemy's entrenched camp and point of retreat across East River to New York, would have destroyed every bark in which he sought to fly, and compelled him to lay down his arms on shore. He fought: his hasty levies were utterly overthrown; some of his generals, his best troops, his artillery taken; the remnant huddled into their entrenched camp after their rout, the pursuers entering it with them. The victors were called back; the enemy was then pent up in a corner of the island, and could not escape. "They are at our mercy, and are ours to-morrow," says the gentle General. Not a ship was set to watch the American force; not a sentinel of ours could see a movement in their camp. A whole army crossed under our eyes in one single night to the mainland without the loss of a single man; and General Howe was suffered to remain in command after this feat, and to complete his glories of Long Island and Breed's Hill, at Philadelphia! A friend, to be sure, crossed in the night to say the enemy's army was being ferried over, but he fell upon a picket of Germans: they could not understand him: their commander was boozing or asleep. In the morning, when the spy was brought to some one who could comprehend the American language, the whole Continental force had crossed the East River, and the empire over thirteen colonies had slipped away.

The opinions I had about our chief were by no means uncommon in the army; though, perhaps, wisely kept secret by gentlemen under Mr. Howe's immediate command. Am I more unlucky than other folks, I wonder? or why are my imprudent sayings carried about more than my neighbours'? My rage that such a use was made of such a victory was no greater than that of scores of gentlemen with the army. Why must my name forsooth be given up to the Commander-in-Chief as that of the most guilty of the grumblers? Personally, General Howe was perfectly brave, amiable, and good-humoured.

"So, Sir George," says he, "you find fault with me, as a military man, because there was a fog after the battle on Long Island, and your friends, the Continentals, gave me the slip! Surely we took and killed enough of them; but there is no satisfying you gentlemen amateurs!" and he turned his back on me, and shrugged his shoulders, and talked to some one else. Amateur I might be, and he the most amiable of men; but if King George had said to him, "Never more be officer of mine," yonder agreeable and pleasant Cassio would most certainly have had his desert.

I soon found how our Chief had come in possession of his information regarding myself. My admirable cousin, Mr. William Esmond—who of course had forsaken New York and his post, when all the Royal authorities fled out of the place, and Washington occupied it,—returned along with our troops and fleets; and, being a gentleman of good birth and name, and well acquainted with the city, made himself agreeable to the newcomers of the Royal army, the young bloods, merry fellows, and macaronis, by introducing them to play-tables, taverns, and yet worse places, with which the worthy gentleman continued to be familiar in the New World as in the Old. Coelum non animum. However Will had changed his air, or whithersoever he transported his carcase, he carried a rascal in his skin.

I had heard a dozen stories of his sayings regarding my family, and was determined neither to avoid him nor seek him; but to call him to account whensoever we met; and, chancing one day to be at a coffee-house in a friend's company, my worthy kinsman swaggered in with a couple of young lads of the army, whom he found it was his pleasure and profit now to lead into every kind of dissipation. I happened to know one of Mr. Will's young companions, an aide-de-camp of General Clinton's, who had been in my close company both at Charleston, before Sullivan's Island, and in the action of Brooklyn, where our General gloriously led the right wing of the English army. They took a box without noticing us at first, though I heard my name three or four times mentioned by my brawling kinsman, who ended some drunken speech he was making by slapping his fist on the table, and swearing, "By——, I will do for him, and the bloody rebel, his brother!"

"Ah! Mr. Esmond," says I, coming forward with my hat on. (He looked a little pale behind his punch-bowl.) "I have long wanted to see you, to set some little matters right about which there has been a difference between us."

"And what may those be, sir?" says he, with a volley of oaths.

"You have chosen to cast a doubt upon my courage, and say that I shirked a meeting with you when we were young men. Our relationship and our age ought to prevent us from having recourse to such murderous follies" (Mr. Will started up, looking fierce and relieved), "but I give you notice, that though I can afford to overlook lies against myself, if I hear from you a word in disparagement of my brother, Colonel Warrington, of the Continental Army, I will hold you accountable."

"Indeed, gentlemen! Mighty fine, indeed! You take notice of Sir George Warrington's words!" cries Mr. Will over his punch-bowl.

"You have been pleased to say," I continued, growing angry as I spoke, and being a fool therefore for my pains, "that the very estates we hold in this country are not ours, but of right revert to your family!"

"So they are ours! By George, they're ours! I've heard my brother Castlewood say so a score of times!" swears Mr. Will.

"In that case, sir," says I, hotly, "your brother, my Lord Castlewood, tells no more truth than yourself. We have the titles at hone in Virginia. They are registered in the courts there; and if ever I hear one word more of this impertinence, I shall call you to account where no constables will be at hand to interfere!"

"I wonder," cries Will, in a choking voice, "that I don't cut him into twenty thousand pieces as he stands there before me with his confounded yellow face. It was my brother Castlewood won his money—no, it was his brother; d—— you, which are you, the rebel or the other? I hate the ugly faces of both of you, and, hic!—if you are for the King, show you are for the King, and drink his health!" and he sank down into his box with a hiccup and a wild laugh, which he repeated a dozen times, with a hundred more oaths and vociferous outcries that I should drink the King's health.

To reason with a creature in this condition, or ask explanations or apologies from him, was absurd. I left Mr. Will to reel to his lodgings under the care of his young friends—who were surprised to find an old toper so suddenly affected and so utterly prostrated by liquor—and limped home to my wife, whom I found happy in possession of a brief letter from Hal, which a countryman had brought in; and who said not a word about the affairs of the Continentals with whom he was engaged, but wrote a couple of pages of rapturous eulogiums upon his brother's behaviour in the field, which my dear Hal was pleased to admire, as he admired everything I said and did.

I rather looked for a messenger from my amiable kinsman in consequence of the speeches which had passed between us the night before, and did not know but that I might be called by Will to make my words good; and when accordingly Mr. Lacy (our companion of the previous evening) made his appearance at an early hour of the forenoon, I was beckoning my Lady Warrington to leave us, when, with a laugh and a cry of "Oh dear, no!" Mr. Lacy begged her ladyship not to disturb herself.

"I have seen," says he, "a gentleman who begs to send you his apologies if he uttered a word last night which could offend you."

"What apologies? what words?" asks the anxious wife.

I explained that roaring Will Esmond had met me in a coffee-house on the previous evening, and quarrelled with me, as he had done with hundreds before. "It appears the fellow is constantly abusive, and invariably pleads drunkenness, and apologises the next morning, unless he is caned over-night," remarked Captain Lacy. And my lady, I dare say, makes a little sermon, and asks why we gentlemen will go to idle coffee-houses and run the risk of meeting roaring, roystering Will Esmonds?

Our sojourn in New York was enlivened by a project for burning the city which some ardent patriots entertained and partially executed. Several such schemes were laid in the course of the war, and each one of the principal cities was doomed to fire; though, in the interests of peace and goodwill, I hope it will be remembered that these plans never originated with the cruel government of a tyrant king, but were always proposed by gentlemen on the Continental side, who vowed that, rather than remain under the ignominious despotism of the ruffian of Brunswick, the fairest towns of America should burn. I presume that the sages who were for burning down Boston were not actual proprietors in that place, and the New York burners might come from other parts of the country—from Philadelphia, or what not. Howbeit, the British spared you, gentlemen, and we pray you give us credit for this act of moderation.

I had not the fortune to be present in the action on the White Plains, being detained by the hurt which I had received at Long Island, and which broke out again and again, and took some time in the healing. The tenderest of nurses watched me through my tedious malady, and was eager for the day when I should doff my militia coat and return to the quiet English home where Hetty and our good General were tending our children. Indeed I don't know that I have yet forgiven myself for the pains and terrors that I must have caused my poor wife, by keeping her separate from her young ones, and away from her home, because, forsooth, I wished to see a little more of the war then going on. Our grand tour in Europe had been all very well. We had beheld St. Peter's at Rome, and the Bishop thereof; the Dauphiness of France (alas, to think that glorious head should ever have been brought so low!) at Paris; and the rightful King of England at Florence. I had dipped my gout in a half-dozen baths and spas, and played cards in a hundred courts, as my Travels in Europe (which I propose to publish after my completion of the History of the American War) will testify. [Neither of these two projected works of Sir George Warrington were brought, as it appears, to a completion.] And, during our peregrinations, my hypochondria diminished (which plagued me woefully at home); and my health and spirits visibly improved. Perhaps it was because she saw the evident benefit I had from excitement and change, that my wife was reconciled to my continuing to enjoy them; and though secretly suffering pangs at being away from her nursery and her eldest boy (for whom she ever has had an absurd infatuation), the dear hypocrite scarce allowed a look of anxiety to appear on her face; encouraged me with smiles; professed herself eager to follow me; asked why it should be a sin in me to covet honour? and, in a word, was ready to stay, to go, to smile, to be sad; to scale mountains, or to go down to the sea in ships; to say that cold was pleasant, heat tolerable, hunger good sport, dirty lodgings delightful; though she is wretched sailor, very delicate about the little she eats, and an extreme sufferer both of cold and heat. Hence, as I willed to stay on yet a while on my native continent, she was certain nothing was so good for me; and when I was minded to return home—oh, how she brightened, and kissed her infant, and told him how he should see the beautiful gardens at home, and Aunt Theo, and grandpapa, and his sister, and Miles. "Miles!" cries the little parrot, mocking its mother—and crowing; as if there was any mighty privilege in seeing Mr. Miles, forsooth, who was under Doctor Sumner's care at Harrow-on-the-Hill, where, to do the gentleman justice, he showed that he could eat more tarts than any boy in the school, and took most creditable prizes at football and hare-and-hounds.

CHAPTER XCI. Satis Pugnae

It has always seemed to me (I speak under the correction of military gentlemen) that the entrenchments of Breed's Hill served the Continental army throughout the whole of our American war. The slaughter inflicted upon us from behind those lines was so severe, and the behaviour of the enemy so resolute, that the British chiefs respected the barricades of the Americans hereafter; and were they firing from behind a row of blankets, certain of our generals rather hesitated to force them. In the affair of the White Plains, when, for a second time, Mr. Washington's army was quite at the mercy of the victors, we subsequently heard that our conquering troops were held back before a barricade actually composed of cornstalks and straw. Another opportunity was given us, and lasted during a whole winter, during which the dwindling and dismayed troops of Congress lay starving and unarmed under our grasp, and the magnanimous Mr. Howe left the famous camp of Valley Forge untouched, whilst his great, brave, and perfectly appointed army fiddled and gambled and feasted in Philadelphia. And, by Byng's countrymen, triumphal arches were erected, tournaments were held in pleasant mockery of the middle ages, and wreaths and garlands offered by beautiful ladies to this clement chief, with fantastical mottoes and posies announcing that his laurels should be immortal! Why have my ungrateful countrymen in America never erected statues to this general? They had not in all their army an officer who fought their battles better; who enabled them to retrieve their errors with such adroitness; who took care that their defeats should be so little hurtful to themselves; and when, in the course of events, the stronger force naturally got the uppermost, who showed such an untiring tenderness, patience, and complacency in helping the poor disabled opponent on to his legs again. Ah! think of eighteen years before and the fiery young warrior whom England had sent out to fight her adversary on the American continent. Fancy him for ever pacing round the defences behind which the foe lies sheltered; by night and by day alike sleepless and eager; consuming away in his fierce wrath and longing, and never closing his eye, so intent is it in watching; winding the track with untiring scent that pants and hungers for blood and battle; prowling through midnight forests, or climbing silent over precipices before dawn; and watching till his great heart is almost worn out, until the foe shows himself at last, when he springs on him and grapples with him, and, dying, slays him! Think of Wolfe at Quebec, and hearken to Howe's fiddles as he sits smiling amongst the dancers at Philadelphia!

A favourite scheme with our ministers at home and some of our generals in America, was to establish a communication between Canada and New York, by which means it was hoped New England might be cut off from the neighbouring colonies, overpowered in detail, and forced into submission. Burgoyne was entrusted with the conduct of the plan, and he set forth from Quebec, confidently promising to bring it to a successful issue. His march began in military state: the trumpets of his proclamations blew before him; he bade the colonists to remember the immense power of England; and summoned the misguided rebels to lay down their arms. He brought with him a formidable English force, an army of German veterans not less powerful, a dreadful band of Indian warriors, and a brilliant train of artillery. It was supposed that the people round his march would rally to the Royal cause and standards. The Continental force in front of him was small at first, and Washington's army was weakened by the withdrawal of troops who were hurried forward to meet this Canadian invasion. A British detachment from New York was to force its way up the Hudson, sweeping away the enemy on the route, and make a junction with Burgoyne at Albany. Then was the time when Washington's weakened army should have been struck too; but a greater Power willed otherwise: nor am I, for one, even going to regret the termination of the war. As we look over the game now, how clear seem the blunders which were made by the losing side! From the beginning to the end we were for ever arriving too late. Our supplies and reinforcements from home were too late. Our troops were in difficulty, and our succours reached them too late. Our fleet appeared off York Town just too late, after Cornwallis had surrendered. A way of escape was opened to Burgoyne, but he resolved upon retreat too late. I have heard discomfited officers in after days prove infallibly how a different wind would have saved America to us; how we must have destroyed the French fleet but for a tempest or two; how once, twice, thrice, but for nightfall, Mr. Washington and his army were in our power. Who has not speculated, in the course of his reading of history, upon the "Has been" and the "Might have been" in the world? I take my tattered old map-book from the shelf, and see the board on which the great contest was played; I wonder at the curious chances which lost it: and, putting aside any idle talk about the respective bravery of the two nations, can't but see that we had the best cards, and that we lost the game.

I own the sport had a considerable fascination for me, and stirred up my languid blood. My brother Hal, when settled on his plantation in Virginia, was perfectly satisfied with the sports and occupations he found there. The company of the country neighbours sufficed him; he never tired of looking after his crops and people, taking his fish, shooting his ducks, hunting in his woods, or enjoying his rubber and his supper. Happy Hal, in his great barn of a house, under his roomy porches, his dogs lying round his feet; his friends, the Virginian Will Wimbles, at free quarters in his mansion; his negroes fat, lazy, and ragged: his shrewd little wife ruling over them and her husband, who always obeyed her implicitly when living, and who was pretty speedily consoled when she died! I say happy, though his lot would have been intolerable to me: wife, and friends, and plantation, and town life at Richmond (Richmond succeeded to the honour of being the capital when our Province became a State). How happy he whose foot fits the shoe which fortune gives him! My income was five times as great, my house in England as large, and built of bricks and faced with freestone; my wife—would I have changed her for any other wife in the world? My children—well, I am contented with my Lady Warrington's opinion about them. But with all these plums and peaches and rich fruits out of Plenty's horn poured into my lap, I fear I have been but an ingrate; and Hodge, my gatekeeper, who shares his bread and scrap of bacon with a family as large as his master's, seems to me to enjoy his meal as much as I do, though Mrs. Molly prepares her best dishes and sweetmeats, and Mr. Gumbo uncorks the choicest bottle from the cellar. Ah me! sweetmeats have lost their savour for me, however they may rejoice my young ones from the nursery, and the perfume of claret palls upon old noses! Our parson has poured out his sermons many and many a time to me, and perhaps I did not care for them much when he first broached them. Dost thou remember, honest friend? (sure he does, for he has repeated the story over the bottle as many times as his sermons almost, and my Lady Warrington pretends as if she had never heard it)—I say, Joe Blake, thou rememberest full well, and with advantages, that October evening when we scrambled up an embrasure at Fort Clinton and a clubbed musket would have dashed these valuable brains out, had not Joe's sword whipped my rebellious countryman through the gizzard. Joe wore a red coat in those days (the uniform of the brave Sixty-third, whose leader, the bold Sill, fell pierced with many wounds beside him). He exchanged his red for black and my pulpit. His doctrines are sound, and his sermons short. We read the papers together over our wine. Not two months ago we read our old friend Howe's glorious deed of the first of June. We were told how the noble Rawdon, who fought with us at Fort Clinton, had joined the Duke of York: and to-day his Royal Highness is in full retreat before Pichegru: and he and my son Miles have taken Valenciennes for nothing! Ah, parson! would you not like to put on your old Sixty-third coat? (though I doubt Mrs. Blake could never make the buttons and button-holes meet again over your big body). The boys were acting a play with my militia sword. Oh, that I were young again, Mr. Blake! that I had not the gout in my toe; and I would saddle Rosinante and ride back into the world, and feel the pulses beat again, and play a little of life's glorious game!

The last "hit" which I saw played, was gallantly won by our side; though 'tis true that even in this parti the Americans won the rubber—our people gaining only the ground they stood on, and the guns, stores, and ships which they captured and destroyed, whilst our efforts at rescue were too late to prevent the catastrophe impending over Burgoyne's unfortunate army. After one of those delays which always were happening to retard our plans and weaken the blows which our chiefs intended to deliver, an expedition was got under weigh from New York at the close of the month of September, '77; that, could it have but advanced a fortnight earlier, might have saved the doomed force of Burgoyne. Sed Dis aliter visum. The delay here was not Sir Henry Clinton's fault, who could not leave his city unprotected; but the winds and weather which delayed the arrival of reinforcements which we had long awaited from England. The fleet which brought them brought us long and fond letters from home, with the very last news of the children under the care of their good Aunt Hetty and their grandfather. The mother's heart yearned towards the absent young ones. She made me no reproaches: but I could read her importunities in her anxious eyes, her terrors for me, and her longing for her children. "Why stay longer?" she seemed to say. "You who have no calling to this war, or to draw the sword against your countrymen—why continue to imperil your life and my happiness?" I understood her appeal. We were to enter upon no immediate service of danger; I told her Sir Henry was only going to accompany the expedition for a part of the way. I would return with him, the reconnaissance over, and Christmas, please Heaven, should see our family once more united in England.

A force of three thousand men, including a couple of slender regiments of American Loyalists and New York Militia (with which latter my distinguished relative, Mr. Will Esmond, went as captain), was embarked at New York, and our armament sailed up the noble Hudson River, that presents finer aspects than the Rhine in Europe to my mind: nor was any fire opened upon us from those beetling cliffs and precipitous "palisades," as they are called, by which we sailed; the enemy, strange to say, being for once unaware of the movement we contemplated. Our first landing was on the Eastern bank, at a place called Verplancks Point, whence the Congress troops withdrew after a slight resistance, their leader, the tough old Putnam (so famous during the war) supposing that our march was to be directed towards the Eastern Highlands, by which we intended to penetrate to Burgoyne. Putnam fell back to occupy these passes, a small detachment of ours being sent forward as if in pursuit, which he imagined was to be followed by the rest of our force. Meanwhile, before daylight, two thousand men without artillery, were carried over to Stoney Point on the Western shore, opposite Verplancks, and under a great hill called the Dunderberg by the old Dutch lords of the stream, and which hangs precipitously over it. A little stream at the northern base of this mountain intersects it from the opposite height on which Fort Clinton stood, named not after our general, but after one of the two gentlemen of the same name, who were amongst the oldest and most respected of the provincial gentry of New York, and who were at this moment actually in command against Sir Henry. On the next height to Clinton is Fort Montgomery; and behind them rises a hill called Bear Hill; whilst at the opposite side of the magnificent stream stands "Saint Antony's Nose," a prodigious peak indeed, which the Dutch had quaintly christened.

The attacks on the two forts were almost simultaneous. Half our men were detached for the assault on Fort Montgomery, under the brave Campbell, who fell before the rampart. Sir Henry, who would never be out of danger where he could find it, personally led the remainder, and hoped, he said, that we should have better luck than before the Sullivan Island. A path led up to the Dunderberg, so narrow as scarcely to admit three men abreast, and in utter silence our whole force scaled it, wondering at every rugged step to meet with no opposition. The enemy had not even kept a watch on it; nor were we descried until we were descending the height, at the base of which we easily dispersed a small force sent hurriedly to oppose us. The firing which here took place rendered all idea of a surprise impossible. The fort was before us. With such arms as the troops had in their hands, they had to assault; and silently and swiftly, in the face of the artillery playing upon them, the troops ascended the hill. The men had orders on no account to fire. Taking the colours of the Sixty-third, and bearing them aloft, Sir Henry mounted with the stormers. The place was so steep that the men pushed each other over the wall and through the embrasures; and it was there that Lieutenant Joseph Blake, the father of a certain Joseph Clinton Blake, who looks with the eyes of affection on a certain young lady, presented himself to the living of Warrington by saving the life of the unworthy patron thereof.

About a fourth part of the garrison, as we were told, escaped out of the fort, the rest being killed or wounded, or remaining our prisoners within the works. Fort Montgomery was, in like manner, stormed and taken by our people; and, at night, as we looked down from the heights where the king's standard had been just planted, we were treated to a splendid illumination in the river below. Under Fort Montgomery, and stretching over to that lofty prominence, called Saint Antony's Nose, a boom and chain had been laid with a vast cost and labour, behind which several American frigates and galleys were anchored. The fort being taken, these ships attempted to get up the river in the darkness, out of the reach of guns which they knew must destroy them in the morning. But the wind was unfavourable, and escape was found to be impossible. The crews therefore took to the boats, and so landed, having previously set the ships on fire with all their sails set; and we beheld these magnificent pyramids of flame burning up to the heavens and reflected in the waters below, until, in the midst of prodigious explosions, they sank and disappeared.

On the next day a parlementaire came in from the enemy, to inquire as to the state of his troops left wounded or prisoners in our hands, and the Continental officer brought me a note, which gave me a strange shock, for it showed that in the struggle of the previous evening my brother had been engaged. It was dated October 7, from Major-General George Clinton's divisional headquarters, and it stated briefly that "Colonel H. Warrington, of the Virginia line, hopes that Sir George Warrington escaped unhurt in the assault of last evening, from which the Colonel himself was so fortunate as to retire without the least injury." Never did I say my prayers more heartily and gratefully than on that night, devoutly thanking Heaven that my dearest brother was spared, and making a vow at the same time to withdraw out of the fratricidal contest, into which I only had entered because Honour and Duty seemed imperatively to call me.

I own I felt an inexpressible relief when I had come to the resolution to retire and betake myself to the peaceful shade of my own vines and fig-trees at home. I longed, however, to see my brother ere I returned, and asked, and easily obtained an errand to the camp of the American General Clinton from our own chief. The headquarters of his division were now some miles up the river, and a boat and a flag of truce quickly brought me to the point where his out-pickets received me on the shore. My brother was very soon with me. He had only lately joined General Clinton's division with letters from headquarters at Philadelphia, and he chanced to hear, after the attack on Fort Clinton, that I had been present during the affair. We passed a brief delightful night together: Mr. Sady, who always followed Hal to the war, cooking a feast in honour of both his masters. There was but one bed of straw in the hut where we had quarters, and Hal and I slept on it, side by side, as we had done when we were boys. We had a hundred things to say regarding past times and present. His kind heart gladdened when I told him of my resolve to retire to my acres and to take off the red coat which I wore: he flung his arms round it. "Praised be God!" said he. "Oh, heavens, George! think what might have happened had we met in the affair two nights ago!" And he turned quite pale at the thought. He eased my mind with respect to our mother. She was a bitter Tory, to be sure, but the Chief had given special injunctions regarding her safety. "And Fanny" (Hal's wife) "watches over her, and she is as good as a company!" cried the enthusiastic husband. "Isn't she clever? Isn't she handsome? Isn't she good?" cries Hal, never, fortunately, waiting for a reply to these ardent queries. "And to think that I was nearly marrying Maria once! Oh, mercy, what an escape I had!" he added. "Hagan prays for the King, every morning and night, at Castlewood, but they bolt the doors, and nobody hears. Gracious powers! his wife is sixty if she is a day; and oh, George! the quantity she drinks is..." But why tell the failings of our good cousin? I am pleased to think she lived to drink the health of King George long after his Old Dominion had passed for ever from his sceptre.

The morning came when my brief mission to the camp was ended, and the truest of friends and fondest of brothers accompanied me to my boat, which lay waiting at the riverside. We exchanged an embrace at parting, and his hand held mine yet for a moment ere I stepped into the barge which bore me rapidly down the stream. "Shall I see thee once more, dearest and best companion of my youth?" I thought. "Amongst our cold Englishmen, can I ever hope to meet with a friend like thee? When hadst thou ever a thought that was not kindly and generous? When a wish, or a possession, but for me you would sacrifice it? How brave are you, and how modest; how gentle, and how strong; how simple, unselfish, and humble; how eager to see others' merit; how diffident of your own!" He stood on the shore till his figure grew dim before, me. There was that in my eyes which prevented me from seeing him longer.

Brilliant as Sir Henry's success had been, it was achieved, as usual, too late: and served but as a small set-off against the disaster of Burgoyne which ensued immediately, and which our advance was utterly inadequate to relieve. More than one secret messenger was despatched to him who never reached him, and of whom we never learned the fate. Of one wretch who offered to carry intelligence to him, and whom Sir Henry despatched with a letter of his own, we heard the miserable doom. Falling in with some of the troops of General George Clinton, who happened to be in red uniform (part of the prize of a British ship's cargo, doubtless, which had been taken by American privateers), the spy thought he was in the English army, and advanced towards the sentries. He found his mistake too late. His letter was discovered upon him, and he had to die for bearing it. In ten days after the success at the Forts occurred the great disaster at Saratoga, of which we carried the dismal particulars in the fleet which bore us home. I am afraid my wife was unable to mourn for it. She had her children, her father, her sister to revisit, and daily and nightly thanks to pay to Heaven that had brought her husband safe out of danger.

CHAPTER XCII. Under Vine and Fig-Tree

Need I describe, young folks, the delights of the meeting at home, and the mother's happiness with all her brood once more under her fond wings? It was wrote in her face, and acknowledged on her knees. Our house was large enough for all, but Aunt Hetty would not stay in it. She said, fairly, that to resign her motherhood over the elder children, who had been hers for nearly three years, cost her too great a pang; and she could not bear for yet a while to be with them, and to submit to take only the second place. So she and her father went away to a house at Bury St. Edmunds, not far from us, where they lived, and where she spoiled her eldest nephew and niece in private. It was the year after we came home that Mr. B, the Jamaica planter, died, who left her the half of his fortune; and then I heard, for the first time, how the worthy gentleman had been greatly enamoured of her in Jamaica, and, though she had refused him, had thus shown his constancy to her. Heaven knows how much property of Aunt Hetty's Monsieur Miles hath already devoured! the price of his commission and outfit; his gorgeous uniforms; his play-debts and little transactions in the Minories;—do you think, sirrah, I do not know what human nature is; what is the cost of Pall Mall taverns, petits soupers, play even in moderation—at the Cocoa-Tree; and that a gentleman cannot purchase all these enjoyments with the five hundred a year which I allow him? Aunt Hetty declares she has made up her mind to be an old maid. "I made a vow never to marry until I could find a man as good as my dear father," she said; "and I never did, Sir George. No, my dearest Theo, not half as good; and Sir George may put that in his pipe and smoke it."

And yet when the good General died (calm, and full of years, and glad to depart), I think it was my wife who shed the most tears. "I weep because I think I did not love him enough," said the tender creature: whereas Hetty scarce departed from her calm, at least outwardly and before any of us; talks of him constantly still, as though he were alive; recalls his merry sayings, his gentle, kind ways with his children (when she brightens up and looks herself quite a girl again), and sits cheerfully looking up to the slab in church which records his name and some of his virtues, and for once tells no lies.

I had fancied, sometimes, that my brother Hal, for whom Hetty had a juvenile passion, always retained a hold of her heart; and when he came to see us, ten years ago, I told him of this childish romance of Het's, with the hope, I own, that he would ask her to replace Mrs. Fanny, who had been gathered to her fathers, and regarding whom my wife (with her usual propensity to consider herself a miserable sinner) always reproached herself, because, forsooth, she did not regret Fanny enough. Hal, when he came to us, was plunged in grief about her loss; and vowed that the world did not contain such another woman. Our dear old General, who was still in life then, took him in and housed him, as he had done in the happy early days. The women played him the very same tunes which he had heard when a boy at Oakhurst. Everybody's heart was very soft with old recollections, and Harry never tired of pouring out his griefs and his recitals of his wife's virtues to Het, and anon of talking fondly about his dear Aunt Lambert, whom he loved with all his heart, and whose praises, you may be sure, were welcome to the faithful old husband, out of whose thoughts his wife's memory was never, I believe, absent for any three waking minutes of the day.

General Hal went to Paris as an American General Officer in his blue and yellow (which Mr. Fox and other gentlemen had brought into fashion here likewise), and was made much of at Versailles, although he was presented by Monsieur le Marquis de Lafayette to the Most Christian King and Queen, who did not love Monsieur le Marquis. And I believe a Marquise took a fancy to the Virginian General, and would have married him out of hand, had he not resisted, and fled back to England and Warrington and Bury again, especially to the latter place, where the folks would listen to him as he talked about his late wife, with an endless patience and sympathy. As for us, who had known the poor paragon, we were civil, but not quite so enthusiastic regarding her, and rather puzzled sometimes to answer our children's questions about Uncle Hal's angel wife.

The two Generals and myself, and Captain Miles, and Parson Blake (who was knocked over at Monmouth, the year after I left America, and came home to change his coat, and take my living), used to fight the battles of the Revolution over our bottle; and the parson used to cry, "By Jupiter, General" (he compounded for Jupiter, when he laid down his military habit), "you are the Tory, and Sir George is the Whig! He is always finding fault with our leaders, and you are for ever standing up for them; and when I prayed for the

King last Sunday, I heard you following me quite loud."

"And so I do, Blake, with all my heart; I can't forget I wore his coat," says Hal.

"Ah, if Wolfe had been alive for twenty years more!" says Lambert.

"Ah, sir," cries Hal, "you should hear the General talk about him!"

"What General?" says I (to vex him).

"My General," says Hal, standing up, and filling a bumper. "His Excellency General George Washington!"

"With all my heart," cry I, but the parson looks as if he did not like the toast or the claret.

Hal never tired in speaking of his General; and it was on some such evening of friendly converse, that he told us how he had actually been in disgrace with this General whom he loved so fondly. Their difference seems to have been about Monsieur le Marquis de Lafayette before mentioned, who played such a fine part in history of late, and who hath so suddenly disappeared out of it. His previous rank in our own service, and his acknowledged gallantry during the war, ought to have secured Colonel Warrington's promotion in the Continental army, where a whipper-snapper like M. de Lafayette had but to arrive and straightway to be complimented by Congress with the rank of Major-General. Hal, with the freedom of an old soldier, had expressed himself somewhat contemptuously regarding some of the appointments made by Congress, with whom all sorts of miserable intrigues and cabals were set to work by unscrupulous officers who were greedy of promotion. Mr. Warrington, imitating perhaps in this the example of his now illustrious friend of Mount Vernon, affected to make the war en gentilhomme took his pay, to be sure, but spent it upon comforts and clothing for his men, and as for rank, declared it was a matter of no earthly concern to him, and that he would as soon serve as colonel as in any higher grade. No doubt he added contemptuous remarks regarding certain General Officers of Congress army, their origin, and the causes of their advancement: notably he was very angry about the sudden promotion of the young French lad just named—the Marquis, as they loved to call him—in the Republican army, and who, by the way, was a prodigious favourite of the Chief himself. There were not three officers in the whole Continental force (after poor madcap Lee was taken prisoner and disgraced) who could speak the Marquis's language, so that Hal could judge the young Major-General more closely and familiarly than other gentlemen, including the Commander-in-Chief himself. Mr. Washington good-naturedly rated friend Hal for being jealous of the beardless commander of Auvergne; was himself not a little pleased by the filial regard and profound veneration which the enthusiastic young nobleman always showed for him; and had, moreover, the very best politic reasons for treating the Marquis with friendship and favour.

Meanwhile, as it afterwards turned out, the Commander-in-Chief was most urgently pressing Colonel Warrington's promotion upon Congress; and, as if his difficulties before the enemy were not enough, he being at this hard time of winter entrenched at Valley Forge, commanding five or six thousand men at the most, almost without fire, blankets, food, or ammunition, in the face of Sir William Howe's army, which was perfectly appointed, and three times as numerous as his own; as if, I say, this difficulty was not enough to try him, he had further to encounter the cowardly distrust of Congress, and insubordination and conspiracy amongst the officers in his own camp. During the awful winter of '77, when one blow struck by the sluggard at the head of the British forces might have ended the war, and all was doubt, confusion, despair in the opposite camp (save in one indomitable breast alone), my brother had an interview with the Chief, which he has subsequently described to me, and of which Hal could never speak without giving way to the deepest emotion. Mr. Washington had won no such triumph as that which the daredevil courage of Arnold and the elegant imbecility of Burgoyne had procured for Gates and the northern army. Save in one or two minor encounters, which proved how daring his bravery was, and how unceasing his watchfulness, General Washington had met with defeat after defeat from an enemy in all points his superior. The Congress mistrusted him. Many an officer in his own camp hated him. Those who had been disappointed in ambition, those who had been detected in peculation, those whose selfishness or incapacity his honest eyes had spied out,—were all more, or less in league against him. Gates was the chief towards whom the malcontents turned. Mr. Gates was the only genius fit to conduct the war; and with a vaingloriousness, which he afterwards generously owned, he did not refuse the homage which was paid him.

To show how dreadful were the troubles and anxieties with which General Washington had to contend, I may mention what at this time was called the "Conway Cabal." A certain Irishman—a Chevalier of St. Louis, and an officer in the French service—arrived in America early in the year '77 in quest of military employment. He was speedily appointed to the rank of brigadier, and could not be contented, forsooth, without an immediate promotion to be major-general.

Mr. C. had friends at Congress, who, as the General-in-Chief was informed, had promised him his speedy promotion. General Washington remonstrated, representing the injustice of promoting to the highest rank the youngest brigadier in the service; and whilst the matter was pending, was put in possession of a letter from Conway to General Gates, whom he complimented, saying, that "Heaven had been determined to save America, or a weak general and bad councillors would have ruined it." The General enclosed the note to Mr. Conway, without a word of comment; and Conway offered his resignation, which was refused by Congress, who appointed him Inspector-General of the army, with the rank of Major-General.

"And it was at this time," says Harry (with many passionate exclamations indicating his rage with himself and his admiration of his leader), "when, by heavens, the glorious Chief was oppressed by troubles enough to drive ten thousand men mad—that I must interfere with my jealousies about the

Frenchman! I had not said much, only some nonsense to Greene and Cadwalader about getting some frogs against the Frenchman came to dine with us, and having a bagful of Marquises over from Paris, as we were not able to command ourselves;—but I should have known the Chief's troubles, and that he had a better head than mine, and might have had the grace to hold my tongue.

"For a while the General said nothing, but I could remark, by the coldness of his demeanour, that something had occurred to create a schism between him and me. Mrs. Washington, who had come to camp, also saw that something was wrong. Women have artful ways of soothing men and finding their secrets out. I am not sure that I should have ever tried to learn the cause of the General's displeasure, for I am as proud as he is, and besides" (says Hal), "when the Chief is angry, it was not pleasant coming near him, I can promise you." My brother was indeed subjugated by his old friend, and obeyed him and bowed before him as a boy before a schoolmaster.

"At last," Hal resumed, "Mrs. Washington found out the mystery. 'Speak to me after dinner, Colonel Hal,' says she. 'Come out to the parade-ground, before the dining-house, and I will tell you all.' I left a half-score of general officers and brigadiers drinking round the General's table, and found Mrs. Washington waiting for me. She then told me it was the speech I had made about the box of Marquises, with which the General was offended. 'I should not have heeded it in another,' he had said, 'but I never thought Harry Warrington would have joined against me.'

"I had to wait on him for the word that night, and found him alone at his table. 'Can your Excellency give me five minutes' time?' I said, with my heart in my mouth. 'Yes, surely, sir,' says he, pointing to the other chair. 'Will you please to be seated?'

"'It used not always to be Sir and Colonel Warrington, between me and your Excellency,' I said.

"He said, calmly, 'The times are altered.'

"'Et nos mutamur in illis,' says I. 'Times and people are both changed.'

"'You had some business with me?' he asked.

"'Am I speaking to the Commander-in-Chief or to my old friend?' I asked.

"He looked at me gravely. 'Well,—to both, sir,' he said. 'Pray sit, Harry.'

"'If to General Washington, I tell his Excellency that I, and many officers of this army, are not well pleased to see a boy of twenty made a major-general over us, because he is a Marquis, and because he can't speak the English language. If I speak to my old friend, I have to say that he has shown me very little of trust or friendship for the last few weeks; and that I have no desire to sit at your table, and have impertinent remarks made by others there, of the way in which his Excellency turns his back on me.'

"'Which charge shall I take first, Harry?' he asked, turning his chair away from the table, and crossing his legs as if ready for a talk. 'You are jealous, as I gather, about the Marquis?'

"'Jealous, sir!' says I. 'An aide-de-camp of Mr. Wolfe is not jealous of a Jack-a-dandy who, five years ago, was being whipped at school!'

"'You yourself declined higher rank than that which you hold,' says the Chief, turning a little red.

"'But I never bargained to have a macaroni Marquis to command me!' I cried. 'I will not, for one, carry the young gentleman's orders; and since Congress and your Excellency chooses to take your generals out of the nursery, I shall humbly ask leave to resign, and retire to my plantation.'

"'Do, Harry; that is true friendship!' says the Chief, with a gentleness that surprised me. 'Now that your old friend is in a difficulty, 'tis surely the best time to leave him.'

"'Sir!' says I.

"'Do as so many of the rest are doing, Mr. Warrington. Et tu, Brute, as the play says. Well, well, Harry! I did not think it of you; but, at least, you are in the fashion.'

"'You asked which charge you should take first?' I said.

"'Ch, the promotion of the Marquis? I recommended the appointment to Congress, no doubt; and you and other gentlemen disapprove it.'

"'I have spoken for myself, sir,' says I.

"'If you take me in that tone, Colonel Warrington, I have nothing to answer!' says the Chief, rising up very fiercely; 'and presume that I can recommend officers for promotion without asking your previous sanction.'

"'Being on that tone, sir,' says I, 'let me respectfully offer my resignation to your Excellency, founding my desire to resign upon the fact, that Congress, at your Excellency's recommendation, offers its highest commands to boys of twenty, who are scarcely even acquainted with our language.' And I rise up and make his Excellency a bow.

"'Great heavens, Harry!' he cries—(about this Marquis's appointment he was beaten, that was the fact, and he could not reply to me), 'can't you believe that in this critical time of our affairs, there are reasons why special favours should be shown to the first Frenchman of distinction who comes amongst us?'

"'No doubt, sir. If your Excellency acknowledges that Monsieur de Lafayette's merits have nothing to do with the question.'

"'I acknowledge or deny nothing, sir!' says the General, with a stamp of his foot, and looking as though he could be terribly angry if he would. 'Am I here to be catechised by you? Stay. Hark, Harry! I speak to you as a man of the world—nay, as an old friend. This appointment humiliates you and others, you say? Be it so! Must we not bear humiliation, along with the other burthens and griefs, for the sake of our country? It is no more just perhaps that the Marquis should be set over you gentlemen, than that your Prince Ferdinand or your Prince of Wales at home should have a command over veterans. But if in appointing this young nobleman we please a whole nation, and bring ourselves twenty millions of allies, will you and other gentlemen sulk because we do him honour? 'Tis easy to sneer at him (though, believe me, the Marquis has many more merits than you allow him); to my mind it were more generous, as well as more polite, of Harry Warrington to welcome this stranger for the sake of the prodigious benefit our country may draw from him—not to laugh at his peculiarities, but to aid him and help his ignorance by your experience as an old soldier: that is what I would do—that is the part I expected of thee—for it is the generous and manly one, Harry: but you choose to join my enemies, and when I am in trouble you say you will leave me. That is why I have been hurt: that is why I have been cold. I thought I might count on your friendship —and—and you can tell whether I was right or no. I relied on you as on a brother, and you come and tell me you will resign. Be it so! Being embarked in this contest, by God's will I will see it to an end. You are not the first, Mr. Warrington, has left me on the way.'

"He spoke with so much tenderness, and as he spoke his face wore such a look of unhappiness, that an extreme remorse and pity seized me, and I called out I know not what incoherent expressions regarding old times, and vowed that if he would say the word, I never would leave him. You never loved him, George," says my brother, turning to me, "but I did beyond all mortal men; and, though I am not clever like you, I think my instinct was in the right. He has a greatness not approached by other men."

"I don't say no, brother," said I, "now."

"Greatness, pooh!" says the parson, growling over his wine.

"We walked into Mrs. Washington's tea-room arm-in-arm," Hal resumed; "she looked up quite kind, and saw we were friends. 'Is it all over, Colonel Harry?' she whispered. 'I know he has applied ever so often about your promotion——'

"'I never will take it,' says I. And that is how I came to do penance," says Harry, telling me the story, "with Lafayette the next winter." (Hal could imitate the Frenchman very well.) "'I will go weez heem,' says I. 'I know the way to Quebec, and when we are not in action with Sir Guy, I can hear his Excellency the Major-General say his lesson.' There was no fight, you know we could get no army to act in Canada, and returned to headquarters; and what do you think disturbed the Frenchman most? The idea that people would laugh at him, because his command had come to nothing. And so they did laugh at him, and almost to his face too, and who could help it? If our Chief had any weak point it was this Marquis.

"After our little difference we became as great friends as before—if a man may be said to be friends with a Sovereign Prince, for as such I somehow could not help regarding the General: and one night, when we had sate the company out, we talked of old times, and the jolly days of sport we had together both before and after Braddock's; and that pretty duel you were near having when we were boys. He laughed about it, and said he never saw a man look more wicked and more bent on killing than you did: 'And to do Sir George justice, I think he has hated me ever since,' says the Chief. 'Ah!' he added, 'an open enemy I can face readily enough. 'Tis the secret foe who causes the doubt and anguish! We have sat with more than one at my table to-day, to whom I am obliged to show a face of civility, whose hands I must take when they are offered, though I know they are stabbing my reputation, and are eager to pull me down from my place. You spoke but lately of being humiliated because a junior was set over you in command. What humiliation is yours compared to mine, who have to play the farce of welcome to these traitors; who have to bear the neglect of Congress, and see men who have insulted me promoted in my own army? If I consulted my own feelings as a man, would I continue in this command? You know whether my temper is naturally warm or not, and whether as a private gentleman I should be likely to suffer such slights and outrages as are put upon me daily; but in the advancement of the sacred cause in which we are engaged, we have to endure not only hardship and danger, but calumny and wrong, and may God give us strength to do our duty!' And then the General showed me the papers regarding the affair of that fellow Conway, whom Congress promoted in spite of the intrigue, and down whose black throat John Cadwalader sent the best ball he ever fired in his life.

"And it was here," said Hal, concluding his story, "as I looked at the Chief talking at night in the silence of the camp, and remembered how lonely he was, what an awful responsibility he carried, how spies and traitors were eating out of his dish, and an enemy lay in front of him who might at any time overpower him, that I thought, 'Sure, this is the greatest man now in the world; and what a wretch I am to think of my jealousies and annoyances, whilst he is walking serenely under his immense cares!'"

"We talked but now of Wolfe," said I. "Here, indeed, is a greater than Wolfe. To endure is greater than to dare; to tire out hostile fortune; to be daunted by no difficulty; to keep heart when all have lost it; to go through intrigue spotless; and to forgo even ambition when the end is gained—who can say this is not greatness, or show the other Englishman who has achieved so much?"

"I wonder, Sir George, you did not take Mr. Washington's side, and wear the blue and buff yourself," grumbles Parson Blake.

"You and I thought scarlet most becoming to our complexion, Joe Blake!" says Sir George. "And my wife thinks there would not have been room for two such great men on one side."

"Well, at any rate, you were better than that odious, swearing, crazy General Lee, who was second in command!" cries Lady Warrington. "And I am certain Mr. Washington never could write poetry and tragedies as you can! What did the General say about George's tragedies, Harry?"

Harry burst into a roar of laughter (in which, of course, Mr. Miles must join his uncle).

"Well!" says he, "it's a fact that Hagan read one at my house to the General and Mrs. Washington and several more, and they all fell sound asleep!"

"He never liked my husband, that is the truth!" says Theo, tossing up her head, "and 'tis all the more magnanimous of Sir George to speak so well of him."

And then Hal told how, his battles over, his country freed, his great work of liberation complete, the General laid down his victorious sword, and met his comrades of the army in a last adieu. The last British soldier had quitted the shore of the Republic, and the Commander-in-Chief proposed to leave New York for Annapolis, where Congress was sitting, and there resign his commission. About noon, on the 4th December, a barge was in waiting at Whitehall Ferry to convey him across the Hudson. The chiefs of the army assembled at a tavern near the ferry, and there the General joined them. Seldom as he showed his emotion, outwardly, on this day he could not disguise it. He filled a glass of wine, and said, 'I bid you farewell with a heart full of love and gratitude, and wish your latter days may be as prosperous and happy as those past have been glorious and honourable.' Then he drank to them. 'I cannot come to each of you to take my leave,' he said, 'but shall be obliged if you will each come and shake me by the hand.'

General Knox, who was nearest, came forward, and the Chief, with tears in his eyes, embraced him. The others came, one by one, to him, and took their leave without a word. A line of infantry was formed from the tavern to the ferry, and the General, with his officers following him, walked silently to the water. He stood up in the barge, taking off his hat, and waving a farewell. And his comrades remained bareheaded on the shore till their leader's boat was out of view.

As Harry speaks very low, in the grey of evening, with sometimes a break in his voice, we all sit touched and silent. Hetty goes up and kisses her father.

"You tell us of others, General Harry," she says, passing a handkerchief across her eyes, "of Marion and Sumpter, of Greene and Wayne, and Rawdon and Cornwallis, too, but you never mention Colonel Warrington!"

"My dear, he will tell you his story in private!" whispers my wife, clinging to her sister, "and you can write it for him."

But it was not to be. My Lady Theo, and her husband too, I own, catching the infection from her, never would let Harry rest, until we had coaxed, wheedled, and ordered him to ask Hetty in marriage. He obeyed, and it was she who now declined. "She had always," she said, "the truest regard for him from the dear old times when they had met as almost children together. But she would never leave her father. When it pleased God to take him, she hoped she would be too old to think of bearing any other name but her own. Harry should have her love always as the best of brothers; and as George and Theo have such a nurseryful of children," adds Hester, "we must show our love to them, by saving for the young ones." She sent him her answer in writing, leaving home on a visit to friends at a distance, as though she would have him to understand that her decision was final. As such Hal received it. He did not break his heart. Cupid's arrows, ladies, don't bite very deep into the tough skins of gentlemen of our age; though, to be sure, at the time of which I write, my brother was still a young man, being little more than fifty. Aunt Het is now a staid little lady with a voice of which years have touched the sweet chords, and a head which Time has powdered over with silver. There are days when she looks surprisingly young and blooming. Ah me, my dear, it seems but a little while since the hair was golden brown, and the cheeks as fresh as roses! And then came the bitter blast of love unrequited which withered them; and that long loneliness of heart which, they say, follows. Why should Theo and I have been so happy, and thou so lonely? Why should my meal be garnished with love, and spread with plenty, while yon solitary outcast shivers at my gate? I bow my head humbly before the Dispenser of pain and poverty, wealth and health; I feel sometimes as if, for the prizes which have fallen to the lot of me unworthy, I did not dare to be grateful. But I hear the voices of my children in their garden, or look up at their mother from my book, or perhaps my sick-bed, and my heart fills with instinctive gratitude towards the bountiful Heaven that has so blest me.

Since my accession to my uncle's title and estate my intercourse with my good cousin Lord Castlewood had been very rare. I had always supposed him to be a follower of the winning side in politics, and was not a little astonished to hear of his sudden appearance in opposition. A disappointment in respect to a place at court, of which he pretended to have had some promise, was partly the occasion of his rupture with the Ministry. It is said that the most August Person in the realm had flatly refused to receive into the R-y-l Household a nobleman whose character was so notoriously bad, and whose example (so the August Objector was pleased to say) would ruin and corrupt any respectable family. I heard of the Castlewoods during our travels in Europe, and that the mania for play had again seized upon his lordship. His impaired fortunes having been retrieved by the prudence of his wife and father-in-law, he had again begun to dissipate his income at hombre and lansquenet. There were tales of malpractices in which he had been discovered, and even of chastisement inflicted upon him by the victims of his unscrupulous arts. His wife's beauty and freshness faded early; we met but once at Aix-la-Chapelle, where Lady Castlewood besought my wife to go and see her, and afflicted Lady Warrington's kind heart by stories of the neglect and outrage of which her unfortunate husband was guilty. We were willing to receive these as some excuse and palliation for the unhappy lady's own conduct. A notorious adventurer, gambler, and spadassin, calling himself the Chevalier de Barry, and said to be a relative of the mistress of the French King, but afterwards turning out to be an Irishman of low extraction, was in constant attendance upon the Earl and Countess at this time, and conspicuous for the audacity of his lies, the extravagance of his play, and somewhat mercenary gallantry towards the other sex, and a ferocious bravo courage, which, however, failed him on one or two awkward occasions, if common report said true. He subsequently married, and rendered miserable a lady of title and fortune in England. The poor little American lady's interested union with Lord Castlewood was scarcely more happy.

I remember our little Miles's infantile envy being excited by learning that Lord Castlewood's second son, a child a few months younger than himself, was already an ensign on the Irish establishment, whose pay the fond parents regularly drew. This piece of preferment my lord must have got for his cadet whilst he was on good terms with the Minister, during which period of favour

Will Esmond was also shifted off to New York. Whilst I was in America myself, we read in an English journal that Captain Charles Esmond had resigned his commission in his Majesty's service, as not wishing to take up arms against the countrymen of his mother, the Countess of Castlewood. "It is the doing of the old fox, Van den Bosch," Madam Esmond said; "he wishes to keep his Virginian property safe, whatever side should win!" I may mention, with respect to this old worthy, that he continued to reside in England for a while after the Declaration of Independence, not at all denying his sympathy with the American cause, but keeping a pretty quiet tongue, and alleging that such a very old man as himself was past the age of action or mischief, in which opinion the Government concurred, no doubt, as he was left quite unmolested. But of a sudden a warrant was out after him, when it was surprising with what agility he stirred himself, and skipped off to France, whence he presently embarked upon his return to Virginia.

The old man bore the worst reputation amongst the Loyalists of our colony; and was nicknamed "Jack the Painter" amongst them, much to his indignation, after a certain miscreant who was hung in England for burning naval stores in our ports there. He professed to have lost prodigious sums at home by the persecution of the Government, distinguished himself by the loudest patriotism and the most violent religious outcries in Virginia; where, nevertheless, he was not much more liked by the Whigs than by the party who still remained faithful to the Crown. He wondered that such an old Tory as Madam Esmond of Castlewood was suffered to go at large, and was for ever crying out against her amongst the gentlemen of the new Assembly, the Governor, and officers of the State. He and Fanny had high words in Richmond one day, when she told him he was an old swindler and traitor, and that the mother of Colonel Henry Warrington, the bosom friend of his Excellency the Commander-in-Chief, was not to be insulted by such a little smuggling slave-driver as him! I think it was in the year 1780 an accident happened, when the old Register Office at Williamsburg was burned down, in which there was a copy of the formal assignment of the Virginia property from Francis Lord Castlewood to my grandfather Henry Esmond, Esquire. "Oh," says Fanny, "of course this is the work of Jack the Painter!" And Mr. Van den Bosch was for prosecuting her for libel, but that Fanny took to her bed at this juncture, and died.

Van den Bosch made contracts with the new Government, and sold them bargains, as the phrase is. He supplied horses, meat, forage, all of bad quality; but when Arnold came into Virginia (in the King's service) and burned right and left, Van den Bosch's stores and tobacco-houses somehow were spared. Some secret Whigs now took their revenge on the old rascal. A couple of his ships in James River, his stores, and a quantity of his cattle in their stalls were roasted amidst a hideous bellowing; and he got a note, as he was in Arnold's company, saying that friends had served him as he served others; and containing "Tom the Glazier's compliments to brother Jack the Painter." Nobody pitied the old man, though he went well-nigh mad at his loss. In

Arnold's suite came the Honourable Captain William Esmond, of the New York Loyalists, as aide-de-camp to the General. When Howe occupied Philadelphia, Will was said to have made some money keeping a gambling-house with an officer of the dragoons of Anspach. I know not how he lost it. He could not have had much when he consented to become an aide-de-camp of Arnold.

Now, the King's officers having reappeared in the province, Madam Esmond thought fit to open her house at Castlewood and invite them thither —and actually received Mr. Arnold and his suite. "It is not for me," she said, "to refuse my welcome to a man whom my Sovereign has admitted to grace." And she threw her house open to him, and treated him with great though frigid respect whilst he remained in the district. The General gone, and, his precious aide-de-camp with him, some of the rascals who followed in their suite remained behind in the house where they had received so much hospitality, insulted the old lady in her hall, insulted her people, and finally set fire to the old mansion in a frolic of drunken fury. Our house at Richmond was not burned, luckily, though Mr. Arnold had fired the town; and thither the undaunted old lady proceeded, surrounded by her people, and never swerving in her loyalty, in spite of her ill-usage. "The Esmonds," she said, "were accustomed to Royal ingratitude."

And now Mr. Van den Bosch, in the name of his grandson and my Lord Castlewood, in England, set up a claim to our property in Virginia. He said it was not my lord's intention to disturb Madam Esmond in her enjoyment of the estate during her life, but that his father, it had always been understood, had given his kinsman a life-interest in the place, and only continued it to his daughter out of generosity. Now my lord proposed that his second son should inhabit Virginia, for which the young gentleman had always shown the warmest sympathy. The outcry against Van den Bosch was so great that he would have been tarred and feathered, had he remained in Virginia. He betook himself to Congress, represented himself as a martyr ruined in the cause of liberty, and prayed for compensation for himself and justice for his grandson.

My mother lived long in dreadful apprehension, having in truth a secret, which she did not like to disclose to any one. Her titles were burned! the deed of assignment in her own house, the copy in the Registry at Richmond, had alike been destroyed—by chance? by villainy? who could say? She did not like to confide this trouble in writing to me. She opened herself to Hal, after the surrender of York Town, and he acquainted me with the fact in a letter by a British officer returning home on his parole. Then I remembered the unlucky words I had let slip before Will Esmond at the coffee-house at New York; and a part of this iniquitous scheme broke upon me.

As for Mr. Will: there is a tablet in Castlewood Church, in Hampshire, inscribed, Dulce et decorum est pro patria mori, and announcing that "This marble is placed by a mourning brother, to the memory of the Honourable William Esmond, Esquire, who died in North America, in the service of his King." But how? When, towards the end of 1781, a revolt took place in the

Philadelphia Line of the Congress Army, and Sir Henry Clinton sent out agents to the mutineers, what became of them? The men took the spies prisoners, and proceeded to judge them, and my brother (whom they knew and loved, and had often followed under fire), who had been sent from camp to make terms with the troops, recognised one of the spies, just as execution was about to be done upon him—and the wretch, with horrid outcries, grovelling and kneeling at Colonel Warrington's feet, besought him for mercy, and promised to confess all to him. To confess what? Harry turned away sick at heart. Will's mother and sister never knew the truth. They always fancied it was in action he was killed.

As for my lord earl, whose noble son has been the intendant of an illustrious Prince, and who has enriched himself at play with his R——l master: I went to see his lordship when I heard of this astounding design against our property, and remonstrated with him on the matter. For myself, as I showed him, I was not concerned, as I had determined to cede my right to my brother. He received me with perfect courtesy; smiled when I spoke of my disinterestedness; said he was sure of my affectionate feelings towards my brother, but what must be his towards his son? He had always heard from his father: he would take his Bible oath of that: that, at my mother's death, the property would return to the head of the family. At the story of the title which Colonel Esmond had ceded, he shrugged his shoulders, and treated it as a fable. "On ne fait pas de ces folies là!" says he, offering me snuff, "and your grandfather was a man of esprit! My little grandmother was éprise of him: and my father, the most good-natured soul alive, lent them the Virginian property to get them out of the way! C'etoit un scandale, mon cher, un joli petit scandale!" Oh, if my mother had but heard him! I might have been disposed to take a high tone: but he said, with the utmost good-nature, "My dear Knight, are you going to fight about the character of our grandmother? Allons donc! Come, I will be fair with you! We will compromise, if you like, about this Virginian property!" and his lordship named a sum greater than the actual value of the estate.

Amazed at the coolness of this worthy, I walked away to my coffee-house, where, as it happened, an old friend was to dine with me, for whom I have a sincere regard. I had felt a pang at not being able to give this gentleman my living of Warrington—on-Waveney, but I could not, as he himself confessed honestly. His life had been too loose, and his example in my village could never have been edifying: besides, he would have died of ennui there, after being accustomed to a town life; and he had a prospect finally, he told me, of settling himself most comfortably in London and the church. [He was the second Incumbent of Lady Whittlesea's Chapel, Mayfair, and married Elizabeth, relict of Hermann Voelcker, Esq., the eminent brewer.] My guest, I need not say, was my old friend Sampson, who never failed to dine with me when I came to town, and I told him of my interview with his old patron.

I could not have lighted upon a better confidant. "Gracious powers!" says Sampson, "the man's roguery beats all belief! When I was secretary and factotum at Castlewood, I can take my oath I saw more than once a copy of the deed of assignment by the late lord to your grandfather: 'In consideration of the love I bear to my kinsman Henry Esmond, Esq., husband of my dear mother Rachel, Lady Viscountess Dowager of Castlewood, I, etc.'—so it ran. I know the place where 'tis kept—let us go thither as fast as horses will carry us to-morrow. There is somebody there—never mind whom, Sir George—who has an old regard for me. The papers may be there to this very day, and O Lord, O Lord, but I shall be thankful if I can in any way show my gratitude to you and your glorious brother!" His eyes filled with tears. He was an altered man. At a certain period of the port wine Sampson always alluded with compunction to his past life, and the change which had taken place in his conduct since the awful death of his friend Doctor Dodd.

Quick as we were, we did not arrive at Castlewood too soon. I was looking at the fountain in the court, and listening to that sweet sad music of its plashing, which my grandfather tells of in his memoirs, and peopling the place with bygone figures, with Beatrix in her beauty; with my Lord Francis in scarlet, calling to his dogs and mounting his grey horse; with the young page of old who won the castle and the heiress—when Sampson comes running down to me with an old volume in rough calf-bound in his hand, containing drafts of letters, copies of agreements, and various writings, some by a secretary of my Lord Francis, some in the slim handwriting of his wife my grandmother, some bearing the signature of the last lord; and here was a copy of the assignment sure enough, as it had been sent to my grandfather in Virginia. "Victoria, Victoria!" cries Sampson, shaking my hand, embracing everybody. "Here is a guinea for thee, Betty. We'll have a bowl of punch at the Three Castles to-night!" As we were talking, the wheels of postchaises were heard, and a couple of carriages drove into the court containing my lord and a friend, and their servants in the next vehicle. His lordship looked only a little paler than usual at seeing me.

"What procures me the honour of Sir George Warrington's visit, and pray, Mr. Sampson, what do you do here?" says my lord. I think he had forgotten the existence of this book, or had never seen it; and when he offered to take his Bible oath of what he had heard from his father, had simply volunteered a perjury.

I was shaking hands with his companion, a nobleman with whom I had had the honour to serve in America. "I came," I said, "to convince myself of a fact, about which you were mistaken yesterday; and I find the proof in your lordship's own house. Your lordship was pleased to take your lordship's Bible oath, that there was no agreement between your father and his mother, relative to some property which I hold. When Mr. Sampson was your lordship's secretary, he perfectly remembered having seen a copy of such an assignment, and here it is."

"And do you mean, Sir George Warrington, that unknown to me you have been visiting my papers?" cries my lord.

"I doubted the correctness of your statement, though backed by your lordship's Bible oath," I said with a bow.

"This, sir, is robbery! Give the papers back!" bawled my lord.

"Robbery is a rough word, my lord. Shall I tell the whole story to Lord Rawdon?"

"What, is it about the Marquisate? Connu, connu, my dear Sir George! We always called you the Marquis in New York. I don't know who brought the story from Virginia."

I never had heard this absurd nickname before, and did not care to notice it. "My Lord Castlewood," I said, "not only doubted, but yesterday laid a claim to my property, taking his Bible oath that———"

Castlewood gave a kind of gasp, and then said, "Great heaven! Do you mean, Sir George, that there actually is an agreement extant? Yes. Here it is—my father's handwriting, sure enough! Then the question is clear. Upon my o———well, upon my honour as a gentleman! I never knew of such an agreement, and must have been mistaken in what my father said. This paper clearly shows the property is yours: and not being mine—why, I wish you joy of it!" and he held out his hand with the blandest smile.

"And how thankful you will be to me, my lord, for having enabled him to establish the right," says Sampson, with a leer on his face.

"Thankful? No, confound you. Not in the least!" says my lord. "I am a plain man; I don't disguise from my cousin that I would rather have had the property than he. Sir George, you will stay and dine with us. A large party is coming down here shooting; we ought to have you one of us!"

"My lord," said I, buttoning the book under my coat, "I will go and get this document copied, and then return it to your lordship. As my mother in Virginia has had her papers burned, she will be put out of much anxiety by having this assignment safely lodged."

"What, have Madam Esmond's papers been burned? When the deuce was that?" asks my lord.

"My lord, I wish you a very good afternoon. Come, Sampson, you and I will go and dine at the Three Castles." And I turned on my heel, making a bow to Lord R———, and from that day to this I have never set my foot within the halls of my ancestors.

Shall I ever see the old mother again, I wonder? She lives in Richmond, never having rebuilt her house in the country. When Hal was in England, we sent her pictures of both her sons, painted by the admirable Sir Joshua Reynolds. We sate to him, the last year Mr. Johnson was alive, I remember. And the Doctor, peering about the studio, and seeing the image of Hal in his uniform (the appearance of it caused no little excitement in those days), asked who was this? and was informed that it was the famous American General—General Warrington, Sir George's brother. "General Who?" cries the Doctor, "General Where? Pooh! I don't know such a service!" and he turned his back and walked out of the premises. My worship is painted in scarlet, and we have replicas of both performances at home. But the picture which Captain Miles and the girls declare to be most like is a family sketch by my ingenious neighbour, Mr. Bunbury, who has drawn me and my lady with Monsieur Gumbo following us, and written under the piece, "SIR GEORGE, MY LADY, AND THEIR MASTER."

Here my master comes; he has poked out all the house-fires, has looked to all the bolts, has ordered the whole male and female crew to their chambers; and begins to blow my candles out, and says, "Time, Sir George, to go to bed! Twelve o'clock!"

"Bless me! So indeed it is." And I close my book, and go to my rest, with a blessing on those now around me asleep.

THE END

Printed in Great Britain
by Amazon